Count Baldassare Castiglione

THE BOOK OF
THE COURTIER

Edited by
VIRGINIA COX
Christ's College, Cambridge

EVERYMAN
J. M. DENT · LONDON
CHARLES E. TUTTLE
VERMONT

First published in Everyman's Library in 1974
This edition first published in Everyman in 1994

J. M. Dent
Orion Publishing Group
Orion House, 5 Upper St Martin's Lane,
London WC2H 9EA
and
Charles E. Tuttle Co. Inc.
28 South Main Street,
Rutland, Vermont 05701, USA

Typeset in Sabon by Deltatype, Ellesmere Port, South Wirral
Printed in Great Britain by
The Guernsey Press Co. Ltd, Guernsey, C. I.

British Library Cataloguing-in-Publication Data
is available upon request.

ISBN 0 460 87502 7

Everyman, I will go with thee,
and be thy guide

CONTENTS

Note on the Author   vii
Note on the Translator and Editor   viii
Chronology of the Life and Times of Castiglione and Hoby   x
Introduction   xvii
List of Principal Speakers   xxxii
Note on the Text   xxxvi

THE BOOK OF THE COURTYER
To the Reader by Thomas Sackevylle   2
The Epistle of the Translator by Thomas Hoby   3
A Letter of Syr J. Cheekes to Thomas Hoby   10
The Epistle of the Author by Count Baldassare Castiglione   12
The First Booke   19
The Second Booke   97
The Thirde Booke   207
The Fourth Booke   289
A Letter to the Lady Victoria Columna Marquess of
    Pescara by the Author   365
The Chiefe Conditions and Qualities in a Courtier   367
The Chief Conditions and Qualityes in a Waytyng
    Gentylwoman   372

Notes   375
Castiglione and His Critics   409
Suggestions for Further Reading   426
Acknowledgements   427

NOTE ON THE AUTHOR

COUNT BALDASSARE CASTIGLIONE was born in 1478, at his family's estate at Casatico, near Mantua. He received a thorough humanistic education in Mantua, where he was related through his mother to the ruling Gonzaga dynasty, and at the brilliant and ill-fated court of Lodovico Sforza in Milan. After the death of his father in 1499, he returned to Mantua and entered the service of the Marquis Francesco Gonzaga, transferring, however, in 1504, to that of Guidobaldo da Montefeltro, Duke of Urbino. The years that followed, until Guidobaldo's death in 1508, were later described by Castiglione as the happiest of his life and it is in Urbino in this period that the dialogues of *The Courtier* (*Il Cortegiano*) are set. The composition of the dialogue, a fifteen-year process, was begun around 1513 in Rome, where Castiglione were serving as ambassador to Guidobaldo's successor, Francesco Maria della Rovere. When the latter was deprived of his dukedom in 1516 by Pope Leo X, Castiglione transferred back into the service of the Mantuan court, in the same year beginning his brief but apparently happy marriage to Ippolita Torelli, tragically terminated by his wife's death at the age of twenty in 1520. The following year, he took holy orders and, in 1524, shortly after the election of Pope Clement VII, he was appointed papal envoy to the court of the Emperor Charles V in Spain. The appointment was a prestigious but an unenviable one: Castiglione found himself in the firing-line in the mounting hostilities between the papacy and the empire that culminated in the Sack of Rome by Imperial troops in 1527. The event earned him the suspicion of the Pope, but, by the time of his death in 1529, a reconciliation had been effected and, already bishop-elect of Avila at his death, it does not seem improbable that, had he lived, he would have attained the rank of cardinal, like several others among the ex-courtiers of Urbino. The news of his death was reputedly greeted by Charles V with the remark: '*Yo os digo que es muerto uno de los mejores caballeros del mundo*' ('I tell you that one of the finest knights in the world is dead').

NOTE ON THE TRANSLATOR AND EDITOR

THOMAS HOBY was born in 1530 in Leominster, Herefordshire. He studied from 1545 at St John's College, Cambridge, an institution then in the vanguard of scholarship and Protestant theology. In 1547, he travelled to Strasbourg, where he lodged with the theologian Martin Bucer, proceeding from there to Italy. There he spent the following two years, the first in Venice and Padua, where he attended the famous University, the second in travels that took him to Tuscany, Rome, Naples and – very unusually for an English traveller in this period – down through Calabria to Sicily. In 1550, he returned to England and shortly afterwards entered the service of William, Marquis of Northampton, for whose wife, Elizabeth Brooke, he undertook to translate the third book of *The Courtier*, with its delineation of the qualities of the perfect court lady and discussion of the equality of women. Hoby's career was abruptly interrupted in 1553 by the accession to the throne of the Catholic Mary Tudor; the following year, like many other Protestants, he left the country, fearing persecution, and it was in Padua, where a distinguished colony of Marian exiles had gathered, that he completed his translation of the remaining three books of *The Courtier*. In 1555, Hoby returned to England and spent the remainder of Mary's reign in retirement on his family's estates, where, in 1558, he married Elizabeth Cooke, one of five famously learned sisters, one of whom was the wife of Sir William Cecil, another the mother of Sir Francis Bacon. The accession of Elizabeth I, the same year, reopened the possibility of a public career, and, with his connection with Cecil, Elizabeth's chief secretary, Hoby was well placed to exploit it. He was appointed ambassador to France in 1566 and knighted shortly before his departure. The same year, however, brought his early death, at the age of thirty-six.

VIRGINIA COX is a lecturer in Italian at the University of Cambridge and a fellow of Christ's College, Cambridge. She is the author of *The Renaissance Dialogue: Literary Dialogue in its Social and Political Contexts, Castiglione to Galileo* (Cambridge, 1992) and is currently working on the Renaissance debate on the status of women.

CHRONOLOGY OF THE LIVES OF CASTIGLIONE AND HOBY

Year	Age	Life
1478		Castiglione born, Casatico
1490	11	Sent to stay with relatives in Milan; pursues humanistic studies and attends court of Lodovico Sforza
1499	20	Death of father; enters service of Marquis of Mantua
1503	24	First military experience, accompanying Marquis on campaign against the Spanish in Naples
1504	25	Transfers to service of Guidobaldo da Montefeltro, Duke of Urbino
1506	27–8	Writes *Thyrsis* with Cesare Gonzaga; sent to England to receive Order of the Garter on behalf of Guidobaldo
1508	29	Death of Guidobaldo; succession of Francesco Maria della Rovere
1509–12	30–3	Serves in papal forces under Francesco Maria della Rovere in campaigns in Romagna and Emilia

CHRONOLOGY OF THEIR TIMES

Year	Artistic Events	Historical Context
1484	Botticelli, *Birth of Venus*	
1485		Battle of Bosworth; Henry VII establishes Tudor dynasty
1492	Deaths of Piero della Francesca and Lorenzo de' Medici	Columbus's voyage to America; election of Pope Alexander VI; conquest of Granada
1494	Deaths of Poliziano (Politian) and Boiardo	French invasion of Naples begins Wars of Italy; downfall of Medici in Florence
1495	Leonardo begins *Last Supper*	
1499	Fernando de Rojas, *La Celestina*	Fall of Milan to the French; beginning of Cesare Borgia's campaigns
1502	Michelangelo working on *David*	
1503	Josquin des Prez in Ferrara	Election of Pope Julius II
1508	Michelangelo begins Sistine Chapel	League of Cambrai against Venice
1509		Accession of Henry VIII of England

Year	Age	Life
1513	34	Sent to Rome as resident ambassador of Urbino; begins composition of *The Courtier*
1516	37	Return to court of Mantua; marriage to Ippolita Torelli; first version of *The Courtier* complete
1517	38	Birth of first child, Camillo
1518	39	Birth of second child, Anna; draft of second version of *The Courtier*
1519	40	Sent to Rome as resident ambassador of Mantua
1520	41	Death of wife after birth of third child, Ippolita
1521	42	Second version of *The Courtier* complete
1524	45	Accepts post as papal nuncio to Spain from Pope Clement VII; begins work on final version of *The Courtier*
1527	48	Final version of *The Courtier* complete
1528	49	Publication of *The Courtier* by heirs of Aldo Manuzio, Venice
1529	50	Dies, Toledo
1530		Hoby born, Leominster

Year	Artistic Events	Historical Context
1511	Raphael completes Stanza della Segnatura; Erasmus, *In Praise of Folly*	
1512	Raphael, *Julius II*	Restoration of Medici
1513	Machiavelli, *The Prince*	Election of Pope Leo X
1515		Accession of Francis I in France
1516	Ariosto, *Orlando Furioso*; More, *Utopia*	Death of Ferdinand the Catholic
1517		Luther displays 95 theses in Wittenberg
1519	Death of Leonardo	Election of Emperor Charles V; Magellan's voyage
1521	Rosso Fiorentino, Volterra *Deposition*	Death of Pope Leo X
1523	Titian working on *Bacchus and Ariadne*	Election of Pope Clement VII
1525	Tyndale, translation of New Testament	French defeat at Battle of Pavia
1527	Death of Machiavelli	Sack of Rome; fall of Medici in Florence
1529		Treaty of Cambrai;
1530		Restoration of Medici
1531	Elyot, *Boke named the Governor*	
1532	Holbein settles in England	
1533		Henry VIII divorces Catherine of Aragon

Year	Age	Life
1545	15	Attends St John's College, Cambridge
1547	17	Travels to Strasbourg; stays with Martin Bucer
1548–50	18–20	Attends Padua University; travels in Italy
1551	21	Enters service of William Parr, Marquis of Northampton
1552	22	Studies law in Paris; translates Book III of *The Courtier* on request of his patron's wife
1554–5	24–5	Second stay in Padua; completes translation of *The Courtier*
1558	28	Marries Elizabeth Cooke
1560	30	Birth of first child, Edward
1561	31	Publication of *The Courtyer*
1562	32	Birth of second child, Anne
1564	34	Birth of third child, Katharine
1566	36	Sent as ambassador to France; dies, Paris; birth of fourth child, Thomas Postumus

Year	Artistic Events	Historical Context
1534	Rabelais, *Gargantua*	Act of Supremacy; election of Paul III
1535		Execution of More
1538	Titian, *Venus of Urbino*	
1539		Dissolution of the monasteries
1541	Michelangelo completes *Last Judgment*	
1543	Copernicus's exposition of heliocentric cosmology	
1545	Ascham, *Toxophilus*	Opening of Council of Trent
1547	Michelangelo starts work on St Peter's	Accession of Edward VI
1550	Vasari, *Lives of the Artists*	
1552	Rabelais, *Quart Livre*	
1553		Accession of Mary Tudor
1556	Death of Aretino	Abdication of Charles V
1558	Cellini begins autobiography	Accession of Elizabeth I
1559		Treaty of Cateau-Cambrésis ends religious wars in Europe
1561	Sackville and Norton, *Gorboduc*	
1563	Veronese completes *Marriage at Cana*	Closure of Council of Trent
1564	Death of Michelangelo; birth of Galileo	

INTRODUCTION

The argument

'The best book ever written on good breeding'; a guide to 'the minuter decencies and inferior duties': the faint praises of Samuel Johnson, written two and a half centuries after the first publication of *The Book of the Courtier*, give a good indication both of the durability of the ideal of behaviour defined in the work and, perhaps more strikingly, of the superficiality with which it has often been read.[1] In this respect, *The Courtier* has been its own worst enemy: the urbanity and lightness of tone of Castiglione's dialogue, and the very incisiveness with which it calibrates what Johnson calls 'the minuter decencies', have often obscured, especially for readers remote in place and time from the society that produced it, the scope and moral gravity of the less 'minute' questions it raises. The task of 'forming the perfect courtier in words' is presented in *The Courtier* as a game: a trivial pursuit devised by the courtiers of the tiny dukedom of Urbino, in the Italian Marches, to while away four evenings in early March in 1507. A parlour game, then, but, in the best Renaissance tradition of *serio ludere*, a game that strays blithely into some of the most crucial and contentious areas of debate of the day.

The section of *The Courtier* that would have the greatest influence on subsequent Italian and European culture is Book I, which deals with the attributes and accomplishments required of the perfect courtier. The resulting figure is a seductive distillation of the medieval ideal of the perfect knight and the humanistic model of the cultivated man. The courtier, it is established, should be of noble birth, handsome, modest and virtuous; skilled in his 'principal profession' of arms, but also versed in classical letters; fluent and eloquent in speech; trained in music and in the practice and appreciation of the visual arts. In addition to these concrete accomplishments, moreover, he should possess the less tangible quality of 'grace': an attribute which may appear to be a natural endowment, but which, it is argued, may be acquired even by those not naturally graceful, through a self-conscious avoidance of 'affectation' – the appearance of striving too hard for effect – and a cultivation of the corresponding virtue of *sprezzatura* or nonchalance.

The speaker in the first book is the Veronese nobleman Lodovico da Canossa; in the second, another courtier, Federico Fregoso, is given the task of explaining how the courtier should put into practice all the 'good qualities' with which Canossa has endowed him. The change of subject and speaker signals the introduction of a new and less ideal perspective: as Fregoso emphasises, in a world riven by envy and beguiled by appearances, in which meretricious mediocrity is frequently preferred over solid merit, the courtier cannot simply rely on his native good qualities to win him success. He must not only possess all the virtues Canossa has given him; he must also know how to exploit them, constructing his persona with the self-conscious artistry of a painter composing a canvas. The difference between the perspectives of the speakers of the first two books of *The Courtier* is perhaps most tellingly illustrated by their sharply differing attitudes to military valour. For Canossa (p. 43), the test of true courage is consistency: the courtier should act with equal valour in all circumstances, even when he knows his actions will go unobserved and unrewarded. Fregoso is distinctly more pragmatic (p. 109): alert, as ever, to appearances, he recommends that the courtier should reserve his most spectacular acts of valour for contexts in which they are most likely to be noted.

Much of Fregoso's advice in the second book is concerned with this need for the courtier to 'script' his behaviour for an audience whose infinitely manipulable impressions are the key to his professional success. Unsurprisingly, his recommendations do not go unchallenged, and much of the debate in the book is concerned with the question of the degree to which this kind of 'image-management' may compromise the courtier's integrity. Is it right, for example, that, as Fregoso advises, the courtier should under-play his expertise in certain fields, in order to manipulate his audience into inferring from his unexpected prowess in these 'second-string' activities that his skills in the areas in which he does admit to competence are greater than they actually are? Is it legitimate for the courtier to stoop to such stratagems or, as one of Fregoso's listeners indignantly suggests, is this kind of dissimulation unworthy of a man of integrity (p. 148)? The problem of integrity becomes especially pressing where the courtier's relations with the prince are concerned: a central issue in the dialogue, which is raised here for the first time. It may be acceptable and professionally necessary for the courtier to feign an unfelt enthusiasm for the prince's favourite pastimes, even if these things are alien to his nature (p.120). But what of his behaviour in more serious matters? What degree of real moral autonomy does he retain? How should he act when the prince's orders – and his own career interests – conflict with his sense of what is right?

These painful questions are left unanswered by a hard-pressed Fregoso and the question of the courtier's moral status is abandoned for the moment, to resurface in the first half of Book 4. The concluding part of the second book is taken up with a discussion of wit and humour, appropriately delegated to the comic dramatist Bernardo Dovizi da Bibbiena. This section of *The Courtier*, with its long anthology of witty sayings, does not tend to arouse the same enthusiasm now as it did among early readers like Ben Jonson: the 'life' and 'quickness' he found there are qualities that often seem conspicuously lacking.[2] The interest of this part of the dialogue today lies mainly elsewhere, in its vivid portrayal of Italian court society, and especially in its evocation of the brittle, doomed brilliance of the papal court on the eve of the Reformation.

The second book ends with a brief but intense dispute on the legitimacy of jokes that impugn women's chastity, which raises the question of the double standard in sexual morality. This leads in turn to a more general discussion of the moral status of women: are they moral imbeciles who must be cowed into chastity by force in the interests of ensuring a legitimate succession, or rational subjects as capable of correct moral choices as men? The question, unsurprisingly, provokes a lively response from the women present, and a speaker sympathetic to their cause, Giuliano de' Medici, is conscripted to establish the dignity of their sex by fashioning the perfect 'lady of the court' the following evening. This enterprise, in the circumstances, could hardly fail to prove controversial; and, indeed, when Giuliano insists that the female courtier should display the same moral virtues and practise the same intellectual pursuits as her male counterpart, his misogynist opponents, led by the *enfant terrible* of the group, Gaspare Pallavicino, are quick to react. The extended debate on women's equality that follows is one of the most interesting and original episodes of the dialogue, its originality undiminished by the existence of a previous humanist tradition of debate on the issue. The fact that the question first arises in the very concrete context of a debate on the double standard is highly significant, in view of the abstract and academic character of many Renaissance discussions of women's equality. The resonances of this initial dispute in Book 2 continue to be felt in the later debate, firmly anchoring its abstruse discussions of Aristotelian biology and its cataloguing of the heroines of classical history and myth to the realities of sexual jealousy and economic and political interest on which the complex superstructure of misogynist thought was built.

The third book ends with a discussion of the ways in which the 'lady of the court' should conduct herself in love, stressing the need for extreme circumspection on her part in the interests of her reputation and concluding, in a significant departure from the adulterous traditions of medieval courtly love literature, that courtship could only be condoned where there was a possibility of its leading to marriage. In the first draft of *The Courtier* (1513–16), the treatise ended at this point, but, in his two substantial later revisions (1518–21 and 1524–7), Castiglione added the material ultimately gathered in the fourth book. In the final version, the third book closes in a dramatic fashion, with a declaration by one of the courtiers, Ottaviano Fregoso, that the task of forming the courtier is anything but complete.

The first half of the fourth book is devoted to Fregoso's substantiation of this claim. What is missing from the previous formulation, he argues, is an end that can justify the courtier's existence, which must serve some higher purpose than that of amusing himself and those around him. The courtly skills allocated to the courtier in the first two books are here redefined simply as a means to the end of winning the prince's confidence, in order to guide him to virtue and wise government. Fregoso's move is a bold one, as he is happy to acknowledge: by transforming the courtier into the prince's mentor, he has significantly extended the usual conception of his role. The effect of his gambit is to raise dramatically the stakes of the 'game' of defining the courtier, embarked on in such a light-hearted spirit at the beginning of the dialogue. The question of the courtier's moral integrity, so equivocally established in the earlier books of *The Courtier*, is transformed here from a matter of conscience to a crucial factor in the health of the state.

The attribution of a vicarious political role to the courtier, in the second version of *The Courtier*, is often regarded as reflecting the progress of Castiglione's own aspirations as he advanced in his courtly career. The last section of the dialogue, added in the final revision, of the 1520s, can, similarly, be related to the author's decision to enter the Church. The first and second versions of the dialogue had been wholly secular in perspective, unequivocally focused on the problems of life in the world. The final version adds a spiritual dimension to the figure of the courtier, with an eloquent dissertation by Pietro Bembo – intellectually the most distinguished of the courtiers in the dialogue – on Platonic love as a means of ascent to the contemplation of divine beauty and truth. The addition is an inspired one, supplying a Platonic, contemplative counterpoint to the preceding, largely Aristotelian discussion of the courtier's role in the active life and providing a magnificent climax to the book in Bembo's final rapt hymn to divine love. It is not, however, permitted to alter the tone of the work definitively: the deliberately anti-climactic scene that follows Bembo's ecstasy of contemplation brings the dialogue back to the mortal world it has fleetingly abandoned. As Bembo's speech ends, his listeners realise that the night has passed without their noticing and open the casements to discover the morning star, Venus, fading in the dawn. The moment is one of unforced lyric power, but the dialogue's civilised and lightly melancholy realism will not allow any such intimation of transcendence to be more than a momentary epiphany. The dialogue ends as it opened, with a scene of flirtatious sparring on a subject – women's equality with men – which promises endless discussions to come.

The historical context

It is easy to forget, while reading the urbane conversations recounted in *The Courtier*, that the period of the dialogue's composition was one of the most turbulent in Italian history. The period from 1494 to 1530 in Italy witnessed the most intense stage in the struggles collectively known as the Wars of Italy, in which the European powers, most significantly France and Spain, fought for control over the peninsula, aided in their ambitions by the disunity and self-seeking of the constellation of states into which Italy was divided. The Wars and the loss of Italian independence they signalled were experienced by Italian intellectuals as a profound collective trauma, whether the rout of the Italian states was attributed to the justified wrath of God, the blind vicissitudes of Fortune or – as most famously in Machiavelli's *Prince* – to the political myopia and military incompetence of her leaders.

The Courtier has frequently been castigated by critics for its idealised portrayal of the Italian ruling classes in a period in which, as it has been pointed out, 'princes and courtiers were the leading sicknesses of Italian society'.[3] It would be misleading to assert, however, that the uglier realities of the Italian situation are entirely absent from the work. References to Italy's military humiliations are distributed at intervals throughout the dialogue: a discussion on the relative merits of arms and letters tackles the claim that an excessive attention to learning had contributed to Italy's military failures (p. 79); the innocuous subject of dress provokes further bitter reflections on Italy's reduction to servitude (p. 131); finally, in Book 4, the possibility is even confronted that precisely the kind of refined living prescribed for the courtier in the previous three books is responsible for the softening of character that has reduced the Italian name to opprobrium (p. 295). Nor are the political failings of Italian leaders passed over in silence: although Castiglione does not miss an opportunity to lavish praise on his patrons, when Ottaviano Fregoso comes to generalise about the quality of Italian leadership in Book 4 (pp. 296–9), his speech is a woeful catalogue of the vanity, moral decadence and ill government that Castiglione had had the opportunity to observe at close quarters in his diplomatic career.

The idealised portrayal of court society contained in *The Book of the Courtier* is not, therefore, without internal flaw-lines that enable the reader to calibrate its relation to the realities it excludes. What is more, the prefaces to each book and the dedicatory letter serve to characterise Castiglione's portrait of Urbino as a memorial to a lost Arcadia, rather than as an accurate representation of a contemporary seat of power. The prefatory letter to De Silva and the preface to Book 4 list the toll of the protagonists of the work who have since died, while the letter to De Silva, written twenty years after the date of the setting of the dialogue, represents the author in Spain in a 'wildernes full of sorow', as the survivor of a vanished age. Though the tragedies mentioned are individual, the sense of loss extends to the whole society described: *The Courtier* has been described, with justice, as in some sense a 'posthumous' work, in that in the two decades that had passed between 1507, when the dialogues are set, and 1528, when they were published, the world of the independent Italian courts they portray had become a political anachronism.

The age of Guidobaldo at Urbino, then, has something of the status of a myth in *The Courtier*, of a personal and collective Golden Age (it is perhaps relevant to recall that in the dramatic eclogue, *Thyrsis*, that Castiglione composed in 1506 with Cesare Gonzaga, the Urbino court is figured in Arcadian imagery). It is important, however, not to exaggerate the elements of nostalgia and evasion in a work that is also notable for its pragmatic concern with the techniques of worldly success. Along with its epigraphs to the dead, Castiglione's preface to Book 4 contains a list of the courtiers who had issued from the 'Trojan horse' of Urbino to achieve positions of authority elsewhere – many in the Church, which was consolidating its position as the most conspicuous arena for talent in Italy. It is a premise – or a promise – of *The Courtier* that the behavioural ethos it elaborates will provide a formula for social success in contexts far removed from the court of Urbino in 1507. That that promise was not regarded as vain by its readers is proved by the subsequent fortunes of the dialogue, which went through over a hundred editions in the century following its publication and was translated into five other languages. The immense popularity of the work testifies to Castiglione's skill in identifying and codifying precisely the qualities needed by the administrative classes of the courts of Europe: qualities quite different from those defined by the chivalric codes of the medieval feudal nobility. Along with the more practical and prescriptive courtesy books that followed it, *The Courtier* transmitted to Europe a behavioural ideal that would become an integral part of Western culture, surviving in a modified guise in the French seventeenth-century ideal of the *honnête homme* and, most influentially perhaps, in the English notion of the 'gentleman'.

The literary context

If *The Book of the Courtier* stands at the head of a new tradition of European courtesy literature, it may also be seen as the culmination of an earlier Italian humanist tradition. The movement of intellectual and educational reform known as humanism – though it was not a term used in the period – is often seen as starting with Francesco Petrarca, or Petrarch (1304–74), who articulated many of the values later humanists would adopt as their own. The impetus of the movement was a powerful drive to disinter the literature and thought of classical antiquity – a heritage which the humanists represented as having lain buried and ignored throughout the benighted epoch that had followed the disintegration of the Roman Empire. A 'dark age', then, followed by a 'renaissance', a rebirth: the dominant metaphors in this historiographical scheme give a vivid sense of the urgency and moral seriousness with which the humanists embarked on their recovery of classical learning.

One aspect of humanism, of relevance here, is the emphasis it placed on the active life (*vita activa*): the life of social and political engagement, traditionally contrasted with the contemplative life. Reacting against the scholastic philosophy that dominated the universities and which they perceived as pedantic, obfuscatory and remote from reality, the humanists turned to the writings of the great Roman moralists and rhetoricians, notably Cicero and Quintilian, to forge a new learning and a new educational syllabus directed towards problems of ethics and civic life. It is from this tradition of humanist writing that *The Courtier* arises, and, in its values and emphases, its classical sources and the manner in which it deploys these sources, Castiglione's dialogue has much in common with earlier, humanist works that had sought to define the qualities necessary in the *vita activa*.

One great difference between Castiglione's text and those of most of his humanist predecessors is, however, the fact that *The Courtier* is written in the vernacular, rather than in Latin. The humanists' enterprise of recovering classical culture had had an important linguistic component: in the century following Petrarch's death, a prodigious amount of energy was devoted to the task of restoring Latin to a Ciceronian purity and purging it of its 'barbarous' post-classical accretions. This intense dedication to Latin was accompanied by a relative neglect of the vernacular: a neglect which reflected, in some cases at least, an active contempt for the conceptual and expressive poverty of the language of the 'people'. By the last two decades of the fifteenth century, however, vernacular literature was beginning a revival, most notably in Lorenzo de' Medici's Florence, where the drive to recover the great heritage of medieval Tuscan literature was partly inspired by nationalist sentiment and imperialist ambition, but also in the northern courts, especially Lodovico Sforza's Milan. By 1501, when the first critical edition of an Italian text, Petrarch's *Rime*, issued from the presses of the great humanist publisher Aldo

Manuzio, vernacular literature had clearly established its right of residence within the humanist republic of letters. In the following decades, fierce debate would persist over the issue of the correct form of the Italian literary language, but the older question of whether the vernacular was a worthy vehicle for literature could be considered – in spite of some lingering resistance – definitively solved.

Castiglione belonged to the generation that witnessed this triumph of the vernacular. It was a generation that included some of the most important and influential Italian writers of any age: Niccolò Machiavelli and his younger Florentine contemporary, the historian and political philosopher Francesco Guicciardini; Lodovico Ariosto, the great Ferrarese poet and dramatist, author of the *Orlando Furioso*; and the poet and literary critic Pietro Bembo, a speaker in *The Courtier*. None of these writers' work can be fully understood outside the tradition of neo-Latin humanism: in differing ways and to different extents, the writings of all bear the mark of their humanist education. These writers' 'translation' of the humanist heritage is, however, a remarkably free one: acutely conscious of the demands of the new audiences they were addressing and alive to the new circumstances in which they were writing, Castiglione and his contemporaries drew on the heritage of humanism to create something radically new.

This process of absorption and innovation is very obvious in *The Courtier*. Castiglione's debt to humanism has already been noted: it is apparent, to look no further, in his choice of the dialogue form, one of the many classical literary genres revived by the humanists. Classical thought, mediated through the humanist experience, shapes *The Courtier* at a far deeper level than can be grasped simply by registering the work's many explicit allusions to classical literature and history: even a notion as apparently newly minted as that of *sprezzatura* – the deceptive air of effortlessness Castiglione identifies as so essential to the courtier's ethos – in fact has a long and complex genealogy in classical aesthetic thought and rhetorical theory. This is not to say, however, as has sometimes been suggested, that *The Courtier* is simply a work of compilation: a jigsaw of classical fragments in a neo-classical frame. The perfect courtier of the dialogue may be cut from the same cloth as the Roman ideal of the orator, as Castiglione signals with a series of self-conscious echoes of Cicero's *De oratore*. But the courtier is by no means a simple modern-day replica of Cicero's orator: forged in the distinctive environment of the court, in which an individual's standing depended less on the stable coin of office than on the fluctuating currency of the prince's favours, Castiglione's courtier is a more equivocal figure, more flexible and protean, less clear-cut in his values; more self-conscious in his management of the image, the 'face' he knows to be his fortune. It would not be difficult to find anticipations of these developments in Castiglione's sources, particularly in that portion of classical rhetorical theory that deals with the need for the legal orator to tailor the character he projects to the different audiences he is addressing. In rhetorical theory, however, this 'accommodation' is a localised forensic strategy. In *The Courtier* it has been translated into a mode of being, a guiding principle of the courtier's existence.

The dialogue

Castiglione's deployment of the dialogue form he inherited from his classical and humanist forebears is another good example of the way in which he conducts his own dialogue with his sources. *The Courtier*'s formal debt to classical dialogue is clearly signalled at the beginning of the work, when Castiglione announces his decision to adopt the dialogue form in words that echo a passage from the opening of Cicero's *De oratore* (p. 22). Any anticipation these words may arouse of a direct imitation of Cicero, however, is immediately dispelled by what follows. In many respects, in fact – its use of a game as a structuring device, its introduction of women speakers, its frequent tone of flirtatious gallantry – *The Courtier* is closer to the traditions of the medieval courtly literature that remained a strong presence in Renaissance court culture than to the soberer conventions of Ciceronian and humanist dialogue.

An important formal influence, in this respect, is Bembo's dialogue on love, *Gli Asolani* (1505), set in the tiny court of the Queen of Cyprus at Asolo, near Venice. Unlike Bembo, however, who follows Boccaccio's *Decameron* in giving invented names to his interlocutors, Castiglione adheres to the Ciceronian convention of using identifiable contemporary figures as speakers. This formal choice is a significant one: in *The Courtier*, as in *De oratore*, the identity of the speakers plays an important role in the dialogue's persuasive strategy, inscribing the ideal of the courtier or orator within a recognisable historical reality. The speakers of *The Courtier* act as living exemplars of the virtues prescribed for the perfect courtier and guarantors of the attainability of what might otherwise seem an impossible ideal. When Lodovico da Canossa refused the offer of time to prepare his speech and effortlessly improvises an evening's worth of profoundly meditated good sense, he is demonstrating the virtue of *sprezzatura* before he has even coined a term for it. Similarly, when he and the speakers who succeed him preface their performances with a ritual acknowledgement of their ignorance and inadequacy to the task, they are exemplifying that urbane self-deprecation that is another of the courtier's essential qualities.

The dialogue form in *The Courtier*, then, has an important exemplary function, allowing Castiglione to demonstrate the art of courtiership at the same time as he defines it. This is true in another sense as well: the adoption of a pseudo-documentary form of dialogue – one that purports to represent an actual, historical conversation – allows Castiglione, as author, to display the same qualities of modesty and *sprezzatura* as have just been observed in his speakers. By presenting his reflections on the courtier in the form of a dialogue among the courtiers of Urbino, Castiglione modestly shrugs off the achievement and the labour of his authorship, casting himself in the humbler and more 'amateur' role of a transcriber of other men's words. We may not precisely believe in this claim, but its *sprezzatura* is disarming; and the immense popularity the pseudo-documentary dialogue enjoyed in subsequent Italian court literature is a testimony to the appeal this manner of authorial self-presentation held for Castiglione's culture.

These considerations do not, of course, exhaust the question of the function of dialogue in *The Courtier*. The gestures of diffidence just examined, on the part of both the author and the speakers of the dialogue, are not only displays of courtly etiquette but also expressions of a genuine sense of the difficulties involved in adjudicating on a subject as complex and as open to debate as the correct forms of social behaviour. As Canossa observes at the beginning of his description of the perfect courtier: 'In everye thynge it is so harde a matter to knowe the true perfeccion, that it is almoste unpossible . . . by reason of the varietie of judgementes . . . and thus dooeth everye man prayse or dysprayse accordynge to hys fansye' (p. 37). In view of this difficulty, Canossa announces, he will limit himself to expressing what he is conscious can only be a partial and inadequate truth, leaving his listeners to judge for themselves:

And for as much as the trueth . . . is oftentymes hid, and I take not upon me to have this knowleage [i.e. the ability to discern the truth], I cannot praise but that kynde of Courtyers which I set most by, and allow that whiche semeth unto me most nigh the trueth, in my smal judgement. The which you shal folowe if ye thinke it good, or els sticke to youre owne, yf it shal vary from mine. Neither will I (for all that) stand stiffe that mine is better then yours, for not onelye one thynge maie seme unto you, and an other to me, but also unto my self it may appere sometime one thing, sometime another (p. 38).

The problem articulated by Canossa is, of course, the same as that faced by Castiglione; and the solution the latter adopts, as author, is similar to that of his speaker. When Castiglione announces his intention to express his views on the courtier not, as is usual in didactic contexts, in the form of a 'certaine order or rule of appointed preceptes', but rather by recounting 'certaine reasoninges [discussions] that were debated in times past betwene men verye excellent for that purpose' (p. 22), he is expressing a commitment to the same kind of open-ended collective enquiry that Canossa instigates with his free canvassing of his listeners' dissent. *The Courtier* does not present us with an 'authorised version' of the subjects it discusses: with its succession of speakers, each bringing a subtly different perspective to bear on the courtier, Castiglione's dialogue is capable, like Canossa, of thinking 'sometime one thing, sometime another'. There are passages, of course, when the dialogue does read more prescriptively than others, and localised debates in which it is not difficult to detect where the author's sympathies lie. Where the more integral moral issues of the dialogue are concerned, however, no one view is permitted to dominate: on questions like the legitimacy of dissimulation or the balance to be achieved between self-interest and the pursuit of higher ends, it is impossible to distil a single authorial position out of *The Courtier*'s complex dialectic of views, each inevitably coloured by the sediment of individual speakers' experiences and prejudices. The structure of *The Courtier* may encourage us to see the fourth book, with its elevated vision, as, in some sense, superseding what has gone before. This movement towards closure is by no means an absolute one, however: Ottaviano Fregoso's and even Bembo's eloquent speeches are punctuated with expressions of scepticism from their listeners and the less idealistic interventions of earlier speakers retain a troubling resonance to the end. *The Courtier* has been read in the centuries since its publication as anything from a cynical primer for self-advancement to a lofty celebration of human dignity and a paean to an ideal society. The very variety of the readings it has attracted is a testimony to the subtlety and *sprezzatura* with which Castiglione uses the dialogue form to dramatise the interplay of ideas.

Hoby's translation

It is an irony of the reception of *The Courtier* that this calculatedly unmagisterial dialogue appears to have been read predominantly as a handbook, a practical manual of morals and manners. This tendency is interestingly reflected in the apparatus provided by sixteenth-century editors such as Lodovico Dolce, whose 1552 edition of *The Courtier*, with its abstracts of the argument of the four books and its peremptory marginal notes summarising the 'lessons' of each page, effectively converts Castiglione's dialogue into precisely that 'certaine order or rule of appointed preceptes' that its author had determined not to write.

Sir Thomas Hoby's *Courtyer*, of 1561, with its appendices summarising the 'chiefe conditions and qualities' of the courtier and the court lady, is a good example of this prescriptive and practically oriented trend in the reception of *The Courtier*. Hoby's appendices make curious reading: cut loose from their context in the dialogue and transformed into a packaged and digestible form, the parts of the courtier add up to strikingly less than their sum. Particularly noteworthy is the way in which the appendices reduce the moral complexities of the dialogue into hard-and-fast maxims: Book 2's notably fluid and at times Machiavellian discussion of the conflicts between personal integrity and service, for example, is summarised in the three rules that the courtier must not 'waite upon or serve a wycked and naughtye person'; must not 'seeke to come up by any naughtie or subtill practise'; and must not 'committ any mischevous or wicked fact at the wil and commaundement of his Lorde' (p. 370; compare pp. 123–7). Of course, there may be an element of censorship here: the high moral tone of these recommendations is characteristic of Hoby's presentation of *The Courtier*, and reveals his affinities with Tudor writers on education like Sir Thomas Elyot or Roger Ascham, who championed the adoption in England of the kind of broad-ranging humanistic education Castiglione recommends for the courtier as a means of reforming and regenerating English political and cultural life.

hoby's preface shows the same keen sense of the social benefits of humanist learning; and it is in a tone of patriotic pride that he announces that, through his agency, Castiglione's courtier 'is beecome an Englishman'.

What kind of Englishman does the courtier make? Hoby is a scrupulous and sensitive translator, and his *Courtyer* is a remarkable achievement, one of the first English translations that can be considered a classic in its own right. It does not, however – as it scarcely could – entirely reproduce the flavour of the Italian original: despite his stated intent to 'folow the very meaning and woordes of the Author', *The Courtier*'s English translator is working within such a different linguistic and cultural reality that the resulting translation is, inevitably, in some sense, a new work. Hoby's language is consistently more concrete than Castiglione's and often considerably more colourful: Castiglione's '*sciocchi*' ('fools') become 'untowardely asseheads'; and we find 'blind buzzards' for '*ciechi*' ('blind people'); 'too loving wormes' for '*troppo amorevoli*' ('over-affectionate') and, somewhat outrageously, 'arsiversy' for '*al contrario*' ('the wrong way round'). These cases are extreme ones, of course, but a similar, though more low-key, intensification of meaning can be found in translations like 'roote out' for '*levare*' ('remove'), 'thrust out wordes' for '*lassano venir le parole*' ('let words out') or 'as long as there is any meat styrring' for '*fin che in tutto non . . . sono levate ancora le vivande*' ('until all the food has been taken away'). The cumulative effect is of a work less sober and stately than the original, more vivid: a work in which the blows of fortune are withstood not so much with a 'courageous spirit' ('*valoroso animo*') as with a 'boulde stomake'.

These differences apart, there are few instances in Hoby's *Courtyer* of significant deviations from the sense of the original, except for occasional mistranslations which will be identified in my notes. One significant exception occurs on the last page of the dialogue, in the passage describing the courtiers' departure at dawn from the Duchess's apartments: where the original has the last exchange of banter taking place simply 'when they were about to leave the room' ('*quando erano per uscir dalla camera*'), Hoby's translation expands this into the phrase 'as they were now passing out at the great chambre doore'. The amendment is a good indication of one great merit of Hoby's translation, which comes through also in his brilliantly colloquial rendering of the speakers' repartee: that imaginative engagement with the scenes he is describing that gives his *Courtyer* an immediacy and vibrancy no modern translation can match.

VIRGINIA COX

References

1. For references, Castiglione and His Critics in this volume, note 8.
2. *Timber or Discoveries made upon Men and Matter* (1641), in *Works*, ed. C. H. Hereford and P. and E. Simpson (Oxford, 1954): 8, 632–3.
3. Lauro Martines, *Power and Imagination. City-States in Renaissance Italy* (New York, 1979): 329.

LIST OF PRINCIPAL SPEAKERS

Minor figures in the dialogue are identified in notes 26, 27, 29, 30, 78, 84, 95 and 198.

Aretino, Unico (1458–1535)

Bernardo Accolti, better known as Unico Aretino, was a Tuscan poet, the son of the humanist Benedetto Accolti. His skill at extemporising made him much in demand at the courts of Milan, Urbino and Mantua, where his much-vaunted doomed love for the Duchess of Urbino was a source of great amusement to the Marchioness Isabella d'Este.

Bari, Roberto da (d. *c.* 1513) ('M. Roberto')

Roberto dei Massimi was an Apulian nobleman, connected with the court of Mantua as well as that of Urbino. Affectionately characterised in *The Courtier* as a wit and gallant, he appears to have been a particularly close friend of Castiglione, who recommended him to his mother in a letter of 1511 as someone he loved 'like a brother'.

Bembo, Pietro (1470–1547) ('M. Peter')

Although a Venetian patrician and destined by family tradition to a political career in the Republic, Bembo instead made a spectacular career in the courts on the strength of his literary talents. After his Urbino period (1506–12), he was appointed to the prestigious office of Secretary to Pope Leo X; subsequently, after a long period of literary retirement in Padua, he returned to Rome in 1539 as a cardinal under Pope Paul III. Bembo was the most prominent literary figure of his age: a noted Latin stylist and chief proponent of the Ciceronianism attacked by Erasmus, and the author, in the vernacular, of a vastly influential corpus of Petrarchist love poetry and two important dialogues on love and on language and literary style (see notes 17 and 284). There is a portrait of him in later life by Titian in the National Gallery of Washington.

Bibbiena, Bernardo (1470–1520) ('M. Bernarde')

The lowest-born of the major speakers in the dialogue, the Florentine Bernardo Dovizi da Bibbiena made his career through the patronage of Giovanni de' Medici, whom he accompanied into exile from Florence in 1494. Bibbiena embarked on a diplomatic career in Rome during the papacy of Julius II and, by 1513, was in a position of sufficient power to engineer Giovanni's accession to the papacy as Leo X: a service for which he was rewarded with a cardinalate and the office of papal treasurer. Celebrated for his wit, Bibbiena was the author of an important early comedy *La Calandria* (1513). He is also remembered as a friend and patron of Raphael, a copy of whose portrait of him is in the Pitti Palace, Florence.

Canossa, Lodovico da (1475–1532) ('Count Lewis')

Canossa was a Veronese nobleman, related through his mother to Castiglione and to the Duchess of Urbino, whose court he joined in 1496. He made a spectacular career from 1513 as papal envoy to France, where he enjoyed the favour of King Francis I, who in 1516 gave him the Bishopric of Bayeux, one of the richest sees in France. This period marked the high point of his career: his relations with Pope Leo X soon deteriorated and, in 1520, he transferred to the service of the French king. Forced to retire from his diplomatic career through ill-health in 1528, he was deprived of the Bishopric of Bayeux and returned for his last years to Italy, forfeiting his right to his possessions in France.

Fregoso, Federico (1480–1541) ('Syr Fridericke' and other spelling variants)

Fregoso was the son of the Genoese statesman Agostino Fregoso and Gentile, an illegitimate daughter of Federico da Montefeltro, who took her children to live with her half-brother, Duke Guidobaldo of Urbino, after the family was exiled from Genoa in 1488. Like many of the Urbino courtiers, Fregoso made his career in the Church: he was appointed Archbishop of Salerno and Bishop of Gubbio in the period of *The Courtier* (1508–9) and towards the end of his life (1539) was made a cardinal by Pope Paul III.

Fregoso, Ottaviano (c. 1477–1524) ('L. Octavian')

The brother of Federico (see above), like him, he spent the first decade of the sixteenth century at the court of Urbino, where he had important military responsibilities. In 1513, with Spanish assistance, he became doge of his home city of Genoa, but, after secret negotiations with the French, he renounced the title for that of viceroy to Francis I. Fregoso was captured by the Imperial forces under the Marquis of Pescara after the French defeat at Bicocca in 1522 and imprisoned in Ischia, where he died two years later, despite the efforts of, among others, Castiglione and the Duchess of Urbino to secure his release.

Frigio, Niccolò ('Frisio', 'Phrisio')
Frigio was a courtier of Pope Julius II, of German origin, who in 1510 became a Carthusian monk in Naples. A letter addressed to him by Castiglione, probably from the period in which *The Courtier* is set, confirms that he held the misogynist sentiments attributed to him in Book III of the dialogue.

Gonzaga, Cesare (1475–1512) ('L. Cesar')
Cesare Gonzaga was a member of a minor branch of the ruling family of Mantua, and related to both Castiglione and the Duchess of Urbino. A diplomat and poet (he collaborated with Castiglione on the pastoral *Thyrsis* of 1506), he died in Bologna in 1512, fighting the French.

Gonzaga, Elisabetta (c. 1471–1526) ('The Dutchesse')
Elisabetta was the sister of Francesco Gonzaga, Marquis of Mantua, and, from 1486, the wife of Guidobaldo da Montefeltro. She was much respected by her contemporaries for her virtue and the dignity with which she withstood her misfortunes, including two periods of exile and a childless marriage to the reputedly impotent Guidobaldo. There is a portrait of her, by an unknown artist, in the Uffizi, Florence.

Medici, Giuliano de' (1479–1516) ('L. Julian')
The youngest son of Lorenzo de' Medici ('il Magnifico'), Giuliano was in exile with the rest of his family from 1494 and resident in Urbino on a near-permanent basis from 1505 to 1512. After his brother Giovanni's accession to the papacy as Leo X in 1513, Giuliano was made lord of Florence; in 1515, he married Philiberte of Savoy, an aunt of Francis I of France, and was made Duke of Nemours. A cultivated man and a patron of the arts, he was the original dedicatee of Machiavelli's *Prince*, though his brief political career showed him to be very far from the kind of ruthless figure Machiavelli admired. There is a portrait of him by Allori in the Uffizi, Florence.

Ortona, Morello de' Ricciardi da ('M. Morello')
Little is known about this figure, characterised with a certain irony in *The Courtier* as a rather crusty aging gallant, though there is evidence that he held a position of some prominence at Urbino as one of Guidobaldo's military lieutenants.

Pallavicino, Gaspare (1486–1511) ('L. Gaspar' 'L. Gasper')
A Lombard nobleman, Pallavicino was, with Francesco Maria

della Rovere, one of the youngest members of the circle portrayed in *The Courtier*, and is characterised as impetuous, provocative and outspoken.

Pio, Emilia (d. 1528) ('L. Emilia')

Emilia Pio came from a noble Emilian family famed for its learning and patronage of the arts: the poet Veronica Gambara was her niece, the humanist Alberto Pio her cousin. She came to Urbino in 1487, on her marriage to Antonio da Montefeltro, the illegitimate son of Duke Federico, and remained at Urbino after her husband's death in 1500, the inseparable companion of the Duchess. The liveliness and caustic wit attributed to her in *The Courtier* are testified by other sources, and it is tempting to believe the legend that she died refusing the sacraments and disputing a passage of Castiglione's newly published dialogue with another of its speakers, Lodovico da Canossa.

Francesco Maria della Rovere (1490–1538) ('L. Generall')

Francesco Maria della Rovere was the son of Duke Guidobaldo's sister Giovanna and of Giovanni della Rovere, the younger brother of Pope Julius II. In 1502, he was made Prefect of Rome: the title by which he is referred to in the dialogue. Francesco Maria was adopted as heir by the childless Guidobaldo and succeeded to the Duchy in 1508, succeeding Guidobaldo, as well, as Captain-General of the papal army. He was notorious for two murders: that of the lover of his widowed sister in 1507 and that of Cardinal Alidosi in 1511 (see note 151): a crime later used by Pope Leo X as a pretext for depriving him of his Dukedom in 1516 (he was restored to it in 1522). There is a portrait of him in later life by Titian in the Uffizi, Florence.

NOTE ON THE TEXT

No manuscript of Hoby's *Courtyer* is known. The text reproduced here is that of the first edition, published by William Seres in 1561, in the accurate transcription made by Sir Walter Raleigh for his edition of the dialogue in the Tudor Translations series, published in London by David Nutt, in 1900. It differs from the text of some other modern editions based on the edition of John Wolfe (London, 1588), which incorporates numerous – and sometimes very unhappy – editorial amendments. The only amendment that has been made to Raleigh's text is the addition of the chapter divisions that have become conventional in modern Italian editions of the dialogue and that have become the standard means of reference in secondary literature. Hoby's occasional mistranslations are noted in the footnotes, and words and phrases that may present difficulties for modern readers are elucidated by means of a literal translation of the relevant passage in the Italian original.

THE BOOK OF
THE COURTIER

To the Reader.

These royall kinges, that reare up to the skye
Their Palaice tops, and decke them all with gold:
With rare and curious woorkes they feed the eye:
And showe what riches here great Princes hold.
A rarer work and richer far in worth,
Castilios hand presenteth here to the,
No proud ne golden Court doth he set furth
But what in Court a Courtier ought to be.
The Prince he raiseth houge and mightie walles,
Castilio frames a wight of noble fame:
The kinge with gorgeous Tyssue claddes his halles,
The Count with golden vertue deckes the same,
Whos passing skill lo Hobbies pen displaise
To Brittain folk, a work of worthy praise.

The LORD HENRY HASTINGES[2]
sonne and heire apparant to the noble
Erle of Huntyngton.

Themistocles the noble Athenien[3] in his banishement
entertayned moste honourablie with the king of Persia,
willed upon a time to tell his cause by a spokesman,
compared it to a piece of tapistrie, that beyng spred
abrode, discloseth the beautie of the woorkemanship,
but foulded together, hideth it, and therfore
demaunded respite to learne the Persian tunge to tell his
owne cause: Right so (honorable Lorde) this Courtier
hath long straid about this realme, and the fruite of him
either little, or unperfectly received to the commune
benefite: for either men skilful in his tunge have delited
in him for their owne private commoditie, or elles he
hath eftsones spoken in peecemeale by an interpreter to
suche as desired to knowe his mynde, and to practise his
principles: the which how unperfect a thing it is,
Themystocles and experience teache. But nowe, though
late in deede, yet for al that at length, beside his three
principal languages, in the which he hath a long time
haunted all the Courtes of Christendome,[4] hee is
beecome an Englishman (whiche many a longe tyme
have wyshed, but fewe attempted and none atchieved)
and welwilling to dwell in the Court of Englande, and in
plight to tel his own cause. In whose commendation I
shall not neede to use any long processe of woordes, for
he can so well speak for himself, and answere to the
opinion men have a long time conceived of him, that
whatsoever I shoulde write therein, were but labour in
waste, and rather a diminishing, then a setting foorth of
his woorthinesse, and a great deale better it were to
passe it over with silence, then to use briefenesse. Onely
for the litle acquaintaunce I have with him, and for the
general profit is in him, my desier is he should nowe at
his firste arrivall, a newe man in this kinde of trade,
be well entertained and muche honoured. And

forsomuche as none, but a noble yonge Gentleman, and
trayned up all his life time in Court, and of worthie
qualities, is meete to receive and enterteine so worthy a
Courtier, that like maye felowship and gete estimation
with his like, I do dedicate him unto your good
lordeship, that through your meanes, and under your
patronage he maye be commune to a greate meany. And
this do I not, for that I suppose you stande in neede of
any of his instructions, but partly because you may see
him confirme with reason the Courtly facions, comely
exercises, and noble vertues, that unawares have from
time to time crept in to you, and already with practise
and learning taken custome in you: and partly to gete
him the more aucthoritie and credite throughe so
honorable a Patrone. For no doubt, if you beseene
willingly to embrace him, other yonge and Courtly
Gentlemen will not shonn hys company: and so both he
shall gete him the reputation now here in Englande
which he hath had a good while since beyonde the sea,
in Italy, Spaine and Fraunce, and I shal thinke my smal
travayle wel imployed and sufficiently recompensed.
The honour and entertainment that your noble
Auncestours shewed Castilio the maker, whan he was
in this realme to be installed knight of the Order for the
Duke his Maister,[5] was not so muche as presently both
he, and this his handywoorke shall receive of you.
Generally ought this to be in estimation with all degrees
of men: for to Princes and Greate men, it is a rule to rule
themselves that rule others, and one of the bookes that a
noble Philosopher exhorted a certaine kyng to provide
him, and diligently to searche, for in them he shoulde
finde written suche matters, that friendes durst not utter
unto kinges:[6] To men growen in yeres, a pathway to the
behoulding and musing of the minde, and to whatsoever elles is meete for that age: To yonge Gentlemen, an
encouraging to garnishe their minde with morall
vertues, and their bodye with comely exercises, and
both the one and the other with honest qualities to
attaine unto their noble ende: To Ladyes and Gentle-
women, a mirrour to decke and trimme themselves with
vertuous condicions, comely behaviours and honest
enterteinment toward al men: And to them all in
general, a storehouse of most necessary implements for

the conversacion, use, and training up of mans life with
Courtly demeaners. Were it not that the auncientnesse
of tyme, the degree of a Consul, and the eloquence of
Latin stile in these our daies beare a greate stroke, I
knowe not whether in the invention and disposition of
the matter, as Castilio hath folowed Cicero, and
applyed to his purpose sundrye examples and pithie
sentences out of him, so hee maye in feate conveyaunce
and lyke trade of writing, be compared to him: but well
I wotte for renowme among the Italians, he is not
inferiour to him. Cicero an excellent Oratour, in three
bookes of an Oratour unto his brother, facioneth such a
one as never was, nor yet is like to be: Castilio an
excellent Courtier, in thre bookes of a Courtyer unto his
deere friende, facioneth such a one as is harde to finde
and perhappes unpossible. Cicero bringeth in to dispute
of an Oratour, Crassus, Scevola, Antonius, Cotta,
Sulpitius, Catulus, and Cesar his brother, the noblest
and chiefest Oratours in those dayes: Castilio to reason
of a Courtier, the Lorde Octavian Fregoso, Syr
Fridericke his brother, the Lorde Julian de Medicis, the
L. Cesar Gonzaga, the L. Francescomaria Della
Roveré, Count Lewis of Canossa, the L. Gaspar
Pallavicin, Bembo, Bibiena, and other most excellent
Courtiers, and of the noblest families in these dayes in
Italy, whiche all afterwarde became Princes,
Cardinalles, Bishoppes and greate Lordes, and some yet
in lyfe.[7] Both Cicero and Castilio professe, they folowe
not any certayne appointed order of preceptes or rules,
as is used in the instruction of youth, but call to
rehearsall, matters debated in their times too and fro in
the disputacion of most eloquent men and excellent
wittes in every woorthy qualitie, the one company in the
olde tyme assembled in Tusculane, and the other of late
yeeres in the newe Palaice of Urbin. Where many most
excellent wittes in this realme have made no lesse of this
boke, then the Great Alexander did of Homer, I cannot
sufficiently wonder that they have not all this while
from tyme to tyme done a commune benefite to profite
others as well as themselves. In this pointe (I knowe not
by what destinye) Englishemen are muche inferiour to
well most all other Nations: for where they set their
delite and bende themselves with an honest strife of

matching others, to tourne into their mother tunge, not onely the wittie writinges of other languages, but also of all the Philosophers, and all Sciences both Greeke and Latin, our men weene it sufficient to have a perfecte knowledge, to no other ende, but to profite themselves, and (as it were) after muche paynes in breaking up a gap, bestow no lesse to close it up againe, that others maye with like travaile folowe after. And where our learned menne for the moste part holde opinion, to have the sciences in the mother tunge, hurteth memorie and hindreth lerning, in my opinion, they do full yll consider from whence the Grecians first, and afterwarde the Latins fet their knowledge. And without wading to any farther reasons that might be alleaged, yf they will marke well the trueth, they shall see at this daye, where the Sciences are most tourned into the vulgar tunge, there are best learned men, and comparing it wyth the contrarie, they shall also finde the effectes contrarie. In Italye (where the most translation of authors is) not onely for Philosophy, Logike, Humanitie and all liberall Sciences bothe in Greeke and Latine (leaving a parte Barbarus, Naugerius, Sannazarus, Bembus, Lazarus[8] and the rest that of very late dayes floryshed) Genua, Tomitanus, Robertellus, Manutius, Piccolhomineus,[9] are presently verye singular, and renowmed throughout all Christendome: but also for the same in the vulgar tunge with litle or no sight at al in the Latin, Aretino, Gelli[10] (a tayler in Florence) the L. Victoria Columna, the L. Dionora Sanseverina, the L. Beatrice Loffreda, Veronica Gambera, Virginea Salvi[11] and infinite other men and women are moste famous throughout Italy, whose divine woorkes and excellent stile bothe in rime and prose geve a sufficient testimonye, not onely of their profounde knowledge and noble wit, but also that knowledge may be obtained in studying onely a mannes owne native tunge. So that to be skilfull and exercised in authours translated, is no lesse to be called learning, then in the very same in the Latin or Greeke tunge. Therefore the translation of Latin or Greeke authours, doeth not onely not hinder learning, but it furthereth it, yea it is learning it self, and a great staye to youth, and the noble ende to the whiche they oughte to applie their wittes, that with diligence and studye have attained a

perfect understanding, to open a gap for others to folow
their steppes, and a vertuous exercise for the unlatined
to come by learning, and to fill their minde with the
morall vertues, and their body with civyll condicions,
that they maye bothe talke freely in all company, live
uprightly though there were no lawes, and be in a
readinesse against all kinde of worldlye chaunces that
happen, whiche is the profite that commeth of
Philosophy. And he said wel that was asked the
question, How much the learned differed from the
unlearned. 'So much' (quoth he) 'as the wel broken and
ready horses, from the unbroken.' Wherefore I wote not
how our learned men in this case can avoide the saying
of Isocrates, to one that amonge soundrye learned
discourses at Table spake never a woorde: 'Yf thou bee
unlearned, thou dooest wiselye: but yf thou bee learned,
unwyselye,' as who should saye, learnyng is yll
bestowed where others bee not profited by it. As I
therefore have to my smal skil bestowed some labour
about this piece of woorke, even so coulde I wishe with
al my hart, profounde learned men in the Greeke and
Latin shoulde make the lyke proofe, and everye manne
store the tunge accordinge to hys knowledge and delite
above other men, in some piece of learnynge, that we
alone of the worlde maye not bee styll counted barbarous in oure tunge, as in time out of minde we have
bene in our maners. And so shall we perchaunce in time
become as famous in Englande, as the learned men of
other nations have ben and presently are. And though
the hardnesse of this present matter be suche, and myne
unskylfulnesse to undertake this enterprise so greate,
that I myghte with good cause have despaired to bringe
to an ende it, that manye excellente wittes have
attempted, yet coulde I not chouse but yelde to the
continual requestes and often perswasions of many
yong gentlemen, which have may chaunce an opinion
that to be in me, that is not in deed, and unto whom in
any reasonable matter I were skilfull in, neyther I coulde
nor ought of duetie to wante in fulfillyng their desire.
Notwithstanding a great while I forbare and lingered
the time to see if anye of a more perfect understanding
in the tunge, and better practised in the matter of the
booke (of whom we want not a number in this realm)

woulde take the matter in hande, to do his countrey so great a benefite: and this imagination prevailed in me a long space after my duetie done in translating the thirde booke (that entreateth of a Gentlewoman of the Courte) perswaded therto, in that I was enfourmed, it was as then in some forwardness by an other, whose wit and stile was greatly to be allowed, but sins prevented by death he could not finish it. But of late beeyng instantly craved upon a fresh, I whetted my stile and settled my self to take in hand the other three bookes (that entreat of the perfection of a Gentilman of the Court) to fulfill their peticion in what I am able, having time and leyser therto, the which I have done, though not in effect, yet in apparance and that in a great deale shorter time, then the hardness of the matter required. And where it shall not perhappes throughly please by reason my smalle understandyng in the tung, and less practise in the matters herin conteined, is not of force to give it the brightness and full perfection in this our tung that it hath in the Italian, it shal suffice yet that I have showed my self obedient in the respect a manne ought to have toward his betters: and no more can they avoid the blame to charge me withall, then I to undertake it. Beside that, I have declared my good will and well meaning no less then if my counning were greater, and could extend much farther. But paraventure the rudeness of this shall be an encouragyng of some other to give the onset upon other matters with a better ripeness of style and much more aptness, and so shall this yet somewhat profit both wayes. But the estimation it must gete by your Honour, is the principall cause that setteth it out, and maketh it worne with the handes of heedfull readers: for in case you cheerfullye receive it, men will recken it good: yf you alow it, worthy to be practised: yf you commend it, woorthie to pass from hand to hand. Therfore emong the other good opinions men generally houlde of you, let it not be the least, that they may houlde also no less of this that you alowe and commende. And so shall you show undeserved kindness, I, bounden dutie, and all others good will to imbrace and to welcome it out of Italy into Englande. And thus shall Castilio be esteamed such a one as he is indeede, and wexe familiar with all men, that of late was knowen of

verie fewe, and so mangled wyth varietye of judgementes, that he was (in a maner) maymed, and lost a
good peece of his estimation. But in case judgementes
now feint, or mine interpretation seeme not pithie but
rude, not proper, but colde, there is no more imperfection in this *Courtier*, then in Cirus himself in the
translation of Xenophon into the Italian[12] or anie other
tung, the one as necessarie and proper for a Gentilman
of the Court, as the other for a king. And I shall desire
my labour may so be taken well in worth, as I have
endevoured my self to folow the very meaning and
woordes of the Author, without being mislead by
fansie, or leaving out any percell one or other, wherof I
knowe not how some interpreters of this booke into
other languages can excuse themselves, and the more
they be conferred, the more it will perchaunce
appeere.[13] Wherfore receive you this, as a token of my
good will, and so receive it, that the frute, what ever it
be, maye be acknowleaged at your handes: and you,
pass the expectation of men in this, as in all other
thinges, which, no doubt, is very great of you: and I, to
acknowleage this benifit, where my habilitie stretcheth
to nothyng elles, shall at the least evermore wishe unto
your Lordshipp longe lief, that you may go forwarde, as
you do, in these beginninges, whiche promise a luckie
ende, to the honour of your self, comefort of your
friendes, and forwardness of the commune weale of
your countrey. 1556. Your L. most bounden,

THOMAS HOBY

A LETTER OF SYR J. CHEEKES[14]
To his loving frind Mayster
THOMAS HOBY

For your opinion of my gud will unto you as you wriit, you can not be deceived: for submitting your doinges to mi judgement, I thanke you: for taking this pain of your translation, you worthilie deserv great thankes of all sortes. I have taken sum pain at your request cheflie in your preface, not in the reading of it for that was pleasaunt unto me boath for the roundnes of your saienges and welspeakinges of the saam, but in changing certein wordes which might verie well be let aloan, but that I am verie curious in mi freendes matters, not to determijn, but to debaat what is best. Whearin, I seek not the besines haplie bi truth, but bi mijn own phansie, and shew of goodnes.

I am of this opinion that our own tung shold be written cleane and pure, unmixt and unmangeled with borowing of other tunges, wherin if we take not heed by tijm, ever borowing and never payeng, she shall be fain to keep her house as bankrupt. For then doth our tung naturallie and praisablie utter her meaning, when she bouroweth no counterfeitness of other tunges to attire her self withall, but useth plainlie her own, with such shift, as nature, craft, experiens and folowing of other excellent doth lead her unto, and if she want at ani tijm (as being unperfight she must) yet let her borow with suche bashfulnes, that it mai appeer, that if either the mould of our own tung could serve us to fascion a woord of our own, or if the old denisoned wordes could content and ease this neede, we wold not boldly venture of unknowen wordes. This I say not for reproof of you, who have scarslie and necessarily used whear occasion serveth a strange word so, as it seemeth to grow out of the matter and not to be sought for: but for mijn own defens, who might be counted overstraight a deemer of thinges, if I gave not thys accompt to you, mi freend and wijs, of mi marring this your handiwork. But I am called awai, I prai you pardon mi shortnes, the rest of mi saienges should be but praise and exhortacion in this your doinges, which at moar leisor I shold do better. From my house in Woodstreete the 16 of July, 1557.

Yours assured

JOAN CHEEK

Francesco-
maria della
Roveré.

After the Lorde Guidubaldo of Montefeltro Duke of
Urbin was departed out of this life, certein other
Gentilmen and I that had bine servauntes to him,
continued in servyce wyth Duke Francesco-maria Della
Roveré hys heire and successor in the state: and whyle
the savour of the vertues of Duke Guidubaldo was fresh
in my mynde, and the great delite I took in those yeeres
in the loving companie of so excellent Personages as
then were in the Court of Urbin: I was provoked by the
memorie therof to write these bookes of the *Courtier*.
The which I accomplished in a fewe dayes, myndinge in
time to amende those faultes that spronge of the desire
that I had speedilie to paye this debt. But fortune now
manie yeeres hath always kept me under in suche
continuall travayles, that I coulde never gete leyser to
bringe it to the passe that my feeble judgement might be
throughlie satisfied withall. At such time therfore as I
was in Spayne, being advertised out of Italy how the

L. Vittoria
Colonna.

Lady Vittoria Colonna Marquesse of Pescara,[16] unto
whom in foretime I had graunted a Copie of this booke,
contrarie to her promise, had made a great part of it to
be copied out: it greeved me somwhat whether I would
or no, standinge in doubt of the sundrie inconveniences
that in the like cases may happen. Yet had I a hope that
the witt and wisdome of that Lady (whose troth I have
alwaies had in reverence, as a matter from above) was
sufficient to provide, not to be harmfull unto me my
beeinge obedient to her commaundement. At last I hard
an yncklinge that part of the booke was rief in Naples in
many mens handes: and as men are always desirous of
noveltie, it was thought that they attempted to imprint
it. Wherfore I, amased at this mischaunce, determined
wyth my self to overlooke by and by that litle in the
booke that time served me therto, with entent to set it

abrode, thinking it lesse hurtful to have it somwhat corrected with mine owne hande, then much mangled with an other mannes. Therfore to have this my pourpose take effect, I tooke in hande to reade it over afresh, and sodeinlie at the first blush by reason of the title, I tooke no litle grief, which in proceadinge forward encreased much more, remembringe that the greater part of them that are brought in to reason, are now dead. For beside those that are mentioned in the Proheme of the last booke, M. Alphonsus Ariosto him self is dead, unto whom the booke was dedicated, a noble yonge Gentilman, discreete, full of good condicions, and apt unto every thing meete for one livinge in court. Likewise Duke Julian de Medicis, whose goodnesse and noble Courtesy deserved to have bene a longer time enjoyed of the world. Also M. Bernard, Cardinall of S. Maria in Portico, who for his livelie and pleasant promptness of witt, was most acceptable unto as manie as knew him, and dead he is. The Lord Octavian Fregoso is also dead, a man in oure tymes verie rare, of a most noble courage, of a pure lief, full of goodnesse, witt, wisdome and Courtesie, and a verie frende unto honour and vertue, and so worthy prayse, that his verie ennemies could say none other of hym, then what sounded to his renoume: and the mishappes he hath borne out with great steadinesse, were sufficient inoughe to geve evidence, that fortune, as she hath alwayes bene, so is she in these dayes also an enemie to vertue. There are dead in like maner manie other that are named in this boke, unto whom a man wold have thought that nature had promised a verie longe lief. But the thinge that should not be rehersed wythout teares is, that the Dutchesse she is also dead. And if my minde be troubled with the losse of so manye frindes and good Lordes of myne, that have left me in this lief, as it were in a wildernes full of sorrow, reason would it should with much more grief beare the heavinesse of the Dutchesse death, then of al the rest, bicause she was more woorth then all the rest, and I was much more bounde unto her then unto all the rest. Therfore for leesinge time to bestowe that of dutye I ought upon the memorye of so excellent a Ladye, and of the rest that are no more in lief, provoked also by the jeopardye of the

M. Alphonsus Ariosto.

Duke of Nemours.

Cardinal of S. Maria in Portico.

Duke of Genua.

Dutchesse of Urbin.

booke, I have made him to be imprinted, and setforth in such sort, as the shortnes of time hath served me. And bicause you had no acqueintance, neither with the Dutches, nor with any of the rest that are dead, saving only with Duke Julian, and with the Cardinal of S. Maria in Portico, while they lived, therfore to the entent, in what I can do, you may have acqueintance with them after their death, I send unto you this booke, as a purtraict in peinctinge of the Court of Urbin: not of the handiwoorke of Raphael, or Michael Angelo, but of an unknowen peincter, and that can do no more but draw the principall lines, without settingfurth the truth with beawtifull coulours, or makinge it appeere by the art of Prospective that it is not. And wher I have enforced my self to setforth together with the communication the propreties and condicions of such as are named in it, I confess I have not only not fully expressed, but not somuch as touched the vertues of the Dutchesse. Bicause not onlye my stile is unsufficient to express them, but also mine understanding to conceive them. And if in this behalf, or in anie other matter woorthy reprehention (as I know well there want not manie in the booke) fault be found in me, I will not speake against the truth. But bicause men somtime take such delite in finding fault, that they find fault also in that deserveth not reproof, unto some that blame me bicause I have not folowed Boccaccio,[17] nor bound my self to the maner of the Tuscane speach used nowadayes, I will not let to say, for all Boccaccio was of a fine witt, according to those times, and in some part writt with great advisement and diligence: yet did he write much better whan he lett him self be guided with witt and his owne naturall inclination, without anie other maner studie or regarde to polish his writinges, then whan with al travaile and bent studye he enforced him self to be most fine and eloquent. For his verie favourers affirme that in his own matters he was far deceived in judgement, litle regarding such thinges as have gotten him a name, and greatlye esteaminge that is nothing woorth. Had I then folowed that trade of writing which is blamed in him by such as praise him in the rest, I could not have eschewed the verye same reprooffes that are laied to Boccaccio himself as touching this. And I had deserved somuch the more, for that his errour was then, in beleavyng he did well, and mine should be nowe, in knowinge I do amisse. Again if I had folowed that trade which is reckened of many to be good, and was litle regarded of him, I should appeere in folowing it to disagree from the judgement of him whom I folowed: the which thing (in mine opinion) were an inconvenience. And beeside yf this respect had not moved me, I could not folowe him in the matter, forsomuch as he never wrott any thing in treatise like unto these bookes of the *Courtier*: and in the tunge, I ought not in mine advise, bicause the force or rule of speach doeth consist more in use, then in anye thinge els: and it is always a vice to use woordes that are not in commune speach. Therfore it was not meete I should have used many that are in Boccaccio, which in his time were used, and now are out of use emonge the Tuscanes them selves. Neyther would I binde my self to the maner of the Tuscane tunge in use nowe a dayes, bicause the practising emonge sundrye Nations, hath alwayes bene of force to transport from one to an other (in a maner) as merchaundise, so also new woordes, which afterward remaine or decaye, according as they are admitted by custome or refused. And this beside the record of auntient writers, is to be evidently seene in Boccaccio, in whom there are so manie woordes French, Spanish, and provincial, and some perhappes not well understood of the Tuscanes in these dayes, that whoso woulde pick them out, should make the booke much the lesser. And bicause (in mine opinion) the kinde of speach of the other noble Cities of Italy, where there resorte men of wisdome, understandinge and eloquence, which practise great matters of government of states, of letters, armes, and diverse affayres, ought not altogether to be neglected for the woordes whiche in these places are used in commune speach: I suppose that they maye be used welinough, writing such as have a grace and comlynesse in the pronuntiation, and communly counted good and of propre signification, though they be not Tuscane, and have also their origion out of Italy. Beeside this in Tuscane they use many woordes cleane corrupte from the Latin, the which in Lumbardye and in the other partes of Italy remaine wholl and without any

THE
EPISTLE
OF THE
AUTHOR

New
Woordes.

Derived
wordes from
the Latin.

chaunge at al, and they are so universallye used of everye man, that of the best sorte they are allowed for good, and of the commune people understood with out difficulty. Therfore I thinke I have committed no errour at all, yf in writing I have used any of these, and rather taken the wholl and pure woord of mine owne Countrey, then the corrupt and mangled of an other. Neyther doeth that rule seeme good unto me, where many say the vulgar tung, the lesse it is like unto the Latin, the more beawtiful it is: and I can not perceive why more authoritie should consist in one custome of speach, then in an other. For if Tuscane be sufficient to authorise corrupt and mangled Latin woordes, and to geve them so great a grace, that mangled in such sort everye man may use them for good (the which no man denieth) should not Lumbardy or any other countrey have the authoritye to allow the very Latin woordes that be pure, sounde, propre and not broken in any part so, but they may be well borne: and assuredly as it may be called a rash presumption to take in hand to forge new wordes, or to set up the olde in spite of custome: so is it no lesse, to take in hande against the force of the same custome to bring to naught, and (as it were) to burye alive such as have lasted nowe many yeeres, and have ben defended from the malice of the time with the shield of use, and have preserved their estimation and dignitye, whan in the warres and turmoiles of Italy, alterations were brought up both of the tunge, buildinges, garmentes and maners. And beeside the hardnesse of the matter, it seemeth to be (as it were) a certein wickednesse. Therfore where I have not thought good in my writing to use the wordes of Boccaccio which are used no more in Tuscane, nor to binde my self to their law that think it not lawful to use them that the Tuscanes use not nowadayes, me thynke I ought to be held excused. But I suppose both in the matter of the booke and in the tunge, forsomuch as one tung may help an other, I have folowed Authores asmuch woorthie praise, as Boccaccio. And I beleave it ought not to be imputed unto me for an errour, that I have chosen to make my self rather knowen for a Lumbard, in speaking of Lumbard, then for no Tuscan, in speaking of tomuch Tuscan. Bicause I wil not do as

Theophrastus did, which for speaking tomuch the meere
Athenian tunge, was of a simple olde woman knowen
not to be of Athens.[18] But bycause in thys point there is
sufficyent talke in the first booke, I will make no more a
do. And to avoid al contention I confesse to my
faultfinders, that I have no knowleage in this their
Tuscan tunge so hard and secrete: and I say that I have
written it in mine owne, and as I speak, and unto such as
speake as I speake: and so I trust I have offended no
man. For I beleave it is forbed no man that is, to wryte
and speake in his owne tunge, neyther is anye man
bound to reade or heare that contenteth hym not.
Therfore if they will not reade my *Courtier*, they shall
offende me nothing at all. Other say, bicause it is so
hard a matter and (in a maner) unpossible to finde out a
man of such perfection, as I would have the Courtier to
be, it is but superfluous to write it: for it is a vaine thing
to teach that can not be learned. To these men I
answere, I am content, to err with Plato, Xenophon,
and M. Tullius,[19] leaving apart the disputing of the
intelligible world and of the Ideas or imagined fourmes:
in which number, as (according to that opinion) the
Idea or figure conceyved in imagination of a perfect
commune weale, and of a perfect king, and of a perfect
Oratour are conteined: so is it also of a perfect Courtier.
To the image wherof if my power could not draw nigh
in stile, so much the lesse peynes shall Courtiers have to
drawe nigh in effect to the ende and marke that I in
writing have set beefore them. And if with all this they
can not compasse that perfection, such as it is, which I
have endevoured to expresse, he that cummeth nighest
shall be the most perfect: as emong many Archers that
shute at one marke, where none of them hitteth the
pinn, he that is nighest is out of doubt better then the
rest. Some again say that my meaning was to facion my
self, perswading my self that all suche qualities as I
appoint to the Courtier are in me. Unto these men I will
not cleane deny that I have attempted all that my mynde
is the Courtier shoulde have knowleage in. And I thinke
who so hath not the knowleage of the thinges intreated
upon in this booke, how learned so ever he be, he can
full il write them. But I am not of so sclender a judgment
in knowing my self, that I wil take upon me to know

THE
EPISTLE
OF THE
AUTHOR
Cicero in
Bruto.

Courtier.

what soever I can wish. The defence therfore of these accusations and peraventure of many mo, I leave for this once, to the judgement of the commune opinion: bicause for the most part the multytude, though they have no perfect knowleage, yet do they feele by the instinct of nature a certein savour of good and ill, and can geve none other reason for it: one tasteth and taketh delite, an other refuseth and is against his stomake.

Therfore if the booke shall generally please, I wil count him good, and think that he ought to live: but if he shall displease, I will count him naught, and beleave that the memorye of him shall soone perish. And if for all this mine accusers will not be satisfied with this commune judgemente, let them content them selves with the judgement of time, which at length discovereth the privie faultes of every thing: and bicause it is father to truth and a judge without passion, it accustometh evermore to pronounce true sentence of the life or death of writynges.

THE FIRST BOOKE

OF THE COURTYER OF COUNT
BALDESSAR CASTILIO
UNTO MAISTER
ALPHONSUS ARIOSTO[20]

[I] I have a longe time doubted with my self (most loving M. Alphonsus) which of the two were harder for me, either to denye you the thinge that you have with suche instance manye tymes required of me, or to take it in hande: bicause on the one side me thoughte it a verye harde matter to denye anye thynge, especiallye the request beinge honest, to the personne whom I love deerlye, and of whom I perceyve my selfe ˙deerlye beloved. Againe on the other syde, to undertake an enterpryse whiche I do not knowe my selfe able to brynge to an end, I judged it uncomely for him that wayeth due reproofes so much as they oughte to be wayed. At length after muche debatynge, I have deter-mined to prove in this behalfe what ayde that affection and great desyre to please, can brynge unto my dilygence, whyche in other thynges is wonte to encreace the laboure of menne. You then require me to wryte, what is (to my thynkynge) the trade and maner of Courtyers, whyche is most fyttynge for a Gentilman that lyveth in the Court of Princes, by the whiche he maye have the knoweleage howe to serve them perfectlye in everye reasonable matter, and obtaine thereby favour of them and prayse of other men. Fynallye, of what sort he ought to be that deserveth to be called so perfect a Courtyer, that there be no wante in him: wherefore I, considering this kinde of request, say, that in case it shoulde not appeare to my selfe a greater blame to have you esteame me to be of smal friendshippe, then all other men of litle wysdome, I woulde have ryd my handes of this laboure, for feare leaste I shoulde bee counted rashe of all such as knowe, what a harde matter it is, emonge suche diversitye of maners, that are used in the Courtes of Christendome, to picke out the perfectest trade and way, and (as it were) the floure of this Courtiership. Because use maketh us manye times to delite in, and to set litle by the self same thinges: wherby somtime it proceadeth that maners, garmentes, cus-tomes, and facions whiche at sometyme have beene in price, becumme not regarded, and contrarywyse the not regarded, becumme of price. Therfore it is manifestlye to be descerned, that use hath greater force then reason, to brynge up newe inventions emonge us, and to abolishe the olde, of the whiche who so goeth about to judge the perfection, is often tymes deceyved. For which consideration, perceyvinge this and manye other lettes in the matter propounded for me to write upon, I am constreyned to make a peece of an excuse, and to open playnelye that this errour (yf it may be termed an errour) is commune to us both, that if anye blame happen to me about it, it may be also partned with you. For it ought to be reckned a no lesse offence in you to laye uppon me a burden that passeth my strengthe, then in me to take it upon me. Let us therfore at length settle oure selves to begin that is oure purpose and drifte, and (if it be possible) let us facion suche a Courtier, as the Prince that shalbe worthye to have him in his servyce, although hys state be but small, maye notwythstandynge be called a myghtye Lorde. We will not in these bookes folow any certaine order or rule of appointed preceptes, the whiche for the moste part is wont to be observed in the teaching of anye thinge whatsoever it be: but after the maner of men of olde time, renuinge a gratefull memorye, we will repeat certaine reasoninges that were debated in times past betwene men verye excellent for that purpose. And althoughe I was not there present, but at the time when they were debated, it was my chaunce to be in Englande,[21] yet soone after my retourne, I hearde them of a person that faythfullye reported them unto me. And I will endevoure my selfe, for so muche as my memorye wyll serve me, to call them perticularly to remembraunce, that you maye see what, men worthy greate commendacion, and unto whose judgement a man maye in everye poynt geve an undoubted credyt, have judged and beleved in this matter. Neyther shall we swarve from the pourpose to arryve in good order at the ende unto the whiche all oure communication is directed, yf wee disclose the cause of the reasoninges that hereafter folowe.

Situation of Urbin.

[II] As everye man knoweth the lytle Citye of Urbin is sytuated upon the side of the Appennine (in a maner) in the middes of Italy towardes the Golf of Venice. The

which for all it is placed emonge hylles, and those not so
pleasaunt as perhappes some other that we behoulde in
manye places, yet in this point the element hathe bene
favourable unto it, that all aboute, the countrye is verye
plentyfull and full of fruites: so that beside the hol-
somenesse of aer, it is verye aboundant and stored wyth
all thinges necessarye for the lief of man. But amonge
the greatest felycityes that men can recken it to have, I
counte thys the chief, that now a longe tyme it hath
alwayes bene governed with very good Princes, although in the commune calamyties of the warres of
Italy it remayned also a season with out anye at all.[22]
But without searching further of this we maye make a
good proofe wyth the famous memorye of Duke
Fridericke,[23] who in his dayes was the light of Italy.
Neyther do we want true and verye large testimonies yet
remayninge of his wisdome, courtesye, justice, liberalitye, of his invincible courage and pollycy of warr. And
of this do his so many vyctoryes make proofe, chyeflye
his conquerynge of places impregnable, his sodeyne
redynesse in settynge forwarde to geve battaile, his
putting to flyght sundrye tymes wyth a small numbre,
verie great and puissaunte armyes, and never susteined
losse in any conflict: so that we may, not without cause,
compare hym to manye famous men of olde time. This
man emong his other deedes praisworthy, in the hard
and sharpe situation of Urbin buylt a Palaice, to the
opinion of many men, the fayrest that was to be founde
in all Italy, and so fornished it with everye necessary
implement belonging therto, that it appeared not a
palaice, but a Citye in fourme of a palaice, and that not
onelye with ordinarie matters, as Silver plate, hanginges
for chambers of verye riche cloth of golde, of silke and
other like, but also for sightlynesse: and to decke it out
withall, placed there a wonderous number of auncyent
ymages of marble and mettall, verye excellente peinctinges and instrumentes of musycke of all sortes, and
nothinge would he have there but what was moste rare
and excellent. To this with verye great charges he
gathered together a great number of most excellent and
rare bookes, in Greke, Latin and Hebrue, the which all
he garnished wyth golde and sylver, esteaming this to be
the chieffest ornament of his great palaice. [III] This

Mare
Adriaticum.

Duke
Frydericke.

The palaice
of Urbin.

duke then folowing the course of nature when he was
lxv. yeares of age, as he had lived, so did he end his lief
with glorye. And left Duke after him a childe of x.
yeares, havynge no more male, and wythout mother,
who hight Guidubaldo.[24] Thys chylde as of the state, so
did it appeare also that he was heyre of all his fathers
vertues: and sodenly wyth a marveylous towardnes
beeganne to promise so much of himselfe, as a manne
woulde not have thought possyble to be hoped of a man
mortall. So that the opinyon of men was, that of all
duke Friderickes notable dedes there was none greater
then that he begat suche a son. But fortune envyinge this
so great vertue, wythall her myght gainstoode this so
gloryous a beginnynge, in suche wyse that before duke
Guidubaldo was xx. yeares of age, he fell sicke of the
gout, the which encreasinge uppon him wyth most
bitter paynes, in a short tyme so nummed hym of all hys
members, that he coulde neyther stande on foote nor
move hymselfe. And in this maner was one of the beste
favoured and towardlyest personages in the world
deformed and marred in his greene age. And beside, not
satisfyed with thys, fortune was so contrarye to him in
all his pourposes, that verye sildome he brought to passe
any thynge to hys minde. And for all he had in him
moste wise counsayle, and an invincible courage, yet it
seemed that whatsoever he tooke in hande bothe in
feates of armes and in everye other thynge small or
greate, it came alwayes to yll successe. And of thys make
proofe his manye and dyvers calamityes, which he
always bore out with suche stoutenesse of courage, that
vertue never yelded to fortune. But wyth a boulde
stomake despising her stormes, lyved wyth great dig-
nytye and estimation emonge all men: in sickenesse, as
one that was sounde, and in adversitye, as one that was
most fortunate. So that for all he was thus diseased in
his bodye, he served in time of warre wyth most
honourable enterteinmente under the most famous
kinges of Naples, Alphonsus and Ferdinande the yonger. Afterward with Pope Alexander the VI. with the
lordes of Venice and Florence. And when Julius the II.
was created Pope, he was then made generall Captayne
of the Churche: at whych tyme proceadynge in hys
accustomed usage, he sett hys delyte above all thynges

Guidubaldo
Duke of
Urbin.

Troubled
with the
goute.

His ill lucke.

Hys service
with princes
and commune
weales.

to have hys house furnished with most noble and valyaunte Gentylmen, wyth whom he lyved very famylyarly, enjoying theyr conversation, wherein the pleasure whyche he gave unto other menne was no lesse, then that he receyved of other, because he was verye wel seene in both tunges, and together wyth a lovynge behavyour and plesauntnesse he had also accompanied the knowleage of infinite thinges. And beside this, the greatnesse of his courage so quickened hym, that where he was not in case with hys personne to practise the feates of Chivalrye, as he had done longe before, yet dyd he take verye great delyte to behoulde them in other men, and with his wordes sometyme correctinge, and otherwhyle praysinge everye man accordynge to hys desertes, he declared evydentlye howe greate a judgement he hadde in those matters. And upon this at Tylt, at Tourneye, in rydynge, in playinge at all sortes of weapon, also in inventing devyces, in pastymes, in musicke, fynallye in all exercises meete for noble Gentilmen, everye manne stryved to showe hymselfe suche a one, as myght deserve to bee judged woorthye of so noble an assemblye. [IV] Therfore were all the houres of the daye devyded into honourable and pleasaunt exercyses, aswell of the bodye as of the mydne. But because the Duke used continuallye, by reason of his infirmytye, soone after supper to go to his rest, everye man ordinarelye, at that houre drewe where the Dutchesse was, the Lady Elizabeth Gonzaga. Where also continuallye was the Lady Emilia Pia, who for that she was endowed with so livelye a wytt and judgement as you knowe, seemed the maistresse and ringe leader of all the companye, and that everye manne at her receyved understandinge and courage. There was then to be hearde pleasaunte communication and merye conceytes, and in every mannes countenaunce a manne myght perceyve peyncted a lovynge jocoundenesse. So that thys house truelye myght well be called the verye mansion place of Myrth and Joye. And I beleave it was never so tasted in other place, what maner a thynge the sweete conversation is that is occasioned of an amyable and lovynge companye, as it was once there. For leavynge aparte what honoure it was to all us to serve suche a Lorde, as he whom I declared unto you right

His propreties and qualityes.

Elizabeth Gonzaga dutchesse of Urbin.

L. Emilia Pia.

nowe, everye man conceyved in his minde an high contentacyon* everye tyme we came into the dutchesse sight. And it appeared that this was a chaine that kept all lincked together in love, in suche wise that there was never agrement of wyll or hearty love greater betweene brethren, then was there beetweene us all. The lyke was beetweene the women, with whom we hadde suche free and honest conversation, that everye manne myght commune, syt, daly, and laugh with whom he had

lusted. But such was the respect which we bore to the Dutchesse wyll, that the selfe same libertye was a verye great bridle. Neither was there anye that thought it not the greatest pleasure he coulde have in the worlde, to please her, and the greatest griefe to offende her. For this respecte were there most honest condicions coupled with wonderous great libertye, and devises of pastimes and laughinge matters tempred in her sight, besyde most wyttye jestes, with so comelye and grave a majesty, that the verye sober moode and greatnesse that dyd knyt together all the actes, woordes and gestures of the Dutchesse in jesting and laughynge, made them also that had never seene her in their lief before, to count her a verye greate Ladye. And all that came in her presence havyng this respect fyxed in their breast, it seemed she had made them to her becke: so that every man enforced himself to folowe this trade, takynge (as it were) a rule and ensample of faire condicions at the presence of so greate and so vertuous a Lady. Whose most excellent qualities I entend not nowe to expresse, for it is neyther my pourpose, and againe they are well inoughe knowen to the worlde, and muche better then I am able either with tunge or with pen to endite. And such as would perhaps have lien hid a space, fortune, as she that wondreth at so rare vertues, hath thought good with many adversities and temptatyons of miseries to disclose them, to make trial therby that in the tender breast of a woman, in companye wyth synguler beawtye, there can dwell wysdome, and stoutenes of courage, and all other vertues that in grave men them selves are most seldome. [V] But leavynge this apart, I say that the maner of all the Gentilmen in the house was

---

* contentacyon: pleasure, contentment.

immedyatelye after supper to assemble together where the dutchesse was. Where emonge other recreations, musicke and dauncynge, whiche they used contynuallye, somctyme they propounded feate questions,* otherwhyle they invented certayne wytty sportes and pastimes, at the devyse sometyme of one sometyme of an other, in the whych under sundrye covertes, often tymes the standers bye opened subtylly theyr imaginations† unto whom they thought beste. At other tymes there arrose other disputations of divers matters, or els jestinges with prompt inventions. Manye tymes they fell into pourposes,[25] as we nowe a dayes terme them, where in thys kynde of talke and debating of matters, there was wonderous great pleasure on all sydes: because (as I have sayde) the house was replenyshed wyth most noble wyttes. Emonge whych (as you knowe) were moste famous the Lord Octavian Fregoso, Sir Friderick his brother, the L. Julian de Medicis, M. Peter Bembo, the L. Cesar Gonzaga, Count Lewis of Canossa, the L. Gaspar Pallavicin, the L. Lodovicus Pius, M. Morello of Ortona, Peter of Naples, M. Robert of Bari, and infynyte other moste woorthye knyghtes and Gentylmen.[26] Beesyde these there were manye that for all ordinarilye they dwelled not there, yet spent they most of their tyme there, as, M. Bernard Bibiena, Unico Aretino, Johnchristopher Romano, Peter Mount, Therpander, M. Nicholas Phrisio,[27] so that thither ran continually poetes, musitiens, and al kinde of men of skyll, and the excellentest in every faculty that were in al Italy. [VI] After pope Iulius the II.[28] had with his owne presence by the ayde of the Frenchmen brought Bolonia to the obedyence of the Apostolyke Sea again, in the yeare MDVI. in hys retourn toward Roome he tooke Urbin in his way, where he was receaved as honorably as was possible, and with as sumptuous and costlye preparation, as coulde have bine in any other Citie of Italy whatsoever it be. So that beeside the Pope, all the Cardinalles and other Courtyers thought themselves throughly satisfied. And some there were that provoked

Noble personages in the Court of Urbin.

---

* feate questions: intriguing problems for discussion.
† opened subtylly theyr imaginations: revealed their thoughts in figurative language.

wyth the sweetenesse of this companye, after the Pope and the Court was departed, contynued manye dayes together in Urbin. At which time they did not onely proceade in their accustomed trade of disportinge and ordinary recreations, but also every man sett to his helpinge hande to augment them somewhat, and especially in pastymes, which they had up almost everye nyght. And the order therof was such, that assoone as they were assembled where the Dutches was, every man satt him downe at his will, or as it fell to his lot, in a circle together, and in sittinge were devyded a man and a woman, as longe as there were women, for alwayes (lightlye)* the number of men was farr the greater. Then were they governed as the Dutchesse thought best, whiche manye times gave this charge unto the L. Emilia.

So the daye after the Pope was departed, the companye beeinge gathered to the accustomed place, after muche pleasaunt talke, the Dutchesse pleasure was that the L. Emilia should beginne these pastimes: and she after a litle refusing of that charge, sayd in this maner: Syth it is your pleasure (Madam) I shall be she that must give the onsett in oure pastimes this night, bicause I ought not of reason disobey you, I thinke meete to propounde a pastyme,† whereof I suppose shall ensue little blame, and lesse travayle. And that shall be to have every man, as nigh as he can, propounde a devyse not yet hearde of, then shall we chuse out such a one as shall be thought meete to be taken in hande in this companye.

And after she had thus spoken, she tourned her unto the L. Gaspar Pallavicin, willynge him to propounde his: who immediatlye made answere: But first (madam) you must beeginne to propound yours.

Then saide the L. Emilia: I have alreadye done. But your grace must commaunde hym (Madam) to be obedient.

Then the Dutchesse laughynge: To thintent (quoth she) every man shal obey you, I make you my deputy, and give unto you all mine aucthority.

[VII] It is surely a great matter, aunswered the L.

Divises of pastimes.

---

* alwayes (lightlye): almost always.
† propounde a pastyme: suggest a game.

GASPAR, that it is alwaies lawfull for women to have this privilege, to be exempt and free from paines takyng, and truelye reason woulde we should in any wise knowe why.* But bicause I will not be he that shall geve example to disobey, I shal leave thys untill an other time, and will speake of that I am nowe charged withall, and thus I beginne. Mine oppinion is, that oure mindes, as in other thinges, so also in lovynge are diverse in judgemente, and therefore it chaunceth often tymes, that the thynge whyche is most acceptable unto one, is most abhorred of an other. Yet for all that they alwayes agree in that everye man counteth most deere the wight beloved. So that many times the overmuch affection in lovers doth so deceive their judgemente, that they weene the person whom they love, to be so garnished wyth all excellent vertues and wythout faulte, that he hath no peere in the worlde. But bycause the nature of man doth not admytte suche full perfectyons, and there is no mann that hath not some defaulte or want in hym, it can not be sayde that suche as these be are not deceyved, and that the lover doeth not become blynde as touchynge the beloved. I would therefore oure pastyme should be thys nyghte to have everye manne open what vertues he would principally the persone he loveth should be indowed with all. And seeyng it is so necessarilye that we all have some spotte, what vyce he woulde also have in hym: to see who can fynde out most prayse woorthye and manlye vertues, and most toller-able vyces, that shoulde be least hurtefull bothe to hym that loveth, and to the wyghte beloved.

After the L. Gaspar hadde thus spoken, the L. Emilia made a signe unto the Lady Constaunce Fregosa,[29] bicause she was next in order, to folow: who was now about to speak, whan the DUTCHESSE sodeinlye said: Seinge the L. Emilia will not take the paine to fynde out some pastime, reason willeth that the other Ladyes should be partakers of the same privilege, and be also fre from this burden for this night: especially seing there are so manye men in place, for assure your self we shall want no pastimes.

The L. Gaspars devise.

The L. Constance Fregosa.

---

* reason woulde we should in any wise knowe why: it would be very interesting to know the reason why.

So shall we do, aunswered the L. EMILIA, and puttinge the L. Constance to silence tourned her to the L. CESAR GONZAGA, that sat next her, commaunding him to speak, and thus he began: [VIII] Whoso wyll diligentlye consider all our doynges, he shall fynde always in them sundrye imperfections. And that happeneth, bicause nature doth varye, as well in this, as in all other thinges. Unto one she hath geven the lyght of reason in one thyng, and unto an other, in an other thyng. Therefore it commeth to passe, where one man knoweth that an other knoweth not, and is ignoraunte in the thyng that the other hath understandynge in, eche man doth easilye perceyve the errour of hys felow, and not hys owne, and we all think oure selves to be verye wyse and peradventure in that poynt most, wherein we are most foolysh. So that we have seene by experience in this house manye men whyche at the beegynnynge were counted most wise, in processe of tyme were knowen to be most foolysh. Whiche hath proceaded of no other thyng but of oure owne dilygence, lyke, as it is sayde to be in Pulia of them that are bitten with a Tarrantula, about whom men occupye manye instrumentes of musicke, and wyth sundrye sounes goe searchynge out, untyll the humor that maketh this dysease by a certayn concordance it hath wyth some of those sounes, feling it, doth sodeinly move, and so stirreth the pacient, that by that styrrynge he recovereth hys health agayne. In lyke maner we, whan we have felt some privie operacion of folye we provoke it so subtillye, and with suche sundry perswasions, and so divers wayes that at length we understand whether it tended. Afterward the humour knowen, we so stir it that always it is brought to the perfection of open foly. And some is wexed foolish in verses, some in musicke, some in love, some in daunsinge, some in makynge antiques,* some in rydinge, some in playnge at fence, everye man accordinge to the moine of his mettall, wherby hath ensued (as you know) marveylous great pastime. I houlde therfore for certeine, that in everye one of us there is some seede

The L. Cesar Gonzagas devise.

A kind of spiders, whiche beyng dyvers of nature cause divers effectes, some after their biting.

fal a singyng, some laugh, some wepe, some watche, some sweate: and this disease is onely cured with instrumentes of musick, whiche must never cease until the diseased beynge constrained with

---

* makynge antiques: devising *moresche* (the elaborate choreographed mimes popular in the period, often performed as interludes between the acts of plays).

of folye, the which beyng stirred may multiplye (in a maner) infinite. Therefore I would this night our pastime were to dispute upon this matter: and that everye man myght say his mynde, seeynge I must be openly foolysh, in what sort of foly I am foolysh, and over what matter, judginge it the issue for the sparkles of folye that are daylye sene to proceade from me. And let the lyke be sayd of all the rest, kepinge the order of oure devises, and let everye man do his best to grounde his opinion upon some sure signe and argument, and so by this our pastime shall everye one of us get profite, in that we shal know our defaultes, and then shall we the better take heede. And in case the veyne of folye whiche we shall discover, be so ranke that it shall appeare to us past remedy, we will set therto oure helpynge hande, and according to the doctrine of Frier Marian, wee shal gaigne a soule whiche shalbe no smal gaigne. At this devise there was much laughing, and none could refraine from speakinge. One sayde, I shoulde be founde foolysh in imagining. An other, in viewinge. An other sayde, he was alreadye become foolysh for love: and suck lyke matters.

the melodye thereof to fall a daunsinge with long exercise over-commeth the force of this poyson.

Frier Marian.

[IX] Then frier SERAPHIN[30] after his maner, laughing: This (quoth he) should be to tedious a matter. But if you wyll have a pretye pastime, let every man tel his opinion, how it cummeth that (in a maner) all women abhorre rattes, and love serpentes, and you shall see that none will hit upon it, but I, that knowe this misterye by a straunge means.

Frier Sera-phin.

And nowe began he to enter into his triflyng tales, but the L. Emilia commaunded him to silence, and over-scipping the Lady that satt there, made a signe to UNICO ARETINO that was next in order, and he without looking for anye more biddyng, I (quoth he) would gladlye be a judge of aucthoritye that I might with all kinde of tourment bolte out the truth of offenders: and that, to discover the deceytes of an ungrate woman, who with the eies of an angel, and hearte of a Serpent, never agreeth her tunge with her mynde, and with a feygned deceyvable compassion, purposeth nothyng els but to make Anatomie of hartes. Neither is there in all the sandie countrey of Libia to be found so venomous a serpent that is so desirous of mans bloud, as is this false

Unico Aret-inos devise.

creature. Which not onely for the sweetnesse of voice
and pleasant soune of woordes, but also for her eyes, for
her laughing, for her countenaunce, and for all her
gestures is a most perfect meremayden.[31] Therfore
seying it is not lawfull for me, as I would, to use chaines,
ropes, or fier, to understand a matter of trouth, my
desire is to compasse the knowledge of it with a miryc
pastyme, whiche is this: That every man shoulde
expresse his fansye what the S dothe signify that the
dutchesse carieth in her foreheade. For although this be
also an artificial covert, the better to beguile, perhappes
there may be an interpretacion whiche she never
thought upon. And who knoweth whether fortune,
with pity behoulding the tormentes of men, hath stirrid
her with this small token to discover against her wyll the
inwarde desire she hathe to slea and bury alyve in
calamitie hym that honoureth and serveth her. The
dutchesse laughed: and Unico, perceiving she would
have excused her self of thys interpretacion, No (quoth
he) speake you not (madam) for it is not your turne to
speake nowe.

The L. EMILIA then tourned her and sayd: M. Unico,
there is none of us all here that geveth not place to you in
everye thyng, and especiallye in knowynge the disposicion of the Dutchesse. And as you by your dyvyne wit
knowe her better then all the rest, so do you love her
better then al the rest, whych lyke byrdes of a feble
sight, that cannot looke stedfastlye into the circle of the
Sunne, cannot so well perceyve the perfection of it.
Therfore all laboure were in vaine in cleeryng of thys
doubt, savyng your judgement alone. Thys interprise
then is reserved onely to you, as unto him that alone can
brynge it to an ende, and none other.

Unico, after he had pawsed a while being stil called
upon to say his fansy, at length rehersed a rime upon the
aforesaide matter, expoundynge what signified the
letter S, the which many judged to be made at the first
sight. But bicause it was more witty and better knitt
then a man would have beleved the shortnes of time
required, it was thought he had prepared it before.

[X] So after mens favourable voyce geven in the
praise of this rime, and after sufficient talke, the L.
OCTAVIAN FREGOSO whose tourne was then next,

began in this sorte smilyng: My lordes, if I should say unto you that I never felt passion of love in my daies, I am sure the Dutchesse and the L. Emilia, althoughe they beleved it not in deede, yet would they make semblant to beleve it, and would saye that it proceded bicause I mistrusted I should never frame any woman to love me. The which trulye I have not hytherto proved with such instance, that of reason I should dispare to obtain it once. Neither have I forborne the doynge of it, bicause I set so much by my self and so litle by women, that I thinke none worthye to bestowe my love and service upon. But rather amased at the continual bewailings of some lovers, that with their palenes, sorow, and silence, it appeareth they have evermore their owne discomfort painted in their eyes. And if they speake, accompany-inge everye woorde with certeyne treblefolde syghes, they reason of nothing elles, but of teares, of tour-mentes, of desperacions, and of longyng for death. So that whansoever any sparckle of love hath beegonne to kyndle in my breast, I have by and by enforced my self wyth all dyligence to quenche it, not for anye hatred that I have conceyved agaynst women (as these Ladyes suppose) but for myne owne health. On the other side, I have knowen some other cleane contrarye to these sorowfull, whiche do not onelye avaunce and content theymselves with the cherefull lookes, lovinge woordes, and sweete countenances of their ladies, but also sauce their sorowes with sweetenesse, so that they count the debates, the angers and the disdeignes of them, moste sweete. Therefore these men seme unto me to be much more then happy, for whereas they fynde so muche sweetenesse in the amorous disdeignes, whiche some men recken much more bytter then death, I beleve in lovyng gestures they should feele that wonderfull blisse, whyche we seeke for in vayne in thys worlde. Therefore would I oure pastyme were this nyght to have everye manne shew, where there muste be a dysdeygne againste hym in the person beloved, what the cause should be that should make the persone conceive thys disdeygne. For if there be anye here that have proved those sweete disdeignes, I am sure they wil desire for courtesy one of these causes that make them so sweet. And perhappes I shall with a better will proceade

The L. Octavian Fregosos devise.

somewhat farther in love, in hope that I shall also fynde thys sweetenesse, where as some finde bitternesse, and so shall not these Ladies geve me anye more this slaunderous reporte, that I am not in love.

[XI] This pastime was muche praysed, and therefore dyd everye man setle himselfe to reason uppon this matter. But the Lady Emilia holdyng her peace, M. PETER BEMBO, that satt next in order, spake in this maner: My Lordes, this pastime that the L. Octavian hath propounded hath raysed no smal doubt in my mind, where he hath resoned of the disdiegnes of love, the whiche though they be sondry, yet unto me have they alwaies bin most bitter. Neither do I beleve that I can learne any sauce that shalbe sufficient to sweten them. But peradventure they are the more and the lesse bitter according to the cause wherof they arrise. For I have in my daies (I remember) seene the woman whom I served, stirred against me, eyther upon a vaine suspicyon that she conceyved her self of my trustinesse, or elles upon some other false opinyon that had bine put into her head by some mennes report to my hindraunce, so that I beleaved no grief might be compared to myne. And me thought that the greatest sorowe I felt was to suffer wythout deservyng, and to sustayne this affliction, not for any offence of mine, but for the small love that was in her. At other times I saw her disdeignefull for some oversight of mine, and knew that her anger proceaded of myne offence, and at that instante I judged the former vexation to be verye lyght in comparison to that whych I felt then. And me thought to be in displeasure, and that for myne owne trespas, wyth the persone whom onelye I coveted and with suche diligence sought to please, was the greatest torment of all other. Therefore woulde I oure pastyme were to have everye man declare his opinion, where there must be a disdeigne agaynst hym in the person beloved, of whom he woulde the cause of this disdeigne shoulde have his beeginning, whether of her or of him selfe: to know which is the greater grief, eyther to dysplease the wight beloved,* or to receyve dyspleasure of the wyght beloved.

M. Peter Bembos devyse.

* the wight beloved: the object of his love.

[XII] Every man looked what the L. Emilia woulde make aunswere to this, but without anye woord speakyng to Bembo, she tourned her and made a signe to SIR FRIDERICK FREGOSO to shew his devyse. And he incontinentlye beegan thus: Madam, I woulde it were lawfull for me, as the maner is manye tymes to remytte me to the judgement of an other, for I for my part woulde wyth all my heart allowe some of the pastymes that have bine already propounded by these Lordes, bicause in deede me thinke they would be worth the hearing. Yet least I shoulde breake the order, thys I saye: who so woulde take in hande to praise oure Court, leaving a part the desertes of the dutchesse, which ghostly spirite,* with her influence, is sufficient to drawe from the earth up into heaven the simplist wittes in the worlde, he might wel do it without suspicion of flattery. For peradventure in all Italy a man shall have muche a do to fynde out so many gentlemen and noble personages that are so worthy, and besyde the principall profession of Chivalrye so excellent in sundry thinges, as are presently here. Therfore if in any place men may be founde that deserve the name of good Courtyers, and can judge what belongeth to the perfeccion of Courtyership, by reason a man may beleve them to be here. To disgrace therefore many untowardly asseheades, that through malepertnes thinke to purchase them the name of a good Courtyer, I would have suche a pastime for this night, that one of the company myght bee picked out who should take in hand to shape in woordes a good Courtyer, specifying all suche condicions and particuler qualities as of necessitie must be in hym that deserveth this name. And in suche thinges as shall not appere necessarie, that it may be lawfull for every man to replye against them, as the maner of Philosophers schooles is against him that kepeth disputacions.

Syr Friderick proceaded styll forwarde in his talke, whan the L. EMILIA interruptyng hym, sayde: If it bee my L. the dutchesse pleaser, this shall be our pastime for this once.

The DUTCHESSE aunswered: I am wel pleased. Then

S. Friderick Fregosos divise.

Good Courtyers in the court of Urbin.

* ghostly spirite: divine virtue.

(in maner) all the company began to say both to the dutchesse, and among themselves that this was the trimmest pastyme they could have, and without looking for answere the one of the other thei craved upon the LADY EMILIA to appoint who shoulde first beginne. Who tournynge her towarde the dutchesse, sayde: Commaunde you (madam) whom shall please you to take this enterprise in hande, for I wyll not by chousing more one then an other, declare my selfe to judge in this behalf, whom I thinke to be better skilled then the rest, and so do wrong to some.

The DUTCHESSE aunswered: Make you this choise your selfe, and take hede that in disobeying you bee not a president to the rest to be disobedient.

[XIII] Then the LADY EMILIA saide laughyng unto Lewis count of Canossa: Therefore for leesyng any more tyme, you (Count) shall be he that shall take this enterprise uppon hym in fourme and maner as Syr Friderick hath declared. Not for that we knowe ye are so good a Courtyer that you have at your fingers endes that belongeth thereto: but because in repeatinge everye thing arsiversy, as we hope ye wyll, we shall have somuch the more pastyme, and everye one shall be able to answere you, where if an other more skilfull then you should take it in hande, there should bee nothing sayde againste hym for tellyng the trueth, and so shoulde we have but a colde pastime.

The COUNT aunswered by and by: We neede not feare (madam) that we shal wante contrarying in wordes againste hym that telleth the trueth, as longe as you bee here. And after they had laughed a whyle at this answer, he proceded on: But truely I would with all my hearte bee ridde of this burthen, for it is to hard for me. And I know that to be most true in me which you have spoken in jest: namelye, that I have no understandynge in that belongeth to a good Courtyer. And this dooe I not seeke to prove with anye other tryall, for seeyng I dooe not the deedes, a manne may judge I understande it not, and I beleve I am the lesse to bee blamed. For oute of doubte* it is a woorse matter not to dooe well, then not to understande howe to dooe it. Yet seynge youre

---

* oute of doubte: without a doubt.

pleaser is, that I shall take the charge uppon me, I can
not, nor wyll refuse it, for withstandyng youre order
and judgemente, the which I knowe is muche better
then myne.

Then the L. CESAR GONZAGA: Because it is nowe
(quoth he) well forwarde in nyghte, and have here redy
for us other sortes of pastimes, peradventure it shoulde
not bee amysse to deferre this resonynge untyll to
morowe, and the Counte shall have leysure to thynke
better uppon that he hathe to saye: for in verye deede to
entreate uppon suche a matter at the fyrste syghte, it is a
harde thynge.

Then aunswered the COUNT: I wyll not dooe as he
dyd, that strypped himself into his dublette, and leaped
lesse grounde then he didde before in his Coate. And me
thynke my lucke is good that it is late, because the
shortenesse of tyme shall make me use fewe woordes,
and the sodeinnesse of the matter shall so excuse me,
that it shall be lawfull for me to speak withoute blame
whatsoever commeth firste to mynde. Because I wyll
not therefore carye this burthen of duetye anye longer
uppon my shoulders, this I saye: In everye thynge it is so
harde a matter to knowe the true perfeccion, that it is
almoste unpossible, and that by reason of the varietie of
judgementes. Therefore manye there are, that delite in a
manne of muche talke, and hym they call a pleasaunt
felowe. Some wyll delite more in modestie, some other
wyll fansye a manne that is actyve and always doynge:
other, one that sheweth a quietnes and a respecte in
every thynge. And thus dooeth everye man prayse or
dysprayse accordynge to hys fansye, always coverynge
a vyce with the name of the next vertue to it, and a
vertue with the name of the nexte vice: as in calling him
that is sawcye, bolde: hym that is sober, drie: hym that
is seelye, good: hym that is unhappye, wittie:* and
lykewyse in the reste. Yet doe I thinke that eche thing
hath his perfeccion, althoughe it be hid, and with
reasonable dyscourses myght be judged of hym that

The true per-
feccion in
thinges.

Vice cloked
with the
name of a
vertue, and
contrariwise.

---

* calling him that is sawcye, bolde: hym that is sober, drie:
hym that is seelye, good: hym that is unhappye, wittie: calling an
arrogant and overbearing man, free-spoken; a modest man, dull; a
fool, good-hearted; an unprincipled man, shrewd and practical.

hath knowlege in the matter. And for as much as the trueth (as I have sayd) is oftentymes hid, and I take not upon me to have this knowlege, I cannot praise but that kynde of Courtyers which I set most by, and allow that whiche semeth unto me most nigh the trueth, in my smal judgement. The which you shal folowe if ye thinke it good, or els sticke to youre owne, yf it shal vary from mine. Neither will I (for all that) stand stiffe that mine is better then yours, for not onelye one thynge maie seme unto you, and an other to me, but also unto my self it may appere sometime one thing, sometime another. [XIV] I wyll have this our Courtyer therfore to be a Gentleman borne and of a good house. For it is a great deale lesse dyspraise for him that is not born a gentleman to faile in the actes of vertue then for a gentleman. If he swarve from the steppes of his auncestours, he stayneth the name of his familie, and doeth not onely not get, but loseth that is already gotten. For noblenesse of birth is (as it were) a clere lampe that sheweth forth and bringeth into light, workes bothe good and badde, and enflameth and provoketh unto vertue, as wel with the feare of slaunder, as also with the hope of praise. And wheras this brightnesse of noblenesse dothe not discover the workes of the unnoble, they have a wante of provocation and of feare of slaunder, and they recken not themselves bounde to wade anye further then their auncestours did before theym, whereas the noble of birthe counte it a shame not to arrive at the leaste at the boundes of their predecessours set foorth unto them. Therefore it chaunceth alwaies (in a maner) bothe in armes and in all other vertuous actes, that the moste famous menne are gentlemen. Because nature in every thing hath depely sowed that privie sede, which geveth a certain force and propertie of her beginning, unto whatsoever springeth of it, and maketh it lyke unto her selfe. As we see by exaumple not onely in the race of horses and other beastes, but also in trees, whose slippes and graftes alwayes for the moste parte are lyke unto the stocke of the tree they came from: and yf at any time they grow out of kind, the fault is in the husbandman. And the lyke is in men, yf they bee trayned up in good nourtour, moste commonlye they resemble them from

The facioning of a Courtyer.

A Gentleman borne.

Gentlemen of most prowesse.

Good bringing up in youthe.

whom thei come and often times passe them, but yf they have not one that can well trayn them up, thei growe (as it were) wylde, and never come to their ripenesse. Truth it is, whether it be through the favour of the starres or of nature, some there are borne endowed wyth suche graces, that they seeme not to have bene borne, but rather facioned with the verye hande of some God, and abounde in all goodnesse bothe of bodye and mynde. As againe we see some so unapte and dull, that a man wyl not beleve, but nature hath brought them into the worlde for a spite and mockerie. And lyke as these with continual diligence and good bringyng up for the most parte can bring small fruite: even so the other with litle attendance clime to the full perfeccion of all excellency. Marke me the Lorde Hyppolitus da Este Cardinall of Ferrara,[32] he hath hadde so happye a birthe, that his person, his countenaunce, his woordes, and all his gestures are so facioned and compact with this grace, that among the moste aunciente prelates (for all he is but yonge) he dothe represente so grave an aucthoritie, that a man woulde weene he were more meete to teache, then nedefull to learne. Likewise in company with menne and women of all degrees, in sportynge, in laughynge, and in jestynge he hath in hym a certayne sweetenesse, and so comely demeanours, that whoso speaketh with hym or yet beholdeth hym, muste nedes beare him an affeccion for ever. But returnyng to our purpose I saye, that betwene thys excellent grace, and that fonde foolyshnesse there is yet a meane, and they that are not by nature so perfectly furnished, with studye and diligence maye polishe and correct a great part of the defaultes of nature. The Courtyer therfore, besyde noblenesse of birthe, I wyll have hym to be fortunate in this behalfe, and by nature to have not only a wytte, and a comely shape of persone and countenance, but also a certain grace, and (as they saie) a hewe,* that shal make him at the first sight acceptable and lovyng unto who so beholdeth him. And let this be an ornament to frame and accompanye all his actes, and

Some borne full of graces and comelines.

Some borne very asseheds.

Hypolitus da Este brother to the Duke of Ferrarra.

---

* a hewe. The term in the original is colloquial and hard to translate: *un sangue*, literally 'a blood'; perhaps here 'an aura'.

to assure men in his looke, suche a one to bee woorthy the companye and favour of every great man.

[XV] Here without any longer tariyng the L. GASPAR PALLAVICIN saide: That our pastime may have the fourme and maner agreed upon, and least it shoulde appeare that we litle esteme the aucthoritie geven us to contrary you, I say (in mine advise) that this noblenesse of birthe is not so necessarie for the Courtyer.[33] And if I wiste that anye of you thought it a straunge or a newe matter, I woulde alledge unto you sondrye, who for all they were borne of moste noble bloude, yet have they bene heaped full of vyces: and contrarywise, many unnoble that have made famous their posteritie. And yf it be true that you sayde before, that the privie force of the firste seede is in everye thynge, we shoulde al bee in one maner condicion, for that we had all one selfe begynnynge, and one shoulde not bee more noble then an other. But besyde the diversityes and degrees in us of highe and lowe, I beleve there bee manye other matters, wherein I judge fortune to be the chief, because we see her beare a stroke in al worldlyc thinges, and (as it were) take a pastime to exalt many times whom pleaseth her without any desert at all, and burie in the botomles depth the most worthy to be exalted. I confirme your saying as touching the happines of them that are borne abounding in all goodnes both of minde and bodie: but this is seen aswel in the unnoble, as in the noble of birthe, for nature hath not these so subtile distinctions: yea (as I have sayde) we se many times in persons of most base degree, most high giftes of nature. Therefore seing this noblenes is gotten neither with force, nor art, but is rather a praise of oure ancestours then our own, me think it a strange opinion that the parentes of our Courtyer being unnoble, his good qualities should be defaced, and these oure good condicions whiche you have named should not be sufficient to bring him to the top of al perfeccion: that is to say, wit, beauty of fisnamy, disposicion of person, and that grace which at the first sight shal make him moste acceptable unto all men.

[XVI] Then aunswered COUNT LEWIS: I denie not, but in men of base degree may reigne the very same vertues that are in gentlemen. But to avoyd rehersal of that we have already said, with many other reasons that might be alleged in commendacion of noblenesse, the which is evermore honored of al men because it standeth with reason that good should spring of good, forsomuch as our entent is to facion a Courtyer without ani maner default or lack in hym, and heaped with all praise, me thinke it a necessarye matter to make him a gentleman, as well for many other respects, as also for the common opinion, which by and by doeth leane to noblenesse.* For where there are two in a noble mans house which at the first have geven no proofe of themselves with woorkes good or bad, assoone as it is knowen that the one is a gentleman borne, and the other not, the unnoble shall be muche lesse estemed with everye manne, then the gentleman, and he must with much travaile and long time imprint in mennes heades a good opinion of himselfe, whiche the other shal geat in a moment, and onely for that he is a gentleman: and howe waightye these imprintinges are every man may easily judge. For, to speake of our selves: we have seen menne come to thys house, whiche for all they were fooles and dulwitted, yet had they a report through all Italye of great Courtyers, and though at length they were discovered and knowen, yet manye daies did thei beguyle us, and mainteyned in oure myndes that oppinion of themselves, whiche at the fyrste they found there imprinted, although they wrought accordyng to their small skil. We have seen other at the fyrste in very smal estimacion, and afterwarde in the ende have acquited themselves marveilous well. And of these errors there are divers causes and among other the obstinatenes of princes, whiche to prove mastries† oftentimes bend themselves to favor him, that to their seeming, deserveth no favour at all, and manye tymes in deede they are deceyved. But because thei have alwaies many that counterfait them, a very great report dependeth upon their favor, the which moste

Noblenes of birthe in estimacion with all men.

The imprintinges or conceivinges of the mind with expectacion.

The yl inclynacion of princes in favouring them that deserve it not.

---

* the common opinion, which by and by doeth leane to noblenesse. The phrase is slightly mistranslated: the original has 'the prestige that automatically attaches to nobility, in everybody's eyes'.

† to prove mastries: to show that they can work miracles.

commonly judgements folow. And if thei find any thing that semeth contrary to the common opinion, thei ar in doubt for deceiving themselves, and alwaies loke for some matter secretly because it semeth, that these general

We be moved to passions without anye manifest cause why.

opinions ought to be founded upon a trothe, and arise of reasonable causes. And forsomuch as our mindes are very apte to love and to hate: as in the sightes of combates and games and in all other kinde of contencion one with an other, it is seene that the lookers on many times beare affeccion without any manifest cause why, unto one of the two parties, with a gredy desire to have him get the victorie, and the other to have the overthrow. Also as touching the opinion of mens qualities, the good or yll reporte at the first brunt moveth oure mynde to one of these two passions: therefore it commeth to passe, that for the moste part we judge with love or els with hatred. You see then of what importance this first imprinting is, and howe he ought to endevoure himself to get it good in princes, if he entende to be set by, and to purchase him the name of a good Courtyer. [XVII] But to come to some

Armes the Courtyers chiefe profession.

particularitie, I judge the principall and true profession of a Courtyer ought to be in feates of armes, the which above all I will have hym to practise lively, and to bee knowen among other for his hardinesse, for his acheving of enterprises, and for his fidelitie toward him whom he serveth. And he shall purchase himselfe a name with these good condicions, in doing the dedes in everie time and

That he take no folie.

place: for it is not for him to feint at any time in this behalfe without a wonderous reproche. And even as in women honestye once stained dothe never retourne againe to the former astate: so the fame of a gentleman that carieth weapon, yf it once take a foile* in any litle point through dastardlines† or any other reproche, doeth evermore continue shameful in the worlde and full of ignoraunce.‡ Therefore the more excellent our Courtyer shalbe in this arte, the more shall he bee worthy praise: albeit I judge not necessarye in hym so perfect a knowledge of thynges and other qualities that is requisite

---

* yf it once take a foile: if it suffers the slightest blemish.
† dastardlines: cowardice.
‡ ignoraunce. A mistranslation: the original has 'ignominy'.

a capitaine. But because this is overlarge a scope of matters, we wyll holde oure selves contented (as wee have sayde) with the uprightnesse of a well meaning minde, and with an invincible courage, and that he alwaies shew himself such as one: for many times men of courage are sooner knowen in small matters then in greate. Often times in daungers that stande them upon, and where many eyes be, ye shall see some that for all their hearte is dead in their bodie, yet pricked with shame or with the company, go forwarde (as it were) blindfield and do their dutie. And God knoweth bothe in matters that little touche them, and also where they suppose that without missynge they may convey themselves from daunger, how they are willing ynough to slepe in a whole skinne. But suche as think themselves neither marked, seen, nor knowen, and yet declare a stout courage, and suffer not the leaste thyng in the worlde to passe that maie burthen them, they have the courage of spirite whiche we seke to have in our Courtyer. Yet will we not have him for al that so lustie to make braverie in woordes, and to bragge that he hathe wedded his harneys for his wife, and to threaten with suche grim lookes, as we have seene Berto[34] do oftentimes. For unto suche maie well be saide that a worthie Gentlewoman in a noble assembly spake pleasauntly unto one, that shall be namelesse for this tyme, whome she to shewe hym a good countenance, desired to daunce with her, and he refusing both that, and to heare musick and many other entertainmentes offred him, alwaies affirming suche trifles not to be his profession, at last the Gentlewoman demaundyng him, What is then your profession? He aunswered with a frowning looke: To fight.

Then saide the Gentlewoman: Seing you are not nowe at the warre nor in place to fight, I woulde thinke it beste for you to bee well besmered and set up in an armorie with other implementes of warre till time wer that you should be occupied, least you waxe more rustier then you are.

Thus with muche laughinge of the standers by she left him with a mocke in his foolishe presumpcion. He therefore that we seeke for, where the enemies are, shall shewe himselfe moste fierce, bitter, and evermore with

Cowardes sometime hardie.

Who have the stoutenesse of courage.

A stout-herted man.

the firste. In everie place beside, lowly, sober, and circumspecte, fleeing above all thinge bragginge and unshamefull praising himself, for therewith a man alwaies purchaseth himself the hatred and yll will of the hearers.

[XVIII] And I, aunswered the L. GASPAR, have knowen few men excellent in any thing whatsoever it bee, but they praise them selves. And me thinke it may wel be borne in them: for he that is of skill, whan he seeth that he is not knowen for his woorkes of the ignoraunte, hath a disdeigne that his connynge should lye buried, and needes muste he open it one waie, least he should bee defrauded of the estimation that belongeth to it, whiche is the true rewarde of vertuous travailes. Therefore among the auncient writers he that muche excelleth doeth sildome forbeare praisyng hymself. They in deede are not to be borne withall that havyng no skill in theym, wyll prayse themselves: but we wyll not take our Courtyer to be suche a one.

Then the COUNT: Yf you have well understoode (quoth he) I blamed the praysynge of a mans selfe impudently and without respecte. And surelye (as you saye) a man ought not to conceyve an yll oppinion of a skilfull man that praiseth hymselfe dyscretely, but rather take it for a more certaine witnes, then yf it came out of an other mans mouth. I agree well that he, whiche in praising himselfe falleth not into errour, nor purchaseth himself lothsomenes or hatred of the hearers, is moste discrete: and beside the praises whiche he geveth himselfe, deserveth the same of other men also, because it is a very harde matter.

Then the L. GASPAR: This (quoth he) muste you teache us.

The COUNT aunswered: Emong the auntient writers there hathe not also wanted that hathe taught it.[35] But in mine opinion, all doth consist in speaking such thynges after a sort, that it maye appeare that they are not rehearsed to that ende: but that they come so to purpose, that he can not refrayne tellyng them, and alwaies seemynge to flee his owne prayse tell the trueth. But not as those lustie laddes dooe, that open their mouthe and thruste oute woordes at aventure they care not how. As within these few dayes one of oure

In what sort
a man maye
praise him-
selfe.

company beyng pusshed throughe the thygh with a
pyke at Pysa, thought that it was the bytynge of a flie.
And an other sayde that he occupied no lookynge glasse
in his chamber, because in hys rage he was so terrible to
beholde, that in lookynge upon his owne countenaunce
he shoulde put himself into much feare.

At this every one laughed. But the L. CESAR
GONZAGA saide unto them: At what laugh you? Knowe
ye not that the great Alexander, hearing a certayne
Philosophers oppinion to be that there were infinite
worldes, fell in weping: and when he was asked the
question why he wept, he aunswered: Because I have
not yet one in hande, as thoughe his mynde was to have
them all.[36] Dooe you not thynke that this was a greater
braverie, then to speak of the fly biting.

So was Alexander a greater person then he that so
sayde, aunswered the COUNT. But excellent men in very
deede are to be helde excused, whan they take muche
upon them: because he that undertaketh great enterprises muste have a boldnesse to dooe it, and a
confidence of hym selfe, and not of a bashfull or
cowardly mynde, but yet sober in woordes: shewing as
though he tooke lesse upon hym then he dothe in deede,
so that his taking upon him do not extend unto
rashnesse.

[XIX] Here the Count respetyng a while, M.
BERNARD BIBIENA saide merelye: I remember you
saide before, that this oure Courtyer oughte of nature to
have a faire comelynesse of fisnamye and person, with
the grace that oughte to make hym so amyable. As for
the grace and beautie of fisnamie, I thynke not the
contrary but they are in me, and therefore doe so many
women burne for the love of me, as you knowe. But for
the comelynesse of persone, I stande somewhat in
doubte, and especiallye by reason of my legges here, for
me thinke in deede thei are not so wel made as I could
wishe thei wer: the body and the rest is meetely wel.
Therfore declare som what more particularly this
comelines of person, what it should be, that I may be
out of this doubt and set my heart at reste.

Whan thei had a while laughed at this, the COUNT
sayde: Certes, the grace of the fisnamy, may wel be said
to be in you without any lye. And no other exaumple

Brave
roysters.

Anaxagoras.

doe I alledge but this, to declare what maner thing it
shoulde bee: for undoubtedly we see your countenaunce
is most acceptable and pleasant to beholde unto every
man, although the proporcion and draughtes* of it be
not very delicate, but it is manly and hath a good grace
withall. And this qualitie have many and sundrye
shapes of visages. And suche a countenaunce as this is,

will I have our Courtyer to have, and not so softe and
womanishe as many procure to have, that do not onely
courle the hear, and picke the browes, but also paumpre
themselves in every point like the most wanton and

dishonest women in the worlde: and a man would
thinke them in goyng, in standing, and in all their
gestures so tender and feint, that their members were
ready to flee one from an other, and their woordes they
pronounce so drawningly,† that a man would weene
they were at that instant yelding up the ghost: and the
higher in degree the men are they talke withall, the more
they use suche facyons. These men, seing nature (as they
seeme to have a desire to appeare and to bee) hath not
made them women, ought not to be esteamed in place of
good women, but like common Harlottes to be
banished, not onely out of pryncee courtes, but also
oute of the companye of Gentlemen. [XX] To come

therefore to the qualitie of the person, I say he is well, if
he bee neither of the least, nor of the greatest sise. For
bothe the one and the other hath with it a certayne
spytefull wonder,‡ and suche men are marveyled at,
almoste, as muche as men marveile to beholde
monstrous thynges. Yet if there must needes be a

defaulte in one of the two extremities, it shall be lesse
hurtfull to bee somewhat of the least, then to excede the
common stature in height. For men so shut up§ of
bodie, beside that manye tymes they are of a dull wit,
they are also unapte for all exercyses of nimeblenesse,
whiche I much desire to have in the Courtyer. And
therefore will I have him to bee of a good shape, and
well proporcioned in his lymmes, and to shewe

* proporcion and draughtes: features.
† so drawningly: in such a languishing tone.
‡ spytefull wonder: displeasing extraordinariness.
§ so shut up: so enormous.

strength, lightnes, and quickenesse, and to have understandyng in all exercises of the bodie, that belonge to a
man of warre. And herein I thinke the chief point is to
handle well all kynde of weapon both for footeman and
horseman, and to know the vauntages in it. And
especially to be skilfull on those weapons that are used
ordinarily emong gentlemen, for beside the use that he
shall have of them in warre, where peradventure nedeth
no great connyng, there happen often times variaunces
betwene one gentleman and an other, whereupon
ensueth a combat. And manye tymes it shall stande him
in stede to use the weapon whiche he hath at that instant
by his side, therefore it is a very sure thing to be skilfull.
And I am none of them whiche saye, that he forgetteth
his conning whan he commeth to the poynte: for to
abide by,* whoso loseth his conning at that time,
sheweth that he hath firste loste his heart and his spirites
for feare. I think also it will serve his turne greatly, to
know the feate of wrastling, because it goeth much
together with all weapon on foote. [XXI] Againe it is
behouffull bothe for him selfe and for his frendes, that
he have a foresight in the quarelles and controversies
that may happen, and let him beware of the vauntages,†
declarynge alwaies in everye pointe bothe courage and
wisedome. Neither let him runne rashely to these
combattes, but whan he muste needes to save his
estimation withall: for beside the great daunger that is
in the doubtfull lotte, hee that goeth headlonge to these
thynges and without urgent cause, deserveth verye great
blame, although his chaunce bee good. But whan a man
perceiveth that he is entred so farre that hee can not
drawe backe withoute burdeyn, hee muste, bothe in
suche thinges he hath to doe before the combat and also
in the combat be utterlye resolved with hymselfe, and
always shewe a readinesse and a stomake. And not as
some dooe, passe the matter in arguing and pointes, and
having the choise of weapon, take suche as have neyther
poynte nor edge. And arme themselves as thoughe they
shoulde goe against the shotte of a Cannon. And
weening it sufficyent not to be vanquished, stande

To be a man
of warre.

To handle
al kind of
weapon.

Fightinge
maketh not a
man to forget
his fence.

Wrastlynge.

To knowe
what is
to be done
in quarrels
whan they
happen.

Not rashe to
fight com-
battes.

Howe a man
ought to be-
have himself
in fightyng a
combatte.

* to abide by: without a doubt.
† beware of the vauntages: be shrewd in assessing the situation.

alwaies at their defence and geve grounde, in so muche that they declare an extreme faint hert, and are a mocking stocke to the verye chyldren. As those two of Ancona: that a while a goe fought a combat beside Perugia, and made them to laughe that looked on.

And what were they? quoth the L. GASPAR PALLAVICIN.

The L. CESAR aunswered: Cousins Germains* of two sisters.

Then said the COUNT: At the combat a man would have thought them naturall brethren, then he went forwarde. Also men occupie their weapon oftentimes in tyme of peace aboute sondrie exercises, and gentlemen are seen in open showes in the presence of people, women and Princes. Therefore will I have our Courtyer

A perfecte horseman.

a perfecte horseman for everye saddle. And beside the skyll in horses and in whatsoever belongeth to a horseman, let him set all his delite and dylygence to wade in everye thyng a litle farther then other menne, so that he maye bee knowen among al menne for one that is excellente. As it is reade of Alcibiades, that he excelled

Alcibiades excelled other nations in theyr owne feates.

all other nations wheresoever he came, and everye manne in the thynge he hadde moste skyll in. So shall this our Courtyer passe other menne, and everye manne in his owne profession. And because it is the peculyer

Property of Italians.

prayse of us Italians to ryde well, to manege wyth reason, especiallye roughe horses, to runne at the rynge and at tylte, he shall bee in this amonge the beste Italyans. At tourneymente, in kepyng a passage, in

Property of Frenchmen.

fightinge at barriers, he shall be good emong the best Frenchmen. At *Joco di canne*,[37] runninge at Bull,

Property of Spaniardes.

casting of speares and dartes, he shall be amonge the Spaniardes excellent. But principallye lette hym accompanye all his mocion wyth a certayne good judgemente and grace, yf he wyll deserve that generall favour whiche is so muche set by. [XXII] There bee also manye other exercises, the whiche thoughe they depende not throughlye upon armes, yet have they a greate agreemente with them, and have in them muche manlye activitie. And of them me thinke huntynge is one of the

huntyng.

chiefest, for it hath a certaine lykenesse with warre, and

---

* Cousins Germains: first cousins.

truelye a pastyme for great men, and fitte for one lyvyng
in courte. And it is founde that it hath also bene muche
used amonge them of olde tyme. It is meete for hym also   Swimming.
to have the arte of swimming, to leape, to runne, to cast   Leapyng.
the stone: for beside the profite that he maie receyve of   Runnyng.
thys in the warres, it happeneth to hym manye tymes to   Castyng the
make proofe of himselfe in suche thynges, whereby he   stone.
getteth hym a reputacion, especiallye among the multitude, unto whom a man muste sometyme applye
hymselfe. Also it is a noble exercyse and meete for one
lyvyng in courte to play at tenyse, where the disposition   Playe at
of the bodye, the quickenesse and nimeblenesse of   tenyse.
everye member is much perceyved, and almoste whatsoever a manne can see in all other exercises. And I
recken vautyng of no lesse prayse, which for all it is   Vawting.
peynefull and harde, maketh a man more light and
quicker then any of the rest: and beside the profite, yf
that lightnesse be accompanyed with a good grace, it
maketh (in my judgemente) a better showe then anye of
the reste. If our Courtyer then be taught these exercises
more then indifferently well, I beleve he may sette a syde
tumblyng, clymynge upon a corde, and suche other   Tumblynge
matters that taste somewhat of jugglers crafte, and doe   not fit for a
lytle beseeme a Gentleman. But because we can not   Gentleman.
always endure emonge these so paynefull doynges,
besyde that the contynuaunce goeth nyghe to geve a
manne hys fyll, and taketh awaye the admyracion that
menne have of thynges sildome seen, we muste contynuallye alter oure lyfe with practysynge sondrye
matters. Therefore wyll I have oure Courtyer to   To frame
descende manye times to more easye and pleasaunt   himself to the
exercyses. And to avoyde envye and to keepe companye   company.
pleasauntlye with every man, let him do whatsoever
other men do: so he decline not at any time from
commendable dedes, but governeth himselfe with that
good judgemente that will not suffer hym to enter into
any folye: but let him laugh, dalie, jest, and daunce, yet
in such wise that he maie alwayes declare himselfe to
bee wittie and discrete, and everie thynge that he doeth
or speaketh, let him doe it with a grace.

   [XXIII] Truelye, saide then the L. CESAR GONZAGA,
the course of this communicacion shoulde not be
stopped: but if I shoulde houlde my peace, I should not

satisfie the libertie whiche I have to speake, nor the
desyre that I have to understand one thing. And let me
be pardoned if where I ought to speake against, I
demaund a question: because I suppose I maie lawfully
do it after the example of M. Bernard, who for the to
great desire he hadde to be counted a welfavoured man,
hath offended agaynst the lawes of our pastime in
demaunding without speakinge against.

Behoulde I beseeche ye, saide then the Dutchesse,
howe one errour bringeth in a great sorte. Therfore who
so offendeth and geveth yll example, as M. Bernard
hathe done, deserveth to be punished not onely for his
owne offence, but for other mens also.

Then aunswered the L. Cesar: Therefore must I
(madam) escape punishmente, for that M. Bernard
ought to bee punished for his owne offence and mine
bothe.

Naye (quoth the Dutchesse) you oughte to have
bothe double punishmente. He for his offence, and for
beynge an occasion for you to commit the lyke: and you
for your offence and for taking hym for a president that
dyd offende.

I have not hytherto offended, madam, answered the
L. Cesar. Therefore because I wyll leave the whole
punishmente for M. Bernard I wyll kepe silence.

And nowe he held his peace, whan the L. Emilia
aunswered: Say what pleaseth you, for (by the
dutchesse leave) I perdone thys faulte, and whosoever
shall offende in so small a trespace.

Upon that the Dutchesse said: I am well pleased.
But take ye heede that ye deceive not your selfe,
thinking peradventure to be better reported of for
mercy then for justice. For in perdoning the offendour
to muche, ye do wrong to him that doeth not offende.
Yet wyll not I have my rigour at this time in accusing
your mercye to be the cause that we shall lose the
hearing of this the L. Cesars demaund.

So he, after the dutches and the L. Emilia had made a
signe to him, sayde by and by: [XXIV] If I do well beare
in mind, me thynke (Count Lewis) you have this night
oftentimes repeted, that the Courtier ought to accompany all his doinges, gestures, demeaners, finally al his
mocions with a grace, and this, me think, ye put for a

sauce to every thing, without the which all his other properties and good condicions were litle woorth. And I beleve verely that every man would soone be perswaded therin, for by the vertue of the worde a man may saye, that whoso hath grace is gracious.* But bicause you have saide sundry times that it is the gift of nature and of the heavens, and againe where it is not so perfect, that it maye with studye and diligence be made muche more, they that be borne so happye and so welthye with such a treasure (as some that we se) me thynke therin they have litle nede of anye other teacher, because the bountifull favour of heaven doeth (as it were) in spite of them, guide them higher then they covet, and maketh them note onely acceptable, but marveylous unto all the world. Therefore I do not reason of this, because the obtainynge of it of our selves lyeth not in our powre: but such as by nature have onely so much, that they be apte to beecome gratious in bestowinge labour, exercise, and diligence, I would faine knowe with what art, with what learning, and by what meane they shall compasse this grace, aswel in the exercises of the bodye (wherin ye thinke it so necessarie a matter) as in all other thynges that they dooe or speake. Therfore as you have in praysinge thys qualytye to us engendred (I beleve) in al a fervent thirst to come by it, by the charge ye received of the L. Emilia, so with teaching it us, ye are bound to quenche it.

[XXV] Bound I am not (quoth the COUNT) to teache you to have a good gracc, nor anye thing els, saving only to shew you what a perfect Courtyer ought to be. Neither will I take upon me to teach you this perfeccion, sins a while a goe, I said, that the Courtier ought to have the feate of wrastlyng and vawtinge, and such other thinges, the which howe I should be able to teache them not having learned them my selfe, I am sure ye knowe it all. It sufficeth that as a good souldyer cann speake his minde to an armourer of what facion, of what temper

Grace.

* whoso hath grace is gracious. The original phrase (*chi ha grazia, quello è grato*) contains a pun on the two meanings of the word 'grazia', which can refer either to the quality of grace or to favour (as in the phrase 'to be in someone's good graces'). The meaning is, then, approximately, 'whoever is graceful finds favour'.

and goodnesse he will have his harneys, and for all that cannot teache him to make it, nor to hammer or temper it: so perhaps I am able to tel you what a perfect Courtyer ought to be, but not to teach you how ye should doe to be one. Notwithstanding to fulfill your request in what I am able, althoughe it be (in maner) in a proverbe that Grace is not to be learned, I say unto you, whoso mindeth to be gracious or to have a good grace in the exercises of the body, (presupposing first that he be not of nature unapt) ought to begin betimes, and to learne his principles of cunning men. The which thyng how necessarie a matter Philip king of Macedonie thought it, a man may gather in that his wil was that Aristotel so famous a philosopher, and perhappes the greatest that ever hath bine in the world, should be the man that should instruct Alexander his sonne in the first principles of letters. And of men whom we know nowadayes, mark how wel and with what a good grace Sir Galiazzo Sanseverino[38] M. of the horse to the Frenche king, doth all exercises of the body: and that because, besyde the naturall disposition of person that is in him, he hath applyed all his study to learne of cunning men, and to have continually excellent men about hym, and of every one to chuse the best of that they have skill in. For as in wrastling, in vawting, and in learning to handle sundry kinde of weapons he hath taken for his guide oure M. Peter Mount, who (as you know) is the true and only maister of al artificiall force and sleight: so in ridyng, in justyng, and in everye other feate, he hath alwayes had before his eyes the most perfectest that hath ben knowen to be in those professions: [XXVI] he therfore that wil be a good scolar, beside the practysing of good thinges, must evermore set al his diligence to bee lyke his mayster, and (if it were possible) chaunge himself into him. And when he hath had some entrey,* it profiteth hym much to behould sondrye men of that profession: and governing hymselfe with that good judgement that must alwayes be hys guyde, go about to pyke out, sometyme of one and sometyme of an other, sundry matters. And even as the

Grace not to be learned.

Aristotle the first that taught the great Alexander.

S. Galeazzo Sanseverino.

A good scoler must seeke to be like his maister.

---

* when he hath had some entrey: when he has already made some progress.

bee in the greene medowes fleeth alwayes aboute the
grasse chousynge out flowres:[39] so shall our Courtyer
steale thys grace from them that to hys seming have it,
and from ech one that percell that shal be most worthy
praise. And not do, as a frende of ours, whom you al
know, that thought he resembled much kyng
Ferdinande the yonger of Aragon, and regarded not to
resemble hym in anye other poynt but in the often
lyftyng up hys head, wrying therewythall a part of hys
mouth, the whych custome the king had gotten by
infyrmitye. And manye such there are that thynke they
doe much, so they resemble a great man in somewhat,
and take many tymes the thynge in hym that woorst
becommeth hym. But I, imagynyng with my self
oftentymes how this grace commeth, leaving a part such
as have it from above, fynd one rule that is most general
whych in thys part (me thynk) taketh place in al thynges
belongyng to man in worde or deede above all other.
And that is to eschew as much as a man may, and as a
sharp and daungerous rock, Affectation or curiosity
and (to speak a new word) to use in every thyng a
certain Reckelesness,[40] to cover art withall, and seeme
whatsoever he doth and sayeth to do it wythout pain,
and (as it were) not myndyng it. And of thys do I beleve
grace is muche deryved, for in rare matters and wel
brought to passe every man knoweth the hardnes of
them, so that a redines therin maketh great wonder.
And contrarywise to use force, and (as they say) to hale
by the hear, geveth a great disgrace, and maketh every
thing how great so ever it be, to be litle estemed.
Therfore that may be said to be a very art that appeereth
not to be art, neyther ought a man to put more diligence
in any thing then in covering it: for in case it be open, it
loseth credit cleane, and maketh a man litle set by.* And
I remember that I have reade in my dayes, that there
were some most excellent Oratours, which among
other their cares, enforced themselves to make every
man beleve that they had no sight in letters,[41] and
dissemblinge their conning, made semblant their
orations to be made very simply, and rather as nature
and trueth lead them, then study and arte, the whiche if

How grace
is to be
atteined.

A generall
rule.

To avoid
curiositie.

Reckelesnes.

To cover art.

---

* litle set by: thought none too highly of.

To seme not
to mynde the
thing a man
doeth excel-
lently well.

it had bene openly knowen, would have putte a doubt in the peoples minde, for feare least he beguiled them. You may see then howe to shewe arte and suche bent study taketh away the grace of every thing. Which of you is it that laugheth not when our M. Peterpaul daunseth after his owne facion with such fine skippes and on tipto without moving his head, as though he were all of wood, so heedfullie, that truely a man would weene he counted his paces? What eye is so blind that perceiveth not in this the disgrace of curiosity,* and in many men and women here present the grace of that not regarded agylitie and slighte conveyaunce† (for in the mocions of the bodye manye so terme it) with a kinde of speaking or smiling, or gesture, betokening not to passe upon it, and to minde anye other thinge more then that,‡ to make him beleve that loketh on that he can not do amisse?

[XXVII] Here M. BERNARD BIBIENA not forbearing any longer, sayde: You may se yet that our M. Robert hath found one to praise his maner of daunsing, though the reste of you set litle by it. For if this excellency doeth consist in Reckelesnes, and in shewing not to passe upon and rather to minde anye other thing then that a man is in hande withall, M. Robert hath no peere in the worlde. For that men should wel perceive that he litle mindeth it, manye tymes his garmentes fall from hys backe, and his slippers from his feete, and daunseth on still without taking uppe againe anye of both.

Then aunswered the COUNT: Seyng you will nedes have me speake, I wyll saye somewhat also of oure vices. Do you not marke, this that you call in M. Robert Reckelesnes, is a verie curiositie?§ for it is well knowen that he enforceth himself with al diligence possible to make a show not to minde it, and that is to minde it to much. And bicause he passeth certain limites of a meane, that Reckelesnes of his is curious, and not comly, and is a thing that commeth cleane contrarye to

* curiosity: affectation.
† not regarded agylitie and slighte conveyaunce: disdainful ease.
‡ not to passe upon it, and to minde anye other thinge more then that: not to regard it, and to have one's mind on anything except what one is doing.
§ curiositie: affectation.

passe from the dryfte,* (that is to wit) to cover arte. Therfore I judge it a no lesse vyce of curiositye to be in Reckelesness (which in it selfe is prayse worthye) in lettynge a mans clothes fal of his backe, then in Preciseness (whiche likewise of it self is praise worthy) to carie a mans head so like a malthorse for feare of ruffling his hear, or to keepe in the bottome of his cappe a looking glasse, and a combe in his sleeve, and to have alwayes at his heeles up and down the streetes a page with a spunge and a brushe: for this maner of Preciseness and Reckelesness are to much in the extremitie, which is alwaies a vice and contrarie to that pure and amiable simplicitie, which is so acceptable to mens mindes. Marke what an yll grace a man at armes hath, when he enforceth himselfe to goe so bolt upright setled in saddle (as we use to say after the Venetian phrase)† in comparison of an other that appeareth not to mind it, and sitteth on horseback so nimbly and close as though he were on fote. How much more do we take pleaser in a gentilman that is a man at armes, and how much more worthy praise is he if he be modest, of few wordes, and no bragger, then an other that alwayes craketh of him self, and blaspheming with a bravery seemeth to threaten the worlde. And this is nothing els but a curiositie to seeme to be a roister. The lyke happeneth in all exercises, yea in everye thinge in the worlde that a man can doe or speak.

Precisenesse.

[XXVIII] Then said the L. JULIAN: This in like maner is verified in musicke: where it is a verye greate vice to make two perfecte cordes, the one after the other, so that the verye sence of our hearing abhorreth it, and often times deliteth in a seconde or in a seven, which in it selfe is an unpleasaunt discord and not tollerable: and this proceadeth because the continuance in the perfit tunes engendreth urkesomnesse, and betokeneth a to curious harmonye the whyche in mynglyng therwythall the unperfect is avoyded wyth makynge (as

Musicke.

---

* that commeth cleane contrarye to passe from the dryfte: that has precisely the opposite effect to that which is intended.

† as we use to say after the Venetian phrase. A mistranslation: the original has 'as we say, in the Venetian manner' (the reference is to the Venetians' famously awkward style of riding, also alluded to at p. 162).

it were) a comparason, whereby oure eares stande to listen and gredely* attend and tast the perfecte, and are otherwhyle delyted wyth the disagrement of the seconde or seven, as it were with a thing lytle regarded.

Behould ye then, answered the COUNT, that curiousnesse hurteth in thys as well as in other thynges. They say also that it hath bene a proverbe emonge some most excellent peincters of old time, that To muche diligence is hurtfull, and that Apelles[42] found fault with Protogenes because he coulde not keepe his handes from the table.†

To much diligence hurtfull.

Then sayd the L. CESAR: The very same fault (me think) is in our Frier Seraphin that he cannot kepe his handes from the table, especially as long as there is any meat styrryng.

The COUNT laughed and went forward: Apelles meanyng was, that Protogenes knew not when it was well, whych was nothyng els but to reprehend hys curyousnesse in hys workes. Thys vertue therfore contrarye to curiosity whych we for thys tyme terme Reckelesnes, besyde that it is the true fountain from the whych all grace spryngeth, it bryngeth wyth it also an other ornamente, whych accompanyinge anye deede that a man doeth, how lytle so ever it be, doeth not onely by and by open the knowledge of hym that doth it, but also many times maketh it to be estemed much more in effect then it is, because it imprinteth in the myndes of the lookers on an opinyon, that whoso can so sleyghtly do well, hath a great deale more knowledge then indeede he hath: and if he wyll apply hys study and dilygence to that he doeth, he myght do it much better. And to repete even the verye same examples, marke a man that taketh weapon in hande: yf goyng about to caste a darte, or houldyng in hys hand a sworde or any other waster,‡ he setleth hym self lightsomely (not thinking upon it) in a ready aptnesse wyth such activity, that a man would weene hys bodye and all his members were naturally setled in that disposition and without

A manne is thought manye times to be more cunning then he is in deede.

---

* gredely: avidly.
† table: here, 'painting' (though the word *tavola* also means 'table', hence Cesare Gonzaga's pun).
‡ waster: weapon.

any payne, though he doeth nothing els, yet doeth he declare hymself unto everye man to be most perfect in that exercise. Lykewyse in daunsinge, one measure,* one mocion of a bodye that hath a good grace, not beyng forced, doeth by and by declare the knowledge of him that daunseth. A musitien, yf in singing he roule out but a playne note endinge in a dooble relise† wyth a sweete tune, so easily that a man would judge he did it at aventure, in that point alone he doeth men to understand that his knowledge is far greater then it is indeede. Oftentymes also in peinctinge, one lyne not studyed upon, one draught with the pensel sleightly drawen, so it appeareth the hand without the guiding of any study or art, tendeth to his mark, according to the peincters purpose, doth evidently discover the excellency of the workman, about the opinion wherof every man afterwarde contendeth accordyng to his judgement. The like happeneth also, in a maner, about every other thing. Therfore shall our Courtyer be esteemed excellent, and in everye thyng he shall have a good grace, and especially in speaking, if he avoide curiositye: into which errour many men runne, and some time more then other, certain of our Lumbardes, which after a yeeres travaile abrode, come home and begin by and by to speake the Romayne tunge, somtime the Spanish tunge, or the Frenche, and God wotteth howe. And all this proceadeth of an over greater desier to show much knowledge: and in this wise a man applyeth hys studye and diligence to gett a most odyous vice. And truelye it were no small travayle for me, if I should use in this communycatyon of oures, those aunciant Tuscane wordes, that are not in use amonge the Tuscanes nowe a dayes, and beesyde that, I beleeve everye manne would laughe at me.

[XXIX] Then spake SYR FREDERICK: In deede reasoning together as wee nowe dooe, peradventure it were not well done to use those auntient Tuscane woordes: for (as you say) they would be a lothsomnesse both to the speaker and to the hearer, and of manye they should not be understoode without muche a doe. But he that shoulde write, I would thinke he

A slight trick betokeneth knowledge.

Men that wil be deemed to be wel languaged.

Auncient Tuscane woordes.

---

* measure: step.   † relise: ornament.

committed an errour in not using them: bicause they
gave a great grace and aucthoritie unto writinges, and
of them is compact a tonge more grave and more full
of majestie, then of the newe.

I knowe not, answered the COUNT, what grace and
aucthority those wordes can geve unto writinges that
ought to be eschewed, not only in the maner of speach
that we now use (which you your self confesse) but also
in any other maner that can be imagined. For if anye
man, of howe good a judgement so ever he were, had to
make an oration of grave matters in the verye Counsell
chamber of Florence which is the head of Tuscane: or
els to common privately with a person of estimacion in
that city about waightye affaires: or also with the
familiarst frend he hath about pleasaunt matters: or
with women or gentilmen about matters of love, either
in jesting or daliyng, banketting, gaming, or where ever
els: or in any time or place, or purpose, I am assured he
would flee the using of those auntient Tuscane
wordes.[43] And in usyng them, beside that he should be a
laughing stock, he should bringe no small lothesomenesse* to hym that heard them. Therfore me thinke it a
straunge matter to use those wordes for good in writing,
that are to be eschewed for naughtie in everie maner of
speache: and to have that whiche is never proper in
speache, to be the proprest way a man can use in
writing, forsomuch as (in mine opinion) wrytyng is
nothinge elles, but a maner of speache, that remaineth
stil after a man hath spoken, or (as it were) an Image, or
rather the life of the woordes. And therfore in speache,
whiche as soone as the soune is pronounced vanisheth a
way, peradventure somthinges are more to be borne
withall, then in writinge. Because writinge keepeth the
woordes in store, and referreth them to the judgemente
of the reader, and geveth tyme to examyne them depely.
And therefore reason willeth that greater diligence
should be had therein to make it more trimme and
better corrected: yet not so, that the written wordes
should be unlike the spoken, but in writing to chuse
oute the fayrest and proprest of significacion that be
used in speaking. And if that should be lawful in

Marginal notes:

Old wordes to
be eschewed
both in speak-
ing and
writing.

What wryt-
yng is.

---

* lothesomenesse: irritation, annoyance.

writing, which is not lawfull in speaking, there should arise an inconvenience of it (in my judgement) very great: namely, that a man myght use a greater libertie in the thinge, where he ought to use most diligence, and the labour he bestoweth in writing, in stede of furtherance should hinder him. Therfore it is certain, whatsoever is allowed in writing, is also allowed in speaking: and that speache is moste beautifull that is like unto beautifull writinges. And I judge it much more behoufful to be understoode in writing then in speaking, because they that write are not alwaies presente with them that rede, as they that speake with them that speake. Therfore would I commende him, that beside the eschewing of many auncient Tuskane woordes, would applye himself also to use bothe in writing and speakyng, suche as now a daies are in use in Tuscane and in other partes of Italy, and that have some grace in the pronunciation. And (in my minde) whoso foloweth any other trade is not assured not to runne into that curiositie so muche blamed, whiche we have spoken of before.

[XXX] Then spake SIR FREDERICK: I cannot denye you, Count Lewis, that writinge is not a maner of speaking. But this I saie, if the wordes that are spoken have any darkenesse in them, that communicacion perceth not the minde of him that heareth: and passing without being understoode, wexeth vaine and to no purpose: the whiche dothe not happen in writyng, for if the woordes that the writer useth bring with them a litle (I will not saie diffycultie) but covered subtilty, and not so open, as suche as be ordinarily spoken, they geve a certain greater aucthoritye to writing, and make the reader more hedefull to pause at it, and to ponder it better, and he taketh a delyte in the wittinesse and learning of him that writeth, and with a good judgement, after some paines takyng, he tasteth the pleaser that consisteth in harde thinges. And if the ygnoraunce of him that readeth bee suche, that he cannot compasse that difficultie, there is no blame in the writer, neither ought a man for all that to thinke that tunge not to bee faire. Therefore in writing, I houlde opinion it is necessarie for a man to use the Tuscane wordes, and only such as have bene used among the auncient

What is allowed in wryting, is allowed in speaking.

Why writing oughte to bee more understoode then speaking.

Tuskans: for it is a great testimoniall and approved by tyme, that they bee good and of pithie signification in that thei be applyed to. And beside this they have that grace and majesty that antiquitie geveth not only to woordes, but unto buildinges, ymages, peinctinges, and to everye thyng that is of force to* preserve it. And many times with this onely brightnes and dignitie they make the fourme of sentences very fair, and through the vertue and elegancie thereof, every matter howe base so ever it be, maie be so decked oute, that it maie deserve verye great commendacion. But this youre custome, that you make so muche a doe of, appeareth unto me very daungerous, and many times it maie be naught.†

So manye Cities so many diverse maner of speaches in Italy.

And if anye vice of speache be taken up of many ignorant persones, me thinke for all that it oughte not to be receyved for a rule, nor folowed of other. Besides this, customs be manye and divers, and ye have not a notable Citye in Italy that hath not a divers maner of speache from all the rest. Therefore if ye take not the paines to declare whiche is the best, a manne maye as well geve hym selfe to the Bergamask tunge, as to the Florentine, and to folowe youre advyse it were no

The Berga-mask tunge the moste barbarous in Italy.

erroure at all. Me semeth then who so wyll be out of doubte and well assured, it is requisite for him to determyne with hym selfe to folowe one, that by al mens accorde is judged good, and to take him for a guyde alwaies and for a shielde againste suche as wyll goe about to fynde faulte, and that I thinke oughte to bee none other, (I meane in the vulgar tunge) but Petrarca

Petrarca.

Boccaccio.

and Boccaccio: and who so swarveth from these two, goeth at all aventure,‡ as he that walketh in the darke without lyght, and therefore many times strayeth from the right waye. But wee are so hardye nowadayes, that wee disdeigne to do as other good menne of auncient tyme have done: that is to saye, to take dylygente heede

Imitation.

Virgil.

to folowinge,§ without the whiche I judge no man canne wryte well. And me thinke Virgill declarethe a greate triall of this, whoo for all that with his so devine a witte and judgemente he tooke all hope from his

---

* of force to: capable of.   † naught: a bad thing.
‡ at all aventure: gropingly.   § folowinge: imitation.

posteritye for anye to folowe him at anye tyme, yet would he folow Homer.

[XXXI] Then the L. GASPER PALLAVICIN: This disputacion (quoth he) of writinge in verye deede is woorthe the hearinge: yet were it more to oure purpose, if you woulde teache in what sorte the Courtier ought to speake, for me thinke he hath more neede of that, and he serveth his tourne oftner with speakyng then with wrytinge.

The L. JULIAN aunswered: There is no doubt, but so excellent and so perfect a Courtier hath nede to understand both the one and the other, and without these two qualyties paraventure all the rest should not be much woorthye prayse: therefore if the Count will fulfill hys charge, he shall teache the Courtier not onelye to speake but also to write well.

Then said the COUNT: I will not (my Lorde) undertake this enterprise, for it shoulde be a greate folye for me to teache an other that I understand not my self. And thoughe I were skillfull in it, yet can I not see howe I shoulde thinke to do the thing in so fewe woordes, which greate Clearkes have scase done wyth such great study and diligence, unto whose writings I would remit our Courtyer, if it were so that I wer bounde to teache him to write and to speake.

The L. CESAR then said: The L. Julian meaneth the speaking and writing of the vulgar tunge, and not Latin, therfore those writinges of great Clearkes are not for oure purpose. But you muste shewe us in this behalfe as muche as you knowe, as for the reste, ye shalbe held excused.

I have already sayde, aunswered the COUNT. But in reasoning upon the Tuskane tunge, perhappes it were rather the L. Julians part, then any mans els to geve judgement in it.

The L. JULIAN saide: I cannot, nor of reason ought to speake against him that saith the Tuskane tunge is fairer then al the rest. Trueth it is, there are many wordes in Petrarca and Boccaccio worne out of use now a daies: and suche would I never use neither in speakyng nor in writyng, and peradventure they themselves if thei were nowe alive would use them no more.

Then spake SIR FREDERICK: No doubt but they

Woordes in Petrarca, and in Boccaccio not to be used.

would use them still. And you Lordes of Tuscane ought to renue your tunge, and not to suffer it decaye, as you do, for a man may saie nowe, that there is lesse knowledge in Florence, then in manye other places of Italy.[44]

Then aunswered M. BERNARD: Those woordes that are no more in use in Florence, doe styl continue among the men of the countrey, and are refused of the gentlemen for woordes corrupt and decayed by antiquitie.

[XXXII] Then the DUTCHESSE: Let us not swarve (quoth she) from our firste purpose, but lette us make Count Lewis teache the Courtyer to speake and to write well, be it Tuscane or what ever els.

The COUNT aunswered: I have alreadye spoken (madam) what I knowe. And I suppose the verye same rules that teache the one, maye also serve to teache the other. But sins ye commaunde me: I will make aunswere unto Syr Frederick what commeth in my head, for I am of a contrary opinion to him. And paraventure I shal be drieven to answere somewhat more darkely then will be allowed, but it shall be as muche as I am hable to saie. And first I say, that (to my judgement) this our tunge, whiche we name the vulgar tunge, is tender and newe, for al it hath bene now used a long while. For in that Italy hathe bene, not onely vexed and spoyled, but also inhabited a long time with barbarous people, by the great resort of those nations, the Latin tunge was corrupted and destroyed, and of that corruption have spronge other tunges. The whiche lyke the ryvers that departe from the toppe of the Appennine and runne abrode towarde the two seas: so are they also divided; and some died with the Latin speach have spred abrode sundrye waies, some into one part, and some into another, and one dyed with barbarousnesse hath remayned in Italy. This then hath a long time bene among us out of order and dyverse, because there was none that would bestow diligence about it, nor write in it, ne yet seke to geve it brightnesse or anye grace. Yet hath it bene afterwarde broughte into better frame in Tuscane, then in the other partes of Italye. And by this it appeareth that the flowre of it hath remained there ever since those first times, because that nation hath kept

The vulgar tunge of Italy is a new tunge.

How the Italian tunge was corrupted.

proper and sweete accentes in the pronunciation and an
order of grammer, where it was meete, more then the
other. And hath had three noble writers, whiche wittily
bothe in the woordes and termes that custome did
allowe in their time, have expressed their conceites and
that hath happened (in my mind) with a better grace to
Petrarca in maters of love, then to any of the other.
Where there arose afterwarde from time to time, not
onely in Tuscane, but in al Italy, among gentlemen
brought up in court, in armes and in letters, some studye
to speake and to write more finely then they did in that
first rude age, whan the turmoyle of the miseries that
arose through barbarous nations was not as yet quieted,
many woordes have bene left out* as well in Florence it
selfe, and in all Tuscane, as in the residue of Italy, and
other brought in, in their stead, and made in this behalfe
the alteration that happeneth in all worldly thinges: the
whiche also hath evermore chaunced in other tunges.
For in case those auncient Latin writinges had lasted
hitherto, we shoulde see that Evander and Turnus[45]
and the other Latins in those dayes spake otherwise
then dyd afterwarde the laste kinges of the Romaines
and the fyrste Consules. You may see the verses song by
the Salii wer scantly understoode of their posteritie:[46]
but because it was so ordeyned by the first inventours of
it, they were not altered for reverence of religion. So
from time to time Oratours and Poets forsoke manye
woordes that had bene used amonge their predecessours: for Antonius, Crassus, Hortensius, and Ciccro
eschewed manye that Cato had used, and Virgill many
of Ennius,[47] and so did the reste. For albeit they had
antiquitie in great reverence, yet did they not esteme
them somuch, that they woulde bee so bounde to them,
as you wil have us nowe. Yea, where they thoughte
good, they spake agaynst them, as Horace, that sayeth,
his predecessours dyd foolyshlye praise Plautus,[48]
which would† that we should have the aucthoritie to
bring up newe woordes. And Cicero in manye places
reprehendeth manye of his predecessours, and to blame
S. Galba, he sayeth that his Oracions smelled of
antiquitie.[49] And affirmeth that Ennius also in some

Petrarca.
Dante.
Boccaccio.

Speaches
chaunge from
time to time.

The priestes
Mars.

Men never
delited in
wordes worne
out with time.

Horace.

Cicero.

* left out: abandoned.
† The subject is still Horace.

pointes set lytle by his predecessours, so that yf we wyll folow them of olde tyme, we shall not folowe them. And Virgil that you saye folowed Homer, folowed hym not in the tunge.* [XXXIII] Therfore woulde I (for my parte) alwayes shonne the use of those auncient woordes, except it wer in certayne clauses, and in them very seldome. And (in my judgement) he that useth them otherwise, committeth a no lesse errour, then whoso would to folowe them of olde time, fede upon maste,† where he hath nowe aboundaunce of corne founde oute. And because you saie the auncient woordes onely with the brightnesse of antiquitie decke oute so highlye every matter, how base so ever it be, that it maye make it woorthy great commendacion: I saie unto you that not of these auncient woordes onely, but of those that be good in dede, I make so smal accompt, **Woordes without faire sentences litle worthe.** that I suppose without the juyce of fair sentences‡ thei ought of reason to be litle set by. For to divide the sentences from the woordes, is the deviding of the soule from the body, the which cannot be done, neither in the one nor in the other, without destruccion ensue upon it. That therfore which is the principal mater and **Knowledge necessarie to speake and write well.** necessary for a Courtyer to speak and write wel, I beleve is knowledge. For he that hath not knowledge and the thing in his minde that deserveth to be understood, can neither speak nor write it. Then must he couch in a good order that he hath to speake or to write, and afterward **What words oughte to be.** expresse it wel with wordes: the which (if I be not deceived) ought to be apt, chosen, clere, and wel applyed, and (above al) in use also among the people: for very suche make the greatnes and gorgeousnes of an Oracion, so he that speaketh have a good judgement and heedfulnes withal, and the understanding to pike such as be of most proper significacion, for that he entendeth to speake and commend, and tempring them like wexe after his owne mynde, applyeth them in suche parte and in suche order, that at the firste showe they maie set furth and doe men to understand§ the dignitie and brightnes of them, as tables of peincting placed in

* in the tunge: where language is concerned.
† maste: acorns.   ‡ sentences: sentiments, thoughts.
§ doe men to understand: display.

their good and naturall light. And this do I saie as well
of writing as of speaking, wherein certayne thinges are
requisite that are not necessary in wryting, as a good
voyce, not to subtyll or soft, as in a woman: nor yet so
boysterous and roughe, as in one of the Countrey, but
shrill, clere, sweete and wel framed with a prompt
pronunciacion and with fitte maners and gestures,
which (in my minde) consiste in certain mocions of al
the body not affected nor forced, but tempred with a
manerly countenance and with a moving of the eyes,
that may geve a grace and accord with the words, and
(asmuch as he can) signify also with gestures the entent
and affeccion*of the speaker. But al these thinges wer in
vain and of smal accompte yf the sentences expressed by
the wordes should not be fair, witty, subtil, fine and
grave according to the mater.

[XXXIV] I doubt, said the M. MORELLO, if this
Courtyer speake with suche finenesse and gravity
among us, there wil be some that wil not understand
him.

Nay, every one shall understand him, answered the
COUNT, for finenes hindreth not the easines of understanding. Neither wil I have him to speak alwaies in
gravity, but of pleasant matters, of mery conceites, of
honest divises, and of jestes according to the time, and
in al notwithstanding after a pithy maner, and with
redines and varietie without confusion, neither shall he
in anye part show vanity or childish foly. And whan he
shal then commune of a matter that is dark and hard, I
wil have him both in woordes and sentences wel
pointed, to expresse his judgement, and to make every
doubt clere and plain after a certaine diligent sort
without tediousnesse.† Likewise (whan he shal see
time‡) to have the understanding to speake with
dignitie and vehemency, and to raise those affections§
which oure mindes have in them, and to enflame or
stirre them accordinge to the matter: sometime

Thynges
necessary in
spekinge.

The voyce.

The
sentences.

What he
muste speake
of.

To speake to
raise affec-
tyons.

---

* affeccion: feelings, emotion.
† without tediousnesse: without difficulty to the reader.
‡ when he shal see time: when the occasion demands.
§ to raise those affections: stirring those emotions.

with a simplicitye of suche meekenesse of mynde, that a man woulde weene nature her self spake, to make them tender and (as it wer) dronken with sweetenesse: and with suche conveiaunce of easinesse, that whoso heareth him, maye conceyve a good oppinion of himselfe, and thinke that he also with very litle a doe, mighte attaine to that perfection, but whan he commeth to the proofe shall finde himselfe farre wide. I would have oure Courtyer to speake and write in that sort, and not onely choose gorgeous and fine woordes out of every parte of Italye, but also I would judge him woorthy praise to use some of those termes bothe Frenche and Spanishe, whiche by oure custome have bene admitted. Therfore it should not mislike me, fallyng so to purpose, to say, *Vauntcourrour*: to saye, to acertain, to aventure: to saye, to perce through a body with talke, meaning thereby to use a familiaritie wyth him, and to grope him to geat of him some perfect knoweledge: to saie, a royall gentleman, a nete man to be about a Prince, and suche other termes,* so he maie thinke to be understoode. Sometime I would have him take certain woordes in an other significacion then that is proper to them, and wrasting them to his purpose (as it were) graffe them lyke a graffe of a tree in a more luckye stocke, to make them more sightly and faire, and (as it were) draw the matters to the sense of the verye eyes, and (as they saie) make them felte wyth hande, for the delyte of him that heareth, or readeth. Neyther woulde I have him to sticke to forge newe also, and with newe figures of speache, deriving them featly from the Latins, as the Latins in olde tyme, derived from the Grecians. [XXXV] In case then of suche learned men bothe of good witte and judgement, as now a dayes may be piked out among us, there were some that would bestow their travail to write after the maner that we

Certaine termes out of the French and Spanishe, which sound not so wel in Englishe nor can be applied to oure phrase.

Woordes in an other sygnificacion.

To forge new wordes.

---

* The examples of foreign borrowings given in the original are *'primor'* ('excellence'); *'accertare'* ('to hit the mark'); *'avventurare'* ('to risk'); *'ripassare una persona con ragionamento'* ('to sound someone out' or literally, as Hoby recognises, 'to run someone through with words'); *'un cavaliere senza rimproccio'* ('a perfect gentleman'); *'attillato'* ('smartly dressed'); and *'creato d'un principe'* ('someone in the service of a prince').

have spoken of, in this tongue thinges worth the
readinge, wee shoulde soone see it in good frame and
flowinge with termes and good phrases, and so copious
that a man might as well write in it as in anye other
tongue: and thoughe it were not the meere auntient
Tuscane tongue, yet shoulde it be the Italian tongue,
commune, plentifull, and variable, and (as it were) like
a delicious gardein ful of sundrie flowres and frutes.
Neyther shoulde this be a newe matter: for of the foure
tongues that were in use amonge the Greeke writers,[50]
pikinge out of everye* worde, moodes and rules as they
thought meete, they raysed therby an other, whiche was
named the Commune tongue, and afterward all fyve   **V. tunges of**
they called with one name the Greeke tongue. And   **Greece.**
albeit the Athenian tongue was more fine, purer, and
eloquenter then the rest, yet did not the good writers
that were not of Athens borne, so affect it, but in the
stile of writing, and (as it were) in the smack and
propretie of their naturall speache they were welinough
knowen: neither were they anye whit the lesse
regarded for all that, but rather such as would appeere
over mere Athenians wer blamed for it. Amonge the
Latin writers in like case manye there were in their
dayes much setbye that were no Romanes althoughe
there appeared not in them that propre and peculiar
purenesse of the Romane tongue, whiche menne of an
other nation can verie seldome attaine. In times past T.   **T. Livius.**
Livius was not neglected, althoughe some one sayde he
founde in him mere Padowan:[51] nor Virgil, for that he   **Virgill.**
was reprehended that he spake not Romane. And (as
you know) there were also read and much setbye in
Roome manie writers of Barbarous nations. But we
more precise a great deale then they of olde time, do
binde our selves with certaine new lawes out of
purpose: and having the brode beaten waye beefore
oure eyes, seeke through gappes to walke in unknowen
pathes. For in oure owne tounge, whose office is (as all
others) to expresse well and clearlye the conceites of the
minde, we delite in darkenesse, and callinge it the vulgar   **The vulgar**
tounge, will use in it woordes, that are not onely not   **tunge ought**
understoode of the vulgar people, but also of the best   **not to be**
                                                         dark.

* of everye: out of each of the four languages.

sort of menne and that men of learninge, and are not used in any part, not regarding that all good wryters of olde time blamed such woordes as were refused of custome, the which you (in my mind) do not well knowe, for somuche as you say, if any vice of speache be taken up of many ignorant parsons, it ought not to be called a custome nor received for a rule of speache. And (as at other tymes I have hard you say) ye wil have again in the stead of Capitolio, we should say Campidoglio:

for Hieronymo, Girolamo: Aldace, for Audace: and for Patrone padrone:[52] and such corrupt and mangled wordes, because they have bene founde so written by some ignorant Tuscane of olde time, and because the men of the countrey speak so in Tuscane now a dayes. The good use of speache therefore I beleve ariseth of men that have wytte, and with learninge and practise have gotten a good judgement, and with it consent and agree to receave the woordes that they think good, which are knowen by a certaine naturall judgement, and not by art or anye maner rule. Do you not knowe

that figures of speach which give suche grace and brightnesse to an Oration, are all the abuse of Grammer rules, but yet are receaved and confirmed by use, because men are able to make no other reason but that they delite, and to the verye sence of our eares it appeareth they bringe a lief and a sweetenesse? And this

beleave I is good custome, which the Romanes, the Napolitans, the Lombardes, and the rest are as apt to receave, as the Tuscanes. [XXXVI] Truth it is, in everye

tounge some thinges are alwayes good, as easinesse to be understoode, a good ordre, varietie, piked sentences,* clawses wel framed: and on the other side Affectation, and the other contrary to these are to be shonned. But of woordes some there are that last a good tyme and afterwarde wexe stale and cleane lose their grace: other some take force and creepe into estimation, for as the seasones of the yeare make leaves and fruites to fal, and afterward garnish the trees a freshe with other: evenso, doth time make those first wordes to fall, and use maketh other to springe afreshe and giveth theim grace and estimation, untill they in like sorte

---

* piked sentences: fine insights.

consumed by lytle and lytle with the envyous biting of tyme come to their end, because at the last both we and whatsoever is oures, are mortall.[53] Consider with your selves that we have no more any knoweleage of the Osca tunge. The Provinciall tung, that (a man may say) the last day was renowmed of noble writers,[54] now is it not understoode of the inhabitantes of the countrey. I beleave therefore (as the L. Julian hath said), that wer Petrarca, and Boccaccio, at this present in lief, they would not use many woordes that we see in their writinges. Therfore (in mine opinion) it is not well done to folow them therin. Yet do I muche commende them that can folowe that ought to be folowed: but notwithstanding I beleve it be possible ynough to write well without folowyng, and especiallye in this our tunge, wherin we may be helped by custome, the which I wyll not take upon me* in the Latin.

[XXXVII] Then Sir Friderick: Why, wil you (quoth he) custom should be more appriced in the vulgar tunge, then in the Latin?

Naye, bothe in the one and the other (answered the Count) I judge custome ought to be the maistresse. But forsomuche as those menne, unto whom the Latin tunge was as proper, as is the vulgar tunge nowe to us, are no more in the world, we must learne of their writinges that they learned by use and custome: neyther doeth auncyent speach signifye anything els but an auncyent custome of speach: and it wer a fond matter to love the auncient speach for nothing elles but to speake rather as men did speake, then as menne doe speake.

Did not they then of olde time folowe? aunswered Sir Fridericke.

I beleave, quoth the Counte, many did folowe, but not in every point. An if Virgill had altogether folowed Hesiodus,[55] he should not have passed him nor Cicero, Crassus, nor Ennius, his predecessors. Behould Homer, who is so auntient that he is thought of many to be the first heroical Poet aswell of time, as also of excellencie of phrase: and whom wyll you have him to have folowed?

Tunges decayed with time.

Auntient speach. Auntient custome of speache.

Olde writers did not imitate in all pointes.

* the which I wyll not take upon me: something I would not venture to say.

Some other, aunswered SIR FRIDERICK, more auntient then he was, whiche we heare not of, by reason of tomuch antiquitie.

Whom will you say then Petrarca and Boccaccio folowed, said the COUNT, whiche (a man may say) were but thre dayes agoo in the world?

I knowe not, answered SIR FRIDERICKE, but it is to be thoughte they in lyke wise bent their minde to folowinge, thoughe wee knowe not of whom.

The COUNT aunswered: A man maye beleave that they that were folowed, were better then they that did folowe: and it were to great a wonder that their name and renowme (if they were good) should so soone be cleane lost. But I beleave their verye maister was witt, and their owne naturall inclination and judgement. And therat no man ought to wonder, for (in a maner) alwayes a manne by sundrye wayes may clime to the toppe of all perfection. And their is no matter, that hath not in it many thinges of like sort unlike the one to the other, which for al that among them selves deserve a like praise. Mark me musick, wherin are harmonies somtime of base soune and slowe, and otherwhile very quicke and of newe divises, yet do they all recreat a man: but for sundrye causes, as a manne may perceive in the maner of singinge that Bidon[56] useth, which is so artificiall, counninge, vehement, stirred, and suche sundrye melodies, that the spirites of the hearers move al and are enflamed, and so listening a man would wene they were lifte up in to heaven. And no lesse doeth our Marchetto Cara move in his singinge, but with a more softe harmonye, that by a delectable waye and full of mourninge sweetnesse maketh tender and perceth the mind, and sweetly imprinteth in it a passion full of great delite. Sundrye thinges in lyke maner do equally please oure eyes somuche, that a man shall have muche a do to judge in whiche they most delite. Behould in peincting Leonard Vincio, Mantegna, Raphael, Michelangelo, George of Castelfranco:[57] they are all most excellent dooers, yet are they in working unlike, but in any of them a man wold not judge that there wanted ought in his kind of trade: for every one is knowen to be of most perfection after his maner. The like is of many Poets both Greeke and Latin, which being diverse in writing

A man may write well without imitation.

Musick.

Sundry sortes of musike and all delite.

Sundry peincters perfit in sundrie kinde of trades.

are alike in praise. Oratours also have alwaies had such
a diversitye emong them, as (in a maner) everye age*
hath brought forth and set by one sort of Oratours
peculiar for that time, which have bene unlike and
disagreing not only to their predecessours and folowers
but also emong themselves. As it is written emonge the
Grecians, of Isocrates, Lysias, Eschines and many other,
al excellent, but yet like unto none saving themselves.
And emong the Latins, Carbo, Lælius, Scipio
Affricanus, Galba, Sulpitius, Cotta, Graccus, Marcus
Antonius, Crassus, and so many, that it should be long
to repete them, all good and moste diverse one from an
other.[58] So that whoso could consider all the Oratours
that have bene in the worlde, he should finde so manye
Oratours, so many kindes of speach. Me thynke I
remember also that Cicero in a place bringeth in
Marcus Antonius to say unto Sulpitius that ther are
many that folow no man, and yet clime they to a high
degree of excellency.[59] And speaketh of certein that had
brought up a new stile and phrase of speaking faire, but
not used of the Oratours of that time wherin they
folowed none but themselves. Therfore he affirmeth
also that maisters shoulde consider the nature of their
scolers, and taking it for their guide, direct and prompt
them in the way that their witt and naturall inclination
moveth them unto. For this cause therfore, Sir
Fridericke, do I beleve if a man have not an inclination
unto some author whatsoever he be, it were not wel
done to force him to folowing. Bicause the vertue of that
disposicion of his, soone feinteth and is hindered, by
reason that it is a stray out of the way in which he would
have profited, had he not bene stopped in it. I knowe not
then how it will stande wel, in steade of enriching this
tunge, and of gevyng it majestye and light, to make it
poore, sclender, bare and dark, and to seeke to shut it
up into so narrowe a rowme, that everye man should be
compelled to folow onely Petrarca and Boccaccio,[60]
and that we should not also in that tung, credit
Laurence de Medicis, Francis Diaceto, and certein
other[61] that notwithstanding are Tuscanes, and perhappes of no lesse learning and judgement then Petrarca

Greeke
oratours.

Latin
oratours.

So manye
oratours so
many kindes
of speach.

De Oratore
lib. i.

Lib. ii.

An errour to
imitate none
but Boccaccio
and Petrarca.

---

* (in a maner) everye age: almost every era.

and Boccaccio. And truly it should be a great miserye to stoppe without wading any farther then almost the first that ever wrote: and to dispaire, that so many and so noble wittes shall never find out any mo then one good maner of speach in the tung that unto them is proper and naturall. But now a dayes there be some so scrupulous, that (as it were) with a religion and high misteries of this their Tuscane tung, put as manye as heareth them in such dread, that they bring in like case many gentilmen and learned men into such an awe, that they dare not open their mouth: and confesse plainly, that they can not speak the tung which thei have learned of their nurses, even from their cradel. But in this point (me think) we have spoken tomuch. Therfore let us now procead in our communication of the Courtier.

[XXXVIII] Then answered SIR FRIDERICK: But first I will saye this lytle, whiche is that I denye not but the opinions and wittes of men are divers emong themselves: neither doe I judge it comlye for one that is vehement and quicke of nature to take in hand to write of soft and quiet matters. Nor yet for an other that is severe and grave to write of mery conceits. For in this point (me think) it is reason every man should apply him self to his own proper inclination, and of this I beleve spake Cicero, when he said that maisters should have a consideration to the nature of their scholers, least they should doe like the yll husbandmanne, that sometime in a soyle that is good onely for vynes will sowe graine. But it wyll not sinke into my head why in a perticuler tunge, that is not so proper unto all menne, as are discourses and conceites, and many other operations, but an invencion contained under certaine termes, a man may not with more reason folowe them that speake best, then speake at al aventure.* And that, as in the Latin tunge a manne ought to apply himselfe to bee in the tunge lyke unto Virgil and Cicero, rather then Silius and Cornelius Tacitus,[62] so in the vulgar tunge why it were not better to folowe the tunge of Petrarca and Boccaccio then any mannes els: and therin expresse well his owne conceites, and so applye himselfe as (Cicero saith) to his owne naturall inclination. And thus

* at al aventure: at random.

shall the difference whiche you saye is betwene the good
Oratours, be found to consist in the senses and not in
the tunge.*

Then the COUNT: I feare me (quoth he) we shall enter
into a large sea, and leave oure first purpose of the
Courtyer. But I would knowe of you, wherin consisteth the goodnes of this tunge?

SIR FRIDERICKE aunswered: In keping well the
propertie of it: and in taking it in the significacion (using
the same stile and measur) that al such have done as
have written wel.

Wherin con-
sisteth the
goodnesse of
the tung.

I would know then, quoth the COUNT, whether this
stile and measure which you speake of, arise of the
sentences† or of the wordes?

Of the wordes, answered SIR FRIDERICK.

Do you not think then, quoth the COUNT, that the
wordes of Silius and Cornelius Tacitus are the very
same that Virgil and Cicero use? and taken in the same
signification?

SIR FRIDERICKE aunswered: They are the very same
in dede, but some yll applyed and dyverslye taken.

The COUNT aunswered: In case a manne shoulde
pyke out of a booke of Cornelius and of Silius, al the
woordes placed in other signification then is in Virgil
and Cicero, (whiche shoulde bee verye fewe) woulde
you not then saye that Cornelius in the tounge were
equall with Cicero, and Silius with Virgil?

[XXXIX] Then the L. EMILIA: Me thinke (quoth
shee) thys youre dysputation hathe lasted to longe, and
hathe been verye tedyouse, therefore it shall bee best to
deferre it untill an other tyme.

Sir Fridericke began still to make aunswere, but the
L. Emilia alwayes interrupted hym.

At laste the COUNT saide: Manye will judge of styles
and talke of numbers and measures,‡ and of folowing,§
but they cannot doe me to understande what maner a
thinge stile and measure is, and wherin folowing
consisteth. Nor why, thinges taken out of Homer or any

Many talkers
of imitation.

---

* in the senses and not in the tunge: in what they say, rather than
the language they use.
† sentences: meaning, thoughts.
‡ measures: rhythm.   § folowing: imitation.

other, are so well couched in Virgil, that they appeare rather amplyfied then folowed, and peradventure the occation thereof is that I am not able to conceive it. But because a great argument that a man understandeth a thinge, is the understanding that he hath to teach it, I feare me they themselves have small understanding in it, and praise Virgil and Cicero, because they heare them praised of many, not for that they knowe the difference betwene them and others, whiche out of peradventure* consisteth not in the observation of two, or three, or of tenne woordes used after a divers maner from other. In Salust, in Cesar, in Varro,[63] and in other good writers, there are founde some termes applyed otherwise then Cicero applyeth them, and both the one and the other doeth welinough. Bicause in so triflynge a matter the goodnesse and perfection of a tunge doeth not consiste as Demosthenes answered Eschines well that had taken him up, demaundinge him of certaine woordes which he hadde used and yet were not auntient, what monsters or wonderous matters they were? Wherat Demosthenes laughed, and answered him, that the fortunes of Grece depended not upon them.[64] Even so would I passe full litle if a Tuscane should reprehende me for speaking rather *Satisfatto*, then *Sodisfatto*: and *Honorevole*, then *Horrevole*: and *Causa*, then *Cagione*: and *Populo*, then *Popolo*, and such other matters.

Then arose SIR FRIDERICK upon his feete and saide: I besech ye give the hearing of these few woordes.

The L. EMILIA answered laughing: Uppon my displeasure I forbid anye of you to talke any more in this matter, for I will have you to breake it of untill an other night. But you Count, proceade you in your communication of the Courtyer, and let us see how good a memory you have: for I beleve, if ye can knitt it agayne where you brake of, ye shall not do a litle.

[XL] Madam, answered the COUNT, me think the thrid is broken in sunder, but if I be not deceyved, I trowe we saide that pestylent curiositie doth alwayes geve an il grace unto al thinges: and contrarywise simplicity and Reckelesness a marvailous good grace. In commendation wherof and in dispraise of curiosity,†

Demosthenes aunswer to Eschines.

Diversitie of certain Tuscane wordes with the rest of Italy.

* out of peradventure: most certainly.
† curiosity: affectation.

many other thinges might be said, yet wil I alleage but
one mo, and then have done. All women generally have
a great desire to be, and when they canne not be, at the
least to appear beawtyfull. Therfore where nature in
some part hath not done her devoyr therin, they
endeavour them selves to supply it with art. Of this
ariseth the trymming of the face, with such studye
and many times peines, the pilling* of the browes and
forehead, and the usynge of all those maner wayes, and
the abydyng of such lothsomenesse,† as you women
beleave are kepte very secret from men, and yet do all
men know them.

> Women that
> peincte them
> selves to seme
> faire to men.

The LA. CONSTANCE FREGOSA laughed at this, and
said: You shoulde do much better to go forward in your
communication, and declare how a man may attein a
good grace, and speak of courtynge,‡ then to discover
the faultes of women wythout purpose.

Nay it is much to purpose, answered the COUNT,
bicause these defaultes that I talke of take this grace
from you: for they proceade of nothing els but of
curiousnesse, wherby ye discover openlye unto everye
man the over great desire that ye have to be beawtiful.
Do you not marke howe much more grace is in a
woman, that if she doth trim her self, doeth it so
scarcely and so litle, that whoso behouldeth her,
standeth in doubt whether she be trimmed or no: then
in an other so bedawbed, that a man woulde wene she
had a viser on her face and dareth not laugh for making
it chappe: nor at any tyme chaungeth her colour, but
whan she apparayeleth her self in the morninge, and all
the rest of the daye standeth lyke an image of woodde
without movinge, shewinge her self onely in torche
light, as craftye marchaundmen do their clothes in their
darke lightes? How much more then doeth a man delite
in one, I meane not foule, that is manyfestlye seene she
hath nothinge uppon her face, though she be not so
white nor so red, but with her naturall colour somewhat
wan, sometime with blusshinge or through other

> Women that
> bestowe no
> payne in set-
> tnge out
> themselves.

* pilling: plucking.
† abydyng of such lothsomenesse: putting up with so much
trouble.
‡ courtynge: the art of courtiership.

chaunce dyed with a pure rednes, with her hear by happe out of order and ruffled, and with her simple and naturall gestures, without shewing her self to bestow diligence or study, to make her faire? This is that not regarded pureness which best pleaseth the eyes and mindes of men, that stande alwayes in awe to be deceived by art. Whyte teeth is a good sight in a woman, for sence they are not in so open sight as is the face, but most communly are hid, a man may think she bestoweth not so much laboure about them, to make them white, as she doeth in the face: yet who so shoulde laughe without cause purposly to show them, should discover the art, and for all their faire whitenesse should appeare unto all men to have a very yll grace, as Egnatius in Catullus.[65] The like is in the handes, which being delicate, smooth and faire, yf they be shewed bare at a tyme whan occasyon is to occupye them, and not of purpose to showe the beawtye of them, they leave a very great desire of themselves, and especiallye after they are covered with gloves agayne, for a manne would judge that in puttynge them on againe she passeth not and lytle regardeth whether they be in sighte or no, and that they are so fayre rather by nature, then by anye studye or dilygence. Have ye not hadde an eye otherwhyle, whan eyther in the stretes goynge to Churche, or in anye other place, or in sportyng, or by any other chaunce it happeneth that a woman lyfteth up her clothes so high, that she sheweth her foote, and sometime a litle of her pretye legge unwittinglye? And seemeth shee not to you to have a verye good grace, yf ye beholde her then with a certayne womanlye disposition, cleanlye and precise, with her shooes of vellute, and her hose sittynge cleane to her legge? Truely it deliteth me much, and I beleve all of you, for everye manne supposeth that Preciseness in so secret a place and so sildom seen, to be unto that woman rather natural and propre then forced, and that thereby she thinketh to gett her no commendation at all. [XLI] In such sort is curiousenesse avoyded and covered, the which you maye nowe conceyve howe contrarye it is, and taketh awaye the grace of everye operation and deede, aswell of the bodye as of the minde, whereof hitherto we have spoken but litle, and yet ought it not to be omitted, for as the minde is muche

White teath.

Faire handes.

Clenlye and precise in places sildome seene.

The minde.

more worthye then the bodye, so deserveth it also to bee
better decked and polished. And howe that ought to be
in oure Courtyer (leavyng a parte the preceptes of so
manye wyse Phylosophers that wryte in this matter and
define the vertues of the minde, and so subtillye dyspute
of the dignitye of them) wee will expresse in fewe
wordes, applyinge to our pourpose, that it is sufficient
he be (as they terme it commonlye) an honest manne
and welmeaning: for in this is comprehended the
goodnesse, the wisdome, the manlynesse and the
temperaunce of the mynde, and all other qualityes that
belonge to so worthye a name. And I recken hym onely   To applye a
a true morall Phylosopher that wyll be good, and to   mans good
that, he needeth fewe other preceptes then that will of   will is pro-
his. And therefore saide Socrates well, that he thought   feting.
his instructions hadde broughte foorth good fruite whan
by them he hadde provoked anye one to applye hys wyll
to the knoweleage and learnynge of vertue. For they
that are come to the pointe that they covette nothynge
more then to be good, do easily attayne the understandynge of all that beelongeth thereto: therefore
herein we wyll make no more a do. [XLII] But besyde
goodnesse, the true and principall ornament of the
mynde in everye manne (I beeleave) are letters, although
the Frenchmen know onelye the noblenesse of armes,   The French
and passe for nothing beside: so that they do not onelye   menne make
not sett by letters, but they rather abhorre them, and all none ac-
learned men they count verie rascalles, and they think it   compte of
a great vilany whan any one of them is called a clarke.   learning.

Then aunswered the L. JULIAN: You say very true,
this errour in deede hath longe reigned among the
Frenchemen. But if Monseigneur Angoulism[66] have so   Francis I.
good luck that he may (as men hope) succede in the   French king.
Croun, the glory of armes in Fraunce doeth not so
florishe nor is had in suche estimation, as letters wilbe, I
beleave. For it is not long sins I was in Fraunce, and saw
this Prince in the Court there, who semed unto me
beside the handsomenesse of personne and beawty of
visage, to have in his countenance so great a majestie,
accompanyed neverthelesse with a certayne lovelye
courteisy, that the realme of Fraunce should ever seeme
unto him a small matter. I understoode afterward by
many gentilmen both French and Italian, very much of

the most noble condicions, of the greatnesse of courage, prowesse and liberalitie that was in him: and emonge other thinges, it was tolde me that he highly loved and esteemed letters, and had in verie great reputation all learned men, and blamed the Frenchemen themselves that their mindes were so farr wide from this profession, especially having at their doores so noble an universitye as Paris is, where all the world resorteth.

Universitye
of Paris.

Then spake the COUNT: It is great wonder that in these tender yeres only by the provocation of nature, contrary to the maner of the countrey, he hath geven himself to so good a way. And because subjectes folow alwaies the condicions of the higher powers, it is possible that it may come to passe (as you say) that the Frenchmen will yet esteeme letters to be of that dignity that they are in deed. The which (if they wil geve ear ther to) they may soone be perswaded, forsomuch as men ought to covet of nature nothing so much and that is more proper for them, then knowleage: which thing it wer a great folly to say or to holde opinion that it is not alwaies good. [XLIII] And in case I might commune with them, or with other that were of a contrarie opinion to me, I would do my diligence to show them, how much letters (which undoubtedlye have bene graunted of God unto men for a soveraigne gift) are profytable and necessarye for our lief and estimation. Neyther should I want the examples of so many excellent capitaines of old time, which all joyned the Ornament of letters, with the prowesse of armes.[67] For (as you know) Alexander had Homer in such reverence, that he laide his *Ilias* always under his beddes head: and he applied diligentlye not these studies onely, but also the speculations of Philosophye under the discipline of Aristotle. Alcibiades encreased his good condicions and made them greater with letters, and with the instructions of Socrates. Also what dyligence Cesar used in studye, those thinges which he hath so divinely written him self, make triall. It is said that Scipio Africanus caried alwayes in his hande the bookes of Xenophon, wherein under the name of Cyrus he instructeth a perfect king. I could recite unto you Lucullus, Sylla, Pompeius, Brutus, and many other Romanes and Gretians, but I will do no more but make

Knowleage.

Howe
the great
Alexander
esteamed
Homer, Plu-
tarck, in
the life of
Alexander.

Alcibiades
Socrates
scholar.

J. Cesar.

Scipio
Africanus.
Paidia Xeno-
phontis.

mencion of Hanibal, which being so excellent a
captaine (yet for all that of a fierce nature, and voide of
all humanitye, an untrue dealer, and a despiser of men
and of the Gods) had also understanding in letters, and
the knowleage of the Greeke tunge. And if I be not
deceived (I trowe) I have read in my time that he left a
booke behind him of his owne makynge in the Greeke
tunge. But this kynd of talke is more then nedeth, for I
knowe all you understand howe much the Frenchemen
be deceived in houlding opinion letters to do anye hurt
to armes. You knowe in great matters and aventurous
in warres the true provocation is glory: and whoso for
lucres sake or for any other consideration taketh it in
hand (beside that he never doeth anye thynge woorthy
prayse) deserveth not the name of a gentleman, but is a
most vile marchaunt. And every man maye conceive it
to be the true glorye, that is stored up in the holy
treasure of letters, excepte such unlucky creatures as
have had no tast therof. What minde is so fainte, so
bashefull and of so base a courage, that in reading the
actes and greatnesse of Cesar, Alexander, Scipio,
Hannibal, and so many other, is not incensed with a
most fervent longing to be like them: and doth not
preferre the getting of that perpetuall fame, before this
rotten life that lasteth twoo dayes? Which in despite of
death maketh him lyve a greate deale more famous then
before. But he that savoureth not the sweetnesse of
letters, cannot know how much is the greatnesse of
glorye, which is a longe whyle preserved by them, and
onely measureth it with the age of one or two men, for
farther he beareth not in minde. Therfore can he not
esteme this shorte glorye so much as he woulde do that,
which (in a maner) is everlastinge, yf by his ill happe he
wer not barred from the knowleage of it. And not
passing upon it so much, reason perswadeth and a man
may well beleave he wyll never hasard hym self to come
by it, as he that knoweth it. I would not nowe some one of
the contrarye parte shoulde alleage unto me the contrarye
effectes to confute mine opinion with all: and tell me how
the Italians with their knowleage of letters have shewed
small prowesse in armes from a certaine time hitherto,
the which neverthelesse is to true.[68] But in very dede a
man may well saye that the offence of a few, hath

*Hannibal
learned.*

Glorye.

*In letters the
true glorye.*

*Noble
courages
enflamed in
readying the
actes of
famous cap-
taines.*

*The un-
learned knowe
not glorye.*

*Why the un-
learned seeke
not to be
famous.*

*Italians faint
in armes.*

brought (beside the great damage) an everlasting reproche unto all other. And the very cause of our confusion, and of the neglecting of vertue in our mindes (if it be not clean dead) proceaded of them. But it were a more shamefull matter unto us to publishe it, then unto the Frenchmen the ignoraunce in letters. Therfore it is better to passe that over with silence that cannot be rehersed without sorow, and leaving this purpose into the which I am entred against my will, retourne againe unto oure Courtier, [XLIV] whom in letters I will have to bee more then indyfferentlye well seene, at the leaste in those studyes, which they call Humanitie, and to have not only the understandinge of the Latin tunge, but also of the Greeke,[69] because of the many and sundrye thinges that with greate excellencye are written in it. Let him much exercise hym selfe in poets, and no lesse in Oratours and Historiographers, and also in writinge bothe rime and prose, and especiallye in this our vulgar tunge. For beside the contentation* that he shall receive thereby himselfe, he shall by this meanes never want pleasaunt intertcinments with women which ordinarylye love such matters. And if by reason either of his other busines beside, or of his slender studie, he shall not attaine unto that perfection that hys writinges may be worthye much commendation, let him be circumspect in keeping them close, least he make other men to laugh at him. Onely he may show them to a frend whom he may trust, for at the leastwise he shall receive so much profite, that by that exercise he shall be able to geve his judgement upon other mennes doinges. For it happeneth verye sildome, that a man not exercised in writinge, how learned so ever he be, can at any tyme know perfectly the labour and toile of writers, or tast of the sweetenes and excellencye of styles, and those inner observations that often times are found in them of olde tyme. And besyde that, those studyes shall make him copyous,† and (as Aristippus aunswered that Tiran) bould to speake uppon a good grounde wyth everye manne.[70] Notwithstanding I wyll have oure Courtier to keepe faste in his minde one lesson, and that is this, to be alwaies wary both in this and in every other point, and

The Courtier ought to be learned.

In humanity.

In the Latyn and Greeke tung.

In poetes.

In oratours.

In Historiographers.

In writynge ryme and prose.

What is to be done of a mans writinges.

The not practised can not judge.

Dionisius.

---

* contentation: pleasure.   † copyous: articulate.

rather fearefull then bould, and beware that he perswade not him self falsely to knowe the thing he
knoweth not indede. Because we are of nature al the
sort of us much more gredy of praise then is requisite,
and better to our eares love the melody of wordes
sounding to our praise, then any other song or soune
that is most sweete. And therfore manye tymes, lyke
the voices of Meremaydens, they are the cause of
drownyng him that doeth not well stoppe his eares at
such deceitfull harmonie. This daunger being perceived,
there hath bene among the auncient wise men that hath
written bookes, howe a manne should know a true
friend from a flatterer. But what availeth it? If there be
many of them (or rather infinit) that manifestly perceive
there are flatterers, and yet love hym that flattereth
them, and hate him that telleth them the trothe, and
often times (standinge in opinion that he that praiseth
them is to scace in his woordes) they themselves helpe
him forward, and utter such matters of themselves, that
the most impudent flatterer of all is ashamed of. Let us
leave these blinde busardes in their owne erroure, and
make oure Courtyer of so good a judgement, that he
will not be geven to understand blacke for white, nor
presume more of him selfe then what he knoweth very
manifestlye to be true, and especially in those thinges,
which (yf he beare well in minde)* the L. Cesar
rehearsed in his divise of pastimes,† that we have manye
tymes used for an instrument to make many become
foolysh. But rather, that he may be assured not to fall
into anye errour, where he knoweth those prayses that
are geven him to be true: let hym not so openly consent
to them, nor confirme them so without resistance, but
rather with modesty (in a maner) denye them cleane,
shewyng alwayes and countynge in effect, armes to be
his principall profession, and al the other good qualities
for an ornament thereof, and pryncypallye amonge
souldiers, least he be like unto them that in learnyng will
seeme men of warr, and among men of warr, learned. In
this wise for the reasons we have said he shal avoyde

*To be rather
warie then
bould in all
thinges.*

*The wordes
of flatterers
sweete.*

*Men take
no hede to
flatterers.*

*Men flatter
themselves.*

*How he
should avoid
flatterers.*

*Letters an
ornamente
of armes.*

---

* yf he beare well in minde. A mistranslation or misprint: if you
[ye] remember.
† divise of pastimes: his suggestion for a game.

curyousnesse, and the meane thinges which he taketh in hand, shal appeare very great.

[XLV] Here M. PETER BEMBO answered: I know not (Count Lewis) howe you will have this Courtier, being learned and of so many other vertuous qualities, to count every thing for an ornament of armes, and not armes and the reste for an ornamente of letters. The whyche wythout other addicyon are in dignitie so muche above armes, as the minde is above the bodye: because the practising of them belongeth properly to the mind even as the practising of armes dooeth to the body.

Armes belong to the mind and body both.

The COUNT answered then: Nay the practisinge of armes beelongeth aswel to the mind as to the body. But I wold not have you (M. Peter) a judge in this cause, for you would be to partial to one of the partes. And forsomuch as this disputation hath already bene tossed a longe time by moste wise men, we neede not to renew it, but I count it resolved upon armes side, and wil have our Courtier (since I have the facioning of him at mi wil) think thus also. And if you be of a contrary opinion, tary til you heare a disputation, where it may be as well lawfull for him that taketh part with armes, to use his armes, as thei that defend letters use in the defence the very same letters.

Oh (quoth M. PETER) you rebuked the Frenchmen before for setting litle by letters, and declared what a great light of glory they shew unto men and how they make them immortal: and now it seemeth you are in an other opinion. Do you not remember that:

Petrarca: Son. 155.

Alexander. Homer.

The great Macedo, when he proched neer
  Fiers Achils famous Toumb, thus said and sight:
O happy Prince that found a Tromp so cleer,
  And happy he that praysd so worthy a wight.[71]

Quint. Curt. lib. 2.

And if Alexander envied Achilles not for his deedes but for his fortune that gave him so great luck to have his actes renowmed by Homer, a man may gather he estemed more the letters of Homer then the armes of Achilles. What other judge then or what other sentence looke you for, as touching the dignity of armes and letters, then that which was geven by one of the greatest capitaines that ever were?

[XLVI] The Count answered: I blame the Frenchmen because they think letters hurt the profession of
armes: and I hould opinion that it is not so necessary for
any man to be learned, as it is for a man of war. And
these two pointes linked together and aided the one by
the other (which is most fit) wil I have to bee in the
Courtier. Neyther doe I thinke my self for this to be in
an other opinion,* but (as I have said) I will not dispute:
whiche of them is most worthy praise, it sufficeth that
learned men take not in hande at anye time to praise any
but great men, and glorious actes, which of themselves
deserve prayse by their proper essentiall vertues from
whence they arrise. Beside that, they are a most noble
Theme for writers, which is a great ornament, and
partly the cause of continuance of writinges, that
paraventure should not be so much read and set by, if
there wanted in them noble matter, but counted vaine
and of smal reputation. And if Alexander envied
Achilles bicause he was praised of him that did it, yet
doth it not consequently folowe that he esteamed letters
more then armes. Wherin if he had knowen himself so
farr wide from Achilles, as in writing he thought al they
would be from Homer that should go about to write of
him, I am sure he would muche sooner have desired wel
doing in himself then wel speaking in an other. Therfore
think I that this was a close praise of himself, and a
wishing for that he thought he had not, namelye the
high excellency of a writer, and not for that he thought
with himself he had already obtayned, that is to say, the
prowess of armes, wherin he counted not Achilles any
whit his superiour, wherefore he called him happye, as
it were signifiyng, where his fame in foretime was not so
renowmed in the worlde, as was the fame that by so
divyne a Poeme was cleere and excellent, it proceaded
not for that his prowes and desertes were not such and
worthy so much praise: but it arose of fortune that had
before hand prepared for Achilles that miracle of nature
for a glorious renowme and trompet of his actes. And
peradventure again he minded thereby to stirr up some
noble wit to wryte of himself, declaring thereby how
acceptable it should be to him, forsomuch as he loved

The Courtyer
a manne of
warre and
learned.

Glorious
actes a noble
Theme.

Alexander
thought not
himself in-
feriour to
Achilles.

What Alex-
ander ment
by calling
Achilles
happy.

* to be in an other opinion: to be contradicting myself.

and reverenced the holye monumentes of letters: about
the which we have now spoken sufficient.

Nay more then sufficient, aunswered the L.
LODOVICUS PIUS. For I beleve there is never a vessell in
the worlde possible to be founde so bigge that shalbe
able to receive al the thinges that you wil have in this
Courtyer.

Then the COUNT: Abide yet a while (quoth he) for
there be manye other thinges to be had in him yet.

PETER OF NAPLES aunswered: After this maner
Crassus de Medicis* shal have great avantage of M.
Peter Bembo.

[XLVII] At this they all laughed. And the COUNTE
beginning a freshe: My Lordes (quoth he) you must
thinke I am not pleased with the Courtyer if he be not
also a musitien, and beside his understanding and
The Courtyer   couning upon the booke,† have skill in lyke maner on
a musitien.   sundrye instruments. For yf we waie it well, there is no
ease of the labours and medicines of feeble mindes to be
founde more honeste and more praise worthye in tyme
of leyser then it. And princypally in Courtes, where
(beside the refreshing of vexacyons that musicke
bringeth unto eche man) many thynges are taken in
hande to please women withal, whose tender and soft
breastes are soone perced with melody and fylled with
swetenesse. Therefore no marvaile that in the olde times
and nowe a dayes they have alwayes bene enclined to
musitiens, and counted this a moste acceptable foode of
the mynde.

Then the L. GASPAR: I beleve musicke (quoth he)
together with many other vanities is mete for women,
and paradventure for some also that have the lykenes of
men, but not for them that be men in dede: who ought
not with suche delicacies to womannishe their mindes,
and brynge themselves in that sort to dread death.

Speake it not, answered the COUNT. For I shall enter
into a large sea of the praise of Musicke, and call to

---

* Crassus de Medicis. Hoby misses the joke here: the figure
referred to (probably a servant of the Medici family), is nicknamed
Grasso ('Fatty'), and his capacities as a receptacle for courtierly
attributes are being contrasted with those of the much slighter
Bembo.
† couning upon the booke: reading music.

rehearsal howe much it hath always bene renowmed emong them of olde time, and counted a holy matter: and how it hath bene the opinion of most wise Philosophers that the world is made of musick, and the heavens in their moving make a melody,[72] and our soule framed after the very same sort, and therfore lifteth up it self and (as it were) reviveth the vertues and force of it with musick: wherfore it is written that Alexander was sometime so fervently styrred with it, that (in a maner) against his wyll he was forced to arise from bankettes and runne to weapon, afterward the musitien chaunging the stroke and his maner of tune, pacified himself againe and retourned from weapon to banketting. And I shall tell you that grave Socrates whan he was well stricken in yeares learned to playe uppon the harpe. And I remember I have understoode that Plato and Aristotle will have a man that is well brought up, to be also a musitien:[73] and declare with infinite reasons the force of musicke to be to very great purpose in us, and for many causes (that should be to long to rehearse) ought necessarilye to be learned from a mans childhoode, not onely for the superficial melodie that is hard, but to be sufficient to bring into us a newe habite that is good, and a custome enclyning to vertue, whiche maketh the minde more apt to the conceiving of felicitie, even as bodely exercise maketh the bodie more lustie, and not onely hurteth not civyl matters and warrelyke affaires, but is a great staie to them. Also Lycurgus in his sharpe lawes allowed musicke. And it is read that the Lacedemons, whiche were valiaunt in armes, and the Cretenses used harpes and other softe instrumentes: and many most excellent captaines of olde time (as Epaminondas) gave themselves to musicke: and suche as had not a syght in it (as Themistocles) were a great deale the lesse set by. Have you not read that among the first instruccions which the good olde man Chiron taught Achilles in his tender age, whome he had brought up from his nurse and cradle, musick was one? And the wise maister would have those hands that should shed so muche Troyan bloude, to be oftentimes occupied in playing upon the harpe?[74] What souldyer is there (therefore) that will thinke it a shame to folow Achilles, omitting many

Musick in estimation in olde time.

Alexander styrred with musicke.

Xenofant. musitien.

Socrates beyng olde lerned upon the harpe.

Why musick is good.

Lycurgus. The Lacedemons. The Cretenses.

Epaminondas. Themistocles the lesse estemed for not beyng a musitien.

Chiron.

Achilles a musitien.

other famous captaines that I could alledge? Do ye not then deprive our Courtyer of musicke, which doth not onely make swete the mindes of men, but also many times wilde beastes tame: and whoso savoureth it not, a manne may assuredly thinke him not to be wel in his wittes. Beholde I praye you what force it hath, that in times paste allured a fishe to suffer a man to ride upon him throughe the tempestious sea. We maie see it used in the holy temples to render laude and thankes unto God, and it is a credible matter that it is acceptable unto him, and that he hath geven it unto us for a most swete lightning of our travailes and vexations. So that many times the boisterous labourers in the fieldes in the heate of the sunne beguyle theyr paine with rude and cartarlyke singing. With this the unmanerly countrey-woman that aryseth before daye oute of her slepe to spinne and carde, defendeth her self* and maketh her labour pleasant. This is the moste swete pastime after reigne, wind, and tempest unto the miserable mariners. With this do the wery pilgromes comfort themselves in their troublesome and long viages. And often tymes prisoners in adversitie, in fetters, and in stockes. In lyke maner for a greater proofe that the tunablenes of musicke (though it be but rude) is a very great refreshing of al worldly paines and griefs, a man would judge that nature hath taughte it unto nurses for a speciall remedye to the contynuall waylinges of sucking babes, whiche at the soune of their voice fall into a quiete and sweete sleepe, forgetting the teares that are so proper to them, and geven us of nature in that age for a gesse of the reste of oure life to come.

[XLVIII] Here the Count pausing a whyle the L. JULIAN saide: I am not of the L. Gaspars opinion, but I beleve for the reasons you alledge and for many other, that musicke is not onelye an ornament, but also necessarie for a Courtyer. But I woulde have you declare how this and the other qualities whiche you appoint him are to be practised, and at what time, and in what sorte. Because many thinges that of them selves bee worthie praise, oftentimes in practisyng theym out of season seeme moste foolish. And contrarywise, some

[margin notes]

Wielde beastes delyte in musicke.

Dolphines delyte in musicke.

Musicke acceptable to God.

Labourers.

Countrey-women.

Mariners.
Pilgroms.

Prisoners.

Suckyng babes.

---

* defendeth her self: the phrase 'from sleep' has been omitted.

thinges that appere to be of smal moment, in the wel
applying them, are greatly estemed.

[XLIX] Then saide the COUNT: Before we enter into
this matter, I will talke of an other thing, whiche for that
it is of importaunce (in my judgemente) I beleve our
Courtyer ought in no wise to leave it out. And that is the
cunning in drawyng, and the knowledge in the very arte
of peincting.[75] And wonder ye not if I wish this feat in   Peincting.
him, whiche now a dayes perhappes is counted an
handycraft and ful litle to become a gentleman, for I   Gentlemens
remember I have read that the men of olde time, and   children
especially in all Greece would have Gentlemens   learned to
children in the schooles to apply* peincting, as a matter   peinct.
both honest† and necessary. And this was received in
the firste degree of liberal artes, afterwarde openly   Peincting
enacted not to be taught to servauntes and bondmen.   forbid to
Emong the Romanes in like maner it was in very great   bondmen.
reputacion, and thereof sprong the surname of the most
noble family of Fabii, for the first Fabius was surnamed   Fabius
Pictor, because in dede he was a most excellent peinter,   Pictor.
and so addicted to peincting, that after he had peincted
the walles of the temple of Health, he writte therein hys   The temple of
name thinking with himselfe, that for all he was borne   health.
in so noble a familye whiche was honoured with so
many titles of Consulshippes and triumphes and other
dignities, and was learned and well seene in the lawe,
and reckened among Oratours, to geve also an encrease
of brightnesse and an ornament unto his renowme, by
leavyng behynde him a memorie that he had bene a
peinter.[76] There have not in lyke maner wanted many
other of notable famylyes that have bene renowmed in
this art, of the which (beside that in it selfe it is moste
noble and worthye) there ensue manye commodities,
and especiallye in warre to drawe oute countreys,   Necessarye
plattefourmes, ryvers, brydges, castelles, houldes,   warre.
fortresses, and suche other matters, the which thoughe
a manne were hable to kepe in mynde (and that is a
harde matter to doe) yet can he not shewe them to others.
And in verye dede who so esteameth not this arte, is (to
my seemyng) farre wyde from all reason: forsomuche as
the engine of the worlde that we behoulde with a large

* apply: study.   † honest: honourable.

The world and peincting.

sky, so bright with shining sterres, and in the middes, the earth environed with the Seas, severed in partes wyth Hylles, Dales, and Rivers, and so decked with suche diverse trees, beawtifull flowres and herbes, a man maye saye it to be a noble and a great peincting, drawen wyth the hande of nature and of God: the whych whoso can folow in myne opinion he is woorthye much commendacion. Neyther can a man atteyne to thys wythout the knoweledge of manye thinges, as he well knoweth that trieth it. Therefore had they of olde time in verye great estimation both the art and the artificers, so that it came to the toppe of all excellencye. And of this maye a man gather a sufficient argument at the auntient ymages of marble and mettall, whyche at thys daye are to be seene. And though peincting be a diverse matter from carving,* yet do they both arise of one self fountayne (namelye) of a good patterne.[77] And even as the ymages are divine and excellent, so it is to be thought peinctinges were also, and so much the more, for that they conteine in them a greater workemanshipp.

Auntient ymages.

Carving.

[L] Then the L. EMILIA tourning her unto Johnchristopher Romano[78] that sat ther among the rest: How thinke you (quoth she) to this judgement, will you graunt that peincting conteineth in it a greater workmanship, then carving?[79]

JOHNCHRISTOPHER answered: In my mynde carving is of more travaile, of more art, and of a more dignitye then peincting.

Then said the COUNT: Bicause ymages are more durable, perhappes a man may say that they are of a more dignity. For sith they are made for a memory, they better satisfy the effect why thei be made, then peincting. But beside memory, both peincting and carving are made also to set out a thing, and in this point hath peincting a great deale the upper hande, the which though it be not so longe lastyng (to terme it so) as carving is, yet doth it for al that endure a long tyme, and for the while it lasteth, is much more sightly.

Then aunswered JOHNCHRISTOPHER: I beleave verelye you thynke not as ye speake, and all this do you

* carving: sculpture (see note 257).

for your Raphaelles sake.[80] And peradventure to, you
judge the excellency you know to be in him in peincting
to be of such perfection, that carvynge in marble cannot
come to that degree. But weye with your selfe, that this
is the praise of the artificer and not of the art. Then he
proceaded: And I judge also both the one and the other
to be an artificiall folowing of nature. But yet I know
not how you can say, that the trueth and property that
nature maketh, cannot be folowed better in a figure of
marble or mettall, wherin the members are all round,
proporcioned and measured as nature her self shapeth
them, then in a Table, where men perceyve nothing but
the outwarde syght and those coulours that deceive the
eyes: and say not to me that being, is not nigher unto the
trueth then seeming. Again, I judge carving in marble
much harder, bicause if ye make a fault it cannot be
amended again, for marble cannot be joyned together,
but ye must be drieven to make a newe image, the which
happeneth not in peincting, for a man may alter, put to,
and diminish, alwaies making it better.

[LI] The COUNT said laughing: I speake not for
Raphaelles sake, neither ought you to think me so
ignoraunt a person, but I understand the excellency of
Michelangelo, of you your selfe, and of other men in
carvyng of marble, but I speak of the art and not of the
artificers. And you say wel, that both the one and the
other is the folowing of nature. But for al that, it is not
so, that peinting appeareth and carving is: for although
images are all round like the lively patterne, and
peinctyng is onely seene in the outward apparance, yet
want there manye thynges in ymages, that want not in
penctinges, and especiallye lightes and shadowes, for
fleshe geveth one light, and Marble an other, and that
doth the Peincter naturally folow with cleare and
darke, more and lesse, as he seeth occasion, which the
graver in marble can not doe. And where the Peincter
maketh not his figure round, he maketh the muscules
and the members in round wise, so that they go to meete
with the partes not seen, after such a maner, that a man
may very well gather the peincter hath also a knowleage
in them and understandeth them. And in this poynt he
must have an other craft that is greater to frame those
membres, that they may seeme short and diminishe

Raphael.

Why carving
is harder then
peinctyng.

Michelange.

Prospective.

accordinge to the proportion of the sight by the way of prospective, which by force of measured lines, coulours, lightes and shadowes discover unto you also in the outward sight of an upright wal the plainnesse and farnesse, more and lesse, as pleaseth him. Think

Wherin the peincter pleasseth the Carver.

you it agayn a triflynge matter to counterfeyt naturall coulours, flesh, clothe, and all other couloured thinges? This can not now the graver in marble do, ne yet express the grace of the sight that is in the black eyes or in azurre with the shininge of those amorous beames. He can not show the coulour of yelow hear, nor the glistring of armour, nor a darke nyght, nor a Sea tempest, nor those twincklinges and sperkeles,* nor the burninge of a Citye, nor the rising of the mornyng in the coulour of roses with those beames of purple and gold. Finallye he can not show the skye, the sea, the earth, hilles, woddes, medowes, gardeines, rivers, Cityes, nor houses, which the peincter doeth all. [LII] For this respect (me thinke) peincting is more noble, and conteyneth in it a greater workemanshippe then graving in marble. And among them of olde tyme I beleve it was in as high estimation as other thinges, the which is also to be discerned by

Remnants of peinctinge in Roome.

certayn litle remnantes that are to be sene yet, especiallye in places under ground in Roome,[81] but much more evidentlye may a man gather it by olde wrytinges, wherein is so famous and so often mention both of the workes and workemen, that by them a man maye understande in what high reputation they have bene alwaies with Princes and Commune weales.[82] There-

Alexander loved Appelles.

fore it is read that Alexander loved highlye Appelles of Ephesus, and somuch, that after he had made him draw out a woman of his, naked, whom he loved most deerly, and understandinge that this good peincter, for her marveylous beauty was most fervently in love with her, without any more a do, he bestowed her upon him.

Alexanders gift to Appelles.

Truely a woorthy liberalitye of Alexander, not to geve onelye treasures and states, but also his owne affections and desires, and a token of very great love towarde Appelles, not regarding (to please him with all) the displeasure of the woman that he highly loved, who it is

---

* twincklinges and sperkeles. A mistranslation: the original has 'flashes of lightning'.

to be thought was sore agreved to chaunge so great a
king for a peincter. There be manye other signes
rehersed also of Alexanders good will toward
Appelles, but he shewed plainlye in what estimation he
had him, whan he commaunded by open proclamation
no other peincter shoulde be so hardy to draw out his
picture. Here could I repete unto you the contentions of
manye noble peincters with the greatest commendation
and marvaile (in a maner) in the world. I coulde tel you
with what solemnitie the Emperours of old time decked
out their tryumphes with peinctinges, and dedicated
them up in haunted* places and how deere it cost them.
And that there wer some Peincters that gave their
woorkes freely, seeming unto them no golde nor silver
was inough to value them. And how a table† of
Protogenes was of such estimation, that Demetrius
lying encamped before Rhodes, where he might have
entred the citie by setting fier to the place where he wiste
this table was, for feare of burning it, staid to bid them
battaile, and so he wan not the city at al. And how
Metrodorus a Philosopher and a most excellent
peincter was sent out of Athens to L. Paulus to bringe up
his children and to deck out his triumph he had to make.
And also manye noble writers have written of this art,
which is a token great inough to declare in what
estimation it hath bene. But I will not we procede any
farther in this communication. Therfore it sufficeth
onely to say that our Courtier ought also to have a
knowledge in peincting, since it was honest and profitable, and much set by in those daies whan men were of a
more prowesse then they are now. And thoughe he
never geat other profite or delite in it (beside that it is a
helpe to him to judge of the ymages both olde and new,
of vessels, buildings, old coines, cameses,‡ gravings and
such other matters) it maketh him also understand the
beawtye of livelye bodies, and not onely in the
sweetenesse of the fisnamy, but in the proportion of all
the rest, aswell in men as other living creatures. Se then
how the knowleage in peinctinge is cause of verye great
pleasure. And this let them think that do enjoy and view

Onely
Appelles
drewe out
his picture.

Estimation
of
peincting.

A table wherin
Bacchus was
peinted.

Metrodorus.

Profite of
peincting.

* haunted: public.   † table: painting.
‡ cameses: cameos.

Lovers ought
to have a
sight in it.

the beauty of a woman so throughly that they think
them selves in paradise, and yet have not the feate of
peinctinge: the which if they had, they would conceive a
farre greater contentation, for then should they more
perfectly understand the beauty that in their brest
engendreth such hartes ease.

[LIII] Here the L. CESAR laughed and saide: I have not
the art of peincting, and yet I knowe assuredly I have a
far greater delyte in behoulding a woman in the world
then Appelles himselfe that was so excellent whom ye
named right now, could have if he wer nowe in lief
again.

Affection
or love.

The COUNT answered: This delite of yours proceadeth not wholy of the beawty, but of the affection
which you perhappes beare unto the woman. And if you
wil tell the troth, the first time you beheld that woman,
ye felt not the thousandeth part of the delite which ye
did afterward, though her beauty wer the very same.
Therfore ye may conceive how affection beareth a
greater stroke in your delite then beauty.

I deny not that (quoth the L. CESAR): but as delite
ariseth of affection, so doth affection arise of beauty,
therfore a man may say for al that, that beauty is the
cause of delite.

The COUNT aunswered: There may be other thinges
also that beside beawty often times enflame our mindes,
as maners, knowledge, speach, gestures and a thousand
mo (which peradventure after a sort may be called
beauty to) and above all the knowing a mans self to be
beloved: so that without the beautys you reason of, a
man may be most ferventlye in love, but those loves that
arise onelye of the beauty which we dyscerne super-
ficially in bodyes, without doubt will bring a farre
greater delite to him that hath a more skill therein then
to him that hath but a litle. Therfore retourning to our
pourpose, I beleve Appelles conceived a far greater joy in

Campaspes.

behoulding the beawty of Campaspes then did
Alexander, for a man maye easilye beleeve that the love
of them both proceeded of that beawtye, and perhaps
also for this respect Alexander determined to bestowe
her upon him, that (in his minde) could knowe her more
perfectlye then he did. Have you not read of the five

V. doughters
of Croton.

daughters of Croton, which among the rest of the

people, Zeusis the peincter chose to make of all five one   Zeusis.
figure that was most excellent in beawty,[83] and wer
renowmed of many Poets, as they that wer alowed for
beawtifull of him that ought to have a most perfect
judgment in beawty?

[LIV] Here the L. Cesar, declaring him self not
satisfied nor willing to consent by any meanes, that any
man coulde tast of the delite that he felt in beholding the
beawty of a certein woman, but he him self, began to
speake: and then was there hard a great scraping of feet
in the floore with a cherme of loude speaking, and upon
that every man tourninge him selfe about, saw at the
Chambre doore appeare a light of torches, and by and
by after entred in the L. Generall with a greate and   L. Francisco-
noble traine, who was then retourned from accom-   maria della
paninge the Pope a peece of the way. And at his first   Rovère.
entry into the Palaice demaundinge what the Dutches
did, he was certefied what kind of pastime they had in
hande that night, and howe the charg was committed to
Count Lewis to entreat of courting.* Therfore he hasted
him as much as he could to come betime to heare
somewhat. And assone as he had saluted the Dutchesse
and setled the reste that were risen up at his comminge,
he satte hym downe in the circle amonge them and
certein of the chiefe of his traine, amonge which were
the marquesse Phebus of Ceva, and Ghirardin brethern,
M. Hector of Roome, Vincent Calmeta, Horace
Floridus and many other.[84]

And whan al was whist,† the L. GENERAL said: My
Lordes, my comminge shoulde bee to hurtefull, if I
should hindre such good communication as I gesse was
even now emong you. Therfore do you me not this
injurie to deprive both youre selves and me of this
pleasure.

Then aunswered COUNT LEWIS: I beleave (my Lorde)
silence ought rather to please all parties then speakinge.
For seinge it hath bene my lot this night before all other
to take this travaile in hande, it hath nowe weried me in
speakinge and I werie all the rest in hearinge: because
my talke hath not bene worthye of this companye, nor

* to entreat of courting: to speak on the art of courtiership.
† whan al was whist: since no-one spoke.

sufficient ynoughe for the waightinesse of the matter I have bene charged withall, wherin sins I have litle satisfied my self, I recken I have muche lesse satysfied others. Therfore (my Lorde) your lucke hath bene good to come at the latter end, and nowe shal it be wel done to geve the enterprise of that is behind to an other that may succede in my roume. For whosoever he be, I knowe well he will much better acquite him selfe then I should do if I went forwarde with it, beinge thus wery as I am.

[LV] This will I in no wise permit, aunswered the L. JULIAN, to be deceived of the promise ye have made me. And I knowe well the Lord Generall will not be against the understandinge of that point.

And what promise was that? quoth the COUNT.

The L. JULIAN answered: To declare unto us in what sort the Courtyer ought to use those good condicions and qualities which you say are meete for him.

The LORDE GENERALL, though he wer but a child in yeares, yet was he wise and discreete more then a man would think belonged unto those tender yeares of his, and in every gesture he declared with a greatnesse of minde a certaine livelinesse of wit, which did sufficiently pronosticate the excellente degree of honoure, and vertue whereunto afterwarde he ascended. Wherfore he said incontinentlye:* If all this be behinde yet to be spoken of (me thinke) I am come in good season. For understandinge in what sort the Courtier muste use his good condicions and qualities, I shall knowe also what they are, and thus shall I come to the knowleage of al that have bene spoken hitherto. Therfore sticke not (Count) to pay this debt, being alreadye discharged of one part therof.

I should not have so greate a debt to discharg, answered the COUNT, if the peynes were equallye devided, but the faulte hath bene, in gevinge a Ladye authoritye to commaunde, that is to partial.

And so smiling he beheld the LADY EMILIA, which said immediatly: You ought not to complain of my partialyty, yet sins ye do it against reason, we wil give one part of this honor, which you call peynes, unto an other: and tourninge her unto Sir Friderick Fregoso,

* incontinentlye: at once.

You (quoth she) propounded this devise* of the Courtier, therfore reason willeth ye should say somewhat in it: and that shalbe to fulfill the L. Julians request, in declaring in what sort, maner and time the Courtier ought to practise his good condicions and qualityes, and those other thinges which the Count hath said are meete for him.

Then SIR FRIDERICK: Madam (quoth he) where ye will sever the sort, the time and the maner of good condicions and qualityes and the well practisinge of the Courtyer, ye will sever that can not be sundred: for it is these thinges that make the condicions and qualityes good and the practising good. Therfore sins the Count hath spoken so much and so wel, and also said somwhat of these circumstances, and prepared for the rest in his mind that he had to say, it were but reason he should go forward untill he came to the ende.

The LADY EMILIA aunswered: Set the case you were the Count your self, and spake that your mind geveth you he would do, and so shall all be well.

[LVI] Then said CALMETA: My Lordes, sins it is late, least Sir Friderick should find a scuse to utter that he knoweth, I beleve it were wel done to deferre the rest of the communication untill to morowe, and bestowe the small time that remayneth about some other pastyme without ambicion. The which being agreed upon of all handes, the Dutches willed the Lady Margaret and the Lady Constance Fregosa to shew them a daunce. Wherefore Barletta immediatly, a very pleasaunt musitien and an excellent daunser, who continually kept al the Court in mirth and joy, began to play upon his instrumentes, and they hande in hande, shewed them a daunce or twoo with a verye good grace and greate pleasure to the lookers on: that doone, because it was farre in nighte, the Dutches arrose uppon her feete, and so every man taking his leave reverentlye of her, departed to his reste.

---

* propounded this devise: suggested this game.

THE SECOND BOOKE

OF THE COURTYER OF COUNT
BALDESSAR CASTILIO
UNTO MAISTER
ALPHONSUS ARIOSTO

[I] Not without marveile many a time and often have I considered wyth my self howe one errour should arise, the which bicause it is generallye seene in olde men, a man may beleave it is proper and naturall unto them: and that is, how (in a maner) all of them commend the times past, and blame the times present: dispraising our doinges and maners: and whatsoever they dyd not in their youthe: affirmynge moreover every good custome and good trade of lyving, every vertue, finally ech thing to declyne alwayes from yll to worse. And in good sooth it seemeth a matter very wide from reason and worthye to be noted, that rype age whiche with long practise is wont to make mennes judgementes more perfecte in other thynges, should in this behalf so corrupt them, that they should not discerne, yf the world wexed worse and worse, and the fathers were generally better then the children, we should long ere this tyme have ben come to that utmost degree of yll that can not wexe worse. And yet doe we see not onely in our dayes, but also in tymes past that this hath alwaies ben the peculier vyce of that age. The which is to be manifestlye gathered by the writynges of manye most auntient aucthours, and especyally comedy writers, whiche expresse better then the rest, the trade of mannes lyfe. The cause therefore of this false opinion in old menne, I beleve (in mine opinion) is, for that, yeares wearing away, cary also with them many commodities, and emonge other take away from the bloud a greate part of the lyvely spirites that altereth the complection,[85] and the instrumentes wexe feeble, wherby the soule worketh her effectes. Therfore the sweete flowers of delite vade away in that season out of oure heartes, as the leaves fall from the trees after harvest, and in steade of open and cleere thoughtes there entreth cloudy and troublous heavinesse accompanied with a thousand heart grieffes: so that not onely the bloude, but the mind is also feble, neither of the former pleasures receyveth it anye thynge elles but a fast memorye and the print of the beloved

An errour in age.

The cause of the errour.

Tyme of
youth.

time of tender age, which whan we have upon us, the
heaven, the earth, and ech thing to our seeming
rejoiceth and laugheth alwayes about our eyes, and in
thought (as in a savoury and pleasaunt gardein)
florisheth the sweete spring time of mirth, so that
peradventure it were not unprofitable, when now in the
colde season, the Son of our lief (taking away from us
oure delites) beginneth to draw towarde the Weste, to
lose in like case therwithal the mindefulnesse of them,
and to find out (as Themistocles sayth) an art to teach us

Senses of
the body.

to forget:[86] for the sences of oure bodye are so
deceyvable, that they beguile many times also the
judgment of the mind. Therefore (me thinke) olde men
be like unto them, that saylinge in a vessell out of a
haven, behoulde the ground with their eyes, and the
vessell to ther seeminge standeth styll and the shore
goeth: and yet is it cleane contrarye; for the haven and
likewise the time and pleasures continue still in their
astate, and we with the vessell of mortalitye flying
away, go one after an other through the tempestuous
sea that swaloweth up and devoureth al thinges, neither
is it graunted us at any time to come on shore again, but
alwaies beaten with contrary windes, at the end we
break our vessell at some rocke. Because therefore the

The mind of
olde age.

minde of old age is without order subject to* many
pleasures, it can not taste them: and even as to them that
be sycke of a feaver whan by corrupt vapours they have
lost theyr taste, all wines appeare moste bitter, though
they be precious and delicate in dede: so unto olde men
for there unaptenes (wherein notwithstanding desier
fayleth them not) pleasures seeme without taste and
colde, much differing from those they remember they
have proved in foretyme, althoughe the pleasures in
themselves be the selfe same. Therfore when they feele
themselves voide of them, it is a griefe, and they blame
the time present for yll, not perceyvinge that this
chaunge proceadeth of themselves and not of the tyme.
And contrarywyse whan they call to minde the
pleasures past, they remember therwithall the time they
had them in, and therfore commend it for good, because
to their weening it carieth with it a savour of it, which

* is without order subject to: is ill-adapted to.

they felt in them whan it was presente, by reason that in effecte our mindes conceyve an hatred against all thynges that have accompanyed oure sorowes, and love suche as have accompanied oure pleasures. Upon this it commeth that unto a lover it is most acceptable sometime to beholde a window though it be shutte, because otherwhiles it may be hys chaunce to see his maistresse there: in like maner to see a rynge, a letter, a gardein or anye other place or what ever other thynge he supposeth hathe bene a wittinge testimoniall of his pleasures. And contrariwise, often times a faire trymmed and well decked chamber is abhorred of him that hath bene kept prysoner in it, or abidde therin any other sorow. And in my dayes I have knowen some that will never drinke of a cup like unto that wherin in their sickenesse they had taken a medicin. For even as that windowe, ringe or letter, doeth bring to the minde a sweete remembraunce unto the one that somuch pleaseth him, for that he imagineth it was a percell of his pleasures, so unto the other the chamber or cuppe seemeth to bringe with the memory his sicknes or imprisoninge againe. The verye same cause (I beleave) moveth old men to praise the times past and discommend the present. [II] Therfore as they talke of other thynges, so do they also of Courtes, affirminge suche as have bene in their memory to be much more excellent and farre better furnished with notable men, then we see them to be that are now a dayes. And immediatly whan they entre into this kinde of talke, they beginne to extoll with infinyte praises the Courtes of Duke Philip, or of Duke Borso, and declare the sayinges of Nicholas Piccininus[87] and reherse that in those tymes a man should very sildome have hearde of a murther committed, and no combattes, no craftes nor deceites: but a certaine faithful and loving good meaning among all men and an upright dealing. And in Courtes at that time there reigned suche good condicions and such honestie that the Courtyers were (in a maner) religious folke:* and woe unto him that shoulde have spoken an yll word of an other, or made but a signe otherwyse then honestly to a woman. And on the other

Thinges beloved that accumpanye pleasures.

Old mens opinion of Courtes.

---

* (in a maner) religious folke: like monks.

side, they say in these dayes every thing is cleane contrary, and not onelye that brotherlye love and manerlye conversation loste emonge Courtiers, but also in Courtes there reigneth nothynge elles but envye and malyce, yll maners, and a most wanton lyfe in every kinde of vice: the women enticefull past shame, and the men womanishe. They disprayse also the apparaile to be dishonest* and to softe. To be shorte, they speake against infinite thinges, emonge the whiche many in very dede deserve to be discommended, for it cannot be excused, but there are many yll and naughtie menne emonge us, and this oure age is muche more full of vices then was that whiche they commende. But (me thinke) they doe full yll skanne the cause of this difference, and they bee fonde persones, because they woulde have all goodnesse in the worlde withoute anye yll, whiche is unpossible. For synce yll is contrarie to good, and good to yll, it is (in a maner) necessarie by contrarietye and a certayne counterpese the one shoulde underproppe and strengthen the other, and where the one wanteth or encreaseth, the other to want or encrease also: beecause no contrarye is wythoute hys other contrarye. Who knoweth not that there shoulde bee no Justyce in the worlde, were it not for wronges? no stoutenesse of courage, were there not feynthearted? nor continency, were there not incontinencie? nor health, were there not sickenes? nor trueth, were there not lyes? nor happynesse were there not mischaunces? Therefore Socrates saieth well in Plato that he marveyleth that Esope made not an Apologus or fable, wherein he mighte have feigned that God, since he coulde never coople pleasure and sorowe together, might have knit them with an extremitie, so that the beginninge of the one shoulde have beene the ende of the other.[88] For we see no pleasure can delite us at anye time if sorow goeth not beefore. Who can love rest well onlesse he have firste felte the griefe of weerinesse? Who savereth meate, drinke, and sleepe, if he have not firste felt hunger, thirste, and watchinge? I beleave therfore passions and dyseases are geven to menne of nature, not principallye to make them subject to them, for it wer not mete that

Envie.
Women wanton.

Men womanish.
Aparaile.

Contraries.

Socrates.
Esopus.

One contrarie foloweth an other.

---

* dishonest: indecorous, unseemly.

she, whiche is the mother of all goodnesse, shoulde by
her owne purposed advise give us so manye evilles, but
since nature doth make healthe, pleasure and other
goodnesse, consequentlye after these, were joyned
diseases, sorowes and other evilles. Therfore since
vertues were graunted to the worlde for a favoure and
gifte of nature, by and by were vices by that lincked
contrariéty necessarily accompanied with them: so that
the one encreasing or wanting, the other must in like
maner encrease or want. [III] Therfore when our olde
men praise the Courtes of times past because there were
not in them so vitious men, as some that are in oures,
they doe not knowe that there were not also in them so
vertuous men, as some that are in oures: the which is no
wonder, for no yll is so evill, as that which arriseth of
the corrupte seede of goodnesse. And therfore where
nature now bringeth forth muche better wyttes then she
didde tho, even as they that bee geven to goodnesse doe
muche better then didde those of theyr tyme, so also
they that be geven to yll doe muche woorse. Therefore it
is not to bee saide, that suche as absteyned frome doinge
ill because they knewe not howe to doe it, deserved in
that case anye praise: for althoughe they dyd but a lyttle
yll, yet dydde they the woorste they knewe. And that the
wittes of those tymes were generally much inferiour to
these now a dayes, a man may judge by all that hath
proceaded from them, letters, peynctynges, statues,
buildinges and al other thinges. Again these olde men
discommende many thynges in us, which of themselves
are neyther good nor badde, onelye because they did
them not: and say it is no good sight to see yonge men
on horsebacke aboute the stretes and especially upon
Mules,* nor to weare furres, nor syde garmentes in
winter, nor to weare a cappe before a man be at the least
xviii. yeares of age, and such other matters, wherin truly
they be much deceyved. For these facions (beside that
they be commodious and profitable) are brought up by
custome, and generallye men delite in them, as at that
time they were contented to goe in their jacket, in their
breechelesse hose and in their lowe shoes with lachettes,

Better wittes
now then in
foretime.

Thinges
neither good
nor badd.

Facions setby
in the olde
tyme.

* upon Mules. The original (*nelle mule*) is more likely to mean
'while wearing mules' (slippers).

and (to appeere fine) carye all day longe a hauke upon their fiste, without pourpose, and daunce without touching a womans hand, and used many other facions, the which as they are nowe stale, so were they at that time muche set by. Therefore may it be lawefull for us also to followe the custome of our times, without controulment of these olde men, whiche going about to praise themselves, say: Whan I was xx. yeares olde I laye wyth my mother and sisters, nor a great while after wiste I what women ment: and nowe children are not so soone crepte oute of the shell, but they knowe more naughtynesse, then they that were come to mans state did in those dayes: neither be they aware in so sayinge that they confirme our children to have more wit then their olde men. Let them leave therfore speakinge against our times, as full of vyces: for in takinge awaye them, they take also away the vertues. And let them remember that among the good men of auncient time, when as the glorious wittes florished in the world, which in very dede were of most perfection in every vertue, and more then manlye,* there were also manye moste mischevous, which if they had still lived, shoulde have excelled oure yll men somuch in ill, as those good men in goodnes, and of this do all Histories make full mention. [IV] But unto these olde men I weene I have made a sufficient aunswer. Therfore we will leave aparte this discourse, perhappes to tedious, but not altogether out of pourpose: and beeing sufficient to have declared that the Courtes of oure time are worthy no lesse praise, then those that old men commend so much, we wil attende to our communication that was had about the Courtier, wherby a man may easely gather, in what degre the Court of Urbin was emonge the reste, and what maner a Prince and Lady they were that had suche noble wyttes attendying upon them, and howe fortunate all they might call themselves that lyved in that familiar felowship. [V] Whan the day folowinge therefore was come, there was great and sundrye talke betweene the Gentlemen and Ladies of the courte upon the disputacion of the night beefore: which arrose a greate parte of it, upon the L. Generalles greedy desire,

The sayinge of olde men.

Noble wittes in the Court of Urbin.

---

* more then manlye: superhuman.

to understande asmuch as had bene said in the matter, who had enquired it almoste of everye manne: and (as it is alwaies wont to come to passe) it was reported unto him sundrye wayes, for some praised one thing, some an other, and also emong many there was a contencion of the Countes oune meaning,* for everye man did not so fullye beare in minde the matters that had bene spoken.

Therfore almost the whole day was spent about talking in this, and assone as night drue on, the L. Generall commaunded meate to be set on the borde, and toke all the Gentelmen with him, and immediatlye after supper he repayred to the DUTCHES side: who beehouldinge so great a companye assembled sooner then they had done at other times, saide: Me thinke, it is a great weight, Sir Friderick, that is layd upon your shoulders, and a greate expectacion that you must satisfy.

Here not tariynge for Sir Friderickes answere, And what greate weight (I beseche ye) is it? said then UNICO ARETINO. Who is so foolishe that whan he can do a thinge, will not do it in a fit and due time?

Reasoning in this wise about the matter, every man satte him downe in his wonted place and maner with very heedfull expectacion of the propounded talke.

[VI] Then SIR FRIDERICK tourninge him to Unico: Doe you not think then, M. Unico (quoth he) that I am laden this night with a great and peinful burden, since I must declare in what sorte, maner and time, the Courtier hath to practise hys good condicions and qualities, and to use those other thinges that are alreadie saide to be mete for him?

Me thynke it is no great matter, answered UNICO: and I beleve a good judgement in the Courtyer is sufficient for al this, which the Count saide well yesterday nighte that he oughte to have: and in case it be so, without any other preceptes, I suppose he may practyse welynough the thynge that hee knoweth in due time and after a good sorte. The whiche to bring more particularly into rule were to harde a matter, and

---

* there was a contencion of the Countes oune meaning: there was a disagreement over what the Count had said.

perhappes more then nedeth, for I know not who is so fonde to go about his fence,* whan the rest be in their musicke: or to goe about the streetes daunsing the Morisco, though he could doe it never so well: or goinge aboute to comfort a mother that had buried her childe, to beginne to talke with her of pleasant matters and mery conceites. I beleve surely no gentleman will do this, onlesse he wer cleane out of his wittes.

Me think (M. Unico) quoth SIR FRIDERICK then, ye harpe to muche uppon youre extremities. For it happeneth otherwhile a man is so fonde that he remembreth not himself so easilye,† and oversightes are not all alike. And it may be, that a man shall abstaine from a common foly which is to manifest, as that is you speake of, to go daunce the Morisco in the market place, and yet shal he not refraine from praising himself out of purpose, from using a noysome sawcinesse, from casting out otherwhile a worde thinking to make men laughe, whiche for that it is spoken out of time will appeare colde and without any grace, and these oversightes often times are covered with a certaine veile that suffereth a manne not to forget who dothe them, onlesse he take no heede to them:‡ and although for many causes our sight descerneth but litle, yet for ambicions sake it is darkened in especyall, for every man willingly setteth forth himselfe in that he perswadeth himself he knoweth, whether this perswasion of his bee true or false. Therefore the well behaving of a mannes selfe in this case (me think) consisteth in a certain wisedome and judgement of choise, and to knowe more and lesse what encreaseth or diminisheth in thinges, to practise them in due time or out of season. And for all the Courtyer be of so good a judgement that he can descerne these differences, yet shall he the sooner compasse that hee seketh, if his imagination be opened

To observe time.

---

* fence: weapon practice.
† it happeneth otherwhile a man is so fonde that he remembreth not himself so easilye: it is sometimes possible to act in an inappropriate way without its being so obvious.
‡ a certaine veile that suffereth a manne not to forget who dothe them, onlesse he take no heede to them: a kind of veil, that prevents the person guilty of them from recognising his errors, unless he thinks very carefully about it.

with some rule, and the wayes shewed him, and (as it were) the places where he should ground himself upon, then yf he should take him self onely to the gencraltie. [VII] Forsomuche as therefore the Count yesterday night entreated upon Courtyership so copiously and in so good a maner, he hath made me (truely) conceive no small feare and doubte that I shall not so throughly satisfie this noble audience in the matter that lieth upon me to discourse in, as he hath done in that was his charge. Yet to make my self partener in what I maye of his praise, and to be sure not to erre (at the least in thys part) I will not contrarie him in any point. Wherefore agreing to his opinions, and beside the reste, as touchynge noblenes of birthe, wit and disposition of person and grace of countenaunce, I say unto you that to gete hym prayse worthely and a good estimation with all men, and favour with suche great men as he shal attende upon, me thinke it behouffull he have the understanding to frame all hys life and to set foorth his good qualities generally in company with al men without purchasing himself envy. The whiche howe harde a matter it is of it selfe, a man maye consider by the sildomenesse of suche as are seen to attain to that point: because we are al the sort of us in very dede more enclined of nature to dispraise faultes, then to commende thinges well done. And a man would thinke that many by a certain rooted malice, although they manifestly descerne the goodnes, enforce themselves with al study and diligence to finde in us either a faulte or at the leaste the likenes of a fault. Therefore it behoveth oure Courtyer in all his doinges to be charie and heedfull, and what so he saith or doeth to accompany it with wisedome, and not onely to set his delite to have in himself partes and excellent qualities, but also to order the tenour of his life after suche a trade,* that the whole may be answerable unto these partes, and see the selfe same to bee alwayes and in every thing suche, that it disagree not from it selfe, but make one body of all these good qualities, so that everye deede of his may be compact and framed of al the vertues, as the Stoikes say the duetie of a wiseman is: although not withstanding

To set forthe good qualities.

Manye bent to finde faultes.

Stoici.

* trade: fashion.

alwaies one vertue is the principall, but all are so knit and linked one to an other, that they tende to one ende, and all may bee applyed and serve to every purpose.

To set out one qualytie with another. Therefore it behoveth he have the understandynge to set them forth, and by comparason and (as it were) contrariety of the one, sometime to make the other the better knowen: as the good peincters with a shadow make the lightes of high places to appeere, and so with light make lowe the shadowes of plaines, and meddle divers coulours together, so that throughe that diversitie bothe the one and the other are more sightly to beholde, and the placing of the figures contrarie the one to the other is a helpe to them to doe the feate that the peincters mynde is to bring to passe. **Lowelinesse.** So that lowlines* is muche to be commended in a Gentleman that is of prowesse and well seene in armes: and as that fearcenesse seemeth the greater whan it is accompanied with sobermoode,† even so dooeth sobermood encrease and shewe it selfe the more through fiercenesse. Therefore little speaking, muche dooing, and not praising a mannes owne selfe in commendable deedes, dissemblyng them after an honeste sorte, dooeth encrease both the one vertue and the other in a person that can discreatly use this trade: and the like is to be said in all the other good qualities. **Generall rules.** Therefore will I have our Courtyer in that he doeth or saieth to use certaine general rules, the whiche (in my minde) containe briefly asmuch as belongeth to me to speake. And for the first and chief lette him avoid (as the Count saide wel in that behalf yester night) above all thinges curiositie.‡ **Avoid curiositye. Circumstances.** Afterwarde let him consider wel what the thing is he doth or speaketh, the place wher it is done, in presence of whom, in what time, the cause why he doeth it, his age, his profession, the ende whereto it tendeth, and the meanes that may bring him to it: and so let him apply himselfe discreatly with these advertisementes to whatsoever he mindeth to doe or speake.

[VIII] After Syr Fridericke had thus saide, he seemed to staye a whyle.

Then said M. MORELLO of Ortona: Me thinke these

---

* lowlines: mildness.
† sobermoode: modesty.
‡ curiositie: affectation.

your rules teache but litle. And I for my parte am as skilfull now as I was before you spake them, althoughe I remember I have harde them at other times also of friers with whom I have bene in confession, and I weene they terme them circumstances.

Then laughed SYR FRIDERICKE and said: If you doe well beare in mynde, the Counte willed yesternighte that the chief profession of the Courtyer should bee in armes, and spake very largely in what sorte he shoulde do it, therefore will we make no more rehearsall thereof: yet by our rule it may be also understoode, that where the Courtyer is at a skirmishe, or assault, or battaile upon the land, or in such other places of enterprise, he ought to worke the matter wisely in seperating himself from the multitude, and undertake his notable and bould feates which he hath to do with as litle company as he can, and in the sighte of noble men that be of most estimation in the campe, and especially in the presence and (if it wer possible) beefore the very eyes of his king or greate parsonage he is in service withal: for in dede it is mete to set forth to the shew thinges well done. And I beleave even as it is an yll matter to seke a false renoume, and in the thing he deserveth no praise at all, so is it also an yll matter to defraude a mans self of his due estimation, and not to seke that praise, which alone is the true reward of vertuous enterprises. And I remember I have knowen of them in my time that for all they wer of prowesse, yet in this point they have shewed themselves but grossheaded, and put their life in as great hasard to go take a flock of shiepe, as in being the formost to scale the walles of a batred towne, the which our Courtyer wil not doe if he beare in minde the cause that bryngeth him to the warre, which ought to be onely his estimation.* And if he happen moreover to be one to shewe feates of Chivalrie in open sightes at tilt, turney, or *Joco di canne* or in any other exercise of the person, remembryng the place where he is, and in presence of whom, he shall provide before hand to be in his armour no lesse handsome and sightly then sure, and feede the eyes of the lookers on wyth all thinges that he shall thinke may

An example of the circumstances.

Praise to be sought for.

Grosheaded persons.

The cause to venture life is estimacion. Open showes.

Readie in his armour.

---

* estimation: honour, glory.

A horse well
trimmed.
Wittye
inventions.
Not of the
laste to come
furthe.

Q. Roscius
comœdus.

A respect to
the talke of
armes.

geve him a good grace, and shall do his best to gete him
a horse sett out with fair harneis and sightly trappinges,
and to have proper devyses, apt poesies, and wittie
inventions that may drawe unto him the eyes of the
lookers on, as the Adamant stone doth yron. He shall
never be among the last that come furth into the listes to
shewe themselves, considering the people, and especially women take muche more hede to the fyrste then to
the last: because the eyes and mindes that at the
begynning are greedy of that noveltye, note everye lyttle
matter and printe it,* afterward by continuaunce they
are not onely full, but weery of it. Therefore was there a
noble Stageplaier in olde tyme that for this respecte
would alwaies be the first to come furth to playe his
parte.[89] In like maner also if our Courtier do but talke
of armes, he shal have an eie to the profession of them
he talketh withall and according to that frame himselfe,
and use one maner of talke with men, and an other with
women: and in case he will touche any thing sounding
to his own praise, he shall do it so dissemblinglye as it
wer at a chaunce and by the way and with the
discretion and warinesse that count Lewis shewed us
yesterday. [IX] Do you not nowe thinke (M. Morello)
that our rules can teache somewhat? Trowe you not
that friende of ours I tould you of a fewe dayes agoe had
cleane forgotten with whom he spake, and why? Whan
to entertein a gentilwoman whom he never saw before,
at his first entring in talke with her, he began to tell how
many men he had slain and what a hardie felow he was,
and how he could play at twohandsworde and had
never done untill he hadde taught her howe to defende
certeine strokes with a Pollaxe being armed and how
unarmed, and to shewe howe (in a mannes defence) to
lay hande uppon a dagger, so that the poore gentilwoman stood upon thornes, and thought an houre a
thousande yeare till she were got from him, for feare
least he would go nigh to kil her as he had done those
other. Into these errours runne they that have not an eye
to the circumstances whiche you saye ye have heard of
Friers. Therfore I say of the exercises of the body, some
there are that (in maner) are never practised but in open

* printe it: are struck by it.

shewe, as runninge at Tilt, Barriers, *Joco di Canne*, and
all the reste that depende uppon Armes. Therefore
whan oure Courtyer taketh any of these in hande, firste
hee muste provide to bee so well in order for Horse,
Harneys, and other fournitures beelongynge thereto,
that he wante nothinge. And if he see not hym selfe
throughelye fournyshed in all poyntes, lette him not
meddle at all. For if he dooe not well, it can not bee
scused that it is not his profession. After thys, he oughte
to have a great consideration in presence of whom he
sheweth himselfe, and who be his matches. For it were
not meete that a Gentilman shoulde be present in
person and a doer in such a matter in the countrey,
where the lookers on and the doers were of a base sort.

[X] Then saide the L. GASPAR PALLAVICIN: In our
countrey of Lumbardy these matters are not passed
uppon,* for you shall see there yonge Gentilmen upon
the holy dayes come daunce al the day long in the Sunne
with them of the countrey, and passe the time with them
in casting the barre, in wrastling, running and leaping.
And I beleve it is not ill done. For no comparason is
there made of noblenesse of birth, but of force and
slight, in which thinges many times the men of the
countrey are not a whit inferiour to Gentilmen, and it
seemeth this familiar conversation conteineth in it a
certein lovely freenesse.

This daunsing in the son, answered SYR FRIDERICKE,
can I in no case away withall:† and I can not see what a
man shal gain by it. But whoso wyll wrastle, runne and
leape with men of the countrey, ought (in my judgement) to do it after a sorte: to prove himselfe and (as
they are wonte to saye) for courtesie, not to trye maistry
with them: and a man ought (in a maner) to be assured
to get the upper hand, elles let him not meddle with al,
for it is to ill a sight and to foule a matter and without
estimation to see a Gentilman overcome by a Cartar
and especially in wrastling. Therfore I beleve it is wel
done to abstaine from it, at the leastwise in the presence
of many, because if he overcome, his gaine is small, and

Well pro-
vided for
open
showes.

How to prac-
tise feates
with men of
the countrey.

---

* are not passed uppon: are not taken so seriously (the original has
'in Lombardy, we are not so fussy about that kind of thing').
† can I in no case away withall: I do not like at all.

his losse in being overcome very great. Also they play at
tenise (in maner) alwaies in open sight, and this is one of
the commune games which the multitude with their
presence muche set furth. I will have oure Courtier
therfore to do this and all the rest beside handlyng his
weapon, as a matter that is not his profession: and not
seeme to seeke or loke for any praise for it, nor be
acknowen that he bestoweth much study or time about
it, although he do it excellently well. Neither shall he be
like unto some that have a delite in musicke, and in
speaking with whom soever alwaies whan he maketh a
pause in their talke, begine in a voice as though they
would sing. Other walking in the stretes or in the
churches, go alwayes daunsing. Other meetyng in the
market place or whersoever anye friende, make a
gesture as though they would play at fence, or wrastle,
according as their delite is.

Here, said the L. CESAR GONZAGA, we have in
Roomé a yong Cardinal that doeth better then so,
whiche feeling him selfe lusty of person leadeth as
manye as come to visit him (though he never sawe them
before) into a gardein, and is very instant uppon them to
strippe themselves into their dublet to leape with him.

[XI] SYR FRIDERICKE laughed, afterwarde he proceaded on: There be some other exercises that may be
done both openly and privately, as dauncyng: and in
this I beleve the Courtier ought to have a respecte,* for
yf he daunseth in the presence of many and in a place ful
of people, he must (in my mind) keepe a certain dignitie,
tempred notwithstanding with a handsome and sightly
sweetnesse of gestures, and for all he feeleth himself
very nimble and to have time and measure at will, yet let
him not enter into that swiftnesse of feete and doubled
footinges, that we see are very comely in oure Barletta,
and peradventure were unseemely for a Gentilman,
although privately in a chamber together as we be
nowe, I will not saye but he maye do both that, and also
daunce the morisco and braulles, yet not openlye onlesse
he were in a maske.† And though it were so that all

---

* in this I beleve the Courtier ought to have a respecte: I think the
courtier should take account of this.
† maske: costume, disguise.

menne knewe him, it skilleth not, for there is no way to that, if a man will shewe himselfe in open sightes about such matters,* whether it be in armes, or out of armes. Because to be in a maske bringeth with it a certaine libertie and lycence, that a man may emong other thinges take uppon him the fourme of that he hath best skill in, and use bente studye and preciseness about the principall drift of the matter wherin he will shewe himselfe, and a certaine Reckelesness aboute that is not of importaunce, whiche augmenteth the grace of the thinge, as it were to disguise a yonge man in an olde mannes attire, but so that his garmentes be not a hindraunce to him to shew his nimblenes of person. And a man at armes in fourm of a wield shepehearde, or some other suche kinde of disguisinge, but with an excellent horse and wel trimmed for the purpose. Because the minde of the lookers on runneth furthwith to imagine the thing that is offered unto the eyes at the first shew, and whan they behold afterward a farre greater matter to come of it then they looked for under that attire, it deliteth them and they take pleasure at it. Therefore it were not meete in such pastimes and open shewes, where they take up counterfaiting of false visages, a prince should take upon him to be like a prince in dede, because in so doing, the pleasure that the lookers on receyve at the noveltye of the matter should want a great deale, for it is no noveltie at all to any man for a prince to bee a prince. And whan it is perceyved that beside his beinge a prince, he wil also beare the shape of a prince, he loseth the libertie to do all those thinges that are out of the dignity of a prince. And in case there should any contencion happen especially with weapon in these pastimes, he mighte easily make men beleave that he keepeth the persone of a prince because he will not be beaten but spared of the rest: beside that, doing in sport the very same he should do in good earnest whan neede required, it woulde take away

To be in maske.

Maner of disguising.

The prince in maske not to take the shap of a prince.

* And though it were so that all menne knewe him, it skilleth not, for there is no way to that, if a man will shewe himselfe in open sightes about such matters: and even if his disguise is not absolute and he can still be recognised, this is not a problem; on the contrary, if he is to appear in public doing this kind of thing . . . this is the best way to do it.

his authoritye in deede and would appeere in lyke case
to be play also. But in this point the prince stripping
himself of the person of a prince, and minglinge
himselfe equallye with his underlinges (yet in suche wise
that he maye bee knowen) with refusynge superioritye,
lette him chalenge a greater superioritie, namelye, to
passe other men, not in authoritie, but in vertue, and
declare that his prowes is not encreased by his being a
prince. [XII] Therefore I saye that the Courtier ought in
these open sightes of armes to have the self same
respect according to his degree. But in vauting,

*In some exer-
cises flee the
multitude.
People have
sone their
fill.*

wrastling, running and leaping, I am well pleased he flee
the multitude of people, or at the least be sene very
sildome times. For there is nothing so excellent in the
world, that the ignorant people have not their fil of, and
smallye regard in often beholding it. The like judgement
I have in musike: but I would not our Courtier should
do as many do, that assone as they come to any place,
and also in the presence of great men with whom they
have no acquaintance at al, without much entreating

*Some set out
them selves
unadvisedly.*

sett out themselves to shew asmuch as they know, yea
and many times that thei know not, so that a man
would weene they cam purposely to shew themselves
for that, and that it is their principall profession.

*How to shew
musike.*

Therfore let oure Courtier come to shewe his musike as
a thing to passe the time withall, and as he wer enforced
to doe it, and not in the presence of noble menne, nor of
any great multitude. And for all he be skilfull and doeth
wel understand it, yet wil I have him to dissemble the
study and peines that a man must needes take in all
thinges that are well done. And let him make semblante
that he estemeth but litle in himself that qualitie, but in
doing it excellently wel make it muche estemed of other
menne.

[XIII] Then saide the L. GASPAR PALLAVICIN: There
are manye sortes of musike aswell in the brest,* as upon
instrumentes, therfore would I gladly learne whiche is
the best, and at what time the Courtyer ought to
practise it.

Pricke song.

Me thinke, answered SIR FRIDERICK, pricksong† is a

* in the brest: vocal.
† pricksong. The original has 'singing from the book'
('sightreading').

faire musicke, so it bee done upon the booke surely and
after a good sorte. But to sing to the lute is muche better,
because al the sweetenesse consisteth in one alone, and
a manne is muche more heedefull and understandeth
better the feate maner and the aer or veyne of it, whan
the eares are not busyed in hearynge any moe then one
voyce: and beesyde everye lyttle erroure is soone
perceyved, whiche happeneth not in syngynge wyth
companye, for one beareth oute an other. But syngynge
to the Lute wyth the dyttie[90] (me thynke) is more
pleasaunte then the reste, for it addeth to the wordes
suche a grace and strength, that it is a great wonder.
Also all instrumentes with freates are ful of harmony,
because the tunes of them are very perfect, and with
ease a manne may do many thinges upon them that fil
the minde with the sweetnesse of musike. And the
musike of a sette of Violes doth no lesse delite a man, for
it is verie sweete and artificiall. A mannes breste* geveth
a great ornament and grace to all these instrumentes, in
the which I wil have it sufficient that our Courtyer have
an understanding. Yet the more counninger he is uppon
them, the better it is for him, withoute medlynge muche
with the instrumentes that Minerva and Alcibiades
refused,[91] because it seemeth they are noisome. Nowe
as touchyng the time and season whan these sortes of
musike are to be practised: I beleve at all times whan a
man is in familiar and loving company, having nothing
elles a doe. But especiallye they are meete to bee
practised in the presence of women, because those
sightes sweeten the mindes of the hearers, and make
them the more apte to bee perced with the pleasantnesse
of musike, and also they quicken the spirites of the verye
doers. I am well pleased (as I have saide) they flee the
multitude, and especially of the unnoble. But the
seasoning of the whole muste bee discreation, because
in effect it wer a matter unpossible to imagine all cases
that fall. And if the Courtyer be a righteous judge of
himselfe, he shall apply himselfe well inough to the
tyme, and shall discerne whan the hearers mindes are
disposed to geve eare and whan they are not. He shall
knowe his age, for (to saie the trueth) it were no meete

Margin notes: To synge to the lute. Singinge with dittie. Instrumentes with freates. A sette of violes. A mannes brest. Shalmes. Dulcimers. Harpe. Time to practise musike. Discreation.

* breste: voice.

Olde men.

matter, but an yll sight to see a man of eny estimation being olde, horeheaded and toothlesse, full of wrinckles, with a lute in his armes playing upon it and singing in the middes of a company of women, although he coulde doe it reasonablye well. And that, because suche songes conteine in them woordes of love, and in olde men love is a thing to bee jested at: although otherwhile he seemeth emonge other miracles of his to take delite in spite of yeres to set a fier frosen herts.

[XIV] Then answered the L. JULIAN: Doe you not barr poore olde men from this pleasure (Syr Fridericke), for in my time I have knowen men of yeeres have very perfect brestes and most nimble fingers for instrumentes, much more then some yong men.

I go not about, quoth SYR FRIDERICKE, to barr olde men from this pleasure, but I wil barr you these Ladies

How olde men should practise musike.

from laughing at that folie. And in case olde men wil sing to the lute, let them doe it secretly, and onely to ridde their mindes of those troublesome cares and grevous disquietinges that oure life is full of: and to taste of that excellency which I beleve Pythagoras and Socrates favoured in musike. And set case they exercise it not at all: for that* thei have gotten a certain habit and custome of it, they shal savour it muche better in hearing, then he that hath no knowledge in it. For like as the armes of a smith that is weake in other thinges, because they are more exercised, be stronger then an other bodyes that is sturdy, but not exercysed to worke with his armes: even so the eares that be exercised in musike do muche better and sooner descerne it, and with much more pleasure judge of it, then other, how good and quicke soever they be that have not bene practised in the varietie of pleasant musike: because those musical tunes perce not, but withoute leaving anye taste of themselves passe by the eares not accustomed to heare them although the very wilde beastes feele some delite in melodye. This is therfore the pleasure meete for olde men to take in musike. The self same I say of daunsing, for in deed these exercises oughte to bee lefte of before age constraineth us to leave them whether we will or no.

* set case . . . for that: even though . . . because.

It is better then, aunswered here M. MORELLO, halfe chafed, to excepte all olde men and to saie that only yong men are to be called Courtiers.

Then laughed SYR FRIDERICKE and said: Note (M. Morello) whether suche as delite in these matters, yf they bee not yonge men, do not study to appere yonge, and therfore dye their hear and make their beard grow* twise a weeke, and this proceadeth upon that nature saith to them in secrete, that these matters are not comely but for yong men.

Olde men that will seme yonge against nature.

All the Ladies laughed, because thei knew these wordes touched M. Morello, and he seemed somwhat out of pacience at the matter.

[XV] Yet are there other enterteinments with women, saide immediatly SYR FRIDERICKE, meete for olde men.

And what be these, quoth M. MORELLO, to tell fables?

And that to, answered SYR FRIDERICKE. But every age (as you know) carieth with him his thoughtes, and hath some peculiar vertue and some peculier vice. And old men for al they are ordinarily wiser then yong men, more continent, and of a better foresight, yet are they withall more lavish in wordes, more greedie, harder to please, more fearfull, alwayes chafyng in the house, sharpe to their children, and will have every man wedded to their will. And contrarywise, yonge men are hardy, easie to be entreated, but more apt to brawling and chiding, waveringe and unstedfast, that love and unlove all at a time: geven to all their delites, and ennemies to them that tell them of their profit. But of all the other ages, mans state is moste temperate, whiche hath nowe done with the curst prankes† of youth, and not yet growen to auncienty. These then that be placed (as it were) in the extremities, it is behouffull for them to knowe howe to correct the vices with reason, that nature hath bredde in them. Therefore oughte olde men to take heede of muche praising themselves, and of the other vices, that we have said are proper to them, and suffre the wisdome and knowledge to beare stroke in

The nature of olde men.

The nature of yong men.

Mans state moste temperate.

The behaviour of olde men.

---

* make their beard grow: shave.
† curst prankes: this is much more emphatic than the original, which simply has 'the flaws of youth'.

them that they have gotten by long experience, and be (as it were) Oracles, to the whiche everye man should haunt for counsaile, and have a grace in utteringe that they knowe, applying it aptlye to the purpose, accompanying with the grace of yeeres a certaine temperate and meery pleasauntnesse. In this wyse shall they be good Courtiers, and be well entertayned wyth menne and women, and everye man will at all tymes be glad of their companye, without syngynge or daunsynge: and whan neede requireth they shall showe their prowesse in matters of weighte. [XVI] The verye same respecte and judgemente shall yonge menne have, not in keepynge the facion of olde menne (for what is meete for the one, were not in all poynctes so fitte for the other, and it is a commune sayinge, To muche gravytee in yonge menne is an yll signe), but in correctynge the natural vices in them. Therfore delite I in a yonge manne, and especiallye a man at armes, if he have a certayne sagenesse in him and few woordes, and somewhat demure, wythoute those busye gestures and unquyete manners whyche we see so manye tymes in that age: for they seeme to have a certayne gyfte above other yonge menne. Beesyde that, thys mylde beehavyour conteyneth in it a kynde of syghtelye* fiersenesse, because it appeereth to bee sturred, not of wrathe but of judgemente, and rather governed by reason then appetyte: and thys (in manner) alwayes is knowen in al menne of stomacke, and we see it lykewyse in brute beastes, that have a certayne noble courage and stoutenesse above the reste: as the Lion and the Egle, neither is it voide of reason,† forsomuche as that violente and sodeyne mocyon withoute woordes or other token of coler whyche wyth all force bursteth oute together at once (as it were the shotte of a gunn) from quietnesse, whyche is contrarye to it, is muche more violente and furious, then that whiche encreaseth by degrees and wexeth hott by little and little. Therefore suche as goynge aboute‡ some enterpryse, are so full of woordes, that they leape and skip and can not stande styll, it appeereth they be

The behaviour
of yonge
menne.

Sagenesse.

Noble corrage
in brute
beastes.

---

* syghtelye: disciplined, controlled.
† neither is it voide of reason: and this is no accident.
‡ goynge about: when about to undertake.

ravyshed in those matters,* and (as oure M. Peter
Mount sayeth well) they doe like children, that goinge
in the nighte singe for feare, as though that synginge of
theirs shoulde make them plucke up their spirites to be
the boulder. Even as therfore in a yonge man a quiet and
ripe youthe is to be commended, because it appeareth
that lightnesse (whiche is the peculiar vice of that age) is   Lightnesse.
tempred and corrected: even so in an olde man a grene
and lively olde age is much to be esteamed, because it
appeareth that the force of the minde is so much, that it
heateth and geveth a certein strength to that feeble and
colde age, and mainteineth it in that middle state, which
is the better part of our life. [XVII] But in conclusion al
these good qualities shal not suffise oure Courtyer to
purchase him the general favour of great men, Gentle-
men and Ladies, yf he have not also a gentle and lovynge   Behaviour in
behaviour in his daily conversation. And of this I beleve   dailye con-
verely it is a hard matter to geve anye maner rule, for the   versation.
infinit and sundry matters that happen in practising
one with an other: forsomuch as emong al the men in   So many men
the world, there are not two to be found that in every   so many
point agree in mind together. Therfore he that must be   mindes.
pliable to be conversant with so many, oughte to guide
himselfe with hys own judgement. And knowing the
difference of one man and an other, every day alter
facion and maner accordyng to the disposition of them
he is conversant withall. And for my part I am not able
in this behalf to geve him other rules then the aforesaid,
whiche oure M. Morello learned of a child in confessing
him self.

Here the L. EMILIA laughed and said: You would rid
your handes of peines taking (Syr Fridericke) but you
shall not escape so, for it is youre parte to minister talke
untill it be bed time.

And what if I have nothing to saye (madam)? Howe
then? aunswered SIR FRIDERICKE.

The L. EMILIA said: We shal nowe trie your wit. And
if al be true I have heard, there have bene men so wittie
and eloquent, that thei have not wanted matter to make
a booke in the praise of a flie, other in the praise of a

* it appeereth they be ravyshed in those matters: lose their fire
when it comes to the point.

quartaine fever, an other in the praise of bauldnes,[92] doth not your hert serve you to finde oute somwhat to saie for one nyghte of Courting?

We have already, answered SYR FRIDERICKE, spoken asmuch as wil go nigh to make two bokes. But since no excuse shal serve me, I wil speak until you shal think I have fulfilled though not my duety, yet my poure. [XVIII] I suppose the conversation which the Courtier ought chiefly to be pliable unto with al diligence to get him favour, is the very same that he shal have with his prince. And although this name of conversation bringeth with it a certain equalitie that a man would not judge can reigne betweene the maister and the servaunt, yet will we so terme it for this once. I will have our Courtyer therfore (beside that he hath and doeth daily geve men to understande that he is of the prowesse which we have said ought to be in him) to turne al his thoughtes and force of minde to love, and (as it were) to reverence the Prince he serveth above al other thinges, and in his wil, maners and facions, to be altogether pliable to please him.

Here without anye lenger staye, PETER OF NAPLES saide: Of these, Courtyers noweadayes ye shall finde ynow, for (me thinke) in fewe wordes ye have peincted us out a joly flatterer.

You are farre deceived, answered SYR FRIDERICKE, for flatterers love not their Lordes nor their friendes, the whiche I saie unto you I will have principally in our Courtyer: and to please him and to obey hys commaundementes whom he serveth, may be done without flattery, for I meane the commaundementes that are reasonable and honest, or suche as of themselves are neyther good nor bad, as is gaming and pastime, and geving himself more to some one exercise then to an other. And to this will I have the Courtyer to frame himselfe, though by nature he were not enclined to it: so that whansoever his lorde looketh upon him, he may thinke in his minde that he hath to talke with him of a matter that he will be glad to heare. The which shal come to passe if there bee a good judgement in him to understand what pleaseth his prince and a wit and wisdom to know how to applie it, and a bent wil to make him pleased with the thing which perhappes by

Conversation with his prince.

To please his prince.

Flatterers.

His behaviour in his princes presence.

nature should displease him. And havinge these principles, he shal never be sad before his prince nor
melancholy, nor so solein as many, that a man would
weene wer at debate with their Lordes, whiche is truly
an hateful matter. He shall not be yll tunged, and
especiallye againste his superiours, whiche happeneth
often times: for it appeereth that there is a storme in
courtes that carieth this condicion with it, that alwaies
looke who* receyveth most benifittes at his Lordes
handes, and promoted from very base degree to high
astate, he is evermore complaynynge and reporteth
woorst of hym: which is an uncomly thing, not onely
for suche as these be, but even for such as be yll handled
in deede. Oure Courtier shall use no fonde sausinesse.
He shall be no carier about of trifling newes. He shall not
be overseene† in speakinge otherwhile woordes that
may offende, where his entent was to please. He shall
not be stubborne and full of contencion, as some busy
bodyes that a man would weene had none other delite
but to vexe and stirr men like flyes, and take uppon
them to contrarie every man spitefullye without respect.
He shall be no babbler, not geven to lyghtenesse, no
lyar, no boaster, nor fonde flatterer, but sober, and
keapinge hym alwayes within his boundes, use continually, and especially abrode, the reverence and respecte
that beecommeth the servaunte towarde the mayster.
And shall not do, as many that meetinge a Prince how
great soever he be, yf they have once spoken with him
beefore, come towarde him with a certaine smilynge
and frindly countenaunce, as though they would make
of one their equall, or showe favour to an inferiour of
theirs. Very sildome or (in maner) never shall he crave
any thinge of his Lorde for himselfe, least the lorde
having respect to denie it him for him selfe, should
happen to graunte it him with dyspleasure, which is farr
worse. Againe in suinge for others, he shall discreatly
observe the times, and his suite shall be for honest and
reasonable matters, and he shall so frame hys suite, in
leavinge out those poinctes that he shall knowe wil
trouble him, and in making easie after a comely sort the

Not yl
tunged.

The most
made of worst
reporters.

Not saucye.
No pratler
of newes.
Not stub-
borne.

No babbler.
No lyar.
No boaster.
No flatterer.

The behaviour
of some fonde
persons to-
ward great
men.

Why he shall
not sue for
him selfe.

His sute for
others.

* alwaies looke who: the man who.
† overseene: careless.

lettes, that his Lord wil evermore graunt it him: and though he denie it, he shall not think to have offended him whom he ment not to doe, for, because greate menne often times after thei have denied request to one that hath suid to them with great instance, thinke the person that laboured to them so earnestly for it, was very greedy of it, and therefore in not obtaining it, hath cause to beare him yll will that denied him it, and upon this suspicion thei conceive an hatred against that person, and can never afterwarde brooke him nor aforde him good countenance. [XIX] He shall not covet to presse into the chamber or other secrete places where his Lord is withdrawen, onlesse he be bed, for all he be of great authoritie with him: because great men often times whan thei are privatly gotten alone, love a certain libertie to speake and do what thei please, and therefore will not be seene or herd of any person that may lightly deeme of them, and reason willeth no lesse. Therfore suche as speake against great menne for making of their chamber persons of no great qualitie in other thinges but in knowing how to attende about their person (me thinke) commit an errour: because I can not see why they should not have the libertie to refresh their mindes, whiche we oure selves would have to refreshe ours. But in case the Courtyer that is inured with weightie affaires, happen to bee afterwarde secretely in chamber with him, he oughte to chaunge his coate and to differr grave matters till an other time and place, and frame himself to pleasante communicacion, and suche as his lorde will bee willing to geve eare unto, least he hinder that good moode of his. But herein and in al other thinges, let him have an especial regard, that he be not combrous to him. And let him rather looke to have favour and promotion offred him, then crave it so openly in the face of the worlde, as manye dooe, that are so greedy of it, that a man would weene the not obtaynynge it, greeveth them as muche as the losse of lyfe: and yf they chaunce to enter into anye displeasure, or elles see other in favoure, they are in suche anguishe of mynde, that thei can by no meanes dissemble the malice, and so make al men laugh them to scorne: and many times thei are the cause that great men favour some one, only to spite them withal. And afterward if

The imagi-
nacyon of
princes.

He shall not
presse into
secret places.

Greate men
should make
of their cham-
ber men of no
greate estima-
tion.

Not to sue for
promotions.

The griefe of
some for
anger.

thei happen to enter in favour that passeth a meane, they are so dronken in it, that thei know not what to do for joy: and a man would wene that thei wist not what wer become of their feete and handes, and (in a maner) are ready to cal company to behoulde them and to rejoice with them, as a matter they have not bene accustomed withal. Of this sort I wil not have our Courtyer to be. I would have him esteame favour and promotion, but for al that, not to love it so much, that a man should thinke he could not live without it. And whan he hath it, let him not shew himself new or straunge in it: nor wonder at it whan it is offred him: nor refuse it in such sort as some, that for very ignorance receive it not, and so make men beleve that thei acknowledge themselves unworthy of it. Yet ought a man alwaies to humble himself somewhat under his degree, and not receive favour and promocions so easilye as thei be offred him, but refuse them modestlye, shewing he much estemeth them, and after such a sort, that he may geve him an occasion that offreth them, to offer them with a great deale more instance: because the more resistance a man maketh in such maner to receive them, the more doeth he seeme to the prince that geveth them to be estemed, and that the benefite whiche he bestoweth is so muche the more, as he that receiveth it seemeth to make of it, thinking himself much honoured therby. And these are the true and perfect promotions that make men esteamed of such as se them abrode: because whan they are not craved, everye man conjectureth they arrise of true vertue, and so muche the more, as they are accompanied with modestie.

[XX] Then said the L. CESAR GONZAGA: Me thinke ye have this clause oute of the Gosspell where it is written: Whan thou art bed to a mariage, go and sit thee downe in the lowest rowme, that whan he commeth that bed thee, he may saie, Friende come higher, and so shal it be an honour for thee in the sight of the gestes.[93]

SYR FRIDERICKE laughed and said: It were to great a sacrilege to steale out of the Gospell. But you are better learned in scripture then I was aware of: then he proceaded. See into what daunger they fal sometime, that rashly before a great manne entre into talke unrequired: and manye times that Lord to skorne them

The wye of some in a meane authorityre.

Behaviour in receivynge promotion.

Promotions not begged.

The rashnes of some.

withall, maketh no aunswere and tourneth his head to the other hand: and in case he doeth make aunswere, every man perceyveth it is done full skornfullye.

To deserve favour.

Therfore to purchase favour at great mens handes, there is no better waye then to deserve it. Neyther must a manne hope when he seeth an other in favour with a Prince, for whatsoever matter, in folowinge his steppes to come to the same, because every thing is not fitt for every man. And ye shal finde otherwhile some one that by nature is so readie in his meerye jestes, that what ever he speaketh bringeth laughter with it, and a man would weene that he were borne onlye for that: and if another that hath a grave facion in him, of howe good a witt so ever he be, attempt the like, it will be very colde and without any grace, so that he will make a man abhorre to heare him, and in effect will be like the asse, that to counterfeyt the dogg would play with his maister.[94] Therefore it is meete eche man knowe himselfe and his own disposicion, and applye himselfe thereto, and consider what thynges are mete for him to folow, and what are not.

Not to counterfait other mens doings.

Some ready in their jestes.

[XXI] Before ye go anye farther, saide here M. VINCENT CALMETA,[95] if I have well marked, me thaught ye said right now, that the best way to purchase favour, is to deserve it: and the Courtier oughte rather to tarie till promotions bee offered him, then presumpciously to crave them. I feare me least this rule bee litle to purpose, and me thinke experience doeth us very manifestly to understande the contrarye: because noweadayes very fewe are in favoure with Princes but such as be malapert.* And I wote well you can be a good witnesse of some, that perceivyng themselves in smal credite with their Princis, are come up only with presumption. As for such as come to promotion with modestie, I for my parte know none, and if I geve you respite to bethink your self, I beleve ye wil finde out but fewe. And if you marke the French Court, which at this day is one of the nobleste in al Christendome, ye shal find that al such as are generally in favour there, have in them a certein malapertnesse, and that not onely one with an other, but with the king himselfe.

* malapert: arrogant and grasping.

Do you not so say, answered SYR FRIDERICKE, for in Fraunce there are very modest and courtious gentlemen. Truth it is, that they use a certein libertie and familiaritie without ceremonies, which is proper and natural unto them, and therefore it ought not to be termed malapertnesse. For in that maner of theirs, although they laugh and jeste at suche as be malapert, yet do they sett muche by* them that seeme to them to have any prowesse or modesty in them.

The Frenche gentlemen without ceremonies.

CALMETA answered: Marke the Spaniardes that seme the very maisters of Courtly facions, and consider how many ye find that with women and great men are not moste malapert, and so muche woorse then the Frenchemen, in that at the fyrste showe they declare a certein modesty. And no doubt but they be wise in so doing, because (as I have said) the great men of our time do al favour suche as are of these condicions.

Spaniardes.

[XXII] Then answered SYR FRIDERICK: I can not abide (M. Vincent) that ye should defame in this wise the great men of our time, because there be many notwithstanding that love modesty: the which I do not say of it self is sufficient to make a man esteamed, but I saie unto you, whan it is accompanied with great prowesse it maketh him muche esteamed that hath it. And though of it self it lye styll,† the woorthye deedes speake at large, and are much more to be wondred at, then if they were accompanied with presumption or rashnes. I will not nowe denie but many Spaniardes there be full of malapertnesse: but I saie unto you, they that are best esteamed, for the moste part are very modest. Agayne some other there be also so cold, that they flee the company of menne to out of measure, and passe a certein degree of meane: so that they make men deeme them either to fearfull or to high minded.‡ And this doe I in no case allowe, neyther would I have modestie so drye and withered, that it shoulde become rudenesse. But let the Courtier, whan it commeth to pourpose, be well spoken, and in discourses uppon states, wise and expert: and have such a judgement that

Many Spaniardes be sawcye.

What modestie ought to be.

* sett muche by: appreciate.
† lye styll: does not advertise itself.
‡ high minded: proud.

he maye frame himselfe to the manners of the countrey where ever he commeth. Then in lower matters, let him bee pleasauntly disposed, and reason* well uppon everye matter, but in especiall tende alwayes to goodnesse. No envious person, no caryar of an yll tunge in his head: nor at anye tyme geven to seeke prefarmente or promotion anye naughtie waye, nor by the meane of anye subtyll practise.

Then saide CALMETA: I wyll assure you all the other waies are muche more doubtfull and harder to compasse, then is that you discommende: because now a dayes (to rehearse it againe) great menne love none but such as be of that condicion.

Do you not so say, answered then SYR FRIDERICKE, for that were to plaine an argumente that the greate menne of our tyme were all vitious and naughte, whiche is untrue, for some there be that bee good. But if it fell to oure Courtyers lott to serve one that wer vitious and wycked, assoone as he knoweth it, let him forsake hym, least he taste of the bytter peine that all good menne feele that serve the wicked.

What he must do in service with the wicked.

We muste praie unto God, answered CALMETA, to helpe us to good, for whan wee are once with them, wee muste take them with all theyr faultes, for infinite respectes constraine a Gentleman after he is once entred into service with a Lorde, not to forsake him.[96] But the yll lucke is in the begynnyng: and Courtyers in this case are not unlyke unluckye foules bread up in an yl vale.

Me thinke, quoth SYR FRIDERICKE, duetye oughte to prevayle beefore all other respectes, but yet so a gentleman forsake not his Lorde at the warre or in anye other adversitie, and bee thought to doe it to followe Fortune, or because he wanted a meane to profitte by, at al other times I beleve he maye with good reason, and oughte to forsake that service, that among good men shall put hym to shame, for all men will imagine that he that serveth the good, is good, and he that serveth the yll, is yll.

Whan a man may forsake his maister.

[XXIII] I woulde have you to clere me of one doubt that I have in my head, quoth then the L. LODOVICUS PIUS, namely, whether a gentleman be bound or no,

* reason: speak.

while he is in his Princis service, to obey him in all
thinges which he shal commaund, though they were
dishonest and shamefull matters.

Howe and in
what princis
are to be
obeied.

In dishoneste matters we are not bounde to obey any
body, aunswered SYR FRIDERICKE.

And what (replyed the L. LODOVICUS PIUS) if I be in
service with a Prince who handleth me well, and hopeth
that I will do any thing for him that may be done, and he
happen to commaunde me to kyll a man, or any other
like matter, ought I to refuse to do it?

You ought, answered SYR FRIDERICKE, to obey your
Lorde in all thinges that tende to his profitt and honour,
not in suche matters that tende to his losse and shame.
Therefore yf he shoulde commaunde you to conspire
treason, ye are not onely not bounde to doe it, but ye are
bounde not to doe it, bothe for your owne sake and for
being a minister of the shame of your Lorde. Truth it is,
many thinges seeme at the first sight good, which are il:
and many ill, that not withstanding are good. Therefore
it is lawfull for a man sometyme in his Lordes service to
kill not one manne alone, but tenne thousande, and to
do many other thinges, which if a man waye them not as
he ought, will appeare yll, and yet are not so in deede.

Then aunswered the L. GASPAR PALLAVICIN: I
beseche you let us heare you speake somwhat in this
case, and teach us how we maie descerne thinges good
in dede, from suche as appeare good.

I pray you pardon me, quoth SYR FRIDERICKE, I will
not at this time enter into that, for there were to muche
to be saide in it: but all is to be referred to your
discretion.

[XXIV] Clere ye me at the least of another doubt,
replied the L. GASPAR.

And what doubt is that? quoth SYR FRIDERICKE.

This aunswered the L. GASPAR: I would know where
I am charged by my maister in expresse wordes in an
interprise or businesse what ever it be, what I have to do
therein: if I, at the deede doynge thinkynge wyth my
selfe in doynge it more or lesse, or otherwise then my
commission, to bringe it more prosperouslye to passe
and more for his profit that gave me that commission,
whether ought I to govern my selfe accordinge to the
first charge withoute passinge the boundes of the

Whether a
man maie
folow a part
of his owne
mind in a
commission.

commission, or elles do the thinge that I judge to be best?

Then answered SIR FRIDERICK: In this pointe I woulde geve you the judgemente with the example of Manlius Torquatus,[97] whiche in that case for overmuch affeccion slue his sonne, if I thoughte hym woorthy great praise, which (to saie the troth) I doe not: although againe I dare not discommende him, contrarye to the opinion of so manye hundreth yeeres. For oute of doubte, it is a daungerous matter to swarve from the commaundementes of a mannes superiours, trusting more in his owne judgemente then in theirs, whom of reason he ought to obey: because if his imagination faile him and the matter take yll successe, he renneth into the errour of disobedience, and marreth that he hath to doe, without any maner excuse or hope of pardon. Againe in case the matter come well to passe accordinge to his desier, he muste thanke his fortune, and no more a doe. Yet in this sorte a custome is brought up to set litle by the commaundementes of the superiour poures. And by his example that bryngeth the matter to good passe, which paraventure is a wise man and hath discoursed with reason and also ayded by fortune, afterwarde a thousand other ignoraunt persons and light headed will take a stomake to aventure in matters of moste importaunce to doe after their owne waye, and to appere wise and of authoritie, wil swarve from the commission of their heades, whiche is a very yll matter, and often times the cause of infinite errours. But I beleave in this point, the person whom the matter toucheth ought to skanne it depely, and (as it were) put in a balaunce the goodnesse and commoditie that is like to ensue unto him in doing contrarie to that he is charged, admytting his purpose succede according to his hope: and counterpese on the other side the hurt and discommoditie that arriseth, if in doing otherwise then he is commaunded, the matter chaunce to have yll successe: and knowing that the hurt may be greater and of more importance, if it succeede yll, then the profitt, if it happen well, he ought to refrain, and in every point to observe his commission. And contrarywise, if the profitt be like to bee of more importaunce, if it succeede well, then the hurte, if it happen amisse, I beleve he may with good reason take in hand to do the thing that

T. Manlius Torq. caused his sonne to be slaine for fighting contrary to commaundement.

Commaundementes of the superioure poures are to be obeyed.

What he that receiveth a charge ought to doe.

reason and judgement shall sette before him, and leave somewhat a side the very fourme of the commission, after the example of good marchaunt men, that to gaine much, adventure a litle, and not much, to gaine a litle. I allowe well that he have a regarde to the nature of the Lorde he serveth, and according to that, frame hymselfe. For in case he be rigorous (as many suche there are) I woulde never counsell him, if he were my friende, to varye in any parcell from the appointed order, least it happen unto him, as a maister Inginner of Athens was served, unto whom P. Crassus Mutianus[98] being in Asia and going aboute to batter a towne, sent to demaunde of him one of the two shipmastes that he had sene in Athens to make a Ramm to beate down the walles, and sayde he woulde have the greater. Thys Inginner, as he that was verye counnynge in deede, knewe the greater woulde not verye well serve for thys pourpose, and because the lesser was more easy to bee caried, and also fytter to make that ordinaunce, he sent that to Mutianus. After he had understoode how the matter passed, he sente for the poore Inginner and asked hym why he obeyed hym not, and not admyttynge anye reason he coulde alleage for hymselfe, made hym to bee strypped naked, beaten and whipped with roddes, so that he died, seemyng to hym in steede of obeying him, he would have counsailed him: therefore with suche rigorous men, a man muste looke well to his doynges. [XXV] But lette us leave a parte nowe this practyse of the superiours, and come downe to the conversation that a manne hath with his equalles or somewhat inferiours, for unto them also must a manne frame hymselfe, because it is more universallye frequented, and a manne findeth himselfe oftner emonge them, then emong his superiours. Although ther be some fonde persons that beeing in companye with the greatest friende they have in the worlde, if they meete wyth one better apparailed, by and by they cleave unto him: and yf an other come in place better then he, they doe the like unto him. And againe, whan the Prince passeth throughe the market place, through churches, or other haunted* places, they make all men geve them rowme

The nature of the L. to be considered.

The crueltye of Mutianus.

Conversacion with a mannes equalles.

Some felowship them selves alwayes with the best apparailed.

* haunted: public.

Men that will
seeme to be
in favour.

with their elbowes tyll they come to their heeles,* and
thoughe they have nothing to saie to him, yet wyll they
talke with him and keape him with a long tale, laugh,
clappe the handes, and nod the head, to seeme to have
weightie businesse, that the people maye see they are in
favoure. But because these kynde of menne vouchesafe
not to speake but with great menne, I wyll not we
should vouchsafe to speake of them.

[XXVI] Then the L. JULIAN: Since ye have (quoth he)
made mention of these that are so ready to felowshippe
themselves with the wel apparailed, I would have you to
shew us in what sorte the Courtier shoulde apparayle
hymself, what kind of garment doeth beste become
hym, and howe he shoulde fitte himselfe in all his
garmentes aboute his bodye: beecause we see infinite
varietie in it, and some are arayed after the Frenche
facion, some after the Spanyshe attier, an other wyll
seeme a Dutcheman.† Neyther wante wee of them also
that wil cloth themselves lyke Turkes: some weare
beardes, other dooe not. Therefore it were a good deede
in this varietie, to shewe howe a manne shoulde chouse
oute the beste.

Of raiment
and apparail.

SYR FRIDERICKE saide: In verye deede I am not able to
geve anye certeyne rule aboute rayment, but that a man
should frame himselfe to the custome of the moste. And
since (as you saye) this custome is so variable, and
Italians are so desirous to take up other mennes facions,
I beleave every manne maye lawfullye apparaile himselfe at his pleasure. But I knowe not by what destinye it
commeth that Italy hathe not, as it was wonte to have, a
facion of attier knowen to bee the Italian facion, for
although the bringing up of these new facions maketh
the first‡ to appeere very grosse, yet were they peraventure a token of libertie, where these have bene a
pronosticate of bondage, the which (me thinke) now is
plainly ynough fulfilled. And as it is written, when
Darius[99] the yere before he fought with Alexander had
altered his swerd he wore by his side, which was a
Persian blade, into the facion of Macedony, it was

Caldæi.

---

* come to their heeles: work their way to the prince's side.
† a Dutcheman: a German.
‡ the first: the previous ones.

interpreted by the Sothsayers, how this signified, that
they into whose facion Darius had altered the fourme of
his Persian blade should become rulers of Persia: even
so where we have altered our Italian facions into
straunge, me thinke, it signified, that all they into whose
facions oures wer chaunged, should come in to over-
runne us: the whiche hathe been to true, for there is not
nowe a nation lefte that hath not made us their prey, so
that there remaineth little behinde to prey upon, and yet
for all that cease they not to prey still.[100] [XXVII] But I
wyll not enter into communication of sorowe: therefore
it shalbe wel to speake of the raiment of our Courtyer,
the whiche so it be not out of use, nor contrary to his
profession, in the rest (I thinke) it will do welynough, so
the wearer be satisfied withall. Truth it is, that I woulde
love it the better yf it were not extreme in anye part, as
the Frenchman is wont to bee sometyme over longe, and
the Dutchmanne overshorte, but as they are bothe the
one and the other amended and broughte into better
frame by the Italians. Moreover I will houlde alwayes
with it, yf it bee rather somewhat grave and auncient,*
then garishe. Therefore me thinke a blacke coulour hath
a better grace in garmentes then any other, and though
not throughly blacke, yet somwhat darke, and this I
meane for his ordinary apparaile. For there is no doubt,
but upon armour it is more meete to have sightly and
meery coulours, and also garmentes for pleasure, cut,
pompous and riche. Likewise in open showes about
triumphes, games, maskeries, and suche other matters,
because so appointed there is in them a certein livelinesse and mirth, which in deede doeth well sette furth
feates of armes and pastimes. But in the rest I coulde
wishe they should declare the solemnitie that the
Spanyshe nation muche observeth, for outwarde
matters manye times are a token of the inwarde.

Then saide the L. CESAR GONZAGA: I woulde not
sticke muche at this, for so a gentleman be of woorthinesse in other matters, his garmentes neyther encrease
nor minishe reputation.

SYR FRIDERICK answered: Ye saie true. Yet whiche of
us is there, that seeing a gentleman go with a garment

Side notes:
Italy a prey to
all nations.

Frenchemen
use long
wastes.
Dutchmen
short.
Grave
apparaile.
Blacke
coulour.
Coulours
upon armour.

Solemnitie
of Spaniardes.

* auncient: sober, restrained.

upon his backe quartred with sundry coulours, or with so many points tyed together, and al about with lases and fringes set overthwart, will not count him a very disard* or a commune jestar?

Neither disard, quoth M. PETER BEMBO, nor jestar woulde a man count him, that had lived any while in Lumbardy, for there they go all so.

Why then, aunswered the DUTCHESSE smylyng, if they go all so, it ought not to bee objected to them for a vice, this kinde of attier being as comely and proper to them, as it is to the Venetians to weare their longe wyde sleeves,[101] and to the Florentines, their hoodes.

I speake no more of Lumbardy, quoth SYR FRIDERICKE, then of other places, for in every nation ye shall finde bothe foolishe and wyse. But to speake that I thinke is most requisite as touching apparaile, I will have the Courtier in all his garmentes handsome and clenlye, and take a certain delite in modest Precisenesse, but not for all that after a womanish or lyghte maner, neither more in one point, then in an other, as we see many so curious about their hear, that they forget all the rest. Other delite to have their teeth faire. Other in their beard. Other in buskines.† Other in cappes. Other in coyffes. And so it commeth to passe, that those fewe thinges whiche they have clenly in them, appeere borowed ware, and all the rest, whiche is most fonde, is knowne to be their owne. But this trade wil I have our Courtier to flee by my counsel, with an addition also, that he ought to determine with himselfe what he will appeere to be, and in suche sort as he desireth to bee esteamed so to apparaile himselfe, and make his garmentes helpe him to be counted suche a one, even of them that heare hym not speake, nor see him doe anye maner thyng.

Delites of men.

[XXVIII] I thinke it not meete, quoth then the L. PALLAVICIN, neyther is it used emong honest menne to judge mennes conditions by their garmentes, and not by their woordes and deedes, for many a manne might be deceived: and this proverb arriseth not without cause: The habit maketh not the Monke.

---

* disard: madman.
† buskines: 'boots' in the original.

I say not, answered SYR FRIDERICK, that menne
shoulde geve a resolute judgement by this alone, of
mennes conditions, and that they are not knowen by
wordes and deedes, more then by the garmentes. But I
saie that the garment is withall no small argument of the
fansie of him that weareth it, although otherwile it
appeere not true.* And not this alone, but all the
behaviours, gestures and maners, beeside wordes and
deedes, are a judgement of the inclination of him in
whom they are seene.

The garment
judgeth the
mynde.

And what thynges be those, aunswered the L.
GASPAR, that you fynde we maye geve judgement upon,
that are neyther woordes nor deedes.

Then said SYR FRIDERICK: You are to subtill a
Logicien, but to tell you as I meane, some Operations
there are that remayne after they are done, as buylding,
writynge, and suche other: some remayn not, as these
that I meane now.[102] Therefore doe I not counte in this
pourpose, goynge,† laughyng, lookyng, and suche
matters to bee Operations, and notwithstandyng outwardly doe geve many times a knowledge of that is
within. Tell me, dyd you not geve your judgemente
upon that friende of oures we communed of this
morning paste, to bee a foolishe and light person,
assoone as you sawe he wried his head and bowed his
bodye, and invited with a cheerfull countenaunce the
companye to put of their cappes to him? So in like
maner whan you see one gase earnestely with his eyes
abashed,‡ lyke one that had lytle witt: or that laugheth
so fondly as do those dombe menne, with the great
wennes in theyr throte, that dwell in the Mountaines of
Bergamo, thoughe he neyther speake ne doe anye thinge
elles, will you not counte him a verye foole? Ye may see
then that these beehaviours, maners and gestures,
whiche I mynde not for this time to terme Operations,
are a great matter to make menne knowne. [XXIX] But
me thynke there is an other thyng that geveth and
dimynisheth muche reputation: namely, the choyse of

Operations.

Gozzuti,
men in the
mountaines
with great
bottles of flesh
under their
chin, through
the drinking
of snow water.

Choise of
friendes.

* although otherwhile it appeere not true: although sometimes the
impression is a false one.
† goynge: walking.
‡ abashed: staring.

friendes, with whom a manne must have inwarde conversation. For, undoubtedly reason wylleth that suche as are coopled in streicte amitie and unseparable companye, should be also alike in wyll, in mynde, in judgemente, and inclination. So that who so is conversaunt wyth the ignoraunt or wycked, he is also counted ignoraunt and wycked. And contrariwise he that is conversaunt with the good, wyse, and dyscreete, he is reckened suche a one. For it seemeth by nature, that everye thing doeth willingly felowshippe with his lyke. Therefore I beleave that a man oughte to have a respect in the first beeginning of these frendshippes, for of two neere friendes, who ever knoweth the one, by and by he ymagineth the other to bee of the same condition.

Then aunswered M. PETER BEMBO: To bee bounde in frendshyppe with suche agreemente of mynde as you speake of, me thynke in deede a manne ought to have great respect, not onely forgetting or leesing reputation, but because nowe adaies ye finde very fewe true friendes. Neyther doe I beleave that there are any more in the world, those Pylades and Orestes, Theseus and Perithous, nor Scipio and Lælius,[103] but rather it happeneth dailye, I wote not by what destinye, that two friendes whiche many yeeres have lyved together with most hartie love, yet at the ende beguile one an other, in one maner or other, either for malice, or envye, or for lightnesse, or some other yll cause: and eche one imputeth the faulte to his felow, of that whiche perhappes both the one and the other deserveth. Therfore because it hath happened to me more then once to bee deceived of hym whom I loved beste, and of whom I hoped I was beloved above anye other person, I have thought with my selfe alone other while to bee well done,* never to put a mannes trust in any person in the worlde, nor to geve himselfe so for a prey to friend how deere and loving so ever he wer, that without stoppe a manne shoulde make him partaker of all his thoughtes, and he woulde his owne selfe: because there are in our mindes so many dennes and corners, that it is unpossible for the witt of manne to knowe the dissymulations

---

* I have thought with my selfe alone other while to bee well done: I have sometimes thought to myself that it would be a good idea.

that lye lurking in them. I beleave therefore that it is well done to love and awaie with one more then another, according to the desertes and honesty: but not for all that so to assure a mannes selfe, with this sweete bait of frendship, that afterwarde it shoulde be to late for us to repente.

[XXX] Then SYR FRIDERICKE: Truely (quoth he) the losse shoulde bee much more then the gain, if that high degree of friendshippe shoulde bee taken from the felowshippe of manne, whiche (in mine opinion) ministreth unto us all the goodnes conteined in our life: and therefore wyll I in no case consente to you, that it is reasonable, but rather I can finde in my heart to conclude, and that with moste evident reasons, that without this perfect friendship, men were much more unluckie, then all other livyng creatures. And albeit some wicked and prophane taste of this holye name of friendship, yet is it not for all that to be so rooted oute of mennes mindes, and for the trespasse of the yll, to deprive the good of so great a felicitie. And I beleave verely for my parte, there is here emong us moe then one couple of friends, whose love is indissoluble and without any guile at all, and to endure untill death, with agreement of will, no lesse then those menne of olde time, whom you mentioned right nowe. And so is it alwaies, whan beside the inclination that commeth from above, a man chouseth him a friende lyke unto himselfe in conditions. And I meane the whole to consist emong the good and vertuous menne, because the friendship of the wicked, is no friendshippe. I allowe well that this knott, which is so streicte, knitt or binde no mo then two, elles were it in a hasarde: for (as you knowe) three instrumentes of musike are hardlier brought to agree together then two. I woulde have our Courtier therefore to finde him oute an especiall and hartie friende, if it were possible, of that sort we have spoken of. Then according to their desertes and honesty, love, honour, and observe all other menne, and alwaies do hys beste to felowshippe himselfe with menne of estimation that are noble and knowen to bee good, more then with the unnoble and of small reputation, so he be also beloved and honoured of them. And this shall come to passe if he be gentle,

Frendshippe necessarye for the lyfe of man.

Frendshippe of two together.

A mans duetie
towarde his
friend.

lowely, freeherted, easie to be spoken to, and sweete in
company, humble and diligent to serve, and to have an
eye to his friendes profitt and estimation, as wel absente
as present, bearing with their naturall defaultes that are
to be borne withall, without breaking with them upon a
small grounde, and correcting in himselfe such as
lovingly shall bee toulde him, never prefarring himselfe
before other menne in seeking the hyghest and chiefe
rowmes of estimation, neither in doing as some that a
manne would weene despised the worlde, and with a
noysome sharpnes will tell every manne his duetie, and
beside that they are full of contention in every trifling
matter, and out of tyme, they comptroule* whatsoever
they doe not themselves, and alwaies seeke cause to
complaine of their friendes, which is a most hatefull
thing.

[XXXI] Here whan Sir Friderick had made a stay, the
L. GASPAR PALLAVICIN saide: I would have you to
expresse somewhat more particularlye this conversation with friendes, then you doe, for in deede ye keepe
your self to muche in the generall, and touch unto us
thinges (as it were) by the waie.

Howe by the waye? aunswered SYR FRIDERICKE.
Woulde you have me to tell you also the verye woordes
that a manne muste use? Suppose you not then we have
sufficientlye communed of this?

I thynke yea, aunswered the L. GASPAR. Yet doe I
desier to understand also some particular point of the
maner of enterteinment emong menne and women,
whiche (me thynke) is a verye necessary matter, con-
sideryng the moste parte of a mans tyme is spent therein
in Courtes, and if it were alwayes after one maner wyse,
a manne would soone wexe weerye of it.

Me thynke, aunswered SYR FRIDERICKE, we have
geven the Courtier a knowledge in so many thynges,
that he maye well varye his conversation and frame
hymselfe accordynge to the inclination of them he
accompanyeth hymself withall, presupposyng him to be
of a good judgemente, and therewithall to guyde
hymself. And according to the time otherwhile, have an

* comptroule: censor, criticise.

eye to grave matters, and sometyme to pastimes and games.

And what games? quoth the L. GASPAR.

SYR FRIDERICK aunswered: Lette us aske counsel of Frier Seraphin that daily inventeth newe.

But in good earneste, replied the L. GASPAR, doe you not thynke it a vice in the Courtier to plaie at Dice and Cardes?

Dice and Cardes.

I thynke it none, quoth SYR FRIDERICKE, onlesse a man apply it tomuch, and by reason of that, setteth aside other thynges more necessary, or elles for none other entent but to get money, and to beguile his felow, and in his losse, fume and take on so, that it might be thought a token of covetousnesse.

The L. GASPAR answered: And what say you to the game at chestes?*

The play at Chestes.

It is truely an honest kynde of enterteynmente and wittie, quoth SYR FRIDERICK. But me think it hath a fault, whiche is, that a man may be to couning at it, for who ever will be excellent in the playe of chestes, I beleave he must beestowe much tyme about it, and applie it with so much study, that a man may assoone learne some noble scyence, or compase any other matter of importaunce, and yet in the ende in beestowing all that laboure, he knoweth no more but a game. Therfore in this I beleave there happeneth a very rare thing, namely, that the meane is more commendable, then the excellency.

The meane knowledge is best in the play at Chestes.

The L. GASPAR answered: There be many Spaniardes excellent at it, and in many other games, whiche for all that bestowe not muche studye upon it, nor yet lay aside the compassing of other matters.

Beleave not the contrarye, aunswered SYR FRIDERICKE, but they beestowe muche studye upon it, although feiningly. As for those other games ye speake of beeside chestes, paraventure they are like many which I have seen that serve to small pourpose, but onely to make the commune people wonder. Therfore (in mine opinion) thei deserve none other praise or reward, then the great Alexander gave unto him, that standyng a farr of, did so well broch Chiche peason

Spaniardes dissemble their study in the play at Chestes.

* chestes: chess.

upon a nedle.[104] [XXXII] But because fortune, as in manye other thinges, so in the opinion of men seemeth to beare a great stroke, it is somtime seen that a gentleman, how well conditioned ever he be, and endowed with many qualities, shall be litle set by of a great man, and (as thei say) groweth not in favour with him,* and without any cause why, that a man may discearn. Therefore whan he commeth into his presence without any acquaintance before hande, with the reste about him, though he be wittie and ready in his answeres, and showeth himself handsomly wel in his beehaviours, in his conditions and wordes, and in what ever belongeth unto him, yet wil that Lord sett light by him, and rather geve hym an yll countenance, then esteame him: and of this wil arrise that the rest immediatly will frame themselves to their lordes mind, and it shall seeme unto every man that he is litle worth, neyther will any manne regarde hym, or make of him, or laugh at his pleasante sayinges, or set any thing by hym, but will beeginne all to serve him sluttish pranckes, and make him a Cousin,† neyther shall good aunsweres suffyce the poore soule, nor yet the takynge of thynges as spoken in jeste, for even the verye Pages wyll bee at hym, so that were he the fairest condicioned man in the world, he can not chouse but bee thus baited and jested at. And contrariwise, if a Prince bee inclined to one that is moste ignoraunt, that can neither do nor saie any thing, his maners and beehaviours (be they never so fonde and foolish) are many tymes commended with acclamation and wonder of all menne, and it seemeth that all the Courte behouldeth and observeth him, and everye manne laugheth at his boording and certein cartarlike jestes, that shoulde rather move a manne to vomite, then to laughe: so addicted and stiffe menne bee in the opinions that arrise of the favoures and disfavoures of great men. Therefore wil I have our Courtier the best he can (beside his

Some woorthy in deede, smally regarded of great men.

Ignoraunt men otherwhile in favour.

* groweth not in favour with him. The original uses a colloquial phrase, *non gli arà sangue*: 'will get on the wrong side of him', 'fail to hit it off with him'.

† make him a Cousin. In the original, this is *dargli la caccia*: 'to hunt him', literally; or 'to get their knives out for him'.

worthinesse) to help himself with witt and art, and whan ever he hath to goe where he is straunge and not knowen, let him procure there goe first a good opinion of him, beefore he come in person, and so woork, that they maie understand there, howe he is in other places with Lordes, Ladyes and gentlemen in good estimation: because that fame, which seemeth to arrise of the judgementes of many, engendreth a certeine assured confidence of a mans worthinesse, which afterwarde finding mennes mindes so settled and prepared, is easily with deedes mainteined and encreased, beeside that a man is eased of the trouble that I feele, whan I am asked the question, who I am and what is my name.

Good opinion.

[XXXIII] I can not see what this can helpe, aunswered M. BERNARD BIBIENA, for it hath sundry tymes happened unto me, and I beleve to many moe, after I had grounded in my mynde by reporte of manye menne of judgemente a matter to bee of great perfection beefore I had seene it, whan I had once seen it, it feinted* muche, and I was muche deceived in mine imagination, and this proceaded of nothyng elles, but of geving to muche credit to fame and reporte, and of conceivinge in my minde so great an opinion, that measuring it afterwarde with the trueth, the effecte, thoughe it were great and excellente, yet in comparison of that I had imagined of it, seemed very sclender unto me. Even so (I feare me) maye also come to passe of the Courtyer. Therefore I can not see howe it were well done to geve these expectations, and to sende that fame of a man beefore: because oure mindes manye times facion and shape thinges, whiche is unpossible afterwarde to aunswere to and fulfill, and so doeth a man lose more then he gayneth by it.

Report deceiveth.

Here SYR FRIDERICK saide: Thinges that unto you and many moe are lesse in effect than the fame is of them, are for the most part of that sort, that the eye at the first sight maie geve a judgemente of them. As if you have never been at Naples or at Roome, whan you here men commune of it, you imagine muche more of it, then perhappes you find afterwarde in sight. But in the conditions of menne it is not alike, because that you see

The report of thinges that the eye is judge of, may deceyve.

* feinted: disappointed.

outwardly is the least part. Therefore in case the first daie you heare a gentlemanne talke, ye perceive not the worthinesse in him that you had beefore imagined, you doe not so soone lose the good opinion of him, as you doe in the thinges wherein your eye is by and by a judge. But you will looke from day to day, to have him disclose some other hid vertue, keping notwithstanding alwaies that stedfaste imprinting whiche you have, risen by the woordes of so manye. And this man then beeing (as I set case our Courtyer is) of so good qualities, he will every houre strengthen you more and more, to geve credence to that fame, for that with his doinges he shall geve you a cause, and you will ever surmise somwhat more to bee in him, then you see. [XXXIV] And certeinly it can not bee denied, but these first imprintinges, have a very great force, and a man ought to take muche heede to them. And that you may understand of what weight they bee, I saie unto you, that I have knowen in my dayes a gentleman, who albeit he was of sufficient manerly beehaviour and modest conditions and well seene in armes, yet was he not in any of these qualities so excellente, but there were manie as good and better. Notwithstandynge (as lucke served him) it beefell that a gentlewoman entred most fervently in love with him, and this love daily encreasing through declaration that the yonge man made to agree with her in that beehalf, and perceivinge no maner meane how they might come to speake together, the gentlewoman provoked with to greate passyon opened her desire to an other gentlewoman, by whose meane she hoped upon some commodity, this woman neyther in blood nor in beautie was a whitt inferiour to the firste. Uppon this it came to passe that she, perceivynge her talke so effectuallye of this yonge manne, whom she never sawe, and knowinge howe that gentlewoman, whom she wist well was most discreete and of a very good judgement, loved him extreemelye, imagyned furthwyth that he was the fairest, the wisest, the discreetest, and finallie the worthiest manne to be beloved that was in the world: and so without seeinge him fell so deepe in love wyth hym, that she practised what she coulde to come by him, not for her friend, but for her owne selfe, and to make him answerable to her in love, the which she

Thinges in the judgement of the minde.

The first conceiving of a thing in ones minde.

An example what reporte can doe.

brought to passe without anye greate a doe, for (to say the troth) she was a woman rather to be sought upon then to seeke upon others. Now heare a pretye chaunce. It happened no longe time after, that a letter which this last gentlewoman writt unto her lover came to the handes of another, that was a noble woman of excellent qualities and singular beawtye, who beeinge (as the most part of women are) inquisitive and greedie to understande secretes and especyallye of other women, opened the letter, and in readinge it perceyved it was written with an extreeme affection of love. And the sweete woordes full of fire that she reade, firste moved her to take compassyon on that Gentlewoman (for she knew verie well from whom the letter came and to whom it went) afterward they had suche force, that skanning them in her minde, and consideringe what maner a man this was like to be, that could bring that woman into suche love, by and by she fell in love wyth him, and that letter was more effectuall to woorke in thys case, then peradventure it would have bene if it had bene sent her from the yonge man himselfe. And as it chaunceth sometime, poyson prepared in a dishe of meate for some great man, killeth him that tasteth first of it, so thys poore gentlewoman because she was to greedye, dranke of the amorous poyson that was ordeyned for an other. What shall I saye to you? The matter was verie open and spred so abrode, that manie women beeside these, partlye in despite of the other, and partly to do as the other did, bent all their studie and diligence to enjoye his love, and for a season played as children do at Chopchirie,* and the wholl proceaded of the first opinion which that woman conceyved that heard him so praysed of an other.

[XXXV] Nowe the L. GASPAR PALLAVICIN answered here smilinge: You to confirme your judgement with reason, alleage unto me womens doinges, which for the most part are voide of al reason. And in case you would tell all, this good felowe thus favoured of so manie women was some doult, and a man in deede not to be regarded, because the maner of them is alwayes to

Womens dedes out of reason.

---

* as children do at Chopchirie. The original has 'they fought over him for a while as children do over cherries'.

cleave to the woorst, and like sheepe to do that they see
the first do, bee it well or yll: beeside that they be so
spitefull emong themselves, that if he had bene a
monstrous creature they would surelye have stolen him
one from an other.

Here manie began and (in maner) all, to speake
againste the L. Gasper, but the DUTCHESSE made them
all to houlde their peace. Afterward she said smilinge: If
the yll which you speake of women were not so farr
wide from the truth, that in speakinge it, it hurteth and
shameth rather the speaker then them, I would suffer
you to be answered. But I will not have you, in speaking
agaynste you wyth a number of reasons, forsake thys
youre ill custome, because you may be sharplie
punished for this offence of yours:* which shall be with
the ill opinion that all thei wil conceive of you that heare
you talke in this wise.

Then aunswered SYR FRIDERICKE: Saye not, my L.
Gaspar, that women are so voide of reason, though
somtime they applie themselves to love, more through
the judgemente of others then their owne, for great men
and many wyse men doe often times the like. And if it be
lawfull to tell the troth, you your selfe and all we here
have many tymes, and doe at this presente credit the
opinion of others, more then our owne. And that it is
true, not long agoe there were certein verses showed
here, that bore the name of Sanazarus,[105] and were
thought of every bodie very excellent, and praised out
of reason, afterwarde whan they wer certeinly knowen
to bee an other mannes doyng, they loste by and by their
reputation, and seemed worse then meane. And where
there was song in the Dutchesse presence, here a certein
Antheme,† it never delited nor was reckened good, until
it was knowen to be the doing of Josquin de Pris.[106] But
what token will you have more plainer of opinion? Doe

What opinion
doeth.

---

* I will not have you, in speaking agaynste you wyth a number of
reasons, forsake thys youre ill custome, because you may be
sharplie punished for this offence of yours: I prefer *not* to see you
contradicted (as it would be all too easy to do) and persuaded out
of this bad habit of yours, so that your sins against women will
continue to earn you a severe punishment.
† Antheme: 'motet' in the original: Hoby translates it with the
equivalent form in Anglican church music.

you not remember where you your selfe dranke of one self wine, sometime ye said it was most perfect, and an other time, without al taste? and that because you had been perswaded they were two sortes, the one of the Coost of Genua, and the other of this soile: and whan the errour was opened, by no meanes you woulde beleave it: that false opinion was grounded so stifly in your head, whiche arrose notwithstanding of other mennes woordes. [XXXVI] Therefore ought the Courtier diligently to applie in the beeginning to geve a good imprinting* of himself, and consider what a harmefull and deadly thing it is, to runne in the contrarie. And in this daunger more then other menne doe they stande that wil make profession to be very pleasaunt and with this their meerie facion purchase them a certeine libertie, that lawfully they may saye and doe what commeth in their minde, without thinking upon it. For suche men many times enter into certein matters, which whan thei can not gete out again, will afterwarde helpe them selves with raising laughter, and it is done with so yll a grace that it will in no wise frame,† whereby they bring a very great lothsomenesse upon as manie as see or heare them, and they remain very colde and without any grace or countenance. Sometime thinking thereby to bee subtill witted and ful of jestes, in the presence of honourable women, yea, and often times to them themselves, they thrust out filthie and most dishonest woordes: and the more they see them blush at it, the better Courtiers they recken themselves, and styll they laugh at it, and rejoyce emong themselves at thys goodlie vertue they thinke thei have gotten them. But they practise this beastlinesse for none other cause, but to bee counted good felowes. This is the name alone whiche they deeme woorthie praise, and whiche they bragg more of, then of anye thing elles, and to gete it them, thei speak the foulest and shamefullest villanies in the world. Many times they shoulder one an other downe the stayers, and hurle billettes and brickes, one at an others head. They hurle handfulles of dust in mens eyes. Thei cast horse and man into ditches, or

Men that counterfeit to be pleasant.

Filthy talke.

Good felowes.

Ruffianlye pranckes.

---

* imprinting: impression.
† it will in no wise frame: it has no chance of success.

downe on the side of some hill. Then at table, potage, sauce, gelies, and what ever commeth to hande, into the face it goith.[107] And afterwarde laughe: and whoso can doe most of these trickes, he counteth himselfe the best and galantest Courtyer, and supposeth that he hath wonne great glorye. And in case otherwhile they gete a gentleman in these their pleasaunt pastimes, that will not geve himselfe to suche horseplay, they say by and by:* He is to wise, we shall have him a Counseller, he is no good felowe. But I will tell you a worse matter. Some there bee that contende and laye wager, who can eate and drinke more unsaverye and stincking thinges, and so abhorryng and contrary to mans senses, that it is not possible to name them, without very great lothsomenesse.

[XXXVII] And what thinges be those? quoth the L. LODOVICUS PIUS.

SYR FRIDERICK aunswered: Let the Marquesse Phebus tell you, for he hathe often seen it in Fraunce, and peraventure felte it.

The MARQUESSE PHEBUS aunswered: I have seen none of these thinges done in Fraunce more then in Italy. But looke what good thinges the Italyans have in their garmentes, in feastinge, in bancketting, in feates of armes and in every other thinge that belongeth to a Courtier, they have it all of the Frenchmen.

I denie not, answered SYR FRIDERICK, but there are also emong the Frenchmen verye honest and sober gentlemen, and for my part I have knowen manye (without peraventure) worthye all praise. But yet some there are of litle good maner: and to speake generally (me thinke) the Spaniardes agree more wyth Italyans, in condicions, then Frenchmen: because (in my minde) the peculiar quiet gravitie of the Spaniardes is more agreeable to oure nature then the quicke livelinesse that is perceived in the French nation almost in every gesture: which is not to be discommended in them, but is rather a grace, for it is so naturall and propre to them, that there is no maner affecting or curiositie in it. There are many Italians that would faine counterfeit their facion, and can do naught elles but shake the head in speakinge,

Italyans borow of the Frenchmen.

Spaniardes agree wyth Italians in condicions.

Gravitye in Spaniardes.
Livelines in French men.

Frenche facions.

* by and by: at once.

and make a legg* with an yll grace, and when they come
oute of their doores into the Citie, goe so faste that good
footemen canne scant overtake them, and with these
maners they weene themselves good Frenchmen, and to
have of that libertye: whiche (ywisse) chaunseth verie
sildome savinge to suche as are brought up in Fraunce
and have learned that facion from their childhood. The
like is to be said in the knowleag of sundrie tunges,
which I commend much in oure Courtier, and especiallye Spanish and Frenche, because the entercourse of
both the one nation and the other is much haunted in
Italy, and these two are more agreable unto us then any
of the rest, and those two Princes for that they are verye
mighty in war and most riall† in peace, have their Court
alwaies fournished with valiant gentlemen, whiche are
dispersed throughout the world, and againe we must
needes practise with them. [XXXVIII] I wil not now
proceade to speake any more particularly of matters to
well knowen, as that oure Courtier ought not to
professe to be a glutton nor a dronkard, nor riotous and
unordinate in any il condicion, nor filthy and unclenly
in his living, with certaine rude and boysterous beehaviours that smell of the plough and cart a thousand
mile of, for he that is of that sort, it is not only not to be
hoped that he will make a good Courtier, but he can be set
to no better use then to kepe sheepe. And to conclude, I
saye that (to doe well) the Courtier oughte to have a
perfect understandinge in that we have sayde is meete for
him, so that every possible thinge may be easye to him,
and all men wonder at him, and he at no manne: meaning
notwithstanding in this poinct that there be not a
certaine loftye and unmanerlye stubburnnesse, as some
men have that showe themselves not to wonder at the
thinges which other men do, because they take upon
them that they can do them much better: and with their
silence do commend them as unworthy to be spoken of,
and wyll make a gesture (in a maner) as though none
beeside were (I will not say their equall, but) able to
conceyve the understanding of the profoundnes of their
couning. Therfore ought the Courtier to shonn these

To have
sundry
languages.

Some com-
mende not
thynges well
done.

---

* make a legg: bow.
† riall: regal, splendid.

hateful maners, and with gentlenesse and courtesie praise other mens good dedes: and thoughe he perceyve himselfe excellent and farr above others, yet showe that he esteameth not hymselfe for such a one. But because these so full perfections are very sildome founde in the nature of man, and perhappes never, yet ought not a man that perceyveth himself in some part to want, to lay aside his hope to come to a good passe, though he can not reach to that perfect and high excellency which he

Many places to be commended beeside the best.

aspireth unto: because in every art there be manye other places beeside the best, all praiswoorthye: and he that striveth to come by the highest, it is sildome sene that he passeth not the meane. I will have our Courtier therfore, if he find himself excellent in anie thinge beeside armes,

Howe a man should show his couning.

to sett out himselfe, and gete him estymatyon by it after an honest sorte, and be so dyscreete and of so good a judgemente, that he maye have the understandinge after a comelye maner, and with good pourpose to allure men to heare or to looke on that he supposeth himselfe to be excellente in: making semblant alwaies to doe it, not for a bragge and to shewe it for vainglory, but at a chaunce, and rather praied by others, then commyng of his owne free will. And in every thing that he hath to do or to speake, if it be possible, lette him come alwaies provided and thinke on it beefore hande, showyng notwithstanding, the whole to bee done ex tempore, and at the first sight. As for the thinges he hath but a meane skill in, let him touche them (as it were) by the waie, without grounding muche upon them, yet in such wise that a man may beleve he hath a great deale more cunning therin, then he uttereth: as certein Poetes sometime that harped upon verye subtill pointes of Philosophie, or other sciences, and paraventure had

Somtyme a mannes ignoraunce is to be confessed.

small understanding in the matter. And in that he knoweth himself altogether ignoraunt in, I will never have him make any profession at all, nor seeke to purchase him anye fame by it: but rather whan occasion serveth, confesse to have no understanding in it.

[XXXIX] This, quoth CALMETA, would Nicholetto[108] never have done, whiche being a verye excellent Philosopher, and no more skilfull in the lawe then in fleeing,* whan a Governour of Padoa was

* fleeing: flying.

mynded to geve him one of those Lectures in the lawe,
he woulde never yelde at the perswasion of many
Scholars, to deceyve the opinion whiche the governour
had conceived of him, and confesse that he had no
understanding in it: but saide styll that he was not in
this point of Socrates opinion, for it is not a Phylosophers part to saye at anye tyme, that he hath no
understanding.

I say not, aunswered SYR FRIDERICKE, that the
Courtyer should of himself go say he hath no understandyng, without it bee required of hym: for I allowe
not this fondnesse to accuse and debase himselfe. Againe
I remember some otherwhyle that in like sorte doe
willingly disclose some matters, whiche although they
happened perhappes without any faulte of theirs, yet
bring they with them a shadowe of sclaunder, as did a
gentleman (whom you all know) which alwayes whan
he heard any mencion made of the battaile beeside
Parma agaynst kynge Charles, he woulde by and by
declare how he fled away, and a man would weene that
he sawe or understoode nothing elles in that journey.[109]
Afterward talking of a certein famous just, he rehersed
continuallie howe he was overthrowen: and manye
times also he seemed in his talke to seeke how he might
bringe into pourpose to declare that upon a nyghte as he
was goynge to speake with a gentlewoman, he was well
beaten wyth a cudgell. Such triflinge folyes I will not
have our Courtier to speake of. But me thinke whan
occasion is offred to showe his skill in a matter he is
altogether ignoraunte in, it is well done to avoide it. Yf
necessitie compell him, let him rather confesse plainly
his lack of understanding in it, then hasard himself, and
so shall he avoide a blame that manye deserve nowadayes, which I woote not through what corrupte
inward motion or judgemente out of reason, do alwayes
take upon them to practise the thinge they know not,
and lay aside that they are skilfull in: and for a
confirmation of this, I know a very excellent musitien,
which leaving his musike a part hath whollye geven
himselfe to versifiynge, and thynketh hymselfe a great
clearke therin, but in deede he maketh everye man to
laughe him to skorne, and now hath he also cleane lost
his musike. An other, one of the chieffest peincters in

Men utter thinges to their shame many times.

How he should doe in a matter he hath no skil in.

Men that take in hand thinges they have no skill in.

the world, neglectinge his art wherin he was verie
excellent, hath applied himselfe to learne Philosophye,
wherein he hath such straunge conceites and monstrous
fansyes, that withall the peinctinge he hath* he can not
peinct them.[110] And such as these there be infinite.
Some there be that knowing themselves to have an
excellency in one thing, make their principall profession
in an other, in which not withstanding they are not
ignorant, but whan time serveth to show themselves in
that they are most skilfull in, they doe it alwayes verie
perfectlye: and otherwhile it commeth so to passe, that
the companye perceivinge them so couning in that
which is not their profession, they imagine them to be
much better in that thei professe in deede. This art in
case it be coopled with a good judgemente, discon-
tenteth me nothing at all.

[XL] Then answered the L. GASPAR PALAVICIN: I
thinke not this an art, but a verie deceite, and I beleave it
is not meete for him that will bee an honest man to
deceive at anye time.

This, quoth SYR FRIDERICKE, is rather an ornament
that accompanyeth the thinge he doeth, then a deceite:
and though it be a deceite, yet is it not to be disalowed.
Will you not saye also, that he that beateth his felow,
where there be two plaiyng at fence together,
beeguyleth hym, and that is bicause he hath more art
then the other? And where you have a jewell that unsett
seemeth faire, afterward whan it commeth to a gold-
smithes handes that in well setting it maketh it appeere
muche more fairer, will you not saye that the goldsmith
deceiveth the eyes of them that looke on it? And yet for
that deceite, deserveth he praise, for with judgement
and art a couninge hande doeth manie tymes ad a grace
and ornament to yvorie, or to sylver, or to a stone that is
faire in sight, settinge it in golde. We saye not then that
this art or deceite (in case you wyll so terme it) deserveth
anie maner blame. Also it is not ill for a man that
knoweth himselfe skilfull in a matter, to seeke occasyon
after a comelye sorte to showe hys feat therein, and in
lykecase to cover the partes he thynketh scante
woorthye praise, yet notwithstandinge all after a

* withall the peinctinge he hath: for all his skill at painting.

certeine warye dyssymulacion. Doe you not remember
how kinge Ferdinande wythout makinge any showe to
seeke it, tooke occasion verye well to stryppe hymselfe
sometyme into his doblet? and that bicause he knewe he
was verye well made and nymble wythall. And bicause
hys handes were not all of the fairest, he sildome plucked
of hys gloves, and (in maner) never. And fewe there were
that tooke heede to this warinesse of hys. Me thynke also I
have reade, that Julius Cæsar ware for the nones a
garlande of Laurell, to hyde hys baldenesse withall.[111] But
in these matters a manne muste be verye circumspecte and
of a good judgemente least he passe hys boundes: for to
avoyde one errour often tymes a manne falleth into an
other, and to gete him praise, purchaseth blame.

[XLI] Therfore the surest way in the worlde, is, for a
manne in hys lyving and conversation to governe
himself alwaies with a certeine honest meane, whych
(no doubt) is a great and moste sure shield againste
envie, the whiche a manne ought to avoide in what he is
able. I wyll have oure Courtier also take heede he
purchase not the name of a lyar, nor of a vaine person,
whiche happeneth manie tymes and to them also that
deserve it not. Therfore in his communicatyon let him
be alwayes heedefull not to goe out of the lykelyhoode
of truth, yea and not to speake to often those truthes
that have the face of a lye,[112] as manye doe, that never
speake but of wonders, and will be of suche authoritye,
that everye uncredyble matter must be beleaved at their
mouth. Other, at the first entringe into a frendshipp
wyth a newe friende, to gete favour wyth hym, the first
thynge they speake, sweare that there is not a person in
the world whom thei love better, and they are wyllynge
to jeoparde their lyfe for hys sake, and suche other
matters out of reason, and whan they part from hym
makewise to weepe, and not to speake a woorde for
sorowe. Thus bicause they woulde bee counted to
lovynge woormes, they make menne counte them lyars,
and fonde flatterers. But it were to longe a matter and
tedyous to recken uppe all vyces that maye happen in
conversatyon. Therefore, for that I desire in the
Courtyer, it suffyceth to saye (beesyde the matters
rehersed) that he bee suche a one that shall never wante
good communycatyon and fytte for them he talketh

King Fer-
dinand of
Naples.

J. Cæsar.

An honest
meane in
livinge.

No lyar.

wythall, and have a good understandynge with a certein
sweetenesse to refresh the hearers mindes, and with
meerie conceites and Jestes to provoke them to solace
and laughter, so that without beinge at any time
lothesome or satiate he may evermore delite them.
[XLII] Now I hope my L. Emilia wil give me leave to
houlde my peace, which in case she denie me, I shall by
mine owne woordes be convicted not to be the good
courtier I have tould you of, for not only good
communication, which neither at this time nor perhappes at any other ye have heard in me: but also this I
have, such as it is, doeth cleane faile me.

Then spake the L. GENERALL: I will not have this false
opinion to sticke in the heade of anye of us, that you are
not a verye good Courtier, for (to say the truth) this
desire of yours to houlde your peace proceadeth rather
because you would be rid of your peine, then for that ye
want talke. Therfore that it maye not appeare in so
noble assemblye as this is, and in so excellent talke, any
percell be left out, saye you not nay to teach us how we
shoulde use these Jestes you have made mention of, and
showe us the art that beelongeth to all this kinde of
pleasant speach to provoke laughter and solace after
an honest sorte, for (in myne opinion) it is verye
necessary and much to pourpose for a Courtier.

My Lord, answered SYR FRIDERICK, Jestes and
meerie conceites are rather a gifte, and a grace of nature,
then of art, but yet there are some nations more redier in
it then other some, as the Tuscanes, which in deede are
very subtill. Also it appeareth propre to the Spaniardes
to invent meerie conceites. Yet are there manye notwithstanding both of this nation and other also that in
to much babblinge passe sometime their boundes and
wexe unsavery and fonde, because thei have no respecte
to the condicion of the person they commune withall, to
the place where they be, to the time, to the gravitie and
modestye which they ought to have in themselves.

[XLIII] Then answered the L. GENERALL: You denie
that there is any art in Jestes, and yet in speaking against
such as observe them not with modestye and gravitie
and have not respecte to the time and to the person they
commune withal, me thinke ye declare that this may
also be taught and hath some doctrine in it.

These rules my Lorde, answered SYR FRIDERICKE, be so generall that they maye be applied to everie matter, and helpe it forward. But I have said there is no art in Jestes, because (me thinke) they are onlie of two sortes: whereof the one is enlarged in communication that is longe and without interruption: as is seene in some men that with so good an utterance and grace and so pleasantly declare and expresse a matter that happened unto them or that they have seene and hearde, that with their gesture and woordes they sett it beefore a mans eyes, and (in maner) make him feele it with hande, and this peraventure for want of an other terme we may calle Festivitie or els Civilitie. The other sort of Jestes is verie breef, and consisteth only in quicke and subtill saiynges, as manie times there are heard emong us, and in nickes, neyther doeth it appeare that they are of any grace without that litle bitynge, and these emong them of olde time wer also called Saiynges, now some terme them Privie tauntes. I say therfore in the first kinde, whiche is a meerye maner of expressinge, there needeth no art, bicause verye nature her self createth and shapeth menne apt to expresse pleasantly and geveth them a countenaunce, gestures, a voice, and woordes for the pourpose to counterfeit what they luste. In the other of Privie tauntes what can art doe? Sins that quippie ought to be shott out and hit the pricke* beefore a man can descerne that he that speaketh it can thinke upon it, elles it is colde and litle woorth. Therfore (thinke I) all is the woorke of witt and nature.

Cavillatio.

Dicacitas.

Dicta.

Then tooke M. PETER BEMBO the matter in hande, and said: The L. Generall denieth not that you say: namely that nature and witt beare not the chieffest stroke, especiallye as touching invention, but it is certein that in ech mans mind, of howe good a witt soever he be, there arrise conceites both good and badd, and more and lesse, but then judgement and art doeth polishe and correct them, and chouseth the good and refuseth the bad. Therfore laiynge aside that beelongeth to witt, declare you unto us that consisteth in art: that is to weete, of Jestes and meery conceites that move laughter, whiche are meete for the Courtier and whyche

* pricke: target.

are not, and in what time and maner they ought to be used: for this is that the L. Generall demaundeth of you.

[XLIV] Then SIR FRIDERICKE said smilynge: There is never a one of us here that I will not geve place unto in everie matter, and especiallie in Jestinge, onlesse perhappes folies, whiche make menne laugh manie times more then wittie saiynges, were also to be allowed for Jestes.

And so tourning him to Count Lewis and to M. Bernarde Bibiena, he said unto them: These be the maisters of this facultie, of whom in case I must speake of meerie saiynges, I must first learne what I have to saye.

COUNT LEWIS answered: Me thynke you beegin nowe to practise that you saye ye are not skilfull in, whiche is, to make these Lordes laughe in mocking M. Bernarde and me, bicause everye one of them woteth well that the thinge which you praise us for, is much more perfectly in you. Therefore in case you be weerie, it is better for you to sue to the Dutchesse that it would please her to deferr the remnaunt of oure talke till to morowe, then to go about with craft to rid your handes of peines takinge.

Sir Friderick beegan to make answere, but the L. EMILIA interrupted him immediatlye and said: It is not the order that the disputacion shoulde be consumed upon your praise, it sufficeth ye are verie well knowen all. But bicause it commeth in my minde that you (Count) imputed to me yesternyght, that I divided not the paines takinge equallye, it shall be well done that Syr Frydericke reste hym a whyle and the charge of speakynge of Jestes we wyll commytte to M. Bernarde Bibiena, for we doe not onlye knowe hym verye quicke wytted in talkynge wythoute intermission, but also it is not oute of oure memorye that he hath sundrye tymes promysed to wryte of thys matter.[113] And therfore we maye thynke he hath verye well thought uppon it all thys whyle, and ought the better to satysfie us in it. Afterwarde when there shall be sufficientlye spoken of Jestes, Syr Fridericke shall proceede forwarde againe wyth that he hath yet beehinde concerning the Courtier.

Then sayde SIR FRIDERICKE: Madam, I knowe not what I have lefte beehinde anie more, but lyke a

travailer on the waye nowe weerie of the peinefulnesse
of my longe journey at noone tide, I will reste me in M.
Bernardes communication at the sowne of hys woordes,
as it were under some faire tree that casteth a goodlye
shadowe at the sweete roaringe* of a plentifull and
livelye springe: afterward (maye happe) beeinge somewhat refreshed I maye have somewhat elles to saye.

M. BERNARDE answered laughynge: Yf I showe you
the toppe ye shall see what shadowe may be hoped for
at the leaves of my tree.[114] To heare the roaringe of the
livelye sprynge ye speake of, it maye happen bee your
chaunce so to doe, for I was once tourned into a
sprynge: not by anye of the goddes of olde tyme, but by
oure frier Marian. And from that tyme hytherto I never
wanted water.

Then beegan they all to fall in a laughynge, bicause
thys pleasante matter whiche M. Bernarde ment that
happened to him in Roome in the presence of Galeotto
Cardinal of S. Petro in Vincula,[115] was well knowen to
them all.

[XLV] After they had ceased laughinge the L. EMILIA
saide: Leave nowe makynge us laugh wyth practisynge
of Jestes, and teache us howe we should use them, and
whence they are deryved, and what ever elles ye knowe
in thys matter. And for losynge anye more tyme beegyne
oute of hande.

I doubte me, quoth M. BERNARDE, it is late, and leaste
my talke of pleasant matters should seeme unpleasant
and tedyous, perhappes it were good to deferr it tyll to
morow.

Here incontinentlye many made answer that it lacked
yet a good deale of the houre whan they were wont to
leave of reasoning.

Then M. BERNARDE tourning to the Dutchesse and to
the L. Emilia, I wil not refuse this labour (quoth he)
althoughe I be wont to marveile at the bouldnesse of
them that dare take upon them to sing to the lute, whan
our James Sansecondo[116] standeth by, even so ought
not I in the presence of hearers that have much better
understanding in that I have to saye, then I my selfe,
take upon me to entreate of Jestes. Nevertheles least I

---

* sweete roaringe: the original has 'murmuring'.

should show a president to anye of these Lordes to refuse that they shall bee charged withall, I will speake as breeflye as I can possible what commeth in my minde as touching matters that cause laughter, which is so propre to us that to describe a man the commune saiyng is, He is a livinge creature that can laugh: because this laughing is perceived onlie in man, and (in maner) alwaies is a token of a certein jocundenesse and meerie moode that he feeleth inwardlie in his minde, which by nature is drawen to pleasantnesse and coveteth quietnes and refreshing, for whiche cause we see menne have invented many matters, as sportes, games and pastimes, and so many sundrie sortes of open showes. And because we beare good will to suche as are the occasion of this recreation of oures, the maner was emonge the kinges of olde time, among the Romanes, the Athenians and manie other, to gete the good will of the people withall, and to feede the eyes and myndes of the multitude, to make greate Theatres, and other publyque buildinges, and there to showe new devises of pastimes, running of horses and Charettes, fightinges of men together, straunge beastes, Comedies, Tragedies, and daunses of Antique.* Neither did the grave Philosophers shonn these sightes, for manie tymes both in thys maner and at banckettes they refreshed their weeryesome myndes, in those high discourses and divine imaginacions of theirs. The which in lykewyse all sortes of men are wyllinge to doe, for not onlye Ploughmen, Mariners, and all such as are inured wyth harde and boysterous exercises, with hande, but also holye religious men and prisoners that from hour to hour waite for death, goe about yet to seeke some remedy and medicine to refreshe themselves. Whatsoever therefore causeth laughter, the same maketh the minde jocunde and geveth pleasure, nor suffreth a man in that instant to minde the troublesome greeffes that oure life is full of. Therfore (as you see) laughing is very acceptable to all men, and he is muche to be commended that can cause it in due time and after a comlie sort. But what this laughing is, and where it consisteth, and in what maner somtime it taketh the veines, the

Homo animal risibile.

To fede the eyes of the people.

* daunses of Antique: mimes.

eies, the mouth and the sides, and seemeth as though it woulde make us burst, so that what ever resistance we make, it is not possible to kepe it, I will leave it to be disputed of Democritus,[117] the which also in case he woulde promise us, he should not perfourme it. [XLVI] The place therfore and (as it were) the hedspring that laughing matters arrise of, consisteth in a certein deformitie or ill favourednesse, bicause a man laugheth onlie at those matters that are disagreeing* in them-selves, and (to a mans seeminge) are in yll plight, where it is not so in deede.† I wote not otherwise how to expounde it, but if you will beethinke your selfe, ye shall perceive the thinge that a man alwayes laugheth at, is a matter that soundeth not well, and yet is it not in yll syttinge. What kinde of wayes therefore those be that the Courtier ought to use in causing laughter and of what scope, I will assay in what I can to utter unto you as farr as my judgemente can give me, bicause to make men laughe alwayes is not comelie for the Courtier, nor yet in suche wise as frantike, dronken, foolishe and fonde men and in like maner commune jesters do: and though to a mans thinkinge Courtes cannot be without suche kinde of persons, yet deserve they not the name of a Courtier, but eche man to be called by his name and esteamed suche as they are. The scope and measure to make men laughe in tauntinge must also be diligentlye considered: who he is that is taunted, for it provoketh no laughter to mocke and skorne a seelye soule in miserie and calamitie, nor yet a naughtie knave and commune ribaulde, bicause a man would thinke that these men deserved to be otherwise punished, then in jestinge at. And mens mindes are not bent to scoff them in misery, onelesse such men in their mishapp bragg and boast of them selves and have a proude and haughtye stomake. Again a respect must be had to them that are generallye favoured and beloved of everie man, and that beare stroke,‡ bicause in mockinge and scorninge such a one, a man may sometime purchase himselfe

Wherein laughing matters consist.

Considera-tions in jesting.

---

* disagreeing: jarring, incongruous.
† (to a mans seeminge) are in yll plight, where it is not so in deede: seem wrong, but in fact are right.
‡ beare stroke: have power.

Who are to
be jested at.

daungerous enimitie.[118] Therefore it is not amysse to scoff and mocke at vices that are in persons not of such miserye that it should move compassion, nor of suche wickidnesse that a man woulde thinke they deserved not to go on the grounde, nor of such aucthoritie that any litle displeasure of theirs may be a great hindraunce to a man. [XLVII] You shall understande moreover that out of the places* jestinge matters are derived from, a man may in like maner pike grave sentences to praise or

Praise or dis-
praise in the
self woordes.

dispraise. And otherwhile with the self same woordes: as to praise a liberall man that partaketh his gooddes in commune with his friendes, the commune saying is, That he hath is none of his owne. The like may be saide in dispraise of one that hath stolen or compased that he hath by other ill meanes. It is also a commune saiyng, She is a woman of no smalle price,† whan a man will praise her for her vertues, for her wisedome and goodnes. The very same may be said of a woman that loketh to be kept sumptiouslye: but it commeth oftner to pourpose that a man in this case serveth his tourne with the self same places then with the self same woordes. As within these few dayes three Gentilmen standinge at masse together in a Churche where was a gentilwoman one of the three was in love withall, there came a poore beggar and stood before her requiringe her almes, and so with much instance and lamenting with a groning voice repeted manie times his request: yet for all that did she not give him her almes, nor denie it him in making signe to depart in Gods name, but stoode musing with her self as though she mindèd another matter. Then said the gentilman that loved her to his two companions, See what I maye hope for at my maistresse handes, which is so cruell, that she will neither give the poore naked soule dead for hunger, that requireth her with such passion and so instantly, her almes, ne yet leave to depart, so much she rejoyceth to beehoulde with her eyes one that is broughte lowe with

---

* out of the places: from the same situations.
† She is a woman of no smalle price ... loketh to be kept sumptiouslye. The original is more salacious: the phrase is *colei è una donna d'assai*, meaning either 'an impressive woman' or 'a woman had by many'.

misery and that in vaine requireth her reward. One of
the two answered: It is no crueltye, but a privie
admonicion for you to doe you to weete that your
maistresse is not pleased with him that requireth her
with much instance. The other answered: Nay, it is
rather a lesson for him, that although she give not that is
required of her, yet she is willing inough to be suid to.
See here, bicause the gentilwoman sent not the poore
man away, there arrose one saying of great dispraise,
one of modest praise and another of nipping boord. *

[XLVIII] To retourn therfore to declare the kindes of
Jests apperteining to our pourpose, I say (in mine
opinion) there are of three sorts, although Sir Friderick
hath made mention but of two. The one a civill and
pleasant declaration without interruption, which consisteth in the effect of a thing. The other a quicke and
subtill readines, which consisteth in one saiyng alone.
Therfore will we ad a third sort to these, which we call
Boordes or meerie Prankes, wherin the processe is long
and the saiynges short and some deedes [119] with all.†
The firste therfore that consisteth in communication
without interruption are in that sort (in a maner) as
though a man woulde tell a tale. And to give you an
example, whan Pope Alexander the sixte died and Pius
the thirde created, beeinge then in Roome and in the
Palaice youre Sir Anthonye Agnello of Mantua, my L.
Dutchesse, and communynge of the death of the one
and creatyon of the other, and therin makyng sundrie
discourses with certein friendes of his, he said: Sirs, in
Catullus time gates beegan to speake without tunge and
to heare without eares and in that sort discovered
advouteries.‡ Now although men be not of such
worthinesse as they were in those daies, yet perhappes
the gates that are made, a great sorte of them, especiallye here in Roome, of auntient Marble, have the same
vertue they had then. And for my parte I beleave that
these two will cleere us of all our doubtes, in case we
will aske counsell of them. Then those Gentilmen
mused much at the matter and attended to see to what

Ré.

Dicto.

Cicero men-
tioneth not
this last kind
of jestes.

---

* nipping boord: cutting wit.
† deedes: actions.
‡ advouteries: adulteries.

ende it woulde come, whan Sir Anthony folowinge on still up and downe lifte up his eyes, as at a sodeine, to one of the two gates of the hall where they walked: and stayinge a while with his finger he showed his companye the inscriptyon over it, which was Pope

Alexanders name, and at the ende of it was V and I, bicause it should signifie (as ye know) the sixt. And said: See here, this gate sayth Alexander Papa VI. which signifieth he hath bin Pope through the force he hath used, and hath prevailed more thereby then with right and reason.[120] Now let us see if we may of this other understand anye thinge of the newe Bishoppe: and tournyng him as at aventure to the other gate, pointed

to the inscription of one N. two PP. and one V. whiche signifieth Nicholaus Papa Quintus, and immediately he said: Good Lord ill newis, see here this gate saith *Nihil Papa Valet.** [XLIX] See now how this kinde of Jestes is propre and good and how fitting it is for one in Court, whether it be true or false a man saith, for in this case it is lawfull to feigne what a man lusteth wythout blame: and in speakinge the truthe, to sett it furthe with a feat lye, augmentinge or diminishinge according to the pourpose. But the perfect grace and very pith of this, is to set furth so well and without peine not onlie in woordes but in gestures, the thynge a man pourposeth to expresse, that unto the hearers he maye appeere to do before their eyes the thinges he speaketh of. And this expressed maner in this wise hath suche force, that otherwhile it setteth furth and maketh a matter delite verie muche, whiche of it selfe is not verie meerie nor wittie. And althoughe these protestacions neede gestures, and the earnestnesse that a livelie voice hath, yet is the force of them knowen also otherwhile in writing.

Who laugheth not when John Boccaccio in the eight journey† of his hundreth tales declareth howe the priest of Varlungo strayned himselfe to singe a Kyrie and a Sanctus, when he perceived Belcolore was in the Church?[121] These be also pleasant declarations in his tales of Calandrino and manie other. After the same

sort seemeth to be the making a man laughe in counterfeitinge or imitatinge (howe-ever we lyste to

* i.e., 'the pope is useless'.
† journey: day

terme it) of a mans maners, wherin hitherto I have seene
none passe oure M. Robert of Bari.

[L] This were no small praise, quoth M. ROBERT, if it
were true, for then would I surely go about to counterfeite rather the good then the bad: and if I could liken
my self to some I know, I would thinke my selfe a
happye man. But I feare me I can counterfeite nothinge
but what maketh a man laughe, which you said before
consisteth in vice.

M. BERNARDE answered: In vice in deede, but that
that standeth not in yll plight. And weete you well, that
this counterfeitinge we speake of, can not be without
witt, for beeside the maner to applie his woordes and his
gestures, and to set beefore the hearers eyes the
countenance and maners of him he speaketh of, he must
be wise, and have great respect to the place, to the time
and to the persons with whom he talketh, and not like a
commune Jester passe his boundes, which thinges you
wonderfully well observe, and therefore I beleave ye are
skilfull in all. For undoubtedlye it is not meete for a
Gentlemanne to make weepinge and laughing faces, to
make sounes and voices, and to wrastle with himselfe
alone as Berto doeth, to apparaile himself like a lobb of
the Countrey as doeth Strascino,[122] and such other
matters, which do well beecome them, bicause it is their
profession. But we must by the way and privilie steale
this counterfeiting, alwayes keaping the astate of a
gentilman, without speaking filthy wordes, or doing
uncomelye deedes, without making faces and
antiques,* but frame our gestures after a certein
maner, that who so heareth and seeth us, may by our
wordes and countenances imagin muche more then he
seeth and heareth, and upon that take occasion to
laughe. He must also in this counterfeiting take heed of
to much taunting in touching a man, especially in the ill
favourednesse of visage or yll shape of bodye. For as the
mishappes and vices of the bodie minister manie times
ample matter to laughe at, if a man can discreatly
handle it, even so the usinge of this maner to bytingly is
a token not onlie of a commune jester, but of a plaine
ennemy. Therfore must a man observe in this poinct

Gior. ix.
Novel. iii.
and v.

Counter-
feiters of mens
maners.

Nippes that
touch a man.

---

* antiques: bodily contortions.

(though it be hard) the facion of our M. Roberte, as I have said, which counterfeiteth al men and not with out touchinge them in the matters wherein they be faultie and in presence of themselves, and yet no man findeth himselfe agreeved, neyther may a man thinke that he can take it in ill part. And of this I will give you no example, bicause we all see infinit in him dailie. [LI] Also it provoketh much laughter (which nevertheles is conteined under declaration*) whan a man repeteth with a good grace certein defaultes of other men, so they be meane and not worthy greater correction: as foolishe matters sometime symplye of themselves alone, somtime annexed with a litle readie nippinge fondenesse. Likewise certein extreme and curious matters. Otherwhile a great and well forged lye. As few dayes ago oure M. Cesar declared a pretie foolishe matter, which was, that beeyng with the Mayor of this Citie, he saw a Countrey man come to him to complaine that he had an Asse stolen from him, and after he had toulde him of his povertie and how the thief deceyved him, to make his losse the greater he said unto him: Syr if you had seen mine Asse you should have knowen what a cause I have to complaine, for with his pad on his backe a man would have thought him very Tully himself.[123] And one of our train meetinge a herd of Gotes beefore the which was a mightie great Ramm Gote, he stayed and with a merveilous countenaunce, saide: Marke me this Gote, he seemeth a Saint Paul.

The L. GASPER saith he knew an other, whyche for that he was an olde servaunt to Hercules duke of Ferrara, did offre him two pretie boyes which he had, to be hys pages, and these two died both beefore they came to hys service. The which whan the duke understoode, he lamented lovinglie with the father, saiyng that he was verie sorie, bicause whan he sawe them upon a time he thought them handsome and wittie children. The father made answere, Nay My Lorde, you sawe nothing, for within these fewe dayes they were become muche more

Foolish matters.

---

* which nevertheles is conteined under declaration: (another form of humour) which can be included in the same category of witty narration.

handsomer and of better qualities then I woulde ever
have thought, and sange together like a coople of
haukes. And one of these dayes a Doctour of oures
beehouldinge one that was judged to be whipped
aboute the markett place, and taking pitye upon him
bicause the poore soules shoulders bled sore, and went
so soft a pace, as thoughe he had walked about for his
pleasure to pass the time withall he sayd to hym: Goo
on a pace poore felowe that thou mayst be the sooner
out of thy peine. Then he tourninge about and beehouldynge him that so said (in a maner) with a
wonder,* staide a while withoute anye woord, afterwarde he saide: Whan thou art whipped goe at thy
pleasure, for nowe will I goe as I shall thinke good.

You may remember also the foolyshe matter that not
longe a goe the Duke rehersed of the Abbot that
beeynge presente upon a daye whan Duke Fridericke
was talkynge where he shoulde bestowe the greate
quantitye of rubbyshe that was caste up to laye the
foundacyon of thys Palayce, woorkynge dailye upon it,
sayde: My Lorde, I have well beethoughte me where
you shall beestowe it, let there be a great pitt digged and
into that may you have it cast without any more ado.
Duke Fridericke answered him not withoute laughter:
And where shall we beestowe then the quantitie of earth
that shall be cast out of that pitt? The abbot saide unto
him: Let it be made so large that it may well receive the
one and the other. And so for all the Duke repeted
sundrie times, the greater the pitt was, the more earth
should be cast out of it, yet coulde he never make it
sinke into his braine, but it might be made so large that
it mighte receive both the one and the other: and he
answered him nothinge elles but make it so much the
larger. Now see what a good forecast this Abbot had.

The judge-
ment of an
Abbot.

[LII] Then said M. PETER BEMBO: And why tell you
not that, of your great Capitain of Florence that was
beeseaged of the Duke of Calabria within Castellina?[124]
Where there were found upon a day in the towne certein
quarelles† poysoned that had bine shott out of the

---

* beehouldynge him that so said (in a maner) with a wonder:
staring at the man who had spoken, as though in amazement.
† quarelles: arrows.

campe, he wrott unto the Duke, yf the warr should proceade so cruellye, he would also put a medicin upon his gunnstones, and then he that hath the woorst, hath his mendes in his handes.

M. BERNARDE laughed and saide: Yf you houlde not youre peace (M. Peter) I will tell whatsoever I have seene my selfe and hearde of your Venetians, which is not a litle, and especially when they play the riders.

Doe not I beesech ye, answered M. PETER, for I will keepe to my selfe two other verie pretye ones that I knowe of your Florentines.

Siena.

M. BERNARDE saide: They are rather of the Seneses, for it often happeneth emonge them. As within these fewe dayes one of them hearing certein lettres read in the Counsell chamber, in which for avoidinge to often repetition of his name that was spoken of, this terme was manie times put in, *il Prelabato* (which signifieth the aforenamed) he said unto him that read them: Soft, stay there a litle and tell me, this Prelibato what is he? A frinde to oure Communaltye?

M. PETER laughed, then he proceaded: I speake of Florentines and not of Seneses.

Speake it hardly, quoth the L. EMILIA, and bash not* for that matter.

M. PETER said: Whan the Lordes of Florence were in warr against the Pisanes,[125] they were otherwhile out of money by reason of theyr great charges, and laying their heades together upon a daye in the counsell chambre what waye were beste to make provision to serve their tourne withall, after many divises propounded, one of

A Florentines devise.

the auntientest Citizins said: I have founde two wayes, wherby without much travaile we may in a small while come by a good portion of money. Wherof the one is (bicause we have no redier rent then the custome at the gates of Florence) where we have xi. gates, let us with speede make xi. mo, and so shall we double oure revenue. The other way is, to set up a mint in Pistoia and an other in Prato no more nor lesse then is here within Florence: and there doe nothinge elles daye and night but coyne money, and all Ducates of golde, and this

* bash not: don't hold back.

divise (in mine opinion) is the speedier and lesse chargeable.

[LIII] They fell a laughing apace at the subtill divise of this Citizin, and whan laughinge was ceased the L. EMILIA said: Will you (M. Bernarde) suffre M. Peter thus to jeste at Florentines without a revenge?

M. BERNARDE answered smilinge: I pardon him this offence, for where he hath displeased me in jestinge at Florentines, he hath pleased me in obeyinge of you, the which I would alwaies do my selfe.

Then said the L. CESAR: I heard a Brescian speake a jolie grosse matter, whiche beeinge this yeere in Venice at the feast of the Assention, rehersed in a place where I was to certain mates of his, the goodlye matters he had seene there, what sundrie merchaundise, what plate, what sortes of spices, and what cloth and silke there was, then how the Signoria yssued out with a great pompe in Bucentoro to wedd the Sea,[126] in which were so manie gentilmen well apparailed, so manie sortes of instrumentes and melodies that a man woulde have thought it a paradise. And whan one of his companions demaunded him what kynde of musike did please him best of all that he had heard there, he said: All were good, yet emong the rest I saw one blowe in a straunge trumpett, whiche at everye pushe thrust it into his throte more then two handful, and then by and by drew it out again, and thrust it in a freshe, that you never sawe a greater wondre.

Then they all laughed, understandinge the fonde imagination of him that thoughte the blower thruste into his throte that part of the Sagbout that is hid in puttinge it backe againe.

[LIV] Then M. BERNARDE went forward: Those Affectations and curiosities that are but meane, bringe a lothsomnesse with them,* but whan they be done oute of measure they much provoke laughter. As otherwhile whan some men are heard to speake of their auntientrye and noblenesse of birth: sometime women of their beawtie and handsomenesse: as not long ago a Gentilwoman did, which at a great feast beinge verie sad and musing with her self, it was demaunded of her, what she

Sidenote: Upon the ascention daye a great faire in Venice.

A faire vessell of pleasure in Venice made Galliwise. Everye yeere upon the Ascension daye the Duke with all the counsell goith in it a mile or two into the sea, and there casteth a ring of gold into it thinking by this yeerly ceremonye they so marie the Sea that it will never leave the Citye on drie lande.

---

* bringe a lothsomnesse with them: are irritating.

thought upon that should make her so sad. And she made answere, I thought upon a matter whiche as ofte as it commeth into my minde doth muche trouble me, and I can not put it out of my hert: whiche is, where in the daye of generall judgement all bodies muste arrise again and appeere naked beefore the judgement seat of Christ, I can not abide the greef I feele in thinking that mine must also be sene naked. Such Affectacions as these be bicause they passe the degree, doe rather provoke laughter then lothsomnesse. Those feat lyes now that come so well to pourpose, how they provoke laughter ye all knowe. And that friend of oures that suffreth us not to wante, within these fewe dayes rehersed one to me that was very excellent.

Feat lyes.

[LV] Then said the L. JULIAN: What ever it were, more excellenter it can not be, nor more suttler then one that a Tuscane of oures, whiche is a merchaunt man of Luca, affirmed unto me the last day for most certein.

Tell it us, quoth the DUTCHESSE.

The L. JULIAN said smilinge: This merchaunt man (as he saith) beeinge upon a time in Polonia, determined to buie a quantitie of Sables, mindinge to bringe them into Italy and to gaigne greatly by them. And after much practisinge in the matter, where he could not himselfe go into Moscovia bicause of the warr beetweene the kynge of Polonia and the Duke of Moscovia, he tooke order by the meane of some of the Countrey that upon a day apointed certein merchaunt men of Moscovia shoulde come with their Sables into the borders of Polonia, and he promysed also to be there himselfe to bargaine with them. This merchaunt man of Luca travailing then with his companie toward Moscovia, arrived at the river of Boristhenes, which he found hard frosen like a marble stone, and saw the Moscovites, which for suspicion of warr were in doubt of the Polakes, were on the other side, and neerer cam not than the breadth of the river. So after they knewe the one the other, makinge certein signes, the Moscovites beegan to speake aloud and toulde the price how they would sell their Sables, but the colde was so extreme, that they were not understood, bicause the woordes beefore they cam on the other syde where thys merchaunt of Luca was and his interpreters, were congeled in the aere and there

Polonia.

Muscovia.

Boristhenes.

remayned frosen and stopped.[127] So that the Polakes that knew the maner, made no more adoe but kindled a great fire in the middest of the river (for to their seeminge that was the point wherto the voice came hott beefore the frost tooke it) and the river was so thicke frosen that it did well beare the fire. Whan they had thus done the wordes that for space of an houre had bine frosen beegan to thawe and cam doune, making a noyse as doeth the snow from the mounteignes in Maye, and so immediatlye they were well understood, but the men on the other side were first departed, and bicause he thought that those woordes asked to great a price for the Sables, he woulde not bargaine, and so cam awaye without.

[LVI] Then they laughed all. And M. BERNARDE: Truelye (quoth he) thys that I wyll tell you is not so subtill, yet is it a pretye matter, and this it is. Where talke was a fewe dayes ago of the countrey or world newly founde out by the mariners of Portugal, and of straunge beastes and other matters brought from thens, that friend I toulde you of, affirmed that he had seene an Ape, verie divers in shape from such as we are accustomed to see, that played excellently well at Chestes.[128] And emong other times upon a day beefore the king of Portugal the Gentilman that brought herr played at Chestes with herr, where the Ape showed some draughtes* very suttill, so that she put him to his shiftes, at length she gave him Checkemate. Upon this the gentilman beeinge somwhat vexed (as communlie they are all that lose at that game) tooke the kinge in his hande whiche was good and bigg (as the facion is emonge the Portugalles) and reached the Ape a great knocke on the heade. She furthwith leaped aside complayning greatly, and seemed to require justice at the kinges handes for the wrong done her. The gentil-man afterward called her to play with him again, the whiche with signes she refused a while, but at last was contented to play an other game, and as she had done the other time beefore, so did she now drive him to a narrow point. In conclusion: the Ape perceivinge she could give the gentilman the mate, thought with a newe

An ape plaied at chestes.

To lose at chestes vexeth men.

---

* draughtes: moves.

divise she would be sure to escape without any mo knockes, and privilie conveyed her right hande without makinge semblant what her entent was, under the gentilmans left elbowe, leaning for pleaser upon a litle taffata coushin, and snatchinge it slightlie awaye, at one instant gave him with her left hande a mate with a paune, and with her right hande caste the coushin upon her heade to save her from strokes, then she made a gamboll beefore the king joifully, in token (as it were) of her victory. Now see whether this Ape were not wise, circumspect and of a good understanding.

Then spake the L. CESAR GONZAGA: It must needes be that this ape was a Doctour emong other Apes and of much authoritie: and I beleave the commune weale of the Apes of India sent her into Portugall to gete a name in a straunge countrey.

At this every manne laughed, both for the lye and for the addition made to it by the L. Cesar.

[LVII] So proceadinge on in his talke M. BERNARDE said: You have understoode therfore what Jestes are that be of effect and communication without interruption asmuche as cummeth to mynde: therfore it shall be well nowe we speake of such as consist in one sayinge alone, and have a quicke sharpenesse that lyeth breefly in a sentence or in a word. And even as in the first kind of meerie talke a man must in his protestacion and counterfeitinge take heede that he be not like commune jesters and parasites, and such as with fonde matters move menne to laughe, so in this breef kinde the Courtier must be circumspect that he appeere not malitious and venimous and speake tauntes and quippies only for spite and to touch the quick, bicause such men often times for offence of the tunge are chastised in the wholl body. [LVIII] Of those readie Jestes therfore that consist in a short sayinge, such are most livelie that arrise of doubtfulnesse,* though alwais they provoke not laughing, for they be rather praised for wittie, then for matters of laughter.

These two examples are put in Italian,

Come pochi di sono disse' il nostro M. Anniball Palleotto ad uno che' li proponea un maestro per insegnare' Grammatica a suoi figliuoli, et poi che' gliel

* doubtfulnesse: ambiguity, double meaning.

hebbe' laudato per molto dotto, venendo al salario, disse', che' oltre' ai danari volea una camera fornita per habitare e dormire, perche' esso non havea letto. Allhor M. Anniball subito rispose', e come' puo egli esser dotto se non ha letto?*

See howe well he tooke avauntage at the diverse signification of *haver letto* (which is interpreted both to have a bed and to have read). But bicause these doubtfull woordes have a pretie sharpenesse of witt in them, beeing taken in a contrarie signification to that al other men take them, it appeereth (as I have said) that they rather provoke a manne to wondre then to laughe, except whan they be joyned with other kindes of sayinges. The kinde therfore of wittie sayinges that is most used to make men laughe, is whan we give eare to heare one thinge, and he that maketh answere, speaketh an other and is alleaged contrarye to expectacion, and in case a doubt be annexed therwithall, then is it verie wittie and pleasant.

Come' laltr' hieri disputandosi di far un bel mattonato nel camerino della S. Duchessa, dopo molte' parole Voi M. Jo. Christofero diceste, Se' noi potessimo havere' il vescovo di Potentia, e farlo ben Spianare, saria molto a proposito, perche egli e' il piu bel matto nato ch' io vedessi mai. Ogn'un rise molto, perche' dividendo quella parola matto nato faceste' lo ambiguo, poi dicendo che' Si havesse a spianare' un vescovo e metterlo per pavimento d'un camerino fu fuor d'opinione' di chi ascoltava, cosi riusci il motto argutissimo e risibile.†

Sidenote: bicause they have no grace in the English tunge by reason of the doubtfulnesse of the woordes that may be taken two sundry wayes: yet is the Englishe as plentifull of these jestes as any other tunge, wherin Syr Thomas Moore excelled in our time.

Sidenote: Mattonato
A pavement.

Sidenote: Matto nato
A naturall foole.

---

* Just like the joke our friend Annibale Paleotto made the other day to a man who was suggesting a tutor to teach his children Latin. The man was praising this tutor as a very learned man, and then, when he came to discuss the terms of employment, he said that, besides his salary, he would need a room to live and sleep in, because he didn't have a bed ('*letto*'). And Annibale immediately came out with the reply: 'So how can he be learned if he hasn't studied' (or 'if he doesn't have a bed': '*se non ha letto*')?

† Just like the joke you made the other day, Giancristoforo, during a conversation about a brick-work floor ('*mattonato*') that was to be put down in the Duchess's dressing-room; after a long discussion, you said: 'If we could get hold of the Bishop of Potenza and flatten him out, he would do nicely, because I've never seen such a born fool ('*matto nato*').' And it raised a great laugh,

[LIX] But of doubtfull woordes there be manie sortes, therfore must a man be circumspect and chouse out termes verie artificiallye, and leave oute suche as make the Jest colde, and that a man would weene were haled by the heare, or elles (as we have saide) that have to much bitternesse in them. As certeine companions beeinge in a friendes house of theirs, who had but one eye, after he had desired the company to tarye dinner with him, they departed all saving one, that said: And I am well pleased to tarye, for I see a voide roume for one, and so with his fingre poyncted to the hole where his eye had bine. See howe bytter and discourtious this is passynge measure, for he nipped him without a cause and wythout beeinge first pricked himselfe: and he saide the thynge that a man might speake against blinde men.* Suche generall matters delyte not, bicause it appeereth they are thought upon of pourpose. And after thys sorte was the saiynge to one wythout a nose: And where doest thou fasten thy spectakles? Or, wherewithall doest thou smell roses at the time of the yere? [LX] but emong other meerie saiynges, they have a verie good grace that arryse whan a man at the nippynge talke of his felowe taketh the verye same woordes in the self same sence, and retourneth them backe agayne pryckynge hym wyth hys owne weapon. As an attourney in the lawe, unto whom in the presence of the judge his adversarye saide, What barkeste thou? furthwyth he answered: Bycause I see a thief.[129] And of this sorte was also, whan Galeotto of Narni passyng throughe Siena stayed in a streete to enquire for an ynn, and a Senese seeinge hym so corpulente as he was, saide laughinge: Other menne carye their bougettes† beehynde them, and this good felowe caryeth his beefore him. Galeotto answered immediatlye: So must menne do in the Countrey of theeves.[130] [LXI] There is yet an other sorte called in Italian *Bischizzi*, and that consisteth in chaungynge or encreasinge, or diminisshinge of a letter

> *Jestes that are to nipping.*
>
> *To nicke a man with his owne woordes.*
>
> *Catullus answere to Philippus.*
>
> *To chaunge a letter or sillable.*

because of the pun you made by dividing up that word '*mattonato*', and also because the idea of flattening out a bishop and using him as flooring was so unexpected; so the joke was very clever and extremely funny.

* against blinde men: against any blind man.

† bougettes: saddlebags.

or syllable. As he that saide: Thou shouldest be better
learned in the Latrine tunge then in the Greeke. And to
you (madam) was written in the superscription of a
letter, To the Ladye Emilia Impia.[131] It is also a meerye
divise to mingle together a verse or mo, takyng it in an
other meeninge then the Author doeth, or some other
commune sayinge. Sometyme in the verye same
meanynge, but altringe a woorde, as a Gentilman said
that had a foule and scoulinge wief: whan he was asked
the question howe he dyd, answered: Thynke thou thy
selfe, for *Furiarum maxima juxta me cubat*.* And M.
Hierom Donato goynge a visitinge the Stacions of
Roome in Lente,[132] in companye wyth manye other
Gentilmen, mett with a knott of fair Romaine Ladies,
and whan one of those gentilmen had said:

> Quot cœlum stellas, tot habet tua Roma Puellas,

by and by he added:

> Pascua quotque hædos, tot habet tua Roma Cinædos,†

showinge a rout of yonge menne that came on the other
side. And Marcantonio della Torre[133] sayde after the
maner to the Byshoppe of Padoa: Where there was a
Nounrye in Padoa under the charge of a religious
person muche esteamed for hys good lyfe and learnynge, yt happened that thys father hauntinge much to
the Nounrye verie familiarlie, and confessynge often the
Sisters, beegat five of them with chylde, where there
were not passinge five mo in all. And whan the matter
was knowen, the father would have fled, and wist not
howe. The bishoppe caused him to be apprehended,
and upon that, he confessed that he had gotten those
five Nounnes with childe through the temptacion of the
Dyvell, so that the Bishoppe was fullye bent to chastice
him sore. And bicause this man was learned, he had
manye friendes, which altogether assayed to helpe him,
and emonge the rest there went also M. Marcantonio to
entreate for him. The Bishoppe would in no wise give

Marginal notes:
Virgil.
The vii.
churches of
Roome.

Ovid.
Of wanton
dames
Roome hath
like store,
As sterres be
in the skie.
As many
boyes pre-
servde for
love,
As Kiddes in
pastures lie.

---

* A phrase from Virgil's *Aeneid* (VI, 605–6) 'Furiarum maxima
iuxta accubat' ('The greatest of the Furies lies near by') is twisted here
to give the sense 'the greatest of the Furies lies at my side'.
† Hoby translates these lines in his note ('like store': 'as many').
The original line is from Ovid's *Art of Love*, I, 59.

eare to them. At length they beynge instant upon him and commending the gyltie, and excusinge him throughe the commoditie of place, frailtye of manne and manie other causes, the Bishop said: I will do nothing for you, bicause I must make accompt unto God of this. And whan they had replyed again, the Bishop said: What answere shall I make unto God at the day of judgement, whan He shall say unto me *Redde' Rationem villicationis tue*? M. Marcantonio answered him immediatly: Mary my lord the verie same that the Gospell sayth: *Dominé quinque talenta tradidisti mihi, ecce alia quinque superlucratus sum.* Then could not the Bishoppe absteine laughing and he asswaged much his anger and the punishmente that he had ordeined for the offender. [LXII] It is likewise verie pretie to allude to names and to feine somwhat, for that he the talke is of, is so called, or els bicause he doeth some such thinge. As not longe sins Proto da Luca[134] (which as you know is one meerelie disposed) asking the Bishopprike of Calio, the Pope answered him: Doest thou not knowe that *Calio,* in the Spanishe tunge is as muche to say as, I houlde my Peace, and thou art a great prater? Therfore it were unfittinge for a Bishoppe at any time in naminge his title to make a lye, now *Calia,* houlde thy peace then. To this Proto gave an answere, the which although it were not in this sorte yet was it no lesse pretie then this. For after he had often put him in remembrance of this his suite and sawe it take none effect, at last he said: Holye father, in case youre holynesse do give me this bisshoppricke, yt shal not be without a profit to you, for then will I surrender two offices into your handes. And what offices hast thou to surrender into my handes? quoth the Pope. Proto answered: I shall surrender unto you *Officium principale,* and *Officium beatæ Mariæ.** Then coulde not the Pope though he were a verye grave person, absteine from laughinge. An other also in Padoa said Calphurnius[135] was so named, bicause he was wont to heate fourneyses.† And upon a day whan I

Yelde an accompt of thy husbandrie. Lord, thou deliveredst unto me v. talentes, beholde I have gained v. mo.

To allude to names.

Dooble signification of *Calio.*

Dooble signification of *Officium.*

---

* The joke is based on the double meaning of 'office': 'ecclesiastical post' and 'breviary'.
† bicause he was wont to heate fourneyses: the word-play rests on the meaning of the Latin phrase *calescit furnos.*

asked Phedra[136] how it happeneth, where prayer is
made in the Church upon goodfridaye not onlie for
Chrystyans, but also for Paganes and for Jewes, there
was no mention made of the Cardinalles, as there was of
Bishops and other prelates. He answered me, that the
Cardinalles were conteined in the Collet, *Oremus pro
hæreticis et Schismaticis.** And oure Count Lewis saide
that I reprehended a ladie of love for occupyinge a
certein kinde of lye† that shined muche, bicause whan
she was trimmed therwithall, I might see my selfe in her
face, and for that I was yll favoured I coulde not abyde
to looke upon my selfe. In this maner was that M.
Camillo Paleotto[137] saide unto M. Anthonio Porcaro,
whiche reasoninge of a companion of his that under
confessyon had sayde unto the Priest that he fasted with
all his harte, and went to Masse and to holye service and
did all the good deedes in the worlde, said: This felowe
in stead of accusynge prayseth hym self. Unto whom M.
Camillo answered: Nay, he rather confesseth himself of
these matters, bicause he reckeneth the doinge of them
great sinn. Do you not remember how well the L.
Generall said the last daye, whan Johnthomas Galeotto
wondred at one that demaunded two hundreth
Ducates for a horse? for whan Johnthomas saide that he
was not worth a farthinge, bicause among other yll
properties he had, he could not abide weapons, neyther
was it possible to make him come nighe where he sawe
anye, the L. Generall said (willing to reprehende him of
cowardise): Yf the horse hath this propertie that he can
not abide weapons, I marveile he asketh not a thousand
Ducates. [LXIII] Also sometime a man speaketh the
verie same woord, but to another ende then the
commune use is. As, whan the Duke was passing over a
very swift river, he said to the trompetter: Goo on. The
trumpetter tourned him backe with his cappe in his
hande and after a reverent maner, saide: It shalbe
youres my lorde.‡ It is also a pleasant maner of jestinge,
whan a man seemeth to take the woordes and not the
meaninge of him that speaketh. As this yeere a Dutch

* The phrase means 'let us pray for heretics and schismatics'.
† lye: cosmetic.
‡ It shalbe youres my lorde: after you.

man in Roome meetinge in an Eveninge oure M. Phillipp Beroaldo[138] whose Scholar he was, said unto him: *Dominé magister, Deus det vobis bonum sero.* And Beroaldo answered incontinently: *Tibi malum cito.** And Diego dé Chignognes beeinge at table with the Great Capitain,[139] whan an other Spaniarde that satt there had saide, *Vino dios* (calling for wine) Diego answered hym again: *Vino, y nolo conocistes,* to nip him for a marrané.† Also M. James Sadoleto[140] said unto Beroaldo, that had tould him how he wold in any wise go to Bolonia: What is the cause that maketh you thus to leave Roome where there are so manie pleasures, to go to Bolonia full of disquietnesse? Beroaldo answered: I am forced to go to Bolonia for three Countes. And nowe he had lifte up three fingers of hys left hande to alleage three causes of his goynge, whan M. James sodeinlye interrupted hym and said: The three countes that make you goe to Bolonia are, Count Lewis da San Bonifacio, Count Hercules Rangon and the Count of Pepoli. Than they all laughed bicause these three Countes had bine Beroaldoes Scholers and were propre‡ yonge menne and applyed their studie in Bolonia. This kinde of meerye jestinge therfore maketh a man laughe muche, bicause it bryngeth wyth it other maner answeres then a manne looketh for to heare: and oure owne errour doeth naturallye delite us in these matters, whyche whan it deceyveth us of that we looke for, we laughe at it. [LXIV] But the termes of speache and fygures that have anye grace and grave talke, are likewise (in a maner) alwayes comelye in Jestes and meerye pleasantnesse. See howe woordes placed con-trarywyse give a great ornament, whan a contrarye clause is sett agaynste another. The same maner is often times verye meerye and pleasant. As, a Genuesé that was verye prodigall and lavysh in hys expences beeinge reprehended by a usurer, who was most covetous, that

---

* The German's Latin is incorrect: he obviously means to wish Beroaldo, 'God give you good evening' (*buona sera* in Italian); but in fact his greeting translates 'may God give you good late'. Beroaldo's reply means 'and may God give you evil soon'.
† marrané: heretic (from the Spanish term *marrano*: a Jewish or Muslim convert to Christianity).
‡ propre: handsome.

said unto him: And whan wilt thou leave castynge away
thy substance? Then he answered: Whan thou leavest
stealinge of other mens. And bicause (as we have
alreadie said) from the places that we derive Jestes from,
that touch a manne, we may manie times from the verie
same take grave sentences to prayse and commende, it is
a verye comelye and honest maner both for the one and
the other pourpose, whan a man consenteth to and
confirmeth the selfe same thinge that the other
speaketh, but interpreteth it otherwise then he meaneth.
As within these fewe dayes a Priest of the Countrey
sayinge Masse to his parishioners, after he had toulde
them what holye dayes they shoulde have that weeke,
he beegane the generall confession in the name of all the
people, and sayde: I have synned in yll dooynge, in yll
speakynge, in yll thynkynge, and the rest that foloweth,
makynge mentyon of all the deadlye sinnes. Then a
Gossippe of his and one that was verye familyar wyth
the Priest to sporte with hym, saide to the standers bye:
Beare recorde, Sirs, what he confesseth with hys owne
mouth he hath done, for I entende to present him to the
Bishoppe for it. The verye same maner used Sallazza
della Pedrata to honoure a Ladye of love wythall. With
whome entringe in talke, after he had praysed herr
beeside her vertuous qualities for her beawtie also, she
answered him that she deserveth not that praise,
bicause she was now well striken in yeeres. And he then
said to her: That is in you of age, is nothing elles but to
liken you unto the aungelles, whiche were the firste and
are the auntientest creatures that ever God made.
[LXV] Also meerie sayinges are muche to the pourpose
to nippe a man, aswell as grave sayinges to praise one,
so the metaphors be well applyed, and especiallye yf
they be answered, and he that maketh answere continue
in the self same metaphor spoken by the other. And in
this sorte was answered to M. Palla Strozzi,[141] whiche
banished out of Florence, and sendinge thither one of
his about certein affaires, said unto him after a
threatninge maner: Tell Cosmus de Medicis in my name
that The henn sitteth abroodé.* The messenger did the

To enterpret
otherwise
then a man
meaneth.

Palla Strozzi.

Cosimo de
Medici.

---

* sitteth abroode: is brooding (in the context, meditating
revenge).

errand to him, as he was wylled. And Cosmus without
any more deliberacion, answered him immediatlye: Tell
M. Palla in my name again, that Hennes can full yll sitt
abroodé out of the nest. With a metaphor also M.
Camillo Porcaro commended honorablye the Lorde
Marcantonio Colonna, who understandynge that M.

The Lorde
Marcus
Anthonius
Columna.

Camillo in an Oration of hys had extolled certein noble
men of Italy that were famous in marcial prowesse, and
emonge the rest had made most honorable mention of
him, after rendringe due thankes, he said to him: You
(M. Camillo) have done by your friendes as some
merchaunt men play by their money, which findinge a
counterfeit Ducat, to dispatch him away, cast him into a
heape of good ones and so uttre him: even so you, to
honour me withall, where I am litle woorth, have sett
me in company with so excellent and vertuous personages, that through their prowesse, I may peraventure passe for a good one. Then M. Camillo made
answere: They that use to counterfeit Ducates, gylte
them so that they seeme to the eye much better then the
good: therfore if there were to be founde counterfeiters
of menne, as there be of Ducates, a man might have a
juste cause to suspect you were false, beeinge (as you
are) of much more faire and brighter mettall then any of
the rest. You may see that this place is commune both
for the one and the other kinde of Jestes, and so are
manie mo, of the which a man might geve infinite
examples, and especially in grave sayinges. As the great
Capitain[142] saide, whiche (beeinge sett at table and
everye roume filled) sawe two Italian Gentilmen standinge bye that had done him verye good service in the
warr, sodainly he start up and made all the rest to arrise
to give place to those two, and said: Make roume Sirs
for these gentilmen to sitt at their meat, for had not they
bine we should not have had now wherwithall to feade
our selves. He saide also to Diego Garzia that perswaded hym to remove out of a daungerous place that
lay open upon gunnshott: Sins God hath not put feare

Lewis the
XII.

into your mynd, put not you it into myne. And kinge
Lewis, which is nowe Frenche kinge, where it was saide
unto him soone after his creation, that then was the time
to be even with his enemies that had done him so much
injurye while he was Duke of Orleans. He made

answere: That the French kinge hath nothing ado to revenge the wronges done to the Duke of Orleans. [LXVI] A man toucheth also in Jest manye times with a certein gravitie without moving a man to laughe. As Gein Ottomani[143] brother to the great Turke, whan he was prisoner in Roome, he said: Justinge* (as we used it in Italy) seemed to him overgreat a daliaunce, and a tryfle to that should be in deede. And he said, whan it was tould him that kinge Ferdinande the yonger was nimble and quycke of person in renning, leapinge, vautynge and suche matters, in his country slaves used these exercises, but great men learned from their childhood liberalitie and were renowmed for that. And in a maner after the same sort, savinge it had a litle more matter to laughe at, was that the archbishopp of Florence said unto Cardinal Alexandrino: That men have nothinge but Substance, a body and a soul: their Substance is at Lawyars disposynge, their Bodye at Phisitiens, and their Soul at divines.

Then answered the L. JULIAN: A man might ad unto this the saiynge of Nicholetto: which is, that it is seldome seene a Lawyer to go to lawe, nor a Phisitien take medicin, nor a divine a good Christian.

[LXVII] M. BERNARDE laughed, then he proceaded: Of this there be infinite examples spoken by great Princes and verie grave men. But a man laugheth also manye times at comparasons. As oure Pistoia[144] wrott unto Seraphin: I sende thee backe again thy great male† whiche is like thy selfe. If ye remember well Seraphin was muche like a male. Again, there be some that have a pastime to liken menne and women to horses, to dogges, to birdes, an often times to coffers, to stooles, to cartes, to candelstickes, which somtime hath a good grace and otherwhile verye stale. Therfore in this point a man must consider the place, the time, the persones, and the other thinges we have so manie times spoken of.

Then spake the L. GASPAR PALLAVICIN: The comparason that the L. John Gonzaga[145] made of Alexander the Great to M. Alexander his son, was verye pleasant.

Gein
Ottomani.

Comparasons.

---

* justinge: jousting.
† male: suitcase.

I wote not what it was, answered M. BERNARDE.

The L. GASPAR said: The L. John was playinge at dice (as his use is) and had lost a numbre of Ducates and was still on the losinge hande, and M Alexander his sonn, which for all he is a childe delyteth no lesse in playe then his father, stoode verie still to beehould him and seemed verye sad. The Count of Pianella, that was there present with manye other Gentilmen, said: See (my Lorde) M. Alexander is verie heavie for youre losse, and his hert panteth waytinge whan lucke will come to you that he may gete some of your winninges: therfore rid him of this griefe, and beefore ye lose the rest, gyve hym at the least one Ducat that he maye goe playe him too, emonge hys companyons. Then sayde the L. John: You are deceyved, for Alexander thynketh not upon suche a trifle, but as it is wrytten of Alexander the great, while he was a childe, understandinge that Philipp his father had dyscomfited a great armie, and conquered a certein kingdome, he fell in weepinge, and whan he was asked the question whye he wept, he answered, bicause he doubted that his father would conquerr so manye Countryes, that he should have none left for him to conquerr: even so nowe Alexander my sonne is sorye and readye to weepe in seeinge me his father lose, bycause he doubteth that I shall lose so much, that I shall leave him nothinge at all to lose.

[LXVIII] Whan they had a whyle laughed at this M. BERNARDE wente forwarde: A man must take heede also hys jestynge be not wicked, and that the matter extende not (to appeere quycwitted) to blasphemye, and studye therin to invent newe wayes: least herein, where a manne deserveth not onelye blame, but also sharpe punishment, he should appeere to seke a praise, which is an abhominable matter. And therfore suche as these be, that goe about to shew their pregnant witt wyth small reverence to Godward, deserve to be excluded out of everye Gentylmans companye. And no lesse, they that be filthye and bawdye in talke, and that in the presence of women have no maner respect, and seeme to take none other delite but to make women blushe for shame, and upon thys goe seekynge oute meerye and jestynge woordes. As thys yeere in Ferrara at a banckett in presence of manye Ladyes there was a

Blasphemye.

Filthy and baudie persons in talke.

Florentine and a Senese, whiche for the moste parte (as you knowe) are ennemies together. The Senese sayd to nipp the Florentine: We have maryed Siena to the Emperour and given him Florence in dowerye. And this he spake bicause the talke was abrode in those dayes, that the Seneses had given a certein quantitie of money to the Emperour, and he tooke the protection of them upon him. The Florentine answered immediatlye: But Siena shalbe first ridden (after the Frenche phrase, but he spake the Italian worde) and then shall the dowerye afterward be pleaded for at good leyser.* You may see the taunt was wittie, but bicause it was in presence of women it appeered bawdie and not to be spoken.

[LXIX] Then spake the L. GASPAR PALLAVICIN: Women have none other delite but to heare of such matters, and yet will you deprive them of it. And for my part I have bine ready to blushe for shame at woordes which women have spoken to me oftener then men.

And I speake not of such women as these be, quoth M. BERNARDE, but of the vertuous that deserve to be reverenced and honoured of all gentilmen.

The L. GASPAR saide: It were good we might finde out some pretie rule howe to knowe them, bicause moste communlie the best in apparance are cleane contrarye in effect.

Then said M. BERNARDE smylinge: Were not the L. Julian here present that in everye place is counted the protectour of women, I woulde take upon me to answere you, but I will not take his offyce from him.

Here the L. EMILIA in like maner smilinge, said: Women neede no defendoure againste an accuser of so small authoritie. Therfore let the L. Gaspar alone in this his froward opinion, risen more bicause he could never finde woman that was willynge to loke upon him, then for anye want that is in women, and proceade you in youre communication of Jestes.

[LXX] Then M. BERNARDE: Trulye madam (quoth he) me thinke I have named unto you manie places, out of the which a man may pike pleasant and wittie sayinges, which afterward have so much the more grace, as they are set furth with a comelie protestacion.

* leyser: leisure.

Yet may there be alleaged manie other also, as whan to encrease or diminish, thinges be spoken that uncrediblye passe the likelihoode of truth. And of this sort was that Marius da Volterra[146] said by a prelate that thought himselfe so taule a person, that as he went into Saint Peters, he stowped for hittinge his heade againste the greate beame over the porche. Also the L. Julian here saide that Golpino hys servaunte was so leane and drie, that in a morning as he was blowing the fire to kendle it, the smoke bore him up the chimney unto the tonnell, and had gone awaye with him had he not stooke on crosse at one of the holes above. And M. Augustin Bevazzano[147] toulde, that a covetous manne whiche woulde not sell hys corne while it was at a highe price, whan he sawe afterwarde it had a great falle, for desperacion he hanged himself upon a beame in his chamber, and a servaunt of his hearing the noise, made speede, and seeing his maister hang, furthwith cut in sunder the rope and so saved him from death: afterwarde whan the covetous man came to himselfe, he woulde have had hys servaunt to have paide him for his halter that he had cut. Of this sort appeareth to be also that Laurence de Medicis said unto a colde jester: Thou shouldest not make me laugh if thou ticklidest me. The like he answered unto an other foolishe person, who in a morninge had found him in bed verie late and blamed him for sleeping somuche, sayinge unto him: I have now bine in the new and olde markett place, afterward I went oute at the gate of San Gallo to walke about the walles, and have done a thousande other matters, and you are yet in bed. Then said Laurence: That I have dreamed in one houre is more woorth, then al that you have done in foure. [LXXI] It is also pretie whan one reprehendeth a thinge which a man would not thinke he minded to reprehende. As the marquesse Friderick of Mantua oure Dutchesse father, beeinge at table wyth manye gentilmen, one of them after he had eaten up his dishe of broth, said: By your leave my L. marquesse. And whan he had so said, he beegane to suppe up the rest that remayned in the dishe. Then said the marquesse by and by: Aske leave of the swyne, for thou doest me no wronge at all. Also M. Nicholas Leonicus[148] said, to touch a noble manne that was falselye reported to be liberall: Gesse you what liberalitye is in him that doeth not onlye geve awaye hys owne good but other mens also. [LXXII] That is in like maner an honest and comelie kinde of jesting that consisteth in a certein dissimulacion, whan a man speaketh one thinge and privilie meaneth another. I speake not of the maner that is cleane contrarye, as if one shoulde call a dwarf a giaunt: and a blacke man, white: or one most ilfavoured beawtifull, bicause they be to open contraries, although otherwhile also they stirr a man to laughe. But whan with a grave and drie speache in sportinge a man speaketh pleasantlie that he hath not in his minde. As whan a gentilman tould M. Augustin Folietta[149] a loude lye and earnestlye did affirme it, bicause he thought he scase beleaved it. At laste M. Augustin said: Gentilman, if you will ever do me pleaser, be so good to me as to quiet your selfe in case I do not beleave anye thinge you saye. Yet whan he replied again and bound it with an othe to be true, at lengthe he saide: Sins you wyll have me, I am content to beleave it for youre sake, for to saye the trueth I would do a greater thinge for you then this commeth to. In a maner after the same sorte Don Giovanni di Cardona[150] said of one that woulde forsake Rome: In mine opinion thys felowe is yll advysed, for he is so wicked that in abidinge in Rome it maye be his chaunce in time to be made a Cardinall. Of this sorte is also that Alphonsus Santacroce said, whiche a litle beefore havinge certein injuries done him by the Cardinall of Pavia, and walking without Bolonia with certein Gentilmen nighe unto the place of execution, and seeinge one newlye hanged there, tourned him that waye with a certein heavie looke and said so loude that every man might heare him: Thou art a happie man that hast nothinge adoo with the Cardinal of Pavia.[151]

[LXXIII] And the kinde of jestinge that is somewhat grounded upon scoffinge seemeth verie meete for great men, bicause it is grave and wittie and may be used both in sportynge matters and also in grave. Therfore dyd manye of olde time and menne of best estimatyon use it: as Cato, Scipio Affricanus minor. But above all they saye Socrates the Philosopher excelled in it. And in oure time Kynge Alphonsus the first of Aragon:[152] which

Dissimula-cion.

Jesting grounded upon scoffinge meete for great men.

upon a time as he went to diner tooke manye ryche jewelles from his fingers, for wetting them in washing hys handes, and so gave them to him that stoode nexte him as thoughe he had not minded who it was. This servaunt had thought sure the king marked not to whom he gave them, and bicause his heade was busied with more waightie affaires, wold soone forgete them cleane, and therof he tooke the more assurance, whan he sawe the kinge asked not for them again. And whan the matter was passed certein dayes, wekes and monthes without hearinge anye woord of it, he thought surelye he was safe. And so about the yeeres end after this matter had happened, an other time as the kinge was in like maner going to diner, he stepped furth and put out his hande to take the kinges ringes. Then the kinge rounding him in the eare, said: The first is well for thee, these shall be good for an other. See this taunt how pleasant, wittie and grave it is, and woorthie in verie deede for the noble courage of an Alexander. [LXXIV] Like unto this maner grounded upon scoffinge there is also an other kinde, whan with honest woordes, a man nameth a vitious matter or a thinge that deserveth blame. As the great Capitain said unto a Gentilman of hys, that after the journey of Cirignola and whan all thinges were alreadye in safetye, mett him as richelye armed as might be, readye to fight. Then the greate Capitain[153] tourninge to him Don Ugo di Cardona, saide: Feare ye not now any more Sea tempest, for Saint Hermus hath appeered. And wyth thys honeste woorde he gave him a nicke. Bicause you knowe Saint Hermus doeth alwayes appeere unto Mariners after a tempeste and gyveth a token of caulme. And the meaning of the great capitain was, that whan this gentilman appeered it was a signe the daunger was alreadye cleane past. Again M. Octavian Ubaldino[154] beeinge in Florence in companye wyth certein of the best Citizins and reasoninge together of souldiers, one of them asked him whether he knewe Antonello da Forli whiche was then fled out of the state of Florence. M. Octavian answered: I have no great knowledge of him, but I have heard him alwaies reported to be a quick souldier. Then said an other Florentin: It appeereth he is quicke, for he taried not so longe as to aske leave to depart. [LXXV] They be

To name an yll thing with honest woordes.

Frumpes.

also pretie tauntes whan a man of the verie communication of his felowe taketh that he would not, and my
meaning is in that sort, as our Duke answered the
Capitain that lost Saint Leo. Whan this state was taken
by Pope Alexander and given to Duke Valentin,[155] the
Duke beeing in Venice at that time I speake of, manie of
his subjectes came continually to give him secret
information how the matters of state passed, and
emonge the rest, thither came also this Capitain, whiche
after he had excused himselfe the best he coulde, laiynge
the fault in his unluckinesse, he saide: My Lorde doubt
ye not, my hart serveth me yet to woorke a meane that
Saint Leo may be recovered again. Then answered the
Duke: Trouble not thy self any more about that, for in
losinge it thou haste wrought a meane that it may be
recovered again.[156] Certein other sayinges there are
whan a man that is knowen to be wittie speaketh a
matter, that seemeth to proceede of folye. As the last
day M. Camillo Paleotto said by one: That foole, as
soone as he beegane to wexe riche, died. There is like
unto this maner a certein wittie and kinde dissimulacion, whan a man (as I have said) that is wise maketh
semblant not to understande that he doth understande.
As the marquesse Friderick of Mantua, which beeing
sued too by a prating felow that complained upon
certein of his neighbours takinge the Pigions of his
Dovehouse with snares, and helde one continuallye in
his hande hanging by the foote in a snare, which he had
founde so dead, he answered him that there should be a
remedye for it. This felow never satisfied, not once but
manye a time repeted unto him his losse, showinge
alwaies the Pigion so hanged, and saide still: But I
besech you, howe thinke ye (my Lorde) what should a
man do in this matter? The marquesse at length said: By
mine advise the Pigion ought in no wise to be buried in
the Church, for sins he hath so hanged himself, it is to be
thought that he was desperat. In a maner after the same
sorte was that Scipio Nasica said unto Ennius. For
whan Scipio went unto Ennius house to speake with
him and called to him in the streete, a maiden of his
made him answere that he was not at home. And Scipio
heard plainlye Ennius himselfe saye unto his mayden to
tell hym that he was not at home, so he departed.

Pope Alex-
ander VI.
usurped the
dukedome of
Urbin and
gave it to
hys sonne
Cesar Borgia,
communlye
called Duca
Valentino.

Dessimula-
cion.

Within a while after Ennius came unto Scipioes house, and so likewise stoode beneethe and called him. Unto whom Scipio himselfe with a loude voice made answere that he was not at home. Then said Ennius: What, do not I knowe thy voice? Scipio answered: Thou hast smalle Courteysie in thee, the last day I beleaved thy maiden that thou waste not at home, and now wilt not thou beleave me my selfe? [LXXVI] It is also pretie whan one is touched in the verie same matter that he hath first touched his felowe. As Alonso Carillo[157] beeinge in the Spanishe Court and havynge committed certein youthfull partes that were of no great import-ance, was by the kinges commaundement caried to prison, and there abode for one night. The next day he was taken out again, and whan he came to the Palaice in the morninge, he entred into the chamber of presence that was full of gentilmen and Ladies, and jestynge together at this his imprisonment, maistresse Boadilla said: M. Alonso, I tooke great thought for this mishap of yours, for al that knew you were in feare least the kinge wold have hanged you. Then said immediatlye Alonso: Indeede maistresse, I was in doubte of the matter my selfe to, but yet I had a good hope that you would have begged me for your husbande. See howe sharpe and wittie this is. Bicause in Spaine (as in many other places also) the maner is, whan a manne is lead to execution, if a commune harlot will aske him for her husbande, it saveth his life. In this maner also did Raphael the peincter[158] answere two Cardinalles (with whom he might be familiar) which to make him talke, found fault in his hearinge with a table he had made, where Saint Peter and Saint Paul were: saiynge, that those twoo pictures were to red in the face. Then said Raphael by and by: My lordes, wonder you not at it, for I have made them so for the nones, bicause it is to be thought that Saint Peter and Saint Paul are even as red in heaven as you see them here, for verie shame that their Churche is governed by such men as you be. [LXXVII] Also those Jestes are pleasant, that have in them a certein privie semblant of laughter. As whan a husband lamented much and bewayled his wief that had hanged her selfe upon a figgtree, an other came to him and pluckynge him by the slieve, said: Friend, may I receive

To touche in the same matter a man is touched.

The maner of Spaine.

A semblant of laughing.

such pleaser as to have a graff of that figgtree to graff in some stocke of myne Orcharde? There be certein other Jestes that be pacient and spoken softlie with a kinde of gravitie. As a man of the Countrye caryinge a coffer upon his shoulders, chaunced therwithall to gyve Cato a harde pushe, and afterward said: Give roume. Cato answered: Haste thou anye thinge upon thy shoulders beeside that coffer? It is also a matter of laughter whan a man hath committed an errour and to amend it speaketh a matter pourposelye that appeereth foolishe, and yet is applyed to the ende that he hath appointed, and serveth hys tourne therwithall that he seeme not oute of countenaunce and dismayed. As not longe sins two ennemies beeinge together in the Counsell chamber of Florence (as it happeneth often in those Commune weales) the one of them, which was of the house of Altoviti, slept, and he that satt next unto him for a sporte, where his adversarye that was of the house of Alamanni, had said nothinge neyther then nor beefore, stirringe him wyth his elbowe made him awake, and saide unto him: Hearest thou not what such a one saith? Make answere, for the Lordes aske for thine advise. Then did Altoviti all sleepie arrise upon his feete and without anye more deliberation said: My Lordes, I say the cleane contrarye to that Alamanni hath spoken. Alamanni answered: What? I have said nothinge. Altoviti said immediatlye: To that thou wilt speake. In this maner also did youre M. Seraphin the Phisitien here in Urbin saye unto a manne of the Country, which had receyved suche a stroke upon the eye, that in verie deede it was oute, yet thought he beste to go seeke to M. Seraphin for remedie. Whan he saw it thoughe he knewe it was past cure, yet to plucke money out of his handes as that blowe had plucked the eye oute of his heade, he promised him largelye to heale it. And so he was in hande with him everye day for money, puttinge him in comforte that within sixe or seven dayes, he shoulde beegine to see wyth it agayn. The poore countrye manne gave him the litle he had, but whan he sawe him so prolonge the matter, he beegane to finde himself agreeved wyth the Physitien, and sayde that he was nothinge the better, neyther coulde he see anye more wyth that eye, then if he had hadd none at all in hys

With a certein gravitie.

A matter that seemeth foolishe.

Altoviti.

Alamanni.

heade. At length M. Seraphin perceyvynge there was no more to be gotten at hys handes, saide: Brother myne, thou muste have pacience, thou haste cleane lost thine eye and no remedye is there for it, praye God thou lose not thyne other wythall. The Countrye manne seeynge thys, fell in weepynge, and lamented muche and saide: Mayster myne, you have pylled me and robbed me of my money, I will complayne to the Duke, and made the greatest outcryes in the worlde. Then sayde M. Seraphin in a rage and to cleere hymselfe: Ah thou vyllein knave: thou wouldest then have two eyes as Cityzins and honest menne have, wouldest thow? Get thee hence in the Dyvelles name. And these woordes were thrust oute wyth suche furye that the poore selie manne was dismayed, and held his peace, and soft and faire departed in Gods name, thinking that he himselfe had bine in the wronge. [LXXVIII] It is also pretie whan a man declareth or enterpreteth a matter meerilie. As in the Spanishe Court in a morning there came into the Palaice a knight who was very ylfavoured: and his wief, that was verie beawtifull, both apparailed in white Damaske, and the Queene said unto Alonso Carillo: Howe thinke ye Alonso by these two? Madam, answered Alonso, me thinke the Ladye is the Dame, and he the aske, which signifieth a foule person and uglesome. Also whan Raphael de Pazzi[159] sawe a letter that the Priour of Messina had written to a maistresse of his, the superscription whereof was: *Esta carta s' ha da dar a qui en causa mi penar*, Me thinke (quoth he) this letter is directed to Paul Tholossa. Imagine you how the standers bye laughed at it, for they all knew that Paul Tholossa had lent tenn thousand Ducates to the Priour of Messina, and bicause he was verie lavishe in his expences, he could finde no waye to pay his dett. It is like unto this, whan a man geveth familiar admonition in maner of counsell, but dissemblinglie. As Cosmus de Medicis said unto a friend of his that had more riches then wit, and by Cosmus meanes had compassed an office without Florence, and at his settinge furthe askinge Cosmus what way he thought best for him to take to execute this office well: Cosmus answered him: Apparaile thy selfe in scarlate, and speake litle. Of this sort was that Count Lewis said unto one that woulde

To enterpret a matter meerely.

Dame aske.

This letter be geven to the cause of my griefe.

Familiar admonition in maner of counsell.

passe for an unknowen person in a certein daungerous place, and wist not howe to disguise himself, and the Count beeinge demaunded of hys advise therin, answered: Apparaile thy selfe like a Doctour, or in some other rayment that wise men use to weare. Also Jannotto de Pazzi said unto one that minded to make an armynge coat of as manye divers colours as might be invented: Take the woordes and deedes of the Cardinall of Pavia.[160] [LXXIX] A man laugheth also at certein matters disagreeinge. As one said the last daye unto M. Antony Rizzo of a certein Forlivese: Gesse whether he be a foole or no, for his name is Bartholomew. And an other: Thou seekest a rider* and hast no horses. And this man wanteth nothinge but good and a horse.† And at certein other that seeme to agree. As within these few dayes where there was a suspicion that a friend of oures had caused a false advoucion of a benifice‡ to be drawen out, afterward whan an other Priest fell sicke, Antony Torello saide unto him: What doest thou lingre the matter, whie doest thou not sende for thy Clerke and see whether thou cannest hit upon this other benefyce?[161] Likewise at certein that doe not agree. As the last day whan the Pope had sent for M. Johnluke of Pontremolo and M. Dominick dalla Porta, which (as you knowe) are both crookbacked, and made them Auditours, sayinge that he entended to bringe the Rota into a right frame, M. Latin Juvenal[162] saide: Oure holie father is deceived yf he thinke that he can bringe the Rota into a right frame with two crooked persons. [LXXX] Also it provoketh laughter, whan a man graunteth the thinge that is toulde him and more, but seemeth to understande it otherwise. As Capitain Peralta beeinge brought into the listes to fight the combatt wyth Aldana and Capitain Molart[163] that was Aldanas patrine requiringe Peralta to sweare whether

Matters disagreeinge.

That seeme to agree.

That agree not.

The Rota in Roome is suche an other matter as the Court of the Arches in England.

* Thou seekest a rider: the original has 'You are looking for M. Stalla' ('Mr Stable').

† this man wanteth nothinge but good and a horse. This joke (adapted from Cicero) is mangled in translation: the original has 'this man lacks nothing except money and brains' (cervello, not cavallo, 'horse', as Hoby reads it).

‡ a false advoucion of a benifice: i.e. a forged document in which a priest (presumably on his deathbed) signed over a benefice to him.

he had about him any Saint Johns Gosspell or charme
and inchauntmente, to preserve him from hurt. Peralta
swore that he had about him neyther Gosspell nor
inchauntment, nor relike, nor any matter of devocion
wherein he had any faith. Then said Molart, to touch
him to be a marrané:* Well no mo woordes in this, for I
beleave without swearinge that you have no faith also in
Christ. It is pretie moreover to use metaphors at a time
in such pourposes. As oure M. Mercantonio that said to
Botton da Cesena, who had vexed him with woordes:
Botton, Botton, thou shalt one day be the botton, and
the halter shalbe the bottonhole. And also when
Marcantonio had made a comedye whiche was verie
longe and of sundrye actes, the verye same Botton saide
in like maner to Marcantonio: To play your Comedye
ye shall neede for preparation asmuche wood as is in
Sclavonia. M. Marcantonio answered: And for preparation of thy Tragedie thre trees is inoughe.† [LXXXI]
Again a man speaketh a word manie times wherin is a
privie signification farr from that appeereth he wold
say. As the L. Generall here being in company where
there was communication of a Capitain that in deede al
his lief time for the more part had received the
overthrow, and as then by a chaunce wann the victorie:
and whan he that ministred this talke said: Whan he
made his entrie into that towne he was apparailed in a
verie faire crimosin velute coate, which he wore alwaies

An answere
to that a man
hath not said.

after his victories. The L. Generall said: Beelike it is
verie new. And no lesse doeth it provoke laughter, whan
otherwhile a man maketh answere unto that which the
other he talketh withall hath not spoken: or els seemeth
to beleave he hath done that he hath not done, and
should have done it. As Andrew Cosia, when he went to
visit a gentilman that discourtiously suffered him to
stand on his feete and he himselfe satt, saide: Sins you
commaund me sir, to obey you I will sitt, and so satt him
downe. [LXXXII] Also a man laugheth whan one
accuseth himselfe of some trespace. As the last daye
whan I saide to the Dukes Chapplaine, that my Lordes

* marrané: heretic.
† thre trees is inoughe: i.e. three trees are enough to construct the
gibbet on which you will be hanged.

grace had a Chapplaine that coulde say masse sooner*
then he: he answered me, It is not possible. And
roundinge me in the eare,† saide: You shall understande that I say not the third part of the secretes.‡ Also
Biagin Crivello,[164] whan a priest was slain at Millane,
he required his benefice of the Duke, the which he was
minded to bestowe upon an other. At length Biagin
perceyvinge no other reason wold prevaile, And what
(quoth he) if I were the cause of his death, why will you
not geve me his benefice? It hath also manie times a
good grace to wish those thinges that can not be. As the
last day one of our companie beehouldinge all these
Gentilmen here playnge at fence, and he liynge uppon a
bed, said: Oh what a pleasure it were, were this also a
valiaunt mans and a good souldiers exercise. In like
maner it is a pretie and wittie kinde of speakinge and
especially in grave men and of authoritie, to answere
contrarye to that he would, with whom he speaketh but
drilie and (as it were) with a certein doubting and
heedfull consideracion. As in times past Alphonsus the
first Kinge of Aragon,[165] gevinge unto a servaunt of his,
horse, harneis and apparaile, bicause he toulde him
how the night beefore he had dreamed that his high-
nesse had given him all those kinde of matters, and not
longe after, the verie same servaunte said again how he
dreamed that night, that he had given him a good sort§
of royalles,** he answered him: Hensfurthe beleave
dreames no more, for they are not alwaies true. In this
sort also did the Pope answere the Bishop of Cervia,
that to grope his minde saide unto him: Holye father, it
is noysed all Roome over and in the Palice to, that your
holynesse maketh me Governour. Then answered the
Pope: Let the knaves speake what they luste, doubt you
not, it is not true I warrant you. [LXXXIII] I could (my
Lordes) beeside these gather manye other places, from
whiche a manne maye dirive meerye and pleasant
Jestes, as matters spoken with feare, wyth marveyle,

To wish that
cannot be.

A contrarye
answere.

---

* sooner: quicker.
† roundinge me in the eare: whispering in my ear.
‡ the secretes: i.e. the parts of the mass that the priest reads in an
undertone.
§ sort: quantity.
** royalles: the original has 'gold florins'.

with threatninges oute of order, with overmuche furiousnesse: beesyde this, certein newlye happened cases provoke laughter: sometime silence with a certain wonder, at other tymes verie laughter it selfe without pourpose: but me thinke I have nowe spoken sufficient, for the Jestes that consiste in woordes (I beleave) passe not these boundes we have reasoned of. As for such as be in operacion,* though there be infinite partes of them, yet are they drawen into fewe principles. But in both kindes the chief matter is to deceive opinion, and to answer otherwise then the hearer loketh for: and (in case the Jest shal have any grace) it must nedes be seasoned with this deceit, or dissimulacion, or mockinge, or rebukinge, or comparason, or what ever other kinde a man will use. And althoughe all kinde of Jestes move a man to laugh, yet do they also in this laughter make diverse effectes. For some have in them a certein cleannesse and modest pleasantnesse. Other bite sometime privily, otherwhile openlye. Other have in them a certein wantonnesse. Other make one laughe assone as he heareth them. Other the more a man thinketh upon them. Other in laughinge make a man blushe withall. Other stirr a man somewhat to angre. But in all kindes a man must consider the disposition of the mindes of the hearers, bicause unto persons in adversitie oftentimes meery toyes augment their affliction: and some infirmities there be, that the more a man occupieth medicine aboute them, the woorse they wexe. In case therfor the Courtier in jestinge and speakinge meerie conceytes have a respecte to the time, to the persons, to his degree, and not use it to often (for parde it bringeth a lothsomnesse if a man stand evermore about it, all day in all kinde of talke and without pourpose) he maye be called pleasant and feat conceyted.† So he be heedefull also that he be not so bitter and bitinge, that a man mighte conjecture he were an envious person in prickinge without a cause, or for plaine malice, or men of to great authoritie (whiche is lacke of discreation) or of to much miserie (which is

Diverse effectes in jestes.

---

* such as be in operacion: i.e. the earlier type of joke discussed, consisting of a witty narration.
† feat conceyted: ingenious.

crueltye) or to mischevous (which is vanitie) or elles in speakinge matters that may offende them whom he would not offende (which is ignoraunce). For some there be that thinke they are bound to speake and to nippe without regard, as often as they can, howe ever the matter goe afterwarde. And emonge these kinde of persons are they, that to speake a woord which should seeme to come of a readinesse of witt, passe not for staynynge of a woorthie gentilwomans honesty, which is a very naughtie matter and woorthie sore punishment. Bicause in this point women are in the number of selie soules* and persons in miserye, and therfore deserve not to be nipped in it, for they have not weapon to defende themselves. But beeside these respectes he that wilbe pleasant and full of jestinge, must be shaped of a certein nature apt to all kinde of pleasantnesse, and unto that frame his facions, gestures and countenaunce, the which the more grave, steadie and sett it is, somuch the more maketh it the matters spoken to seeme wittie and subtil. [LXXXIV] But you (Sir Fridericke) that thought to rest your selfe under this my tree without leaves and in my withered reasoninges, I beleave you have repented youre selfe, and you recken ye are entred into the baytinge place† of Montefiore.[166] Therfore it shall be well done for you like a wel practised Courtier (to avoide an ill hosterie) to arryse somwhat beefore your ordinarye hour and set forwarde on your journey.

The smalle respett some have in jestinge.

A paltockis ynn.

Nay, answered SIR FRIDERICKE, I am come to so good an hosterie, that I minde to tarye in it lenger then I had thought at the firste. Therfore I will rest me yet a while, untill you have made an ende of all the talke ye have beegone withall. Wherof ye have left oute one percell that ye named at the beeginning: whiche is, Meerie Pranckes,‡ and it were not well done to deceyve the companye of it. But as you have taught us manie pretie matters concerninge Jestes, and made us hardie to use them throughe example of so many singular wittes, great men, Princis, Kinges and Popes, I suppose ye will likewise in Meerie Pranckes so boulden us, that we

---

* selie soules: the wretched.
† baytinge place: inn.
‡ Meerie Pranckes: practical jokes.

maye take a courage to practise some against you your self.

Then said M. BERNARDE smilinge: You shall not be the firste, but perhappes it will not be your chaunce, for I have so manie times bin served with them, that it maketh me looke wel about me: As dogges, after they have bine once scaulded with hott water, are aferd of the colde. How be it sins you will have me to speake somewhat of this to, I beleave I may rid my handes of it in fewe woordes. [LXXXV] And in mine opinion a Meerie Prancke is nothinge elles, but a friendlye deceit in matters that offende not at all or verie little. And even as in Jestynge to speake contrary to expectacyon moveth laughter, so doeth in Meerie Pranckes to doe contrarie to expectacion. And these doe so muche the more delite and are to be praised, as they be wittie and modest. For he that will woorke a Meerie Prancke without respect, doth manie times offende and then arrise debates and sore hatred. But the places that a man may dirive Merie Pranckes from are (in a maner) the verie same that be in Jestes. Therfore to avoide repetition of them, I will say no more but that there be two kyndes of Meerie Pranckes everye one of which may afterwarde be divided into mo partes. The one is, whan any man whoever he be, is deceyved wittilie, and after a feat maner and with pleasantnesse. The other, whan a manne layeth (as it were) a nett, and showeth a piece of a bayte so, that a man renneth to be deceyved of himself. The first is suche, as the Meerie Prancke was, that within these fewe dayes was wrought unto a coople of greate Ladyes (whom I will not name) by the meane of a Spaniarde called Castilio.

Then the DUTCHESSE: And whie (quoth she) will you not name them?

M. BERNARDE answered: Bicause I would not have them to take it in yll part.

Then said the DUTCHESSE again, smilinge: It is not againste good maner sometime to use Meerie Pranckes with great men also. And I have heard of manie that have bine played to Duke Fridericke, to kinge Alphonsus of Aragon, to Queene Isabel of Spaine, and to manie other great Princis, and not onlie they tooke it not in ill part, but rewarded very largely them that plaied them those partes.

What is a
Meerye
prancke.

M. BERNARDE answered: Neyther upon this hope do I entend to name them.

Say as pleaseth you, quoth the DUTCHESSE.

Then proceaded M. BERNARDE and said: Not manie dayes since in the Court that I meane, there arrived a manne of the Countrie about Bergamo, to be in service wyth a Gentilman of the Court: whyche was so well sett oute with garmentes and so finelye clad, that for all hys brynginge up was always keapinge Oxen and could doe nothinge elles, yet a manne that had not hearde him speake woulde have judged him a woorthie Gentilman. And so whan those two Ladies were enfourmed that there was arrived a Spaniarde, servaunt to Cardinall Borgia,[167] whose name was Castilio, a verie wittie man, a musitien, a daunser and the best Courtier in all Spaine, they longed verie much to speake with him, and sent incontinentlye for him, and after they had receyved him honorablye, they caused him to sitt downe, and beegan to entertein him with a verie greate respect in the presence of all menne, and fewe there were present that knew him not to be a Bergamask Cowherd. Therfore seeinge those Ladies enterteine him with such respect, and honour him so muche, they fell all in a laughyng, the more bicause the seelie felowe spake still his natyve language, the meere Bergamaske tunge. But the Gentilmen that divised this Prancke, had first toulde those Ladyes that emonge other thinges he was a great dissembler and spake all tunges excellentlye well, and especiallye the Countrie speache of Lumbardye, so that they thought he feigned, and manie tymes they beehelde the one the other with certein marveilinges, and saide: What a wonderfull matter is this, howe he counterfeyteth this tunge! In conclusion thys communication lasted so longe that everye mans sydes aked for laughinge, and he could not chouse himselfe but uttre so manye tokens of hys noblenesse of birth, that at length those Ladies (but with muche ado) beleaved he was the man that he was in deede. [LXXXVI] Suche Meerie Pranckes we see daily, but emong the rest they be pleasant that at the first make a man agast and after that, ende in a matter of suretie, bicause he that was deceived laugheth at himself whan he perceyveth he was afeard of nothing. As liynge upon a time in Paglia, there chaunced to be in the verie

The woorst speach in all Italy.

Whan a man is afeard of nothing.

Paglia is a
litle village
in the utmost
boundes of
the territorie
of Siena.

same ynn three other good felowes, two of Pistoia and
one of Prato, whiche after supper (as the maner is for
the most part) fell to gamynge. And not longe after, one
of the Pistoiens losinge his reste, had not a farthynge left
him to blesse himselfe, but beegan to chafe, to curse,
and to bann and to blaspheme terriblye, and thus
tearinge of God he went to bed. The other two after they
had played a while, agreed to woorke a Meerie Pranke
with him that was gone to bed. And whan they
perceyved that he was fallen in sleepe, they blew out the
candels and raked up the fire and beegane to speake
aloude, and to make the greatest hurly burlye in the
worlde, makinge wise to contende together about their
game. The one said: Thou tookest the carde under-
neath. The other deniynge it said: Thou hast viede upon
flush,* let us mount:† and suche other matters with
suche noise that he that slept awoke, and hearynge them
at play and talkinge even as though they had seene the
cardes, did a litle open his eyes: whan he sawe there was
no maner light in the chamber, he sayde: What a Dyvell
meane you to crie thus all night? Afterwarde he layed
him downe again to sleepe. The other two companions
gave him no maner answere, but still continued in their
pourpose untill he awoke better and muche wondred,
and whan he saw for certeintie that there was neyther
fire nor anye kinde of lighte and perceyved they played
still and fell in contention, he said: And how can ye see
the cardes without light? The one of the two answered: I
weene thou hast lost thy sight aswel as thy money. Seest
thou not that we have here two candels? He that was in
bed lift up himselfe upon his elbowes and in a maner
angred, said: Eyther I am dronken or blinde, or elles you
make a lye. The two arrose and went to bed darkelong,
laughing and makinge wise to beleave that he went
about to mocke them. And he again saide to them: I tell
you troth I see you not. At length the two beegane to
seeme to wonder much, and the one saide to the other:
By good Lord, I beleave he speaketh in good earnest,
reach me the candell, and lett us see least perhappes he

* Thou hast viede upon flush: you have wagered on four cards of
the same suit.
† mount: deal again.

have some impediment in his sight. Then thought the
poore wretch surelie that he had bine blinde, and
weeping dounright, saide: Oh Sirs, I am blinde: and
furthwith he beegane to call upon our Ladye of Loreto
and to beeseche her to perdon him his blasphemies and
cursinge for the losse of his money. But his two
companions put him in good comforte and saide: It is
not possible but thou shouldest see us. Yt is some fansye
that thou haste conceyved in thine heade. Oh good
lorde, answered the other, it is no fansye, nor I see no
more then if I had never had eyes in my heade. Thy
sighte is cleere inoughe, quoth the two. And the one said
to the other: Marke how well he openeth his eyes? And
how faire they be to looke to? And who wolde beleave
but he coulde see? The poore soule wept faster, and
cried God mercye. In conclusion they said unto him: See
thou make a vow to go divoutlye to our ladye of Loreto
barefoote and barelegged, for that is the best remedie
that may be had. And in the meane space we will goe to
Aquapendente and the other townes here about to seeke
for some Phisitien, and will helpe the in what we can.
Then did the seelie soule kneele upon his knees in the
bed, and wyth aboundance of teares and verie bitter
repentance for his blaspheminge, made a solemne vow
to go naked to our ladye of Loreto and to offre unto her
a paire of eyes of silver, and to eate no flesh upon the
Wenesdaye nor egges upon the Fridaye, and to faste
bread and water every Saturday in worship of our lady:
yf she give him the grace to receyve his sight again. The
two companions entringe into an other chamber,
lighted a candell, and came with the greatest laughter in
the world beefore this poore soule, who for all he was
rid of so great an anguish as you may thinke he had, yet
was he so astonied with his former feare, that he could
not onlye not laugh, but not once speake a woord, and
the two companions did nothinge elles but sturr him,
saiynge that he was bounde to perfourme all those
vowes, for that he had received the grace he asked.
[LXXXVII] Of the other kynde of Meerie Pranckes
whan a man deceyveth himselfe, I will give you none
other example, but what happened unto me my selfe
not longe sins. For this shroftide that is past, my Lordes
grace of Saint Peter ad Vincula,[168] which knoweth full

The greatest
pilgromage
in Italy.

Aquapen-
dente is a
towne of
the Popes
xii. miles
from Paglia.

Whan a man
deceiveth
himselfe.

well what a delite I have whan I am in maskerie to play
Meerie Pranckes with friers, havinge first given order as
he had divised the matter, cam upon a daye with my L.
of Aragon and certein other Cardinalles, to the windowes in the banckes, making wise to stande there to
see maskers passe to and fro, as the maner of Roome is. I
being in maskerie passed bye, and whan I behelde on the
one side of the streete a frier standinge (as it were) in a
studye with himselfe, I judged I had found that I sought
for, and furthwith rann to him, like a greedye hauke to
her preye, and whan I had asked him and he toulde me
who he was, I made semblant to knowe hym, and wyth
manye woordes beegane to make him beleave that the
marshall went about to seeke him for certein complaintes against him, and persuaded him to go with me
to the Chauncerye and there I would save him. The frier
dismayed and all tremblinge seemed as thoughe he wist
not what to do, and said that he doubted taking in case
he should go far from Saint Celso. Still I put him in good
comfort, and saide somuche to him that he leaped up
beehinde me, and then me thought my divise was fully
accomplished. And I beegane to ride my horse by and by
up and downe the merchauntes streete, which went
kicking and winsing. Imagine with your selves now
what a faire sight it was to beehould a frier on
horsebacke beehinde a masker, his garmentes fleeing
abrode and his head shaking to and fro, that a man
would have thought he had bine alwaies falling. With
this faire sight, the gentilmen beegane to hurle egges out
at the windowes,[169] and afterwarde all the bankers and
as many as were there, so that the haile never fell with a
more vyolence from the skye, then there fell egges out
from the windowes, whiche for the moste part came all
upon me. And I for that I was in maskerie* passed not
upon† the matter, and thought verilie that all the
laughinge had bine for the frier and not for me, and
upon this went sundrie times up and downe the Bankes
always with that furye of hell beehinde me. And
thoughe the frier (in maner) weepinge beesought me to
lett him goe downe and not to showe suche shame to the

---

* maskerie: carnival costume.
† passed not upon: did not think about.

weede, yet did the knave afterward privilie cause egges
to be given him by certein Lackayes sett there for the
nones, and makinge wise to greepe me harde for
fallynge,* squised them in my bosome, and many times
on my head, and otherwhile in my forehead, so that I
was foule arayed. Finally whan everie man was weerye
both of laughinge and throwing egges, he leaped downe
from behind me, and plucking his hood backward
showed me a great bushe of heare, and said: M.
Bernarde, I am a horse keaper in the stable at Saint Peter
ad Vincula, and am he that looketh to youre mulett.
Then wiste I not whyche prevayled moste in me, grief,
angre or shame. Yet for the lesse hurt I fled towarde my
lodgynge, and the nexte mornynge I durste not showe
my heade abrode. But the laughynge at that Meerie
Prancke dyd not endure the daye folowynge onelye, but
also lasteth (in a maner) until this daye.

[LXXXVIII] And so whan they had a whyle renewed
the laughinge at rehersynge this agayn, M. BERNARDE
proceaded. It is also a good and pleasant kinde of
Meerie Pranckes, from whens in like maner Jestes are
dirived, whan one beleaveth that a man will do a matter
which he will not in deede. As whan I was in an
Eveninge after supper uppon the bridge of Leo, and
goinge together with Cesar Boccadello sportinge one
with an other, we beegan to take houldfast the one of
the others armes, as though we wold have wrastled,
bicause then we perceyved no man about the bridge,
and beeing in this maner together, there came two
Frenchmen by, which seeing us thus striving, demaunded what the matter ment, and stayed to part us,
thinkinge we had bine at debate in good ernest. Then
said I incontinentlye: Helpe sirs, for this poore gentilman at certein times of the moone is frantike, and see
now how he striveth to cast himselfe of the bridge into
the river. Then did the two renn and layed hande upon
Cesar with me and helde him streict. And he (sayinge
alwayes that I was out of my witt) struggled the more to
winde himself out of their handes, and they greeped him
somuch the harder. At this the people assembled to

To feine the
doinge of a
matter.

---

* makinge wise to greepe me harde for fallynge: pretending to
hold on tight to me so as not to fall.

beehoulde our rufflinge together, and everie manne rann, and the more poore Cesar layed about him with his handes and feete (for he beegane nowe to enter into coler) the more resorte of people there was, and for the greate strength he put, they beleaved verelie that he woulde have leaped into the river, and therfore helde they him the streicter, so that a great thronge of people caried him to the ynn above grounde, all tourmoiled and without his cappe, pale for wrathe and shame that nothinge he spake coulde prevaile, partlye bicause those Frenchmen understood him not, and partly bicause I also cariynge him to the ynn did alwaies bewaile the poore soules ill lucke, that was so wexed out of his witt. [LXXXIX] Now (as we have saide) of Meerie Pranckes a man maye talke at large, but it sufficeth to repete that the places whens thei are dirived be the verie same whiche we have said of Jestes. As for examples, we have infinit whiche we see daylye: and emong the rest there are manye pleasant in the tales of Boccaccio, as those that Bruno and Buffalmacco played to their Calandrino, and to M. Symon:[170] and manie other of women, which in verie deede are wittie and pretie. I remember also I have knowen in my dayes manye that have bine meerilie disposed in this maner, and emonge the rest a Scholar in Padoa borne in Sicilia called Pontius,[171] which seeinge upon a time a man of the countrey have a coople of fatt capons, feininge himselfe to bye them, was at a point with him for the price, and bed him come wyth him to his lodginge, for beeside his price he woulde geve him somwhat to breake his fast withall. And so brought him to a place where was a styple that stoode by himself, alone severed from the Church, that a manne might goe rounde about him, and directlye over againste one of the foure sides of the styple was a lane. Here Pontius, whan he had first beethought himselfe what he had to doe, saide unto the man of the countrey: I have layd these Capons on a wager with a felowe of mine, who saith that this toure compaseth xl. foote, and I say no, and even as I met with thee I had bought this packthrid* to measure it, therefore beefore we go to my lodging I will trie which of us hath wonn

Giornat. viii.
Novel. iii.
Novell. v.
Novell. vi.
Novell. ix.
Giornat. ix.
Novell. iii.
Novell. v.

Pontius a scholar of Padoa.

---

* packthrid: string.

the wager. And in so saiynge he drewe the packthrid out of his sleeve, and put the one ende of it into the man of the countreys hand, and saide: Give here, and so tooke the Capons: and with the other ende he beegane to go about the bell toure, as though he would have measured it, making first the man of the countrey to stand still, and to houlde the packthrid directlye on the contrary side of the toure to that, that was at the head of the lane, where assone as he came, he drove a naile into the walle, to the which he tyed the packthrid, and leavynge it so, went his wayes without anye more a do downe the lane with the Capons. The man of the Countrey stoode still a good while, alwayes lookinge whan he wolde have done measuring. At length after he had said manie times, What do you so longe? he thought he woulde see, and founde that Pontius held not the line, but a naile that was driven into the walle, which onlye remayned for payment of his Capons. Of this sort Pontius played manye Meerie Pranckes. And there have bine also manie other pleasaunt men in this maner, as Gonella, Meliolo, in those dayes, and now our frier Seraphin and frier Marian here and manye well knowen to you all.[172] And in verie deede this kinde is to be praysed in men that make profession of nothinge elles. But the Meerie Pranckes that the Courtier ought to use, must (by myne advyse) be somewhat wyde from immoderate jesting. He ought also to take heed that his Meerie Pranckes tourne not to pilferinge, as we see many naughti-packes,* that wander about the world with divers shiftes to gete money, feining now one matter, now an other. And that they be not to bitter, and above all that he have respect and reverence, aswell in this, as in all other thinges, to women, and especially where the staininge of their honestie shall consist.

Pilferinge.

Reverence
to women.

[XC] Then the L. GASPAR: Trulye, M. Bernarde (quoth he) you are to partiall to these women. And whie will you that men shoulde have more respecte to women then women to men? Set not you asmuch by your honestie, as they do by theirs? Thinke you then that women ought to nippe men both with woordes and mockes in every matter without any regarde, and men

* naughtipackes: wicked men.

shoulde stande with a flea in their eare, and thanke them for it?

M. BERNARDE answered: I say not the contrarye, but women in their Jestes and Meerie Pranckes ought to have the respectes to menne which we have spoken of. Yet I say with more libertie may they touch men of smalle honestie, then men maye them. And that bicause we oure selves have established for a lawe, that in us wanton lief is no vice, nor default, nor anye sclaunder, and in women it is so great a reproch and shame, that she that hath once an yll name, whether the report that goith of her be true or false, hathe loste her credit for ever. Therfore sins the talkinge of womens honestie is so daungerous a matter to offende them sore, I say that we oughte to touche them in other matters and refraine from this. For whan the Jest or Meerie Pranck nippeth to sore, it goith out of the boundes whiche we have alreadye said is fitt for a gentilman.

[XCI] Here M. Bernarde makinge a little stopp, the L. OCTAVIAN FREGOSO saide smylinge: My L. Gaspar can make you an answere to this law which you alleage that we oure selves have made, that yt is not perchaunce so **Women.** oute of reason, as you thynke. For sins women are moste unperfect creatures and of litle or no woorthynesse in respect of menne, it beehoved for that they were not apt to woorke any vertuous deede of them selves, that they should have a bridle put upon them with shame and feare of infamye, that shoulde (in maner) by force **Continencie.** bring into them some good condicion. And continency was thought more necessary in them, then any other, to have assuraunce of children. So that verie force hath driven men with all inventions, pollicies, and wayes possible to make women continent, and (in maner) graunted them in all thinges beeside to be of smalle woorthinesse, and to do the cleane contrarye alwaies to that they ought to do. Therfore sins it is lawfull for them to swarve out of the waye in all other thinges without blame, if we should touch them in those defaultes, wherin (as we have said) they are to be borne withall, and therfore are not unseemelye in them, and passe full litle upon it, we shoulde never move laughter. For you have alreadye said, that Laughter is provoked with certein thinges that are disagreeinge.*

* disagreeinge: incongruous.

[XCII] Then spake the DUTCHESSE: Speake you (my L. Octavian) of women thus, and then complaine that they love you not?

The L. OCTAVIAN answered: I complaine not of it, but rather I thanke them for it, sins in not lovinge of me, they bind not me to love them. Neither do I speake after mine owne opinion, but I say that the L. Gaspar might alleage these reasons.

M. BERNARDE said: Truly women should make a good bargayne, if they coulde make attonementes with suche two greate ennemies as you and the L. Gaspar be.

I am not their ennemye, answered the L. GASPAR, but you are an ennemye to menne. For in case you will not have women touched in this honesty of theirs, you ought aswell to appoynt them a lawe not to touche menne, in that whiche is asmuche shame to us, as incontinencye to women. And why was it not as meete for Alonso Carillo to make the answere which he gave maistres Boadilla of the hope that he had to save his lief, in that she wold take him to husband, as it was for her to say first: All that knew him thought the kinge wold have hanged him.[173] And whie was it not as lawefull for Richard Minutoli to beguile Philippellos wief, and to trane her to that bayne, as it was for Beatrice to make Egano her husbande arrise out of his bed, and Anichin to beeswadell him with a cudgell, after she had lyen a good space with him? And the other that tied the packthrid to her great toe, and made her owne husbande beleave that he was not hymselfe,* sins you saye those Meerie Pranckes of women in Boccaccio are so wittie and pretie.[174]

Boccaccio.
Giornat. iii.
Novell. vi.
Giornat. vii.
Novell. vii.
Giornat. vii.
Novel. viii.

[XCIII] Then said M. BERNARDE smiling: My lordes, forsomuch as my part hath bin to entreat onlie of Jestes, I entende not to passe my boundes therin, and I suppose I have already showed whie I judge it not meete to touch women neyther in woorde nor deede about their honestie, and I have also given them a rule not to nippe men where it greeveth them. But I saye that those Meerie pranckes and Jestes whiche you (my L. Gaspar) alleage, as that Alonso said unto M. Boadilla, althoughe

---

* he was not hymselfe. A mistranslation: the original was 'that she [i.e. the wife] was someone else'.

it somwhat touche honestie, yet doeth it not discontent me, bicause it is fett farr inoughe of,* and is so privie, that it may be simplye† understoode, so, that he might have dissembled the matter, and affirmed that he spake it not to that ende. He spake an other (in mine opinion) verie unseemlie, whiche was: Whan the Queene passed by M. Boadillas house, Alonso sawe peincted with coles all the gate over, suche kinde of dishonest‡ beastes, as are peincted about ynnes in such sundrie wise, and cumminge to the Countesse of Castagneto said unto her: See (madam) the heades of the wielde beastes that M. Boadilla killeth everie daye in huntinge. Marke you this, thoughe it were a wittie metaphor, and borowed of Hunters, that counte it a glorye to have manie wielde beastes heades nayled at their gates, yet is it dishonest and shamefull jestinge. Beeside that, it was not in answeringe, for an answere hath muche more courtesie in it, bicause it is thought that a manne is provoked to it, and it must needes be at a sodeine. But to retourn to our matter of the Meerie Pranckes of women, I say not that they do well to beeguile their husbandes: but I say that some of the deceites whiche Boccaccio recyteth of women, are pretie and wittie inough, and especiallye those you have spoken of your selfe. But in mine opinion the prancke that Richarde Minutoli wrought, doeth passe the boundes, and is muche more bitterer then that Beatrice wrought. For Richarde Minutoli tooke muche more from Philippellos wief, then did Beatrice from Egano her husbande: bicause Richarde with that privie pollicie enforced her, and made her to do of herself that she wolde not have done: and Beatrice deceyved her husbande to do of herself that she lusted.

[XCIV] Then saide the L. Gaspar: For no other cause can a manne excuse Beatrice but for love, whiche ought to be alowed aswell in men as in women.

Then answered M. Bernarde: Trulye the passions of love bringe with them a great excuse of everye fault, yet judge I (for my part) that a Gentilman that is in love,

---

* fett farr inoughe of: oblique enough.
† simplye: innocently.
‡ dishonest: obscene.

ought aswell in this point as in all other thynges, to be
voide of dissimulation, and of an upright meaninge.
And if it be true that it is such an abhominable profit
and trespace to use tradiment against a mans verie
ennemye: consider you how muche more haynous that
offence is againste a person whom a man loveth. And I
beleave ech honest lover susteyneth such peynes, such
watchinges, hasardeth himselfe in suche daungers,
droppeth so manie teares, useth so manie meanes and
wayes to please the woman whom he loveth, not
cheeflye to come bye her body, but to winn the fortresse
of that minde, to breake in peeces those most harde
Diamondes, to heate that colde yce, that lye manye
times in the tender brestes of these women. And this do I
beleave is the true and sounde pleasure, and the ende
wherto the entent of a noble courage is bent. And for my
part trulye (were I in love) I wold like it better to know
assuridlye that she whom I loved and served loved me
again with hert, and had bent her minde towarde me,
without receiving any other contentation, then to
enjoye her and to have my fill of her againste her owne
will, for in that case I shoulde thinke my selfe maister of
a deade carcase. Therfore suche as compase their
desires by the meane of these Meerie Pranckes, which
maye perhappes rather be termed Tradimentes* then
Meerie Pranckes, do injurye to other, and yet receyve
they not for all that the contentacion which a man
should wishe for in love, possessynge the bodie without
the will. The like I saye of certein other that in love
practise enchauntmentes, sorceries, and otherwhile
plaine force, sometime meanes† to cast them in sleepe
and suche like matters. And knowe for a sooth, that
gyftes also diminishe muche the pleasures of love,
bicause a man maie stand in doubt whether he be
beloved or no, but that the woman maketh a countenance to love him, to fare the better by him: therfore ye
see that the love of Ladies and great women is
esteamed, bicause it appeereth that it can arrise of none
other cause, but of perfect and true love, neyther is it to
be thoughte that a great Ladye wyll at anye tyme showe

Love without
dissimulation.

Tradiment
against one
beloved.

The true end
of lovers
desires.

Unhonest
lovers.

Gyftes in
love.

---

* Tradimentes: treacheries.
† meanes: potions.

to beare good will to her inferiour, onlesse she love him in verye deede.

[XCV] Then answered the L. GASPAR: I denie not that the entent, the peynes and daungers of lovers ought not principally to have their ende dyrected to the victorye rather of the minde then of the bodye of the woman beloved. But I saye that these deceytes whiche you in men terme Tradimentes, and in women Meerie prankes, are a verie good meane to come to this ende, bicause alwayes he that possesseth the bodie of women, is also maister of the mind. And if you beethinke you well, Philippellos wief after her great lamentatyon for the deceyt wrought her by Richard, knowinge howe muche more savourye the kysses of a lover were then her husbandes, tournynge her rigour into tender affection towarde Richarde, from that daye forwarde loved hym moste deerlye.[175] You maye perceive nowe that his continuall hauntinge, hys presentes, and hys so manye other tokens, whyche had bine so longe a proof of hys good will toward her, were not able to compasse that, that hys beeyinge with her a smalle while did. Nowe see this Meerie Prancke or Tradiment (howe ever you will terme it) was a good waye to wynn the fortresse of that minde.

Then M. BERNARDE: You (quoth he) make a surmise, which is most false, for in case women should alwayes give their minde to him that possesseth their body, there should be none found that wold not love their husbandes more then anye person in the worlde beesyde, where it is seene not to be so. But John Boccaccio was (as you be) without cause an ennemye to women.[176]

[XCVI] The L. GASPAR answered: I am no ennemye of theirs, but (to confesse the troth) fewe menne of woorthynesse there be that generally set any store by women, although otherwhile, to serve their tourne withall, they make wise to the contrarye.

Then answered M. BERNARDE: You doe not onelye injurye to women, but to all menne also that reverence them: notwithstandinge (as I have saide) I will not swarve from my first pourpose of Meerie Pranckes, and undertake suche an enterprise so harde, as is the defence of women against you, that are a valiant Champyon. Therfore I will ende this my communication, whyche perhappes hath byne lenger then needed, but oute of paraventure not so pleasaunt as you looked for. And syns I see the Ladyes so quyet and beare these injuries at youre handes so pacyentlye as they doe, I wyll hensefurth beleave that some parte of that which the L. Octavian hath spoken is true: namely that they passe not to be yll reported of in everye other matter, so theyr honesty be not touched.

Then a greate parte of the women there, for that the Dutchesse had beckened to them so to doe, arrose upon their feete, and ran all laughyng toward the L. Gaspar, as they wold have buffeted him and done as the wood women did to Orpheus,[177] saing continually: Now shall we see whether we passe to be yll spoken of or no.

Orpheus was torne in peeces with women.

[XCVII] Thus partlye for laughinge, and partlye for the risinge of everye one from his seate, yt seemed the sleepe that now beegane to enter into the eyes and heade of some of them departed.

But the L. GASPAR said: See I pray you where thei have not reason on their side, they will prevaile by plaine force, and so end the communication, gevinge us leave to depart with stripes.*

Then answered the L. EMILIA: No (quoth she) it shall not be so: for whan you perceyved M. Bernarde was weerie of his longe talke, you beegan to speake so muche yll of women, thinkinge you shoulde finde none to gainsaye you. But we will sett into the field a fresher knight that shall fight with you, bicause your offence shall not be so long unpunished. So tourninge her to the L. Julian that hitherto had said little, she said unto him: You are counted the protectour of the honour of women, therfore it is nowe hyghe time to showe that you come not by this name for nothinge, and in case ye have not bine woorthelye recompensed at anye time for this profession hitherto, nowe muste you thinke that in puttinge to flight so bitter an ennemy, you shall binde all women to you muche more, and so muche, that where they shall do nothinge elles but rewarde you, yet shall the bondage† still remaine freshe, and never cease to be recompensed.

* with stripes: the worse for wear.
† bondage: obligation, debt.

[XCVIII] Then answered the L. JULIAN: Me thinke (madam) you show great honour to your ennemy, and verie litle to youre defender: for undoubtedlye the L. Gaspar hath said nothing against women, but it hath bine fullye answered by M. Bernarde. And I beleave everye one of us knoweth, that it is meete the Courtier beare verie great reverence towarde women, and a discreete and courtiouse person ought never to touch their honestie neither in boord, nor in good earnest. Therfore to dispute of this so open a trueth, were (in maner) to put a doubt in manifest matters. I thinke wel that the L. Octavian passed his boundes somwhat in sayinge that women are most unperfect creatures and not apt to woorke anye vertuous deede, and of litle or no woorthinesse in respect of men. And bicause manie times credit is geven to men of great authority, although they speake not the full truth, and also whan they speake in boorde, the L. Gaspar hath suffered himselfe to be lead by the L. Octavians woordes to saye that Men of wisdome sett no store by them, which is most false. For I have knowen few

Men of worthines observe women.

men of woorthinesse at anye time that doe not love and observe women, the vertue and consequentlye the woorthinesse of whom I deeme not a jott inferiour to mens. Yet if we should come to this contention, the cause of women were lyke to quaile greatlie, bicause these Lordes have shaped a Courtier that is so excellent and of so manie divine qualities, that whoso hath the understanding to consider him to be such a one as he is, will imagin that the desertes of women can not attaine to that point. But in case the matter should be equally devided, we have first neede of so witty and eloquent a person as is Count Lewis and Sir Fridericke, to shape a gentilwoman of the Palaice with all perfections due to a woman, as they have shaped the Courtier with the perfections beelonging to a man. And then if he that defended their cause were anie thinge wittie and eloquent, I beleave (bicause the truth will be a helpe to him) he may plainlye showe that women are as full of vertues as men be.

The LADYE EMILIA answered: Nay, a great deale more, and that it is so you may see, vertue is the female, and vice the male.*

* The allusion is to the genders of the Italian words, *la virtù* and *il vizio*.

[XCIX] The L. GASPAR then laughed, and tourning him to M. Nicholas Phrisio: What is your judgement, Phrisio (quoth he)?

PHRISIO answered: I am sorie for the L. Julian that he is so seduced with the promises and flatteringe woordes of the L. Emilia to renn into an errour to speake the thinge whiche for hys sake I am ashamed of.

The L. EMILIA answered smilinge: You will sure be ashamed for your owne sake, whan you shall see the L. Gaspar after he is convicted, confesse his owne errour and yours to, and demaunde that pardon whiche we will not graunt him.

Then spake the DUTCHESSE: Bicause it is very late, I will we defar the wholl untill to morow, the more for that I thinke it well done we folow the L. Julians counsell, that beefore we come to this disputacion we maye have a gentilwoman of the Palaice so facioned in all perfections, as these Lordes have facioned the perfect Courtier.

Madam, quoth the L. EMILIA then, I pray God it fall not to oure lott to give this enterprise to anye confederate with the L. Gaspar, least he facion us for a gentilwoman of the Court, one that can do nought elles but looke to the kitchin and spinn.

Then saide PHRISIO: In deede that is an office fitt for herr.

Then the DUTCHESSE: I have a good hope in the L. Julian (quoth she) who will (for the good witt and judgement I knowe he is of) imagyn the greatest perfection that maye be wished in a woman, and in like maner expresse it well in woordes, and so shal we have somewhat to confounde the L. Gaspars false accusations withall.

[C] Madam, answered the L. JULIAN, I wote not whether youre divise be good or no to committ into my handes an enterprise of so great weight, for (to tell you the troth) I thinke not my selfe able inoughe. Neyther am I like the Count and Sir Fridericke, whiche with their eloquence have shaped suche a Courtier as never was, nor I beleave ever shalbe. Yet if your pleasure be so that I shall take this bourden upon me, let it be at the least with those condicions that the other have had before me: namely, that everie man, where he shall thinke good, maye replye against me, and this shall I recken not overthuartinge but aide, and perhappes in correctynge mine erroures we shall finde the perfection of a gentilwoman of the Palaice whiche we seeke for.

I trust, answered the DUTCHESSE, your talke shall be such, that litle may be saide against you. Therfore settle your minde to thynke upon onlie this and facion us suche a Gentilwoman that these our adversaries maye be ashamed to say, that she is not equall with the Courtier in vertue: of whom it shall be well done Sir Friderick speake no more, for he hath but to well sett him furth, especiallye sins we must compare a woman to him.

I have (madam) answered SIR FRIDERICK, litle or nothinge now left to speake of the Courtier, and that I did thinke upon, M. Bernardes Jestes have made me forgete.

If it be so, quoth the DUTCHESSE, assembling together to morow beetimes, we shal have leiser to accomplish both the one and the other. And whan she had so said, they arrose all upon their feete, and takynge their leave reverentlye of the Dutchesse everye man withdrue him to his lodging.

THE THIRDE BOOKE

OF THE COURTYER OF COUNT

BALDESSAR CASTILIO

UNTO MAISTER

ALPHONSUS ARIOSTO

Englisshed at the request of
the Ladye Marquesse of Northampton
in anno 1551

THE THIRDE BOOKE

[I] It is read that Pithagoras verie wittilye and after a suttill maner found out the measure of Hercules bodye, in that he knewe that the space where everye fyve yeeres they kept the games or prices of Olympicus in Achaia nigh unto Elis beefore Jupiter Olympicus Temple, was measured by Hercules himselfe: and appointed a furlonge of grounde there of sixe hundreth and five and twentie of his owne feete: and the other furlonges whiche after his time were caste oute in diverse partes of Greece by his successors, were also of sixe hundreth and five and twentie of their feete, but for all that somewhat shorter then his. Pythagoras knewe furthwith by that proportion how muche Hercules foote was bigger then all other mens feete, and so the measure of his foote once knowen, he gathered that all Hercules bodye proporcionally in greatnesse exceaded all other mens, so muche, as that furlonge, all other furlonges.[178] You may then (gentle M. Alphonsus) by the verie same reason easlie gather by this least parte of all the rest of the bodye, how farr the Court of Urbin excelled all the other in Italy. For if the sportes and pastymes (that are used to none other end but to refresh the werisome mindes after earnest labours) far passed all such as are commonly used in the other Courtes of Italy: what (gesse you) were al the other vertuous practises, wherunto al men had their mindes bent and were full and wholly addicted. And of this I may be boulde to make my vaunt, nothing mistrusting but to be credited therin, consideringe I goe not about to praise so auntient antiquities wherin I might, if I were disposed, feine what I lusted:* but of this I speake, I am able to bring furth manie men of woorthy credence, for sufficient triall, whiche as yet are in lief and have themselves seene and marked well the livinge and conversation of such as in times past excelled in that Court. And I reckon my selfe

Pisis. ad Jovem Olimpicum.

Plin. lib. ii. cap. xxiii. *De natur. histor.*

The Court of Urbin.

* feine what I lusted: invent just what I chose.

bounde (for that lyeth in me to do) to stretch furth my force with all diligence to defende this famous memorie from mortall oblivion, and with my penn to make it live in the mindes of oure posteritie, wherby perhappes in time to come there shall not want that will envie this our time. For there is no manne that readeth of the wonderfull families of times past, but in his mind he conceyveth a certein greater opinion of them that are written upon, then it appeereth those bookes can expresse though they have bine written with perfection: even so do we consider that all the readers of this our travayle (if at the least wise it shall deserve so much favour, that it may come to the sight of noble men and vertuous Ladies) will cast in their minde and thinke for a surety, that the Court of Urbin hath bine muche more excellent and better fournished with notable men, then we are able to expresse in writinge. And in case so much eloquence were in me, as there was prowesse in them, I should nede none other testimonie to make such give full credence to my woordes, as have not seene it.

[II] Whan therfore the companye was assembled in the accustomed place the day folowinge at the due hour, and set with silence, everye man tourned his eyes to Sir Fridericke and to the L. Julian, waytinge whan the one of them would beegine to speake his minde.

Wherfore the DUTCHESSE, after she had bine still a while: My L. Julian (quoth she) every mans desire is to see this your Gentilwoman well set furthe, and if you showe us her not in such maner, that all her beawties maye be discerned, we will suspect that you are jealous over her.

The L. JULIAN answered: Madam, if I reckened her beawtifull, I woulde show you her without any other setting furth, and in suche wise as Paris did beehoulde the three Goddesses.[179] But in case these Ladies be not a helpe to me to trim her (who can do it right well) I doubt me, that not onlye the L. Gaspar and Phrisio, but all the other Lordes here shall have a just cause to speake yll of her. Therfore sins she is yet in some part deemed beawtifull, perhappes it shall be better to kepe her close and see what Sir Friderick hath yet beehind to speake of the Courtier, which (no doubt) is muche more beawtifull then my woman can be.

Minerva.
Juno.
Venus.

That I had in minde, answered SIR FRIDERICKE, is not so necessary for the Courtier, but it may be left out, and no hurt done: yea, it is a contrarye* matter almost to that hitherto hath bine reasoned of.

And what matter is it then? quoth the DUTCHESSE.

SIR FRIDERICKE answered: I was pourposed, in what I coulde, to declare the causes of these companies and ordres of knightes brought up by great Princis under diverse standardes, as is that of Saint Michael in the house of Fraunce, the order of the Garter under the title of Saint George in the house of Englande, the Golden Flice in the house of Burgony,[180] and how these dignities be geven, and in what sort thei that deserve are disgraded from them, how they first came up, who were the founders of them, and to what ende they were ordeined, bicause we see that these knightes in great Courtes are alwayes highlye esteamed. I minded also, if time had suffised me, beside the diversitie of maners used in the Courtes of christian Princes in feasting and appeeringe in open showes, to speake somewhat also of the great Turkes: but much more particularlye of the Sophyes kinge of Persia:[181] for whan I understood by merchaunt men a longe time trafficked in that countrey, the noble men there to be very ful of prowesse and well manered and use in their conversation one with an other, and in womens service, and in all their practisinges much courtesie and great sobrietie, and whan time serveth, in marciall feates, in sportinges, and undertaking enterprises much sumptuousnes, great liberality and braverie, I delited to knowe what order they take in these thinges which they sett most store by, wherin their Pompes consist and braveries of garmentes and armour, wherin they differ from us, and wherin we agree, what kinde of enterteinment their women use, and with what sober mode† they showe favour to who so is in their love service: but to say the truth, it is no fitt time nowe to entre into this talke, especiallye sins there is other to be said, and much more to our pourpose then this.

[III] Yes, quoth the L. GASPAR, both this and many

Marginal notes: Order of S. Michael. Of the Garter. Of the Golden Flise.

Marginal notes: Great Turke. The Sophy.

---

* contrarye: different.
† sober mode: modesty.

other thinges be more to the pourpose, then to facion this gentilwoman of the Palaice, forsomuche as the verie same rules that are given for the Courtier, serve also for the woman, for aswell ought she to have respect to times and places and to observe (asmuche as her weaknesse is able to beare) all the other properties that have bin somuch reasoned upon, as the Courtier. And therfore in steade of this, it were not perhappes amisse to teach some particular pointes that beelong to the service about a Princis person, for no doubt the Courtier ought to know them and to have a grace in doing them. Or els to speake of the way that he ought to take in the bodily exercises, how to ride, to handle weapon, and wrastle, and wherin consisteth the hardnes of these feates.

Then spake the DUTCHESSE, smiling: Princis are not served about their persons with so excellent a Courtier as this is. As for the exercises of bodye and strength and slightnes* of person, we will leave them for M. Peter Mount here to take charge to teache them whan he shall thinke most meete, for presently the L. Julian hath nothinge elles to speake of, but of this woman, whom (me thinke) you nowe beegine to have a feare of, therfore woulde brynge us oute of oure pourpose.

PHRISIO answered: Certein it is, that nowe it is needlesse and out of pourpose to talke of women, especially beeinge yet beehinde somwhat to be spoken of the Courtier, for the one matter ought not to be mingled with the other.

You are in a great errour, answered the L. CESAR GONZAGA, for like as no Court, how great ever it be, can have any sightlinesse, or brightnesse in it, or mirth without women, nor anie Courtier can be gratious, pleasant or hardye, nor at anye time undertake any galant enterprise of Chivalrye onlesse he be stirred wyth the conversacion and wyth the love and contentacion of women, even so in like case the Courtiers talke is most unperfect ever more, if the entercourse of women give them not a part of the grace wherwithall they make perfect and decke out their playing the Courtier.

* slightnes: agility.

The L. OCTAVIAN laughed and saide: Beehoulde a peece of the bayte that bringeth men out of their wittes.

[IV] Then the L. JULIAN tourning him to the Dutchesse: Madam (quoth he) sins it is so youre pleasure, I will speake that commeth to minde, but with verie great doubt to satisfie. And iwisse a great deale lesse peine it were for me to facion a lady that should deserve to be Queene of the world, then a perfect gentilwoman of the Court, for of herr I wote not where to fett any pattern, but for a Queene I should not neede to seeke farr, and sufficient it were for me onlye to imagin the heavenly condicions of a lady whom I know, and through seeynge them, direct all my thoughtes to expresse plainlye with woordes the thynge that manye see with their eyes, and where I could do no more, yet should I fulfill my dutie in naminge her.

Then said the DUTCHESSE: Passe not your boundes (my L. Julian) but minde the order taken, and facion the gentilwoman of the Palaice, that this so woorthie a maistresse maye have hym* that shall woorthelie serve her.

The L. JULIAN proceaded: For a proof therfore (Madam) that your commaundement may drive me to assaye to do, yea the thinge I have no skill in, I shall speake of this excellent woman, as I woulde have her. And whan I have facioned her after my minde, and can afterwarde gete none other, I will take her as mine owne, after the example of Pigmalion.[182] And where as the L. Gaspar hath said, that the verye same rules that are given for the Courtier, serve also for the woman, I am of a contrarye opinion. For albeit some qualities are commune and necessarye aswell for the woman as the man, yet are there some other more meeter for the woman then for the man, and some again meete for the man, that she ought in no wise to meddle withall. The verie same I saye of the exercises of the bodye. But principally in her facions, maners, woordes, gestures and conversation (me thinke) the woman ought to be muche unlike the man. For right as it is seemlye for him to showe a certein manlinesse full and steadye, so doeth it well in a woman to have a tendernes, soft and milde,

*Ovid. lib. xiii.
Metam.*

Wherin the woman should differ from the man.

* hym: her.

with a kinde of womanlie sweetnes in everye gesture of herres, that in goyng, standinge and speakinge what ever she lusteth, may alwayes make her appeere a woman without anye likenes of man. Adding therfore this principle to the rules that these Lordes have taught the Courtier, I thinke well, she maye serve her tourne with manye of them, and be endowed with verye good

In what they agree.

qualities, as the L. Gaspar saith. For many vertues of the minde I recken be as necessary for a woman, as for a man. Likewise noblenesse of birth, avoidinge Affectation or curiositie, to have a good grace of nature in all her doinges, to be of good condicyons, wyttye, foreseeyng, not haughtie, not envious, not yll tunged, not light, not contentious, not untowardlye, to have the knowleage to wynn and kepe the good wyll of her Ladye and of all others, to do well and with a good grace the exercises comely for women. Me thinke well

Beawtie.

beawty is more necessarie in her then in the Courtier, for (to saye the truth) there is a great lacke in the woman that wanteth beawtie. She ought also to be more circumspect and to take better heed that she give no occasion to be yll reported of, and so to beehave her selfe, that she be not onlye not spotted wyth anye fault, but not so much as with suspicion. Bicause a woman hath not so manye wayes to defende her selfe from sclaunderous reportes, as hath a man. But for somuch as Count Lewis hath verye particularly expressed the principall profession of the Courtier, and willeth it to be in Marsiall feates, me thinke also beehouffull to uttre (according to my judgement) what the Gentilwomans of the Palace ought to be: in which point whan I have throughlye satisfied, I shall thinke my self rid of the greatest part of my dutye. [V] Leaving therfore a part

Vertues of the minde.

Commune properties.

the vertues of the minde that ought to be commune to her with the Courtier, as wisdome, noblenes of courage, staidenesse,* and manie mo, and likewise the condicions that are meete for all women, as to be good and discreete, to have the understanding to order her husbandes gooddes and her house and children whan she is maried, and all those partes that beelonge to a

---

* wisdome, noblenes of courage, staidenesse: in more conventional terminology, 'prudence', 'magnanimity' and 'temperance'.

good huswief: I say that for her that liveth in Court, me thinke there beelongeth unto her above all other thinges, a certein sweetnesse in language that may delite, wherby she may gentlie entertein all kinde of men with talke woorth the hearynge and honest, and applyed to the time and place, and to the degree of the person she communeth withall: accompaniyng with sober and quiet maners and with the honestye* that must alwayes be a stay to all her deedes, a readie livelines of wit, wherby she may declare herselfe far wide from all dulnesse: but with such a kinde of goodnes, that she may be esteamed no lesse chaste, wise and courteise, then pleasant, feat conceited and sobre: and therfore must she kepe a certein meane very hard, and (in a maner) dirived of contrarie matters, and come just to certein limites, but not passe them. This woman ought not therfore (to make herself good and honest) be so skemish† and make wise to‡ abhorr both the companye and the talke (though somwhat of the wantonnest) if she be present, to gete her thens by and by,§ for a man may lightlye gesse that she feined to be so coye to hide that in herselfe, whiche she doubted others might come to the knowleage of: and such nice facions are alwaies hateful. Neither ought she again (to showe herself free and pleasant) speake wordes of dishonesty, nor use a certein familiaritye withoute measure and bridle, and facions to make men beleave that of her, that perhappes is not: but beeinge present at suche kinde of talke, she ought to geve the hearinge with a litle blushing and shamefastnes. Likewise to eschew one vice that I have seen reigne in many: namely, to speake and willingly to give ear to such as report ill of other women: for suche as in hearinge the dishonest bee-haviours of other women disclosed, are offended at the matter, and make wise not to credit and (in maner) to thinke it a wonder that a woman should lead an uncleane lief, they make proof that sins this fault seemeth unto them so foule a matter, they commit it

Sweetenesse
in language.

Livelinesse
of witt.

A meane.

Wanton
talke.

To much
familiaritye.

To speake
and give eare
to ill reportes
of other
women.

---

* honestye: chastity.
† skemish: prudish, squeamish.
‡ make wise to: make a show of.
§ gete her thens by and by: leave immediately.

not. But those that go alwaies harking out* the loves of others and disclose them so point by point, and with such joye, it seemeth that they envy the matter, and that their desire is to have all men know it, that the like may not be imputed to them for a trespace, and so they tourne it to certein laughters with a kind of gesture, wherby they make men to suspect at the verie same instant that they take great contentacion at it. And of this arriseth, that men although to their seeming they give diligent ear to it, for the most part conceive an ill opinion of them and have them in verye small reputation, and (to their weeninge) with these beehaviours are enticed to attempt them farther. And many times afterward they renn so farr at rovers,† that it purchaseth them worthely an yll name, and in conclusion are so litle regarded, that men passe not for their companie, but rather abhorr them. And contrariwise, there is no man so shameles and high minded,‡ but beareth a great reverence towarde them that be counted good and honest, bicause that gravitie tempered with knowleage and goodnes, is (as it were) a shield against the wanton pride and beastlines of saucy merchauntes.§ Wherfore it is seen that one woord, a laughter or a gesture of good will (how litle soever it be) of an honest woman, is more set by of every man, then al the toyes and wanton gestures of them that so lavishly show small shamefastnesse. And where they leade not in deede an uncleane lief, yet wyth those wanton countenaunces, babblinge, scornfulnesse, and suche scoffynge condicions they make men to thinke they do. [VI] And forsomuch as wordes that are not grounded upon some pithie foundacion, are vaine and childishe, the Gentilwoman of the Palaice, beeside her discreation to understand the condicion of him she talketh withall, to entertein him honestlye, must needes have a sight in manie thinges, and a judgemente in her communication to pike out such as be to pourpose for the condicion of him she talketh withall, and be heedefull that she speake

Honest women esteamed with all men.

Beehaviour in talke.

---

* harking out: prying into.
† renn so farr at rovers: reach such a point of shamelessness.
‡ high minded: insolent, louche.
§ saucy merchauntes: the insolent.

not otherwile where she wold not, woordes that may offende him. Let her beeware of praysing her selfe undiscreatly, or beeinge to tedious that she make him not weerie. Let her not go mingle with pleasant and laughing talke, matters of gravitie: nor yet with grave, Jestes and feat conceites. Let her not foolishlye take upon her to know that she knoweth not, but soberly seeke to be esteamed for that she knoweth, avoiding (as is saide) Curiositie in all thinges. In this maner shall she be indowed with good condicions, and the exercises of the body comlie for a woman shall she do with an exceading good grace, and her talke shall be plentuous and ful of wisdome, honesty, and pleasantnesse: and so shall she be not only beloved but reverenced of all men, and per-happes woorthie to be compared to this great Courtier, aswel for the qualities of the minde as of the bodye.

[VII] Whan the L. Julian had hitherto spoken, he helde his peace, and settled himselfe as thoughe he had made an ende of his talke.

Then said the L. GASPAR: No doubt (my L. Julian) but you have decked gaily out this Gentilwoman, and made her of an excellent condicion: yet me seemeth that you have gone generallye inough to woorke, and named in her certein thinges so great, that I thinke in my minde you are ashamed to expounde them, and have rather wished them in her, after the maner of them that somtime wishe for thinges unpossible and above nature, then taught them. Therfore woulde I that you declared unto us a little better, what exercises of the bodye are meete for a Gentilwoman of the Palaice, and in what sorte* she ought to entertein, and what those many thinges be whiche you saye she ought to have a sight in: and whether wisedome, noblenesse of courage, staidnesse and those manye other vertues that you have spoken of, your meaninge is should helpe her about the overseeinge onlie of her house, children and hous-houlde (the which neverthelesse you will not have her principall profession) or els to entertein, and to do these exercises of the body with a good grace: and in good felowship take heede ye put not these seelie† vertues to

Curiositie.

* in what sorte: how.
† seelie: poor.

so vyle an occupation that they may be ashamed of it.

The L. JULIAN laughed and said: You can not chouse (my L. Gaspar) but still you must uttre youre yll stomake againste women. But certes me thought I had spoken sufficient, and especiallie beefore such audience, that I beleave none here, but understandeth concernynge the exercises of the body, that it is not comlye for a woman to practise feates of armes, ridinge, playinge at tenise, wrastling, and manye other thynges that beelonge to men.

Then said UNICO ARETINO: Emonge them of olde time the maner was that women wrastled naked with men,[183] but we have lost this good custome together with manye mo.

The L. CESAR GONZAGA replied to this: And in my time I have seene woman playe at tenise, practise feates of armes, ride, hunt, and do (in a maner) all the exercises beeside, that a gentilman can do.

[VIII] The L. JULIAN answered: Sins I may facion this woman after my minde, I will not onelye have her not to practise these manlie exercises so sturdie and boisterous, but also even those that are meete for a woman, I will have her to do them with heedefulnesse and with the soft mildenesse that we have said is comelie for her.

Daunsing.
Singinge.
Speculation
of musike.
Instrumentes
of musike.

And therfore in daunsynge I would not see her use to swift and violent trickes, nor yet in singinge or playinge upon instrumentes those harde and often divisions* that declare more counninge then sweetenesse. Likewise the instrumentes of musike which she useth (in mine opinion) ought to be fitt for this pourpose. Imagin with your selfe what an unsightly matter it were to see a woman play upon a tabour or drumm, or blowe in a flute or trompet, or anye like instrumente: and this bicause the boisterousnesse of them doeth both cover and take away that sweete mildenes which setteth so furth everie deede that a woman doeth. Therfore whan

How she
should come
to showe her
feates.

she commeth to daunse, or to show any kinde of musike, she ought to be brought to it with suffringe her self somewhat to be prayed, and with a certein bashfulnes, that may declare the noble shamefastnes that is contrarye to headinesse. She ought also to frame her

* harde and often divisions: frequent and dramatic dynamic contrasts.

garmentes to this entent, and so to apparaile herself that
she appeere not fonde* and light. But forsomuch as it is
lefull and necessary for women to sett more by their
beawty then men, and sundrie kindes of beawtie there
are, thys woman ought to have a judgement to knowe
what maner garmentes set her best out, and be most fitt
for the exercises that she entendeth to undertake at that
instant, and with them to arraye herselfe. And where
she perceyveth in her a sightlye and cheerfull beawtye,
she ought to farther it with gestures, wordes and
apparaile, that all may betoken mirth. In like case an
other that feeleth herself of a milde and grave disposition, she ought also to accompany it with facions of
the like sort, to encrease that that is the gift of nature. In
like maner where she is somwhat fatter or leaner then
reasonable sise, or wanner, or browner, to helpe it with
garmentes, but feiningly asmuch as she can possible,
and keapinge herselfe clenlye and handsome, showe
alwaies that she bestoweth no pein nor diligence at all
about it. [IX] And bicause the L. Gaspar doeth also aske
what these manye thinges be she ought to have a sight
in, and howe to entertein, and whether the vertues
ought to be applyed to this enterteinment, I saye that I
will have her to understande that these Lordes have
wylled the Courtier to knowe: and in those exercises
that we have saide are not comelye for her, I will at the
least she have that judgement, that men can have of the
thinges which they practise not, and this to have
knowleage to praise and make of Gentilmen more and
lesse accordinge to their desertes. And to make a breef
rehersall in fewe woordes of that is alreadye saide, I
will that this woman have a sight in letters, in musike, in
drawinge or peinctinge, and skilfull in daunsinge, and
in divising sportes and pastimes, accompaniynge with
that discreete sobermode† and with the givinge a good
opinion of herselfe, the other principles also that have
bine taught the Courtier. And thus in conversation, in
laughing, in sporting, in jestinge, finally in every thinge
she shall be had in very great price, and shall entertein
accordingly both with Jestes and feat conceites meete

Garmentes.

Beawtie.

A judgement
in exercises
not meete for
her.

Qualities for
a Gentil-
woman.

* fonde: foolish.
† sobermode: modesty.

Vertues.

for her, everie person that commeth in her company. And albeit staidnes, noblenes of courage, temperance, strength of the minde, wisdome and the other vertues a man wold thinke beelonged not to entertein, yet will I have her endowed with them all, not somuch to entertein (although notwithstanding they may serve therto also) as to be vertuous: and these vertues to make her suche a one, that she may deserve to be esteamed, and al her doinges framed by them.

[X] I wonder then, quoth the L. GASPAR smilinge, sins you give women both letters, and staidnesse, and noblenesse of courage and temperance, ye will not have them also to beare rule in Cities and to make lawes, and to leade armies, and men to stand spinning in the kitchin.

The L. JULIAN answered in like maner smiling: Perhappes to, this were not amisse, then he proceaded. Do you not know that Plato (which in deede was not very friendly to women) giveth them the overseeing of Cities, and all other marciall offices he appointeth to men?[184] Thinke you not there were manye to be found that could aswel skill in ruling Cities and armies, as men can? But I have not appointed them these offices, bicause I facion a waiting gentilwoman of the Court, not a queene. I se wel you wold covertly have up again the sclaunderous report that the L. Octavian gave women yesterday: namely, That they be moste unperfect creatures, and not apt to woorke anye vertuous deed, and of verie litle woorthiness and of no value in respet of men. But surelye both he and you should be in verie great errour if ye thought so.

[XI] Then saide the L. GASPAR: I wyll not have up again matters alreadye past, but you woulde faine presse me to speake some worde that might offende these Ladies mindes, to make them my foes, as you with flattringe them falselye will purchase their good will. But they are so wise above other, that they love trueth better (althoughe it make not so muche with them*) then false praises: neyther take they it in yll part for a man to saye, that Men are of a more woorthiness, and they will not lett† to confesse that you have spoken great wonders,

* althoughe it make not so muche with them: although it is not so flattering to them.
† let: fail, hesitate.

and appointed to the gentilwoman of the Palaice certein fonde unpossible matters, and so many vertues that Socrates and Cato and all the Philosophers in the worlde are nothinge to her. For to tell you the plaine trothe, I marveile you were not ashamed somuch to passe youre boundes, where it ought to have suffised ye to make this gentilwoman of the Palaice beawtifull, sober, honest, welspoken, and to have the understandinge to entertein without renninge in sclaunder, with daunsinge, musike, sportes, laughing, Jestes, and the other matters that we see daily used in Court: but to go about to give her the knowleage of all thinges in the worlde, and to appoint her the vertues that so syldome times are seene in men, yea and in them of old time, it is a matter that can neyther be held withall nor scantlye heard. Now that women are unperfect creatures and consequently of less woorthiness then men, and not apt to conceive those vertues that they are, I pourpose not to affirme it, bicause the prowesse of these Ladies were inough to make me a lyer. Yet this I saye unto you, that most wise men have left in writing, that nature, bicause she is alwaies set and bent to make thinges most perfect, if she coulde, woulde continuallye bring furth men, and whan a woman is borne, it is a slacknes or default of nature, and contrary to that she would do.[185] As it is also seene in one borne blinde, lame, or with some other impediment, and in trees manye frutes that never ripen: even so may a woman be said to be a creature brought furth at a chaunce and by happe, and that it is so, marke me the woorkes of the man and the woman, and by them make your proof of the perfection of ech of them. Howbeit sins these defaultes of women are the wite of nature that hath so brought them furthe, we ought not for this to hate them, nor feint in havinge lesse respect to them then is meete, but to esteame them above that they are, me thinketh a plaine errour.

A woman the default of nature.

[XII] The L. JULIAN looked the L. Gaspar would have proceaded on still, but whan he sawe nowe that he helde his peace, he said: Of the unperfectnes of women me thinke you have alleaged a verye cold reason, wherunto (albeit may happ it were not now meete to entre into these subtil pointes) I answere accordinge to the opinion of him that is of skill, and accordinge to the truth, that

Substantia non recipit maius aut minus.

Substance in what ever thinge it be, can not receive into it more or less: for as no stone can be more perfectlye a stone, then an other: as touchinge the beeinge of a stone: nor one blocke more perfectlie a blocke, then an other: no more can one man be more perfectlye a man then an other, and consequently the male kinde shall not be more perfect, then the female, as touchinge* his formall substance: for both the one and the other is conteined under the Species of *Homo*, and that wherein they differ is an accidentall matter and no essentiall. In case you will then tell me that the man is more perfecte then the woman, thoughe not as touchinge the essentiall, yet in the Accidentes, I answere that these accidentes must consist eyther in the bodye or in the minde: yf in the bodye, bicause the man is more sturdier, nimbler, lighter, and more abler to endure travaile, I say that this is an argument of smalle perfection: for emonge men themselves such as abounde in these qualities above other, are not for them the more esteamed: and in warr, where the greatest part of peinfull labours are and of strength, the stoutest are not for all that the moste set bye. Yf in the mind, I say, what ever thinges men can understande, the self same can women understande also: and where it perceth the capacitie of the one, it may in likewise perce the others. [XIII] Here after the L. Julian had made a litle stopp, he proceeded smilinge: Do you not know that this principle is helde in Philosophy, Who so is tender of flesh is apt of mind? Therfore there is no doubt, but women beeing tenderer of flesh, are also apter of minde, and of a more enclined witt to musinges and speculations, then men. Afterward he folowed on: But leaving this a part, bicause you said that I should make my proof of the perfection of ech of them by the woorkes, I saye unto you, if you consider the effectes of nature, you shall finde that she bringeth women furth as they be, not at a chaunce, but fittlye necessary for the ende. For albeit she shapeth them of bodye not stoute and of a milde minde, with manye other qualities contrarye to mens, yet doe the condicions of eche of them stretch unto one self ende, concerning the self same profit. For even as

Homo both man and woman.

* as touchinge: where . . . is concerned.

through that weake feeblenes women are of a lesser
courage, so are they also by the verye same more warie.
Therfore moothers nourish up children and fathers
instruct them, and with manlines provide for it abrode,
that they* with carefull diligence store up in the house,
which is no lesse praise. In case you wil then consider the
auntient Histories (albeit men at all times have bine verie
sparing in writinge the prayses of women)[186] and them of
latter dayes, ye shall finde that continually vertue hath
raigned aswell emong women as men: and that suche
there have bine also that have made warr and obteined
glorious victories, governed realmes with great wisdome
and justice, and done what ever men have done. As
touchinge sciences, do you not remember ye have read of
so manie that were well seene in Philosophie? Other, that
have bine most excellent in Poetrye? Other, that have
pleaded, and both accused and defended beefore Judges
most eloquentlye? Of handicraftes, longe it were to
reherse, neither is it needfull to make any rehersall therof.
If then in the essentiall substance the man is no more
perfect then the woman, nor yet in the Accidentes (and of
this beeside reason, the experiences are seene) I wote not
wherein this his perfection shoulde consist. [XIV] And
bicause you saide that Natures entent is alwaies to bring
furth thinges most perfect, and therfore if she could,
would alwayes bringe furth a man, and that the bringing a
woman furth is rather a default and slackenesse of nature,
then her entent, I answere you that this is ful and wholly to
be denied, neither can I see whie you maye saye that
nature entendeth not to bringe furth women, without
whom mankind can not be preserved, wherof nature
herself is more desirous then of anye thinge elles, bicause
through the meanes of this felowship of male and female
she bringeth furth children, that restore the received
benifites in their childhood to their fathers in their olde
dayes, in that they nourishe them: afterwarde they renue
them, in beegettinge them selves also other children, of
whom they looke in their old age to receive it, that beeing
yonge they beestowed uppon their fathers: whereby

Women have
acheved great
enterprises.
Women
learned.
In philo-
sophie.
In poetrie.
In Rheto-
ricke.

---

* with manlines provide for it abrode, that they: men, with
their strength, acquire wealth outside the home, which women
then . . .

nature (as it were) tourning her about in a circle, fulfilleth an everlastingnesse, and in this wise geveth an immortalitie to mortall men. Sins then to this, the woman is as needefull as the man, I can not discern for what cause the one is made by happ more then the other. Truth it is that Nature entendeth alwaies to bringe furth matters most perfect, and therfore meaneth to bring furth man in his kinde, but not more male then female. Yea were it so that she alwayes brought furth male, then shoulde it withoute peraventure be an unperfectnesse: for like as of the bodye and of the soule there arriseth a compounde more nobler then his partes, whiche is, man: even so of the felowshippe of male and female there arriseth a compounde preservinge mankinde, without which the partes were in decaye, and therfore male and female by nature are alwaies together, neither can the one be without the other: right so he ought not to be called the male, that hath not a female (accordinge to the definition of both the one and the other) nor she the female that hath not a male. And for somuch as one kinde alone betokeneth an imperfection, the divines of olde time referr both the one and the other to God: wherfore Orpheus said that Jupiter was both male and female:[187] and it is read in Scripture that God facioned male and female to his likeness. And the Poetes manie times speaking of the Goddes, meddle the kindes together.

Male can not be without female.

[XV] Then the L. GASPAR: I woulde not (quoth he) we should entre into these subtill pointes, for these women will not understande us. And albeit I answere you with verie good reasons, yet will they beleave, or at the leaste make wise to beleave that I am in the wrong, and furthwith will geve sentence as they lust. Yet sins we are entred into them, only this will I saye, that (as you know, it is the opinion of most wise men) the man is likened to the Fourme, the woman to the Mattier:[188] and therfore as the Fourme is perfecter then the Mattier, yea it giveth him his beeing, so is the man much more perfect then the woman. And I remember that I have heard (whan it was) that a greate Philosopher in certein Problemes of his saith: Whens commeth it that naturally the woman alwaies loveth the man, that hath bine the first to receive of her, amorous pleasures? And

Fourme.

Mattier.

Aristot.
i. *Physic.* xviii.

contrariwise the man hateth the woman that hath bine
the first to coople in that wise with him? and addinge
therto the cause, affirmeth it to be this: For that in this
act, the woman receyveth of the man perfection, and the
man of the woman imperfection: and therfore everie
man naturallye loveth the thinge that maketh him
perfect, and hateth that maketh him unperfect. And
beeside this a great argument of the perfection of the
man, and of the imperfection of the woman, is, that
generallye everye woman wisheth she were a man, by a
certein provocation of nature, that teacheth her to
wishe for her perfection.

[XVI] The L. JULIAN answered sodeinlye: The seelie
poore creatures wish not to be a man to make them
more perfect, but to have libertye, and to be ridd of the
rule that men have of their owne authoritie chalenged
over them. And the similitude which you give of the
Mattier and Fourme, is not alike in everye point:
bicause the woman is not made so perfect by the man, as
is the Mattier by the Fourme, for the Mattier receiveth
his beeinge of the Fourme, and can not stande without
it: yea the more Mattier Fourmes have, the more
imperfection they have withall, and severed from it, are
most perfect: but the woman receiveth not her beeinge
of the man, yea as she is made perfect by the man, so
doeth she also make him perfect: wherby both the one
and the other come together to beegete children: the
whyche thinge they can not do any of them by them
selves. The cause then of the continuall love of the
woman towarde the first that she hath bine with, and of
the hatred of the man towarde the first woman, I will
not affirme to be that youre Philosopher alleageth in his
Problemes, but I impute it to the surenesse and stable-
nesse of the woman, and waveringe of the man, and that
not without naturall reason: for sins the male is
naturallye hott, by that qualitie he taketh lightnesse,
stirring and unstedfastnes, and contrariwise the woman
throughe colde, quietnesse, steadie waightinesse, and
more earnest imprintinges.

[XVII] Then the L. EMILIA tourninge her to the L.
Julian: For love of God (quoth she) come once out of
these your Mattiers and Fourmes and males and
females, and speake so that you maye be understoode:

for we have heard and very well understoode the ill that the L. Octavian and the L. Gaspar have spoken of us: but sins we understande not nowe in what sort you stand in our defence, me thinke therfore that this is a straiynge from the pourpose, and a leavinge of the yvell imprintinge in everye mans minde that these our ennemies have given of us.

Give us not this name, answered the L. GASPAR, for more meter it were for the L. Julian, whiche in givinge women false prayses, declareth that there are none true for them.

The L. JULIAN saide then: Doubt ye not (madam) all shall be answered to. But I will not raile upon men so without reason, as they have done upon women. And if perchaunce there were any one here that meant to penn this our talke, I wolde not that in place where these Mattiers and Fourmes were understoode, the argumentes and reasons which the L. Gaspar alleageth against you shoulde be seene unanswered to.

I wote not, my L. Julian, quoth then the L. GASPAR, howe in this you can denie, that the man is not throughe his naturall qualities more perfect then the woman, whiche of complexion is colde and the man hott, and

Heat muche perfecter then colde.

muche more nobler and perfecter is heate then colde, bicause it is active and furth bringinge: and (as you know) the element* poureth downe here emonge us onlye heate, and not colde, which perceth not the woorkes of nature: and therfore beciuse women are colde of complexion, I thinke it is the cause of their feinthertednes and fearfulnesse.[189]

[XVIII] Will you still, answered the L. JULIAN, entre into subtill pointes? you shall perceive your self at everye time to come into a greater pecke of troubles:

Heate.

and that it is so, herken to. I graunt you, that heat in it self is more perfect then colde, but this foloweth not in meddled matters and compounded, for in case it were so, the body that were most hot should be most perfect: whiche is false, bicause temperate bodies be most perfect. I do you to weete moreover, that the woman is

Women cold of complexion.

of complexion colde in comparason of the man: which for overmuch heat is far wide from temper: but as

* the element: the heavens.

touching herself, she is temperate, or at the least neerer
to temper then the man, bicause she hath that moisture
within her of equall portion with the natural heat,
which in the man through overmuch drouth doth
sooner melt and consume away. She hath also suche a
kinde of colde that it resisteth and comforteth the
naturall heate, and maketh it neerer to temper, and in
the man overmuch heat doth soone bring the natural
warmth to the last degree, the which wanting nourishment, consumeth away: and therfore, bicause men in
generacion sooner waxe dry then women, it happeneth
oftentimes that they are of a shorter lief. Wherfore this
perfection may also be geven to women, that living
longer then men, they accomplish it, that is the entent of
nature more then men. Of the heat that the element
poureth downe upon us, we talke not nowe, bicause it is
diverse in signification to it whiche we entreat upon: the
which sins it is nourisher of all thinges under the sphere
of the moone aswell hott as colde, it can not be
contrarye to colde. But the fearfulnes in women
although it beetokeneth an imperfection, yet doth it
arrise of a praiswoorthie cause, namely the subtilnes
and readines of the spirites, that convey spedely the
shapes to the understanding, and therfore are they
soone out of pacience for* outward matters. Full well
shall you see many times some men, that dread neither
death nor any thing els, yet are they not for all that to be
called hardy, bicause they know not the daunger, and
goe furth like harbraines where they see the way open,
and cast no more with them selves, and this proceadeth
of a certein grosnes of the dulled spirites: therfore a
fond person can not be said to be stoutherted, but verie
courage in deede commeth of a propre advisement and
determined will so to doe, and to esteame more a mans
honestie and dutye, then all the perils in the worlde, and
althoughe he see none other waye but death, yet to be of
so quiet an hert and minde that his senses be not to seeke
nor amased, but do their duty in discoursing and
beethinkinge, even as though they were most in quiet.
Of this guise and maner we have seene and heardsay
many great men to be, likewise manie women, which

Why the
woman is
more tem-
perat then
the man.

Men sooner
drie then
women.

The perfec-
tion of women
above men.

Fearfulnesse
in women.

Heady
persons.

Courage.

---

* therfore are they soone out of pacience for: for this reason, they
are easily disturbed by.

both in olde time and presentlie have showed stoutenes of courage, and brought matters to passe in the world woorthie infinite praise, no lesse then menne have done.

[XIX] Then said PHRISIO: These matters beegan, whan the first woman in offending made others to offend also against God, and for inheritance left unto mankinde death, afflictions, sorowes, and all other miseries and calamityes, that be felt nowe adayes in the worlde.

Eve.

The L. JULIAN answered: Sins you will also farther youre pourpose with entringe into scripture, doe you not knowe that the same offence was in like maner amended by a woman? Whiche hath profited muche more then she hindred us, so that the trespace acquited with so woorthye a deede, is counted moste happye. But I pourpose not now to tell you, how much in dignitie all creatures of mankinde be inferiour to the virgin our Lady, for meddlinge holye matters with these our fonde reasoninges: nor reherse howe manye women with infinite stedfastnes have suffred cruell death under Tirannes for the name of Christ: nor them that with learninge in disputacion have confuted so manye Idolatrers. And in case you will answere me, that this was a miracle and the grace of the holy ghost, I say unto you that no vertue deserveth more praise, then that which is approved by the testimonie of God. Manye other also of whom there is no talke, you your self maye looke upon, especially in readinge Saint Hierom, which setteth out certein of his time with such wonderfull prayses, that they might suffise the holyest man that can be.[190] [XX] Imagin then how many there have bine of whom there is made no mention at all: bicause the seelie poore soules are kept close without the pompous pride to seeke a name of holinesse emong the people, that now a dayes many men have, accursed Hypochrites, which not minding, or rather setting smalle store bye, the doctrine of Christ, that willeth a man whan he fasteth, to annoint his face, that he maye appeere not to faste, and commaundeth prayer, almes deedes, and other good woorckes, to be done, not in the markett place, nor Sinagoges, but in secrete, so that the left hande knowe not of the right, they affirme no treasure in the world to be greater, then to give a good example, and

Our Lady.

S. Hierom.

Religious men.

thus hanging their head aside and fastning their eyes
upon the grounde, spreadinge a report about, that they
will not once speake to a woman, nor eate anye thinge
but raw herbes, smokye,* with their side garmentes all
to ragged and torne, they beeguile the simple: but for all
that, they absteine not from falsifiynge willes, sowinge
mortall hatred beetweene man and wief, and otherwhile poison: usinge sorcery, inchauntmentes and al
kinde of ribaldrie, and afterward alleage a certein
authoritie of their owne heade, that saith: *Si non caste,
tamen caute*, and with this weene to heale everye greate
sore, and with good reason to perswade hym that is not
heedefull that God forgiveth soone all offences how
heynous ever they be, so they be kept close and no ill
example arriseth of them. Thus with a veile of holinesse,
and this mischevous devise, manie times they tourne all
their thoughtes to defile the chaste minde of some
woman, often times to sowe variance beetweene
brethren, to governe states, to set up the one and plucke
downe the other, to chop of heades, to imprison and
banish menne, to be ministers of the wickednesse, and
(in a maner) the storers and hoorders up of the
robberies that many Princes commit. Other past shame
delite to seeme delicate and smothe, with their croune
minionlye† shaven, and well clad, and in their gate lift
up their garment to show their hose sit cleane, and the
handsomnesse of person in makinge courteisie. Other
use certein bye lookes and gestures even at masse,
whiche they houlde opinion beecome them wel, and
make men to beehoulde them: mischeevous and wicked
menne, and cleane voide not onlye of all religion but of
all good maner. And whan their naughty lief is laide to
them, they make a Jest at it, and give him a mocke that
telleth them of it, and (as it were) count their vises a
prayse.

Then said the L. Emilia: Suche delite you have to
speake yll of Friers, that ye are fallen into this talke
without all pourpose. But you commit a great offence to
murmur against religious persons, and without any
profit ye burden youre conscience: for were it not for them,

---

* smokye: filthy.
† minionlye: daintily.

that they pray unto God for us, we shoulde yet have far greater plages then we have.

Then laughed the L. JULIAN and said: Howe gessed you so even (Madam) that I spake of Friers, sins I named them not?[191] But forsooth this that I saye, is not called murmuringe, for I speake it plaine and openlye. And I meane not the good, but the bad and wicked, of whom I have not yet spoken the thousandeth part of that I know.

Speake you not now of Friers, answered the L. EMILIA: for I thinke it (for my part) a greevous offence to give eare to you, and for hearing you any more, I will gete me hens.

[XXI] I am well pleased, quoth the L. JULIAN, to speake no more of this. But to retourn to the prayses of women, I saye that the L. Gaspar shall not finde me out any notable man, but I will finde his wief or sister or daughter of like merite and otherwhile above him. Beeside that, manie have bine occasion of infinite goodnesse to their men, and sometime broken them of manye erroures. Therfore sins women are (as we have declared) naturallye as apt for the selfe same vertues, as men be, and the proof therof hath bine often seene, I wote not whye, in givinge them that is possible they maye have and sundrie times have had and still have, I ought to be* deemed to speake wonders, as the L. Gaspar hathe objected against me: consideringe that there have ever bine in the worlde and still are, women as nigh the woman of the Palaice whom I have facioned, as men nigh the man whom these Lordes have facioned.

Then said the L. GASPAR: Those reasons that have experience against them (in my minde) are not good. And ywisse, yf I shoulde happen to aske you what these great women are or have bine, so worthy praise, as the great men whose wives, sisters, or daughters they have bine, or that have bine occasion of anye goodnesse, or such as have broken them of their erroures, I beeleave it woulde combre you shreudlye.

[XXII] Surely, answered the L. JULIAN, none other thinge coulde combre me, but the multitude of them: and if time served me, I woulde tell you to this pourpose

Women not inferiour to men.

---

* I ought to be: I should be.

the Hystories of Octavia wief to Marcus Antonius and
sister to Augustus. Of Porcia daughter to Cato and wief
to Brutus. Of Caia Cecilia wief to Tarquinius Priscus.
Of Cornelia daughter to Scipio, and of infinite other,
which are most knowen.[192] And not onelye these of oure
Countrey, but also Barbariens, as that Alexandra
whiche was wief to Alexander Kinge of the Jewes,[193]
who after the death of her husbande, seeinge the people
in an uprore, and alreadye runn to weapon to slea the
two children whiche he had left beehinde hym, for a
revenge of the cruell and streict bondage that their
father had alwayes kept them in, she so beehaved
herselfe, that sodeinlye she asswaged that just furye,
and in a moment, with wisdome made those myndes
favourable to the children, whyche the father in manye
yeeres with infinit injuries had made their most
ennemies.

Tell us at the leaste, answered the L. EMILIA, howe
she dyd.

The L. JULIAN saide: She perceiving her children in so
great a jeopardye, immediatlye caused Alexanders
bodye to be caste oute into the middes of the markett
place: afterwarde calling unto her the Citizins, she said,
that she knewe their mindes were set on fire wyth moste
juste furye againste her husbande: for the cruell injuries
whiche he wickedlye had done them, deserved it: and
even as whan he lyved, she dyd her best alwayes to
withdrawe hym from so wicked a lief, so nowe she was
readie to make a triall therof, and to helpe them to
chastise him even deade, asmuch as she might, and
therfore should take that bodye of his and give it to be
devoured of Dogges, and rente it in peeces in the
cruellest maner they coulde imagin. But yet she desired
them to take pitye uppon the innocent chyldren, that
coulde not onelye be in no fault, but not so muche as
weettynge of their fathers yll doynges. Of such force
were these woordes, that the ragynge furye once
conceyved in all that peoples myndes was sodainlye
asswaged, and tourned into so tender an affection, that
not onelye with one accorde they chose those children
for their heades and rulers, but also to the deade corps
they gave a most honourable buryall.

Here the L. JULIAN made a little pause, afterwarde he

Octavia.
Porcia.
Cecilia.
Cornelia.

Alexandra.
Egesipp. lib. 1.
cap. 12.

*She asswaged
the furye of
the people.*

Laodice.

Harmonia.

Obstinacie
called sted-
fastnesse.

Epicharia.

Leena bitt in
sunder her
tunge and
spitt it in the
face of Hippias
the Tiran.
Plin. lib. 34.
cap. 8.

proceaded: Knowe you not that Mithridates wyef and
Systers showed a farre lesse feare of death, then
Mithridates him selfe? And Asdruballes wief, then
Asdrubal himselfe? Know you not that Harmonia
daughter to Hiero the Syracusan, woulde have died in
the burninge of her Countrye?[194]

Then Phrisio: Where obstinacye is bent,* no doubt
(quoth he) but otherwhile ye shall find some women
that will never chaunge pourpose, as she that coulde no
lenger call her husbande pricklouse, with her handes
made him a signe.[195]

[XXIII] The L. Julian laughed and said: Obstinacy
that is bent to a vertuous ende, ought to be called
stedfastnesse, as in Epicharia a libertine of Roome,
whiche made privie to a great conspiracie againste
Nero, was of such stedfastnesse, that beeinge rent with
all the most cruell tormentes that could be invented,
never uttred any of the partners: and in the like perill
manie noble gentilmen and Senatours fearfullye
accused brethren, friendes, and the deerest and best
beloved persons to them in the worlde.[196] What saye
you of this other, called Leena? In whose honoure the
Athenians dedicated before the castle gate a lionesse of
mettall without a tunge, to beetoken in her the steady
vertue of silence. For she beeinge in like sort made privie
to a conspiracye against the Tirannes, was not agast at
the death of two great men her friendes, and for all she
was torne with infinite and moste cruell tormentes,
never disclosed any of the conspiratours.[197]

Then saide the L. Margaret Gonzaga:[198] Me
seemeth that ye make to breef rehersall of these
vertuous actes done by women. For although these our
ennemies have heard them and read them, yet they
make wise not to knowe them, and would faine the
memorye of them were loste. But in case ye will doe us
to understande them, we will at the least honour them.

[XXIV] Then answered the L. Julian: With a good
will. Now wil I tell you of one, that did suche a deede as
I beeleave the L. Gaspar himself will confesse that verie
fewe menne doe. And beegane. In Massilia there was in
times past an usage, whiche is thought came out of

* bent: concerned.

Greece: and that was, that openlye there was poyson layed up meddled wyth Cicuta, and it was lefull for him to take it that alleaged to the Senate that he ought to be rid of his lief for some discommoditie that he felt therin, or elles for some other juste cause: to the entent that who so had suffered to much adversitie or tasted over great prosperitie, he might not continue in the one, or chaunge the other. In the presence therfore of Sextus Pompeius——

Cicuta a venimous herbe horrible of savour, one kinde wherof is supposed to be hemlocke.

Here PHRISIO not tariynge to have the L. Julian proceade farther: This, me seemeth (quoth he) is the beeginninge of some longe tale.

Then the L. JULIAN tourninge him to the L. Margaret, said: See, Phrisio will not suffre me to speake. I would have toulde you now of a woman, that after she had showed the Senate that she ought of right to die, glad and without any feare, tooke in the presence of Sextus Pompeius the poyson with such stedfastnesse of minde and with such wise and lovinge exhortations to hers, that Pompeius and all the rest that beeheld in a woman suche knowleage and stedinesse in the tremblinge passage of death, remayned (not without teares) astonied with great wonder.[199]

[XXV] Then the L. GASPAR smiling: And I again remember (quoth he) that I have read an Oration, wherin an unfortunate husband asketh leave of the Senate to die, and alleageth that he hath a just cause, for that he can not abide the continuall weerisomnes of his wives chattinge, and had leiffer drinke of that poison which you say was laied up openly for these respectes, then of his wives scoldinges.

The L. JULIAN answered: How many seelie poore women should have a just cause to aske leave to die, for abidinge, I will not say the yll woordes, but the most yvell deedes of their husbandes? For I know some my self, that in this worlde suffre the peines which are said to be in hell.

Bee there not againe, trow you, answered the L. GASPAR, manye husbandes that are so tourmented with their wives, that everye hour they wishe for death?

And what displeasure, quoth the L. JULIAN, can women doe their husbandes, that is so without remedy, as those are which husbandes do their wives? which though not for love, yet for feare are obedient to their husbandes.

Sure it is in deede, quoth the L. GASPAR, that the litle they do well otherwhile, commeth of feare, for fewe there are in the world that secretlye in their minde hate not their husbandes.

Nay, cleane contrarye, answered the L. JULIAN: and in case you will remembre what you have read, it is to be seene in all Histories, that alwaies (in a maner) wives love their husbandes better then they their wives. Whan have you ever seene or read that a husbande hath showed such a token of love towarde his wief, as did Camma towarde her husbande?[200]

I wote not, answered the L. GASPAR, what she was, nor what token she showed.

Nor I, quoth PHRISIO.

The L. JULIAN answered: Give eare. And you (my L. Margaret) looke ye beare it well awaye. [XXVI] This Camma was a most beawtifull yonge woman, indowed with suche modestie and honest condicions, that no lesse for them, then for her beawty she was to be wondred at: and above other thinges with all her hert she loved her husband, who had to name Synattus. It happened that an other Gentilman of greater authoritie then Synattus, and (in a maner) head ruler and Tirann of the Citie where they dwelled, fell in love with this yonge woman: and after he had longe attempted by all wayes and meanes to compasse her, and all but loste labour, beethinkinge himselfe that the love she bore her husbande, was the onlye cause that withstood his desires, he caused this Synattus to be slayne. Thus instant upon her afterwarde continuallye, other frute coulde he never gete of her, then what he had beefore. Wherfore this love daily encreasinge, he was fullye resolved to take her to wief, for all in degree she was muche inferiour to him. So suite beeinge made to her friendes by Sinoris (for so was the lover named) they tooke in hande to perswade her to be contented wyth it: declaring that to agree therto, was verye profitable, and to refuse it, perilous for her and them all. She after she had a while gainsaied them, at length made answere that she was contented. Her kinsfolke brought this tidinges to Sinoris, which passing measure glad, gave

Camma.

An example of the true love of a wief toward her husbande. Plutarc.

order to have this mariage made out of hande. After they were then both come for this pourpose solemnlye into the Temple of Diana, Camma had caused to be brought to her a certein sweet drinke whiche she had made, and so beefore the image of Diana in the presence of Sinoris she dranke the one moitie.* Afterwarde, with her owne hand (for this was the usage in mariages) she gave the remaine to the bridegrome, whiche dranke it cleane up. Camma assone as she sawe her device take effect, kneeled her downe verye joyfull before the image of Diana, and said: Oh Goddesse, thou that knowest the bottome of my hert, be a good witnesse to me, howe hardlye after my deere husbande deceased, I have refreined from killinge my selfe, and what peines I have susteined to endure the greef to live in this bitter lief, in whiche I have felt none other joye or pleasure, but the hope of the revenge whiche I perceyve nowe is come to effect. Therfore wyth gladnesse and contentation I go to finde out the sweete companye of that soule, whiche in lyef and death I have alwayes more loved then mine owne selfe. And thou Caytif, that weeneddest to have bine my husbande, in steade of a mariage bed, give ordre to prepare thee a grave, for of thee do I here make a sacrifice to the shadowe of Synattus. Synoris amased at these woordes, and alreadye feelynge the operation of the poyson within him that put him to great peine, proved many remedies, but all prevayled not. And Camma had fortune so favourable on her side, or what ever els, that beefore she died, she had knowleage that Sinoris was deade. Whan she hearde of that, with verye great contentation she layed her upon her bed, with her eyes to heaven, continuallye callynge upon the name of Synattus, and saying, Oh most sweete mate, sins nowe I have bestowed for the last tokens upon thy death, both teares and revenge, and perceive not that I have anye thinge yet beehinde to doe for thee here, I flee the world and this without thee a cruell lief, which for thy sake onlye in times past was deere to me. Come therefore and meete me (oh my Lorde) and embrace as willinglie this soule, as she willinglye commeth to thee. And speakinge these woordes, and with her armes spred, as thoughe

* moitie: half.

she woulde at that instant have embraced him, died. Say now Phrisio, what thinke you by this?

PHRISIO answered: Me thinke you woulde make these Ladies weepe. But let us sett case this was true, I say unto you that we finde no more such women in the worlde.

An other
example of
fressher
yeeres.

[XXVII] The L. JULIAN saide: Yes, that there be, and that it is so, give eare. In my dayes there was in Pisa a gentilman whose name was M. Thomas, of what house, I remember not, for all I heard my father often times tell it, which was his great friend. This M. Thomas then,

Thomaso
Lucchese.

passinge upon a daye in a litle vessell from Pisa towarde Sicilia about his affaires, was overtaken with certein foistes* of Moores, that were on the backe of him unawares and beefore the governours of the vessell had espied them. And for all the men within, defended them selves well, yet bicause they were but fewe and the ennemies manie, the vessell with as manie as were on borde was taken by the Moores, some hurt, some whole, as fell to their lotte, and emonge them M. Thomas, whiche had played the man and slaine with his owne hande a brother of one of the Capitaines of those foystes: for which matter the Capitain full of wrathe, as you maye conjecture by the losse of his brother, woulde have him for his prisoner, and beatinge and buffetinge him daily, brought him into Barbary, where in great misery he determined to kepe him alive his captive and with muche drugerye. All the rest, some one waye, some

M. Argentin.

an other, within a space were at libertye, and retourned home, and brought tidinges to his wief, called M. Argentin, and children, of the hard lief and great affliction which M. Thomas lived in, and was like without hope to live in continuallye, onlesse God wonderfullye helped him. The which matter whan she and they understoode for a certaintie, attemptinge certein other wayes for hys deliveraunce, and where he himselfe was fullye resolved to ende his lief, there happened a carefull affection and tender pitie so to quicken the witt and courage of a sonne of his called Paul, that he had respect to no kind of daunger, and determined eyther to die or to deliver his father. The

---

* foistes: pirate ships.

which matter he brought to passe and with suche privie
conveiaunce, that he* was first in Ligurno beefore it
was knowen in Barbarye that he was parted thens. Here
hens M. Thomas (beeinge arrived in safetye) writ to his
wief, and did her to weete his settinge at libertie, and
where he was, and how the next daye he hoped to see
her. The honest Gentilwoman filled with so great and
sodeine joye, that she shoulde so shortlye aswell
throughe the zeale as prowesse of her sonne, see her   Inordinate
husbande whom she loved so much, where she once   affection.
surelye beleaved never to have seen him again, after she
had read the letter she lifted her eyes to heaven and
calling upon the name of her husbande, fell starke dead
to the grounde, and with no remedie done to her, did the
departed soule retourn to the body again. A cruell sight,
and inoughe to temper the willes of men and to
withdrawe them from covetinge to ferventlye superfluous joyes.

[XXVIII] Then said PHRISIO smilinge: What know
you whether she died for sorowe or no, understanding
her husbande was comminge home?

The L. JULIAN answered: Bicause the rest of her lief
was nothinge agreeable therto.† But I weene rather the
soule could not tary the lingering to see him with the
eyes of her bodye, and therfore forsooke it, and drawen
out thens with covetinge, fled by and by where in
readinge the letter, her thought was fled.

The L. GASPAR said: It may be that this woman was
overloving, bicause women in everie thinge cleave
alwayes to the extremitie, which is yll. And see, for that
she was overloving she did yll to herselfe, to her
husbande and to her children, in whom she tourned into
bitternesse the pleasure of that daungerous and desired
libertie of his. Therfore you ought not to alleage her for
one of the women, that have bine the cause of so great
goodnesse.

The L. JULIAN answered: I alleage her for one of them
that make trial that‡ there are wives whiche love their

---

* he: i.e. the father.
† the rest of her lief was nothinge agreeable therto: that would
have been out of keeping with the rest of her life.
‡ make trial that: testify to the fact that.

husbandes. For of such as have bine occasion of great profittes in the world I coulde tell you of an infinite number, and reherse unto you so auntient, that welnighe a man wolde judge them fables. And of suche as emong men have bine the inventors of suche kinde of matters, that they have deserved to be deemed Goddesses, as, Pallas, Ceres, the Sybilles, by whose mouth God hath so oftentimes spoken and discovered to the world matters to come. And such as have taught verye great men, as, Aspasia, and Diotima the which also with sacrifice drove of a plague tenn yeeres that shoulde have fallen in Athens.[201] I coulde tell you of Nichostrata mother to Evander, whiche showed the Latins their letters. And of an other woman also that was maistres to Pindarus Liricus. And of Corinna and Sappho, which were most excellent in Poetrie:[202] but I wil not seeke matters so far of, I say unto you that leaving the rest apart, of the greatnes of Roome perhappes women were a no lesse cause then men.

This, quoth the L. GASPAR, were good to understande.

[XXIX] The L. JULIAN answered: Herken to it then.[203] After Troye was wonn, manye Trojans, that in so great a destruction escaped, fled some one way, some another: of whiche, one part, that by manye Sea stormes were tossed and tumbled, came into Italy in the coost where the Tever entreth into the Sea: so landing to provide for their necessaries, beegane to goe a forraginge about the Countrie. The women that taried beehinde in the shippes, imagined emonge themselves a profitable divise, that shoulde make an ende of their perilous and longe Seawandringe, and in steade of their lost Countrey recover them a new. And after they had layed their heades together, in the mens absence, they sett fire on the shippes, and the firste that beegane this woorke was called Roma. Yet standinge in feare of the mens displeasure that were retiringe backe again, they went to meete with them, and imbracing and kissing in token of good will, some their husbandes, some their next a kinn, they asswaged that first brunt: afterwarde they disclosed to them quietlye the cause of their wittie enterprise.* Wherfore the Trojans, on the one side, for

Marginal notes:

Aspasia loved and taught the eloquent Pericles Duke of Athens. Nichostrata. Hermione. Corinna. Sappho.

Women the cause of the greatnes of Roome.

Tiberis.

Roma.

---

* wittie enterprise: wise plan.

neede, and one the other for beeinge courteiouslye
receyved of the inhabitauntes, were very well pleased
with that the women had done, and there dwelled with
the Latins in the place where afterward was Roome.
And of this arrose the auntient custome emonge the
Romanes, that women meetinge their kinsfolke, kissed
them. Now ye see what a helpe these women were to
give the beeginninge to Roome. [XXX] And the Sabine
women were a no lesse helpe to the encrease of it, then
were the Trojane to the first beeginning:[204] for whan
Romulus had purchased him the generall hatred of al
his neighboures, for the ravine* that he made of their
women, he was assayled with warre on all sides, the
which for that he was a valiaunt man, he soone rid his
handes of with victorie: onlye the warr with the Sabines
excepted, which was verie sore, bicause Titus Tatius
kinge of the Sabines was verye puissant and wise.
Wherupon after a sore bickeringe beetweene the
Romanes and Sabines, with verie great losse on both
sides, preparynge for a freshe and cruell battaile, the
Sabine women clad in blacke, with their heare scattred
and haled, weepinge, comfortlesse, without feare of
weapons now bent to give the onsett, came into the
middes beetweene their fathers and husbandes, bee-
seachinge them not to file their handes with the bloode
of their fatherinlawes and sonninlawes, and in case it
were so that they repined at this aliaunce, thei should
bend their weapons against them: for much better it
were for them to die, then to live widowes or fatherles
and brotherlesse, and to remembre that their children
had bine begotten of such as had slaine their fathers, or
they them selves of such as had slaine their husbandes.
With these pitifull waylinges, manie of them caried in
their armes their yonge babes, of whom some beegane
alreadie to leuse their tunge and seemed to call and
sport with their graundfathers, unto whom the
women showinge furth their nephewes† and weeping,
said: Beehoulde youre owne bloode that in such rage ye
seeke to shed with youre owne handes. Of suche force
was in this case the affection and wisedome of the

An auntient
custome
emonge the
Romanes.

Women a
helpe to the
encrease of
Roome.

T. Tatius.

---

* ravine: abduction.
† nephewes: in the original, 'children'.

women, that there was not onlye concluded beetwene the two Kinges ennemies together, an indissoluble frendship and league, but also (which was a more wonderfull matter) the Sabines came to dwell in Roome, and of two peoples was made one, and so did this accorde much encrease the strength of Roome: thanked be the wise and couragious women whiche were so rewarded of Romulus, that partinge the people into thirtie bandes, gave them the names of the Sabine women.

30 curiæ.

[XXXI] Here the L. JULIAN pausinge a while, and perceyvinge that the L. Gaspar spake not: Trowe you not (quoth he) that these women were occasion of goodnes to their men, and helped to the greatnesse of Roome?

The L. GASPAR answered: No doubt, they were woorthie much praise. But in case you woulde aswell tell the faultes of women, as their well doinge, you woulde not have kept hid, that in this warr of T. Tatius a woman betrayed Roome, and taught the ennemies the waye to take the Capitolium, wherby the Romanes were welnighe all undone.[205]

Sp. Tarpeius daughter corrupted with money by T. Tatius.

The L. JULIAN answered: You mention me one ill woman, and I tell you of infinite good. And beeside the afore named, I coulde applye to my pourpose a thousand other examples of the profit done to Roome by women, and tell you whie there was once a Temple buylded to Venus armata, and an other to Venus calva,[206] and howe the feast of Handmaydens was instituted to Juno, bicause the Handmaidens once delivered Roome from the guiles of the ennemies.[207] But leavinge all these thinges a part, that couragious act for discoveringe the conspiracye of Catilina, for whiche Cicero is so praised, had it not cheeflye his beeginninge of a commune woman, which for this may be said to have bin the occasion of al the good that Cicero boasteth he did the commune weale of Roome?[208] And in case I had sufficient time, I would (may happe) showe you also that women have oftentimes corrected men of manye vices: but (I feare me) my talke hath alreadye bine overlong and combrous. Therfore sins I have accordinge to my pour fulfilled the charge that these Ladies have geven me, I meane to give place to him that

Venus armata.

Venus calva.

Fulvia.

shall speake more woorthier matters to be heard, then I can.

[XXXII] Then the L. EMILIA: Do you not deprive (quoth she) women of the true praises due unto them. And remember thoughe the L. Gaspar and perchaunce the L. Octavian to, heare you with noisomnesse, yet doe we and these other Lordes herken to you with pleasure.

Notwithstandinge the L. JULIAN woulde there have ended, but all the Lordes beegane to entreat him to speake. Wherfore he saide laughinge: Least I should provoke my L. Gaspar to be mine enemy any more then he is, I will but breefly tell you of certein that come into my minde, leavinge manye that I could recite unto you. Afterward he proceeded: Whan Philipp Demetrius sonne,[209] was about the Citie of Scio, and had layed siege to it, he caused to be proclaymed, that what ever bondemen woulde forsake the Citie and flee to him, he promised them liberty and their maisters wives. The spite of women for this so shamefull a proclimation was such, that they came to the walles with weapon, and fought so fierslye, that in a smalle time they drove Philipp awaye with shame and losse, which the men could not do. These selfe same women beeing with their husbandes, fathers and brethren that went into banishment, after they came into Leuconia, did a no lesse glorious act, then this was. For the Erythreans that were there with their federates, made warr against these Sciotis, which not able to houlde out, came to accorde with composition to depart onlye in their doblet and shirt out of the Citie. The women hearinge of this so shamefull a composition, were muche offended, revilinge them, that leavinge their weapons, they would issue out like naked men emonge their ennemies. And whan they made answere that it was alreadie so condicioned, they willed them to carye their shield and speare, and leave their clothes, and answere their ennemies that this was their arraye. And in so doinge by their womens counsell, they covered a greate part of the shame, which they coulde not cleane avoide. Likewise whan Cirus had discomfitted in battaile the armye of the Persians, as they rann awaye, in their fleeinge they mett with their women without the gates, who comminge to them, saide: Whither flee ye you cowardes? Entende

Philippus kinge of Macedonia sonne to Demetrius.

The stout hert of women.

ye perhappes to hide you in us from whens ye came? These and suche like woordes the men hearinge, and perceiving howe muche in courage they were inferiour to their women, were ashamed of themselves, and retourning backe again to their ennemies fought with them a freshe and gave them the overthrowe.

[XXXIII] Whan thc L. JULIAN had hitherto spoken, he stayed, and tourning him to the Dutchesse, said: Now (Madam) you will licence me to houlde my peace.

The L. GASPAR answered: It is time to houlde your peace, whan you knowe not what to saye more.

The L. JULIAN saide smiling: You provoke me so, that ye maye chaunce be occupied all night in hearing the praises of women. And ye shall understande of manye Spartane women that much rejoyced at the glorious death of their children: and of them that forsooke them or slue them with their owne handes whan they hard they used dastardlinesse.[210] Again how the Saguntine women in the destruction of their Countrey, tooke weapon in hand against Hanniballes souldiers. And how the armie of the Dutch men vanquished by Marius, their women not obteininge their suite to live free in Roome in service with the virgins vestalles, killed themselves everie one with their younge children. And a thousand mo that al auntient Histories are full of.

Then said the L. GASPAR: Tushe (my L. Julian) God woteth how these matters passed, for those times are so farr from us, that many lyes may be toulde, and none there is that can reprove them.

[XXXIV] The L. JULIAN said: In case you will measure in everye time the woorthinesse of women with mens, ye shall finde that they have never bine nor yet presently are any whit inferiour to men. For leavinge apart those so auntient, if ye come to the time whan the Gothes raigned in Italy, ye shall finde that there was a queene emong them Amalasunta that ruled a long while with marveilous wisdome. Afterward Theodolinda, queene of the Longobardes, of singuler vertue. Theodora Empresse of Greece. And in Italy emong manye other was a most singuler Lady the Countesse Matilda, whose praises I leave to be toulde of Count Lewis, bicause she was of his house.[211]

Nay, quoth the COUNT, it is youre part, for you

Amalasunta.
Theodolinda.

Theodora.
Countesse
Matilda.

knowe it is not meete that a man shoulde praise his owne.

The L. JULIAN continued on: And how many famous in times past finde you of this most noble house of Montefeltro? Howe manye of the house of Gonzaga, of Este and Pij? In case we will then speake of the time present, we shall not neede to seeke Examples farr fett, for we have them in the house. But I will not serve my pourpose with them whom we see in presence, least ye should seeme for courteisie to graunt me it, that in no wise ye can denye me. And to goe oute of Italye, remembre ye, in oure dayes we have seene Ann Frenche Queene a verye great Ladye, no lesse in vertue then in State: and if in justice and mildenesse, liberalitye and holynesse of lief, ye lust to compare her to the Kinges Charles and Lewis (whyche had bine wyef to bothe of them) you shall not finde her a jott inferiour to them.[212] Beehoulde the Ladye Margaret daughter to the Emperour Maximilian, whyche wyth great wysedome and justyce hitherto hath ruled and still doeth her State.[213] [XXXV] But omitting all other, tell me (my L. Gaspar) what kinge or what Prince hath there bine in our dayes, or yet many yeeres beefore in Christendome, that deserveth to be compared to Queene Isabel of Spaine?[214]

The L. GASPAR answered: Kinge Ferdinande her husbande.

The L. JULIAN saide: This will I not denie. For sins the Queene thought him a woorthie husbande for her and loved and observed him somuch, yt can not be said nay, but he deserved to be compared to her. And I thinke well the reputacion he gote by her was a no lesse dowerie then the kingdome of Castilia.

Nay, answered the L. GASPAR, I beleave rather of manie of kinge Ferdinandes actes Queene Isabel bore the praise.

Then saide the L. JULIAN: In case the people of Spaine, the Nobles, private persons, both men and women, poore and rich, be not al agreed together to lye in her praise, there hath not bine in our time in the world a more cleere example of true goodnesse, stoutnes of courage, wisdome, religion, honestie, courteisie, liberalitie, to be breef, of all vertue, then Queene Isabel.

Urbin.
Mantua.
Ferrara.

Ann French
Queene.

L. Margaret.

Isabel
Queene of
Spaine.

Praise of her.

And where the renoume of that Ladye in everie place and with all Nations is verye great, they that lived with her and were present at all her doinges, do all affirme this renoume to be spronge of her vertue and desertes. And whoso will waye her actes, shall soone perceive the truth to be so. For leavinge apart infinite thinges that make triall of this, and might be toulde, if it were our pourpose, everye man knoweth that in the first beginninge of her reigne, she founde the greatest part of Castilia possessed by great Astates:* yet recovered she the wholl again, so justly and in such sort that they dispossessed themselves continued in a great good affection, and were willing to make surrender of that they had in possession. It is also a most knowen thinge with what courage and wisedome she alwaies defended her realmes from most puissant ennemies. And likewise to her alone may be geven the honour of the glorious conquest of the kingdome of Granada,[215] whiche in so longe and sharpe a warr against stubborne ennemies, that fought for their livelode, for their lief, for their law, and to their weening in Goddes quarell, declared evermore with counsell and with her owne person somuch vertue and prowesse, as perhappes in oure time fewe Princis have had the stomake, not onlye to folowe her steppes, but to envie her. Beeside this, all that knewe her, report that there was in her suche a divine maner of government, that a man woulde have weened that her will onlye was almost inoughe to make everye man without any more businesse,† to do that he ought: so that scase durst a man in his owne home and in secrete commit any thinge that he suspected woulde displease her. And of this a great part was cause the wonderfull judgement which she had in knowinge and chousinge ministers meete for the offices she entended to place them in. And so well could she joigne the rigour of justice with the mildenesse of mercye and liberalitie, that there was no good person in her dayes that coulde complaine he had bine smallye rewarded, ne anye yll, to sore punisshed. Wherfore emonge her people toward

---

* Astates: i.e. great noblemen.
† without any more businesse: without her having to insist.

her, there sprange a verie great reverence dirived of love
and feare, which in all mens mindes remayneth still so
settled, that a man woulde thinke they looked that she
should beehoulde them from heaven, and there above
eyther praise or dyspraise them. And therfore with her
name, and with the wayes which she ordeined, those
Realmes are still ruled, in wise that albeit her lief
wanteth, yet her authoritie lyveth, like a whiele that
longe swynged about with violence,* keepeth the same
course a good while after of it self, though no man move
it anye more. Consider you beeside this (my L. Gaspar)
that in oure time all the great men of Spaine and
renowmed in what ever thinge, have bine made by
Queene Isabel. And the great Capitain Gonsalve   Ferdinando
Ferdinande was more setbye for it, then for all his   Gonsalvo.
famous victories and excellent and couragious actes,
that in peace and warr have made him so notable and
famous, that in case fame be not unkinde, she will for
ever spred abrode to the worlde his immortall prayses,
and make proof that in oure age we have had fewe
Kinges or great Princis, that by him have not bine
surmounted in noble courage, knowleage and all
vertue. [XXXVI] To retourn therfore to Italye, I saye
unto you that we have not wanted here also moste
excellent Ladies. For in Naples we have two Queenes,   Queenes
and not longe a go in Naples likewyse died the other   of Naples.
Queene of Hungarye, as excellent a Ladye as you
knowe anye, and to be compared well inoughe to the   Queen of
mightye and glorious kinge Mathew Corvin her   Hungary.
husbande.[216] Likewise the Dutchesse Isabell of Aragon
most woorthie sister to kinge Ferdinande of Naples,   Dut. Isabel
which as golde in the fire, so in the stormes of   of Aragon.
fortune
hath she showed her vertue and prowesse.[217] If you will
come into Lumbardy, you shall marke the Ladye Isabell
marquesse of Mantua, whose moste excellent vertues   Isabel Marq.
shoulde receyve great wronge in speakinge of them so   of Mantua.
temperatelye, as whoso will speake of them in this place
must be driven to do.[218] I am sorye moreover that you
all knew not the Dutchesse Beatrice of Millane her   Dut. Beatrice
sister, that you might never again wonder at a womans   of Millane.
wit.[219] And the Dutches Elionor of Aragon Dutches of   Dut. Elionor
                                                         of Ferrara.

* like a whiele that longe swynged about with violence: like a
wheel set in motion forcefully.

Ferrara, and mother to both these Ladies whom I have named, was suche a one, that her moste excellent vertues gave a good triall to all the worlde, that she was not onlye a woorthie daughter to a kinge, but also deserved to be a Queene over a farr greater State then all her auncestours possessed.[220] And to tell you of an other: Howe manie menne knowe you in the worlde, woulde abide the bitter strokes of fortune so pacientlye, as Queene Isabell of Naples hath done?[221] Whiche for all the losse of her kingdome, banishment and deathe of kinge Fridericke her husbande and two sonnes, and imprisonment of the Duke of Calabria her eldest, yet still showeth her selfe a Queene: and so beareth out the myserable inconveniences of wretched povertie, that every man maye see, thoughe she hath chaunged fortune, yet hathe she not altered condicion. I omitt the naminge unto you of infinite other great Ladies, and also women of lowe degre, as many Pisanes that in defence of their country against Florentines, have declared that noble courage without any feare of death, that the most invincible courages coulde doe that ever were in the worlde: wherfore certein of them have bine renowmed by many noble Poetes.[222] I coulde tell you of certein most excellent in letters, in musicke, in peinctinge, in carvinge, but I wil not any more go searching out emonge these examples, whiche are most knowen to you all. It sufficeth that if in youre myndes ye thinke upon women whom you youre selves knowe, it shall be no harde matter for you to understande, that they are not most commonlye in prowesse or woorthinesse inferiour to their fathers, brethren and husbandes: and that manye have bine occasion of goodnesse to menne, and manie times broken them of manye of their vices. And where presentlye there are not founde in the worlde those great Queenes that go to conquer farr Countreys, and make great buildinges, Piramides and Cities, as Thomiris Queene of Scithia, Artemisia, Zenobia, Semiramis, or Cleopatra,[223] no more are there also men like unto Cæsar, Alexander, Scipio, Lucullus, and the other noble Romane Capitanes.

[XXXVII] Say not so, answered then PHRISIO laughing, for presently there are more found like Cleopatra or

Queene Isabel
of Naples.

Pisanes.

Semiramis, then ever there were. And thoughe they have not so many states, poures and riches, yet there wanteth not in them good wil to counterfeit them at the least in giving themselves to pleasure, and satisfying al their lustes asmuche as they may.

The L. JULIAN said: You will ever Phrisio passe your boundes. But in case there be found some Cleopatres, there want not for them infinit Sardanapalles,[224] whiche is much woorse.

Make not this comparason, quoth the L. GASPAR then, I beleave not that men are so incontinent, as women be: and where they were so, yet shoulde it not be woorse. For of the incontinencye of women arrise infinite inconveniences, that do not of mens. And therfore (as it was well said yesterday) they have wisely ordeined that it may be lawfull for them to be out of the way without blame in all other thinges, that they maye applye their force to kepe them selves in this one vertue of chastitie, without the which children were uncertein, and the bonde that knitteth all the world together by bloode and by the love that naturallye ech man hath to that is borne him, shoulde be lewsed. Therfore a wanton lief in women is lesse to be borne withall then in men, that carie not their children nine monthes in their bodye.

[XXXVIII] Then answered the L. JULIAN: Doubtlesse these be pretie argumentes that ye make, I merveile you put them not in writinge. But tell me. For what cause is it ordeined that a wanton lief shoulde not be so shamefull a matter in men as in women? Consideringe if they be by nature more vertuous and of greater prowesse, they maye also the easelier kepe themselves in this vertue of continencie: and children should be no more nor lesse certein, for if women were geven to wanton living, so men were continent, and consented not to the wantonnesse of women, they emonge themselves and without anye other helpe could not beare children. But if you wil tel the troth, you your self know, that we have of our owne authority claymed a libertie, wherby we will have selfe same offences in us verye light and otherwhile woorthie praise, and in women not sufficientlye to be punished, but with a shamefull death, or at the least everlastinge sclaunder. Therfore sins this

These queenes gave themselves to all their appetites.

Sardanapalus a king in Assiria monstrous in all kinde of lecherie.

The wanton lief of men make women unchast.

Men have calenged a libertye.

opinion hath taken root, me thinketh it a meete matter to punish them in like maner sharpely, that with lyes bringe up a sclaunder upon women. And I beleave that everie worthie gentilman is bounde to defende alwaies with weapon, where neede requireth, the truth: and especially whan he knoweth any woman falslye reported of to be of litle honestie.

[XXXIX] And I, answered the L. GASPAR smilinge, do not onlye affirme to be everye worthye gentilmans dutye that you saye, but also take it for great courtesy and honestie to cover some offence that by mishappe or overmuch love a woman is renn into. And thus you may see that I am more on womens side, where reason beareth me oute, then you be. I denie not that men have taken a litle libertie, and that bicause they know by the commune opinion, that to them wanton living is not so sclaunderous as to women, which through the weakenes of their kinde, are muche more enclined to appetites, then men: and in case they absteine other-while from satisfiynge their lustes, they doe it for shame, not that will is not moste readye in them, and therfore have men layed uppon them feare of sclaunder for a bridle, to keepe them (in a maner) whether they will or no in this vertue, without the whiche (to saye the trothe) they were litle to be set bye: for the world hath no profit by women, but for gettinge of children. But the like is not of men, whiche governe Cities, armies, and doe so manye other waightye matters, the whiche (sins you will so have it) I will not dispute, how women coulde do, yt sufficeth they do it not. And whan it was meete for men to make triall of their continencie, aswell howe they passed women in this vertue, as in the rest, althoughe you graunt it not. And about this, will not I reherse unto you so many Histories or fables, as you have done, I remit you to the continencie onlie of two most mightie personages, youthfull and upon their victorye, whiche is wont to make haute* men of lowest degree.[225] And the one is, the great Alexander toward the most beawtiful women of Darius his ennemie and discomfited. The other, Scipio, unto whom beeinge xxiiii. yeeres of age, and havinge wonn by force a Citie

The conti- nencie of Alexander to- ward Darius wief and daughters. Q. Curt. lib. iii.

Carthago nova.

The conti- nency of

* haute: insolent.

in Spaine, there was brought a most beawtiful and noble Damisell taken emonge manye other. And whan Scipio understoode that she was affiansed to a Lorde of the Countrey, he did not only absteine from all dishonest act towarde her, but undefiled restored her to her husband and a large gift withall. I coulde tell you of Xenocrates, which was so continent, that a most beawtifull woman lyinge naked by his side and dalying with him and using all the wayes she coulde (in which matters she was verie well practised) she had never the pour to make him once showe the least signe of wantonnesse, for all she bestowed a wholl night about it. And of Pericles that did no more but heare one prayse with overmuche earnestnesse the well favourednesse of a boye, and he tooke him up sharplye for it.[226] And of manye other most continent of their owne free wil, and not for shame or feare of punishment, that compelleth the greatest part of women to kepe them selves upright in this vertue, whiche notwithstandinge deserve much praise withall: and whoso falselye bringeth up of them a sclaunderous report of uncleannesse of lyvinge, is worthie (as you have said) very sore punishment.

[XL] Then spake the L. CESAR whiche had helde his peace a good while: Judge you in what sort the L. Gaspar speaketh in the dispraise of women, whan these are the matters that he speaketh in their praise. But if the L. Julian will give me leave, that I maye in his steade answere him certein few matters, as touchinge where (in mine opinion) he hath falselye spoken against women, it shall be good for him and me bothe. For he shall rest him a while, and shall afterward the better go forwarde to speake of some other perfection of the Gentilwoman of the Palaice, and I shall have a good tourne that I have occasion to execute jointlye with him this dutie of a good knight, whiche is to defende the truth.

Mary I besche you, answered the L. JULIAN: for me thinke I have alreadye fulfilled accordinge to my poure, that I ought, and this communication nowe is out of the pourpose that I went about.

The L. CESAR then beegane: I will not nowe speake of the profit that the worlde hath by women beeside the bearinge of children, for it is well inoughe declared howe necessarye they be, not onlye to oure beeinge, but

Scipio toward a yong Ladye betrothed to Allucius a lord among the Celt-iberians.

Xenocrates.

Pericles re-prehended Sophocles for sayinge *O puerum pulchrum.*

also to oure well beeinge. But I saye (my L. Gaspar) that in case they be as you affirme more inclined to appetites, then men, and notwithstandinge absteine more then men (which you your selfe graunt) they are so much the more woorthie praise, as their kinde is lesse able to withstande naturall appetites. And if you saye they do it for shame, I can not see but for one vertue you give them two. For in case shame can doe more in them then appetite, and throughe it refraine from yll doynge, I esteame this shame (which in conclusion is nothinge els but feare of sclaunder) a moste sildome vertue and reigninge in verie fewe menne. And if I coulde without infinite reproche to menne, tell howe manye of them be drowned in unshamefastnesse and impudencye (whiche is the vice contrarie to this vertue) I shoulde infect these devoute eares that heare me. And for moste part these kinde of injurious persons both to God and nature, are menne wel stricken in yeeres, which professe some preesthoode, some Philosophye, some divinitie, and rule Commune weales with suche Catoes gravitie in countenance,[227] that it maketh an outwarde showe of all the honestye in the worlde, and alwaies alleage woman kinde to be most incontinent, where they at no time finde them selves more agreeved, then at the want of their naturall lustynesse, that they may satisfie their abominable desires, whiche still abide in the minde after nature hath taken them from their bodye, and therfore manye times finde oute wayes, where force preveyleth not. [XLI] But I will not tell farther. It suffyceth for my pourpose ye graunt that women absteine more from uncleane livinge, then menne. And sure it is, that they are not kept short with any other bridle, then what they put upon them selves. And that it is true, the moste part of them that be kept under with overstreict looking to, or beaten of their husbandes or fathers, are lesse chaste, then they that have some libertye. But generallye a great bridle to women, is the zeale of true vertue and the desire of good name, whyche manye that I have knowen in my dayes more esteame, then their owne lief. And in case you wil tell the troth, everie one of us hath seene most noble yonge menne, discreete, wise, of prowes and welfavoured, spend many yeeres in lovinge, sparinge for nothinge that might entice, tokens, suites, teares: to be short, whatsoever may be imagined, and all

Shame.

Injurious persons to God and nature.

Zeale of true vertue and good report.

but lost labour. And if it might not be tould me that my
condicions never deserved I shoulde be beloved, I
woulde alleage my self for a witnesse, which more then
once throughe the unchaungeable and overstedfaste
honestie of a woman was nighe deathes doore.

The L. GASPAR answered: Marveile you not therat,
for women that are suid to, always refuse to fulfill his
request that suith to them, but those that are not suid to,
sue to others.

[XLII] The L. CESAR said: I never knewe them that
have bine suid to by women, but manye there be that
perceivinge they have attempted in vaine and spent their
time fondlye, renn to this noble revenge, and saye that
they had plentie of the thinge whiche they did but caste
in their minde. And to their weeninge, to report yll and
to studye for inventions how to bringe up sclaunderous
tales of some woorthie gentilwoman, is a kinde of
Courtiers.* But these kinde of persons that knavishelye
make their vaunt of anye woman of price, be it true or
false, deserve very sore correction and punishment. And
if it be otherwhile bestowed upon them, it can not be
saide howe muche they are to be commended that do
this office. For in case they tell lyes, what mischiefe can
be greater then to take from a woorthy woman with
guile the thinge which she more esteameth then her lief?
And no other cause, but that ought to make her
renowmed with infinite prayses. If again, it be true they
say, what peine can suffice so trayterous a person, that
rendreth suche ingratitude in recompence to a Gentilwoman, whiche wonne with his false flattringes,
feigned teares, continuall suites, bewaylinges, craftes,
deceites, and perjuries hath suffred her selfe to be lead to
love overmuche, afterward without respect,† hath given
herselfe unheedfullie for a praye to so wycked a spirit?
But to answere you beeside to this wonderfull continencye of Alexander and Scipio which you have
alleaged, I saye, that I will not denie but eche of them
did a deede woorthie much praise. Notwithstandinge

Sclaunderous
persons of
womens
honesties.

---

* a kinde of Courtiers: there may be a word missing here. The
original has *cortegiania* ('courtiership' or 'courtlinesse').
† respect: reserve.

least ye should saye that in rehersinge to you auntient matters, I toulde you fables, I will alleage a woman of oure time of base degree, who notwithstanding showed a farr greater continency then anye of these two great astates. [XLIII] I say unto you therfore that I knewe once a welfavoured and tender yonge woman, whose name I tell you not, for givynge matter to manye leude persons to report yll, whiche assone as they understande a woman to be in love, make an yll descantinge upon it. She therfore beloved of a woorthie and faire condicioned yonge Gentilman, was bent with hert and minde to love him. And of this not I alone, unto whom of her owne accord she uttered trustfullye the wholl matter, no otherwise then if I had bine, I will not say a brother, but an inward* sister of herres, but all that beehelde herr in companye of the beloved yonge man, were well weettinge of her passion. She thus ferventlye lovinge, as a most loving minde coulde love, continued two yeeres in suche contynencie, that she never made anye token to this yonge man of the love that she bore him, but suche as she coulde not hide from him. At no time she woulde speake with him, nor receive any letters from him or tokens, where there never passed daye but she was tempted with both the one and the other. And howe she longed for it, that wote I well, for yf otherwhile she coulde privilie gete anye thinge that had bine the yonge mans, she was so tender over it, that a manne woulde have thought that of it had spronge her lief and all her joye. Yet woulde she never in so long a time content him with other, then to beehoulde him and be seene of him again, and somtime happening to be at open feastes, daunce with him as she did with others. And bicause there was no great difference in their degree, she and the yonge man coveted that so great a love might have a luckye ende, and be man and wief together. All the men and women in the Citie desired the same, savinge her cruell father, which of a weywarde and straunge opinion minded to beestowe her upon an other more welthie. And this was not by the unluckye mayden otherwise gainstoode, then with most bitter teares. And after this unfortunate mariage was

An example of true continencye.

* inward: close, intimate.

concluded with great compassion of the people there, and despaire of the poore lovers, yet did not this stroke of fortune serve to roote up so grounded a love in the hert of ech other but lasted afterwarde the terme of three yeeres, albeit she full wiselye dissembled it, and sought everye waye to cutt in sunder those desires, whiche now were past hope. And in this while she folowed on still in her set pourpose of continencye, and perceivinge she could not honestly have him, whom she worshipped in the world, she chose not to have him at all, and continued in her wont not to accept messages, tokens nor yet his lookes. And in this resolved determination the seelie soule vanquished with moste cruell affliction, and wexed through longe passion verie feint, at the three yeeres ende, died. Rather woulde she forgoo her contentacions and pleasures so much longed for, finally her lief, then her honestie. And yet wanted she no meanes nor wayes to fulfill her desire most secretlye, and without perill either of sclaunder or anye other losse. And for all that, refrained she from the thinge of herselfe that she so muche coveted, and for the whiche she was so continuallye attempted by the person whom alone in the world her desire was to please. And to this was she not driven for feare or anye other respect, but onlye for the zeale of true vertue. What will you say of an other? that for six monthes almost nightlye laye with a moste deere lover of herres, yet in a gardein full of most savoury fruites, tempted with her owne most fervent longinge and with the petitions and teares of him that was moore deere to herr then her owne selfe, refrayned from tastinge of them. And for all she was wrapped and tyed* in the streict chaine of those beloved armes, yet never yelded she herselfe as vanquished, but preserved undefiled the floure of her honestie. [XLIV] Trowe you not (my L. Gaspar) that these be deedes of continencye alike to Alexanders? Whiche most ferventlye inamored not with the women of Darius, but with this renowme and greatnesse, that pricked him forwarde with the spurres of glorye to abide peines and

An other example of a mayden.

---

* wrapped and tyed. Moral disapproval may lie behind Hoby's omission of the word *ignuda* ('naked'), which follows this phrase in the original.

daungers to make himself immortall, set at nought not onelie other thinges, but hys owne lief, to gete a name above all men? and do we marveile with suche thoughtes in his hert that he refrayned from a thinge whiche he coveted not greatlye? for sins he never sawe those women beefore, it is not possible that he shoulde be in love with them at a blushe, but rather perhappes abhorred them for Darius his ennemies sake. And in this case everie wanton act of his towarde them, had bine an injurye and not love. And therfore no great matter if Alexander, whiche no lesse with noblenes of courage then marciall prowesse subdued the world, abstained from doing injury to women. The continency in like

Scipio.

case of Scipio is doubtlesse much to be commended, yet if ye consider wel, not to be compared to these two womens: for he in like maner also refrayned from a thing that he coveted not, beeinge in his ennemies countrey, a fresh Capitain, in the beeginning of a most weightie enterprise, leaving beehind him in his Countrie such expectacion of himself, and having beeside to give accompt to rigorous judges, that often times chastised not only the great, but the least offences of al, and emong them he wist well he had enemies, knowing also if he had otherwise done, bicause she was a noble damsel and espoused to a noble man, he should have purchased him so many enemies and in such sort, that many wold have driven of and perchaunce have set him cleane beeside his victory.[228] Thus for so many respectes and so weighty, he absteined from a light and hurtfull appetite, in showing continency and a freeherted wel-meaning, the which (as it is written) gote him all the hartes of that people: and an other armie stood him in steade with favour to vanquish mens hertes, whiche perhappes by force of armes had bine invincible. So that this maye rather be termed a warlike pollicie, then pure continencie: albeit beeside, the report of this matter is not

Cn. Nœvius.
Val. Antiates.

all of the purest, for some writers of authoritie affirme that this Damsell was enjoyed of Scipio in the pleasures of love: and of this I tell you ye maye depose upon.

[XLV] PHRISIO said: Perhappes ye have founde it in the Gospell.

I have seene it my self, answered the L. CESAR, and therfore I have a much more certeintye of this, then you

or anye man els can have that Alcibiades arrose no
otherwise from Socrates bed then children do from their
fathers beddes:[229] for to saye the truth, a straunge place
and time was bed and night to view with fixed minde the
pure beawty which is said Socrates loved without anye
unhonest desire, especiallye lovinge better the beawtie
of the minde, then of the bodye: but in boyes, not in old
men, for all they were wiser. And in good sooth a better
example could not have bine pyked out to praise the
continencie of men, then this Xenocrates, which occupied in his studye fastned and bound by his profession,
whiche is Philosophie, that consisteth in good maners,
and not in wordes, old, cleane spent of his natural
lustinesse, nothinge able, no not in makinge profer to be
able, refrayned from a commune haunted woman,[230]
which for the names sake might abhorr him. I woulde
sooner have beleaved he had bine continent, if he had
declared any token to have bine come to his right senses
again, and in that case have used continencie: or elles
abstained from the thinge which olde men covett more
then the battailes of Venus, namelye from wine. But to
establishe well continencie in olde age, it is written that
he was full and laden with it.[231] And what can be saide
to be more wider from the continencie of an olde man,
then dronkennesse? And in case the shonning of Venus
matters in that slow and colde age deserveth so much
praise, how much should it deserve in a tender mayden,
as those two I have tould you of? Of whiche the one
most streictlye bridlinge all her senses, not onlie denied
her eyes their light, but also toke from the hart those
thoughtes, whiche alone had bine a moste sweete foode
a longe time to kepe him in lief. The other ferventlye in
love, beeinge so often times alone in the armes of him
whom she loved more a great deale then all the world
beeside, fightinge against her owne self and against
him that was more deere to her then her owne selfe,
overcame that fervent desire, that many times hath and
doth overcome so manie wise men. Trow ye not nowe
(my L. Gaspar) that writers may be ashamed to make
mention of Xenocrates in this case, and to recken him
for chaste? where if a man coulde come bye the
knowlage of it, I wold lay a wager that he slept al that
night until the next day diner time, like a dead body

Alcibiades
was Socrates
scholer the
welfavouredst
yonge boy in
al Athens.

Xenocrates.

Lais of
Corinth.

Olde men
desyrous
of wine.

buried in wine: and for all the stirringe that woman made, coulde not once open his eyes, as though he had bine cast into a dead slepe.

[XLVI] Here all the men and women laughed, and the L. EMILIA: Surelye, my L. Gaspar (quoth she) yf you will beethinke your selfe a litle better, I beleave you shall finde out some other prety example of continencye alike unto this.

The L. CESAR answered: Is not this other (thinke ye Madam) a goodly example of continencye which he hath alleaged of Pericles? I muse much that he hath not aswell called to rehersall the continencie and pretie saiyng that is written of him that a woman asked to great a summ of for one night, and he answered her, that he minded not to bye repentance so deere.[232]

They ceased not laughinge, and the L. CESAR, after he had stayed a while: My L. Gaspar (quoth he) perdon me, yf I tell troth. For in conclusion these be the wonderful continencies that men write of themselves, accusinge women for incontinent, in whom are dailye seene infinit tokens of continencie. And certesse if ye ponder it aright, there is no fortresse so impringable, nor so well fensed that beeinge assaulted with the thousandeth part of the inginnes and guyles that are practised to conquer the steadie mind of a woman, would not yelde up at the first assault. How manye trained up by great astates and enriched throughe them and advaunced to great promotion, having in their handes their fortresses, houldes and Castles, wherupon depended their whol state, their lief and al their gooddes, without shame or care to be named Traiters, have disloyallye given them to whom they ought not? And would God in our dayes there were suche scarcitie of these kinde of persons, that we might not have much more a do to find out some one, that in this case hath done that he ought, then to name suche as have failed therin. See you not so many other that daily wander about to kill men in thickettes, and rovinge by sea, onlye to robb mens money? Howe manye Prelates make marchaundise with the goodes of the Churche of God? How manye Lawiers falsifie testaments? What perjuries make they? How many false evidences, onlye to gete money? How manye Phisitiens poison the diseased,

Demosthenes answer to Lais of Corinth that asked him xxiiii. li. for one night.

Trayters.

Theeves.

Prelates.

Lawyers.

Phisitiens.

onlye for it? Howe manye again for feare of death do
most vile matters? And yet all these so stiff and hard
battayles doeth a tender and delicate yonge woman
gainstande manye times, for sundrye there have bine,
that have chose rather to dye then to lose their honesty.

[XLVII] Then said the L. GASPAR: These (my L.
Cesar) bee not, I beleave, in the world nowadayes.

The L. CESAR answered: And I will not alleage unto
you them of olde time. But this I say, that manye might
be found out, and are daily, that in this case passe not
for* death. And nowe it commeth into my mynde that
whan Capua was sacked by the French men[233] (which is
not yet so longe since, but you may full well beare it in
minde) a well favoured yong gentylwoman of Capua,   Examples of
beeinge lead out of her house where she had bine taken   the chastitie
by a companye of Gascoignes, whan she came to the   of women.
ryver that renneth by Capua, she feigned to plucke on
her shoe, insomuch that her leader lett her goe a litle,
and she streight waye threw herselfe into the river.
What will you saye of a poore Countrey wenche, that   Ulturno.
not manye monthes ago at Gazuolo beeside Mantua
gone into the fielde a leazinge† with a sister of herres,
sore a thirst entred into a house to drinke water, where
the good man of the house, that was yonge, seeinge her
meetlye welfavoured and alone, takynge her in his
armes, firste wyth faire woordes, afterwarde with
threatninges attempted to frame her to do his pleasure,
and where she strived still more obstinatelye, at length
with manye blowes and by force overcame her. She thus
tossed and sobbinge, retourned into the fielde to her
sister, and for al the instance that she made uppon herr,
woulde never disclose to herr what oultrage she received
in that house, but still drawinge homewarde, and
showinge herselfe apeaced by litle and litle, and to
speake without desturbance, she gave her certein
instructions. Afterward when she came to the Olio,   Olio.
whiche is the river that renneth by Gazuolo, keapinge
her somewhat a louf from her sister, that knew not nor
imagined that she minded to do, sodeinlye cast her self
into it. Her Sister sorowfull and weepinge, folowed

* passe not for: think nothing of.
† a leazinge: to gather corn.

downe by the rivers side as faste as she coulde, whiche caried her a good pace awaye, and everye time the poore soule appeared above water, her sister threw in to her a corde that she had brought with her to binde the corne withall. And for al the corde came to her handes more then once (for she was yet nigh inoughe to the bancke) the stedfast and resolved girl alwaies refused it and pushed it from her. And thus shonninge all succour that might save her lief, in a short space died. She was neyther stirred by noblenes of blood, nor by feare of death or sclaunder, but onlye by the greef of her lost maidenheade. Nowe by this you may gather, howe manye other women doe deedes moste woorthye memorye, sins (as a manne maye saye) three dayes a go, this hath made such a triall of her vertue, and is not spoken of, ne yet her name knowen. But had not the death folowed at that time of the Bishop of Mantua uncle to oure Dutchesse, the bancke of the Olio in the place where she cast herselfe in, had nowe bine garnished with a verie faire sepulture, for a memorie of so glorious a soule, that deserved somuch the more cleere renowme after death, as in lief it dwelled in an unnoble bodye.[234]

[XLVIII] Here the L. CESAR tooke respit a while, afterwarde he set forwarde: In my dayes also in Roome there happened a like chaunce, and it was, that a welfavoured and well borne yonge Gentilwoman of Roome, beeinge longe folowed after of one that showed to love her greatly, wold never please him with any thing, no not somuch as a looke. So that this felow by force of money corrupted a waitinge woman of herres, who desirous to please him to fingre more money, was in hande with her maistresse upon a daie, no great holye day, to go visit Saint Sebastianes Church. And giving the lover intelligence of the wholl, and instructinge him what he had to doe, lead the yonge Gentilwoman into one of the darke Caves under grounde, that whoso go to Saint Sebastianes are wont to visit. And in it was the yonge man first closely hid, whiche perceivinge himselfe alone with her whom he loved somuche, beegane everye waye to exhort her with as faire language as he could, to have compassion upon him, and to chaunge her former rigour into love. But whan he sawe all his prayers

A chaunce that happened to a gentil-woman in Roome.

One of the vii. Churches of Roome ii. miles without the City.

coulde take none effect, he tourned him to threatninges.
And whan they prevayled not, he all to beate her. In the
ende he was full and wholye bent to have his pourpose,
if not otherwise, by force, and therin used the helpe of
the naughtye woman that had brought her thither. Yet
coulde he never do so muche as make her graunt to him,
but in woordes and deedes (althoughe her force was but
small) alwaies the seelye yonge woman defended herselfe
in what she coulde possible. So that what for the spite he
conceived, whan he sawe he coulde not gete his will,
and what for feare least the matter shoulde come to her
kinsfolkes eare and make him punished for it, this
mischevous person wyth the aide of the woman that
doubted* the same, strangled the unluckye yonge
woman, and there left her, and rennynge his waye
provided for himselfe for beeinge founde out again. The
waiting woman blinded with her owne offence, wist not
to flee, and beeinge taken upon certeine susspitions,
confessed the wholl matter, and was therfore punished
accordinge to her desertes. The body of the constante
and noble gentilwoman with great honoure was taken
out of the cave and caried to buriall within Roome, with
a garlande of Laurell about her heade, accompanied
with an infinit number of men and women: emong
whiche was not one that brought his eyes to his home
again without teares. And thus generallye of all the
people was this rare soule no lesse beewayled then
commended. [XLIX] But to tell you of them that you
your selfe know, remembre you not that ye have heard   Lady Fœlix
tel, as the Lady Fœlix della Rovere[235] was on her   della Rovere.
journey to Saona, doubting least certein sailes that were
descried a farr of, had bine Pope Alexanders vesselles
that pursuid her, was utterlye resolved, if they had made
towarde her, and no remedie to escape, to cast herself
into the Sea. And this is not to be thought that she did
upon anye lightnesse, for you aswell as any man, do
know with what a witt and wisedome the singuler   Praise of the
beawtie of that Ladye is accompanied. I can no lenger   Dutches that
keepe in silence a woorde of our Dutchesse, who livinge   lead a widowes
xv. yeeres in companye with her husbande, like a   lief with the
widowe, hath not onlye bine stedfast in not uttringe this   Duke.

* doubted: feared.

to anye person in the world, but also whan she was perswaded by her owne friendes to forsake this widowheade, she chose rather to suffer banishment, poverty, and al other kinde of misery, then to agree to that, which all other men thought great favour and prosperitie of fortune.

And as he still proceaded in talkinge of this, the DUTCHESSE saide: Speake of somwhat els, and no more ado in this matter, for ye have other thinges inoughe to talke of.

The L. CESAR folowed on. Full well I know that you wil not denie me this (my L. Gaspar) nor you Phrisio.

No doubtlesse, answered PHRISIO: but one maketh no number.

[L] Then saide the L. CESAR: Truth it is that these so greate effectes and rare vertues are seene in few women. Yet are they also that resist the battailes of love, all to be wondred at, and such as otherwhile be overcome deserve muche compassion. For surelye the provocations of lovers, the craftes that they use, the snares that they laye in waite are suche and so applyed, that it is to great a wonder, that a tender girle should escape them. What daye, what hour passeth at anye time that the yonge woman thus layed at is not tempted by her lover with money, tokens, and al thinges that he can imaginn may please her? At what time can she ever looke out at a window, but she seeth continuallye the earnest lover passe by? With silence in woordes, but with a paire of eyes that talke. With a vexed and feint countenance. With those kindled sighes. Often times with most abundant teares. Whan doeth she at any time yssue out at her doores to Church or any other place, but he is alwaies in the face of her? And at everye tourning of a lane meeteth her in the teeth, with such heavy passion peinted in his eies that a man wold weene that even at that instant he were ready to die? I omitt his precisenesse in sundrye thinges, inventions, meery conceites, undertaking enterprises, sportes, daunses, games, maskeries, justes, tourneimentes, the which thinges she knoweth al to be taken in hand for her sake. Again, in the night time she can never awake, but she heareth musike, or at the least that unquiet spirit about the walles of her house casting furth sighes and lamentable

The carefull diligence of lovers.

voices. If by a hap she talketh with one of her waiting women about her, she (being already corrupted with money) hath straight way in a readinesse some pretye token, a letter, a rime, or some such matter to present her in the lovers behalf: and here entring to pourpose, maketh her to understand how this selie soule burneth, how he setteth litle by his owne lief, to do her service, and how he seeketh nothing of her but honesty, and that only his desire is to speake with her. Here then for all hard matters are founde out remedies, counterfeit kayes, laders of ropes, wayes to cast into sleepe, a trifling matter is peincted out,* examples are alleaged of others that do much woorse: so that every matter is made so easy, that she hath no more trouble, but to say, I am content.† And in case the poore soule maketh resistaunce but a while, they plye her with suche provocations, and finde suche meanes, that with continuall beatynge at, they breake in sunder that is a lett to her. And many there be that perceiving they can not prevaile with faire woordes, fall to threatninges, and say that they wil tell their husbandes they are, that they be not. Other bargain bouldlye with the fathers and many times with the husbandes which for money or promotions sake give their owne daughters and wives for a prey against their wil. Other seeke by inchauntmentes, and witchcraftes to take from them the liberty that God hath graunted to soules, wherin are seene wonderfull conclusions.‡ But in a thousand yeere I coulde not repeate all the craftes that men use to frame women to their willes, which be infinit. And beeside them which every man of himselfe findeth out, there hath not also wanted that hath wittily made bookes, and beestowed great study to teache how in this beehalfe women are to be deceived.[236] Now judge you how from so manye nettes these simple dooves can be safe, tempted with so sweete a bayte. And what great matter is it then, in case a woman knowinge her self somuch beeloved and worshipped many yeeres together, of a noble and faire condicioned yong man,

---

* a trifling matter is peincted out: the thing is made out to be of trifling importance.
† content: willing.
‡ wonderfull conclusions: miraculous results.

which a thousand times a day hasardeth his lief to serve her, and never thinketh upon other but to please her with the continuall beatinge whiche the water maketh whan it perceth the most hard marble stone, at length is brought to love him? Is this (thinke you) so haynous a trespace, that the seelye poore creature taken with so manye enticementes, deserveth not, if the woorst should fal, the perdon that many times murtherers, theves, fellones and traiters have? Wil you have this vice so uncomperable great, that bicause one woman is found to renn into it, all women kinde shoulde be cleane despised for it, and generallye counted voide of continencye? Not regardinge that manye are founde moste invincible, that against the continuall flickeringe provocations of love are made of Diamondes, and stiff in their infinite steadinesse, more then the rockes against the surges of the Sea?

[LI] Then the L. Gaspar whan the L. Cesar stayed talkinge, beegan to make him answere, but the L. OCTAVIAN smilinge: Tushe, for love of God (quoth he) graunt him the victory, for I know ye shall doe small good, and me thinke I see you shall not onlye make all the women youre ennemies, but also the more part of the menne.

The L. GASPAR laughed and said: Nay, the women have rather great cause to thanke me. For had not I contraryed the L. Julian and the L. Cesar, they shoulde not have come to the knowleage so manye prayses as they have given them.

Then saide the L. CESAR: The prayses which my L. Julian and I have given women, and many mo beeside, were most knowen, therfore they have bine but

Women.

superfluous. Who woteth not that without women no contentation or delite can be felt in all this lief of ourse? whiche (sett them aside) were rude and without all sweetenesse, and rougher then the lief of forest wilde beastes? Who knoweth not that women rid oure hartes of al vile and dastardlye imaginations, vexations, miseries, and the troublesome heavinesse that so often times accompanieth them? And in case we will consider the truth, we shall know moreover as touchinge the

The opera-
tions of love.

understanding of great matters, that they do not stray our wittes, but rather quicken them, and in warr make men past feare and hardie passinge measure. And certesse it is not possible, that in the hart of man, where once is entred the flame of love, there should at any time reigne cowardlynesse.* For he that loveth, alwaies coveteth to make himself as lovely as he can, and evermore dreadeth that he take no foyle, that should make him litle set by of whom he desireth to be much set by: and passeth not to go a thousande times in a daye to his death, to declare himselfe woorthye of that love. Therfore whoso coulde gather an armie of lovers, that shoulde fight in presence of the ladies they loved, shoulde subdue the wholl world, onlesse against it on the contrarie part there were an other armie likewise in love. And to abide by,† the houldinge out of Troye x. yeeres against all Greece, proceaded of nothinge elles but of certein lovers, whiche whan they entended to issue out abrode to fight, armed themselves in the presence of their Ladies, and many times they helped them themselves, and at their settinge furth rounded‡ them some certein woord, that set them on fire and made them more then men. Afterward in fightinge they wist well that they were beeheld from the walles and Toures by the Ladies, wherfore they deemed every bould enterprise that they undertooke, was commended of them, whiche was the greatest rewarde to them that they coulde have in the worlde. Manye there be that houlde opinion that the victorye of kinge Ferdinande and Isabell of Spaine, against the kinge of Granada was cheeflye occasioned by women, for the moste times whan the armye of Spaine marched to encounter with the ennemyes, Queene Isabel set furth also with all her Damselles: and there were manye noble gentilmen that were in love, who til they came within sight of the enemies, alwaies went communing with their Ladies. Afterwarde echone takinge his leave of his, in their presence marched on to encountre with the ennemies, with that fiersenesse of courage, that love and desire to showe their Ladies that they were served wyth valiaunt men, gave them. Wherupon it beefell manye

Why Troy withstoode all Greece x. yeeres.

Women the cause of the conquest of the kingdom of Granada.

---

* cowardlynesse: baseness.
† to abide by: certainly.
‡ rounded: said.

times that a very few gentilmen of Spaine put to flight and slue an infinit number of Moores, thanked be the courteious and beloved women. Therfore I wote not (my L. Gaspar) what weywarde judgement hath lead you to dispraise women. [LII] Do you not see that of all comelye exercises and whiche delite the worlde, the cause is to be referred to no earthlye thynge, but to women? Who learneth to daunce featlye for other, but to please women? Who applyeth the sweetenesse of musicke for other cause, but for this? Who to write in meeter, at the least in the mother tung, but to expresse the affections caused by women? Judge you howe manye most noble Poemes we had bine without both in Greeke and Latin, had women bine smallye regarded of Poetes. But leavinge all other a part, had it not bine a verye great losse, in case M. Francis Petrarca, that writt so divinlye his loves in this oure tunge, had applied his minde onlye to Latin matters: as he woulde have done, had not the love of the Damsell Laura sometime strayed him from it? I name not unto you the fine wittes that are nowe in the worlde, and here present, whiche dailye bringe furthe some noble frute, and notwythstandynge take their grounde onlye of the vertue and beawtye of women. See whether Salomon myndynge to write mysticallye verye highe and heavenlye matters, to cover them wyth a gracious veile, did not feigne a fervent Dialogue full of the affection of a lover with his woman, seeminge to him that he coulde not fynde here beeneth emonge us anye lykenesse more meete and agreeinge wyth heavenlye matters, then the love toward women: and in that wise and maner minded to gyve us a litle of the smacke of that divinitye, whiche he bothe for hys understandynge and for the grace above others, had knowleage of.[237] Therefore thys needed no disputacyon (my L. Gaspar) or at the least so manye woordes in the matter. But you in gainsaiynge the truth have hindred the understandinge of a thousande other pretie matters and necessary for the perfection of the gentilwoman of the Palaice.

The L. GASPAR answered: I beleave there can no more be said. Yet if you suppose that the L. Julian hath not garnished her throughlye with good condicions, the fault is not in him, but in him that hath so wrought that

Women the cause of worthie qualities.

Francesco Petrarca.

Salomon.

there are no mo vertues in the worlde: for all that there be, he hath beestowed uppon her.

The DUTCHESSE saide smilinge: Well, you shall see that the L. Julian will yet finde out mo beeside.

The L. JULIAN answered: In good sooth (Madam) me seemeth I have sufficientlye spoken. And for my part I am well pleased wyth this my woman. And in case these Lordes will not have her as she is, let them leave her to me.

[LIII] Here whan all was whist, SIR FRIDERICKE saide: My L. Julian, to give you occasion to saye somewhat elles, I will but aske you a question, as touchynge that you have willed to be the principall profession of the Gentilwoman of the Palayce. And this it is, that I longe to knowe howe she shoulde beehave herselfe in a point that (to my seemynge) is moste necessarye. For albeit the excellent qualityes whiche you have geven her conteine in them discretion, knowledge, judgemente, sleight, sobermoode,* and so manye other vertues, wherebye of reason she ought to have the understandynge to entertein everye manne and in all kinde of pourpose, yet thinke I notwithstandynge above any other thing that it is requisite for her to knowe what beelongeth to communication of love. For even as everye honest Gentilmanne for an instrument to obteine the good will of women, practyseth those noble exercises, precise† facions and good maners whyche we have named, even so to this pourpose applyeth he also hys woordes, and not onlye whan he is stirred thereto by some passion, but often times also to do honour to the woman he talketh withall, seemynge to him that to declare to love her is a witnes that she is woorthie of it, and that her beawtie and woorthynesse is suche, that it enforceth everie manne to serve her. Therfore woulde I knowe, howe this woman in suche a case shoulde beehave herselfe uprightlye, and howe to answere him that loveth her in deed, and how him that maketh false semblant: and whether she ought to dissemble the understandinge of it, or be answerable, or shonn the matter, and howe to handle herselfe.

Entertein-
ment.

To talke of
love.

---

* sleight, sobermoode: tact, modesty.
† precise: elegant.

[LIV] Then said the L. JULIAN: It were first needefull to teach her to knowe them that make semblant to love, and them that love in deede: afterward for beeinge answerable in love or no, I beeleave she ought not to be guided by any other mans will, but by her owne self.

SIR FRIDERICKE saide: Teach you her then what are the moste certein and surest tokens to descerne false love from true, and what triall she shal thinke sufficient to content herselfe withall, to be out of doubt of the love shewed her.

The L. JULIAN answered smiling: That wote not I, bicause men be nowadayes so craftye, that they make infinite false semblantes, and sometime weepe, whan they have in deede a greater lust to laughe. Therefore they shoulde be sent to the constant Ile under the Arch of faithfull lovers.[238] But least this woman of mine (which is my charge and no mans elles, bicause she is my creature) should renn into those erroures whiche I have seene manye other renn into, I would saye that she should not be light of credence that she is beloved: nor be like unto some, that not onlie make not wise* they understande him not that communeth with them of love, be it never so farr of,† but also at the first woorde accept all the prayses that be given them: or elles denie them after such a sort, that it is rather an alluringe for them to love them they commune withall, then a withdrawinge of themselves. Therfore the maner of enterteinment in reasoninge of love that I will have my woman of the Palaice to use, shall be alwaies to shonn beeleavinge that whoso talketh of love, loveth her anye whitt the more. And in case the Gentilman be (as manye suche there are abrode) malapert, and hath smalle respect to her in his talke, she shall shape him such an answere, that he shall plainly understande she is not pleased withall. Again, if he be demure and useth sober facions and woordes of love covertlie, in suche honest maner, as I beeleave the Courtier whom these Lordes have facioned will doe, the woman shall make wise not to understand him, and shal draw his woordes to another sense, seekinge alwaies sobrely with the

* make not wise: do not pretend.
† farr of: obliquely.

discretion and wisdome that is alreadye said becommeth her, to stray from that pourpose.* But in case the communication be such that she can not feigne not to understande it, she shall take the wholl (as it were) for a meerie divise, and make wise that she knoweth it is spoken to her rather to honour her withall, then that it is so in deede, debasinge her desertes and acknowleginge at the Gentilmans courtesie the prayses which he geveth her: and in this sort she shall be counted discreete, and shall be on the surer hande for† beeinge deceived. Thus me seemeth the Gentilwoman of the Palaice ought to behave herself in communication of love.

[LV] Then SIR FRIDERICK: You debate this matter, my L. Julian (quoth he) as though it were requisite, that all suche as speake with women of love, shoulde tell lyes, and seeke to deceive them, the whiche in case it were so, I woulde say your lessons were good. But if this gentilman that enterteineth, loveth in very deede, and feeleth the passion that so tourmenteth mens hertes sometime, consider you not in what peine, in what calamitie and death ye put him in, whan at no time you will that the woman shall beeleave him in any thinge he saith about this pourpose? Shall othes, teares, and so many other tokens then, have no force at all? Take heede (my L. Julian) least a manne may thinke that beeside the naturall crueltye whiche manie of these women have in them, you teach them yet more.

The L. JULIAN answered: I have spoken, not of him that loveth, but of him that enterteineth with communication of love, wherein one of the necessariest pointes is, that woordes be never to seeke: and true lovers as they have a burninge hart, so have they a colde tunge, with broken talke and sodeine silence. Therfore (may happ) it were no false principle to saye: He that loveth much, speaketh litle. Howbeit in this I beleave there can be given no certein rule, by reason of the diversity of mens maners. And I wote not what I should say, but that the woman be good and heedfull, and alwaies

* to stray from that pourpose: to change the subject.
† on the surer hande for: safer from.

beare in mynde, that men may with a great deale lesse daunger declare themselves to love, then women.

[LVI] The L. GASPAR said laughinge: Why (my L. Julian) wil not you that this your so excellent a woman shall love again, at the least whan she knoweth certeinlye she is beeloved? consideringe if the Courtier were not loved again, it is not likelye he woulde continue in lovinge her: and so shoulde she want manye favours, and cheefly the homage and reverence, wherwithal lovers obey and (in a maner) woorship the vertue of the women beloved.

In this, answered the L. JULIAN, I will not counsel her. But I say pardee to love, as you now understand, I judge it not meete, but for unmaried women.[239] For whan this love can not ende in matrimonye, the woman muste needes have alwaies the remorse and pricking that is had of unlefull matters, and she putteth in hasarde to staine the renowme of honestie, that standeth her so much upon.

Then answered SIR FRIDERICKE smilinge: Me thinke (my L. Julian) this opinion of yours is verie soure and crabbed, and I beleave you have learned it of some Frier Preacher, of them that rebuke women in love with lay men, that their part may be the more. And me seemeth you sett over hard lawes to maried women, for manye there be that their husbandes beare verye sore hatred unto without cause, and nipp them at the hert, sometime in lovinge other women, otherwhile in woorkinge them all the displeasures they can imagin. Some are compelled by their fathers to take olde men full of diseases, uglesome and weywarde, that make them lead their lief in continual misery. And in case it were leful for such to be divorsed and severed from them they be ill coopled withal, perhappes it were not to be alowed that they should love any other then their husband. But whan eyther through the sterres, theyr enemies, or through the diversitie of complexion, or anie other casualtie it befalleth, that in bed, whiche ought to be the nest of agreement and love, the cursed furie of hell soweth the seede of his venime, which afterwarde bryngeth furth disdeigne, susspition and the pricking thornes of hatred, that tourmenteth those unluckie soules bound cruelly together in the fast lincked chaine

Maried women.

that can not be broken but by death, why will not you have it lefull for this woman to seeke some easement for so harde a scourge, and give unto an other that which her husbande not onelye regardeth not, but rather cleane abhorreth? I houlde well, that suche as have meete husbandes and be beloved of them, ought not to do them injurie: but the other in not lovinge him that loveth them do them selves injurie.

Nay, they do themselves injurie in lovinge other beeside their husbande, answered the L. JULIAN. Yet sins not loving is not many times in our will, if this mishap chaunce to the woman of the Palaice, that the hatred of her husbande or the love of an other bendeth her to love, I will have her to graunt her lover nothing elles but the minde: nor at any time to make him any certein token of love, neither in woorde nor gesture, nor any other way that he may be fully assured of it.

[LVII] Then saide M. ROBERT OF BARI smilinge: I appeale (my L. Julian) from this judgement of youres, and I beleave I shall have many felowes. But sins you will teach this currishnesse* (that I maye terme it so) to maried women, will ye also have the unmaried to be so cruell and discourtious, and not please their lovers at the least in somewhat?

In case my woman of the Palaice, answered the L. JULIAN, be not maryed, myndinge to love, I wyll have her to love one, whom she maye marye, neyther will I thinke it an offence if she showe him some token of love. In which matter I will teache her one generall rule in fewe woordes, and that is, That she showe him whom she loveth all tokens of love, but such as may bring into the lovers minde a hope to obtein of her any dishonest matter. And to this she must have a great respect, bicause it is an errour that infinit women renn into, which ordinarilye covett nothinge somuch as to be beawtifull: and bicause to have manye lovers they suppose is a testimonye of their beawtie, they do their best to winn them as many as they can. Therfore often times they renn at rovers in beehaviours of small modestie, and leavinge the temperate sobermoode†

How maidens shoulde love.

A generall rule.

---

* currishnesse: boorishness; lack of civility.
† sobermoode: modesty.

that is so sightlye in them, use certein wanton countenaunces, with baudie woordes and gestures full of
unshamefastnesse, houldinge opinion that menne
marke them and give eare to them willyngly for it, and
with these facions make themselves beloved, which is
false: bicause the signes and tokens that be made them,
sprynge of an appetite moved by an opinion of
easinesse, not of love. Therfore will not I that my
woman of the Palaice with dishonest beehaviours
should appeere as though she wold offre herselfe unto
whoso wyll have her, and allure what she can the eyes
and affection of who so beehouldeth her: but with her
desertes and vertuous condicions, with amiablenesse
and grace drive into the mind of whoso seeth her the
verye love that is due unto every thinge woorthy to be
beloved: and the respect that alwaies taketh awaye
hope from whoso mindeth anye dishonest matter. He
then that shall be beloved of such a woman, ought of
reason to houlde himselfe contented with everye litle
token, and more to esteame a looke of herres with
affection of love, then to be altogether maister of an
other. And to such a woman I wote not what to ad
more, but that she be beloved of so excellent a Courtier,
as these Lordes have facioned, and she likewise to love
him, that both the one and the other may have ful and
wholy his perfection.

The love
of honest
women.

[LVIII] After the L. Julian had thus spoken he helde
his peace, whan the L. GASPAR laughinge: Now (quoth
he) you can not complaine that the L. Julian hath not
facioned this woman of the Palaice most excellent. And
if perdee there be any suche to be found, I say that she
deserveth well to be esteamed equall with the Courtier.

The L. EMILIA answered: I will at all times be bounde
to finde her, whan you finde the Courtier.

M. ROBERT said then: Doubtlesse it can not be saide
nay, but the L. Julians woman whiche he hath facioned
is most perfect. Yet in these her last properties as
touching love, me seemeth notwithstanding that he
hath made her somwhat over crabbed, and especially
where he will have her in woordes, gestures and
countenance to take cleane away all hope from the
lover, and settle him as nigh as she can in despaire. For
(as all menne know) the desires of man stretch not to

suche kinde of matters, whereof there is no hope to be
had. And althoughe at times some women there have
bine, that perhappes bearing themselves loftie of their
beawtie and woorthinesse: the first woorde they have
said to them that communed with them of love hath
bine, that they should never looke to come bye anye
thinge of them that liked them:* yet in countenaunce,
and daliance together they have afterward bine more
favourable to them, so that with their gentle deedes they
have tempred in part their proude woordes. But if this
woman both in woordes, deedes and beehaviours take
hope quite awaye, I beeleave our Courtier, if he be wise,
will never love her, and so shall she have this imperfection, that she shall be without a lover.

[LIX] Then the L. JULIAN: I wyll not (quoth he) have
my woman of the Palaice to take away the hope of every
thinge, but of dishonest matters, that which, in case the
Courtier be so courteious and discreete, as these Lordes
have facioned him, he will not onelye not hope for, but
not once motion.† For if beawtie, maners, witt, good-   *Honest love.*
nesse, knowleage, sobermoode, and so manye other
vertuous condicions which we have given the woman,
be the cause of the Courtiers love towarde her, the ende
also of this love must needes be vertuous: and if
noblenesse of birth, skilfulnes in marciall feates, in
letters, in musike, gentlenesse, beeing both in speach
and in beehaviour indowed with so many graces, be
the meanes wherwithall the Courtier compaseth the
womans love, the end of that love must needes be of the
same condicion that the meanes are by the whiche he
commeth to it. Beeside that, as there be in the world   *Sundrye*
sundrie kindes of beawtye, so are there also sundrie   *kindes of*
desires of men: and therfore it is seene that manie,   *beawtye.*
perceivinge a woman of so grave a beawtie that goinge,
standinge, jestinge, dalyinge, and doinge what she
lusteth, so tempreth al her gestures, that it driveth a
certein reverence into whoso behouldeth her, are agast
and a ferde to serve her: and rather drawn with hope,
love those garishe‡ and enticefull women, so delicate

---

* looke to come bye anye thinge of them that liked them: hope to
get from them any of those things they desired.
† not once motion: the original has 'not even desire'.
‡ garishe: lovely.

and tender, that in their woordes, gestures and countenance declare a certein passion somewhat feeble,*
that promiseth to be easely brought and tourned into
love. Some to be sure from deceytes, love certein other
so lavishe both of their eyes, woordes and gestures, that
they do what ever first commeth to minde, with a
certein plainesse that hideth not their thoughtes. There
want not also manye other noble courages, that
seeminge to them that vertue consisteth about hard
matters (for it is over sweete a victorie to overcome that
seemeth to an other impringable) are soone bent to love
the beawties of those women, that in their eyes,
woordes and gestures declare a more churlish gravitie
then the rest for a triall that their prowesse can enforce
an obstinate minde, and bende also stubborne willes
and rebelles against love, to love. Therfore suche as
have so great affiance in themselves, bicause they recken
themselves sure from deceit, love also willinglye certein
women, that with a sharpenesse of wit, and with art it
seemeth in their beawtie that they hide a thousande
craftes. Or elles some other, that have accompanied
with beawty a certein skornefull facion in few wordes,
litle laughing, after a sort as though (in a maner) they
smallye regarded whoso ever behouldeth or serveth
them. Again there are founde certein other, that
vouchesafe not to love but women that in their
countenaunce, in their speach and in all their gestures
have about them all hansomnesse, all faire condicions,
all knowleage, and all graces heaped together, like one
floure made of all the excellencies in the worlde.
Therfore in case my woman of the Palaice have scarsitie
of these loves proceadinge of an yll hope, she shal not
for this be without a lover: bicause she shal not want
them that shalbe provoked through her desertes and
through the affiance of that prowesse in themselves,
wherby they shal knowe themselves worthy to be
beloved of her.

[LX] M. Robert still spake against him, but the
DUTCHESSE toulde him that he was in the wronge,
confirminge the L. Julians opinion: after that she added:
We have no cause to complaine of the L. Julian, for

* feeble: languishing.

doubtlesse I thinke that the woman of the Palaice whom he hath facioned, maye be compared to the Courtier, and that with some avauntage: for he hath taught her to love which these Lordes have not done their Courtier.

Then spake UNICO ARETINO: It is meete to teache women to love, bicause I never sawe anye that coulde doe it, for almoste continuallye all of them accompanye their beawtye with crueltye and unkindnesse toward suche as serve them most faithfullye, and whiche for noblenesse of birth, honestie and vertue deserved a rewarde for theyr good will: and yet manye times geve themselves for a prey to most blockish* and cowardly men and verye assheades, and which not only love them not, but abhor them. Therfore to shon these so foule oversightes, perhappes it had bin well done first to have taught them to make a choise of him that should deserve to be beloved, and afterward to love him. The whiche is not necessarye in men, for they knowe it to well of themselves: and I my selfe can be a good witnesse of it, bicause love was never taught me, but by the divine beawty and most divine maners of a Lady, so that it was not in my will not to woorshippe her: and therfore needed I therin no art nor teacher at all. And I beleave that the like happeneth to as manie as love truly. Therfore the Courtier hath more neede to be taught to make him beloved then to love.

[LXI] Then said the L. EMILIA: Do you now reason of this then, M. Unico.

UNICO answered: Me thinke reason woulde that the good will of women shoulde be gotten in servinge and pleasinge them. But it, wherin they recken themselves served and pleased, I beleave must be learned of women themselves, whiche oftentimes covett suche straunge matters, that there is no man that would imagin them, and otherwhile they themselves wote not what they should longe for: therfore it were good you (Madam) that are a woman, and of right ought to know what pleaseth women, shoulde take thys peine, to do the worlde so great a profit.

Then saide the L. EMILIA: For somuch as you are generallye most acceptable to women, it is a good

Beawtifull
women cruell.

---

* blockish: stupid.

likelihoode that you knowe al the waies how their good will is to be gotten. Therfore is it pardee meete for you to teach it.

Madam, answered UNICO, I can give a lover no profitabler advise then to procure that you beare no stroke* with the woman whose good will he seeketh. For the smalle qualities which yet seemed to the world sometime to be in me, with as faithfull a love as ever was, were not of suche force to make me beloved, as you to make me be hated.

[LXII] Then answered the L. EMILIA: God save me (M. Unico) for once thinking and much more for workinge anye thinge that should make you be hated. For beeside that I should doe that I ought not, I shoulde be thought of a sclender judgement to attempt a matter unpossible. But sins ye provoke me in this sort to speake of that pleaseth women, I will speake of it, and if it displease you, laye the fault in your selfe. I judge

Howe to
obtein the
good will of
women.

therfore, that whoso entendeth to be beloved, ought to love and to be lovely:† and these two pointes are inoughe to obtein the good will of women. Nowe to answere to that which you lay to my charge, I say that everie manne knoweth and seeth that you are moste lovelie. Mary whether ye love so faithfullye, as you saye ye do, I am verye doubtfull and perhappes others to. For, your beeing over lovely, hath bine the cause that you have bine beloved of many women: and great rivers divided into manye armes beecome smalle brookes: so love likewise scattered into mo then one bodye hath smalle force. But these your continuall complaintes and accusinge of the women whom you have served of unkindenesse (which is not likely, consideringe so manye desertes of yours) is a certein kind of discretion, to cloke the favours, contentations and pleasures whyche you have received in love, and an assurance for the women that love you and that have given themselves for a prey to you, that you will not disclose them. And therfore are they also wel pleased, that you should thus openlye showe false loves to others, to cloke their true. Wherfore if haplye those women that you nowe make

* beare no stroke: have no influence.
† lovely: lovable.

wise to love, are not so light of beleaf, as you would they
were, it happeneth bicause this your art in love
beeginneth to be discovered, and not bicause I make
you to be hated.

[LXIII] Then said M. UNICO: I entende not to attempt
to confute your wordes, bicause me seemeth it is aswell
my destiny not to be beleaved in truth, as it is yours to be
beleaved in untruth.

Saye hardlye M. Unico, answered the L. EMILIA, that
you love not so, as you woulde have beleaved ye did.
For if you did love, all your desires should be to please
the woman beloved, and to will the selfe same thinge
that she willeth, for this is the lawe of love. But your   The lawe
complaininge somuche of her, beetokeneth some   of love.
deceite (as I have said) or els it is a signe that you will
that, that she willeth not.

Nay (quoth M. UNICO) there is no doubt but I will
that, that she willeth, which is a signe I love her: but it
greeveth me bicause she willeth not that, that I will,
which is a token she loveth not me, according to the
verie same lawe that you have alleaged.

The L. EMILIA answered: He that taketh in hande to
love, muste please and applye himself full and wholy
to the appetites* of the wight beloved, and accordinge
to them frame hys owne: and make his owne desires,
servauntes: and hys verye soule, like an obedient
handmaiden: nor at anye tyme to thynke upon other,
but to chaunge his, if it were possible, into the beloved
wightes, and recken this his cheef joy and happinesse,
for so do they that love trulye.

My cheef happinesse were jumpe, answered M.
UNICO, if one will alone ruled her soule and myne both.

It lieth in you to do it, answered the L. EMILIA.

[LXIV] Then spake M. BERNARDE interruptinge
them: Doubtlesse, who so loveth trulye, directeth all his
thaughtes, without other mens teachinge, to serve and
please the woman beloved. But bicause these services of
love are not otherwhile well knowen, I beleave that
beeside lovinge and servinge, it is necessary also to make
some other showe of this love, so manifest, that the
woman may not dissemble to know that she is beloved:

* appetites: desires.

yet with such modesty, that it may not appeere that he beareth her litle reverence. And therfore you (Madam) that have beegone to declare howe the soule of the lover ought to be an obedient handmayden to the beloved, teach us withall, I besech you, this secrete matter, which me thinke is most needefull.

The L. CESAR laughed and said: If the lover be so bashfull, that he is ashamed to tell it her, let him write it her.

To this the L. EMILIA said: Nay, if he be so discreete, as is meete, beefore he maketh the woman to understand it, he ought to be out of doubt to offende her.

Then saide the L. GASPAR: All women have a delite to be suide to in love, althoughe they were mynded to denye the suite.

The L. JULIAN said: You are muche deceyved. For I woulde not counsell the Courtier at anye time to use this way, except he were sure not to have a repulse.

[LXV] What shoulde he then do? quoth the L. GASPAR.

The L. JULIAN answered: In case you will needes write or speake to her, do it with such sobermoode, and so warilye, that the woordes maye firste attempt the minde, and so doubtfullye touch her entent and will, that they maye leave her a way and a certein issue to feine the understandinge that those woordes conteine love: to the entent if he finde anye daunger, he maye draw backe and make wise to have spoken or written it to an other ende, to enjoye these familiar cherishinges and daliances with assuraunce, that oftentimes women showe to suche as shoulde take them for frendshippe, afterwarde denye them assone as they perceyve they are taken for tokens of love. Wherefore suche as be to rashe and venture so saucilie with certein furies and plunges, oftentimes lose them, and woorthilie: for it displeaseth alwaies every honest gentilwoman, to be litle regarded of whoso without respect seeketh for love at her beefore he hath served her. [LXVI] Therfore (in my minde) the way which the Courtier ought to take, to make his love knowen to the woman me thinke should be to declare them in signes and tokens more then in woordes. For assuredlye there is otherwhile a greater affection of love perceyved in a sigh, in a respect, in a feare, then in a

Howe a man should disclose his love to a woman.

thousande woordes. Afterwarde, to make the eyes the trustye messangers, that maye carye the ambassades of the hart: bicause they oftentimes declare with a more force what passion there is inwardlye, then can the tunge, or letters, or messages, so that they not onlye disclose the thaughtes, but also manye tymes kendle love in the hert of the person beloved. For those lively spirites[240] that issue out at the eyes, bicause they are engendred nigh the hart, entring in like case into the eyes that they are leveled at, like a shaft to the pricke, naturallye perce to the hart, as to their restynge place and there are at truste with those other spirites: and with the moste subtill and fine nature of bloode whyche they carie with them, infect the bloode about the hart, where they are come to, and warme it: and make it like unto themselves, and apt to receive the imprintinge of the image which they have caried away with them. Wherfore by litle and litle comminge and goinge the waye through the eyes to the hart, and bringinge backe with them the tunder and strikinge yron of beawtie and grace, these messangers kendle with the puffinge of desire the fire that so burneth, and never ceaseth consuminge, for alwayes they bringe some matter of hope to nourishe it. Therfore it may full well be said, that the eyes are a guide in love, especiallye if they have a good grace and sweetenesse in them, blacke, of a cleere and sightlye blackenesse, or elles gray, meery and laughinge, and so comely and percinge in beehouldinge, as some, in which a man thinketh verilie that the wayes that give an issue to the spirites are so deepe, that by them he maye see as farr as the hart. The eyes therefore lye lurkinge like souldiers in warre lyinge in wayte in bushment, and if the fourme of all the bodye be welfavoured and of good proportion, it draweth unto it and allureth whoso beehouldeth it a farr of, until he come nigh: and assoone as he is at hande, the eyes shoote, and like sorcerers, beewitch, and especiallie whan by a right line they sende their glisteringe beames into the eies of the wight beloved at the time whan they do the like, bicause the spirites meete together, and in that sweete encounter the one taketh the others nature and qualitye: as it is seene in a sore eye, that beehoulding steadily a sound one, giveth him his disease. Therfore me thinke oure Courtier may in this wise open a great percel of the love to his woman. Truth it is that in case the eyes be not governed with art, they discover manie times the amorous desires more unto whom a man woulde least: for through them (in a maner) visibly shinefurth those burninge passions, whiche the lover mindinge to disclose onlie to the wight beloved, openeth them manie times also unto whom he woulde most soonest hide them from. Therfore he that hath not lost the bridle of reason, handleth himselfe heedefullye, and observeth the times and places: and whan it needeth, refrayneth from so stedfast bee-houldinge, for all it be a most savourie foode, bicause an open love is to harde a matter.

Open love.

[LXVII] COUNT LEWIS answered: Yet otherwhile to be open it hurteth not: bicause in this case manye times men suppose that those loves tende not to the ende which everie lover coveteth, whan they see there is litle heede taken to hide them, and passe not whether they be knowen or no: and therfore with deniall a man chalengeth him a certein libertye to talke openly and to stande without susspition with the wight beloved: whiche is not so in them that seke to be secrete, bicause it appeereth that they stande in hope of, and are nighe some great rewarde, whiche they woulde not have other men to knowe. I have also seene a most fervent love springe in the hart of a woman towarde one, that seemed at the firste not to beare him the least affection in the world, onlye for that she heard say, that the opinion of many was, that they loved together. And the cause of this (I beleave) was, that so generall a judgement seemed a sufficiente witnesse, that he was woorthie of her love. And it seemed (in a maner) that report brought the ambassade on the lovers beehalfe muche more truer and worthier to be beleaved, then he himselfe coulde have done with letters, or woordes, or any other person for him: therfore sometime this commune voice not onlye hurteth not, but farthereth a mans purpose.

The L. JULIAN answered: Loves that have report for their messanger, are verye perilous to make a man pointed to with a finger. And therfore who ever

entendeth to walke this race* warilye, needes must he
make countenaunce to have a great deale lesse fire in his
stomake, then in deede he hath, and content himselfe
with that, that he thinketh a trifle, and dissemble his
desires, jeolosies, afflictions and pleasures, and manye
times laugh with mouth whan the hart weepeth, and
showe himself lavishe of that he is most covetous of: and
these thinges are so harde to be done, that (in a maner)
they are unpossible. Therfore if oure Courtier would
folowe my counsell, I would exhort him to kepe his
loves secrete.

[LXVIII] Then said M. BERNARDE: You must then
teach it him, and me thinke it is muche to pourpose: for
beeside privie signes that some make otherwhile so
closely, that (in a maner) without any gesture, the
person whom they covett, in their countenance and eyes
reade what they have in the hert, I have sometime heard
betweene two lovers a long and a large discourse of
love, wherof yet the standers by could not plainlye
understand any particuler point, nor be out of doubt
that it was of love, suche was the discreation and
heedefulnesse of the talker: for without makinge anie
maner showe that they were not willinge to be hearde,
they rounded† privilye the wordes onlie that were most
to pourpose, and al the rest they spake aloude, which
might be applied to divers meaninges.

Then spake SIR FRIDERICK: To reason thus in
peecemeale of these rules of secretnesse, were a takinge
of an infinit matter in hand: therfore would I that we
spake somwhat rather how the lover shoulde keepe and
maintein his Ladies good wil, which me thinke is much
more necessary.

[LXIX] The L. JULIAN answered: I beleave the
meanes that serve him to compasse it, serve him also to
kepe it, and all this consisteth in pleasinge the woman
beloved, without offending her at any time. Therfore it
were a hard matter to give any certein rule, bicause
whoso is not discrete, infinit wayes committeth oversightes, whiche otherwhile seeme matters of nothing,
and yet offende they much the womans minde. And this

*To maintein
good will.*

---

* walke this race: take this path.
† rounded: said, whispered.

happeneth more then to others, to suche as be mastred with passion: as some that whenso ever they have opportunitie to speake with the woman they love, lament and beewaile so bitterlye, and covett manye times thinges so unpossible, that through this unreasonablenesse they are lothed of them. Other, if they be prickcd with anye jeolosie, stomake the matter so greevouslye, that without stopp they burst oute in raylinge upon him they suspect, and otherwhile* it is without trespace eyther of him or yet of the woman, and will not have her speake with him, nor once tourne her eyes on that side where he is. And with these facions manye tymes, they do not onlye offende the woman, but also they are the cause that she bendeth herselfe to love him. Bicause the feare that a lover declareth to have otherwhile least his Ladye forsake him for the other, beetokeneth that he acknowleageth himself inferiour in desertes and prowesse to the other, and with this opinion the woman is moved to love him. And perceyvinge that to put him out of favour he reporteth ill of him, although it be true, yet she beleaveth it not, and notwythstandinge loveth him the more.

[LXX] Then saide the L. CESAR: I confesse that I am not so wise that I coulde refrayne speakynge yll of my felow lover, except you coulde teache me some other better waye to dispatche him.

The L. JULIAN answered smilinge: It is saide in a Proverbe, Whan a mans ennemye is in the water uppe to the middle, lette him reache him his hande, and helpe him from daunger: but whan he is up to the chinn, set his foote on his head and drowne him out of hand. Therefore certein there be that playe so with their felow lovers, and untill they have a sure meane to dispatche them, go dissembling the matter, and rather show themselves friendes then otherwise. Afterward whan occasion serveth them so fitlye, that they know they may overthrowe them with a sure riddaunce, reportinge all yvell of them, be it true or false, they doe it without sparynge, with art, deceite and all wayes that they can imagin. But bicause I woulde not lyke that oure Courtier shoulde at anye tyme use anye deceyte, I

An Italian proverbe.

---

* otherwhile: sometimes.

woulde have him to withdrawe the good will of his
maistresse from his felowlover with none other arte, but
with lovinge, with servinge, and with beeinge vertuous,
of prowesse, discreet, sober, in conclusion with
deservinge more then he, and with beeinge in everye
thynge heedfull and wise, refrayninge from certein
leude folies, into the which often times manye
ignoraunt renn, and by sundrie wayes. For in times past
I have knowen some that in writinge and speakinge to
women used evermore the woordes of Poliphilus,[241]
and ruffled so in their subtill pointes of Rhetoricke, that
the women were oute of conceit with their owne selves,
and reckened themselves most ignoraunt, and an houre
seemed a thousand yeere to them, to ende that talke and
to be rid of them. Other, bragg and boast to by yonde all
measure. Other speake thinges manie times that
redounde to the blame and damage of themselves, as
some that I am wont to laughe at, which make
profession to be lovers, and otherwhile say in the
companye of women: I never founde woman that ever
loved me, and are not weetinge* that the hearers by and
by† judge that it can arrise of none other cause, but that
they deserve neither to be beloved, nor yet so much as
the water they drinke, and count them assheades, and
would not love them for all the good‡ in the worlde:
seeming to them that in case they should love them, they
were lesse worth, then all the rest that have not loved
them. Other, to purchase hatred to some felowe lover of
theirs, are so fonde that in like maner in the companye
of women they saye: Such a one is the luckiest man in
the worlde, for once,§ he is neyther welfavoured, nor
sober, nor of prowess,** neyther can he do or say more
then other menne, and yet all women love him, and renn
after him, and thus uttringe the spite they beare him for
this good lucke, althoughe neyther in countenaunce nor
deedes he appeereth lovelye, yet make they them
beleave that he hathe some hid matter in him, for the

Howe a
womans good
will is to be
drawen from
a mans rivale.

Men that
professe to be
to lovinge in
woordes.

The fondnes
of some
lovers.

* are not weetinge: do not realise.
† by and by: at once.
‡ good: the original has 'gold'.
§ for once: even though.
** neyther welfavoured, nor sober, nor of prowess: neither
handsome, nor intelligent, nor brave.

whiche he deserveth the love of so manie women, wherfore the women that heare them talke of him in this wise, they also upon this beleaf are moved to love him muche more.

[LXXI] Then COUNT LEWIS laughed and saide: I assure you our Courtier if he be discreete, will never use this blockishenes, to gete him the good will of women.

The L. CESAR GONZAGA answered: Nor yet an other that a Gentilman of reputation used in my dayes, who shal be namelesse for the honour of men.

The DUTCHESSE answered: Tell us at the least what he did.

Blockish over sightes.

The L. CESAR said: This manne beeinge beloved of a great Lady, at her request came privilye to the towne where she laye. And after he had seene her and communed with her, as long as they thought meete and had time and leyser therto, at his leave takinge with many bitter teares and sighes in witnesse of the extreme greef he felt for this departinge, he required her to be alwaies mindfull of him. And afterward he added withall, that she woulde discharge his ynn, for sins he came thither at her request, he thought meete that he should not stand to the charges of his beeing there himself.

Then beegan all the Ladies to laugh, and said that he was most unwoorthy of the name of a Gentilman: and many were ashamed with the selfe shame that he himselfe shoulde woorthilye have felt, if at anye time he had gotten so muche understandynge, that he might have perceyved so shamefull an oversight.*

Then tourned the L. GASPAR to the L. Cesar and said: Better it had bine to have omitted the rehersal of this matter for the honour of women, then the naming of him for the honour of men. For you may well imagin what a judgement that great Ladie had in lovinge so unreasonable a creature. And perhappes to, of manye that served her, she chose him for the most discreatest, leavinge beehinde, and showinge ill wil unto them that he was not woorthie to wayte upon.

COUNT LEWIS laughed and saide: Who woteth whether he was discreate in other thinges or no, and

* oversight: error.

was out of the waye onlye about ynnes? But many times for overmuch love men committ great folies. And if you will tell the truth, perhappes it hath bine your chaunce to commit mo then one.

Love maketh men commit great folies.

[LXXII] The L. CESAR answered smilinge: Of good felowshippe let us not discover oure owne oversightes.

Yet we must discover them, answered the L. GASPAR, that we maye knowe how to amende them, then he proceeded: Now that the Courtier knoweth how to wynn and kepe the good will of his Lady, and take it from his felow lover, you (my L. Julian) are dettour to teache her to kepe her loves secrete.

The L. JULIAN answered: Me thinke I have sufficientlye spoken, therefore gete ye nowe an other to talke of this secreate matter.

Then M. Bernarde and all the rest beegane a freshe to be in hande with him instantlye, and the L. JULIAN said: You will tempt me. Ye are all the sort of you to great Clearkes* in love. Yet if ye desire to know farther, goe and reade Ovid.

And howe, quoth M. BERNARDE, shal I hope that his lessons are any thing worth in love, whan he counselleth and saith that it is very good for a man in the companye of his maistresse to feigne the dronkarde? See what a goodly way it is to gete good will withall. And he alleageth for a pretie divise to make a woman understande that he is in love with her, beeinge at a banckett, to diepe his finger in wine and write it upon the table.[242]

The L. JULIAN said smilinge: In those dayes it was no fault.

And therfore, quoth M. BERNARDE, seeinge so sluttishe a matter was not disalowed of men in those daies, it is to be thought that they had not so courtlye beehaviours to serve women in love, as we have. But let us not omitt oure first pourpose to teache to keepe love secrete.

[LXXIII] Then saide the L. JULIAN: In myne advise to keepe love secrete, the causes are to be shonned that uttre it, whiche are manye: yet one principall, namelye, to be over secrete and to put no person in truste. Bicause everye lover coveteth to make his passions knowen to

To kepe love secrete.

* to great Clearkes: all too expert.

A friende.

the beloved, and beeinge alone, he is driven to make many mo signes and more evident, then if he were aided by some lovinge and faithfull friende. For the signes that the lover himselfe maketh, give a farr greater susspition, then those that he maketh by them that go in message betwene. And forsomuch as men naturallye are greedie to understand, assone as a straunger beeginneth to suspect the matter, he so applieth* it, that he commeth to the knowleage of the truth, and whan he once knoweth it, he passeth not for disclosinge it, yea sometime he hath a delite to do it. Which happeneth not of a friend, who beeside that he is a helpe to him with favour and counsell, doeth many times remedie the oversightes committed by the blinde lover, and alwaies procureth secretnes, and preventeth many matters which he himself can not foresee: beeside the great comfort that he feeleth, whan he maye uttre his passions and greeffes, to a harty friende, and the partening of them likewise encreaseth his contentations.

[LXXIV] Then said the L. GASPAR: There is an other cause that discovereth loves much more then this.

What is that? answered the L. JULIAN.

What dis-
closeth love.

The L. GASPAR said: Vaine greedinesse† joigned with the fondenesse and cruelty of women, which (as you your selfe have saide) procure as muche as they can to gete them a great numbre of lovers, and (if it were possible) they would have them al to burne and make asshes, and after death to retourn to lief, to die again. And thoughe they love withall, yet rejoice they at the tourment of lovers, bicause they suppose that greef, afflictions and the calling every hour for death, is a true witnesse that they are beloved, and that with their beawtie they can make men miserable and happy, and give them life and death, as pleaseth them. Wherfore they feede upon this only foode, and are so gredie over it, that for wanting it they never throughly content lovers, nor yet put them out of hope, but to kepe them still in afflictions and in desire, they use a certein lofty sowernesse‡ of threatninges mingled with hope, and

* applieth: investigates.
† greedinesse: ambition.
‡ lofty sowernesse: imperious severity.

wold have them to esteame a woorde, a countenance or
a beck of theirs for a cheef blisse. And to make men
count them chaste and honest aswel others as their
lovers, they finde meanes that these sharpe and discourtious maners of theirs may be in open sight, for
every man to thinke that they will much woorse handle
the unwoorthy, sins they handle them so, that deserve
to be beloved. And under this beleaf thinking themselves with this craft safe from sclaunder, often times
they lye nightlie with most vile men and whom they
scase knowe. So that to rejoice at the calamitie and
continuall complaintes of some woorthie gentilman,
and beloved of them, they barr themselves from those
pleasures, whiche perhappes with some excuse they
might come bye, and are the cause that the poore lover
by verye debating of the matter is driven to use wayes,
by the which the thinge commeth to light, that with all
diligence shoulde have bine kept most secrete. Certein
other there are, whiche if with deceite they can bringe
manye in beeleaf that they are beloved of them, nourish
emonge them jeolosies with cherishinge and makinge*
of the one in the others presence. And whan they see
that he also whom they love best is now assured and
oute of doubt that he is beloved through the signes and
tokens that be made him, manie times with doubtfull
woordes and feigned disdeignes they put him in an
uncerteintie and nippe him at the verie hart, makinge
wise not to passe for him and to give themselves full and
wholye to the other. Wherupon arrise malicc,
enimities, and infinite occasions of stryfe and uttre
confusion. For needes must a man showe in that case
the extreme passion which he fealeth, althoughe it
redounde to the blame and sclaunder of the woman.
Other, not satisfied with this onlye tourment of jeolosye,
after the lover hath declared all his tokens of love and
faithfull service, and they receyved the same with some
signe to be answerable in good will, without pourpose
and whan it is least looked for, they beegine to
beethinke themselves,† and make wise to‡ beleave that

---

* makinge: making much.
† beethinke themselves: pull back.
‡ make wise to: pretend to.

he is slacked, and feininge newe suspitions that they are not beloved, they make a countenaunce that they will in any wise put him out of their favour. Wherfore throughe these inconveniences the poore soule is constrayned of verye force to beegine a freshe, and to make her signes, as thoughe he beegane his service but then, and all the daye longe passe up and downe through the streete, and whan the woman goith furth of her doores to accompanye her to Churche and to everie place where she goith, and never to tourne hys eyes to other place. And here he retourneth to weepinge, to sighes, to heavie countenance, and whan he can talke with her, to swearing, to blaspheminge, to desperation, and to all rages which unhappie lovers are lead to by these wielde beastes, that have greater thirst of blood then the verie Tygres. [LXXV] Such sorowfull tokens as these be are to often sene and knowen, and manie times more of others then of the causer of them, and thus are they in few dayes so published, that a stepp can not be made, nor the leaste signe that is, but it is noted with a thousande eyes. It happeneth then, that longe before there be any pleasures of love beetwext them, they are ghessed and judged of all the world. For whan they see yet their lover nowe nighe deathes doore, cleane vanquished with the crueltye and tourmentes they put him to, determineth advisedlye and in good ernest to draw backe, then beegine they to make signe that they love him hartely, and do him al pleasures and give themselves to him, leaste if that fervent desire should feint in him, the frute of love shoulde withall be the lesse acceptable to him, and he ken them the lesse thanke for doinge all thinges contrarily. And in case this love be already knowen abrode, at this same time are all the effectes knowen in like maner abrode, that come of it, and so lose they their reputation, and the lover findeth that he hath lost time and labour and shortned his life in afflictions without any frute or pleasure, bicause he came by his desires, not whan they should have bine so acceptable to him that they woulde have made him a most happie creature, but whan he set litle or nothinge by them. For his hart was nowe so mortified with those bitter passions, that he had no more sense to taste the delite or contentation offred him.

[LXXVI] Then said the L. Octavian smilinge: You helde your peace a while and refrayned from speakinge yll of women, but now ye have so wel hit them home, that it appered ye waited a time to plucke uppe your strength, like them that retire backeward to give a greater pushe at the encounter. And to say the truth, it is ill done of you, for nowe me thinke ye may have done and be pacified.

The L. Emilia laughed, and tourninge her to the Dutchesse she said: See Madam, our ennemies begine to breake and to square one wyth an other.

Give me not this name, answered the L. Octavian, for I am not your adversarie, but this contention hath displeased me, not bicause I am sorye to see the victory upon womens side, but bicause it hath lead the L. Gaspar to revile them more then he ought, and the L. Julian and the L. Cesar to praise them perhappes somwhat more then due: beeside that through the length of the talke we have lost the understandinge of manye other pretye matters that are yet beehinde to be said of the Courtier.

See, quoth the L. Emilia, whether you be not oure adversarie, for the talke that is past greeveth you, and you would not that this so excellent a Gentilwoman of the Palaice had bine facioned: not for that you have any more to say of the Courtier (for these lordes have spoken already what they know and I beleave neither you, ne any man elles can ad ought therto) but for the malice you beare to the honour of women.

[LXXVII] It is out of doubt, answered the L. Octavian, beeside that is alreadie spoken, of the Courtier, I coulde wishe muche more in him. But sins every man is pleased that he shall be as he is, I am well pleased to, and woulde not have him altered in anye point, savinge in makinge him somwhat more frindlye to women, then the L. Gaspar is, yet not perhappes, so much as some of these other Lordes are.

Then spake the Dutchesse: In any case we must see whether youre witt be suche that it can give the Courtier a greater perfection, then these Lordes have alreadye done: therefore dispose your selfe to uttre that you have in your minde, els will we thinke that you also can not ad unto him more then hath alreadie bine saide, but that you minded to diminish the praises and worthinesse of the gentilwoman of the Palaice, seeing ye judge she is equall with the Courtier, whom by this meane you would have beleaved might be muche more perfect, then these Lordes have facioned him.

The L. OCTAVIAN laughed and said: The prayses and disprayses given women more then due, have so filled the eares and minde of the hearers, that they have left no voide rowme for anye thinge elles to stande in: beeside that (in mine opinion) it is very late.

Then said the DUTCHESSE: If we tarie till to morowe, we shall have more time, and the prayses and dispraises, whiche (you saye) are given women on both sides passinge measure, in the meane season will be cleane out of these Lordes mindes, and so shall they be apte to conceyve the truth that you will tell us. Whan the Dutchesse had thus spoken, she arrose upon her feete, and courteisly dismissing them all, withdrew her to the bedchamber, and everye manne gote him to his rest.

THE FOURTH BOOKE
OF THE COURTYER OF COUNT
BALDESSAR CASTILIO
UNTO MAISTER
ALPHONSUS ARIOSTO

[I] Thinkinge to write oute the communication that was had the fourth night after the other mentioned in the former bookes, I feele emong sundry discourses a bitter thought that gripeth me in my minde, and maketh me to call to remembraunce worldlie miseries and our deceitfull hopes, and how fortune many times in the verie middes of our race, otherwhile nighe the ende disapointeth our fraile and vaine pourposes, sometime drowneth them beefore they can once come to have a sight of the haven a farr of. It causeth me therfore to remember that not long after these reasoninges were had, cruell death bereved our house of three moste rare gentilmen, whan in their prosperous age and forwardnesse* of honour they most florished, and of them the first was the Lord Gaspar Pallavicin, who assaulted with a sharpe disease, and more then once brought to the last cast, although his minde was of suche courage that for a time in spite of death he kept the soule and bodye together, yet did he ende hys naturall course longe beefore he came to his ripe age. A very great losse not in our house onlie and to his friendes and kinsfolke, but to his Countrie and to all Lombardye. Not longe after died the L. Cesar Gonzaga, which to all that were acquainted with him left a bitter and sorowfull remembraunce of his death. For sins nature so sildome times bringeth furth such kinde of men, as she doeth, meete it seemed that she shoulde not so soone have bereved us of him. For undoubtedlye a man maye saye that the L. Cesar was taken from us even at the very time whan he beegane to show more then a hope of himself, and to be esteamed as his excellent qualities deserved. For with manye vertuous actes he alreadie gave a good testimony of his worthinesse, and beeside his noblenesse of birthe, he excelled also in the ornament of letters, of marciall prowesse, and of everye woorthie qualitie. So that for his goodnesse, witt, nature, and knowlege, there was

L. Gaspar
Pallavicin.

L. Cesar
Gonzaga.

* forwardnesse: promise.

M. Robert
of Bari.

nothinge so highe, that might not have bine hoped for at
his handes. Within a short while after, the death of M.
Robert of Bari was also a great heavinesse to the wholl
house: for reason seemed to perswade everie man to
take hevily the death of a yonge man of good beehaviour,
pleasaunt and moste rare in the beawtie of fisnamye and
in the makinge of his person, with as lucky and lively
towardnes, as a man coulde have wished. [II] These men
therfore, had they lived, I beleave would have come to
that passe, that unto whoso had knowen them, they
woulde have showed a manifest proof, how much the
Court of Urbin was worthie to be commended, and
howe fournished it was with noble knightes, in whiche
(in a maner) all the rest have done that were brought up
in it. For trulye there never issued out of the horse of
Troy so many great men and capitaines, as there have
come menne out of this house for vertue verie singular
and in great estimation with al men. For as you knowe

The promot-
inge of certein
mentioned in
the booke.

Sir Fridericke Fregoso was made archebishop of
Salerno. Count Lewis, Bishoppe of Baious. The L.
Octavian Fregoso, Duke of Genua. M. Bernarde
Bibiena, Cardinal of Santa Maria in Portico. M. Peter
Bembo, Secretarye to Pope Leo. The L. Julian was
exalted to the Dukedome of Nemours and to the great
astate he is presentlye in. The Lord Francescomaria
della Roveré, Generall of Roome, he was also made
Duke of Urbin: although a muche more praise may be
given to the house where he was brought up, that in it he
hath proved so rare and excellent a Lorde in all vertuous
qualities (as a man may beehoulde) then that he atteined
unto the Dukedome of Urbin: and no smalle cause
thereof (I thinke) was the noble company where in daily
conversation he alwaies hearde and sawe commendable
nourtour. Therfore (me thinke) whether it be by happe,
or throughe the favour of the sterres, the same cause
that so longe a time hath graunted unto Urbin verie
good governours, doth still continue and bringeth furth
the like effectes. And therefore it is to be hoped that
prosperous fortune will still encrease these so vertuous
doinges, that the happines of the house and of the State
shall not only not diminish, but rather daily
encrease:[243] and therof we see alreadye manye evident
tokens, emonge whiche (I recken) the cheeffest to be,

that the heaven hath graunted suche a Lady as is the
Ladye Eleonor Gonzaga the newe Dutchesse.[244] For if
ever there were coopled in one bodye alone, knowlage,
witt, grace, beawtie, sober conversation, gentilnesse
and every other honest qualitie, in her they are so
lincked together, that there is made therof a chaine,
whiche frameth and setteth furth everie gesture of
herres with al these condicions together. Let us therfore
proceade in our reasoninges upon the Courtyer, with
hope that after us there shall not want suche as shall
take notable and woorthye examples of vertue at the
presente Court of Urbin, as we nowe do at the former.

[III] It was thought therefore (as the L. Gaspar
Pallavicin was wont to reherse) that the next daye after
the reasoninges conteined in the laste booke, the L.
Octavian was not muche seene: for manye deemed that
he had gotten himself out of companye to thinke well
upon that he had to saye without trouble. Therfore
whan the companye was assembled at the accustomed
houre where the Dutchesse was, they made the L.
Octavian to be diligentlye sought for, whiche in a good
while appered not, so that manye of the Gentilmen and
Damselles of the Court fell to daunsynge and to minde
other pastymes, supposynge for that night they shoulde
have no more talke of the Courtyer.

And nowe were they all settled about one thinge or an
other, whan the L. OCTAVIAN came in (almost) no more
looked for: and beehouldinge the L. Cesar Gonzaga and
the L. Gaspar daunsinge, after he had made his
reverence to the Dutchesse, he saide smilinge: I had well
hoped we shoulde have hearde the L. Gaspar speake
some ill of women this night to, but sins I see him
daunce with one, I imagin he is agreede with all. And I
am glad that the controversie, or (to terme it better) the
reasoninge of the Courtier is thus ended.

Not ended, I warrant you, answered the DUTCHESSE,
for I am not suche an ennemye to men, as you be to
women, and therfore I wil not have the Courtier
bereved from his due honour and the fournimentes
whiche you youre selfe promised him yester night.

And whan she had thus spoken, she commaunded
them all after that daunse was ended to place themselves after the wonted maner, the which was done.

L. Eleonor
Gonzaga
Dut. of Urbin.

And as they stoode all wyth heedfull expectation, the L. OCTAVIAN said: Madam, sins for that I wished manye other good qualities in the Courtier, it foloweth by promise that I muste entreate uppon them, I am well willinge to uttre my minde: not with opinion that I can speake all that may be said in the matter, but only so much as shall suffice to roote that oute of your mind, which yester night was objected to me: namely, that I spake it more to withdrawe the prayses from the Gentilwoman of the Palaice, in doinge you falselye to beleave that other excellent qualities might be added to the Courtier, and with that pollicie prefarre him beefore her, then for that it is so in deede. Therfore to frame my selfe also to the houre, which is later then it was wont to be whan we beegane our reasoninges at other times, I will be breef. [IV] Thus continuinge in the talke that these Lordes have ministred, whiche I full and wholye

Thinges good. alowe and confirme, I say, that of thinges which we call good, some there be that simply and of themselves are alwaies good, as temperance, valiant courage, helth, and all vertues that bring quietnesse to mens mindes. Other be good for diverse respectes and for the ende they be applied unto, as the lawes, liberality, riches and other like. I thinke therfore that the Courtier (if he be of the perfection that Count Lewis and Sir Friderick have described him) maye in deede be a good thinge and woorthie praise, but for all that not symplye, nor of himself, but for respect of the ende wherto he may be applied. For doubtlesse if the Courtier with his noble-nesse of birth, comlie beehaviour, pleasantnesse and practise in so many exercises, should bringe furth no other frute, but to be suche a one for himself, I woulde not thinke to come by this perfect trade of Courtiership, that a man shoulde of reason beestowe so much studye and peynes about it, as who so will compase it must do. But I woulde say rather that manie of the qualities appointed him, as daunsing, singinge and sportinge, were lightnesse and vanitie, and in a man of estimation rather to be dispraised then commended: bicause those precise* facions, the setting furthe ones selfe,† meerie

* precise: elegant.

† settinge furth ones selfe: the original has *imprese* (see note p. 25).

talke and such other matters belonginge to enterteinment of women and love (althoughe perhappes manie
other be of a contrary opinion) do many times nothinge
elles but womannish the mindes, corrupt youth, and
bring them to a most wanton trade of livinge: wherupon afterwarde ensue these effectes, that the name of
Italy is brought into sclaunder, and few there be that
have the courage, I will not saye to jeoparde their lief,
but to entre once into a daunger. And without
peradventure there be infinite other thinges, that if a
man beestow his labour and studie about them, woulde
bring furth muche more profit both in peace and warr,
then this trade of Courtiershipp of it self alone. But in
case the Courtiers doinges be directed to the good ende
they ought to be and whiche I meane: me thinke then
they should not onlye not be hurtfull or vaine, but most
profitable and deserve infinit praise. [V] The ende
therfore of a perfect Courtier (wherof hitherto nothinge
hath bine spoken)[245] I beleave is to purchase him, by the
meane of the qualities whiche these Lordes have given
him, in such wise the good will and favour of the Prince
he is in service withall, that he may breake his minde to
him, and alwaies enfourme hym francklye of the trueth
of everie matter meete for him to understande, without
feare or perill to displease him. And whan he knoweth
his* minde is bent to commit any thinge unseemlie for
him, to be bould to stande with him† in it, and to take
courage after an honest sort at the favour which he hath
gotten him throughe his good qualities, to disswade him
from everie ill pourpose, and to set him in the waye of
vertue. And so shall the Courtier, if he have the
goodnesse in him that these Lordes have geven him
accompanied with readinesse of witt, pleasantnesse,
wisdome, knowleage in letters and so many other
thinges, understande how to beehave himself readilye in
all occurrentes to drive into his Princis heade what
honour and profit shall ensue to him and to his by
justice, liberalitie, valiauntnesse of courage, meekenesse and by the other vertues that beelong to a good

*Dastardli-
nesse.*

*The ende of
a Courtier.*

---

* his: i.e. the prince's.
† stande with him: stand up to him (the original has 'dare to
contradict him').

Prince, and contrariwise what sclaunder and damage commeth of the vices contrarie to them. And therfore in mine opinion, as musike, sportes, pastimes, and other pleasaunt facions, are (as a man woulde saye) the floure of Courtlines, even so is the traininge and the helping forward of the Prince to goodnesse and the fearinge him from yvell, the frute of it. And bicause the praise of weldoinge consisteth cheeflye in two pointes, wherof the one is, in chousinge out an ende that our pourpose is directed unto, that is good in deede: the other, the knowleage to find out apt and meete meanes to bringe it to the appointed good ende: sure it is that the mind of him which thinketh to worke so, that his Prince shall not be deceived, nor lead with flaterers, railers and lyers, but shall knowe both the good and the bad and beare love to the one and hatred to the other, is directed to a verye goode ende. [VI] Me thinke again, that the qualities which these Lordes have given the Courtier, may be a good meanes to compasse it: and that, bicause emonge manye vices that we see now a dayes in manye of our Princis, the greatest are ignoraunce and selfe leekinge: and the roote of these two mischeeves is nothing elles but lyinge, which vice is worthelie abhorred of God and man, and more hurtful to Princis then any other, bicause they have more scarsitye then of any thinge elles, of that which they neede to have more plenty of, then of any other thinge: namely, of suche as shoulde tell them the truth and put them in minde of goodnesse: for enemies be not driven of love to do these offices, but they delite rather to have them live wickedly and never to amende: on the other side, they dare not rebuke them openlye for feare they be punished. As for friendes few of them have free passage to them, and those few have a respect to reprehende their vices so freelye as they do private mens: and many times to coorie favour and to purchase good will, they give themselves to nothinge elles but to feede them with matters that may delite, and content their minde, thoughe they be foule and dishonest. So that of friendes they become flatterers, and to make a hande by that streict familiaritie, they speake and woorke alwaies to please, and for the most part open the way with lyes, which in the Princis minde engender ignorance, not of outwarde matters

The floure of courtlines.
The frute of it.
Well doinge.

Lies engender ignorance and self leeking.

Enemies.

Friendes.

Flattery.

onlie, but also of his owne selfe. And this may be said to
be the greatest and fowlest lye of all other, bicause the
ignorant minde deceiveth himself and inwardlie maketh
lyes of himself. [VII] Of this it commeth, that great men,   Great men.
beeside that they never understande the truth of any
thinge, dronken with the licentious libertye that rule
bringeth with it and with abundance of delicacies
drowned in pleasures, ar so far out of the way and their
mind is so corrupted in seeing themselves alwaies
obeyed and (as it were) woorshipped with so much
reverence, and praise, without not onlye anye reproof
at all, but also gainsayinge, that through this
ignoraunce they wade to an extreeme selfe leekinge, so
that afterwarde they admitt no counsell nor advise of
others. And bicause they beleave that the understandinge how to rule is a most easye matter, and to compasse
it there needeth neyther arte nor learninge, but onlye
stoutenesse, they bende their minde and all their
thoughtes to the maintenance of that port they kepe,
thinking it the true happynesse to do what a man
lusteth. Therfore do some abhorr reason and justice,
bicause they weene it a bridle and a certeine meane to
bringe them in bondage and to minishe in them the
contentation and hartes ease that they have to beare
rule, if they should observe it: and their rule were not
perfect nor wholl if they shoulde be compelled to obey
unto dutie and honestie, bicause they have an opinion
that Whoso obeyeth, is no right Lord in deede. Therfore
taking these principles for a president and suffering
them selves to be lead with selfe leekinge, they wexe
loftie, and with a statlye countenance, with sharpe and
cruell condicions, with pompous garmentes, golde and
jewelles, and with comminge (in a maner) never abrode
to be seene, they thinke to gete estimation and
authoritie emong men, and to be counted (almost)
Goddes: but they are (in my judgement) like the   Images of
Colosses that were made in Roome the last yeere upon   horrible
the feast day of the place of Agone, whiche outwardlye   greatnesse.
declared a likenesse of great men and horses of triumph,
and inwardly were full of towe and ragges.[246] But the
Princis of this sort are so muche woorse, as the Colosses
by their owne waightye pese stande upright of them
selves, and they bicause they be yll counterpesed and

without line or levell placed upon unequall grounde, throughe their owne waightinesse overthrowe them selves, and from one errour renn into infinit. Bicause their ignoraunce beeinge annexed with this false opinion that they can not err, and that the port they kepe commeth of their knowlage, leadeth of them every waye by right or by wronge to lay hande upon possessions bouldly, so they maye come bye them. [VIII] But in case they woulde take advisemente to knowe and to woorke that that they ought, they would aswell strive not to reigne as they doe to reigne, bicause they shoulde perceyve what a naughtye and daungerous matter it were for Subjectes that ought to be governed, to be wyser then the Princis that shoulde governe. You may see that ignoraunce in musike, in daunsinge, in ridinge hurteth no man, yet he that is no musitien is ashamed and aferde to singe in the presence of others, or to daunse, he that can not, or he that sitteth not wel a

Ignorance of rules.

horse, to ride: but of the unskilfulnes to govern people arrise so manie yvelles, deathes, destructions, mischeeffes and confusions, that it may be called the deadliest plagu upon the earth. And yet some princes most ignorant in government, are not bashfull nor ashamed to take upon them to govern I wil not say in the presence of foure or half a dosen persons, but in the face of the world: for their degree is sett so on loft, that all eyes beehould them, and therfore not their great vices only, but their least faultes of all are continuallie noted. As yt is written that Cimon was yll spoken of bicause he loved wine, Scipio, sleepe, Lucullus, bancketinges.[247] But wolde God, the Princis of these oure times wolde coople their vices wyth so manie vertues as did they of olde time: which yf they were out of the way in any point, yet refused they not the exhortations and lessons of such as they deemed meete

Princis of olde time were refourm-able.

to correct those faultes: yea they saught with great instance to frame their lief by the rule of notable personages: as Epaminondas by Lisias of Pythagoras sect: Agesilaus by Xenophon: Scipio by Panætius, and infinit others.[248] But in case a grave Philosopher shoulde come beefore enie of our Princes, or who ever beeside, that wolde showe them plainlie and without enie circomstance the horrible face of true vertue and

teache them good maners and what the lief of a good
Prince ought to be, I ame assured they wolde abhorr
him at the first sight, as a most venimous serpent, or
elles they wolde make him a laughinge stocke, as a most
vile matter. [IX] I saye therfore that sins nowadayes
Princis are so corrupt through yl usages, ignorance and
false self leekinge, and that yt is so harde a matter to geve
them the knoweleage of the truth and to bende them to
vertue, and men with lyes and flatterie and such
naughtye meanes seeke to coorie favour wyth them, the
Courtier by the meane of those honeste qualities that
Count Lewis and Sir Friderick have given hym, may
soone,* and ought to go about so to purchase him the
good will and allure unto him the minde of his Prince,
that he maye make him a free and safe passage to
comune with him in every matter without troublinge
him.† And yf he be suche a one as is said, he shall
compase yt with smalle peine, and so may he alwayes
open unto him the truth of everie matter at ease. Besyde
this by litle and litle distille into his minde goodnesse,
and teache him continencie, stoutnesse of courage,
justice, temperance, makinge him to taste what
sweetenesse is hid under that litle bitternesse, which at
the first sight appeereth unto him that withstandeth
vices: which are alwaies hurtfull, displeasant and
accompanied wyth yl report and shame, even as vertues
are profitable, pleasant and praisable, and enflame him
to them with the examples of manie famous Capitanes,
and of other notable personages, unto whom they of old
time used to make ymages of mettal and marble, and   Images in
sometime of gold, and to set them up in commune   the honour
haunted places, aswell for the honoure of them, as for   of men.
an encouragynge of others, that with an honest envie
they might also endevour them selves to reach unto that
glorie. [X] In this wise maye he leade him throughe the
roughe way of vertue (as it were) deckynge yt about
with boowes to shadowe yt and strawinge it over wyth
sightlye flouers, to ease the greefe of the peinfull journey
in hym that is but of a weake force. And sometyme with
musike, somtime with armes, and horses, sometyme
with rymes and meeter, otherwhyle wyth communication of love, and wyth all those wayes that these Lordes

* soone: easily.
† without troublinge him: the original has 'tactfully'.

have spoken of, continuallye keepe that mynde of his
occupyed in honest pleasure: imprintynge notwythstandynge therin alwayes beesyde (as I have said) in
companie with these flickeringe provocations* some
vertuous condicion, and beeguilinge him with a
holsome craft, as the warie phisitiens do, who manye
times whan they minister to yonge and tender children
in ther sickenesse, a medicin of a bitter taste, annoint
the cupp about the brimm with some sweete licour.[249]
The Courtier therfore applyinge to such a pourpose this
veile of pleasure, in everie time, in everie place, and in
everye exercise he shall attaine to his ende, and deserve
muche more praise and recompence, then for anie other
good woorke that he can do in the worlde, bicause there
is no treasure that doeth so universallie profit, as doeth
a good Prince, nor anie mischeef so universallie hurt, as
an yll Prince. Therfore is there also in peine so bitter and
cruell that were a sufficient punishment for those
naughtie and wicked Courtiers, that make their honest
and pleasant maners and their good qualities a cloke for
an ill ende, and by meane of them seeke to come in
favour with their Princis for to corrupte them and to
straye them from the way of vertue and to lead them to
vice. For a man may say, that such as these be, do infect
with deadlie poyson, not one vessel wherof one man
alone drinketh, but the commune fountain that all the
people resorteth to.

[XI] The L. Octavian helde his peace as though he
would have said no more, but the L. GASPAR: I can not
see, my L. Octavian (said he) that this goodnesse of
minde and continincie, and the other vertues whiche
you will have the Courtier to showe his Lord, may be
learned: but I suppose that they are given the men that
have them, by nature and of God. And that it is so, you
may see that there is no man so wicked and of so ill
condicions in the world, nor so untemperate and unjust,
which if he be asked the question, will confesse him self
such a one. But everie man be he never so wicked, is glad
to be counted just, continent and good: which shoulde
not be so, in case these vertues might be learned, bicause
it is no shame not to know the thinge that a man hath

---

* provocations: enticements.

not studied, but a rebuke* it is not to have that which we ought to be indowed withal of nature. Therfore doeth ech man seeke to cover the defaultes of nature, aswell in the minde, as also in the bodie: the which is to be seene in the blinde, lame, crooked and other mayned and deformed creatures. For although these imperfections may be layed to nature, yet doeth it greeve ech man to have them in him self: bicause it seemeth by the testimonie of the self same nature that a man hath that default or blemishe (as it were) for a patent and token of his ill inclination. The fable that is reported of Epimetheus[250] doeth also confirme myne opinion, whiche was so unskilfull in dividinge the gyftes of nature unto men, that he left them much more needie of everye thinge, then all other livinge creatures. Wherupon Prometheus stole the politike wysdome from Minerva and Vulcan that men have to gete their livinge withall. Yet had they not for all that, civill wisdome to gather them selves together into Cities, and the knowleage to live with civility, bicause it was kept in the Castle of Jupiter by most circumspect overseears, whiche put Prometheus in such feare, that he durst not approch nygh them. Wherupon Jupiter takinge pitye upon the miserye of men, that could not felowshipp together for lacke of civill vertue, but were torne in peeces by wielde beastes, he sent Mercury to the earth to carie justice and shame, that these two thinges might fournish Cities and gather Citizins together: and willed that they shoulde be given them, not as other artes were, wherin one counning man sufficeth for manie ignorant, as phisike, but that they should be imprinted in everie man. And ordeyned a lawe, that all such as were without justice and shame, should be banished and put to death, as contagious to the Citie. Beehoulde then (my L. Octavian) God hath graunted these vertues to men, and are not to be learned, but be naturall.

Fable of Epimetheus.

[XII] Then the L. OCTAVIAN somwhat smiling: Will you then, my L. Gaspar (quoth he) have men to be so unfortunate and of so pevish a judgement, that with policie they have found out an art to tame the natures of wield beastes, as beares, wolves, Lions, and may with

* rebuke: reproach.

the same teach a prety bird to fle as a man lust, and retourne back from the wood and from his naturall libertye of his owne accord to snares and bondage, and with the same pollicy can not, or will not finde out artes whereby they maye profit themselves, and with studie and diligence make their mind more perfect? This (in mine opinion) were like as if Phisitiens shoulde studie with all diligence to have the art onlie to heale fellonies in fingers and the read gumme in yonge children, and lay aside the cure of fevers, pleurisie and other sore diseases, the which how out of reason it were everie man may consider. I beleave therfore that the morall vertues are not in us all together by nature, bicause nothinge can at anye time be accustomed unto it, that is naturallie his contrarie: as it is seene in a stone, the whiche though it be cast upward ten thousand times, yet will he never accustome to go up of him selfe.[251] Therfore in case vertues were as natural to us, as heavinesse to the stone, we shoulde never accustome our selves to vice. Nor yet are vices naturall in this sort, for then shoulde we never be vertuous: and a great wickednesse and folie it were, to punishe men for the faultes that came of nature without oure offence: and this errour shoulde the lawes committ, whiche appoint not punishment to the offenders for the trespace that is past, bicause it can not be brought to passe that the thinge that is done, maye not be done, but they have a respect to the time to come, that who so hath offended maye offende no more, or elles with yll president give not a cause for others to offende. And thus yet they are in opinion that vertues maye be learned, whiche is most true, bicause we are borne apt to receive them, and in like maner vices: and therfore there groweth a custome in us of bothe the one and the other throughe longe use, so that first we practise vertue or vice, after that, we are vertuous or vitious. The contrarie is knowen in the thinges that be geven us of nature, for firste we have the pour to practise them, after that, we do practise: as it is in the senses, for first we can see, heere, feele, after that, we do see, heere and feele: although notwithstandinge many of these doinges be also sett oute more sightlye with teachinge. Wherupon good Schoolmaisters do not only instruct their children in letters, but also in good

Vertues may be learned.

A difference beetwene that a man hath by nature and by custome.

nourtour in eatinge, drinkinge, talking, and goinge with certein gestures meete for the pourpose. [XIII] Therfore even as in the other artes, so also in the vertues it is behouffull to have a teacher, that with lessons and good exhortations may stirr up and quicken in us these morall vertues, wherof we have the seede inclosed and buried in the soule,[252] and like the good husbande man, till them and open the waye for them, weedinge from about them the briers and darnell of appetites, which many times so shadow and choke our mindes, that they suffre them not to budd nor to bringe furth the happie frutes, which alone ought to be wished to grow in the hartes of men. In this sort then is naturally in everie one of us justice and shame, which (you saye) Jupiter sent to the earth for all men. But even as a bodye without eyes, how sturdie ever he be, if he remove to anie certein place, often times faileth: so the roote of these vertues that be potentiallie engendred in our mindes, yf it be not aided with teaching, doth often come to nought. Bicause if it shoulde be brought into doinge and to his perfect custome, it is not satisfied (as is said) with nature alone: but hath neede of a politike usage and of reason, whiche maye clense and scoure that soule, takinge away the dymm veile of ignorance, wherof arrise (in a maner) all the erroures in men. For in case good and ill were wel knowen and perceived, every man would alwaies chouse the good and shonn the yl. Therfore may vertue be said to be (as it were) a wisdome and an understanding to chouse the good: and vice, a lacke of foresight and an ignorance that leadeth to judge falsely. Bicause men never chouse the il with opinion that it is ill, but they are deceived through a certein likenesse of good.

Vertue.

Vice.

[XIV] Then answered the L. GASPAR: Yet are there many that know plainlie they do ill, and do it notwithstanding, and that bicause thei more esteame the present pleasure which they feele, then the punishment that they doubt shall fall upon them, as theeves, murtherers and such other.

The L. OCTAVIAN said: True pleasure is alwaies good, and true sorow, evell: therfore these be deceived in taking false pleasure for true, and true sorowe for false: wherupon manye times through false pleasures, they renn into true displeasures. The art therfore that

True pleasure.

True sorow.

teacheth to discerne this trueth from falshood, maye in like case be learned: and the vertue by the which we chouse this good in deede, and not that which falsely appeereth to be, may be called true knowleage, and more available for mans lief, then anye other, bicause it expelleth ignorance, of the which (as I have said) springe all evelles.

True knowleage.

[XV] Then M. PETER BEMBO: I wot not, my L. Octavian (quoth he) how the L. Gaspar should graunt you, that of ignoraunce should springe all evelles, and that there be not manye which in offendinge knowe for certeintie that they do offende, neyther are they anye deale deceived in the true pleasure nor yet in the true sorow: bicause it is sure that such as be incontinent judge with reason and uprightly, and know it, wher unto they are provoked by lust contrary to due, to be ill, and therefore they make resistance and sett reason to matche greedy desire, wherupon arriseth the battaile of pleasure and sorow against judgement. Finally reason overcome by greedie desire far the mightier, is cleane without succour, like a shippe, that for a time defendeth herself from the tempestuous Seastormes, at the end beaten with the to raginge violence of windes, her gables and tacklinges broken, yeldeth up to be driven at the will of fortune, without occupiyng helme or any maner help of Pilott for her safegard. Furthwith therefore commit they the offences with a certein doubtfull remorse of conscience and (in a maner) whether they will or no, the which they would not do, onlesse they knew the thing that they do to be ill, but without striving of reason would ren wholy headlonge after greedy desire, and then shoulde they not be incontinent, but untemperate, which is much woorse.[253] Therfore is incontinencie said to be a diminished vice, bicause it hath in it a part of reason, and likewise continency an unperfect vertue, bicause it hath in it part of affection:* therfore (me thinke) that it can not be said that the offences of the incontinent come of ignorance, or that they be deceived and offende not, whan they know for a truth that they do offende.

Reason.

Incontinency.
Continency.

[XVI] The L. OCTAVIAN answered: Certesse (M.

* affection: passion.

Peter) youre argument is good, yet (in my minde) it is more apparant then true. For although the incontinent offend with that doubtfulnesse, and reason in their minde striveth againste greedye desire, and that that is yll, seemeth unto them to be ill in deede, yet have they no perfect knowleage of it, nor understand it so throughly as nede requireth. Therfore of this, it is rather a feeble opinion in them, then certeine knowleage, wherby they agree to have reason overcome by affection: but if they had in them true knowleage, there is no doubt, but they would not offend: bicause evermore the thinge wherby greedie desire overcometh reason, is ignorance, neyther can true knowleage be ever overcome by affection, that proceadeth from the body and not from the mind, and in case it be wel ruled and governed by reason it becommeth a vertue: yf not it beecommeth a vice. But such force reason hath, that she maketh the sense alwaies to obey and by wonderous meanes and wayes perceth* least ignorance shoulde possesse that, which she ought to have:† so that althoughe the spirites and the sinewes, and the bones have no reason in them, yet whan there springeth in us that motion of minde, that the imagination (as it were) pricketh forward and shaketh the bridle to the spirites, all the members are in a readinesse, the feete to renn, the hands to take or to doe that whiche the minde thinketh upon, and this is also manifestlye knowen in many, which unwittingly otherwhile eate some lothesome and abhorring meat, but so well dressed that to their taste it appeereth moste delicate: afterwarde understandinge what maner thynge it was, it doeth not only greeve them and loth them in their minde, but the bodie also agreeth with the judgement of the minde, that of force they cast that meate up again.

[XVII] The L. Octavian folowed on still in his talke, but the L. JULIAN interruptinge him: My L. Octavian (quoth he) yf I have well understoode, you have said that continencie is an unperfect vertue, bicause it hath

Ignorance.

Reason.

---

* perceth: penetrates.
† least ignorance shoulde possesse that, which she ought to have: except when ignorance holds sway over what is hers [i.e. reason's] by rights.

in it part of affection: and me seemeth that the vertue (where there is in oure minde a variance beetwene reason and greedie desyre) whiche fighteth and giveth the victorye to reason, ought to be reckened more perfect, then that which overcommeth havinge neyther greedie desire nor anie affection to withstand it: bicause (it seemeth) that that minde absteyneth not from yll for vertues sake, but refrayneth the doing it, bicause he hath no will to it.

Then the L. OCTAVIAN: Which (quoth he) wolde you esteame the valianter Capitain, eyther he that hasardeth him selfe in open fight, and notwithstanding vanquisheth his enemies, or he that by his vertue and knowleage weakeneth them in bringinge them in case not able to fight, and so without battaile or anie jeopardie discomfetethe them?

He, quoth the L. JULIAN, that overcommeth with most suretie, is out of doubt most to be praised, so that this assured victorie of his proceade not through the slackenesse of the ennemies.

The L. OCTAVIAN answered: You have judged aright. And therfore I say unto you, that continencie may be compared to a Capitain that fighteth manlie, and though his ennemies be stronge and well appointed, yet geveth he them the overthrowe, but for al that not without much a do and daunger. But temperance free from all disquietinge, is like the Capitain that without resistance overcommeth and reigneth. And havinge in the mynde where she is, not onlie assuaged, but cleane quenched the fire of gredie desire, even as a good Prince in civill warr dispatcheth the sedicious inward ennemies, and giveth the scepter and wholl rule to reason, so in like case this vertue not enforcing the mind, but powringe therinto through most quiet waies a vehement persuasion that may incline him to honestie, maketh him quiet and full of rest, in everie part equall and of good proportion: and on everie side framed of a certein agreement with him self, that filleth him with such a cleare caulmenesse, that he is never out of pacience: and becommeth full and wholy most obedient to reason, and readie to tourn unto her all his motions, and folow her where she lust to leade him, without anie resistance, like a tender lambe that renneth, standeth and goith alwaies

Temperance.

by the ewes side, and moveth only as he seeth her do. This vertue therefore is most perfect, and is cheeflie requisit in Princis, bicause of it arrise manie other.

[XVIII] Then the L. CESAR GONZAGA: I wott not (quoth he) what vertues requisit for Princis may arrise of this temperance, yf it be she that riddeth the mind of affections (as you say) which perhappes were meete for some Monke or Heremite: but I can not see how it should be requisit for a Prince that is couragious, freeharted and of prowesse in marciall feates, for whatsoever is done to him, never to have angre, hatred, good will, disdeigne, lust, nor any affeccion in him: nor how without this he can gete him authoritie emonge the people and souldiers.

The L. OCTAVIAN answered: I have not said that temperance shoulde throughlye ridd and roote oute of mens mindes, affections: neyther shoulde it be well so to do, bicause there be yet in affections some partes good: but that which in affections is corrupt and striving against honestie, she bringeth to obey unto reason. Therfore it is not meete, to ridd the troublesome disquietnesse of the mind, to roote up affections cleane, for this were as if to avoide dronkennesse, there shoulde be an act established, that no man shoulde drinke wine: or bicause otherwhile in renninge a man taketh a fall, everie man should be forbed renning. Marke them that breake horses, they breake them not from their renninge and comminge on loft,* but they will have them to do it at the time and obedience of the rider. The affections therfore that be clensed and tried by temperance are assistant to vertue, as angre, that helpeth manlinesse: hatred against the wicked, helpeth justice, and likewise the other vertues are aided by affections, which in case they were cleane taken away, they woulde leave reason verie feeble and feint, so that it shoulde litle prevaile, like a shipp maister that is without winde in a great caulme. Marvaile ye not then (my L. Cesar) if I have said, that of temperance arrise manie other vertues: for whan a minde is in tune with this harmonie, by the meane of reason he easely receiveth afterward true manlinesse, which maketh him boulde and safe

True manlinesse.

* comminge on loft: leaping.

from all daunger, and (in a maner) above worldly

Justice.

passions. Likewise Justice, an undefiled virgin, friend to sobermode and goodnesse, queene of all other vertues, bicause she teacheth to do that, which a man ought to do, and to shon that a man ought to shonn, and therfore is she most perfect, bicause through her the woorkes of the other vertues are brought to passe, and she is a helpe to him that hath her both for him selfe and for others: without the which (as it is commanlye said) Jupiter him selfe coulde not well govern hys kingdome. Stoutnesse

Stoutnesse of courage.

of courage* doeth also folowe after these, and maketh them all the greater, but she can not stand alone, bicause whoso hath not other vertues can not be of a stoute courage. Of these then wisdome is guide, which

Wisdome.

consisteth in a certein judgement to chouse well. And in this happie chayne are also lincked liberalitie, sump-tuousnesse,† the desire to save a mans estymation, meekenesse, pleasantnesse, courtesie in talke, and manie other which is nowe no time to speake of. But in case oure Courtier wyll do as we have saide, he shall finde them all in his Princis minde: and daylie he shall see springe suche beawtifull floures and frutes, as all the delicious gardeins in the world have not the like: and he

The way to govern well.

shall feele verie great contentacion within him self, whan he remembreth that he hath given him, not the thinges whiche foolish persons give, whiche is, golde, or silver, plate, garmentes, and such matters, wherof he that giveth them hath him self verie great scarsitie, and he that receiveth them exceading great store: but that vertue, which perhappes among all the matters that belong unto man, is the cheeffest and rarest, that is to say, the maner and way to rule and to reigne in the right kinde. Which alone were sufficient to make men happie, and to bring once again into the worlde the golden age, whiche is written to have bine whan Saturnus reigned in the olde time.

The reigne of a good prince.

[XIX] Here whan the L. Octavian paused a litle as though he woulde have taken respite, the L. GASPAR said: Whiche recken you (my L. Octavian) the happiest

---

* stoutnesse of courage: this is the Aristotelian 'magnanimity', greatness of soul.
† sumptuousnesse: magnificence.

government and that were most to pourpose to bring into the world again that golden age whych you have made mention of, eyther the reigne of so good a Prince, or the governance of a good Commune weale?[254]

The L. OCTAVIAN answered: I woulde alwayes prefarr the reigne of a good Prince, bicause it is a government more agreeable to nature, and (if it be lawfull to compare small matters with infinit) more like unto Goddes, whiche one and alone governeth the universall. But leavinge this, ye see that in whatsoever is broughte to passe with the pollicie of man, as armies, great saylinge vesselles, buildynges and other lyke matters, the wholl is committed to one alone, to dyspose therof at his will. Likewise in oure bodye all the membres travaile and are occupied as the hart thinketh good. Beeside this it seemeth meete that people shoulde aswell be governed by one Prince, as manye other livinge creatures be, whom nature teacheth this obedience, as a moste soveraign* matter. Marke ye whether deere, cranes and manye other foules, whan thei take their flight do not alwaies set a Prince beefore, whom they folowe and obey. And bees (as it were) with discourse of reason and with such reverence honour their kinge, as the most obedientest people in the world can do. And therfore this is a verie great argument that the soveraigntie of a Prince is more accordinge to nature, then a Commune weales.

[XX] Then M. PETER BEMBO: And me thinke (quoth he) that sins God hath given us libertie for a soveraigne gifte, it is not reason that it should be taken from us: nor that one man should be partner of it more then an other, which happeneth under the rule of princis, who for the most part keepe their people in most streict bondage.[255] But in Commune weales well in order this libertie is well kept. Beeside that, both in judgementes and in advisementes, it happeneth oftner that the opinion of one alone is false, then the opinion of many, bicause troublous affection either through anger, or throughe spite, or through lust, sooner entreth into the mind of one alone then into the multitudes, whiche (in a maner) like a greate quantitie of water, is lesse subject to

Libertye.

---

* soveraign: salutary.

corruption, then a smalle deale. I saye again that the
example of the beastes and foules doth not make to
pourpose, for both Deere and Cranes and the rest doe
not alwaies sett one and the selfe formost for them to
folowe and obey, but they still chaunge and varie,
givinge this prefarment somtime to one, otherwile to
an other, and in this maner it beecommeth rather the
fourme of a Commune weale, then of a kingdome, and
this maye be called a true and equall libertie, whan they
that somtime commaunde, obey again an other while.
The example likewise of the bees (me thinke) is not
alike, bicause that kinge of theirs is not of their owne
kinde: and therefore he that will give unto men a
worthie head in deede, must be faine to finde him of an
other kinde, and of a more noble nature then mans, if
menne (of reason) shoulde obey him, as flockes and
heardes of cattell that obey, not a beast their like, but a
sheppharde and a hardman, which is a man and of a
more woorthie kinde, then theirs. For these respectes, I
thynke (my L. Octavian) the government of a
Commune weale is more to be coveted, then of a kinge.

[XXI] Then the L. OCTAVIAN: Against your opinion,
M. Peter (quoth he) I will alleage but one reason:
whiche is, that of wayes to rule people well, there be
onlye three kindes. The one a kingdome: the other, the
rule of good men, whiche they of olde tyme called
Optimates, the third, the governance of the people. And
the transgressinge (to terme it so) and contrarie vice that
every one of these is chaunged into beeinge apayred*
and corrupted, is whan the kingdome beecommeth a
Tyrannie: and whan the governance of good men is
chaunged into the handes of a few great men and not
good: and whan the rule of the people is at the
disposition of the communaltye,† whiche making a
meddlie of the ordres,‡ suffreth the governance of the
wholl at the wil of the multitude.²⁵⁶ Of these three yll
governmentes (it is sure) the Tyrannie is the woorst of

Three kindes
of wayes to
rule.

---

* apayred: impaired.
† communaltye: common people (in the original, *plebe*).
‡ making a meddlie of the ordres: inverting the natural social
hierarchy.

al, as it may be proved by many reasons. It foloweth then, that of the three good, the kingdome is the best, bicause it is contrarye to the woorste, for (as you knowe) the effectes of contrarie causes, they be also contrarye emong them selves.

Nowe as touchinge it, that you have spoken of libertye, I answere, that true liberty ought not to be saide to live as a manne will, but to lyve accordynge to good lawes. And to obey, is no lesse naturall, profitable and necessarye, then to commaunde. And some thinges are borne and so appointed and ordeyned by nature to commaunde, as some other to obeysance. Truth it is, that there be two kyndes of bearinge rule, the one Lordlye and forsyble, as maisters over slaves, and in this* doeth the soule commaunde the bodye. The other more milde and tractable, as good Princis by waye of the lawes over their Subjectes, and in this reason commaundeth greedie desire. And ech of these two wayes is profitable: bicause the bodye is created of nature apte to obey the soule, and so is desire, reason. There be also manye menne whose doinges be applied onlye about the use of the body: and such as these be are so farr wide from the vertuous, as the soule from the bodye, and yet bicause they be reasonable creatures, they be so much partners of reason,† as they doe no more but know it, for they possesse it not, ne yet have they the use of it. These therefore be naturallye bondemen, and better it is for them and more profitable to obeye, then to beare swey.

[XXII] Then saide the L. GASPAR: In what maner wise be they then to be commaunded that be discreete and vertuous and not by nature bonde?

The L. OCTAVIAN answered: With that tractable‡ commaundment kinglye and civill. And to such it is well done otherwhile to committe the bearinge of suche offices as be meete for them, that they maye likewise beare swey and rule over others of lesse witt then they be, yet so that the principal governement maye full and

Two kindes of wayes to beare swinge.

How good men be to be ruled.

---

* in this: i.e. in this manner.
† they be so much partners of reason, as: they participate of reason, merely to the extent that.
‡ tractable: benign.

wholye depende uppon the cheef Prince. And bicause
you have said, that it is an easier matter to corrupt the
minde of one, then of a great sort,* I saye, that it is also
an easier matter to finde one good and wise, then a great
sorte. Both good and wise ought a man to suppose a

kinge maye be, of a noble progenie, inclined to vertue of
hys owne naturall motion, and throughe the famous
memorye of his auncestoures, and brought up in good
condicions. And though he be not of an other kinde
then man, as you have saide is emonge the bees, yet yf he
be helped forwarde with the instructions, bringinge up,
and art of the Courtier, whom these Lordes have
facioned so wise and good, he shall be moste wise,
moste continent, moste temperate, moste manlye, and
moste juste, full of liberalitie, majestie, holynesse, and
mercye: finallye he shall be moste glorious and moste
deerlye beloved both to God and manne: throughe
whose grace he shall atteine unto that heroicall and
noble vertue, that shall make him passe the boundes of
the nature of manne, and shall rather be called a Demy

God, then a manne mortall. For God deliteth in and is
the defendour not of those Princis that will folowe and
counterfeit him in showinge great poure, and make
themselves to be woorshipped of menne, but of such as
beeside poure, whereby they are mightye, endevour
themselves to resemble him also in goodnesse and
wisdome, wherby they maye have a will and a knowleage
to doe well and to be his ministers, distributinge for the
beehouf of manne the benifittes and giftes that they
receive of him. Therfore even as in the firmamente the
sonne and the moone and the other sterres show to the

world (as it were) in a glasse a certeine likenesse of God:
so uppon the earth a muche more liker image of God are
those good Princis that love and woorshippe him, and
showe unto the people the cleere light of his justice,
accompanied with a shadowe of the heavenlye reason and
understandinge: and suche as these be doeth God make
partners of his true dealing, rightuousnesse, justice and
goodnesse, and of those other happy benifittes which I can
not name, that disclose unto the worlde a much more
evident proof of the Godhead, then doeth the light

* a great sort: many.

of the sonne, or the continuall tourninge of the firmamente with the sundrye course of the sterres. [XXIII]
It is God therfore that hath appointed the people under
the custodie of Princis, which ought to have a diligent
care over them, that they may make him accompt of it,
as good stewardes do their Lord, and love them and
thinke their owne, all the profit and losse that
happeneth to them, and principally above all thing
provide for their good astate and welfare. Therfore
ought the prince not only to be good, but also to make
others good, like the Carpenters* square, that is not
only straight and just it self, but also maketh straight
and just whatsoever it is occupied about.²⁵⁷ And the
greatest proofe that the Prince is good, is whan the
people are good: bicause the lief of the Prince is a lawe
and ringleader of the Citizins, and upon the con-
dicions† of him must needes al others depende:
neyther is it meete for one that is ignorant, to teach: nor
for him that is out of order, to give order: nor for him
that falleth, to help up an other. Therfore if the Prince
will execute these offices aright, it is requisit that he
apply all his studie and diligence to get knowleage,
afterward to facion within him selfe and observe
unchangeablye in everye thinge the lawe of reason, not
written in papers, or in mettall, but graven in his owne
minde, that it maye be to him alwayes not onlie familier,
but inwarde, and live with him, as a percell of him: to
the intent it may night and day, in everye time and place
admonish him and speake to him within his hart,
riddinge him of those troublous affections that untemperate mindes feele, whiche bycause on the one side
they be (as it were) cast into a moste deepe sleepe of
ignorance, on the other overwhelmed with the
unquietnesse which they feele through their weyward
and blind desires, they are stirred with an unquiet rage,
as he that sleepeth otherwile with straunge and horrible
visions: [XXIV] heaping then a greater poure upon
their noughtie desire, there is heaped also a greater
trouble withall. And whan the Prince can do what he
will, then is it great jeopardie least he will the thing that

The lief of
the kinge a
lawe to the
people.

---

* Carpenters: architects (see note 257).
† condicions: behaviour, life.

Bias sayinge.	he ought not. Therfore said Bias well, that promotions declare* what men be:[258] for even as vesselles while they are emptie, though they have some chinke in them, it can ill be perceived, but if they be filled with licour, they showe by and by on what side the fault is, so
Authorities disclose vices.	corrupt and il disposed mindes syldome discover their vices, but whan they be filled with authoritie. For then they are not able to carie the heavie burdien of poure, but forsake them selves and scatter on every side greedie desire, pride, wrath, solemnesse† and such tirannicall facions as they have within them. Wherupon without
Tirannes.	regard they persecute the good and wise, and promote the wicked. And they can not abide to have frendshippes, assemblies and conferences among Citizins in Cities. But maintein spies, promoters, murtherers and cutthrotes to put men in feare and to make them become feintharted. And they sowe debate and striefe to keepe them in division and weake. And of these maners insue infinit damages and the uttre undoinge of the poore people, and often times cruell slaughter or at the least continuall feare to the Tirannes them selves. For good Princis feare not for them selves but for their sakes whom they rule over: and Tyrannes feare verie them whom they rule over. Therfore the more numbre of people they rule over and the mightier they are, the more is their feare and the more ennemies they have.
Clearus.	How fearefull (think you) and of what an unquiet mind was Clearus Tirann of Pontus every time he went into the market place, or into the theatre, or to anie banket, or other haunted place? For (as it is written) he slept shutt into a chest. Or Aristodemus of Argos? which of his bed had made to him self a prison (or litle better) for in his palaice he had a litle roume hanginge in the aer, and so high that he should clime to it with a ladder, and there slept he with a woman of his, whose mother overnight tooke away the ladder, and in the morning sett it to again.[259] Cleane contrarie to this therfore ought the lief of a good Prince to be, free and safe and as deere to his subjectes as their owne: and so framed, that he may have a parte of both the doinge and beeholdinge‡

* declare: show.
† solemnesse: arrogance.
‡ doinge and beeholdinge: active and contemplative.

lief, asmuche as shall be beehouffull for the benefit of
hys people.

[XXV] Then the L. GASPAR: And whiche of the two
lives, my L. Octavian (quoth he) do you thinke most
meete for a Prince?

The L. OCTAVIAN answered smilinge: Ye thinke
perhappes that I stande in mine owne conceite to be the
excellent Courtier that ought to knowe so manye
matters, and to applye them to the good end I have
spoken of. But remember your selfe, that these Lordes
have facioned him with manie qualityes that be not in
me: therefore let us firste doe our best to finde him out,
for I remytt me to him both in this and in al other
thinges that belong to a good Prince.

Then the L. GASPAR: I thinke (quoth he) that if anye
of the qualities geven the Courtier want in you, it is
rather musike and daunsinge and the rest of smalle
accompt, then such as beelong to the instructing of a
Prince and to this ende of Courtlines.

The L. OCTAVIAN answered: They are not of small
accompt all of them that help to purchase a man the
favour of a Prince, which is necessarie (as we have said)
before the Courtier aventure to teach him vertue, the
which (I trowe) I have showed you may be learned, and
profiteth asmuch as ignorance hurteth, whereof springe
all vices, and speciallye that false leekinge a man hath of
him selfe. Therefore (in minc opinion) I have sufficientlye
said, and perhappes more then my promise was.

Then the DUTCHESSE: We shal be so much the more
bounde (quoth she) to your gentilnesse, as ye shall
satisfye us more then promise. Therfore sticke not to
speake your fansye concerninge the L. Gaspars request.
And of good felowshippe showe us beside whatsoever
you woulde teache your Prince, if he had neede of
instructions: and sett the case that you have throughlye
gotten his favour, so as it maye be lawfull for you to tell
him francklye what ever commeth in your minde.

[XXVI] The L. OCTAVIAN laughed and said: Yf I had
the favour of some Prince that I knowe, and shoulde tell
him franckly mine opinion (I doubt me) I shoulde soone
lose it: beeside that, to teach hym, I should neede firste to
learne my selfe. Notwithstandinge sins it is youre
pleasure that I shall answere the L. Gaspar in this point

Vita con-
templativa.

also, I say, that (in my minde) Princis ought to give them selves both to the one and the other of the two lyves, but yet somewhat more to the beehouldinge:[260] bicause this in them is divided into two partes, whereof the one consisteth in knoweynge well and judgeing: the other in commaundinge aryght, and in suche wyse as it shoulde be done, and reasonable matters*and suche as they have authoritye in, commaunding them to hym, that of reason ought to obeye, and in time and place accordingely. And of thys spake Duke Friderick, whan he said, He that can commaunde, is always obeyed. And to commaunde is evermore the principall office of Princis, which notwithstandinge ought manye times also to see with their eyes and to be present at the deede doynge, and accordinge to the time and the busenesse otherwhile also be doynge them selves, and yet hath all thys a

Vita activa.

part wyth action or practise. But the ende of the actyve or doinge lief ought to be the beehouldinge, as of warr,

How to trade
people.

peace, and of peynes, rest. [XXVII] Therfore is it also the office of a good Prince so to trade† his people and with such lawes and statutes, that they maye lyve in rest and in peace, without daunger and with encrease of welth, and injoye praisablye this ende of their practises and actions, which ought to be quietnesse. Bicause there have bine often times manye Commune weales and Princis, that in warr were alwayes most florishinge and mightie, and immediatlye after they have had peace, fell in decaye and lost their puissance and brightnesse, like yron unoccupied. And this came of nothing elles, but bicause they had no good trade of lyving in peace, nor the knowleage to injoie the benifit of ease. And it is not a matter lawfull to be alwayes in warr without seekinge at the ende to come to a peace: although some Princis suppose that their drift ought principally to be, to bringe in subjection their borderers, and therfore traine up their people in a warlyke wyldenesse of spoyle,‡ and murther, and suche matters: they wage them to

A custome
among the
Scythes.

exercise it, and call it vertue. Wherupon in the olde tyme it was an usage emonge the Scythes, that whoso hadde not slayne some ennemie of his, could not drinke in solemne banckettes of the gobblet that was caried about

* reasonable matters: i.e. in reasonable matters.
† trade: govern.
‡ wyldenesse of spoyle: ferocious thirst for booty.

to his companions. In other places the maner was to reare about ones sepulture so manye Obeliskes, as he that laye there buryed had slain of his ennemies.[261] And all these thinges and many mo, were invented to make men warlike, onlye to bring others in subjection, which was a matter (almost) unpossible, bicause it is an infinite peece of woorke, untill all the worlde be brought under obeysance: and not very reasonable, accordinge to the lawe of nature which will not have, that in others the thinge should please us, whiche in our selves is a greef to us. Therfore ought Princis to make their people warlyke, not for a greedie desire to rule, but to defende themselves the better and their owne people, from whoso woulde attempt to bringe them in bondage, or to do them wrong in any point. Or els to drive out Tirans, and to govern the people well, that were yll handled. Or elles to bringe into bondage them, that of nature were suche, that they deserved to be made bondmen, with entent to govern them well, and to give them ease, rest and peace. And to this ende also ought to be applied the lawes, and al statutes of justice, in punishing the yll, not for malice, but bicause there should be no yll, and least they shoulde be a hinderaunce to the quiet livinge of the good: bicause in very deede it is an uncomelye matter and woorthie blame, that in warr (which of it selfe is nought*) men shoulde showe themselves stout and wise, and in peace and rest (which is good) ignoraunt, and so blockishe that they wiste not howe to injoye a benifit. Even as therfore in warr they ought to bende their people to the profitable and necessarye vertues to come by that ende (which is, peace) so in peace, to come by the end therof also (which is, quietnes) they ought to bend them to honest vertues, which be the end of the profitable. And in this wise shal the subjectes be good, and the Prince shall have manye mo to commende and to rewarde, then to chastise. And the rule both for the subjectes and for the Prince shall be most happye, not Lordly, as the maister over his bondeman, but softe and meeke, as a good father over his good childe.

[XXVIII] Then the L. GASPAR: Gladly (quoth he) woulde I understande what maner vertues these are,

Greate high square stones smaller and smaller unto the top.

Why Princis should make their people warlike.

The ende of the lawes.

* nought: bad.

that be profitable and necessarye in warr, and what honest in peace.

The L. OCTAVIAN answered: All be good and helpe the tourne, bicause they tende to a good ende. Yet cheeflye in warr is much set by that true manlines, which maketh the minde voide from all passions, so that he not onlye feareth not perilles, but passeth not upon them. Likewise steadfastnesse, and pacyence, abidinge with a quiet and untroubled minde all the strokes of fortune. It is beehouffull likewise in warr and at all other times to have all the vertues that beelonge to honestye, as justice, staidnesse, sobermoode:* but muche more in peace and rest, bicause often times men in prospiritie and rest, whan favourable fortune fauneth upon them, wexe unrighteous, untemperate, and suffre themselves to be corrupted with pleasures. Therfore suche as be in this state have verie great neede of these vertues, bicause rest bringeth yll condicyons to soone into mens mindes: wherupon arrose a Proverbe in olde time, that Rest is not to be given to bondmen. And it is thought that the Piramides of Ægipt were made to kepe the people occupied, bicause Unto everie manne, use to abide peynes is most profitable. There be more over manie other vertues, all helpfull, but it sufficeth for this time to have spoken this muche: for if I could teach my Prince and traine him in this maner and so vertuous a bringinge uppe (as we have sett furthe) in doinge it without anye more (I woulde beeleave) that I had sufficientlye well compased the ende of a good Courtier.

[XXIX] Then the L. GASPAR: My L. Octavian (quoth he) bicause you have muche praysed good bringing up, and seemed (in a maner) to beleave that it is the cheef cause to make a man vertuous and good, I would knowe, whether the Courtiers instructing of hys Prince, ought to beegine firste of use and (as it were) daylye facions, that unawares to him may make him to accustome himselfe to weldoinge: or elles whether he ought to beegine it himself in opening unto him with reason the proprety of good and yll, and in makinge him to perceive, beefore he take the matter in hand, which is the good waye and to be folowed, and which the yll, and

Manlinesse.

Steadfast-
nesse.

Rest.

Hugious
great stones
steeplewise.

* staidnesse, sobermoode: temperance, modesty.

to be shonned: finallye whether into that minde of his,
the vertues ought to be driven and grounded with
reason and understanding first, or with custome.

The L. OCTAVIAN said: You bringe me into overlonge
a discourse. Yet bicause you shall not thinke that I will
slacke for that I am not willing to make answere to your
requestes, I saye, that like as the soule and the bodye in
us are two thinges, so is the soule divided into two
partes: whereof the one hath in it reason, and the other
appetite. Even as therefore in generation the body goith
beefore the soule, so doeth the unreasonable part of the
soule go before the reasonable: the whiche is plainlye to
be descerned in yonge babes, who (in a maner)
immediatlye after their birthe uttre angre and fervent
appetite, but afterwarde in processe of time reason
appeereth. Therfore first must the bodye be cherished
beefore the soule: after that, the appetite beefore
reason: but the cherishinge of the bodye for a respect to
the soule, and of the appetite for a respect to reason.[262]
For as the vertue of the minde is made perfecte with
learninge, so is the civill* wyth custome. Therefore
ought there to be a grounde made firste wyth custome,
whiche maye governe the appetites not yet apt to
conceyve reason: and wyth that good use leade them
to goodnesse: afterwarde settle them wyth understandynge, the whyche althoughe she be laste to showe
her light, yet doeth she the more perfectlye make the
vertues to be injoyed of whoso hathe his mynde well
instructed wyth maners, wherein (in mine opinion)
consisteth the wholl.

Reason.
Appetite.

[XXX] The L. GASPAR said: Beefore ye proceade anye
farther, I woulde knowe howe the body should be
cherished: bicause you have saide that we must cherishe
it beefore the soule.

*Cherishing
of the bodye.*

The L. OCTAVIAN answered smiling: Know of these
men that make much of it and are faire and rounde, as
for mine (as you see) it is not half well cherished. Yet
may there also be much said in this beehalf: as, the time
meete for mariage, that children be neither to nigh nor
to farr of from the fathers age: exercises, and bringinge

* civill: i.e. moral (virtue).

up soone after there birth, and in the rest of their lief to make them handsome, towardlie, and livelie.

The L. GASPAR answered: The thing that woulde best please women to make their children handsome and welfavoured (in my minde) were the felowship that Plato will have of them in his Commune weale, and in that wise.[263]

Then the LADY EMILIA smilinge: It is not in the covenaunt (quoth she) that ye shoulde a freshe fall to speake yll of women.

I suppose, answered the L. GASPAR, that I give them a great praise, in sainge that they shoulde desire to have a custome brought up, which is alowed of so woorthye a man.

The L. CESAR GONZAGA said laughing: Let us see whether amonge the L. Octavians lessons (yet I wott not whether he have spoken al or no) this may take place: and whether it were well done the Prince should establish it for a lawe or no.

The few that I have spoken, answered the L. OCTAVIAN, may perhappes be inough to make a good Prince, as Princes go nowadayes. Although if a man would go more narrowly to woorke in the matter, there were muche more for him yet to saye.

Then said the DUTCHESSE: Sins it costeth us nothinge but woordes, show us of good felowshippe that, that woulde come in youre mind to teach your Prince.

[XXXI] The L. OCTAVIAN answered: Manie other matters I woulde teache hym (madam) if I knew them my selfe: and amonge the rest, that he should pike out a certein numbre of Gentilmen emonge his subjectes, of the noblest and wisest, wyth whom he shoulde debate all matters, and give them authority and free leave to uttre their minde francklye unto him without respect: and take suche order wyth them that they maye well perceive, that in everie thinge he woulde knowe the truth and abhorr lyinge. And beeside this Counsell of the nobilitie, I woulde perswade him to chouse out others amonge the people of a baser degree, of whom he shoulde make an honest substanciall Counsell, that shoulde debate with the Counsell of the nobilitye the affaires of the Citye beelonginge to the commune and private astate. And in this wise shoulde be made, of the Prince, as of the head, of the nobilite and communes, as

A counsell of noble men.

A counsell of the commons.

of the membres, one bodie alone knitt together, the
governance wherof should cheeflie depende upon the
Prince, yet shoulde the rest beare a stroke also in it: and
so shoulde this state have the fourme and maner of the
three good governmentes, which is, a kingdome, men of
the best sorte, and the people.[264] [XXXII] Afterward I
woulde showe him, that of cares beelonging to a Prince,
the cheeffest is of justice: for maintenance wherof wise
and well tryed men shoulde be chosen out for officers,
whose wisdome were verie wisdome in deede, accompanied with goodnesse, for elles is it no wisdome, but
craft. And where there is a want of this goodnesse,
alwayes the art and subtill practise of lawyers is nothing
elles, but the uttre decay and destruction of the lawes
and judgementes: and the fault of every offence of theirs
is to be layed in him that put them in office. I would tell
him how that of justice also dependeth the zeale toward
God, which beelongeth unto all men and especiallye to
Princis, who ought to love him above all thinges, and to
direct all their doinges unto him, as unto the true ende:
and (as Xenophon saith)[265] to honoure and love him
alwayes, but much more in prosspiritie, bicause they
maye afterwarde lefullye with a more confidence call to
him for assistance whan they bee in anye adversitye: for
it is not possible to govern either himself or others well,
without the help of God, who unto the good sendeth
otherwhile good fortune for his minister, to helpe them
out of great daungers, sometime adversitye leaste they
shoulde slumber so much in prosperity that they myght
happen to forgete him, or the wisdomc of man, which
manie times redresseth ill fortune, as a good player the
ill chaunces of the dice, with counninge play at tables. I
woulde not forgete also to put the Prince in minde to be
devoute indeede, not superstycious, nor given to the
vanitie of nigromancy and prophecies: for in case he
have accompanied with the wisdome of manne, a
godlye zeale and true religion, he shall also have good
lucke, and God his defendour, who will alwayes
encrease his prospiritie both in peace and warr.
[XXXIII] Beeside, I woulde declare unto him how he
shoulde love his Countrey and his people, keapinge
them not in tomuch bondage, for beeing hated* of them

Cares in a
Prince.

Godly
affections.

To love his
Country and
people.

---

* for beeing hated: to avoid becoming hated.

wherof arrise sedicions, conspiricies, and a thowsand
mischeeves beeside: nor yet in to much libertye, lest he
be set at nought, wherof proceadeth the licencious and
riotus livinge of the people, theft, robberye and murther
withoute anye feare of lawes, often tymes the decay and
uttre destruction of cities and kingdoms. Moreover
how he shoulde love them that be nighest to him from
one degree to an other, observinge among them all in
certein matters a like equalitie, as in justice and libertye,
and in some matters a reasonable partiality as in beeing
liberal, in recompensing, in bestowinge promotions and
honours according to the unequalnesse of desertes,
which ought not alwaies to* exceade, but to be
exceaded with recompences. And that in thus doing he
should not only be beloved, but (in a maner) worshipped of his subjectes, neither should he neede to
commit the gaurde of his person to straungers for his
own (for the better safegard and profit of them selves)
would guarde him with their own person: and ech man
woulde willinglye obey the lawes, whan they shoulde
see him to obey them him self, and bee (as it were) an
uncorrupted keaper and minister of them: and so shall
he make all men to conceive suche an assured confidence of him, that if he shoulde happen otherwhile to go
biyonde them in anye point, everie one woulde know it
were done for a good entent: the self same respect and
reverence they woulde have to his will, as they have to
the lawes. And thus shoulde the Citizens mindes be
tempered in suche sort, that the good woulde not seeke
for more then is requisit, and the badd shoulde not
perishe: bicause manie times abundance of wealth is
cause of great destruction, as in poore Italy, which hath
bine and still is, a prey and bootie in the teeth of
straunge nations, aswell for the ill government, as for
the abundaunce of riches that is in it. Therfore the best
way were, to have the greater part of the Citizins,
neyther verye wealthie, nor verye poore: bicause the
over wealthy many times were stiff necked† and
recklesse, the poore, desperate and pikinge.‡ But the

Equalitye.
Partialitye.

To much
welth.

How to ordre
his citizins.

* ought not alwaies to: should never.
† stiff necked: proud.
‡ pikinge: deceitful, grasping.

meane sort lye not in waite for others, and live with a
quiet minde that none lye in waite for them. And where
this meane sort are the greater number, they are withall
the mightier. And therfore neyther the poore nor riche
can woorke anie conspiracie against the Prince, or
against others, nor move sedicion. Wherfore to avoide
this evyll, the most surest way is universally to maintein
a meane. [XXXIV] I would counsell him therfore to use
these and many other remedies for the pourpose, that in
the minde of the subjectes there springe not a longing
after newe matters and alteracion of state, whiche most
communly they do, either for gain, or elles for promotion that they hope upon, or for losse, or elles for some
toile that they be a ferde of. And these sturres in their
mindes be engendred some time of hatred and despite
that maketh them desperate for the wronges and
unshameful dealing that they receive through the
covetisenesse, pride, and crueltye, or unlefull lust of the
higher powers: otherwhile of a contempt and litle
regard that ariseth in them through the negligence and
ill handlinge and lack of foresight in Princis. And these
two faultes must be prevented with purchasing him the
love of the people, and authoritye, whiche is done in
rewardinge and promotinge the good and in finding
wiselie a remedy, and sometime with rigour, that the
evil and sedicious wexe not great: the whiche thinge is
easier to be stopped beefore they come to it, then to
plucke theym downe againe after they are once on loft.
And I would saye, to restraine the people from renninge
into those inconveniences, there is no better way, then
to keepe them from yll custommes, and speciallye suche
as be put in use and creepe in unawares by litle and litle,
bycause they be secrete infections that corrupte Cities
beefore a manne can not onlye remedye them, but spie
them out. With suche meanes I woulde counsell the
Prince to do his best to preserve his subjectes in quiet
astate, and to give them the gooddes of the mynde, and
of the bodye and of fortune: but them of the bodye and
of fortune, that they maye exercise them of the minde,
whiche the greater and plentier they be, so much the
more profitable be they: that happeneth not in them of
the bodye, nor of fortune: in case therefore the subjectes
bee good and of woorthynesse and well bent to the ende

*Alteracion
of state.*

*Extortion of
the higher
powers.*

*Lacke of
wisdome in
princis.*

*That the
evell wexe
not great.*

Il customes.

*Goodes of the
minde, of the
bodye and of
fortune.*

of happynes, that Prince shall be a verye great Lorde: for that is a true and a greate governement, under the whyche the subjectes be good, well ruled and well commaunded.

[XXXV] Then the L. GASPAR: I suppose (quoth he) that he shoulde be but a smalle Lorde, under whom the subjectes were all good. For in everye place there be fewe good.

The L. OCTAVIAN answered: In case some certeine Circe[266] shoulde tourne into wilde beastes all the Frenche Kinges subjectes, woulde not you thinke him a smalle Lorde for all he reigned over so manye thousande beastes? And contrarywyse yf onelye the Cattell that scattre abrode feadynge aboute oure Mountaignes here, might become wise menne, and valiaunt Gentilmen, woulde not you thinke that heardmenne that shoulde governe them and have them obedient to them, of heardmen were become great Lordes? you maye see then, that not the multytude of Subjectes, but the woorthynesse of them makes Princis greate.

[XXXVI] The Dutchesse, the L. Emilia, and all the rest gave verye diligent ear to the L. Octavians talke for a good while together, but after he had here made a litle stop, as though he had made an end of his talk, the L. CESAR GONZAGA saide: Certesse (my L. Octavian) it can not be saide, but your lessons be good and profitable: yet shoulde I beleave that if ye instructed your prince wyth them, ye deserved rather the name of a good Schoolmaister then of a good Courtier: and he of a good governoure rather then of a good prince. Yet my meaninge is not, but that the care of princis shoulde be to have their people well ruled with justice and good usages, notwithstandinge it maye be sufficient for theym (in my minde) to chouse out good ministers to execute these kinde of matters, but the verie office of them is farr higher. Therefore if I thought myself to be the excellent Courtier that these Lordes have facioned, and in my princis favour, without paraventure I woulde never incline him to any vitious matter: but to atteine unto the good ende (you speake of, and the which I confirme ought to be the frute of the Courtiers travailes and doinges) I woulde endevour to put into his head a

Not the multitude, but the woorthy.

certein greatnesse, wyth that princelye sumptuousnesse, and readynes of courage, and unconquered
prowesse in armes, that shoulde make him beloved and
reverenced of all menne, in suche wise, that for this in
especiall he shoulde be famous and notable to the
worlde. I woulde showe him also, that he ought to
accompanye with his greatnesse a familiar gentle
beehaviour, with a soft and lovelye kindenesse, and
good caste to make muche of his subjectes and
straungers discreatlye more and lesse accordinge to
their desertes, observing alwaies notwithstandinge the
majestye meete for his degre, that shoulde not in anye
point suffre him to diminish his authoritie through
overmuch abaysinge, nor yet purchase him hatred
throughe over soure rigorousnesse: that he ought to be
full of liberality and sumptuous, and give unto everye
manne without stint, for God (as they say) is the
treasurer of freharted princis: make gorgious bankettes,
feastes, games, people pleasinge showes, kepe a great
number of faire horses for profit in war, and for
pleasure in peace, Haukes, Houndes, and all other
matters that beelong to the contentation of great Princis
and the people. As in our dayes we have seene the L.
Francis Gonzaga marquesse of Mantua do, which in
these thinges seemeth rather kinge of all Italy, then
Lorde over one Citie.[267] I would assay also to bring him
to make great buildinges, both for his honour in lief,
and to give a memorie of him to his posteritie, as did
Duke Friderick in this noble Palaice, and nowe doeth
Pope July in the Temple of Saint Peter, and the waye
that goith from the Palaice to his house of pleasure
Belvedere, and many other buildinges,[268] as also the
olde auntient Romanes did, wherof so many remnantes
are to be seene about Roome, Naples, Pozzolo, Baie,
Civita Vecchia, Porto, and also out of Italy, and so
manie other places, which be a great witnes of the
prowes of those divine courages.[269] So did Alexander
the great in like maner, whiche not satisfied with the
fame that he got him worthelie for subduing the world
with marcial prowesse, built Alexandria in Ægipt,
Bucephalia in India, and other Cities in other
Countries: and entended to bringe the mountaigne
Athos into the shape of a man, and in the left hande of

Markq. of
Mantua.

S. Peters
church.

Belvedere.

The great
Alexander.
Plutar.
Athos a hill
in Thracia of
a wonderfull
height.

him to builde a verie large Citie, and in the right a greate
boule, into the whiche should gather al the rivers that
rann from it, and thens shoulde fall downe towarde the
Sea, a pourpose in verie deede princely and meete for the
great Alexander.[270] These thinges (thinke I) my L.
Octavian, beecome a noble and a right Prince, and shall
make him both in peace and warr most triumphant, and
not put him in the heade of such particuler and smalle
matters, and have a respect to take weapon in hande
onelye to conquerr and vanquishe suche as deserve to be
conquered, or to profitt his subjectes withall, or to
dispossesse them that governe not as they ought. For in
case the Romanes, Alexander, Hanniball, and the rest
had had these respectes they should never have reached
to the toppe of the glorye they did.

[XXXVII] The L. Octavian answered then smilinge:
Such as had not these respectes shoulde have done the
better in case they had hadd them: althoughe if ye consider
well, ye shall finde that manie had them, and especiallye
those auntientest of olde time, as Theseus, and
Hercules. And thinke not that Procustes, Scyron,
Caccus, Diomedes, Antheus and Gerion[271] were anye
other then cruell and wicked Tirannes againste whom
these noble couraged Demigoddes kept continual and
mortall war, and therfore, for ridding the world of such

**Tirannes
monstres.**

intollerable monstres (for Tyrannes ought not to be
called by other name) unto Hercules were made
Temples, and sacrifices, and godlye honours given him,
bicause the benefit to roote up Tirannes is so profitable
to the worlde, that who so doeth it, deserveth a farre
greater rewarde, then whatsoever is meete for a mortall
man. And of them you have named, do you not thinke

**Alexander
profited the
vanquished.**

that Alexander did profit with his victories the
vanquished? sins he so traded those barbarous nations
whiche he overcame, with such good maners, that of
wylde beastes he made them men? He built manye
beawtifull Cities in Countreis ill inhabited, plantinge
therin civill kinde of living, and (as it were) coopled Asia
and Europe together with the bonde of amitie and holye
lawes, so that the vanquished by him were more happie
then the rest, bicause emong some he brought in
matrimonie: emong other, husbandrie: emong other,
religion: emonge other, not to sley, but to make muche

of their parentes in their olde age: emong other, the refraining from bedding with their mothers, and a thousand other matters, that might be said for a witnesse of that profit which his victories brought to the world. [XXXVIII] But leaving aside them of olde time, what enterprise were more noble, more glorious, and more profitable then if Christians would bend their force to conquerr the infidelles.[272] Would you not thinke that this warr, prosperously acheved, and beeing the cause of so manye a thousande to be brought from the false sect of Mahumet to the light of the Christian truth, it should be a profit aswel to the vanquished, as to the subduers? And undoubtedly, as Themistocles in time past, being banished out of his Countrey, and imbraced of the king of Persia, and much made of, and honoured with infinit and moste rich giftes, said unto his traine: Oh sirs we had bine undone, had we not bine undone,[273] even so might then the Turkes and the Moores speake the very same with good cause, for that in their losse should consist their welfare. This happinesse therfore (I hope) we shall come to the sight of, if God graunt so long lief to Monseigneur d'Angoulesme that he may come to the Crowne of Fraunce, who showeth suche a hope of him selfe, as foure nightes ago the L. Julian spake of.[274] And to the Crowne of England the L. Henry Prince of Wales, who presentlye groweth under his most noble father, in all kinde of vertue, like a tender ympe* under the shadow of an excellent tree and laden with frute, to renue him much more beawtiful and plentuous whan time shal come, for as our Castilio writeth from thens, and promiseth at hys retourn to tell us more at the full, a man can judge no lesse, but that nature was willing in this Prince to show her counning, planting in one body alone so many excellent vertues, as were sufficient to decke out infinit.[275]

Then said M. Bernard Bibiena: A very great hope of him self promiseth also the L. Charles Prince of Spaine, who not yet fullye tenn yeeres of age, declareth now such a wit, and so certein tokens of goodnes, wisdome, modesty, noble courage and of every vertue, that if the Empire of Christendome (as it is thought) come to his

Margin notes:

Xerxes.

King Francis the first.

Kinge Henry the VIII.

The Emperour Charles the V.

---

* ympe: sapling.

handes, it is to be reckened upon, that he will darken the name of many Emperours of olde time, and in renowme be compared to the most famous that ever were in the worlde.[276]

[XXXIX] The L. OCTAVIAN proceaded: I beeleave therefore that God hath sent suche and so heavenly Princis upon the earth, and made them one like an other in youth, in mightines of armes, in state, in handsomnes and disposition of person, that they may also be minded alike in this good pourpose: and in case anye maner envye or strife of matching others arrise at any time emong them, it shall be, who shall be the first, and most inclined and most couragious in so glorious an enterprise. But let us leave this kinde of talke, and retourne unto our owne. Unto you therfore (my L. Cesar) I say, that such thinges as you would have the Prince to do, be very great and worthye muche praise. But you must understand that if he be not skilfull in that I have saide he ought to have a knowleage in, and have not framed his minde in that wise, and bent it to the waye of vertue, it shall bee harde for him to have the knowleage to be noble couraged, liberall, just, quicke-spirited, wise, or to have any other of those qualities that beelong unto him: neither would I have him to be suche a one for anye other thinge, but to have the understanding to put in use these condicions (for as they that build, be not all good woorkemen,* so they that give, be not all liberall) for vertue never hurteth anye man: and manye there be, that laye hande on other mens gooddes to give, and so are lavish of an other mans substance. Some give to them they ought not, and leave in wretchednesse and miserie such as they be bound to. Other give with a certein yll will and (as it were) with a dispite, so that it is knowen they do it, bicause they can do none other. Other do not onlye not kepe it secrete, but they call witnesse of it, and (in a maner) cause their liberalities to be cried. Other foolishlye at a sodeine emptye the fountain of liberalitye, so that afterwarde they can use it no more. [XL] Therfore in this point (as in all other matters) he must have a knowleage, and govern him self with the wisdome that is a companion unto all the other vertues

Emulation emong Kinges.

Liberalitye.

Knowleage.

---

* woorkemen: the original has 'architects' (see note 257).

whiche for that they are in the midle, be nygh unto the
two extremities, that be vices.[277] Wherefore he that
hath not knoweleage renneth soone into them. For as it
is a harde matter in a circle to find out the pricke in the
centre, whiche is the middle, so is it harde to find out the
pricke of vertue placed in the middle beetwene two
extreme vyces, the one for the overmuch, and the other
for the overlitle, and unto these we are inclined
sometime to the one, sometime to the other, and this is
knowen by the pleasure and greef that is felt within us,
for through the one we doe the thinge that we ought
not, and through the other we leave undone that, which
we ought to do: although pleasure be muche more
daungerous, bicause oure judgement is soone lead by it
to be corrupted. But bicause the perseverance how farr*
a man is wide from the centre of vertue, is a hard matter,
we ought by litle and litle to drawe backe of oure selves
to the contrarie part of this extremytye, whiche we
know we be inclined unto, as they do, that make
straight crooked staves, for by that meane we shall
draw nighe unto vertue, which is placed (as I have said)
in that pricke of the meane: wherby it commeth that by
manye wayes we be wide, and by one alone we do oure
office and dutye: like as Archers by one waye alone hitte
the marke, and by manye mysse the pricke. Therefore
oftentimes a Prince to be gentle and lowelye, doeth
manye thinges contrarie to comelinesse, and so
humbleth him selfe that he is nought sett by. Some other
to show a grave majestye with authoritye according,
beecommeth cruell and untollerable. Some one, to be
counted eloquente, entreth into a thowsande straunge
matters and longe processes with curious woordes
giving ear to hym selfe, so that other men can not for
lothsomenesse heare him. [XLI] Therfore (my L. Cesar)
do you not call a smalle matter anye thing that maye
better a Prince how small so ever it be. Nor thinke that I
judge it to be in the reproofe of my lessons where you
say, that a good Governour were rather instructed
therewithall, then a good Prince: for perhappes there
can not be a greater praise nor more comlye for a Prince,
then to call him a good Governour. Therfore if it

*Vertue in
the middle.
Extremities,
vices.*

*A good
Prince a good
governour.*

* the perseverance how farr: to perceive how far.

shoulde fall to my lott to instruct him, he should have a care not only to govern the matters alreadye spoken of, but also farre lesser, and understande in peecemeale whatsoever belongeth to his people, asmuch as were possible: and never credite nor trust any officer so muche, as to give him the bridle wholy into his handes, and the disposinge of the wholl government. For no man is most apt to all thinges. And much more hurt

Mistrustinge. commeth of the light beeleaf of Princis, then of mistrusting, whiche otherwhile doeth not onlye not hurt, but oftentimes profiteth exceadingly. Yet in this point a good judgement is verye necessarye in a Prince to descern who deserveth to be put in trust, and who not. I woulde he shoulde have a care to understande the doinges and to be an overseear of his officers and

The Prince towarde hys subjectes. ministers. To breake and to ende controversies emonge his subjectes. To take up matters beetwene them and to knitte them together in alliance by mariage. To provide

Citye. so, that the Citye may be all joyned together and agreeinge in amitye, lyke a private house, well peopled, not poore, quiet, and full of good artificers. To show

Marchaunt men. favour to marchaunt men and to helpe them also with stokkes.* To be liberall and honourable in hous-

Hous-keepinge. keepinge† towarde straungers and religious persons.

Superfluous thinges. To tempre all superfluous matters, bicause throughe the offences committed in these thinges, albeit they appeere but small, cities manye times fall in decay: therefore it is reason that the Prince set a stint to the oversumptuous buildinges of private men, bancquettinges, unmesur-

Excesse of women. able doweries of women, their riotous excesse, their pompe in jewelles and apparaile, whiche is nothinge elles but a token of their foly: for (beeside that throughe ambicion and malice that one of them beareth an other, they many times lavish out their livelode and husbandes substance, otherwhile for some pretye jewell or other matter of fansye) sometime they sell their honestie to him that will buye it.

[XLII] Then said M. BERNARDE BIBIENA smilinge: You beegine (my L. Octavian) to take my L. Gaspars and Phrisios part.

---

* stokkes: subsidies.
† houskeepinge: hospitality.

Then the L. OCTAVIAN answered in like maner smilyng: The controversye is ended, and I entende not nowe to renue it. Therfore wil I speake no more of women, but retourn to my prince.

PHRISIO answered: You may now leave him hardely, and be contented to have him suche a one as you have instructed him. For doubtles it wer an easier matter to find out a woman of the qualities the L. Julian hath spoken of, then a prince of the qualities that you would have in him. Therfore (I feare me) he is like the Commune weale of Plato, and we shall never see suche a one, onlesse it bee perhappes in heaven.

The L. OCTAVIAN answered: Thinges possible, though they be hard, yet is it to be hoped that they maye be: therefore maye we yet parhappes see him upon the earth in oure time. For althoughe the heavens be so scante in bringinge furth excellent Princis, that in so manye hundreth yeeres we do scantlye see one, yet may this good lucke happen to us.

Then said COUNT LEWES: I have a good hope of it. For beeside the three great ones that we have named, of whom may be hoped it, that beelongeth to the high degree of a perfect Prince, there be also nowadayes in Italy certein Princes children, which although they be not like to have such powre, may happe will supplye it with vertue: and he that emonge them all declareth a more towardenesse and promiseth of him selfe a greater hope then anye of the reste (me think) is the L. Friderick Gonzaga, sonn and heyr to the marquesse of Mantua, and nephewe to oure Dutchesse here. For beeside the honest inclination to good nourtour and the discreation that he declareth in these tendre yeeres, they that have the bringing upp of him, reporte suche wonderous thinges as touchinge his beeing wittye, desirous of glory, stouthearted, courteious, freeharted, frindlye to justice, so that of so good a beeginning, there can not be loked for but a verye good ende.[278]

Then PHRISIO: Well, no more of this (quoth he) we will pray unto God that we may se this your hope fulfilled.

[XLIII] Here the L. OCTAVIAN tourning him toward the dutches, after a sort as though he had ended as much as he had to saye: You have now heard, madam (quoth

Good Princes verye scant.

L. Friderick Gonzaga Duke of Mantua.

he) what I am able to say of the ende of the Courtier, wherin though I have not satisfied in all pointes, it shall suffice me yet, that I have showed, that some other perfection may be given him beside the matters whych these Lordes have spoken of, who (I beleave) have lefte out both this and what so ever I am able to saye, not bycause they knew it not better then I, but bicause they were loth to take the peynes: therfore will I give them leave to go forward, if they have anye thinge elles lefte beehinde to be saide.

Then said the DUTCHESSE: Beeside that it is late (for within a while it will be time for us to make an ende for this night) me thinke, we ought not to mingle anye other talke with this, wherin you have gathered together suche sundrye and goodlye matters, that concerninge the ende of Courtlinesse, it may be said, that you are not onlie the perfect Courtier whom we seke for, and able to instruct your Prince well, but also (if fortune be so favourable on your side) ye maye be the good Prince your self, whiche shoulde not be withoute great profit to your Countrey.[279]

Then laughed the L. OCTAVIAN and said: Perhappes (madam) were I in that astate, it woulde be with me as it is with manye others that can better saye well, then do well.

[XLIV] Here after a litle debatinge of the matter to and fro emonge the company, with certein contentions tending to the commendacion of that that had bine spoken, and agreeinge on all handes not yet to be bed time, the L. JULIAN saide smilinge: Madam, I am so verie an ennemye to crafte and guile, that needes must I speake against the L. Octavian: who for that he is (as I muche doubt him) a secrete conspiratour with the L. Gaspar againste women, hath overshott himselfe in committing of two errours (in mine opinion) very great: wherof the one is, that meaninge to preferr this Courtier beefore the Gentilwoman of the Palaice, and to make him to passe those boundes that she is not able to reache to, he hath also preferred him beefore the Prince, whiche is most unseemlye. The other, that he hath given him suche an ende, that it is evermore harde and otherwhile unpossible for him to comebye it: and yet whan he doeth come by it, he ought not to have the name of a Courtier.

I can not see, quoth the L. EMILIA, howe it is harde or unpossible for the Courtier to come bye this his ende, nor yet howe the L. Octavian hath prefarred him beefore the Prince.

Graunt it him not, answered the L. OCTAVIAN: for I have not preferred the Courtier beefore the Prince. And as touchinge the ende of Courtlinesse, I dare undertake that I am not overseene* in any point.

Then answered the L. JULIAN: You can not say (my L. Octavian) that alwaies the cause, by the which the effect is such as it is, is no more suche as the effect is. Therfore needes must the Courtier, by whose instruction the prince must be of such an excellencye, be more excellente then the prince: and in this wise shall he be also of a more woorthinesse then the prince himselfe, which is most unsittinge. Then concerninge the ende of Courtlinesse, that which you have spoken may folowe whan there is litle beetwene the age of the prince and the Courtiers: yet verye hardlye, for where there is smalle difference of age, it is likelye there is also smalle difference of knowleage. But in case the prince be olde and the Courtier yong: it is meete that the olde prince knowe more then the yonge Courtier, and where this foloweth not alwaies, it foloweth somtime, and then is the ende which you have appointed to the Courtier unpossible. In case againe the prince be yonge and the Courtier aged, muche a doe shall the Courtier have to wynne him the good will of the prince with those qualities that you have given him. For (to saye the truth) feates of armes and the other exercises beelonge unto yonge menne and be not comelye in age: and musike, daunsinge, feastinges, sportinges, and love, be matters to be laughed at in olde menne, and (me thinke) to an instructer of the lief and maners of a prince, who ought to be a grave person and of authoritie, ripe in yeeres and experience and (if it were possible) a good Philosopher, a good Capitain and to have the knowleage almost of every thinge, they are most unseemly. Wherfore he that instructeth a Prince (I beleve) ought not to be called a Courtier, but deserveth a far greater and a more honorable name. Therfore (my L. Octavian) perdon me

---

* I am not overseene: I have not overstepped the mark.

in case I have opened this your craftye conveiance, which I thinke my self bounde to do for the honour of my woman, whom you would have to be of lesse worthines then this Courtier of yours, and I wil none of that.

[XLV] The L. OCTAVIAN laughed and saide: A more praise it were for the Gentilwoman of the Palaice (my L. Julian) to exalt her so muche that she maye be equall with the Courtier, then so much to debase the Courtier that he shoulde be equall with the Gentilwoman of the Palaice: for it were not unfitt for the woman also to instruct her ladye, and with her to drawe to the same ende of Courtlinesse, whiche I have said is meete for the Courtier with his prince. But you seeke more to dispraise the Courtier, then to praise the Gentilwoman of the Palaice, therfore shall it become me also to take part with the Courtier. Now to make you answere to youre objections, you shall understande that I have not saide, that the instruction of the Courtier ought to be the onelye cause why the Prynce shoulde be such a one, for in case he be not inclined of nature and apt to be suche a one, all diligence and exhortacion of the Courtier were in vaine. As in like maner every good husband man should labour in vaine, that would take in hande to tyll and sowe with good graine the barraine sande of the Sea, bicause this barrainnesse in that place is naturall. But whan to the good seede in a frutefull soile with the temperatnesse of aer and rayne meete for the season of the yeere, there is also applied the diligence of mans husbandinge the grounde, alwaies great abundance of corne is seene to springe plentuouslye: yet for all this, is it not to be saide, that the husbande man alone is the cause of it, although without him all the other thinges do litle or nothinge helpe the pourpose. There be therfore manie Princis, that would be good, in case their myndes were well tylled, and of theym speake I, not of suche as be like the barraine Countrey, and of nature so farr wide from good condicions that no teaching were able to frame their minde to a right trade. [XLVI] And forsomuch as (as we have already said) such custommes and properties be ingendred in us, as oure doinges are, and vertue consisteth in doing and practise, it is not unpossible nor any marveile, that the Courtier should

This ende of the Courtyer serveth also for a Gentil woman with her Lady.

Virtus in actione.

traine his Prince in manye vertues, as justice, liberality,
noble courage, the practisinge wherof he, through his
greatnesse, maye lightlye put in use and make it
custome, whiche the Courtier can not do, bicause he
hath no meanes to practise theym, and thus the Prince
inclined to vertue by the Courtyer, may beecome more
vertuous then the Courtier: beesyde that, you muste
conceyve that the whettstone which cutteth not a whitt,
doeth yet make a toole sharpe: therefore althoughe the
Courtier instructeth his Prince yet (me thinke) it is not
to be said that he is of a more woorthynes then his
Prince. That the ende of this Courtier is harde and
somtime unpossible, and that whan the Courtier doeth
come bye it, he ought not to be named a Courtier, but
deserveth a greater name, I tell you plainlye, that I denye
not this hardenesse, bicause it is no lesse harde to find
out so excellent a Courtier, then to come by such an
ende. Yet by reason (me thinke) the unpossiblenes of the
matter lieth not in the point that you have alleaged. For
in case the Courtier be so yong that he hath not
understanding in the thinge, which he ought to have a
knowleage in, it is not to the pourpose to speake of him,
bicause he is not the Courtier that we entreate upon,
neyther is it possible for him that must have a sight in so
many thinges to be verye yonge. And if it happen
moreover the Prince to be so wise and good of him selfe,
that he needeth no exhortations or counsell of others
(although it be so harde a matter as everye man
knoweth) it sufficeth that the Courtier be such a one, as
if his Prince had neede, he coulde make him vertuous:
and then may he in effect fulfill the other part, not to
suffre him to be deceived, and to worke that evermore
he may understande the truth of everye thinge, and
bolster him against flatterers and raylers, and all suche
as shoulde endevour to corrupt his minde with unhonest delites. And in this wise shall he yet comebye a
part of his ende though he can not practise the wholl,
which can not be justlye layde to him for a fault, sins he
refrayneth the doinge of it upon so good a ground. For
were an excellent Phisitien in place where al were sound
and in helth, a man ought not therefore to saye, that
the Phisitien (althoughe he cured no diseased) wanted
of his end. Wherefore as the Phisitiens respect ought to

The ende of
the Courtier
harde.

The Courtiers
respect, the
vertue of his
Prince.

Olde
Courtiers.

be the helthe of men, even so the Courtiers, the vertue of
his Prince: and it sufficeth them both to have this end
inwardlye grafte in them,* whan the want of uttringe it
outwardelye in practise, is occasioned by the subjecte,
to the whiche thys ende is directed. But in case the
Courtier were so old, that it became him not to be doing
in musike, feastinges, sportinges, marcialfeates, and the
other slightes of the bodye, yet can it not be saide not
wythstandinge, that it were unpossible for him to entre
that way in favour with his Prince: for where his age
taketh awaye the practisinge of those thinges, it taketh
not away the understandinge of them, and if he have
practised them in his youth, it maketh him to have so
muche the more perfect judgement in them, and giveth a
knoweleage to teach theim his Prince so muche the
more perfectlye, as yeares and experience bringe
knowleage of all thinges with them. And thus shal the
aged Courtier, although he exercise not the qualities
that he is indowed withal, comebye his ende at length,
to instructe well hys Prince. [XLVII] And in case you
will not call him a Courtier, it shall nothing offende me,
for nature hath not appointed suche narrowe boundes
to the dignities of men, that one maye not come up from
one to an other: therfore many times meane souldiers
arrise to be Capitaines: private men, kinges: priestes,
Popes: and scolers, maisters: and so with there degree
or dignitie they take their name accordinglye. Wherfore
perhappes a man maye say that to beecome the

Instructer of
a Prince.

Instructer of a Prince were the ende of a Courtier,
althoughe I perceive not who should refuse this name of
a Perfect Courtier, whiche (in my minde) is woorthie
verye great praise. And I can not see but Homer, as he
facioned two most excellent personages for example of
mans lief, the one in practises (whiche was Achilles) the

Achilles.
Ulisses.

other in passions and sufferances (which was Ulisses):
even so in like maner he minded to facion a perfect

Phœnix.

Courtier (whiche was Phœnix)[280] who after rehersall of
his loves and manye other matters of youth, declareth
that he was sent to Achilles by his father Peleus, to be in
his companye and to teache him to speake and to do:

* inwardlye grafte in them: i.e. have it in potential within them.

whiche is nothinge elles but the ende that wee have appointed for oure Courtier. Neyther can I thinke that Aristotel and Plato tooke scorne of the name of a perfect Courtier, bicause it is plainlye to be seene that they practised the deedes of Courtiershippe and gave them selves to this ende, the one with the great Alexander, the other with the kynges of Sicilia.[281] And bicause it is the office of a good Courtier to knowe the nature and inclination of his Prince, and so accordynge to the busynesse and as occasion serveth with slightenesse* to entre in favour with him (as we have saide) by those wayes that make him a sure entry, and afterward bend him to vertue, Aristotel so well knew the nature of Alexander, and with slightnesse framed him selfe so well thereafter, that he was beloved and honoured of him more then a father. Wherfore emong many other tokens that Alexander showed him, for a witnesse of hys good will, he caused Stagira the citye where he was borne once destroied, to be builded new again. And Aristotel, beeside the directinge him to that glorious end, that was to make the worlde onelye a generall countrey,† and all men, as one people, that shoulde live in amitye and agreement together, under one government and one lawe, that (like the sonn) should generallye geve light to all, he instructed hym in the naturall sciences and in the vertues of the minde full and wholy, that he made him most wise, most manlie, moste continent, and a true morall Philosopher, not in woordes onelye, but in deedes. For there can not be imagined a more noble Philosophy, then to bringe to a civill trade of living such wild people as were the inhabitauntes of Bactria and Caucasus, India and Scithia, and to teache them matrimonie, husbandrye, to honour their fathers, to abstaine from robbinge and killinge and from other noughty condicions, and to builde so many most noble Cities in straunge Countries, so that infinit throughe those lawes were brought from a wilde lief to live lyke men. And of these thinges in Alexander the Author was Aristotel in practisinge the wayes of a good Courtier. The which Calisthenes

Aristotell and Plato were Courtiers.

Both the Dionysses.

The office of a good Courtier.

Aristotel wayed the nature of Alexander.

Stagira destroyed by Philip Alexanders father.

---

* slightenesse: dexterity, tact.
† onelye a generall countrey: all one nation.

He rebuked
Alexander
for beeinge
woorshipped
as a god, and
therfore died
upon the rack.
Q. Curt. lib. 8.

coulde not do, for all Aristotel showed him the way of it, who bicause he was a right philosopher and so sharpe a minister of the bare truth without mynglinge it with Courtlinesse, he lost his lief and profited not, but rather gave a sclaunder to Alexander.[282] With the very same way of Courtlinesse Plato framed Dion the Syracusan.[283] But whan he mett afterwarde with Dionysius the Tyrann, like a booke all full of faultes and erroures, and rather needful to be cleane blotted out, then altered or corrected, bicause it was not possible to scrape out of him that blott of tiranny wherwithall he was stained so long together, he would not practise therein the wayes of Courtiership, for he thought they shoulde be all in vaine: the whiche our Courtier ought to do also, if his chaunce be to serve a Prince of so ill a nature, that by longe custome is growen in use with vices, as they that have the consumption of the lunges with their disease. For in this case he ought to forsake his service, least he beare the blame of his Lordes yll practises, or feele the hartgreefe that all good men have which serve the wicked.

The Courtier
oughte not to
serve the
wicked.

[XLVIII] Here whan the L. Octavian had made a staye, the L. GASPAR sayde: I had not thought oure Courtier hadd bene so woorthy a personage. But sins Aristotel and Plato be his mates, I judge no man ought to disdeigne this name anye more. Yet wott I not whether I may beleave that Aristotel and Plato ever daunsed or were musitiens in all their lief time, or practised other feates of chivalrye.

The L. OCTAVIAN answered: Almost it is not lawfull to thinke that these two divine wittes were not skilfull in everye thinge, and therfore it is to be presupposed that they practised what ever beelongeth to Courtlynesse. For where it commeth to pourpose they so penn the matter, that the very craftes maisters them selves know by theyr writinges that they understoode the whol even to the pith and innermost rootes. Wherefore to a Courtier or instructer of a Prince (howe ever ye lust to terme him) that tendeth to the good ende, which we have spoken of, it is not to be said but that all the good qualities which these Lordes have given him do beelonge, though he were never so grave a Philosopher or holie* in his maners: bicause they strive not against

* holie: strict, austere.

goodnesse, discreation, knoweleage and will, in all age, and in all time and place.

[XLIX] Then the L. GASPAR: I remembre (quoth he) that these Lordes yesternight reasoninge of the Courtiers qualities, did alowe him to be a lover, and in makinge rehersall of asmuche as hitherto hath bene spoken, a manne maye pike out a conclusion, That the Courtier (whiche with his worthynesse and credit must incline his Prince to vertue) must in maner of necessitie be aged, for knoweleage commeth verye syldome times beefore yeeres, and speciallye in matters that bee learned wyth experyence: I can not see, whan hee is well drawen in yeeres, howe it wyll stande well wyth hym to be a lover, considerynge (as it hath bine said the other night) Love frameth not with olde men, and the trickes that in yonge men be galauntnesse, courtesie and precisenesse* so acceptable to women, in them are meere folies and fondnesse to be laughed at, and purchase him that useth them hatred of women and mockes of others. Therfore in case this your Aristotel an old Courtier were a lover, and practised the feates that yong lovers do (as some that we have sene in our daies) I feare me, he woulde forgete to teach his Prince: and paraventure boyes would mocke him behinde his backe, and women would have none other delite in him but to make him a jesting stocke.

The Courtier
a lover.

Then said the L. OCTAVIAN: Sins all the other qualities appointed to the Courtier are meete for him, althoughe he be olde, me thinke we shoulde not then barr him from this happinesse to love.

Nay rather, quoth the L. GASPAR, to take this love from him, is a perfection over and above, and a makynge him to lyve happilie out of miserie and wretchednesse.

[L] M. PETER BEMBO said: Remember you not (my L. Gaspar) that the L. Octavian declared the other nighte in his divise of pastymes, although he be not skilfull in love, to knowe yet that there be some lovers, which recken the disdeignes, the angres, the debates and tourmentes whiche they receive of their Ladies, sweete? Wherupon he required to be taught the cause of this

---

* precisenesse: elegance.

sweetenesse. Therfore in case oure Courtier (thoughe he be olde) were kendled with those loves that be sweete without any bitter smacke, he should feele no miserie nor wretchednesse at all. And beeing wise, as we set case he is, he shoulde not be deceived in thinkinge to be meete for him what so ever were meete for yong men, but in lovinge shoulde perhappes love after a sorte, that might not onlye not bringe him in sclaunder but to muche praise and great happinesse, without any lothsomnes at all, the which verie sildome or (in maner) never happeneth to yonge men: and so should he neyther lay aside the teaching of his Prince, nor yet commit any thinge that should deserve the mockinge of boyes.

Then spake the DUTCHESSE: I am glad (M. Peter) that you have not bine muche troubled, in oure reasoninges this night, for now we maye be the boulder to give you in charge to speake, and to teache the Courtier this so happie a love, which bringeth with it neither sclaunder, nor any inconvenience: for perhappes it shall be one of the necessariest and profitablest qualities that hitherto hath bine given him, therefore speake of good felowship asmuch as you know therin.

M. PETER laughed and saide: I would be loth (Madam) where I say that it is lefull for olde men to love, it should be an occasion for these Ladyes to thinke me olde: therefore hardely give ye this enterprise to an other.

The DUTCHESSE answered: You ought not to refuse to be counted olde in knowleage, thoughe ye be yonge in yeeres. Therfore saye on, and excuse your selfe no more.

M. PETER said: Surelye (madam) if I must entreate upon this matter, I must first go aske counsell of my Heremite Lavinello.[284]

The L. EMILIA said then halfe in angre: There is never a one in al the company so disobedient as you be (M. Peter) therfore shoulde the Dutchesse doe well to chastice you somewhat for it.

M. PETER said smilinge: For love of God (madam) be not angrye with me, for I will say what ever you will have me.

Goo to, saye on then, answered the L. EMILIA.

[LI] Then M. PETER after a whiles silence, somewhat settlinge hymselfe as thoughe he shoulde entreat uppon a waightie matter, said thus: My Lordes, to showe that olde menne maye love not onlie without sclaunder, but otherwhile more happilye then yonge menne, I must be enforced to make a litle discourse to declare what love is, and wherein consisteth the happinesse that lovers maye have. Therefore I beseche ye give the hearynge wyth heedefulnesse, for I hope to make you understand, that it were not unsitting for anye man here to be a lover, in case he were xv. or xx. yeeres elder then M. Morello.

Olde men may love without sclaunder.

And here after they had laughed a while, M. PETER proceeded.[285] I saye therefore that accordinge as it is defined of the wise menn of olde time, Love is nothinge elles but a certein covetinge to enjoy beawtie: and forsomuch as covetinge longeth for nothinge, but for thinges knowen, it is requisite that knowleage go evermore before* coveting, which of his owne nature willeth the good, but of him self is blind, and knoweth it not. Therfore hath nature so ordeined, that to every vertue of knowleag ther is annexed a vertue of longing. And bicause in oure soule there be three maner wayes to know, namelye, by sense, reason, and understandinge: of sense, there arriseth appetite or longinge, which is commune to us with brute beastes: of reason arriseth election or choise, which is proper to man: of understanding, by the which man may be partner with Aungelles, arriseth will. Even as therfore the sense knoweth not but sensible matters and that which may be felt, so the appetyte or covetinge onlye desireth the same: and even as the understanding is bent but to beehoulde thinges that may be understoode, so is that wil only fead with spirituall gooddes. Man of nature indowed with reason, placed (as it were) in the middle beetwene these two extremities, may through his choise inclinynge to sense, or reachynge to understandynge, come nigh to the covetinge sometime of the one somtime of the other part. In these sortes therfore may beawtie be coveted, the general name wherof may be applied to al thinges, eyther naturall or artificiall, that

What love is.

Knowleage. Coveting.

Sense. Reason. Understand-inge.

Beawtie.

* go evermore before: always precede.

are framed in good proportion, and due tempre, as their nature beareth. [LII] But speakynge of the beawtie that we meane, which is onlie it, that appeereth in bodies, and especially in the face of mann, and moveth thys fervent covetinge which we call Love, we will terme it an influence of the heavenlie bountifulness, the whiche for all it stretcheth over all thynges that be created (like the light of the Sonn) yet whan it findeth out a face well

The face. proportioned, and framed with a certein livelie agreement of severall colours, and set furth with lightes and shadowes, and with an orderly distaunce and limites of lines, therinto it distilleth it self and appeereth most welfavoured, and decketh out and lyghtneth the subject where it shyneth wyth a marveylous grace and glistringe (like the Sonne beames that strike against beawtifull plate of fine golde wrought and sett wyth precyous jewelles) so that it draweth unto it mens eyes with pleasure, and percing through them imprinteth him selfe in the soule, and wyth an unwonted sweetenesse all to stirreth her and delyteth, and settynge her on fire maketh her to covett him. Whan the soule then is taken wyth covetynge to enjoye thys beawtie as a good thynge, in case she suffre her selfe to be guyded with the judgement of sense, she falleth into most deepe erroures, and judgeth the bodie in whyche Beawtye is descerned, to be the principall cause thereof: wherupon to enjoye it, she reckeneth it necessarye to joigne as inwardlye as she can wyth that bodye, whyche is false:

In possessing the body beawtie is not enjoied. and therefore who so thynketh in possessynge the bodye to injoye beawtie, he is farr deceived, and is moved to it, not wyth true knowleage by the choise of reason, but wyth false opinyon by the longinge of sense. Wherupon the pleasure that foloweth it, is also false and of necessytye full of erroures. And therefore into one of the

They that love sensuallye. two vyces renn all those lovers that satisfye theyr unhonest lustes with the women whom they love: for eyther assone as they be come to the coveted ende, they not onely feele a fulnesse and lothesomnesse, but also conceyve a hatred against the wyght beloved,* as thoughe longinge repented hym of hys offence and acknowleaged the deceite wrought hym by the false

* the wyght beloved: the object of his love.

judgement of sense, that made hym beleave the yll to be good: or elles they contynue in the verye same covetynge and greedynesse, as thoughe they were not in deede come to the ende, whyche they sought for. And albeit throughe the blynde opynyon that hath made them dronken (to their seeminge) in that instante they feele a contentation, as the deseased otherwhile, that dreame they drinke of some cleare spring, yet be they not satisfied, nor leave of so. And bicause of possessing coveted goodnes there arriseth alwayes quietnesse and satisfaction in the possessors minde, in case this were the true and righte end of there covetinge, whan they possesse it they would be at quietnesse and throughlye satisfied, whiche they be not: but rather deceyved through that likenesse, they furthwith retourn again to unbridled covetinge, and with the very same trouble which they felt at the first, they fall again into the raginge and most burninge thirst of the thinge, that they hope in vaine to possesse perfectlye. These kind of lovers therfore love most unluckely,* for eyther they never comebye their covetinges, whiche is a great unluckinesse: or elles if they do comebye them, they finde they comebye their hurt, and ende their myseryes with other great miseries, for both in the beginninge and middle of this love, there is never other thinge felt, but afflictions, tourmentes, greeffes, pining, travaile, so that to be wann, vexed with continuall teares, and sighes, to lyve with a discontented minde, to be alwaies dumbe, or to lament, to covet death, in conclusion to be most unlucky are the propreties which (they saye) beelonge to lovers. [LIII] The cause therfore of this wretchednesse in mens mindes, is principally sense, whiche in youthfull age bereth moste swey, bicause the lustinesse of the fleshe and of the bloode, in that season addeth unto him even so much force, as it withdraweth from reason: therfore doeth it easelye traine the soule to folowe appetite or longinge, for when she seeth her selfe drowned in the earthly prison, bicause she is sett in the office to govern the body, she can not of her self understand plainly at the first the truth of spirituall behouldinge. Wherfore to compasse the understanding

Properties of lovers.

* unluckely: unhappily.

of thinges, she must go begg the beginning at the senses, and therfore she beleaveth them, and giveth ear to them, and is contented to be lead by them, especiallye whan they have so much courage, that (in a maner) they enforce her and bicause they be deceitfull they fyll her with errours and false opinions. Wherupon most communlye it happeneth, that yonge men be wrapped in this sensual love, which is a very rebell against reason, and therfore thei make them selves unwoorthy to enjoy the favoures and benifites, which love bestoweth upon his true subjectes, neither in love feele they any other pleasures, then what beastes without reason do, but much more grevous afflictions. Setting case* therfore this to be so, which is most true, I say, that the contrary chaunseth to them of a more ripe age. For in case they, whan the soule is not nowe so much wayed downe with the bodyly burdein, and whan the naturall burning asswageth and draweth to a warmeth, if thei be inflamed with beawty, and to it bend their coveting guided by reasonable choise, they be not deceived, and possesse beawtye perfectly, and therefor through the possessing of it, alwaies goodnes ensueth to them: bicause beauty is good and consequently the true love of it is most good and holy, and evermore bringeth furth good frutes in the soules of them, that with the bridle of reason restraine the yll disposition of sense, the which old men can much sooner do then yong. [LIV] Yt is not therfore out of reason to say, that olde men may also love without sclaunder and more happily, then yong men: taking notwithstanding this name Olde, not for the age at the pittes brinke, nor when the canelles of the body be so feble, that the soule can not through them worke her feates, but when knowleage in us is in his right strength. And I wil not also hide this from you: namely, that I suppose, where sensuall love in every age is naught, yet in yonge men it deserveth excuse, and perhappes in some case lefull: for although it putteth them in afflictions, daungeres, travailes, and the unfortunatenes that is said, yet are there many that to winne them the good will of their Ladies practise vertuous thinges, which for all they be not bent to a good end, yet

Beawtie.

---

* Setting case: allowing.

are they good of them selves, and so of that much bitternesse they pike out a litle sweetnesse, and through the adversities which they susteine, in the ende they acknowleage their errour. As I judge therfore those yong men that bridle their appetites, and love with reason, to be godlye: so do I houlde excused suche as yelde to sensuall love, wherunto they be so inclined through the weakenesse and frailtie of man: so they showe therin meekenesse, courtesie, and prowesse, and the other worthie condicions that these Lordes have spoken of, and whan those youthfull yeeres be gone and past, leave it of cleane, keapinge alouf from this sensuall covetinge as from the lowermost steppe of the stayers, by the whiche a man may ascende to true love. But in case after they drawe in yeeres once they reserve in their colde hart the fire of appetites, and brynge stoute reason in subjection to feeble sense, it can not bee said how much they are to be blamed: for lyke men without sense they deserve with an everlasting shame to be put in the numbre of unreasonable living creatures, bicause the thoughtes and wayes of sensuall love be farr unsittinge for ripe age.[286]

[LV] Here Bembo paused a while as though he woulde brethe him, and whan all thinges were whist M. MORELLO of Ortona saide: And in case there were some olde man more freshe and lustye and of a better complexion then manye yonge men, whie woulde you not have it lefull for him to love with the love that yonge men love?

The DUTCHESSE laughed and said: Yf the love of yong men be so unluckye, why would you (M. Morello) that old men should also love with this unluckinesse? But in case you were old (as these men say you be) you woulde not thus procure the hurt of olde men.

M. MORELLO answered: The hurt of olde men (me seemeth) M. Peter Bembo procureth, who will have them to love after a sort, that I for my part understande not: and (me think) the possessing of this beawtye, whiche he prayseth so muche, without the body, is a dreame.

Do you beeleave M. Morello, quoth then COUNT LEWIS, that beauty is alwaies so good a thing as M. Peter Bembo speaketh of?

Not I in good sooth, answered M. MORELLO: but I remember rather that I have seene manie beautifull women of a most yll inclination, cruell, and spitefull, and it seemeth that (in a maner) it happeneth alwaies so, for beawtie maketh them proude: and pride, cruell.

COUNT LEWIS said smilinge: To you perhappes they seeme cruell, bicause they content you not with it, that you would have. But cause M. Peter Bembo to teach you in what sort old men ought to covet beawtye and what to seeke at their Ladies handes, and what to content them selves withall: and in not passinge out of these boundes, ye shal se that they shal be neither proud nor cruell: and wil satisfy you with what you shal require.

M. MORELLO seemed then somwhat out of pacience, and said: I will not knowe the thinge that toucheth me not. But cause you to be taught how the yonge men ought to covet this beawty, that are not so fresh and lusty as olde men be.

[LVI] Here SIR FRIDERICKE to pacifie M. Morello and to breake their talke, woulde not suffer Count Lewis to make answere, but interrupting him said: Perhappes M. Morello is not altogether out of the way in saing that beawty is not alwayes good, for the beautye of women is manye times cause of infinit evilles in the worlde, hatred, warr, mortality, and destruction, wherof the rasinge of Troye can be a good witnesse: and beawtiful women for the most part be eyther proude and cruell (as is saide) or unchast, but M. Morello woulde finde no faulte with that. There be also manye wicked men that have the comelinesse of a beautifull countenance, and it semeth that nature hath so shaped them, bicause they may be the redier to deceive, and that this amiable looke were like a baite that covereth the hooke.

Then M. PETER BEMBO: Beleave not (quoth he) but beautie is always good.

Here COUNT LEWIS bicause he woulde retourn again to his former pourpose interrupted him and said: Sins M. Morello passeth not to understand that, which is so necessary for him, teache it me, and showe me howe olde men may come bye this hapinesse of love, for I will not care to be counted olde, so it may profit me.

[LVII] M. PETER BEMBO laughed and said: First will I take the errour out of these gentilmens minde: and

afterwarde will I satisfie you also. So beeginning a fresh:
My Lordes (quoth he) I would not that with speakynge
ill of beawtie, which is a holy thinge, any of us as
prophane and wicked shoulde purchase him the wrath
of God. Therfore to give M. Morello and Sir Fridericke
warninge, that they lose not their sight, as Stesichorus
did,[287] a peine most meete for who so dispraiseth
beawtie, I saye, that beawtie commeth of God, and is
like a circle, the goodnesse wherof is the Centre. And
therefore, as there can be no circle without a centre, no
more can beawty be without goodnesse. Wherupon
doeth verie sildome an ill soule dwell in a beawtifull
bodye. And therefore is the outwarde beawtie a true
signe of the inwarde goodnes, and in bodies thys
comelynesse is imprynted more and lesse (as it were) for
a marke of the soule, whereby she is outwardlye
knowen: as in trees, in whiche the beawtye of the
buddes giveth a testimonie of the goodnesse of the frute.
And the verie same happeneth in bodies, as it is seene,
that Palmastrers* by the visage knowe manye tymes the
condicions, and otherwhile the thoughtes of menne.
And which is more, in beastes also a manne may
descerne by the face the qualitie of the courage, whiche
in the bodye declareth it selfe as muche as it can. Judge
you howe plainlye in the face of a Lion, a horse and an
Egle, a manne shall descerne anger, fiersenesse and
stoutenesse: in Lambes and Doves simplenesse and
verie innocencye: the craftye subtiltye in Foxes and
Wolves, and the like (in a maner) in all other livinge
creatures. [LVIII] The foule therefore for the most part
be also yvell and the beawtifull, good. Therfore it maye
be said that Beawtie is a face pleasant, meerie, comelye,
and to be desired for goodnesse: and Foulness a face
darke, uglesome, unpleasant and to be shonned for yll.
And in case you will consider all thinges, ye shall finde,
that what so ever is good and profitable hath also
evermore the comelinesse of Beawtie. Behoulde the
state of this great Inginn† of the world, which God
created for the helth and preservation of every thing
that was made.[288] The heaven rounde besett with so

A notable
Poet whiche
lost his sight
for writing
against
Helena, and
recanting,
had his sight
restored him
again.

Judgment by
the face.

Beawtie.
Foulnesse.

De Orat.
lib. 3.
The worlde.
The heaven.

---

* Palmastrers: the original has *fisionomi* ('physiognomists').
† Inginn: fabric.

many heavenly lightes: and in the middle, the Earth invironed wyth the Elementes, and uphelde wyth the verye waight of it selfe: the sonn, that compassinge about giveth light to the wholl, and in winter season draweth to the lowermost signe, afterward by litle and litle climeth again to the other part: the Moone, that of him taketh her light, accordinge as she draweth nigh, or goith farther from him: and the other five sterres, that diversly keepe the very same course. These thinges emong them selves have such force by the knitting together of an order so necessarilye framed, that with altering them any one jott, they shoulde be all lewsed,* and the worlde would decaye. They have also suche beawtie and comelinesse, that all the wittes men have, can not imagin a more beawtifull matter. Thinke nowe of the shape of man, which may be called a litle world:[289] in whom every percell of his body is seene to be necessarily framed by art and not by happ, and then the fourme all together most beawtifull, so that it were a harde matter to judge, whether the members, as the eyes, the nose, the mouth, the eares, the armes, the breast and in like maner the other partes: give eyther more profit to the countenance and the rest of the body, or comelinesse. The like may be said of all other livinge creatures. Beehoulde the fethers of foules, the leaves and bowes of trees, which be given them of nature to keepe them in their beeinge, and yet have they withall a verye great sightlinesse. Leave nature, and come to art. What thinge is so necessarie in saylynge vesselles, as the forepart, the sides, the mainyardes, the mast, the sayles, the sterne, owers, ankers, and tacklinges? all these thinges notwithstanding are so welfavoured in the eye, that unto who so beehouldeth them they seeme to have bine found out aswell for pleasure, as for profit. Pillars and great beames uphoulde high buildinges and Palaices, and yet are they no lesse pleasurfull unto the eyes of the beehoulders, then profitable to the buyldinges. When men beegane first to build, in the middle of Temples and houses they reared the ridge of the rouffe, not to make the workes to have a better showe, but bicause the water might the more

The earth.

The sonne.

The moone.

The planettes.

Man.
Aristot.
8. Phisic.

Foules.
Trees.

Shippes.

Buildinges.

The rouffe of houses.

---

* be all lewsed: fall apart.

commodiouslie avoide on both sides: yet unto profit
there was furthwith adjoined a faire sightlinesse, so that
if under the skye where there falleth neyther haile nor
rayne a mann should builde a temple, without a reared
ridge, it is to be thought, that it coulde have neyther a
sightly showe nor any beawtie. [LIX] Beeside other
thinges therfore, it giveth a great praise to the world, in
saiynge that it is beawtifull. It is praised, in saiynge, the
beawtifull heaven, beawtifull earth, beawtifull sea,
beawtifull rivers, beawtifull wooddes, trees, gardeines,
beawtifull Cities, beawtifull Churches, houses, armies.
In conclusion this comelye and holye beawtie is a
wonderous settinge out of everie thinge. And it may be
said that Good and beawtifull be after a sort one selfe
thinge, especiallie in the bodies of men: of the beawtie
wherof the nighest cause (I suppose) is the beawtie of
the soule: the which as a partner of the right and
heavenlye beawtie, maketh sightlye and beawtifull
what ever she toucheth, and most of all, if the bodye,
where she dwelleth, be not of so vile a matter, that she
can not imprint in it her propertye. Therfore Beawtie is
the true monument and spoile of the victorye of the
soule, whan she with heavenlye influence beareth rule
over materiall and grosse nature, and with her light
overcommeth the darkeness of the bodye. It is not then to
be spoken that Beawtie maketh women proude or cruel,
although it seeme so to M. Morello. Neyther yet ought
beawtifull women to beare the blame of that hatred,
mortalytie, and destruction, which the unbridled
appetites of men are the cause of. I will not nowe denye,
but it is possible also to finde in the worlde beawtifull
women unchast, yet not because beawtie inclineth them
to unchast livinge, for it rather plucketh them from it, and
leadeth them into the way of vertuous condicions,
throughe the affinitie that beawtie hath with goodnesse:
but otherwile yll bringinge up, the continuall provocations of lovers, tokens, povertie, hope, deceites, feare, and
a thousande other matters overcome the steadfastnesse,
yea of beawtifull and good women: and for these and like
causes may also beawtifull menn beecome wicked.

[LX] Then said the L. CESAR: In case the L. Gaspars
sayinge be true of yesternight, there is no doubt but the
faire women be more chast then the foule.

And what was my sayinge? quoth the L. Gaspar.

The L. Cesar answered: If I do well beare in minde, your saiynge was, that the women that are suide to, alwaies refuse to satisfie him that suith to them, but those that are not suide to, sue to others. There is no doubt but the beautiful women have alwaies more suyters, and be more instantlye laide at in love, then the foule. Therefore the beawtifull alwayes deny, and consequentlye be more chast, then the foule, whiche not beeinge suied to, sue unto others.

M. Peter Bembo laughed and said: This argument can not be answered to.

Afterwarde he proceaded: It chaunseth also oftentimes, that as the other senses, so the sight is deceyved, and judgeth a face beawtyfull, which in deede is not beawtifull. And bicause in the eyes and in the wholl countenance of some women, a man behouldeth otherwhile a certein lavish wantonnes peincted with dishonest flickeringes,* many, whom that maner deliteth bicause it promiseth them an easines to come by the thing, that they covet, cal it beawty: but in deed it is a cloked unshamefastnes, unworthy of so honorable and holy a name.

M. Peter Bembo held his peace, and those Lordes still were earnest upon him to speake somewhat more of this love and of the waye to enjoy beautye aright, and at the last: Me thinke (quoth he) I have showed plainly inough, that olde men may love more happelye then yonge, whiche was my drift, therfor it belongeth not me to entre anye farther.

Count Lewes answered: You have better declared the unluckinesse of yonge men, then the happynesse of olde menn, whom you have not as yet taught, what waye they must folow in this love of theirs: onelye you have saide, that they must suffre them selves to bee guided by reason, and the opinion of many is, that it is unpossible for love to stand with reason.

[LXI] Bembo notwithstanding saught to make an ende of reasoning, but the Dutchesse desired him to say on, and he beegane thus afreshe: Too unluckie were the nature of man, if oure soule (in the whiche this so

* flickeringes: enticements.

fervent covetinge may lightlie arrise) should be driven
to nourish it with that onelye, whiche is commune to
her with beastes, and coulde not tourn it to the other
noble parte, whiche is propre to her. Therfore sins it is
so your pleasure, I wil not refuse to reason upon this
noble matter. And bicause I know my self unworthy to
talke of the most holye misteries of love, I beseche him
so leade my thought and my tunge so, that I may show
this excelent Courtier how to love contrarye to the
wonted maner of the commune ignorant sort. And even
as from my childhode I have dedicated all my wholl lief
unto him, so also now that my wordes may be answerable
to the same intent, and to the prayse of him: I may
therfore, that sins the nature of man in youthfull age is
so much inclined to sense, it may be graunted the
Courtier, while he is yong, to love sensuallye. But in
case afterwarde also in hys riper yeres, he chaunse to be
set on fire with this coveting of love, he ought to be good
and circumspect, and heedful that he beeguyle not him
self, to be lead willfullye into the wretchednesse, that in
yonge men deserveth more to be pitied then blamed:
and contrarywise in olde men, more to be blamed then
pitied. [LXII] Therfore whan an amiable countenance
of a beautiful woman commeth in his sight, that is
accompanied with noble condicions and honest
behaviours, so that as one practised in love, he wotteth
well that his hewe* hath an agreement with herres,
assoone as he is a ware that his eyes snatch that image
and carie it to the hart, and that the soule beeginneth to
beehoulde it with pleasure, and feeleth within her self
the influence that stirreth her and by litle and litle
setteth her in heate, and that those livelye spirites, that
twinkle out throughe the eyes, put continually freshe
nourishment to the fire: he ought in this beginninge to
seeke a speedye remedye and to raise up reason, and
with her, to fense the fortresse of his hart, and to shutt in
such wise the passages against sense and appetites, that
they maye entre neyther with force nor subtill practise.
Thus if the flame be quenched, the jeoperdye is also
quenched. But in case it continue or encrease, then must

Sense.
Reason.

* hewe: the original has *sangue*, literally 'blood': here perhaps
'nature', 'inner self'.

the Courtier determine (when he perceiveth he is taken) to shonn throughlye all filthinesse of commune love, and so entre into the holye way of love with the guide of reason, and first consider that the body, where that beawtye shyneth, is not the fountaine frome whens beauty springeth, but rather bicause beautie is bodilesse and (as we have said) an heavenlie shyning beame, she loseth much of her honoure whan she is coopled with that vile subject and full of corruption, bicause the lesse she is partner therof, the more perfect she is, and cleane sundred frome it, is most perfect. And as a mann heareth not with his mouth, nor smelleth with hys eares: no more can he also in anye maner wise enjoye beawtye, nor satisfye the desyre that shee stirrith up in oure myndes, with feelynge, but wyth the sense, unto whom beawtye is the verye butt to levell at: namelye, the vertue of seeinge. Let him laye aside therefore the blinde judgemente of the sense, and injoye wyth his eyes the bryghtnesse, the comelynesse, the lovynge sparkles, laughters, gestures and all the other pleasant fournitours of beawty: especially with hearinge the sweetenesse of her voice, the tunablenesse of her woordes, the melodie of her singinge and playinge on instrumentes (in case the woman beloved be a musitien) and so shall he with most deintie foode feede the soule through the meanes of these two senses, which have litle bodelye substance in them, and be the ministers of reason, without entringe farther towarde the bodye with covetinge unto anye longinge otherwise then honest. Afterward let him obey, please, and honoure with all reverence his woman, and recken her more deere to him then his owne lief, and prefarr all her commodities and pleasures beefore his owne, and love no lesse in her the beauty of the mind, then of the bodye: therfore let him have a care not to suffer her to renn into any errour, but with lessons and good exhortations seeke alwaies to frame her to modestie, to temperance, to true honestye, and so to woorke that there maye never take place in her other then pure thoughtes and farr wide from all filthinesse of vices. And thus in sowinge of vertue in the gardein of that mind, he shall also gather the frutes of most beautifull condicions, and savour them with a marveilous good relise. And this shall be the right

Beawtye severed from the body is most perfect.

engendringe and imprinting of beawtye in beawtie, the
whiche some houlde opinion to be the ende of love. In
this maner shall oure Courtier be most acceptable to his
Lady, and she will alwayes showe her self towarde him
tractable, lowlye and sweete in language, and as
willinge to please him, as to be beloved of him: and the
willes of them both shall be most honest and agreeable,
and they consequently shall be most happy.

[LXIII] Here M. MORELLO: The engendringe (quoth
he) of beawtye in beawtye aright, were the engendringe
of a beawtyfull chylde in a beautifull woman, and I
woulde thinke it a more manifest token a great deale
that she loved her lover, if she pleased him with this,
then with the sweetenesse of language that you speake
of.

M. PETER BEMBO laughed and said: You must not
(M. Morello) passe your boundes. I may tell you, it is
not a small token that a woman loveth, whan she giveth
unto her lover her beawtye, which is so precious a
matter: and by the wayes that be a passage to the soule
(that is to say, the sight and the hearinge) sendeth the
lookes of her eyes, the image of her countenance, and
the voice of her woordes, that perce into the lovers hart,
and give a witnes of her love.

M. MORELLO said: Lookes and woordes may be, and
oftentimes are, false witnesses. Therfore whoso hath
not a better pledge of love (in my judgement) he is in an
yll assurance. And surelye I looked still that you would
have made this woman of yours somewhat more
courteyous and free towarde the Courtier, then my L.
Julian hath made his: but (me seemeth) ye be both of the
propretie of those judges, that (to appeere wise) give
sentence against their owne.

[LXIV] BEMBO said: I am well pleased to have this
woman muche more courteyous towarde my Courtier
not yonge, then the L. Julians is to the yong: and that
with good reason, bicause mine coveteth but honest
matters, and therfore may the woman graunt him them
all without blame. But my L. Julians woman that is not
so assured of the modestye of the yonge man, ought to
graunt him the honest matters onlye, and denye him the
dishonest. Therefore more happye is mine, that hath
graunted him whatsoever he requireth, then the other,

that hath parte graunted and parte denyed. And bicause you may moreover the better understande, that reasonable love is more happye then sensuall, I saye unto you, that self same thinges in sensuall ought to be denyed otherwhile, and in reasonable, graunted: bicause in the one, they be honest, and in the other dishonest. Therfore the woman to please her good lover, beside the graunting him merie countenances, familiar and secret talke, jesting, dalying, hand in hand, may also lawfullye and without blame come to kissinge: whiche in sensuall love, according to the L. Julians rules, is not lefull. For

A kisse.

sins a kisse is a knitting together both of body and soule, it is to be feared, least the sensuall lover will be more inclined to the part of the bodye, then of the soule: but the reasonable lover woteth well, that although the mouthe be a percell of the bodye, yet is it an issue for the wordes, that be the enterpreters of the soule, and for the inwarde breth, whiche is also called the soule: and therfore hath a delite to joigne hys mouth with the womans beloved with a kysse: not to stirr him to anye unhonest desire, but bicause he feeleth that, that bonde is the openynge of an entry to the soules, whiche drawen with a coveting the one of the other, power them selves by tourn, the one into the others bodye, and be so mingled together, that ech of them hath two soules, and one alone so framed of them both ruleth (in a maner) two bodyes. Wherupon a kisse may be said to be rather a cooplinge together of the soule, then of the bodye, bicause it hath suche force in her, that it draweth her unto it, and (as it were) seperateth her from the bodye. For this do all chast lovers covett a kisse, as a cooplinge of soules together. And therfore Plato the divine lover saith, that in kissing, his soule came as farr as his lippes to depart out of the body. And bicause the separatinge of the soule from the matters of the sense and the through coopling her with matters of understanding may be beetokened by a kisse, Salomon saith in his heavenlye boke of Balattes, Oh that he would kisse me with a kisse of his mouth, to expresse the desire he had, that hys soule might be ravished through heavenly love to the behouldinge of heavenly beawtie in such maner, that cooplyng her self inwardly with it, she might forsake the body.

[LXV] They stoode all herkening heedfullie to Bembos reasoninge, and after he had staide a while and sawe that none spake, he saide: Sins you have made me to beegine to showe oure not yonge Courtier this happye love, I will leade him yet somewhat farther forwardes, bicause to stande styll at this stay were somewhat perillous for him, consideringe (as we have often times said) the soule is most inclyned to the senses, and for all reason with discourse chouseth well, and knoweth that beawtie not to spring of the bodye, and therfore setteth a bridle to the unhonest desires, yet to beehould it alwaies in that body, doeth oftentimes corrupt the right judgement. And where no other inconvenience insueth upon it, ones absence from the wight beloved carieth a great passion with it: bicause the influence of that beawtie whan it is present, giveth a wonderous delite to the lover, and settinge his hart on fire, quickeneth and melteth certein vertues in a traunce and congeled in the soule, the which nourished with the heat of love, floow about and go bubbling nigh the hart, and thrust out through the eyes those spirites, whiche be most fyne vapoures made of the purest and cleerest parte of the bloode, which receive the image of beawtie, and decke it with a thousande sundrye fournitures.[290] Wherupon the soule taketh a delite, and with a certein wonder is agast, and yet enjoyeth she it, and (as it were) astonied together with the pleasure, feeleth the feare and reverence that men accustomably have towarde holy matters, and thinketh her self to be in paradise. [LXVI] The lover therfore that considereth only the beawtie in the bodye, loseth this treasure and happinesse, assoone as the woman beloved with her departure leaveth the eyes without their brightnes, and consequently the soule, as a widowe without her joye. For sins beawtie is farr of, that influence of love setteth not the hart on fire, as it did in presence. Wherupon the pores be dryed up and wythered, and yet doeth the remembraunce of beawty somwhat stirr those vertues of the soule in such wise, that they seeke to scattre abrode the spirites, and they fyndinge the wayes closed up, have no yssue, and still they seeke to gete out, and so with those shootinges inclosed pricke the soule, and tourment her bitterlye, as yonge children, whan in their tender gummes they beegin to breede teeth. And hens come the teares, sighes, vexations and tourmentes of lovers: bicause the soule is alwayes in affliction and travaile and (in a maner) wexeth woode, untill the beloved beawtie commeth beefore her once again, and then is she immediatlye pacified and taketh breth, and throughlye bent to it, is nouryshed wyth most deintye foode, and by her will, would never depart from so sweete a sight. To avoide therfore the tourment of this absence, and to enjoy beawtie without passion, the Courtier by the helpe of reason muste full and wholy call backe again the coveting of the body to beawtye alone, and (in what he can) beehoulde it in it self simple and pure, and frame it within in his imagination sundred from all matter, and so make it frindlye and lovinge to hys soule, and there enjoye it, and have it with him daye and night, in every time and place, without mystrust ever to lose it: keapinge alwayes fast in minde, that the bodye is a most dyverse thynge from beawtie, and not onlie not encreaseth, but diminisheth the perfection of it. In this wise shall our not yonge Courtier be out of all bitternesse and wretchednes that yong men feele (in a maner) continuallye, as jelousies, suspicions, disdeignes, angres, desperations and certein rages full of madnesse, wherby manye times they be lead into so great errour, that some doe not only beate the women whom they love: but rid them selves out of their lief. He shal do no wrong to the husband, father, brethren or kinsfolke of the woman beloved. He shall not bringe her in sclaunder. He shall not be in case with much a do otherwhile to refraine hys eyes and tunge from discoverynge his desires to others. He shall not take thought at departure or in absence, bicause he shall ever more carye his precious treasure about wyth him shut fast within his hert. And beeside, through the vertue of imagination he shall facion within himself that beawty muche more faire, then it is in deede. [LXVII] But emong these commodities the lover shal finde an other yet far greater, in case he will take this love for a stayer (as it were) to clime up to an other farr higher then it.[291] The whiche he shall bringe to passe, if he will go and consider with himself, what a streict bonde it is to be alwaies in the trouble to beehoulde the beawtie of

one bodye alone. And therfore to come out of this so
narrow a rowme, he shall gather in his thought by litle
and litle so manye ornamentes, that meddlinge all
beawties together, he shall make an universall concept,
and bringe the multitude of them to the unitye of one
alone, that is generally spred over all the nature of man.
And thus shall he beehoulde no more the particuler
beawtie of one woman, but an universall, that decketh
out all bodies. Wherupon beeing made dymm with this
greater light, he shall not passe upon the lesser, and
burnynge in a more excellent flame, he shall litle
esteame it, that he sett great store by at the first. This
stayer* of love, though it be verye noble, and such as
fewe arrive at it, yet is it not in this sort to be called
perfect, forsomuch as where the imagination is of force
to make conveiance and hath no knowleage, but
through those beeginninges that the senses helpe her
wythall, she is not cleane pourged from grosse
darkenesse: and therefore though she do consider that
universall beawtie in sunder and in it self alone, yet doeth
she not well and cleerlye descerne it, nor without some
doubtfulness, by reason of the agreement that the
fansyes have with the bodye. Wherefore suche as come
to thys love, are lyke yonge Birdes almost flushe,
whyche for all they flytter a litle their tender wynges, yet
dare they not stray farr from the neste, nor commytt
theym selves to the wynde and open weather. [LXVIII]
Whan oure Courtier therfore shall be come to this
point, although he maye be called a good and happye
lover, in respect of them that be drowned in the miserye
of sensuall love, yet wil I not have him to set his hart at
rest, but bouldlye proceade farther, folowinge the high
way after his guyde, that leadeth him to the point of true
happinesse. And thus in steade of goinge out of his witt
with thought, as he must do that will consider the
bodilye beawty, he may come into his witt, to behoulde
the beawty that is seene with the eyes of the minde,
which then beegin to be sharpe and thorough seeinge,
whan the eyes of the body lose the floure of their
sightlynesse. Therfore the soule rid of vices, purged
with the studyes of true Philosophie, occupied in

* stayer: stairway.

spirituall, and exercised in matters of understandinge, tourninge her to the beehouldyng of her owne substance, as it were raysed out of a most deepe sleepe, openeth the eyes that all men have, and fewe occupy, and seeth in her self a shining beame of that lyght, which is the true image of the aungelike beawtye partened* with her, whereof she also partneth with the bodye a feeble shadowe: therfore wexed blinde about earthlye matters, is made most quicke of sight about heavenlye. And otherwhile whan the stirringe vertues of the body are withdrawen alone through earnest behouldinge, eyther fast bounde through sleepe, whan she is not hindred by them, she feeleth a certein previe smell of the right aungelike beawtie, and ravished with the shining of that light, beeginneth to be inflamed, and so greedilye foloweth after, that (in a maner) she wexeth dronken and beeside her self, for coveting to coople her self with it, havinge founde (to her wening) the footesteppes of God, in the beehouldinge of whom (as in her happy end) she seeketh to settle her self. And therfore burninge in this most happye flame, she arryseth to the noblest part of her (which is the understanding) and there no more shadowed with the darke night of earthlye matters, seeth the heavenlye beawtye: but yet doeth she not for all that enjoye it altogether perfectlye, bicause she beehouldeth it onlye in her perticular understandinge, which can not conceive the passing great universall beautye: wherupon not throughlye satisfied with this benifit, love giveth unto the soule a greater happines. For like as throughe the perticular beawtye of one bodye he guydeth her to the universall beawtye of all bodies: evenso in the last degree of perfection throughe perticular understandinge he guideth her to the universall understandinge. Thus the soule kindled in the most holye fire of true heavenlye love, fleeth to coople her selfe with the nature of Aungelles, and not onlye cleane forsaketh sense, but hath no more neede of the discourse of reason, for being chaunged into an Aungell, she understandeth all thinges that may be understoode: and without any veile or cloude, she seeth the meine sea of the pure heavenlye beawtye and

---

* partened with: shared with, communicated to.

receiveth it into her, and enjoyeth that soveraigne
happinesse, that can not be comprehended of the
senses. [LXIX] Sins therfore the beawties, which we
dayly see with these our dimm eyes in bodies subject to
corruption, that neverthelesse be nothinge elles but
dreames and most thinne shadowes of beauty, seme
unto us so wel favoured and comely, that oftentimes
they kendle in us a most burning fire, and with such
delite, that we recken no happinesse may be compared
to it, that we feele otherwhile through the only looke
which the beloved countenance of a woman casteth at
us: what happy wonder, what blessed abashement*
may we recken that to bee, that taketh the soules,
whiche come to have a sight of the heavenly beawty?
what sweete flame? What soote† incense maye a mann
beleave that to bee, whiche arriseth of the fountaine of
the soveraigne and right beawtye? Whiche is the origion
of all other beawtye, whiche never encreaseth nor
diminisheth, always beawtyfull, and of it selfe, aswell
on the one part as on the other, most simple, onelye like
it self, and partner of none other, but in suche wise
beawtifull, that all other beawtifull thinges, be beawtifull, bicause they be partners of the beawtie of it. This is
the beawtye unseperable from the high bountye, whiche
with her voyce calleth and draweth to her all thynges:
and not onlye to the indowed with understandinge giveth
understandinge, to the reasonable reason, to the
sensuall sense and appetite to live, but also partaketh
with plantes and stones (as a print of her self) stirring,
and the natural provocation‡ of their properties. So
much therfore is this love greater and happier then
others, as the cause that stirreth it, is more excellent.
And therefore, as commune fire trieth golde and maketh
it fyne, so this most holye fire in soules destroyeth and
consumeth what so ever there is mortall in them, and
relieveth and maketh beawtyfull the heavenlye part,
whyche at the first by reason of the sense was dead and
buried in them. This is the great fire in the whiche (the
Poetes wryte) that Hercules was burned on the topp of

Heavenly
beawtie.

---

* abashement: awe.
† soote: sweet.
‡ provocation: instinct.

A mounteign
betweene
Thessalia and
Macedonia
where is the
sepulchre of
Hercules.

the mountaigne Oeta: and throughe that consumynge
with fire, after hys death was holye and immortall. Thys
is the fyrie bushe of Moses: the divided tunges of fire:
the inflamed Chariot of Helias: whych doobleth grace
and happynesse in their soules that be worthy to see it,
whan they forsake thys earthly basenesse and flee up
into heaven.[292] Let us therefore bende all oure force and
thoughtes of soule to this most holye light, that showeth
us the waye which leadeth to heaven: and after it,
puttynge of the affections we were clad withall at our
comminge downe, let us clime up the stayers, which at
the lowermost stepp have the shadowe of sensuall
beawty, to the high mansion place where the heavenlye,
amiable and right beawtye dwelleth, which lyeth hid in
the innermost secretes of God, least unhalowed eyes
shoulde come to the syght of it: and there shall we fynde
a most happye ende for our desires, true rest for oure
travailes, certein remedye for myseryes, a most health-
full medycin for sickenesse, a most sure haven in the
troublesome stormes of the tempestuous sea of this life.
[LXX] What tunge mortall is there then (O most holy
love) that can sufficientlye prayse thy woorthynesse?
Thou most beawtifull, most good, most wise, art
dirived of the unity of heavenly beautie, goodnesse and
wisedome, and therin doest thou abide, and unto it
through it (as in a circle) tournest about. Thou the most
sweete bonde of the worlde, a meane beetwext
heavenlye and earthlye thynges, wyth a bountifull
tempre bendest the high vertues to the government of
the lower, and tourninge backe the mindes of mortall
men to their beeginning, cooplest them with it. Thou
with agreement bringest the Elementes in one, stirrest
nature to brynge furth, and that, which arriseth and is
borne for the succession of the lief.* Thou bringest
severed matters into one, to the unperfect givest perfec-
tyon, to the unlyke likenesse, to enimitye amitye, to the
Earth frutes, to the Sea calmnesse, to the heaven lyvelie
light. Thou art the father of true pleasures, of grace,
peace, lowlynesse and good will, ennemye to rude
wildenesse and sluggishnesse, to be short, the beginninge
and ende of all goodnesse. And forsomuche as thou

* succession of the lief: perpetuation of life.

delitest to dwell in the floure of beawtyfull bodyes and beawtyfull soules, I suppose that thy abydynge place is nowe here emonge us, and from above otherwhyle showest thy selfe a litle to the eyes and mindes of them that be woorthye to see thee. Therefore vouchesafe (Lorde) to harken to oure prayers, power thy selfe into oure hartes, and wyth the bryghtnesse of thy most holye fire lyghten oure darkenesse, and like a trustie guide in thys blynde mase, showe us the right waye: refourme the falsehoode of the senses, and after longe wandringe in vanitye gyve us the ryght and sounde joye. Make us to smell those spirituall savoures that relieve* the vertues of the understandinge, and to heare the heavenlye harmonie so tunable, that no discorde of passion take place anye more in us. Make us dronken with the bottomelesse fountain of contentation that alwaies doeth delite, and never giveth fill, and that giveth a smacke of the right† blisse unto who so drinketh of the renning and cleere water therof. Pourge wyth the shininge beames of thy light our eyes from mysty ignoraunce, that they maye no more set by mortall beawty, and wel perceive that the thinges which at the first they thought themselves to see, be not in deede, and those that they saw not, to be in effect. Accept oure soules, that be offred unto thee for a sacrifice. Burn them in the livelye flame that wasteth al grosse filthines, that after they be cleane sundred from the body, thei may be copled with an everlastinge and most sweet bonde to the heavenly beawty. And we severed from oure selves, may be chaunged like right lovers into the beloved, and after we be drawen from the earth, admitted to the feast of the aungelles, where fed with immortall ambrosia and nectar, in the ende we maye dye a most happie and livelye death, as in times past died the fathers of olde time, whose soules with most fervent zeale of beehouldinge thou diddest hale from the bodye and coopleddest them with God.

The poetes feigne to be the meate and drinke of the Goddes.

[LXXI] When Bembo had hitherto spoken with such vehemencye, that a man woulde have thought him (as it were) ravished and beeside himselfe, he stoode still

* relieve: quicken.
† right: true.

without once mooving, houldynge his eyes towarde heaven as astonied, whan the LADY EMILIA, whiche together with the rest gave most diligent eare to this talke, tooke him by the plaite of hys garment and pluckinge hym a litle, said: Take heede (M. Peter) that these thoughtes make not your soule also to forsake the bodye.

Madam, answered M. PETER, it shoulde not be the first miracle that love hath wrought in me.

Then the Dutchesse and all the rest beegan a fresh to be instant upon M. Bembo that he woulde proceade once more in his talke, and every one thought he felt in his minde (as it were) a certein sparkle of that godlye love that pricked him, and they all coveted to heare farther: but M. BEMBO: My Lordes (quoth he) I have spoken what the holye furie of love hath (unsaught for) indited* to me: now that (it seemeth) he inspireth me no more, I wot not what to say. And I thinke verelie that love will not have his secretes discovered any farther, nor that the Courtier shoulde passe the degree that his pleasure is I shoulde show him,† and therfore it is not perhappes lefull to speake anye more in this matter.

[LXXII] Surelye, quoth the DUTCHESSE, if the not yonge Courtier be such a one that he can folowe this way which you have showed him, of right he ought to be satisfied with so great a happines, and not to envie the yonger.

Then the L. CESAR GONZAGA: The way (quoth he) that leadeth to this happines is so stiepe (in my mind) that (I beleave) it will be much a do to gete to it.

The L. GASPAR said: I beleave it be harde to gete up for men, but unpossible for women.

The L. EMILIA laughed and said: If ye fall so often to offende us, I promise you, ye shall be no more forgiven.

The L. GASPAR answered: It is no offence to you, in saiynge, that womens soules be not so pourged from passions as mens be, nor accustomed in behouldinges,‡ as M. Peter hath said, is necessary for them to be, that

---

* indited: dictated.
† his pleasure is I shoulde show him: that it pleased him [Love] to have me show him [the courtier].
‡ behouldinges: contemplation.

will tast of the heavenly love. Therefore it is not read
that ever woman hath had this grace: but manie men
have had it, as Plato, Socrates, Plotinus, and manie
other: and a numbre of our holye fathers, as Saint
Francis, in whom a fervent spirite of love imprinted the
most holie seale of the five woundes. And nothinge but
the vertue of love coulde hale up Saint Paul the Apostle
to the sight of those secretes, which is not lawfull for
man to speake of: nor show Saint Stephan the heavens
open.[293]

Here answered the L. JULIAN: In this point men shall
nothinge passe women, for Socrates him selfe doeth
confesse that all the misteries of love which he knew,
were oped unto him by a woman, which was Diotima.
And the Aungell that with the fire of love imprinted the
five woundes in Saint Francis, hath also made some
women woorthy of the same print in our age. You must
remembre moreover that S. Mari Magdalen had manye
faultes forgeven her, bicause she loved muche: and
perhappes with no lesse grace then Saint Paul, was she
manye times through Aungelyke love haled up to the
thirde heaven.[294] And manye other (as I showed you
yesterdaye more at large) that for love of the name of
Chryste have not passed upon lief, nor feared tourmentes, nor any other kinde of death how terrible and
cruell ever it were. And they were not (as M. Peter wyll
have his Courtier to be) aged, but soft and tender
maidens, and in the age, when he saith that sensuall love
ought to be borne withal in men.

[LXXIII] The L. Gaspar began to prepare himself to
speake, but the DUTCHESSE: Of this (quoth shee) let M.
Peter be judge, and the matter shal stand to his verdite,
whether women be not as meete for heavenlie love as
men. But bicause the pleade beetweene you may happen
be to longe, it shall not be amisse to deferr it untill to
morow.

Nay, to nyght, quoth the L. CESAR GONZAGA.

And how can it be to night? quoth the DUTCHESSE.

The L. CESAR answered: Bicause it is daye alreadye,
and showed her the light that beegane to entre in at the
cliftes of the windowes. Then everie man arrose upon
his feete with much wonder, bicause they had not
thaught that the reasoninges had lasted lenger then the

accustomed wont, savinge onelye that they were beegon much later, and with their pleasantnesse had deceived so the Lordes mindes, that they wist not of the going away of the houres. And not one of them felt any heavinesse of slepe in his eyes, the which often happeneth whan a man is up after his accustomed houre to go to bed. Whan the windowes then were opened on the side of the Palaice that hath his prospect toward the high top of Mount Catri, they saw alredie risen in the East a faire morninge like unto the coulour of roses, and all sterres voided, savinge onelye the sweete Governesse of the heaven, Venus,[295] whiche keapeth the boundes of the nyght and the day, from whiche appeered to blowe a sweete blast, that filling the aer with a bytinge cold, begane to quicken the tunable notes of the prety birdes, emong the hushing woodes of the hilles at hande. Wherupon they all, takinge their leave with reverence of the Dutchesse, departed toward their lodginges without torche, the light of the day sufficing.

And as they were now passing out at the great chambre doore, the L. GENERALL tourned hym to the Dutches, and said: Madam, to take up the variance beetweene the L. Gaspar and the L. Julian, we will assemble this night with the judge sooner then we did yesterdaye.

The LADY EMILIA answered: Upon condicion, that in case my L. Gaspar wyll accuse women, and geve them (as his wont is) some false reporte, he wil also put us in suretye to stand to triall, for I recken him a waveringe starter.*

THE ENDE OF CASTILIOS BOOKES OF THE COURTYER.

* waveringe starter: defaulter, fugitive from justice.

A LETTER that the Author writt to the LADY
VICTORIA COLUMNA MARQUESS OF PESCARA,
whom he mentioneth in the Epistle
before his booke.[296]

Most honorable and my verie good Lady, I am much
behouldinge to M. Thomas Tuke[297], bicause he was the
occasion that your Ladishipp hath vouchsafed to write
unto me: which is most acceptable to me, and not
without cause, consideringe I have written so manye
letters and coulde never receive anye answere from you
again, albeit they conteined sundrye matters. Truth it is
indeede, that unmeete it were your L. shoulde write
unto me, onlesse therewithall you used my service and
commaunded me in what I am able to do for you. As
touchinge M. Tuke, I will do as much for him, as shall
lie in me to doe, both for your L. sake that may
commaunde me, and for the brotherlye love that I beare
him. Where M. Gutteriz hath wrytten unto you that I
complayned of you, I wonder nothinge at it, for (to saye
the troth) I uttred my greef a good while sins in a letter
that I wrott unto you your self, as I passed the
mountaignes of Fraunce to come into Spaine. And he
that toulde me the matter that caused it, was my L.
Marquesse of Vasto, who showed me a letter of yours, in
the which you your self confessed the stelth* of the
Courtyer. The whyche thynge I as then tooke in great
good part, doubtynge nothynge but that it shoulde
remayne in youre handes, and be well kept untyll I my
self shoulde come to demaunde it of you. At the last I
was enformed by a Gentilman Neopolitan, who
continueth still here in Spaine, that there were certein
Fragmentes of the poore Courtier in Naples, and he sawe
them in the handes of sundrye men, and he that
scattered it thus abrode reported that he had it of you. It
was some greef to me, as a father that seeth hys chylde
so yll handled: yet afterward yeeldyng to reason, I knew

* stelth: theft.

he deserved not to have anye more store made of him, but (like an untymelye birth) to be left in the hygh waye for the benifit of nature. And so undoubtedly was I determined to do, consideringe yf there were any thinge in the Booke not yll, men woulde have the woorse opinion of it, whan they shoulde see it so out of order. And no diligence shoulde prevaile any more to poolish it and to sett it furth, sins it had lost the thyng, which perhappes at the first was onlye it, that made it esteamed: that is to weete, the noveltye of the matter. And knowinge your saiynge to be true, that the cause of my complaint was verye triflynge, I resolved wyth my selfe, to leave at the least my complaininge, though I coulde not my sorowynge. And that whyche I brake wyth M. Gutteriz (in case it be well wayed) was no complaint. In conclusion others, more bent of a zeale then I was, have enforced me to write hym over again, as the shortnesse of tyme hath served me,* and to sende hym to Venice to be put in print, and so have I done. But if your L. shoulde suspect that the good will whiche I bear you were any deale feinted for this, your judgement shoulde deceyve you, whiche (I beleave) it did never in all youre lief beefore: but rather I recken my selfe more bounde to you, bicause the necessity that drove me to make hast so spedilie to imprint it, hath saved me a great peece of labour, where I was once mynded to have added manye other matters, which coulde be but of small moment as the rest are. And thus shall the reader have the lesse labour and the Author lesse blame. Therefore it is nowe past time eyther for you or me to repent or correct. And thus I take my leave of you. In Burgos the xxi. of Septembre, 1527.

---

* as the shortnesse of tyme hath served me: as far as possible, in the brief time available.

A BREEF REHERSALL OF
THE CHIEFE CONDITIONS AND QUALITIES
IN A COURTIER

To be well borne and of a good stocke.

To be of a meane stature, rather with the least then to high, and well made to his proportion.

To be portly and amiable in countenance unto whoso beehouldeth him.

Not to be womanish in his sayinges or doinges.

Not to praise himself unshamefully and out of reason.

Not to crake and boast of his actes and good qualities.

To shon Affectation or curiosity above al thing in al things.

To do his feates with a slight, as though they were rather naturally in him, then learned with studye: and use a Reckelesness to cover art, without minding greatly what he hath in hand, to a mans seeminge.

Not to carie about tales and triflinge newis.

Not to be overseene in speaking wordes otherwhile that may offende where he ment it not.

Not to be stubborne, wilfull nor full of contention: nor to contrary and overthwart men after a spiteful sort.

Not to be a babbler, brauler or chatter, nor lavish of his tunge.

Not to be given to vanitie and lightnesse, nor to have a fantasticall head.

No lyer.

No fonde flatterer.

To be well spoken and faire languaged.

To be wise and well seene in discourses upon states.

To have a judgement to frame himself to the maners of the Countrey where ever he commeth.

To be able to alleage good, and probable reasons upon everie matter.

To be seen in tunges, and specially in Italian, French and Spanish.

To direct all thinges to a good ende.

To procure where ever he goeth that men may first

conceive a good opinion of him beefore he commeth there.

To felowship him self for the most part with men of the best sort and of most estimation, and with his equalles, so he be also beloved of his inferiours.

To play for his pastime at Dice and Cardes, not wholye for moneis sake, nor fume and chafe in his losse.

To be meanly seene in the play at Chestes, and not overcounninge.

To be pleasantlie disposed in commune matters and in good companie.

To speake and write the language that is most in use emonge the commune people, without inventing new woordes, inckhorn tearmes or straunge phrases, and such as be growen out of use by long time.

To be handesome and clenly in his apparaile.

To make his garmentes after the facion of the most, and those to be black, or of some darkish and sad coulour, not garish.

To gete him an especiall and hartye friend to companye withall.

Not to be ill tunged, especiallie against his betters.

Not to use any fonde saucinesse or presumption.

To be no envious or malitious person.

To be an honest, a faire condicioned man, and of an upright conscience.

To have the vertues of the minde, as justice, manlinesse, wisdome, temperance, staidenesse, noble courage, sobermoode, etc.

To be more then indifferentlye well seene in learninge, in the Latin and Greeke tunges.

Not to be rash, nor perswade hymselfe to knowe the thing that he knoweth not.

To confesse his ignorance, whan he seeth time and place therto, in suche qualities as he knoweth him selfe to have no maner skill in.

To be brought to showe his feates and qualities at the desire and request of others, and not rashlye presse to it of himself.

To speake alwaies of matters likely, least he be counted a lyer in reporting of wonders and straunge miracles.

To have the feate of drawing and peincting.

To daunce well without over nimble footinges or to busie trickes.

To singe well upon the booke.

To play upon the Lute, and singe to it with the ditty.

To play upon the Vyole, and all other instrumentes with freates.

To delite and refresh the hearers mindes in being pleasant, feat conceited, and a meerie talker, applyed to time and place.

Not to use sluttish and Ruffianlike pranckes with anye man.

Not to beecome a jester or scoffer to put anye man out of countenance.

To consider whom he doth taunt and where: for he ought not to mocke poore seelie soules, nor men of authoritie, nor commune ribaldes and persons given to mischeef, which deserve punishment.

To be skilfull in all kynd of marciall feates both on horsbacke and a foote, and well practised in them: whiche is his cheef profession, though his understandinge be the lesse in all other thinges.

To play well at fense upon all kinde of weapons.

To be nimble and quicke at the play at tenise.

To hunt and hauke.

To ride and manege wel his horse.

To be a good horsman for every saddle.

To swimme well.
To leape wel.
To renn well.
To vaute well.
To wrastle well.
To cast the stone well.
To cast the barr well.

} Sildome in open syght of the people but privilye with himselfe alone, or emonge hys friendes and familiers.

To renn well at tilt, and at ring.
To tourney.
To fight at Barriers.
To kepe a passage or streict.
To play at *Jogo di Canne*.
To renn at Bull.
To fling a Speare or Dart.

} These things in open syght to delyte the commune people withall.

Not to renn, wrastle, leape, nor cast the stone or barr with men of the Countrey, except he be sure to gete the victorie.

To sett out himself in feates of chivalrie in open showes
well provided of horse and harness, well trapped, and
armed, so that he may showe himselfe nymeble on
horsbacke.

Never to be of the last that appeere in the listes at justes, or
in any open showes.

To have in triumphes comelic armour, bases, scarfes,
trappinges, liveries, and such other thinges of sightlie
and meerie coulours, and rich to beehoulde, wyth
wittie poesies and pleasant divises, to allure unto him
chefflie the eyes of the people.

To disguise himself in maskerie eyther on horsbacke or a
foote, and to take the shape upon hym that shall be
contrarie to the feate that he mindeth to worke.

To undertake his bould feates and couragious enterprises
in warr, out of companye and in the sight of the most
noble personages in the campe, and (if it be possible)
beefore his Princis eyes.

Not to hasarde himself in forraginge and spoiling or in
enterprises of great daunger and small estimation,
though he be sure to gaine by it.

Not to waite upon or serve a wycked and naughtye
person.

Not to seeke to come up by any naughtie or subtill
practise.

Not to committ any mischevous or wicked fact at the wil
and commaundement of his Lorde or Prince.

Not to folowe his owne fansie, or alter the expresse
wordes in any point of his commission from hys Prince
or Lorde, onlesse he be assured that the profit will be
more, in case it have good successe, then the damage, if
it succeade yll.

To use evermore toward his Prince or L. the respect that
beecommeth the servaunt toward his maister.

To endevour himself to love, please and obey his Prince in
honestye.

Not to covett to presse into the Chambre or other secrete
part where his Prince is withdrawen at any time.

Never to be sad, melancholie or solenn beefore hys Prince.

Sildome or never to sue to hys Lorde for anye thing for
himself.

His suite to be honest and reasonable whan he suyth for
others.

To reason of pleasaunt and meerie matters whan he is withdrawen with him into private and secrete places alwayes doinge him to understande the truth without dissimulation or flatterie.

Not to love promotions so, that a man shoulde thinke he coulde not live without them, nor unshamefastlye to begg any office.

To refuse them after such a comelye sort, that the Prince offrynge hym them, maye have a cause to offre them with a more instance.

Not to presse to his Prince where ever he be, to hould him with a vaine tale, that others should thinke him in favour with him.

To consyder well what it is that he doeth or speaketh, where, in presence of whom, what time, why, his age, his profession, the ende, and the meanes.

The final end of a Courtier, wher to al his good condicions and honest qualities tende, is to beecome an Instructer and Teacher of his Prince or Lorde, inclininge him to vertuous practises: and to be francke and free with him, after he is once in favour in matters touching his honour and estimation, alwayes putting him in minde to folow vertue and to flee vice, opening unto him the commodities of the one and inconveniences of the other: and to shut his eares against flatterers, whiche are the first beeginninge of self leekinge and all ignorance.

His conversation with women to be alwayes gentle, sober, meeke, lowlie, modest, serviceable, comelie, merie, not bitinge or sclaundering with jestes, nippes, frumpes, or railinges, the honesty of any.

His love towarde women, not to be sensuall or fleshlie, but honest and godlye, and more ruled with reason, then appetyte: and to love better the beawtye of the minde, then of the bodie.

Not to withdrawe his maistresse good will from his felowlover with revilinge or railinge at him, but with vertuous deedes, and honest condicions, and with deserving more then he, at her handes for honest affections sake.

OF THE CHIEF CONDITIONS AND QUALITYES
IN A WAYTYNG GENTYLWOMAN

To be well born and of a good house.

To flee affectation or curiositie.

To have a good grace in all her doinges.

To be of good condicions and wel brought up.

To be wittie and foreseing, not heady and of a renning witt.

Not to be haughtie, envious, yltunged, lyght, contentious nor untowardlye.

To win and keepe her in her Ladies favour and all others.

To do the exercises meete for women, comlye and with a good grace.

To take hede that she give none accasion to bee yll reported of.

To commit no vice, nor yet to be had in suspition of any vice.

To have the vertues of the minde, as wisdome, justice, noblenesse of courage, temperance, strength of the minde, continency, sobermoode, etc.

To be good and discreete.

To have the understandinge beinge maried, how to ordre her husbandes substance, her house and children, and to play the good huswyef.

To have a sweetenesse in language and a good uttrance to entertein all kinde of men with communication woorth the hearing, honest, applyed to time and place and to the degree and disposition of the person whiche is her principall profession.

To accompany sober and quiet maners and honesty with a livelie quicknesse of wit.

To be esteamed no lesse chast, wise and courteious, then pleasant, feat conceited and sober.

Not to make wise to abhorr companie and talke, though somewhat of the wantonnest, to arrise and forsake them for it.

To geve the hearing of such kinde of talke with blushing and bashfulnesse.

Not to speake woordes of dishonestye and baudrye to showe her self pleasant, free and a good felowe.

Not to use over much familyaritie without measure and bridle.

Not willinglie to give eare to suche as report ill of other women.

To be heedefull in her talke that she offend not where she ment it not.

To beeware of praysinge her self undiscreatlye, and of beeing to tedious and noysome in her talke.

Not to mingle with grave and sad matters, meerie jestes and laughinge matters: nor with mirths, matters of gravitie.

To be circumspect that she offend no man in her jesting and tauntynge, to appeere therby of a readye witt.

Not to make wise to knowe the thing that she knoweth not, but with sobernesse gete her estimation with that she knoweth.

Not to come on loft nor use to swift measures in her daunsinge.

Not to use in singinge or playinge upon instrumentes to muche devision and busy pointes, that declare more cunning then sweetenesse.

To come to daunce, or to showe her musicke with suffringe her self to be first prayed somewhat and drawen to it.

To apparaile her self so, that she seeme not fonde and fantasticall.

To sett out her beawtye and disposition of person with meete garmentes that shall best beecome her, but as feininglye as she can, makyng semblant to bestowe no labour about it, nor yet to minde it.

To have an understandinge in all thinges belonginge to the Courtier, that she maye gyve her judgemente to commend and to make of gentilmen according to their worthinesse and desertes.

To be learned.

To be seene in the most necessarie languages.

To drawe and peinct.

To daunse.

To devise sportes and pastimes.

Not to be lyghte of creditt that she is beloved, thoughe a man commune familierlye with her of love.

The chief conditions and qualityes in a waytyng gentylwoman.

To shape him that is oversaucie wyth her, or that hath small respecte in hys talke, suche an answere, that he maye well understande she is offended wyth hym.

To take the lovynge communication of a sober Gentylman in an other signifycatyon, seeking to straye from that pourpose.

To acknoweleage the prayses whyche he giveth her at the Gentylmans courtesye, in case she can not dissemble the understandinge of them: debasynge her owne desertes.

To be heedefull and remembre that men may with lesse jeopardy show to be in love, then women.

To geve her lover nothing but her minde, whan eyther the hatred of her husband, or the love that he beareth to others inclineth her to love.

To love one that she may marye withall, beeinge a mayden and mindinge to love.

To showe suche a one all signes and tokens of love, savynge suche as maye put hym in anye dyshonest hope.

To use a somewhat more famylyar conversation wyth men well growen in yeeres, then with yonge men.

To make her self beloved for her desertes, amiablenesse, and good grace, not with anie uncomelie or dishonest behaviour, or flickeringe enticement with wanton lookes, but with vertue and honest condicions.

The final ende whereto the Courtier applieth all his good condicions, properties, feates and qualities, serveth also for a waiting Gentilwoman to grow in favour with her Lady, and by that meanes so to instruct her and traine her to vertue, that she may both refraine from vice and from committing anye dishonest matter, and also abhorr flatterers, and give her self to understand the full troth in every thyng, without entring into self leeking and ignorance, either of other outward thinges, or yet of her owne self.

NOTES

1. Thomas Sackville (1536–1608) is best remembered as the author, with Thomas Norton, of the earliest English tragedy in blank verse, *Gorboduc* (1561). Sackville subsequently made an impressive career at the court of Elizabeth I: he was raised to the peerage in 1567 and later made Lord Treasurer.

2. Lord Henry Hastings (1535–95), a nobleman of strong Protestant sympathies, succeeded his father as 3rd Earl of Northumberland in 1561. His grandfather, the 1st Earl, had been host to Castiglione on his diplomatic visit to England in 1506 (see note 5).

3. The great Athenian general and statesman Themistocles (*c.* 514–449 BC), responsible for the defeat of the Persians at Salamis in 480, was ostracised a decade later and fled to Persia. The source of the anecdote here is Plutarch's *Life of Themistocles*, 29, 3.

4. A Spanish translation of *The Courtier*, by Juan Boscán, was published six years after the dialogue's original publication, in 1534. A French translation, by Jacques Colin, followed in 1537.

5. Castiglione travelled to England in late 1506, just prior to the events recorded in *The Courtier*, to receive the Order of the Garter from Henry VII on behalf of the Duke of Urbino, Guido da Montefeltro.

6. The reference may be to the opening of the oration on government *To Nicocles* by the Greek orator and educationalist Isocrates (fourth century BC) where it is noted that rulers are particularly in need of formal guidance since they lack the honest criticism from friends that is such an important part of private citizens' moral education.

7. On Castiglione's imitation of Cicero's *De oratore*, see Introduction, The literary context. On the successes of the speakers in the dialogue, see Castiglione's introduction to Book IV and the List of Principal Speakers.

8. Ermolao Barbaro (1453–93) was a Venetian statesman and humanist, who produced pioneering studies of Greek and Latin philosophical texts. Andrea Navagero (1483–1529) was another Venetian humanist, appointed official historian to the Republic from 1516. For Jacopo Sannazaro, see note 105; for Pietro Bembo, the List of Principal Speakers. The last figure mentioned, Lazzaro Bonamico (1477/8–1552), was a lecturer in classics at the University of Padua, whose lectures Hoby attended during his stay in Padua in 1549, noting in his diary that

Bonamico was the most celebrated lecturer in the University, 'stipended by the Signiory of Venice with a great stipend'.

9. Hoby's choice of representative contemporary figures reflects his association with the University of Padua, which he visited in 1549 and 1554. His selection also reflects developments in Italian culture since the early years of the century: where the earlier figures listed were distinguished chiefly as humanists and Latin stylists, of these later figures only Paolo Manuzio (1512–74) – the son of the famous humanist publisher, Aldo Manuzio – fits this model, while the others all represent the newly specialised and technical academic culture of the mid-century. Marcantonio Genua (c. 1490–1563) was a leading Paduan philosopher and Aristotelian commentator. Francesco Robortello (1516–67) was another lecturer at Padua, remembered chiefly for his commentary on Aristotle's *Poetics* (1548), a landmark in the development of literary theory. The other two figures mentioned here, Bernardino Tomitano (1517–76) and Alessandro Piccolomini (1508–79), are of particular interest in this context, since both men were associated in the 1540s with the Paduan Accademia degli Infiammati (Academy of the Inflamed, or Inspired), which championed the use of the vernacular in academic fields previously dominated by Latin.

10. Pietro Aretino (1492–1556) and Giambattista Gelli (1498–1563) were unusual figures in a literary culture still dominated by the nobility and bourgeoisie. Aretino, the son of an itinerant cobbler, made a spectacular career in Venice as a proto-journalist and libellist; he was also a dramatist, pornographer and writer of devotional works. Gelli was a Florentine shoemaker, a fervent defender of the use of the vernacular, and the author of several popular dialogues on philosophical themes, which were quickly translated into English.

11. A striking feature of Italian literary culture from the 1540s was the amount of women's writing published, especially lyric poetry: an anthology of women's poetry published in Venice in 1559 contained the work of over fifty poets. Hoby was evidently impressed by the phenomenon and commented in his diary on his visit to Siena in 1550 that 'most of the women are well learned, and write excellentlie well both in prose and verse'. Vittoria Colonna (note 16) and Veronica Gambara, both from prominent noble families, remain among the best-known of Renaissance women poets. The other three poets named here are obscurer figures, though Virginia Salvi, whom Hoby singles out for praise in the diary entry noted above, had a substantial amount of work published.

12. Xenophon's *Cyropaedia* is one of the classical texts cited by Castiglione as models for *The Courtier* (see note 19). Hoby is probably referring here to the translation of the work by Lodovico Domenichi, published in Venice in 1548.

13. Hoby is probably thinking here of Jacques Colin's French translation of 1537, which takes considerable liberties with the text.

14. Sir John Cheke (1514–57) was a fellow of St John's College, Cambridge, tutor to Edward VI and later first Regius Professor of Greek at Cambridge. He was celebrated for his erudition and described by Thomas Nashe as 'the Exchequer of Eloquence, supernaturally traded in all tonges'. Hoby must have encountered him during his time as a student at St John's, and met him again during his second stay in Padua in 1554–5, where he completed his translation of *The Courtier*. Cheke's letter reflects the heated current debate on the legitimacy of foreign borrowings in English: while 'neologisers' like Sir Thomas Elyot defended the practice as a means of enriching the English language, purists like Cheke insisted that the resources of the language were sufficient without turning to alien sources. Cheke's linguistic purism is well illustrated in his translation of the Gospel of St Matthew, where he uses words coined from English stems like 'hundreder' (centurion), 'gain-birth' (regeneration) and 'mooned' (lunatic) in preference to the Latinisms that have prevailed. Hoby treads something of a middle path: while he is not afraid to use Latinisms, he also quite frequently shows a preference for more colloquial English terms, translating 'loquacità', for example, as 'babblinge', 'imitare' as 'to follow' and 'mediocrità' as 'meane' (this last in preference to the term 'mediocrity' used by Elyot in this sense).

15. Miguel de Sylva (c. 1480–1556) was a Portuguese cleric, diplomat and humanist, whom Castiglione probably met when the former was Portuguese ambassador to Rome during the papacy of Leo X.

16. Vittoria Colonna (1490–1547) was a poet, a prominent member of the Catholic Reform movement and the addressee of some of Michelangelo's greatest love poetry. Hoby appends to the end of *The Courtier* a letter of Castiglione's to Colonna of September 1527, confirming the part her 'indiscretion' played in prompting him finally to publish the work.

17. The 1520s were a time of heated debate on the most appropriate form for the Italian literary language and the question is disputed at length in Book I of *The Courtier*. The notion that modern writers should use as their linguistic models the great fourteenth-century Tuscan authors Francesco Petrarca and Giovanni Boccaccio was one particularly associated with Pietro Bembo, who argued the case for it in his influential dialogues *On the Vernacular* of 1525. It should be noted that Castiglione's linguistic practice in *The Courtier* does not entirely accord with his theory: the work underwent substantial linguistic revision prior to publication and, in the published version, its language corresponds closely enough to the norms advocated by Bembo for it to have been proposed later in the century as a model of Tuscan prose.

18. Theophrastus (d. c. 287 BC) was a Greek philosopher, a pupil of Aristotle and his successor as head of the Peripatetic School. The story is told in Cicero's *Brutus*, 46, 172 and Quintilian's *On the Education of the Orator*, 8, 1, 2.

19. The works referred to are Plato's *Republic*, Cicero's *De oratore* (*On the Orator*) and Xenophon's *Cyropaedia*: a fictitious account of the education and the exploits of Cyrus the Great, the founder of the Persian Empire, influential in the Renaissance as an exemplary treatise on kingship.

20. Alfonso Ariosto (1475–1525) was a courtier at the Este court at Ferrara and a distant cousin of the poet Lodovico Ariosto.

21. Castiglione had in fact returned from his visit to England (note 5) a few days prior to Julius II's visit to Urbino.

22. The court of Urbino was forced into exile in Mantua and Venice in 1502–3, when the Duchy was seized by Cesare Borgia, the son of Pope Alexander VI, as part of the latter's design of creating a dynastic state in central Italy.

23. Federico da Montefeltro (1422–82), familiar from the portraits of Piero della Francesca, was one of the most prominent *condottieri* of the fifteenth century and an important patron of the arts. The Palace of Urbino, mentioned below, was built between about 1455 and 1480, and is one of the masterpieces of fifteenth-century Italian architecture. William Thomas, in his *History of Italy* (1549), the earliest English guidebook to Italy, found it 'a very fair house, but not so excellent as the Conte Baldassare in his *Courtesan* doth commend it'.

24. Guidobaldo da Montefeltro (1472–1508) succeeded his father as Duke of Urbino in 1482. He was ousted from the Dukedom by Cesare Borgia in 1502, but restored the following year and appointed commander of the papal army by his uncle, Pope Julius II. Crippled by gout from an early age and rumoured also to be afflicted with syphilis, his marriage to Elisabetta Gonzaga failed to produce an heir.

25. Hoby translates as 'pourposes' the Italian term *imprese*, which can mean 'enterprises' or 'undertakings', but which here signifies 'emblems': symbolic devices consisting of an enigmatic image and a motto, usually in Latin, alluding to the bearer's circumstances or expressing his or her philosophy of life. The invention and decipherment of these devices was one of the favourite pastimes of the Renaissance courts and a substantial literature grew up on the subject.

26. The main figures introduced here are identified in the List of Principal Speakers. Lodovico Pio was Emilia's brother and a captain in the papal forces. Little is known of Pietro da Napoli beside his name.

27. For Bernardo Bibbiena, Unico Aretino and Niccolò Frigio, see List of Principal Speakers; for Giancristoforo Romano and Pietro Monte, notes 78 and 38. Anton Maria Terpandro was a poet and musician with close connections with the court of Urbino.

28. Julius II (Giuliano della Rovere), the subject of Raphael's famous portrait in the National Gallery, London, had been elected Pope in 1503. His close connections with Urbino – his younger brother had married Duke Federico's sister – account to a large extent for the prestige of the

Urbino court in this period. Now chiefly remembered as a great patron of the arts, Julius's domestic political importance lies largely in his reassertion of papal control over the vast area of central Italy known as the Papal States. The Bologna campaign of 1506 referred to here is selected by Machiavelli in Chapter 25 of *The Prince* as the most characteristic example of his reckless but brilliant military leadership.

29. Costanza Fregosa, one of the very few women present to have a speaking role in the dialogue, was the sister of Federico and Ottaviano Fregoso (see List of Principal Speakers) and niece to Duke Guidobaldo.

30. Fra Serafino was a buffoon with close links to the courts of Ferrara, Urbino and Mantua, where he was a particular favourite of the Marchioness, the famous Isabella d'Este. Fra Mariano, mentioned earlier, was Mariano Fetti (1460–1531), a lay member of the Dominican order and perhaps the most successful buffoon of his day, patronised especially by Pope Leo X.

31. Hoby's translation loses the point of the original, which has *sirena* ('siren'): an alternative interpretation of the meaning of the letter 'S' that the Duchess wore on her headband.

32. Ippolito d'Este (1479–1520) was the younger brother of Alfonso I, Duke of Ferrara; created an archbishop at the age of seven and a cardinal at fourteen. He is remembered now as the somewhat unappreciative patron of the great Ferrarese poet Lodovico Ariosto and the dedicatee of the latter's *Orlando Furioso*. A letter to Ippolito from Castiglione of 1520 indicates that he was among the readers to whom the manuscript of *The Courtier* was sent for scrutiny.

33. The question of whether nobility should be defined by birth and wealth with virtue or by virtue alone was the subject of intense debate among fifteenth-century humanists, who tended to incline, for the most part, to the position sustained by Pallavicino here.

34. The 'Berto' referred to appears to have been a court buffoon of the period.

35. The reference is probably to Plutarch's essay, *On Inoffensive Self Praise*.

36. Castiglione's source for this story is probably the popular historical compilation, *Memorable Sayings and Deeds* by the first-century Roman writer Valerius Maximus (Book 8, 14).

37. The *gioco di canne* was a Spanish sport, of Moorish origins, introduced into Italy in the fifteenth century. It involved throwing sticks or javelins: a skill with obvious military applications.

38. Galeazzo Sanseverino (d. 1525) was a mercenary commander who married into the family of Lodovico Sforza ('il Moro'), Duke of Milan, transferring to the service of the French king after Lodovico's deposition in 1499. Pietro Monte, mentioned below, was a military trainer, also associated with the court of Milan, who wrote treatises on duelling and on military technique.

39. The image derives from Horace (*Odes*, 4.2) and was much used in Renaissance discussions of literary imitation to describe writers' assimilation of their sources.

40. This is the famous term *sprezzatura*, coined by Castiglione. Hoby's translations of the term – 'reckelesness' ('heedlessness') and 'disgracing' – do not entirely capture the meaning of the original. 'Nonchalance' is perhaps the best translation, but Castiglione's term, deriving from the verb '*sprezzare*' ('to disdain') has an added inflection of aristocratic contempt for any appearance of effort or strain. Gabriel Harvey, interestingly, in a summary of the passage, uses the term 'negligent diligence', indicating an awareness of one of Castiglione's classical sources for this notion, a passage in Cicero's *Orator*, 78, where 'a certain diligent negligence' (*negligentia diligens*) is identified as one of the charms of Attic oratory (on Harvey's annotations, see essay on Castiglione and His Critics).

41. The reference is probably to Cicero's *De oratore*, 2, 1, 4–5.

42. Apelles was court painter to Alexander the Great and the most famous painter of Ancient Greece. The anecdote here is from Pliny's *Natural History*, 35, 10, 80.

43. On the dispute on language in the period, see above, note 17. Although the debate was concerned with the written language, there is some evidence that some speakers affected archaic Tuscan in speech: in Pierio Valeriano's dialogue *On the Vernacular*, of 1524, a speaker complains that Rome is full of pedants waiting to pounce on anyone using non-Tuscan words.

44. The Florentine language had altered significantly between the fourteenth and the early sixteenth century: a 'deterioration' that led Pietro Bembo, in the first book of his dialogues *On the Vernacular* of 1525, to have one of his speakers remark that, in learning to write Tuscan correctly, it was a positive advantage not to be a native of Tuscany.

45. Evander and Turnus are figures from the legendary prehistory of Rome recounted in Virgil's *Aeneid*: the former, Aeneas' ally, was a Greek exile and the founder of a settlement on the Tiber; the latter, an Italian warrior and Aeneas' most fearsome opponent.

46. The Salian priests (Salii) were members of a Roman religious order dedicated to Mars. The unintelligibility of the ancient hymns they sang on their annual procession through Rome is noted by Horace in his second *Epistle*, 1, 86–7, and by Quintilian, in his *On the Education of the Orator*, 1, 6, 40, in contexts that Castiglione may well have intended his readers to recall: Horace's mention occurs in a passage denouncing those whose uncritical reverence for the art of the past blinds them to the merits of contemporary works, while Quintilian uses the example of the Salian hymns to illustrate the point that linguistic archaisms should be used sparingly to avoid any air of affectation.

47. M. Antonius (143–87 BC), L. Licinius Crassus (140–91 BC) and Q. Hortensius Hortalus (114–50 BC) were all prominent Roman orators; the former two protagonists in Cicero's *De oratore*. Cicero complains in his *Brutus*, 16–18, that the writings of M. Porcius Cato the elder (234–149 BC) are neglected by modern readers because the language has become antiquated. Virgil, the poet of the *Aeneid*, lived from 70 to 19 BC. Quintus Ennius (239–?169 BC) was the author of the epic *Annals*, of which only fragments remain.

48. Horace lived from 65 to 8 BC. His criticism of the Roman comic playwright, Plautus (d. 184 BC), is contained in his *Art of Poetry*, 270–5.

49. Sergius Sulpicius Galba was a younger contemporary of Cato the Elder (second century BC). The reference to Cicero's verdict on him is to a passage in *Brutus*, 21, 82, where it is noted that, despite the great reputation he enjoyed when alive, Galba's surviving works fail to impress and sound more archaic than those of Cato himself.

50. The 'foure tongues' of ancient Greece were more precisely families of dialects: the Attic, Doric, Ionian and Aeolian. In Hellenistic times, a common language or *koinē*, derived from Attic origins, displaced the ancient dialects as the literary language of the Greek empire. This use of the Greek *koinē* as an example of a language created from a fusion of dialect forms may derive from a lost treatise on the Italian language by Vincenzo Colli ('Calmeta'), one of the speakers in *The Courtier*; it is discussed and rejected by Pietro Bembo in his dialogues *On the Vernacular*, 1, 13.

51. This accusation, levelled at Livy by G. Asinius Pollio, is recounted by Quintilian in his *On the Education of the Orator*, 1, 5, 56.

52. In each case, the non-Tuscan version cited is closer to the Latin spelling than the Tuscan: a fact that was frequently cited by non-Tuscan writers as evidence of the 'uncorrupted' state of their dialects, though in fact these forms are to be explained rather by the influence of Latin on orthography. The 'Campidoglio' is the Capitol in Rome; 'Girolamo', 'Jerome'; *'audace'* means 'bold' and *'padrone'*, 'master'.

53. The analogy derives from a famous passage in Horace's *Art of Poetry*, 60–72.

54. The reference is to the poetry of the troubadours, an important influence on early Italian poetry, which was, in this period, beginning to become the object of serious study by philologists like Bembo. Oscan, mentioned earlier, was one of the pre-Roman languages of Southern Italy.

55. Hesiod (*c.* 700 BC) was one of the earliest Greek poets apart from Homer. For Crassus and Ennius, see note 47.

56. Bidon da Asti (Antonio Collebandi) was a French-born singer who worked in the courts of Ferrara and Mantua before joining the papal chapel under Leo X towards the end of the latter's reign. It is probably at this time, around 1520, that Castiglione came to hear him: in an earlier

version of the manuscript, the name cited at this point is that of Alessandro Agricola, a Florentine musician who died in 1506. Marchetto Cara, mentioned below, was a celebrated composer of songs, mainly associated with the court of Mantua, where he enjoyed the enthusiastic patronage of the Marchioness, Isabella d'Este.

57. Castiglione's correspondence testifies to his keen and informed interest in the visual arts, and few would dispute his taste in his selection of the greatest artists of his day. Giorgio da Castelfranco is better known as Giorgione (?1478–1510): a pivotal figure in the development of Venetian art and a major influence on Titian. The choice of Andrea Mantegna, the earliest of the artists mentioned here (active 1441/5, d. 1506) may reflect Castiglione's attachment to the court of Mantua, where Mantegna painted his greatest works.

58. It is telling that Castiglione turns to classical antiquity to exemplify stylistic diversity in literature, where in the case of art and music he had drawn on modern examples. His source here is Cicero, who makes the same point in his *De oratore*, 3, 7, 26–8, and at a number of points in his *Brutus*.

59. The reference is to Cicero's *De oratore*, 2, 23, 98.

60. The purist position under attack in this passage was sustained most authoritatively by Pietro Bembo (see note 17). The omission of any reference to Dante here and in the subsequent discussion of imitation may appear surprising to modern readers, but it reflects an attitude frequent among Castiglione's contemporaries. Pietro Bembo, in his influential dialogue *On the Vernacular* of 1525, while recognising Dante's greatness as a poet, comments disapprovingly on the indecorousness of some of the language he uses in the *Divine Comedy* and advises contemporary writers against using his writings as a linguistic model.

61. The 'modern' writers mentioned here are both Florentine: Lorenzo de' Medici, the effective ruler of Florence from 1469 to 1492, who was not only a great patron of the arts but a considerable lyric poet; and Francesco Cattani da Diacceto (1466–1522), a Florentine writer and Neoplatonist philosopher, whose influence can be detected in Bembo's speech on love in Book 4 of *The Courtier*. Another writer listed here by Castiglione – the great Florentine poet and humanist Angelo Poliziano, or Politian (1454–94) – is unaccountably omitted by Hoby.

62. Silius Italicus was a Silver Latin poet (*c.* 26–101 AD), the author of a vast epic on the Punic Wars discovered in the fifteenth century and first published in 1471. Cornelius Tacitus (born *c.* 56/7 AD), the great historian, extremely influential in the later sixteenth century in particular, is here paired rather incongruously with Silius as an example of linguistic decadence.

63. The writers referred to here are all contemporaries of Cicero's: the historian, G. Sallustius Crispus (Sallust) (*c.* 86–35 BC); Julius Caesar

(100–44 BC), who wrote commentaries on his conquest of Gaul and on the Civil Wars, and the antiquarian and polymath Marcus Terentius Varro (116–27 BC).

64. Demosthenes' rejoinder to Aeschines is reported in Cicero's *Orator*, 26–7.

65. The reference is to Catullus's thirty-ninth poem, satirising a certain Egnatius, whose pride in the whiteness of his teeth is such that he insists on smiling even through court-cases and funerals.

66. Monsieur d'Angoulême (1494–1547), son of the Valois Charles d'Angoulême, succeeded to the French throne as Francis I in 1515. As augured here, he proved a notable patron of learning and the arts, luring a number of Italian artists to France, including, most famously, Leonardo da Vinci.

67. Castiglione's sources here are Plutarch's *Lives*, Cicero's *Tusculan Disputations* and *The Life of Hannibal* by Cornelius Nepos.

68. The reference here is to the humiliations inflicted on the Italians in the Wars of Italy (see Introduction, The historical context).

69. The study of Greek flourished in Italy from the fifteenth century, but it remained far less widely studied than Latin, and it has been pointed out that Castiglione's own knowledge of the language – he studied in Milan in his youth under the emigré scholar Demetrius Chalcondylas – was still something of an exception in his generation.

70. Aristippus was a Greek philosopher (*c.* 430–*c.* 350 BC), a pupil of Socrates and founder of the sceptical Cyrenaic school. The anecdote here comes from Diogenes Laertius's *Lives of the Philosophers*, 1, 8, though Aristippus's interlocutor is not identified there.

71. The Petrarch sonnet of which Hoby translates the first four lines is no. 187, 'Giunto Alessandro alla famosa tomba'. Another source Castiglione is likely to have borne in mind in this passage is Cicero's oration *Pro Archia*.

72. The notion that the celestial spheres made musical sounds as they moved, inaudible to human ears, ('the harmony of the spheres') derives from Pythagoras and is developed by Plato in his *Timaeus*.

73. The relevant passages in Plato and Aristotle are *Republic* 398c–401d, and *Politics* 1338a, 13–30. The anecdote concerning Alexander derives from Plutarch, while that concerning Socrates is found in Valerius Maximus and Quintilian, as well as Diogenes Laertius.

74. Lycurgus (*c.* ninth century BC) was the legendary legislator of Sparta, reputed to have been responsible for all its laws and constitution. Epaminondas was the Theban general who destroyed Spartan supremacy by his victory at Leuctra in 371 BC. On Themistocles, see note 3. Achilles, in legend, was brought up by the centaur Chiron, half-man and half-horse. Castiglione's main sources here are Cicero's *Tusculan Disputations* and the dialogue, *On Music*, then thought to be by Plutarch.

75. Castiglione's recommendation that the courtier study drawing reflects the new prestige accorded in the Renaissance to the visual arts and their practitioners: a development perhaps best exemplified, in Castiglione's time, by the career of Raphael, who, in Giorgio Vasari's words, 'lived more like a prince than a painter'.

76. Castiglione's source here is Pliny's *Natural History*, 35, 19, which also provided Castiglione with evidence of the place of the visual arts in the classical educational curriculum.

77. The word '*disegno*', which Hoby translates as 'patterne', is a key term in Italian Renaissance art theory. It can mean 'drawing' or 'draughtsmanship', but it is also used, as here, in a broader, philosophical sense to designate the intellectual element within artistic creation, the conception of the image to be realised.

78. Giovan Cristoforo Romano (*c.* 1465–1512) was a sculptor, goldsmith and medallist associated with the courts of Milan, Mantua and Urbino.

79. The question of the relative merits of painting and sculpture, known as the *paragone* ('comparison'), was the subject of heated debate in the Italian Renaissance, drawing comment from many of the greatest artists and art theorists of the age. Michelangelo commented sourly, when his opinion on the subject was solicited in 1547, that more time was wasted in talking about these problems than would go into creating works in either medium.

80. Raphael (Raffaello Sanzio, 1483–1520), one of the greatest painters of the Italian Renaissance, was born in Urbino and started his career at the court there. He was a close friend of Castiglione, whose portrait he painted (the work is now in the Louvre).

81. The original has *grotte* (lit. 'caves'). The reference is to the examples of decorative art discovered underground in the remains of Roman architecture, the most striking being those discovered in the late fifteenth century in Nero's Golden House. These Roman decorative forms – known as *grottesche* ('grotesques') from their underground origin – were imitated by Raphael in his decoration of Cardinal Bibbiena's apartments in the Vatican palace (1516), and in Leo X's *loggia*, described by Castiglione in a letter of 1519 as 'perhaps more beautiful than any modern thing now to be seen'.

82. The source of the following anecdotes is, again, Pliny's *Natural History*, 35, 104–5 and 135. Demetrius I of Macedon was a general of Alexander the Great; he besieged Rhodes in 305 BC. Lucius Aemilius Paulus was a Roman consul (181 and 168 BC) and general.

83. The Greek painter Zeuxis, called on to paint a figure of Helen for a temple to the goddess Hera in Croton, in southern Italy, reputedly used as models five beautiful girls of the city, selecting the loveliest features of each. The anecdote was frequently cited in the Renaissance in discussions of the relation between nature and art, and is alluded to by Ariosto

in a famous passage of the *Orlando Furioso* (11, 71). Castiglione's source is probably a passage in Cicero's rhetorical treatise, *De inventione*, 2, 1, 1–3; the same story is found in Pliny's *Natural History*, 35, but with a different setting.

84. The first two figures named here were Piedmontese noblemen, sons of the Marquis of Ceva; they later became infamous for their murder of a member of their family. 'Ettore Romano' has been conjecturally identified with the soldier Ettore Giovenale, later dismissed from the service of Francesco Maria della Rovere after comporting himself dishonourably in battle. Orazio Florido was a soldier and diplomat, a prominent member of the Urbino court under Francesco Maria. For Vincenzo Calmeta, see note 95.

85. The 'vital spirits' were vapours refined from the blood and disseminated around the body through the arteries and nerves; they were conceived of as the means by which the soul acted on the body. The notion occupied an important place within medieval and Renaissance medical and philosophical theory, and entered literary culture through its importance in descriptions of the mechanisms of love.

86. The reference is to Cicero's *De oratore*, 2, 74, 299, where it is recounted that Themistocles (see note 3), asked whether he wished to learn the art of memory, replied that he would prefer to learn how to forget what he wished to forget. It should be noted, however, that, in Cicero, the anecdote is used to a quite different end: to illustrate the prodigiousness of Themistocles' powers of recollection.

87. The figures referred to are Filippo Maria Visconti (1391–1447), the last Visconti ruler of Milan; Borso d'Este (1413–71), ruler of Ferrara and a notable patron of the arts, whose reign had gained a proverbial status as a golden age; and the *condottiere* Niccolò Piccinino (1386–1444), celebrated for his wit.

88. The reference is to Plato's *Phaedo*, 60b.

89. Castiglione's source here is Aristotle's *Politics*, 7, 15, 10.

90. The phrase indicates improvised song or declamatory speech-song over instrumental accompaniment. It is not clear which form of stringed instrument is indicated by the term '*viola*' (Hoby's 'lute'), though it has been suggested that the term refers to the '*viola da mano*', a guitar-like instrument that Castiglione himself seems to have owned and played.

91. The reference is to wind instruments: Minerva is said to have thrown the flute away when she saw her reflection in a spring and realised the effect it had on her face, while Alcibiades, according to Plutarch's *Life*, 2, 4–5, refused to learn the flute as he considered it beneath the dignity of an Athenian citizen to play an instrument that distorted the face so much that the performer's best friends could not recognise him.

92. The rhetorical exercise of paradoxical encomium – the formal

defence of an unexpected, unworthy or indefensible subject – was practised in antiquity and revived by Renaissance humanists. The references here are to the Greek satirist Lucian's praise of a fly, the sophist Favorinus's of quartan fever and the early Christian writer Synesius of Cyrene's of baldness.

93. Gonzaga is adapting, rather loosely, *Luke*, 14:8 and 10.

94. The reference is to one of Aesop's fables.

95. Vincenzo Colli (*c.* 1460–1508), whose pen-name Calmeta probably derives from a character in one of Boccaccio's romances, was a poet and literary critic of some influence, who had been a prominent figure in the court of Milan in the 1490s. In view of his gloomy insistence here on the corruption of modern princes, it is interesting to note that, prior to joining the court of Urbino in 1503, Calmeta was briefly in the service of Cesare Borgia, whose ruthlessness is celebrated by Machiavelli in *The Prince*.

96. Castiglione had every cause to be aware of the difficulties involved in abandoning a prince's service: his own decision to transfer from the service of Francesco Gonzaga, Marquis of Mantua, to that of Guidobaldo da Montefeltro in 1504 had won him the lasting displeasure of the Marquis, who for a considerable time prevented him from entering Mantuan territory even to visit his family. Castiglione's resentment at this treatment is expressed forthrightly in a letter to his mother of March 1507, in which he notes that he is even considering exchanging his estates near Mantua with those of a Bolognese acquaintance.

97. Titus Manlius Torquatus was a Roman consul (fourth century BC) who supposedly executed his son in punishment for the latter's having disobeyed a command not to engage in single combat with the enemy. The example is cited by Aulus Gellius in his *Attic Nights*, 1, 13, in a passage which is Castiglione's source for this whole discussion.

98. Publius Licinius Crassus Mucianus was Roman consul in 131 BC when he fought in Asia Minor against Aristonicus of Pergamus. The anecdote is drawn, like that of Titus Manlius Torquatus, from Aulus Gellius's *Attic Nights*, 1, 13.

99. Darius III of Persia, defeated by Alexander the Great in 333 BC. The source is probably Quintus Curtius, *History of Alexander*, 3, 3, 6.

100. The reference is to the humiliations suffered by the Italians during the Wars of Italy (see Introduction, The historical context).

101. The original uses a Venetian dialect term: '*maniche a cómeo*' (literally, 'elbow sleeves'). It should be remembered that Bembo, the addressee of this riposte, was Venetian in origin.

102. Fregoso is referring to the distinction in Aristotelian ethics between *praxis* (rational activity that is an end in itself) and *poïesis* (activity whose end is some product external to itself). His point is clearer in the original, where the word Hoby translates as 'deedes' is *opere*, which means both 'actions' (deeds) and 'finished works'.

103. The friendships between Orestes and Pylades and Theseus and

Pirithous, in Greek legend, are mentioned in Plutarch's *On Having Many Friends* (99e), which may be Castiglione's source here. The friendship between Caius Laelius Sapiens (consul 140 BC) and Scipio Africanus the younger (*c.* 185–129 BC) is celebrated in Cicero's *On Friendship*.

104. Alexander's reward to the man who excelled at impaling chick-peas on a needle from a distance was a measure of chick-peas.

105. Jacopo Sannazaro (1457–1530) was a Neapolitan poet who wrote in both Latin and Tuscan. He is best known for his influential pastoral, *Arcadia*, written in the 1480s, but first published in 1504.

106. The great Flemish composer Josquin des Prez (*c.* 1440–1521) spent much of his career in Italy, in Milan, Rome and finally Ferrara, where he was *maestro di cappella* from 1503 to 1504.

107. Castiglione does not exaggerate in this account of court table-manners: Vittorio Cian, in his edition of *The Courtier*, cites a vivid eye-witness report of a banquet at the papal court during Carnival in 1513, whose high point was a large-scale food-fight initiated by the jester Fra Mariano.

108. Paolo Nicola Vernia (1420–99) was a philosopher and lecturer at Padua University, where his Averroism brought him into conflict with the Church in the 1480s. He had a reputation as an unbeliever, an eccentric and a perverse wit. For Socrates's protestation that he knew nothing, except the fact that he knew nothing, see Diogenes Laertius's *Lives of the Philosophers*, 2, 32.

109. The word 'journey' here means '(day's) battle'. The anecdote has a personal resonance, since the battle referred to is Fornovo (1495), where Castiglione's father fought and received the wounds from which he would later die.

110. The painter referred to is almost certainly Leonardo da Vinci (1452–1519), who in the last decade of his life virtually abandoned painting to concentrate on his mathematical, scientific and anatomical interests (the word 'philosophy' here is used in its broad Renaissance sense, including what we would now call the sciences).

111. Castiglione's source here is Suetonius's *Life of Caesar*, 45.

112. The phrase echoes a line in Dante's *Inferno*, 16, 124–6.

113. Bibbiena is an appropriate choice for the task, as a famous wit and the future author of one of the most successful vernacular comedies of the early sixteenth century, *La Calandria*, first performed in Urbino in 1513.

114. Bibbiena's allusion is to his baldness.

115. Galeotto della Rovere was the nephew of Julius II and Cardinal of San Pietro in Vincoli. He died in 1508, much mourned at the court of Urbino, with which he had close contacts.

116. Iacopo da Sansecondo was a singer and musician, who performed in the courts of Milan, Ferrara, Mantua and Urbino. Castiglione's letters reveal him to have been a close friend.

117. Democritus (*c.* 460–361 BC) was a Greek atomist philosopher, whose proverbial cheerfulness was traditionally contrasted with Heraclitus's lugubriousness. The passage, and the whole of Castiglione's argument in this section, is closely imitated from Cicero's discussion of humour in Book II of his *De oratore*.

118. The inclusion of the powerful in the category of people who should not be the object of jokes is one of Castiglione's most significant additions to Cicero's theory of humour. It may derive from the Neapolitan humanist Giovanni Pontano's *On Conversation* (*c.* 1499).

119. As Hoby notes, Castiglione's inclusion of the category of practical jokes marks a departure from his source, Cicero's *De oratore*. The attention afforded to practical jokes in *The Courtier* reflects the immense popularity such pranks enjoyed in the period: a popularity that reached its height in Rome during the papacy of the relentlessly jovial Pope Leo X.

120. Alexander VI (Rodrigo Borgia) was Pope from 1492 to 1503. He was notorious for his unscrupulousness and corruption and was said to have bought his way into the papacy. The reference to Catullus is to *Poems*, 67, where the door of a house regales the poet with scurrilous gossip concerning its inhabitants.

121. The lascivious priest of Varlungo is described, in Day 8, Story 2, of Boccaccio's *Decameron*, as straining himself 'like an ass braying' to impress his parishioner Belcolore. The stories in Days 8 and 9 recounting the tricks played on the stooge Calandrino by the Florentine painters Bruno and Buffalmacco contain some of Boccaccio's most celebrated passages of comic description.

122. Niccolò Campani da Siena (1478–1523), known as Strascino after one of his farces, was a comic actor and poet who enjoyed great success at Leo X's court in Rome.

123. Marcus Tullius Cicero, the great Roman orator, was frequently referred to in the period as Tully.

124. The reference is to the siege of Castellina in Chianti in 1478 by Alfonso, Duke of Calabria, in allegiance with papal forces.

125. The reference is to the bitter conflict between Florence and Pisa from 1495 to 1509, which ended with the defeat of the latter.

126. The unusual detail of Hoby's note here reflects the fact that he had seen the Bucentaur himself on his visit to Venice in 1549, when it was sent to greet the Duke and Duchess of Urbino, arriving on an official visit. He mentions in the same place in his diary the 'wonderous greate ceremonie about the marying of the sea'.

127. The inspiration for this tall story may have been a passage in Plutarch's *On How a Man May Become Aware of His Progress in Virtue* (79a), which uses the myth that words freeze in cold climates to describe the effect of Plato's words on his listeners, who heard them when young and only understood them years later. Rabelais draws on the same myth

for the episode in his *Quart Livre*, 55–6, where Pantagruel and his companions defrost the sounds of an entire battle.

128. The East Indies, discovered by Vasco da Gama in 1497, proved, among other things, a valuable source of exotic diplomatic gifts, the most famous being the elephant sent in 1514 as a gift to Pope Leo X. A letter of Castiglione's of 1505 describes the arrival of Portuguese ambassadors in Rome bringing a consignment of exotic animals as a gift to the papal court, including parrots and 'various new breeds of monkey'.

129. As Hoby recognises, this is one of the numerous jokes in Castiglione's anthology translated directly from Cicero's *De oratore* (2, 54, 220).

130. Galeotto of Narni (*c.* 1427–*c.* 1490) was an eccentric humanist and adventurer, who served for a while at the Hungarian court of Matthias Corvinus. He was accused of heresy in 1477 in Venice and forced to give a public retraction in the Piazzetta wearing a crown of devils; the quip recounted here is supposed to have been said as he was led to this punishment.

131. Emilia's surname, 'Pio', is also an adjective meaning 'compassionate'. The transformation into 'Impia' – 'cruel' or 'heartless' – is most likely a gallant reference to her chastity and imperviousness to her admirers' advances. The practice of using the feminine ending for women's surnames was common in this period in Italian.

132. Girolamo Donato (1457–1511) was a Venetian diplomat, noted for his learning and wit. The Roman custom described here is one Hoby had the opportunity to observe when he visited the city in the Jubilee year of 1550. He noted in his diary 'whosoever will receave the full indulgence of this Jubilee must visit the vii principall churches of Roome all in a daie (which he shall have inoughe to do) a foote', continuing caustically, 'with these and like fond traditions is the papall seate cheefely maintained, to call men out of all places in christendome to lighten their purses'.

133. Marcantonio della Torre (*c.* 1480–1511) was a Veronese nobleman, who lectured in medicine and philosophy at Pavia University and in Padua and Venice. He was an important figure in the development of the study of anatomy and his lectures on the subject at Pavia are said to have been attended by Leonardo da Vinci.

134. Proto da Lucca was a buffoon at the papal court in the first decade of the sixteenth century. The 'very grave' Pope in this anecdote is Julius II.

135. Giovanni Calfurnio (d. 1503) was a humanist and lecturer in rhetoric at Padua University.

136. The humanist Tommaso Inghirami (1470–1516), the subject of a famous portrait by Raphael in the Pitti Palace, gained his nickname after a famous youthful performance in the title-role of Seneca's *Phaedra*. He

was appointed to the coveted post of Vatican librarian by Julius II in 1510 and was later made professor of rhetoric at Rome University by Leo X.

137. Camillo Paleotto was a Bolognese nobleman, a lecturer in rhetoric at Bologna University and brother to the Annibale Paleotto mentioned at p. 166. In an earlier version of *The Courtier*, Camillo Paleotto appears among the speakers of the dialogue and, indeed, plays the prominent role in Book 3 given to Giuliano de' Medici in the final version.

138. Filippo Beroaldo the Younger (1472–1518) was a distinguished humanist scholar who followed 'Fedra' Inghirami (see note 136) as papal librarian. He had close links with the Urbino court and defended Francesco Maria della Rovere in the trial following his murder of Cardinal Alidosi (see note 151).

139. The Spanish commander Gonsalvo da Cordoba (1453–1515) earned the name 'The Great Captain' after the part he played in the Spanish reconquest of Granada. An outstanding military strategist and reformer, he won a series of famous victories against the French in the Kingdom of Naples and was made Viceroy of Naples before falling into disfavour with King Ferdinand in 1507.

140. Iacopo Sadoleto (1477–1547) was a distinguished humanist, famed particularly as a Latin stylist, and one of the readers to whom Castiglione submitted the manuscript of *The Courtier* for comments. He was papal secretary under Leo X and Clement VII, and was later created a cardinal by Paul III.

141. Palla Strozzi (1372–1462) was a Florentine noble and a fierce opponent of the Medici family, exiled to Padua for ten years after Cosimo de' Medici came to power in Florence in 1434.

142. For the 'Great Captain', see note 139.

143. Djem or Zizim (1459–95) was the son of Mahomet II and brother of the Sultan Bayezid II. He spent most of his life in prison in France and Italy after a failed attempt to dispossess his brother and died, reputedly poisoned by Pope Alexander VI, in 1495.

144. Antonio Cammilli (1440–1502), known as Pistoia, from his birthplace, was a comic poet, who served the Este in Ferrara and Lodovico Sforza ('il Moro') in Milan. His correspondent is Serafino Aquilano (1466–1500), a peripatetic court poet celebrated for his skill at poetic improvisation.

145. Giovanni Gonzaga (1474–1523) was a soldier and diplomat, uncle to the Marquis Federico Gonzaga whose service Castiglione entered in 1516. The source for the anecdote concerning Alexander the Great is Plutarch.

146. Mario da Volterra (1464–1537) was made Bishop of Aquino by Leo X in 1516; he later became Bishop of Cavaillon, in France. The joke derives from Cicero (*De oratore*, 2, 66, 267).

147. Agostino Bevazzano (d. 1550) was Bembo's secretary at the

papal court and a member of Castiglione's circle during his period in Rome. He is the subject, with Andrea Navagero, of Raphael's double portrait in the Galleria Doria-Pamphili in Rome.

148. Niccolò Leonico Tomeo (1456–1531) was a Venetian-born philosopher, who lectured at the University of Padua from c. 1497–1509. A humanist and a man of broad cultural interests, he was one of the first philosophers to teach Aristotle using the Greek text, rather than translations.

149. Agostino Foglietta was a Genoese nobleman and diplomat, much esteemed by the Medici popes, Leo X and Clement VII. He died in the Sack of Rome in 1527.

150. Don Giovanni di Cardona was a Spanish *condottiere* who fought under Cesare Borgia. The witticism attributed to him here is based on one in *De oratore*, 2, 67, 269.

151. The Cardinal of Pavia referred to here was Francesco Alidosi, a favourite of Julius II and a man, according to Guicciardini, of 'outrageous and infinite vices'. He was stabbed to death in 1511 by the Duke of Urbino, Francesco Maria della Rovere, enraged at a slight on his performance as leader of the papal forces (see the note on Francesco Maria in the List of Principal Speakers). There is another joke at Alidosi's expense at p. 185.

152. Alfonso I ('The Magnanimous') was King of Naples from 1443–1458. Both the anecdotes told about him in *The Courtier* (the other is at p. 187) make reference to his legendary liberality: he was an outstanding patron of learning and established Naples as one of the centres of Renaissance humanism.

153. For the 'Great Captain', see note 139. The battle referred to here took place at Cerignola, in Apulia, in April 1503: the Spanish, under Gonsalvo da Cordoba, defeated the French army led by the Duke of Nemours.

154. Ottaviano Ubaldini (d. 1498) was a nephew of Federico da Montefeltro, famed for his interests in astrology and magic; Antonello da Forlì, a mercenary captain who had fought for Sigismondo Malatesta against Federico. The same anecdote is recounted by the Neapolitan humanist Giovanni Pontano in his *On conversation* (c. 1499).

155. On the occupation of Urbino in 1502 by Cesare Borgia (who was Duke of Valentinois in France), see note 22.

156. The joke is adapted from *De oratore* (2, 67, 273), as are several of those on the following page.

157. The Alonso Carillo mentioned here was a nephew of the fifteenth-century statesman and archbishop of the same name. 'Maistresse Boadilla' is thought to be Beatriz de Bobadilla, Marchioness of Moya, an intimate of Queen Isabella.

158. On Castiglione's friendship with Raphael, see note 80. This joke was one of several that fell victim to the censorship of Antonio

Ciccarelli, who produced a revised edition of the *Cortegiano* on order of the Inquisition in 1584: in Ciccarelli's edition, the setting of the anecdote is transferred to ancient Rome and the subject of the painting becomes Romulus and Remus.

159. Raphael de' Pazzi (1471–1512) was a Florentine soldier who fought under Cesare Borgia and Julius II. He died in the Battle of Ravenna, as, it seems, did Don Pietro de Cuña, the Prior of Messina referred to here.

160. For the Cardinal of Pavia, see note 151. Giannotto de' Pazzi has not been identified.

161. Antonio Torello (d. 1536) was private chamberlain to Julius II and Leo X. The joke is modelled on one in *De oratore*, 2, 70, 183, where it concerns the forgery of a will.

162. Latino Giovenale (1486–1553) was a papal notary and ambassador, known as a connoisseur of antique sculpture and a poet in Latin and the vernacular.

163. The two Spanish soldiers named here, Peralta and Aldana, were personally known to Castiglione, who acted as second to the former in a duel between the two in Parma in 1510. The other figure referred to, Molard, is a Frenchman killed at the battle of Ravenna in 1512.

164. Biagin Crivello was a courtier and intimate of Lodovico Sforza ('il Moro'), Duke of Milan. The same anecdote is reported by Matteo Bandello in his *Novelle* (3, 26), with the significant variant that, in his version, Crivello actually *does* kill the priest.

165. For Alfonso I of Aragon, see note 152.

166. The reference is to an inn near Urbino, notorious for its squalor.

167. Probably Cardinal Francesco Borgia (1441–1511), the son of Pope Calixtus III, created cardinal by his cousin, Alexander VI (Rodrigo Borgia), in 1500.

168. Cardinal Galeotto della Rovere (see note 115). 'My L. of Aragon', mentioned below, is Luigi d'Aragona (1474–1519), the illegitimate son of Ferdinand I of Aragon, another of the aristocratic and worldly young cardinals who played such a prominent role in Italian court life in this period. Via de' Banchi, in which the episode recounted here is said to have taken place, was one of the most fashionable promenades of Rome, in the area of the city restructured under Julius II.

169. The throwing of eggs, both real ones and false ones containing perfumed water, was a popular Carnival custom. Hoby witnessed the more decorous version in Venice at Carnival in 1549 and recorded in his diary the 'casting of eggs into the windows among the ladies full of sweete waters and damaske poulders'.

170. In Boccaccio's Calandrino stories (note 121), the hopelessly naive protagonist is tricked, among other things, into believing himself invisible and convincing himself that he is pregnant. A further *Decameron* story (Day 8, Story 9), concerns a trick played by Bruno and Buffalmacco on the foolish doctor Maestro Simone.

171. 'Pontius' is Caio Caloria of Messina (b. *c.* 1460), a comic poet best known for a Sicilian dialect comedy set in Venice, where he lived in the 1480s.

172. For Fra Serafino and Fra Mariano, see note 30. Pietro Gonella features in several of the stories of the fourteenth-century writer Francesco Sacchetti as a famous buffoon of the court of Ferrara, and it has been suggested that, by Castiglione's time, the name had become a generic one for court jesters. Lodovico Meliolo was the steward of the court of Mantua in the late fifteenth and early sixteenth centuries, famed for his humour.

173. The reference is to the joke recounted on p. 182.

174. The *Decameron* stories in question are, as Hoby rightly notes, Day 3, 6 and Day 7, 7 and 8. In the first, Ricciardo Minutolo tricks the woman he loves into having sex with him in a bath-house, in the belief that he is her husband. In the second, extremely tortuous tale, a Bolognese noblewoman, Beatrice, not only manages to trick her husband Egano into waiting in the garden in the middle of the night, dressed in her clothes, while she has sex with his servant, Anichino, but also arranges things so that the latter can beat her husband on the pretence of defending his honour (a 'strangely malicious' trick, as Boccaccio acknowledges, even by the standards of the *Decameron*). In the last tale, a woman ties a string round her big toe and hangs it out of the window, as a means of communicating to her lover whether her husband is asleep; when the latter discovers the ruse and tries to punish her, she tricks him by substituting her maid for herself in the bed and finally confuses him so much that he loses all grasp on what has happened.

175. The reference is to the *Decameron* story mentioned in the previous note, which ends in the way Pallavicino indicates.

176. Bibbiena is probably thinking here of Boccaccio's misogynist *Corbaccio* ('The Evil Crow'), which enjoyed considerable popularity in the Renaissance.

177. According to one version of the legend, Orpheus died torn to pieces by the women of Thrace during a Bacchanalian orgy. The scene formed the climax of the drama, *Orfeo*, written for the court of Mantua in 1479 by the Florentine poet Angelo Poliziano (Politian).

178. Castiglione's source for the anecdote concerning Pythagoras's calculation of the size of Hercules is the first chapter of Aulus Gellius's *Attic Nights*, rather than Pliny as Hoby suggests.

179. The goddesses were naked. The reference is to the myth of the Judgment of Paris: the Trojan Paris was called on to judge which of the three goddesses Hera (Juno), Aphrodite (Venus) and Athena (Minerva) was most beautiful. He awarded the victory to Aphrodite, with grave consequences for the Trojans.

180. The Order of St Michael was founded by Louis XI of France in 1469; that of the Golden Fleece by Philip the Good, Duke of Burgundy, in 1429 and that of the Garter by Edward III of England in 1344. At the time the dialogue is set, the Duke of Urbino had recently been made a member of the last (note 5).

181. The ruler of the Ottoman empire in this period was Sultan Bayezid II; the king of Persia, Ismail Sufi I (1480–1524), founder of the dynasty that ruled Persia for the next two centuries. In an earlier version of *The Courtier*, Fregoso's proposal for a comparative study of court customs is even more ambitious, extending to the courts of 'those kings newly discovered by the Portuguese and Spanish mariners'.

182. Pygmalion is the legendary king of Cyprus who sculpted a statue of a beautiful woman and fell in love with his own creation. When Aphrodite, goddess of love, answered his prayers and gave life to the statue, he made it his wife.

183. The source for this comment is a passage in Plato's *Republic*, 452b.

184. Plato's opinion, expressed in Book 5 of the *Republic*, was frequently cited in the Renaissance debate on women's moral and intellectual equality with men, often as a counterweight to Aristotle's attribution of a purely domestic role to women in his *Politics*.

185. This notion originates in Aristotle's writings on biology, where it is stated that 'we should look upon the female state as being as it were a deformity, though one which occurs in the ordinary state of nature' (*Generation of Animals*, 775a15). This Aristotelian tenet, assimilated by medieval scholastic philosophers, provided the theoretical underpinning for Renaissance misogynistic thought, in medicine, law and theology, as well as political and ethical thought. As Castiglione was well aware, no argument for women's equality could afford to ignore this doctrine if it wished to be taken seriously; and, in the dispute that follows, he shows himself willing to take on the challenge, even though it involves employing a technical, scholastic terminology quite alien from the normal tone of the dialogue. On the background to the dispute, see Ian Maclean, *The Renaissance Notion of Woman. A Study in the Fortunes of Scholasticism and Medical Science in European Intellectual Life* (Cambridge, 1980).

186. The observation that women's achievements in history have been obscured as a result of the envy or ignorance of male writers is found in other writers of the period, notably Ariosto (*Orlando Furioso*, 20, 2, 7–8; 37, 2, 4–6).

187. Castiglione is probably referring here to a passage in one of the so-called 'Orphic hymns', supposedly composed by the legendary sage Orpheus, in which Zeus is addressed as both 'male' and as 'immortal virgin'. The hymns were translated into Latin by the Florentine philosopher Marsilio Ficino in 1462.

188. It was a central tenet of Aristotelian philosophy that all natural objects were a composite of matter (the physical substance of which they were composed) and form (the principle that determined their nature). Form was regarded as superior to matter, which needed form to complete and perfect it. For the analogy between the relation between form and matter and that between men and women, see, for example, Aristotle's *Physics*, 192a22 ('matter desires form as the female the male').

189. In Aristotelian philosophy, the nature of all material things was regarded as being determined by their particular combination of the four qualities (or contraries) of heat, coldness, dryness and moisture. The qualities of heat and dryness were held to predominate in the constitution of the male, the perfect version of the species, while females were predominantly cold and moist, as the result of a lack of vital heat at the moment of their conception. This physical difference between the sexes was thought to have psychological implications: in his *History of Animals*, 608b7–13, Aristotle describes women's character as more compassionate, more querulous, more shameless, more deceitful and more cowardly than men's.

190. The writings of St Jerome (AD *c.* 340–420), the early Christian scholar, controversialist and translator of the Bible, were much admired in the Renaissance, for their style as well as their content. Jerome's circle had included a number of devoted female acolytes, most notably St Paula and St Eustochium, and his *Epistles* contain numerous admiring references to their virtue (see especially Letter 65).

191. The corruption and hypocrisy of friars was the source of much satirical comment in this period: Machiavelli's comedy *The Mandrake Root*, for example, portrays a grasping friar at the centre of a plot to trick a chaste wife into corruption.

192. Octavia was Mark Antony's wife, abandoned for Cleopatra. Plutarch speaks admiringly, in his life of her husband, of her beauty and intelligence and her dignity in the face of Antony's desertion. Porcia was the daughter of Cato the Younger and the wife of Brutus, Julius Caesar's assassin. Her courage is praised by Valerius Maximus and by Plutarch in his *Life of Brutus*, who relates that, when her husband showed himself reluctant to involve her in the conspiracy, she wounded herself in the arm to prove her strength of character and ability to keep a secret. Caia Cecilia Tanaquil was the wife of one of the early kings of Rome in Roman legend, famed especially for her medical knowledge and power of divination. Cornelia was the daughter of Scipio Africanus the Elder and the mother of the two tribunes, Tiberius and Caius Gracchus. She is praised in Plutarch's lives of the Gracchi for her magnanimity and her dignified behaviour after their deaths and by Cicero (in his *Brutus*) and Quintilian for the learning and eloquence testified by her letters.

193. Alexandra was the wife of Alexander Jannaeus, second king of the

Jews after the Babylonian captivity. Castiglione's source here is the Jewish historian Josephus (b. AD 37/8), in his *Jewish Antiquities*.

194. In his *Life of Lucullus*, Plutarch describes how Mithridates VI, King of Pontus (120–63 BC), fearing defeat by the Romans, gave orders for his wives and sisters to be put to death to save them the shame of captivity. The story of the wife of the Carthaginian general Hasdrubal, who threw herself into the flames of a burning temple along with her two children when the city fell to the Romans during the Third Punic War (146 BC), while her husband pusillanimously surrendered to the victors, is told by Valerius Maximus in his *Memorable Sayings and Deeds*. The third woman mentioned here, Harmonia, was in fact the granddaughter rather than the daughter of Hiero II of Syracuse (d. 215 BC). She was killed along with the other members of the dynasty, after her husband Themistus had been overthrown in a popular uprising. Her story is mentioned by Valerius Maximus in the same chapter as that of Hasdrubal's wife (3, 2, 8), although there, as in Boccaccio's version of the anecdote in his compilation *On Famous Women*, the emphasis falls on the heroism of an unnamed maidservant of Harmonia who offered herself to be killed in place of her mistress and whose courage inspired Harmonia to go willingly to her death.

195. The reference is to a folk-tale of Tuscan origin, concerning a husband so frustrated by his wife's demands for a pair of scissors that he lowers her into a well; even as she sinks into the water, she continues to gesture with her hand. Hoby appears to have misunderstood the story: he translates the Italian '*forbici*' ('scissors') as 'pricklouse' ('tailor').

196. Epicharis, arrested for her involvement in a plot against Nero (in AD 65), throttled herself while on the way to be tortured a second time. The source of the anecdote is Tacitus's *Annals*; it is also recounted in Boccaccio's *On Famous Women*, 41.

197. Leona or Leaena was an Athenian courtesan, tortured to death for her part in the assassination of Hipparchus, brother of the tyrant Hippias, in 514 BC. She is said to have bitten her tongue out rather than betray the identity of the assassins. She is mentioned in Pausanias's *Itinerary of Greece* and in Boccaccio's *On Famous Women*, though the detail of the statue probably derives from Plutarch's account of the story in his essay, *On Talkativeness*.

198. Margherita Gonzaga, already mentioned at the end of Book 1, was the illegitimate daughter of Francesco Gonzaga, Marquis of Mantua, and niece to the Duchess Elisabetta. Her request here formalises the new phase the discussion on women has entered into: the listing of examples of famous women of classical and modern history. The strategy was already, by Castiglione's day, an established part of 'defences of women', figuring, for example, in a number of treatises on the subject written for the courts of Mantua and Ferrara in the late fifteenth century. The most important classical and medieval precedents, on which

Castiglione draws heavily here, are Plutarch's *Brave Deeds of Women* and Boccaccio's *On Famous Women*, already mentioned.

199. The story of the woman of Marseilles is recounted in Valerius Maximus's *Memorable Sayings and Deeds*, 2, 6, 8.

200. The story of Camma, deriving from Plutarch's *Brave Deeds of Women*, is the model for the episode of Drusilla and Tanacro which Ariosto added to the 1532 version of the *Orlando Furioso* (37, 45–75), perhaps influenced by Castiglione's retelling of the story here.

201. Pallas Athene was the Greek goddess of wisdom, daughter of Zeus and Metis. Ceres or Demeter was the goddess of the earth, sister of Zeus and daughter of Cronos and Rhea. The Sybils were mantic priestesses who dwelt in shrines and were consulted for their enigmatic prophecies. Aspasia and Diotima are both mentioned in Plato's dialogues: Aspasia is the cultured courtesan praised in the *Menexenus* for her mastery of rhetoric, while Diotima is the (probably fictitious) priestess from Manitea to whom Socrates attributes his teachings on love in the *Symposium*.

202. Nicostrate was a legendary figure of the prehistory of Rome, said to be the mother (or, in other sources, the wife) of Evander, the exiled king of Arcadia who founded the city of Pallanteum, which later became part of Rome. Her prophetic gifts are mentioned by Plutarch in his *Life of Romulus*, and by Boccaccio, in his *On Famous Women*, where she is credited with the invention of the Latin alphabet. Sappho (sixth century BC) is the famous Greek love poet; Corinna (fifth century), another lyric poet of whose verse a few fragments remain. In one of these, Corinna mentions the 'other woman' referred to here, Myrtis, as the teacher of the poet Pindar.

203. The anecdote on the Trojan women derives from Plutarch's *On the Origins of Roman Customs*, 265c; it is also mentioned in the same author's *Brave Deeds of Women*, 243e–244a.

204. Castiglione's sources for the legend of the Sabine women are Livy's *History of Rome*, I, 12–13, and Plutarch's *Life of Romulus*, 19.

205. In Roman legend, Tarpeia, the daughter of the commander of the fortress on the Capitol, was bribed into betraying the city to Titus Tatius, King of the Sabines, and then was crushed to death by the Sabine invaders when she demanded her reward. Her name survived in the Tarpeian rock near the Capitol, from which criminals were flung. The story is found in a number of sources, including Livy's *History of Rome*, I, 11, and Plutarch's *Life of Romulus*, 17.

206. 'Venus calva' means 'the Bald Venus': one explanation offered for the name is that the temple was built to commemorate an occasion when Roman women cut off their hair to make bow-strings during a siege by the Gauls. The mention of a temple in Rome to the Armed Venus may be due to a confusion on Castiglione's part: his probable source for the detail of the temple to Venus Calva is a passage in the third/fourth-

century Christian writer Lactantius, which also mentions that a temple was built in Sparta dedicated to Venus Armata (*Divine Institutes*, 1, 20).

207. The legend of how Rome was saved from the Latins by slave-girls who took the place of the free-born girls demanded as hostages and then disarmed their hosts is told by Plutarch in his lives of *Romulus*, 29, and *Camillus*, 33, and by the fifth-century Roman writer Macrobius in his *Saturnalia*, 1, 11.

208. L. Sergius Catilina was a Roman aristocrat who conspired to overthrow the republic in 63 BC. The 'commune woman' referred to here is Fulvia, who induced one of the conspirators, her lover, to reveal the plot to Cicero, then consul.

209. The reference is to Philip V of Macedon (237–179 BC). The story is derived from Plutarch's *Brave Deeds of Women*, 245b, as is the account of the bravery of the Persian women that follows.

210. Castiglione's source for the bravery of Spartan women is probably Plutarch's collection, *Famous Sayings of Spartan Women*. The anecdote concerning the German women is told in Valerius Maximus's *Memorable Sayings and Deeds*, 6, 1, 3, with the comment that it was fortunate for Rome that the women's husbands were not possessed of the same courage as their wives. There is a description of Hannibal's siege of Sagunto in Spain in 218 BC in Livy's *History of Rome*, 21, 6–14.

211. Amalasontha (d. 535) was the daughter of Theodoric I, King of the Ostrogoths, and regent of the East Gothic kingdom from her father's death in 526. Theodolinda (d. 625) was the wife of Autharis, king of the Lombards and, in her second marriage, of Agilulph, Duke of Turin. She was famous for her piety and learning and a correspondent of Pope Gregory the Great. Theodora (d. 867) was the wife of Theophilus, Emperor of Constantinople, canonised by the Greek Church. Countess Matilda of Canossa (1046–1115), was the feudal ruler of Tuscany, renowned for her learning and religious zeal.

212. Anne of Brittany (1476–1514) was the daughter of Duke Francis II of Brittany. Her marriages to the French kings Charles VIII and Louis XII united the Dukedom with France. She was celebrated for her virtue, learning and patronage of literature.

213. Margaret of Austria (1480–1530) was the daughter of the Emperor Maximilian I and wife first to Juan of Castile and then to Duke Filiberto of Savoy. After she was widowed for the second time, in 1507, her father, the Emperor Maximilian I, entrusted her with the government of the Low Countries and the education of her nephew, the future Emperor Charles V. She was noted for her patronage of the arts, and was the dedicatee of one of the most influential sixteenth-century defences of women's equality with men, Henricus Cornelius Agrippa's *On the Dignity and Excellence of the Female Sex* (1529).

214. Isabella the Catholic (1451–1504), perhaps the most powerful woman of her day, married Ferdinand of Aragon in 1469, uniting the

kingdoms of Aragon and Castile. The eulogy of her qualities as a ruler that follows was expanded in the final version of the dialogue, written when Castiglione was papal nuncio at the court of her grandson, the Emperor Charles V.

215. The Arab kingdom of Granada was conquered in 1492. A leading part in the campaign was played by the Great Captain, Gonsalvo da Cordoba, mentioned below (see note 139).

216. The Queen of Hungary was the Neapolitan princess Beatrice of Aragon (1457–1508), who married Matthias Corvinus, King of Hungary and, with him, was instrumental in fostering cultural links between Hungary and Italy. She returned to Italy after the annulment of her second marriage, with Ladislav, King of Bohemia. The two queens of Naples mentioned earlier (described by Castiglione as 'remarkable', though Hoby omits the adjective) were probably Giovanna III of Aragon (d. 1517), the widow of Ferdinand I of Naples, and her daughter Giovanna IV (d. 1518), the widow of Ferdinand II.

217. Isabella of Aragon (1470–1524) was the daughter of Alfonso II of Naples and of Ippolita Maria Sforza, daughter of the Duke of Milan. In 1489 she was married to her cousin Giangaleazzo Sforza of Milan, to find that he was increasingly deprived of authority by the regent, Lodovico Sforza 'il Moro'. Her husband died in 1494 and the following year Isabella's family were driven from Naples by the French.

218. This is the famous Isabella d'Este (1474–1539), wife of Francesco Gonzaga, Marquis of Mantua, celebrated for her diplomatic skills, her forceful character and her patronage of the arts. Castiglione was a correspondent of hers and she may have been instrumental in arranging his reconciliation with her husband in 1516.

219. Beatrice d'Este (1457–97) was the sister of Isabella. She was married in 1491 to Lodovico Sforza 'il Moro', already effective ruler of Milan and, from 1494, Duke. Beatrice died in childbirth in 1497 and was deeply mourned by her husband. During her lifetime she had made a mark through her vivacious character, her luxurious tastes and her interest in and patronage of the arts.

220. Eleanora of Aragon (1450–93) was the daughter of Ferdinand I, King of Naples, and the elder sister of Beatrice of Aragon, Queen of Hungary, mentioned above. In 1473, she married Duke Ercole I d'Este.

221. Isabella del Balzo (d. 1533) was the wife of Federico, who became King of Naples in 1496 and was ousted by Franco-Spanish forces in 1501. After her husband's death in exile three years later, she spent her remaining years in relative poverty, dependent on relatives in Gazzuolo and Ferrara.

222. In 1499, the Florentines sent an army under the mercenary captain Paolo Vitelli to attack Pisa, during the siege of which the women acted

with conspicuous bravery. Among the 'many noble Poetes' who celebrated their heroism was Castiglione himself.

223. Tomiris or Thamyris was a legendary warrior queen of the Massagete (not of the Scythians, as Castiglione states here), whose story is told by Herodotus and by Boccaccio in *On Famous Women*. The most famous anecdote associated with her is that of her gory revenge on Cyrus, King of Persia, who had killed her son: after defeating him in battle, she plunged his severed head into a bucket of blood 'to slake his thirst'. Artemisia is probably the queen of Caria in Asia Minor (d. 350 BC), famed for her devotion to the memory of her dead husband Mausolus, to whom she erected a celebrated monumental tomb, the Mausoleum. Zenobia was Queen of Palmyra from AD 266, ruling as regent after the assassination of her husband Odenathus until her defeat by the Romans in AD 273. Boccaccio narrates her life in *On Famous Women*, 98, stressing her military prowess, good government, chastity and erudition, and Sir Thomas Elyot makes her a speaker in his *Defence of Good Women* (1540). Semiramis was a perhaps legendary queen of Assyria, of the thirteenth century BC, whose story is told in Boccaccio's *On Famous Women*, 2. Reigning after the death of her husband, Ninus, she extended the Assyrian empire conquering Egypt, but she remained best-known for her reputed sexual voracity, for which Dante placed her in the circle of the lustful in Hell. Cleopatra (69–30 BC) is the famous last queen of Egypt, the ally and lover of Mark Antony, who committed suicide after the latter's defeat by Octavian.

224. Sardanapalus is the name given by Greek historians to the Assyrian king Asurbanipal, thought to have ruled from 667–626 BC. His name became a byword for luxury and moral decadence, and is used in this sense by Dante in his *Paradiso*, 15, 107.

225. Alexander the Great defeated Darius, the last King of Persia, in 331 BC. His continence in refraining from taking sexual advantage of the king's wife and daughters was praised by Plutarch in his *Life of Alexander*, 21. The similar self-restraint shown by Scipio Africanus when commanding Roman armies in Spain in 210 BC is described by Valerius Maximus in his *Memorable Sayings and Deeds*, 4, 3, 1, who also supplies, in the same chapter, the anecdote concerning the Greek philosopher Xenocrates (d. 314 BC).

226. The story of the rebuke given to the tragedian Sophocles by Pericles, the great fifth-century Athenian statesman and general, comes from Cicero's *De officiis*, 1, 40, 144.

227. The reference is to the proverbial austerity and severity of M. Porcius Cato the elder (AD 234–149), known as Cato the Censor.

228. In the light of this 'political' interpretation of the Scipio and Alexander episodes, it is interesting to note that Machiavelli, in Chapters 17 and 19 of *The Prince*, advises princes that the fundamental rule to observe in avoiding their subjects' hatred is to abstain from interfering with their property and their women.

229. For the episode in question see Plato's *Symposium*, 219d.

230. 'Haunted' means 'public': the woman in the anecdote concerning Xenocrates (see above, p. 249) was a famous prostitute of the day, Phrine.

231. Valerius Maximus, in his account of Xenocrates' chastity (see note 225) includes the detail that the latter was drunk.

232. The anecdote of Demosthenes' retort to Laide, or Taide, is told by Aulus Gellius in his *Attic Nights*, 1, 8, 1–6.

233. Capua was sacked in July 1501 by the French army during the joint Franco-Spanish invasion of the Kingdom of Naples. The 'extraordinarily cruel' outrages perpetuated by the victors against Capuan women are noted by Guicciardini in his *History of Italy*, who reports that some 'fearing death less than the loss of their honour, threw themselves into wells or into the river'.

234. Lodovico Gonzaga, the Duchess's uncle, was bishop of Mantua from 1483 to 1511. In an earlier version of this passage, Castiglione gives the name of the girl as Maddalena Biga.

235. Felice della Rovere (d. *c.* 1536) was the illegitimate daughter of Pope Julius II, married to the lord of Bracciano, Giangiordano Orsini. She had close contacts with the Court of Urbino and was noted for her cultural interests.

236. Castiglione is probably thinking principally of Ovid's *Art of Love*, on which he draws heavily in his own description of lovers' wiles, though it has been suggested that he may also have in mind medieval French works like the *Roman de la Rose* and Andreas Capellanus's *On Love*, as well as the more recent *On the Nature of Love* by Mario Equicola (1495/6).

237. The reference is to the Song of Songs, at this time seen as an allegory of divine love.

238. This is an allusion to an episode in the popular Spanish romance cycle *Amadis of Gaul*, of which the first four volumes, by Garci Rodriguez de Montalvo, were published in 1508. The Isle of Constancy contained a garden at whose entrance stood a statue of a man holding a trumpet which was blown sweetly at the approach of true lovers but with a dreadful sound to repel the false.

239. The strength of the reaction against this statement can be explained by the fact that it represents a decided departure from the tradition of courtly love codified in works like Andreas Capellanus's *On Love*.

240. On the 'vital spirits', see above, note 85.

241. The reference is to the eccentric allegorical romance, *Hypnerotomachia Poliphili* (*The Dream of Polyphilius*), first published in 1499. The work is written in a bizarre mixture of Italian and neologisms derived from Latin and Greek stems. Some idea of the effect of the original can be had from the Elizabethan translation of the work, *The Strife of Love in a Dream* (1592), which contains phrases like

'hemicircubate flexure', 'plemmirulate trammels' and 'quadrangled plaints'.

242. This piece of advice is found in Ovid's *Art of Love*, 1, 567–71; the advice on feigning drunkenness at lines 595–8 of the same book.

243. There is a historical irony in this augury for the continuing success of Urbino: in 1516, shortly after this preface was written, Francesco Maria della Rovere was deposed from the Dukedom (see List of Principal Speakers), and the court spent the following six years in exile.

244. Eleanora Gonzaga (*c.* 1492–1543), the eldest daughter of Francesco Gonzaga and Isabella d'Este, married Duke Francesco Maria della Rovere in 1509.

245. The basis of Fregoso's critique is the Aristotelian notion that it is only when they achieve their proper end (*telos*) that things can be considered complete (see, for example, *Metaphysics*, 1021b, 25).

246. Colossal figures representing classical and modern heroes and allegorical figures were a frequent feature of the triumphal processions of the Renaissance, modelled on records of such events in ancient Rome. 'The place of Agone' is the present-day Piazza Navona, which lies on the site of the Stadium of Domitian, where the 'Agoni Capitolani' (Capitoline Games) were once held. The analogy derives from a passage in Plutarch's *To an Uneducated Ruler*, an important source for this whole first section of Ottaviano's argument.

247. The source for these examples is Plutarch's *To an Uneducated Ruler*, 782. Cimon was the great naval commander responsible for Athens' victories over the Persians in 477–467 BC; Publius Cornelius Scipio Africanus (236–183 BC), the Roman general who defeated Hannibal and brought Spain, Carthage and Asia Minor under Roman rule. Lucius Licinius Lucullus (consul 74 BC) was another Roman general who led a successful campaign in Asia Minor, but is chiefly remembered for his hedonism and extravagance, discussed disapprovingly by Plutarch in his *Life*.

248. Epaminondas (*c.* 420–362 BC) was a Theban general and statesman; Lysis (not Lisias as in the text), a philosopher and follower of Pythagoras who fled from Italy to Thebes to escape persecution. Agesilaus was King of Sparta from 398 to 361 BC, an outstanding commander and friend of the historian Xenophon, who accompanied him on his campaigns in Asia and wrote a panegyric on him. Panaetius was a Stoic philosopher from Rhodes who settled in Rome where he became friendly with the Roman statesman and general Publius Cornelius Scipio Aemilianus (*c.* 185–129 BC). Castiglione's sources here are Cicero's *De oratore*, 3, 34, 139 and Plutarch's essays *Philosophers as Companions to Men in Power* and *Socrates' Personal Deity*.

249. The image of the sweetened medicine-cup derives from Lucretius's *On the Nature of Things*, 1, 936–942.

250. The story of Epimetheus is taken from Plato's *Protagoras*, 320d–322a. The question raised by Pallavicino here, of whether virtue can be taught, is also discussed in another Platonic dialogue, the *Meno*.

251. The example of the stone derives from Aristotle's *Nicomachean Ethics*, 2, 1, as does the notion developed below of virtue as a habit developing through 'longe use'.

252. Although essentially Aristotelian in its emphases, Ottaviano's treatment of virtue shows a tendency to syncretism: this phrase has been identified as an allusion to the Platonic conception of learning as the reawakening of knowledge possessed by the soul during its previous residence in the realm of Ideas, while the notion subsequently developed, of ignorance as the root of moral error, is one particularly identified with Socrates.

253. The distinction between the intemperate and the incontinent man is discussed in Aristotle's *Nicomachean Ethics*, 7, 8–9: both allow themselves to be dominated by their appetites, but the latter, unlike the former, recognises his error and feels remorse for his actions. The same chapters of the *Ethics* contain a further, related distinction, important to the discussion that follows: that between the continent man, who is drawn to self-indulgence, but dominates his appetites and acts according to reason, and the temperate man, whose appetites are naturally moderate (though Ottaviano stresses the possibility of achieving this state through the exercise of reason).

254. The question of the optimum form of government was much discussed in the early sixteenth century, a period that saw the culmination of the trend towards princely government that, over the past three centuries, had transformed Italy's medieval republican city-states into *signorie*. Castiglione's treatment of the problem is interesting: though here, predictably, he slants the discussion in favour of monarchical government, he does later (p. 320–1) have Fregoso recognise the need for some form of counterbalance to the prince's power.

255. Bembo's Venetian origins are relevant to the defence of republicanism he undertakes here (though in fact, in his own life, Bembo showed a preference for life under princely regimes). For fifteen years after the fall of the Florentine republic to the Medici in 1512, and definitively after the short-lived revival of republicanism in Florence between 1527 and 1530, Venice remained the only major power within Italy to retain a republican constitution.

256. This codification of these various types of government, which formed the basis for much Renaissance political discourse, is found in Plato's *Republic* and in Aristotle's *Politics* and *Nicomachean Ethics*, where a preference for monarchy is expressed (*Nic. Ethics*, 8, 10). Aristotle's *Politics* is the principal source for Fregoso's arguments here, including his fundamental point, that some individuals are destined by nature to serve, others to command (*Politics*, 1, 5).

257. Hoby's use of the word 'carpenters' to translate 'architects' (like the earlier 'carving' for 'sculpture') has been cited as evidence of the gulf between English and Italian culture in this period, and specifically of the different status of the visual arts within these two cultures. While it is certainly true that it was in Italy that the arts first began to shrug off their medieval status as crafts and to come to be regarded as liberal and intellectually prestigious pursuits, Hoby's preference for native words over loan-words (note 14) should be borne in mind when considering his choice of these terms.

258. Bias was a Greek thinker of the sixth century BC, one of the so-called Seven Sages. The maxim of his cited here is quoted by Aristotle in the *Nicomachean Ethics*, 1130a, 1–2. The image of the cracked vessels derives from Plutarch's essay *To an Uneducated Ruler*, 782e.

259. The examples derive from Plutarch, *To an Uneducated Ruler*, 781.

260. The question of the relative merits of the active and contemplative life ('doing' and 'beholding', in Hoby's terminology) was one much debated by fifteenth-century humanists. The problem is discussed by Aristotle in his *Politics*, 7, 2–3, and in his *Nicomachean Ethics*, 10, 7–8, where the superiority of the contemplative life is sustained.

261. The examples of the Scythians' 'warlyke wyldenesse' and of the Spanish custom of erecting obelisks to mark a dead soldier's head-count are taken from Aristotle's *Politics*, 1324b, 10–22.

262. Ottaviano's arguments here derive, again, from Aristotle's *Politics*, 7, 15.

263. The reference is to Book V of Plato's *Republic*, where it is suggested that individual households should be banned along with private property, that wives should be held in common and children brought up by the community as a whole.

264. On Castiglione's sources for the three forms of good government, see note 256. The notion (originating in Plato's *Laws*) that the most stable and successful government would be a 'mixed' one, combining elements from all three forms, was one that held considerable appeal for his contemporaries and was claimed as one of the merits of the Venetian constitution.

265. The source is Xenophon's *Cyropaedia*, 1, 6 (see above, note 19).

266. The enchantress of Homer's *Odyssey* (Book X) who turns Odysseus's men into beasts.

267. Francesco Gonzaga (1466–1519) succeeded his father as Marquis of Mantua in 1484. Castiglione served him before his transfer to Urbino in 1504 and returned to his service in 1516 after a long period of mutual mistrust (see note 96). According to one contemporary report, the Marquis kept 200 hunting dogs of different breeds and 150 birds of prey. He and his son, Federico, also enjoyed European fame as breeders of racehorses, a number of which are commemorated by portraits in Giulio Romano's Palazzo del Te.

268. Julius II was the most ambitious of the Renaissance popes in his artistic and architectural patronage. The task of rebuilding St Peter's was entrusted to Donato Bramante in 1506. Bramante was also commissioned to design a triumphal way linking the Vatican and Belvedere, but work on this was abandoned at Julius's death in 1513.

269. Pozzuoli, near Naples, has a famous first-century amphitheatre; Baia, nearby, and Civitavecchia, north of Rome, the remains of Roman baths. Porto, near Rome, was a Roman port, by Castiglione's day a marshy island, where the famous second-century statue known as the Apollo Belvedere was found in 1503.

270. The source for Alexander's architectural achievements and projects is Plutarch's *Life of Alexander*. Alexandria was founded in 332 BC; Bucephalia – named after Alexander's favourite horse – in 327. The project for converting Mount Athos into a giant statue of Alexander carrying a city in his hand was ultimately rejected by the king when it was pointed out to him that the city would have no territory and would be reliant on imports for its provisioning.

271. Procrustes and Sciron, in Greek legend, were brigands with ingenious lines in disposing of their victims: the former placed his on a bed and stretched them or cut them to fit its length, while the latter kicked his into the sea to fatten the turtles he kept. Both were killed by Theseus. The other figures listed, from Roman myth, were all slain by Hercules: Cacus was a giant son of Vulcan who had stolen Hercules' cattle; Diomed, son of Mars, another giant who fed his mares on human flesh; Antaeus, a Libyan giant, son of Gaia, the earth goddess, and invincible as long as he remained in physical contact with the ground; Geryon, the three-headed king of Hesperia whose cattle Hercules stole.

272. Calls for a new crusade against the infidel were not infrequent in Italy in the fifteenth and sixteenth centuries, down to the time of Torquato Tasso's epic *Jerusalem Delivered* (1581). The period witnessed a steady expansion of the Ottoman Empire, which, by the time *The Courtier* was published, had established control over Greece, the Balkans and Egypt.

273. Castiglione's source here is Plutarch's *Life of Themistocles*, 29. For the context, see note 3.

274. 'Monsieur d'Angoulême' is the future Francis I (note 66), thirteen years old at the time the dialogues are set. Castiglione had met him in Italy in the year of his accession (1515) and an earlier version of *The Courtier* contains a dedicatory letter to the French king.

275. Henry VIII (1491–1547) ascended to the English throne in 1509. Castiglione was not alone in his favourable impressions of the humanistically educated young prince, whom he had met, as is indicated in the text, during his visit to the court of Henry VII in 1506–7 (note 5).

276. The future Emperor Charles V (1500–58), whom Castiglione

would later come to know well as papal nuncio to Spain, was only six years old at the time the dialogues are set.

277. The notion that virtue is the disposition to observe the mean between two vicious extremes derives from Aristotle's *Nicomachean Ethics*, 2, 6. Though stated most explicitly here, the principle underlies many of Castiglione's recommendations in *The Courtier*: in Book 1, for example, the newly defined aesthetic virtue of *sprezzatura* is shown to lie between the two extremes of over-preciseness and affected casualness.

278. Federico Gonzaga (1500–40), Marquis and later first Duke of Mantua. Castiglione served him as ambassador to the papal court from his accession in 1519 to the time of his appointment as papal nuncio to Spain in 1524.

279. The suggestion is prophetic: Ottaviano Fregoso became Doge of Genoa in 1513 (see List of Principal Speakers).

280. Phoenix appears in Book 9 of Homer's *Iliad* as appointed by Peleus, King of Phthia to oversee Achilles' upbringing.

281. Aristotle was invited by Philip of Macedonia to educate his son Alexander in 342 BC. The story of his reconstruction of Aristotle's home town of Stagyra is found in Plutarch's *Life of Alexander*. Plato spent three years, from 390 BC, at the court of Dionysius I, tyrant of Syracuse, until he was dismissed. He was recalled by Dion (note 283) after the succession of Dionysius II in 367, but returned to Greece disappointed when he found the tyrant ill-disposed to his teachings.

282. Callisthenes was a pupil and kinsman of Aristotle's, who accompanied Alexander as historian on his Asian campaign, but fell into disfavour when he publicly opposed the proposal that Alexander be worshipped as a god, after the Persian custom, and was ultimately executed on suspicion of conspiracy. The example is an equivocal one: although Castiglione's likely sources, the lives of Alexander by Plutarch and Quintus Curtius, do contain the suggestion that Callisthenes' brusqueness contributed to his downfall, the incident is used to illustrate less the philosopher's failings than Alexander's deterioration into arbitrary rule.

283. Dion (*c.* 408–*c.* 354 BC) was a Syracusan statesman, the brother-in-law of Dionysius I, who became a disciple of Plato during his first residence in Syracuse (note 281). After the succession of Dionysius II, he recalled Plato to Syracuse, in the hope that he could exert a beneficial influence on the new ruler. After the failure of this plan, he opposed Dionysius and finally overthrew him in 356, only to be overthrown himself after two years of rule.

284. Hoby's translation is inaccurate: the original is 'my Lavinello's hermit'. The reference is to the third book of Bembo's dialogue on love, *Gli Asolani* (1505), set at the court of Asolo, near Venice, where, in imitation of Plato's *Symposium*, one of the interlocutors, Lavinello, recounts what he has learned of love from a hermit.

285. The content of the dissertation on love that follows is a blend of Christian and Platonic concepts and imagery, drawn from the works of Plato himself (specifically, the *Symposium* and *Phaedrus*), and from the works of writers like Bembo himself, Francesco Cattani da Diacceto (see note 61) and Marsilio Ficino (1433–99), the founder of Renaissance Neoplatonism and author of an extremely influential commentary on the *Symposium* (1469).

286. A similar condemnation of sensual love in older men is also found in Book III of Bembo's *Asolani*. The future cardinal was rather less rigorous in his practice, however: the three children born of his long-standing liaison with 'la Morosina' (Fausta Morosina della Torre) were born in his mid to late fifties, and after he had taken holy orders.

287. The Greek poet Stesichorus (*c.* 560 BC) wrote two poems on Helen of Troy, one giving the Homeric version of her story, the other a radically revisionist version in which it is denied that she ever went to Troy. A legend, recounted in Plato's *Phaedrus*, 243a–b, told that he was miraculously stricken blind after composing the first poem and that his sight was restored only after he had composed the palinode.

288. The most immediate source for the passage which follows is probably Cicero's *Tusculan Disputations*, 1, 28, 68, though it also echoes passages of Cicero's *Dream of Scipio* and Plato's *Timaeus*. The vision of the cosmos expressed here is, of course, that of the Ptolemaic–Aristotelian system, in which the earth stands immobile at the centre of the universe, circled by great transparent spheres bearing the planets and the sun. Circles and spheres were traditional symbols of perfection and the whole vision is one of a divinely ordered universe.

289. The notion of man as a microcosm (lit. 'small world'), correspond-ing in all his parts to the universe (the 'macrocosm') was central to Renaissance thought. It finds eloquent expression in Sir Walter Ralegh's *History of the World* (1614), 1, 2, 5, in which man is described as 'an abstract or model, or brief story of the universal'.

290. On these 'spirites', see above, note 85.

291. The notion that it was possible to ascend to God through the contemplation of beauty was most influentially expressed in the Renaissance in Marsilio Ficino's commentary on Plato's *Symposium* (1469). Beauty, for Ficino, was a ray emanating from God and radiating down through the angelic intelligences to the material substance of bodies. Through love – defined as the desire for beauty – the human mind could reascend this 'ladder', progressing from the beauty of one particular human body to the beauty of the soul and thence to the beauty of the angelic mind and finally to the source of all beauty in God. True union with God could only be achieved when the soul had separated itself from the body, but Ficino and others believed that this state could be reached by a small number of individuals during life, though imperfectly and only for brief periods of time (see following note).

292. The combination of classical and Biblical *exempla* here is characteristic of the syncretism of Renaissance Neoplatonism. Hercules died after putting on the poisoned shirt of Nestor, sent to him by the jealous Deianeira. In agony, he flung himself onto a burning pyre and passed to immortal life, received by Jove. For the incident of Moses' vision of God in the burning bush, see Exodus, 3; the incident was depicted twice in the Vatican in this period, by Raphael and Giulio Romano. The appearance of tongues of fire over the Apostles' heads at Pentecost is recounted in Acts of the Apostles, 2: 1–4; that of Elijah, carried off in a chariot of fire, in 2 Kings, 2: 11–12.

293. The reference to St Paul's ecstasy is to 2 Corinthians, 12: 2–4; that to St Stephen's to Acts of the Apostles, 7: 55. St Francis of Assisi (1181/2–1226) was the first great saint to receive the stigmata, the miraculous wounds of Christ on his hands, feet and side. Plotinus, mentioned earlier, was the originator of Greek Neoplatonic philosophy (third century AD), and an immense influence on Renaissance Neoplatonism. His attainment of a state of ecstasy through contemplation is described in the last volume of his *Enneads*.

294. St Mary Magdalen was said in an apocryphal tradition to have been uplifted by angels during prayer. The 'third heaven' is the circle of Venus: in Ptolemaic cosmology (note 288), the third of the concentric spheres circling the earth. On Diotima, mentioned earlier, see note 201.

295. The planet Venus – the morning star – was, of course, associated with love: Dante, in the *Paradiso*, places the souls of lovers in the circle of Venus.

CASTIGLIONE AND HIS CRITICS

One of the earliest and most telling testimonies to the impact of *The Courtier* is an observation by the historian and political theorist Francesco Guicciardini in his *Ricordi* (1530), a remarkable series of meditations on political and moral themes:

> When I was young, I used to scoff at the idea of learning music, singing, dancing and other such frivolities. I even made light of fine writing, horsemanship, dressing well, and all those things that seem more decorative than substantial in a man. But later, I wished I had not done so. For although it is not wise to spend too much time cultivating the young toward the perfection of these arts, I have nevertheless seen from experience that these ornaments and accomplishments lend dignity and reputation even to men of ability. It may even be said that whoever lacks them is lacking something important. Moreover, skill in these sorts of entertainment opens the way to the favour of princes, and can sometimes be the path to great profit and advancement for those who excel in them. For the world and princes are no longer as they should be, but as they are.[1]

Guicciardini does not mention *The Courtier* by name, but it can be plausibly surmised that his reading of the work, as well as his experiences as a diplomat, contributed to the change of heart documented here. This admission of the practical value of courtly accomplishments, on the part of a man bred to the sterner republican culture of Florence, gives a good indication of the reasons for the rapid and spectacular success of *The Courtier* in Italy and throughout Europe, while its grudging tone hints at some of the reservations that the dialogue's content provoked even during the period of its greatest acclaim.

The Courtier's reception in Europe was rapid and enthusiastic: within nine years of its first publication, it had been translated into Spanish and French, and translations into German and Latin, as well as English, soon followed. In England, as Hoby acknowledges in his preface, even before his translation was published, *The Courtier* was already widely known in the original and through the

French translation. A copy of the dialogue is known to have been in the possession of Thomas Cromwell in 1530, and it has been plausibly suggested that Sir Thomas Elyot may have been influenced by Castiglione in his *Boke named the Governor* (1531), especially in the sections concerning the need for those destined to high office to study music and art. Whatever the case, the educational value of the work was quickly recognised, and it is in another great Tudor educational treatise, Roger Ascham's *The Scholemaster* (1570), that we encounter the first English critical appraisal of the work after Hoby's preface. Like many of his Protestant contemporaries, Ascham's attitude to 'Papist' Italy was one of profound moral suspicion: in nine days in Venice, he tells us, 'I saw . . . more liberty to sin, than ever I heard tell of in our noble city of London in nine year.' *The Courtier* is, however, exempted from his strictures and is recommended as a convenient means to acquire the polish of an Italian education without the moral dangers of a visit to Italy:

> To ioyne learnyng with cumlie exercises, *Conto Baldesaer Castiglione* in his booke, *Cortegiano*, doth trimlie teach, whiche booke, advisedlie read, and diligentlie folowed, but one year at home in Englande, woulde do a yong ientleman more good, I wisse, then three yeares travell abrode spent in Italie. And I mervell this booke is no more read in the Court, than it is, seying it so well translated into English by a worthie Ientleman Syr *Th. Hobbie*, who was in many wayes well furnished with learnyng, and very expert in knowledge of divers tonges.[2]

The reigns of Elizabeth and James I mark the apex of *The Courtier*'s popularity in England: Hoby's translation was republished three times, in 1577, 1588 and 1603, while Bartholomew Clerke's translation of the dialogue into Latin – in itself evidence of the work's classic status – enjoyed an even greater fortune, with no fewer than six editions between 1571 and 1612. The motives that drew Elizabethan readers to the work were not always as lofty as its humanist enthusiasts like Hoby or Ascham might have hoped: where Hoby had presented his *Courtyer* as a work of morality and stressed the benefits to society of the art of courtiership it taught, there is evidence that his readers were less interested in its moral and political dimensions than in its unparalleled efficacy as a practical handbook to the techniques of success in court life. In a period of unprecedented social mobility and increasing centralisation of power, when the court had become a magnet to ambitious young men seeking to exploit new opportunities for advancement,

The Courtier's seductively idealised but pragmatic and psychologically astute teachings seemed to place the rewards of court service enticingly within reach.

The fascination *The Courtier* held for anyone seeking to make a career in the court is well demonstrated by the dense marginal annotations, stretching over a period of some twenty years, from 1572 to 1594, in the copy of Hoby's *Courtyer* owned by the poet, polemicist, academic and arch social climber Gabriel Harvey. Harvey's emphases in his reading emerge clearly in the summary he drew up on the last page of the volume in 1580 and in the two verse digests of Castiglione's teachings on the courtier and court lady that he published in a collection of his Latin poetry in 1578. Harvey's summary makes an interesting contrast with Hoby's appendices to the *Courtyer*: not only does it neatly shear off the political idealism and spiritual aspirations of Book 4 of the dialogue, but it is uncannily emptied of the moral qualities on which Castiglione's translator had laid such stress:

> Above all things it importeth a Courtier to be gracefull and lovelie in countenance and behaviour, fine and discreet in discourse and interteinment; skilfull and expert in Letters and Arms; active and gallant in every Courtlie Exercise; nimble and speedie of boddie and mind; resolute and valorous in action and profound and invincible in execution, as is possible: and withall ever generously bould, wittily pleasant and full of life in all his sayings and doings. His apparrel must be like himself, cumlie and handsome; fine and cleanlie to avoid contempt, but not gorgeous or statelie to incurr envie or suspicion of pride, vanitie, self-love or other imperfection. Both inside, and outside, must be a faire paterne of worthie, fine and Loovelie Vertu.[3]

The influence of *The Courtier* on Elizabethan culture was complex, profound and capillary: recent studies of George Puttenham's *Arte of English Poesie* (1589) have revealed, for example, the degree to which the categories of courtesy theory shaped the poetic practice and the literary thought of the age.[4] Echoes of Castiglione's dialogue have been detected in many Elizabethan writers, including, inevitably, Shakespeare, but it would be misleading to attempt to gauge the work's influence in terms of direct imitations. By the time Shakespeare was writing, the ideals of courtesy articulated in *The Courtier* and in subsequent Italian courtesy books like Giovanni della Casa's *Galateo* (translated 1576) and Stefano Guazzo's *Civil Conversation* (translated 1581 and 1586), had become so profoundly assimilated within

English polite society that an attempt to trace their influence would be as complex and ultimately frustrating a process as attempting to trace the influence of Hollywood on modern European manners and culture.

The parallel with Hollywood is an apt one, in that it captures the elements of reserve and resistance, as well as the enthusiasm, that characterise the reception of these Italian behavioural ideals outside Italy. The Italophilia that, according to the outraged Ascham, led Englishmen to attend the Italian Church in London 'to heare the Italian tonge naturally spoken' rather than 'to hear Gods doctrine trewly preached', was balanced by an Italophobia that increased as the century developed. The skills in the manipulation of appearances that characterised the Italianate courtier lay dangerously close to outright dissimulation; and the figure of the slippery and unscrupulous courtier became a standard feature of Elizabethan and Jacobean drama, incorporating elements from that other great Italian cultural export, Machiavelli's *The Prince*. Moralists in both France and England condemned the corrupting influence of Italian manners; and, although Castiglione himself escaped some of these censures, as the extract from Ascham's *Scholemaster* cited above testifies, he was sufficiently closely identified with the seductive and equivocal ideals of courtiership for a writer like John Marston, in his *Satires* (1598), to use the name 'the absolute Castilio' to epitomise the polished but empty and superficial court culture he was satirising.[5]

In Italy, as well, in the later sixteenth century, Castiglione was not exempt from criticism, though for rather different reasons. The mood of Italian culture had changed sharply with the Counter-Reformation; and in the relentlessly pious atmosphere of post-Tridentine Rome, features of *The Courtier* that had passed unnoted in Castiglione's day – its occasional jibes at Church corruption and its classicising allusions to Fortune, rather than divine providence, as the arbiter of worldly events – were considered dangerous enough to merit the issue of a bowdlerised edition in 1584, under the aegis of the Inquisition. Another criticism levelled at *The Courtier*, this time from a secular perspective, was that it gave an excessively idealised representation of the life of the courts. This critique was most astutely developed by the poet Torquato Tasso, author of the great epic *Jerusalem Delivered*, and a man who had experienced the crueller realities of court life at first hand. In his dialogue *On the Court* (1585) – composed during its author's confinement in an insane asylum at the instance of his patron, the Duke of Ferrara —Tasso brilliantly analyses the internal contradictions within Castiglione's treatment of the courtier's relation with his master and concludes pessimistically that talent, virtue and learning are a less secure route to success at court than mediocrity, cunning and a slavish and acritical devotion to one's prince.[6]

The Courtier's career as a conduct book appeared in decline by the seventeenth century: there were no further editions in Italy for over a century after 1606 and in England after the last publication of Clerke's Latin version in 1612. The eighteenth century, however, saw a revival of *The Courtier*'s fortunes: Clerke's version was republished with revisions in 1713 and the 1720s saw the publication of two new English translations, both of which were popular enough to merit further editions. It is interesting to note that the work is presented by its new editors not as a historical curiosity but as a still valid guide to polite conduct: even if one, Robert Samber, notes *à propos* of the section on humour, that readers should make allowance for the fact that it reflects the tastes of a society 'whose turns of Wit were of another Gusto', he still goes on to insist that Castiglione's basic rules here will be found as relevant today as they were in the past.[7] Samber's confidence appears to have been justified: Samuel Johnson, according to Boswell, described *The Courtier* as 'the best book ever written on good breeding'; and the same author, in his *Life of Addison* (1781), observes that, if works like *The Courtier* and Casa's *Galateo* are no longer much read, it is only because they have already effected that reformation of manners that their authors intended.[8] Castiglione's treatment of what Johnson calls 'the minuter decencies' of life was securely enough ballasted with morality to escape the censorious response elicited from him by a more recent guide to 'good breeding', Lord Chesterfield's *Letters to His Son*, of 1774. None the less, the influence of *The Courtier* has frequently been detected in this work, which, for Johnson, paired 'the manners of a dancing-master' with 'the morals of a whore'.

The Courtier survived, then, as a conduct book until the eve of the French Revolution, when Romanticism's cult of sincerity triggered its decline into anachronism, made definitive by the anti-élitist sentiment of modern democratic culture. This trajectory was a gradual one, however: the behavioural model proposed by Castiglione was still close enough to modern norms for John Addington Symonds to be able to describe Castiglione's courtier in

1875 as, 'with one or two points of immaterial difference, a modern gentleman, such as all men of education at the present day would wish to be'.[9] Even in the twentieth century, *The Courtier* has not entirely lost the power to shape its readers' conduct that its early enthusiasts so prized. When James Joyce read the book, according to his brother Stanislaw, it had precisely the effect on him that Elizabethan moralists had feared: that of making him 'more polite but less sincere'.[10]

Despite these vestigial remnants of its career as a conduct book, however, the history of the reception to *The Courtier* over the past century and a half has been principally shaped by its status as a crucial document of that controversial cultural–historical era, the Renaissance. It seems appropriate to start any consideration of the modern critical history of *The Courtier* with the work that, more than any other, shaped modern perceptions of that era, Jacob Burckhardt's *The Civilisation of the Renaissance in Italy* (1860). Burckhardt discusses *The Courtier* briefly in his chapter on the social life of the Renaissance, and, consistently with his notion of the Renaissance as the cradle of individualism, his emphasis falls on the courtier's self-perfection rather than on his political role:

> It was for [court] society – or rather for his own sake – that the *cortigiano*, as described to us by Castiglione, educated himself. He was the ideal man of society and was regarded by the civilization of that age as its choicest flower: and the court existed for him rather than he for the court. Indeed, such a man would have been out of place at any court, since he himself possessed all the gifts and the bearing of an accomplished ruler, and because his calm supremacy in all things, both outward and spiritual, implied too independent a nature. The inner impulse which inspired him was directed, though our author does not acknowledge the fact, not to the service of the prince, but to his own perfection.[11]

Burckhardt's vastly influential work initiated a perception of *The Courtier* as one of the quintessential expressions of the Renaissance 'spirit'; a view expressed, with differing emphases, by the editors who, at the turn of the century, launched *The Courtier* on its twentieth-century audience. Sir Walter Raleigh, who edited Hoby's translation in the Tudor Translations series in 1900, describes *The Courtier* as 'an abstract or epitome of the chief moral and social ideas of the age' and one of the fullest expressions of 'that dominant note of the Renaissance, the individualism which subordinated all institutions to the free development of human faculty'. Vittorio Cian, in the introduction to his annotated edition of the work (1894), describes it as reflecting with 'an unparalleled faithfulness and expressive potency', 'the triumphant phase of our Renaissance, when the arts and sciences and all the finest expressions of our Italian spirit shone forth, as in a glorious noontide'.

In the English-speaking world, this phase in *The Courtier*'s reception is most interestingly illustrated by the response to the dialogue of William Butler Yeats, who was introduced to Hoby's *Courtyer* by Lady Gregory in 1904. The dialogue's portrayal of the court of Urbino made a profound and enduring impression on him, as a mythical ideal against which to measure the degraded reality of his day. The Montefetro court is alluded to in *To A Wealthy Man* (1913) as 'that grammar school of courtesies/ where wit and beauty learned their trade/upon Urbino's windy hill.' It is in *The People* (1915), however, that Yeats most eloquently evokes his imagined Urbino, as the locus of a dream existence immeasurably richer than his present life in his own 'unmannerly town':

> I might have climbed among the images of the past
> the unperturbed and courtly images
> evening and morning, the steep street of Urbino
> to where the Duchess and her people talked
> the stately midnight through
> until they stood
> in their great windows, looking at the dawn.
> I might have had no friend that could not mix
> courtesy and passion into one like those
> that saw the wick grow yellow in the dawn . . .

The celebratory reading of *The Courtier* I have been discussing did not go unchallenged in Italy, where Burckhardt's exalted vision of the Renaissance was countered by an equally strong native tradition of regarding the sixteenth century as an age in which Italian literature distanced itself from the vivifying contact with the people and closed itself off into a vacuous Arcadia, dominated by a pedantic cult of form. This position is most influentially exemplified in Francesco De Sanctis's *History of Italian Literature* (1870/1), in which Castiglione is identified as an arch-representative of this decadent trend, typifying that combination of superficial polish and spiritual bankruptcy from which only Machiavelli, among the prose writers of the age, is exempt:

[Giovanni della Casa's] *Galateo* and *The Courtier* are the two best prose-writings of the period, as representations of a polished and elegant society that lived completely on the surface ... and that regarded manners as the most important thing in life. Even the intellect, lax below its show of virility, devoted its energies principally to writing in a mannerly way, to dressing its writing up correctly. Boccaccian and Ciceronian style soon became conventional, a pure mechanism of imitation, not engaging the writer's intellect in any way ... [In philosophy, poetry and prose], the sickness was the same: a passivity or indifference of the intellect, the heart, the imagination – the entire soul ... Amid all this cataclysm of rhetorical prose-writings, Machiavelli's prose made its appearance, as a presentiment of modern writing.[12]

Such flat condemnation was extreme, but elements of this view persisted; and unfavourable comparisons with Machiavelli became almost *de rigueur* in discussions of *The Courtier*. In most versions of the comparison, Machiavelli's 'realism' is contrasted with Castiglione's 'idealism', as in the following extract from one of the most popular and frequently republished student guides to Italian literature:

There is an Olympian air about the court portrayed in this book, which makes one think of a fresco by Raphael, rather than of the real life of the courts as it appears from the history of the period and the writings of Machiavelli and Guicciardini. This is not to say that *The Courtier* is a false book: rather, it portrays for us the lovely appearances, the polite manners, the front of stage of the palaces of the period, while the two great historians reveal what is behind the scenes: the ambitions, the passions, the scheming, the convolutions. *The Courtier* is essentially a decorative and idyllic book: [Guicciardini's] *Ricordi* and [Machiavelli's] *Prince* are realistic or dramatic books, which adhere to the essence of life, in all its complexities and its ugliness.[13]

It is this critical orthodoxy that Joseph A. Mazzeo took as his starting-point in an essay of 1965 that breathed new life into the Burckhardtian conception of *The Courtier*, proposing as the 'true subject' of the dialogue the 'creation of the self as a work of art':

Given the expressed intention of Castiglione – the task of the perfect courtier is in the last analysis that of giving political advice to his ruler – some readers have pointed to the fact that Castiglione is remarkably unrealistic or unconcerned about the way affairs of state were actually conducted. After all, he lived in the same chaotic Italy that Machiavelli inhabited and he too was a diplomat with ample opportunity to see the same truths. This sort of objection can really have no force once we understand that Castiglione's task is that of delineating a *perfect*

Courtier, an ideal type, and not that of drafting a program of action to be implemented at every point. His book is a kind of Utopia, or better, an Arcadia, for it begins with a lament for the deaths of so many of the beautiful and charming people who graced the court of Urbino and created that perfect moment, now gone forever, of which *The Courtier* is an imaginative reconstruction. Whether the events and people of the book ever existed as Castiglione gives them to us is less important than it is for us to understand that they were able to inspire a nostalgic vision of a perfect small society vitally concerned with the perfection of the self.[14]

Mazzeo was still able, in 1965, to describe *The Courtier* as a 'relatively neglected' text, with some justice, at least where the English-speaking world was concerned. Though it was much valued as a historical and cultural document, little attention had been given to *The Courtier* as a work of literature: even an admirer like Raleigh could describe it as 'scarcely among the greatest works of its age'. The past few decades have witnessed a dramatic change in this respect: especially since 1978 when the five-hundredth anniversary of Castiglione's birth inspired a number of conferences and publications, *The Courtier* has attracted a growing amount of respectful critical attention. Recent criticism shows a growing appreciation of its structural complexity and the sophistication of its argument, and few would now dissent from the judgment that it represents one of the finest literary achievements of its age.

Many factors have contributed to this new interest, but one in particular deserves to be mentioned: the important work done in the 1960s by Ghino Ghinassi on the earlier versions of *The Courtier*, culminating with his publication in 1968 of the *Seconda redazione* of the dialogue. Ghinassi's work revealed the extent and scope of Castiglione's revisions, and this – in combination, obviously, with more general trends in critical methodology – has resulted in a number of important developments. One has been an enhanced awareness on the part of critics of Castiglione's meticulous artistry and the sophistication of his fictional mediation of history, which has laid to rest the last relics of the myth of *The Courtier* as a snapshot of Urbino 'from life'. Another, for which the ground had been laid earlier by critics like Vittorio Cian, Erich Loos and Carlo Dionisotti, has been a shift away from the tendency to regard *The Courtier* as a generic expression of the 'Renaissance spirit' towards a closer focus on the precise historical juncture in which *The Courtier* was written. The effect of this latter development might be characterised as that of 'putting the courtier back in

The Courtier': the question the dialogue is addressing is now less often perceived to be the universal one of the perfectibility of human nature than the specific one of the fate of a certain class at a particular moment in history.

This new vision of *The Courtier* has been articulated with exceptional lucidity by Eduardo Saccone, an Italian critic working in the United States, who pits himself explicitly against the Burckhardtian critical tradition epitomised in the quotation from Mazzeo above. For Burckhardt, as has been noted, the courtier was an autonomous, narcissistic aesthetic creation ('the court existed for him rather than he for the court'). For Saccone, by contrast,

> . . . the reality is a different and a dramatic one, from the first. From the first, the formation of the courtier depends crucially on his public, on other people. Self-sufficient perfection, a completely autonomous personality, are not his objectives by any means. The courtier is always fighting on two fronts: that of his competition with his peers and rivals and that of the favour of the prince. From the first – and this is naturally a truism – the courtier cannot exist without the court, which is to say without the favour of the prince who holds court . . . The service of the prince is from the outset – as Burckhardt himself cannot fail to have realized – what he calls the 'inner impulse' that motivated the courtier.[15]

Saccone also tackles another, related component of the traditional critical perception of *The Courtier*: the 'idealism' so frequently counterposed to Machiavelli's 'realism'. The dichotomy, he argues, indicates a misunderstanding of the character of both *The Prince* and *The Courtier*, though one that has worked more particularly to the disadvantage of the latter. In fact, the situation is more complex: 'just as (if we still wish to use these terms) *The Prince*'s realism does not exclude an element of idealism, so *The Courtier*'s so-called idealism is founded on an extremely concrete and historical analysis of reality'.[16] The aim of the courtier, like that of Machiavelli's prince, is ultimately that of survival; and the 'good manners' *The Courtier* prescribes as a means to capture and maintain the prince's favour are, in this sense, as functional as the 'bad manners' Machiavelli teaches the prince. Even the apparently utopian vision of Book 4 can be understood in the light of these pragmatic considerations: the courtier's survival and his grasp on the limited but real power the system permits him depend crucially on the maintenance of that system, which in turn depends on the prince's education to government.

The question of the relation between realism and idealism in *The Courtier* is also addressed by the American historian Lauro Martines (1983), who, along with Marxist-influenced critics like José Guidi, sees Castiglione's dialogue as an articulation of the crisis experienced by the traditional ruling class of Italy during the period of the Wars of Italy as it attempted to come to terms with the reduced political role forced on it by the consolidation of despotic rule throughout Italy and to adjust to the humiliating reality of foreign domination:

> *The Courtier* was written largely between about 1513 and 1518, in the midst of the Italian debacle . . . To talk about courtiers and princes in those years was to talk about leading ailments in Italian society . . . In setting his sights on the courtier, Castiglione was discussing nothing less than leadership in Italy: the qualities, real and desired, of the sort of men who governed states and rode in the forefront of events.[17]

Castiglione's task in *The Courtier*, for Martines, is that of confronting 'the challenge to upper-class identity' in Italy. Although ultimately he fails, as he must do – the last book is 'a fall into undisguised idealism' – his partial success is attributed to his skill in shuffling the real and the ideal in the dialogue, creating the illusion of a solution where in fact no solution existed:

> Much of the work's appeal for the upper classes outside of Italy was in the picture of a relaxed and civilized nobility. The dialogue's swift shifting back and forth between the ideal and the reality made the ideal seem attainable . . . In Italy, under the threat to their commanding identity, upper-class readers clutched the work to themselves because it rescued leadership in a mimesis the idealism of which was disguised as realism, and this was accomplished by means of the dialogue's steering back and forth between ideal forms and the real Italy of the princes. Castiglione won conviction through his literary style and tone. He fostered the illusion of reality by continually raising the question of the work's unreality and then providing immediate disclaimers. Whereas outside of Italy, the dialogue's shifts between ideal and reality seemed to put the ideal within reach, in Italy, the same shifts made the ideal seem real.[18]

A less sweeping perspective is adopted by Daniel Javitch, who stresses the character of *The Courtier* as a practical guide to courtiership, insisting, like Saccone, on the functional dimension of aspects of the ethos of the perfect courtier – flexibility, detachment, indirection – that have traditionally been perceived in a purely aesthetic key:

One of the chief novelties of the *Cortegiano*, and a basic reason for its tremendous fortune in the sixteenth century, is that it set forth an art of conduct tailored to the social and political exigencies of Renaissance despotism. This pragmatic and forward-looking aspect of Castiglione's code had been obscured by modern commentators who have tended to dwell on the book's idealistic, escapist and nostalgic features ... . When Castiglione's speakers recommend various stylistic attributes that the courtier must possess, they rarely, if ever, point out that these attributes are especially desirable because they are pleasing to the prince. One might think that they, rather than their sovereign, are the principal arbiters of graceful conduct at court. This deceptive impression is further reinforced, of course, by the absence of Urbino's ruler, Duke Guidobaldo, from the parlor game taking place in his palace. Appearances to the contrary, however, the ruler is not excluded from the conversations at Urbino ... If we consider the courtier's principal stylistic attributes and try to establish why they are valued, it gradually becomes apparent that these attributes are not simply advocated because they appeal to the social and aesthetic tastes of a courtly elite, but, more importantly, because they are necessary and effective means of maintaining a favorable relationship with the prince.[19]

Javitch's approach reflects a trend among social and cultural historians from which the study of *The Courtier* has greatly benefited: a growing interest in the court as a sociopolitical phenomenon of outstanding importance in European culture. One feature of court culture that has attracted attention is that highlighted by Javitch: the absolute centrality of princely power as the structuring element in all social and cultural activity. Another is the stylised and performative character of court life, which a number of recent critics of *The Courtier* have used as a key to both Castiglione's behavioural theory and his representation of social interaction at the court of Urbino. One such critic is Wayne A. Rebhorn, who combines this approach, however, with a more traditional, idealist conception of *The Courtier*'s ends, which distances him from critics like Javitch and Saccone:

Like many others in the Renaissance, Castiglione conceives social activity as essentially a question of playing a series of roles, each entailing certain predetermined attitudes and modes of activity, status relationships and types of dress and deportment – in other words, each having its appropriate *figurative mask* ... Castiglione wants the aspiring courtier to become aware of what masking involves, of the different roles required by different social situations; and he especially wants his courtier to develop an ideal flexibility, a protean quality which will enable him to shift from role to role with the lightning speed of a quick-change artist. Castiglione mocks those unselfconscious men at the opposite extreme from his ideal, who mechanically perform the parts assigned to them ... offending the ladies by playing the soldier off the battlefield as well as on it. He suggests that such men are more than buffoons, that they are profoundly unfree, enslaved to the tyrant roles they do not understand and cannot manipulate. By contrast, through his understanding of role-playing and his mastery of the myriad forms assumed by human activities, Castiglione's ideally flexible courtier not only achieves social success but the truest sort of freedom as well.[20]

While historicist critics like Frank Whigham have related this 'performative' aspect of *The Courtier*'s behavioural model to the peculiar conditions of life in the Renaissance court, similarities have also been noted between Castiglione's analysis of social interaction and that of modern social anthropologists like Erving Goffman, especially in their shared concern with 'face-work' and 'the presentation of self'. Castiglione's astuteness as a sociologist *avant la lettre* has been increasingly appreciated in recent criticism: as Rebhorn has noted, it is this aspect of the work that sharply differentiates *The Courtier* from other conduct books of the period:

There are vast differences in form between most courtesy books and *Il Cortegiano*. Not only does Castiglione present his teaching through conversations and speeches rather than lists of rules, but he shows himself far more interested in the analysis of behavioural situations and the moral problems they pose than in producing a set of specific prescriptions for social success and ethical behaviour ... As the exception that proves the rule, when Castiglione does urge the courtier to dress in black or at least in dark colours like the Spaniards, he shows himself most interested in defining the social contexts where such dress is and is not appropriate, describing the image it enables the courtier to project and analyzing the psychological effect it has on others.[21]

This is not the only facet of *The Courtier* whose 'modernity' has been noted: one reason for the recent revival of interest in the work is certainly the affinity many critics have detected in it with aspects of contemporary thought. An obvious instance of the way in which contemporary concerns have redirected critical interests is the attention shown recently to the discussion of the status of women in Book 3: an aspect of *The Courtier* that had previously been passed over almost entirely in silence. Critical responses have, however, been mixed here: while some historians of the

Renaissance debate on women, like Linda Woodbridge, consider Castiglione as one of the participants in this debate who came closest to anticipating modern feminist thought, others, often influenced by Joan Kelly's discussion of *The Courtier* in her seminal essay, *Did Women Have a Renaissance?*, have stressed rather those aspects of Castiglione's description of the 'lady of the court' that can be seen as reinforcing gender stereotypes and underlying the historical tendency in this period towards a more rigid differentiation of sex roles. Critics who adopt this second position tend to stress the discrepancy between the theoretical celebration of women's equality with men in Book 3 and the very sharply differentiated roles adopted by the male and female speakers in the dialogue itself. Women are present in the dialogue but silent, excluded from the discussion that 'forms' them: the passive recipients of a discourse elaborated by and for men. As Valeria Finucci has argued, while 'the *Cortegiano* is sometimes so innovative that one could be tempted to see the treatise as an optimistic exaltation of womanhood', in fact 'what is said and what the text shows seldom coincide'.[22]

It is possible to detect other respects in which contemporary concerns have shaped critical responses to *The Courtier*. There has been a new interest, for example, in recent criticism, in the importance accorded to play in *The Courtier*; in its sense of the deceptive nature of reality and the fallibility of human judgment; in its gestures towards the notion of identity as a social fabrication. A critic who exemplifies these new concerns well is Giulio Ferroni, who relates the theatrical and performative character of social interaction in *The Courtier* to the epistemological relativism particularly marked in the earliest version of the dialogue. In a human environment mired by flux and uncertainty, where true knowledge is impossible and all judgments partial and provisional, all social activity must rest on a fragile tissue of collective fictions:

> The discrepancy between 'perfection' and relativity . . . is the determining factor in Castiglione's elaboration of his model of social intercourse. If [the courtier's] perfection . . . is an instrument of social success, it is nonetheless also true that this success must be realized in a space defined by social interchanges which, by their very nature, undermine any possibility of stability or certainty. Social intercourse takes place within a gallery of mirrors, where the stability of the 'truth' is supplanted by 'appearance', 'deception', 'impression', 'opinion' and 'error'. To succeed in society . . . is to establish a grip on these shifting, slippery, ambiguous

categories that govern all human behaviour; and to do this involves being able to impress a strong 'opinion' of oneself onto other people's minds, establishing a solid 'reputation', capable of drawing others' praise and admiration. The able courtier will be one who can bring to converge on himself, in a positive way, the play of fiction and appearance that makes up social intercourse. The 'perfect' courtier will be the one who succeeds best in constructing himself as a pure social image, spun on the thread of the human propensity to error.[23]

Ferroni, as was noted, confines these remarks to the first version of the dialogue, before the addition of the fourth book, with its leaning – or yearning – towards more stable and absolute truths. The challenge of Book 4, and especially Bembo's speech, is confronted in the passage that follows by Richard Lanham, the author of perhaps the most consistently 'postmodern' reading of the work:

> We may think of Bembo's mysticism as completing what has gone before or as contradicting it. If we want a god's eye view, a perspective from the eighth sphere, he provides one, he takes us at least as far as man can. If we doubt that such a perspective exists, we are free to view Bembo as the author of *Gli Asolani*, an outstanding spokesman for the fashionable Platonism – another spokesman for another style. *The Courtier* is a game in which people entertain theories because the theories entertain them. Platonism earns no exemption. If Bembo wants to heat his mind with incredibilities, the conversational framework proves wide enough to contain him. But it does not certify him, any more than it certifies any other attitude. Bembo's search for the center may lead to heaven or to heavenly sentimentality. We choose our own compass points. *The Courtier* shows us how to leave process for essence . . . but it does not itself do so. Sublimity can be thought of as a skill as well as a transport. It may lead back to the game as well as out of it.[24]

The Courtier has emerged from the intense discussion it has sustained over the past few decades looking a very different work from the way it appeared to its enthusiasts in the early years of the century. A work once lauded for its serenity and balance, it is now more likely to be perceived as, in the words of a recent editor, 'a contradictory, lacerated text that, despite continual revisions . . . could never assume a homogeneous, balanced, smooth textual form'.[25] At one time prized chiefly for its representation of a past age of glorious certainties, it is now as frequently appreciated for its painfully clear-sighted anticipation of modern dilemmas. The critical activity of the past decades has wrenched *The Courtier* from the genteel museum existence it once seemed destined to and re-established it as a central text in the intellectual history of the West. It is unwise to make predictions, but the fact that, after almost half a millennium, Castiglione's dialogue has shown such a capacity for reinventing itself augurs well for the future of this rich, complex and provocative text.

REFERENCES

1. *Maxims and Reflections of a Renaissance Statesman* (Ricordi), translated by Mario Domandi, with an introduction by Nicolai Rubenstein (Gloucester, Mass., 1970): 86 (No. 179). (The translation has been slightly amended.)
2. *English Works*, ed. William Aldis Wright (Cambridge, 1904; reprinted 1970): 218.
3. Caroline Ruutz-Rees, 'Some Notes of Gabriel Harvey's in Hoby's Translation of Castiglione's *Courtier*', *P.M.L.A.*, 25 (1910): 634–5.
4. I refer particularly to Daniel Javitch, *Poetry and Courtliness in Renaissance England* (Princeton, 1978).
5. *Certaine Satyres* (1598), ed. A. Davenport (Liverpool, 1961): 68.
6. The dialogue has been translated by Dain A. Trafton as *Tasso's Dialogue on the Court*, in *English Literary Renaissance Supplements*, 2 (1973).
7. *The Courtier*, translated by Robert Samber (London, 1724).
8. James Boswell, *Journal of a Tour to the Hebrides* (1773), in *Boswell's Life of Johnson*, edited by George Birkbeck Hill; revised edition by L. F. Powell (Oxford, 1964): 5, 276; and Samuel Johnson, *Life of Addison*, in *Lives of the English Poets*, edited by George Birkbeck Hill (Oxford, 1905): 2, 92–3.
9. *The Renaissance in Italy*, 3rd edition (London, 1897; reprinted 1926): 1, 145.
10. Richard Ellman, *James Joyce* (Oxford, 1982): 75.
11. *The Civilisation of the Renaissance in Italy*, translated by S. G. C. Middlemore, with an introduction by Peter Burke and notes by Peter Murray (London, 1990), p. 246.
12. *Storia della letteratura italiana*, Ch. 15, in *Opere*, edited by Niccolò Gallo, with an introduction by Natalino Sapegno (Milan and Naples, 1961): 501.
13. Attilio Momigliano, *Storia della letteratura italiana dalle origini ai nostri giorni*, 8th edition (Milan, 1968): 187.
14. *Renaissance and Revolution. The Remaking of European Thought* (New York, 1965): 134.
15. *Le buone e le cattive maniere: letteratura e galateo nel Cinquecento* (Bologna, 1992): 70.
16. Ibid., 82.
17. *Power and Imagination. City-States in Renaissance Italy* (New York, 1979): 329.

18. Ibid., 330.

19. 'Il Cortegiano and the Constraints of Despotism', in Castiglione: the Real and the Ideal in Renaissance Culture, edited by Robert W. Hanning and David Rosand (New York and London, 1983): 17–18.

20. Courtly Performances. Masking and Festivity in Castiglione's 'Book of the Courtier' (Detroit, 1978): 14.

21. Ibid., 19.

22. Valeria Finucci, The Lady Vanishes: Subjectivity and Representation in Castiglione and Ariosto (Stanford, 1992): 40. The essay by Joan Kelly referred to earlier may be found in her Women, History and Theory (Chicago, 1984).

23. 'Sprezzatura e simulazione', in La corte e il 'Cortegiano', edited by Carlo Ossola and Adriano Prosperi (Rome, 1980): 1, 127.

24. The Motives of Eloquence: Literary Rhetoric in the Renaissance (New Haven and London, 1976): 162–3.

25. Amedeo Quondam, preface to Baldassare Castiglione, Il Libro del Cortegiano (Milan, 1981).

ACKNOWLEDGEMENTS

I should like to express my thanks to Peter Burke, of Emmanuel College, Cambridge, for his valuable suggestions concerning the early reception of *The Courtier* and for letting me see the manuscript of his forthcoming study of the fortunes of the dialogue.

SUGGESTIONS FOR FURTHER READING

The best general introduction to Castiglione's life and works, particularly strong on the intellectual context of *The Courtier*, is J. R. Woodhouse, *Baldesar Castiglione: A Reassessment of 'The Courtier'* (Edinburgh: Edinburgh University Press, 1978). A useful collection of essays is *Castiglione: the Real and the Ideal in Renaissance Culture*, edited by Robert W. Hanning and David Rosand (New Haven: Yale University Press, 1983), which includes essays on specialist topics such as music in *The Courtier*, as well as readings of the dialogue by Thomas M. Greene, Daniel Javitch, Eduardo Saccone and others. Other recent monographs in English are Wayne A. Rebhorn's *Courtly Performances. Masking and Festivity in Castiglione's 'Book of the Courtier'* (Detroit: Wayne State University Press, 1978) and Joseph D. Falvo's very thorough *The Economy of Human Relations: Castiglione's 'Libro del Cortegiano'* (New York: Peter Lang, 1992), which includes an up-to-date bibliography of recent secondary literature. Useful introductions to the political and cultural history of the period are *Italy in the Age of the Renaissance, 1380–1530*, by Denys Hay and John Law (London: Longman, 1989), and (on cultural history), Peter Burke, *The Italian Renaissance* (Cambridge: Polity, 1987).

On Hoby's life, see Sir Walter Raleigh's introduction to his edition of *The Courtyer* (London: David Nutt, 1900) and Edgar Powell's edition of his diary, *The Travels and Life of Sir Thomas Hoby* (London: Camden Miscellany, No. 10, 1902). On his translation of *The Courtier*, the best study in English is still probably the chapter on Hoby in F. O. Mathiessen, *Translation: An Elizabethan Art* (Cambridge, Mass., 1931), though a far more comprehensive modern study exists in Italian, by Carmela Nocera Avila. More generally, on the reception of Castiglione and other Italian courtesy theorists in the English court, see Frank Whigham, 'Interpretation at Court: Courtesy and the Performer–Audience Dialectic', in *New Literary History*, 14, 3 (1983): 623–639; also, for a broader survey of the fortunes of the ideal of the courtier in Europe, Sydney Anglo's 'The Courtier, the Renaissance and Changing Ideals', in *The Courts of Europe. Politics, Patronage and Royalty, 1400–1800*, edited by A. G. Dickens (London, 1977). A comprehensive study of *The Courtier*'s reception and influence is forthcoming: Peter Burke's *The Fortunes of 'The Courtier'* (Cambridge: Polity Press, 1995).